Rồng của chợ bơi đen
Dragon of Black Pool Market
NOW OPEN
24 HOUR
affordable food & grocery
Authentic vietnamese coffee
free wi-fi
MW01406349
FEDERAL BUREAU OF INVESTIGA
LA COSA NOSTRA (CHICAGO)
PART # 1 OF 6
PAGES AVAILABLE THIS PART 178
Norte del Valle
Mexico too?
3 dead.
Chauchua?
White Shadows?
Why Chicago???
certain!
uncertain

Culture Watch, Chicago News at Nine

Transcript from Sept. 3, 2011, 21:49 ET

AMANDA KLINE, CULTURE WATCH HOST: I'm here with Chicago businesswoman Cho Chu-tsao. Ms. Cho is president of Genetic Agricultural Products and founder of the Chauchua-American Advocacy Alliance. Ms. Cho, I understand you have some issues with Dr. Cole's study.

CHO CHU-TSAO, CHAUCHUA-AMERICAN ADVOCACY ALLIANCE: Thanks for having me on the show, Amanda. Let me say at the outset, I'm not here as a business owner. I'm here as a proud Chauchua, born and raised in Chicago. Go, Bulls! And you're right. But you're putting it too mildly. The fact is, this study by Henrietta Cole is nothing more than racist pseudoscience. Her so-called findings aren't fit for a phrenologist's dream-journal. The University of Chicago ought to be ashamed.

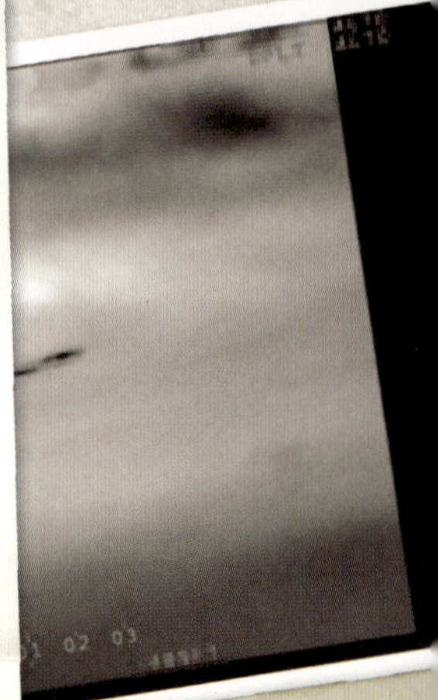

Amity and norms in the Chauchua diaspora

Henrietta Cole, Department of Anthropology, University of Chicago, 1126 E 59th Stre
Chicago, IL 60637, USA. Published in the *Proceedings of the Sixth Annual Conference*
Anthrosocial Institute (October 2011).

ABSTRACT: Interviews with members of Chauchua tribes in the U.S. and in their traditiona homelands in Southeast Asia, cross-referenced with a review of historical literature, reveal distinctive norms that recur across the contexts of cultures into which the Chauchua assimilate. We study Chauchua traditions that take the values of physical strength and psychological dominance that all societies treasure, and embrace them to a hypertrophic degree that excludes ideas of "fondness" or "natural affection." There is no way to say "I love you" in the Chauchua language; the closest analogue would be "I take pleasure in your deference." The Chauchua struggle to maintain cultural identity necessitated an embrace of taboos such as incest and anthropophagy. Tribal hierarchies were established by power display and violence, which extended to interpersonal interactions and shaped emotional rules and semantics. There are no analogs to the concepts of reciprocity and patronage: "If I share my food with you during this time of want, you ought to do a favor for me later." In their place exists a network of threats, expressed with a richly nuanced vocabulary of abuse. Traditional Chauchua relationships do not include amity, only favorite slaves. Most notably, familial amity emerged as a cultural trait only with the influence of surrounding cultures. By Chauchua tradition, kindness is seen as a perversion. Even the weak currying favor from the strong is an alien concept, since it's presumed that the strong simply take what they want without waiting for it to be offered. Weak Chauchua are abused as a matter of course by strong Chauchua, in ever-shifting patterns of allegiance and relative status. At the top are malevolent deities, who are owed not reverence or loyalty, but terrified obedience. Finally, we examine ways in which the Chauchua struggle for cultural identity created an imperative to dominate, betray, and manipulate outsiders, an expectation often expressed in keen attention to the "weaknesses" of compassion-based cultures.

"Shzor – shzong"
– immunity to shock and pain
– psilocylah mushroom spec

Irrawaddy River near the "City of Dagon" (Rangoon?

GA positioning as off-bran painkiller w/o opiod addictiveness if legaliz

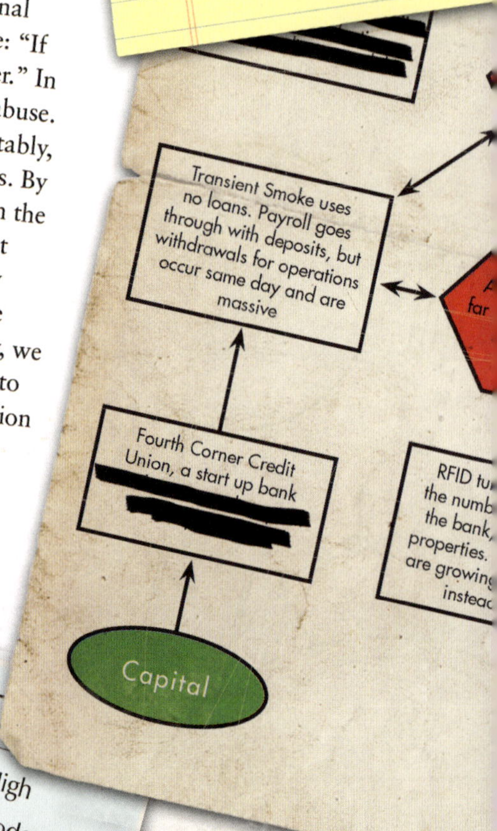

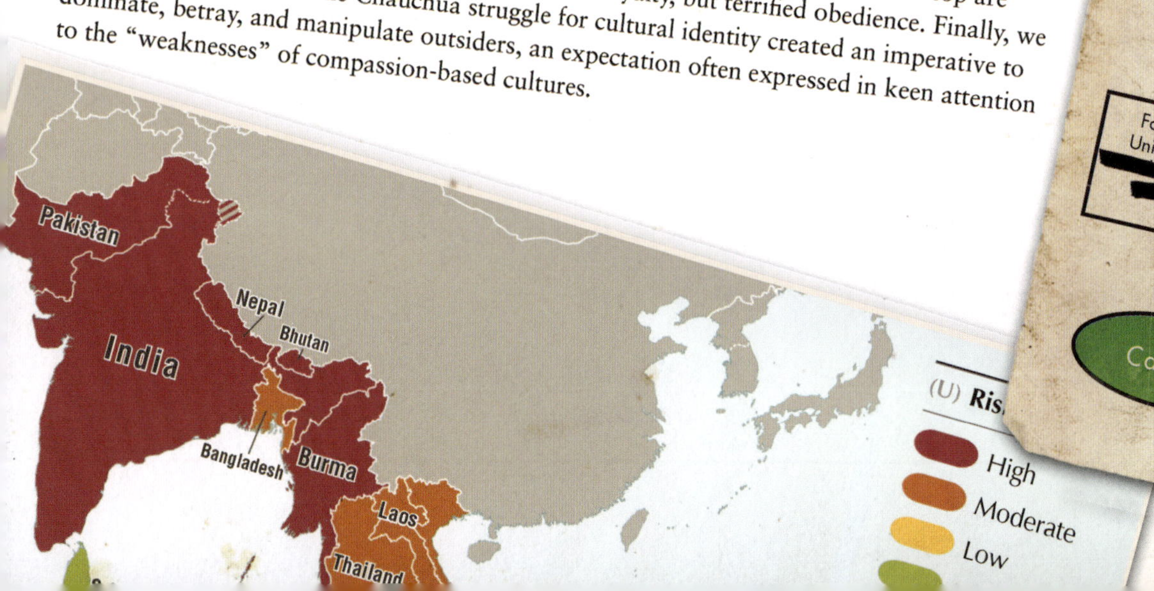

DELTA GREEN

// Handler's Guide //

A Role-Playing Game of Lovecraftian Horror and Conspiracy

ARC DREAM PUBLISHING PRESENTS *DELTA GREEN: HANDLER'S GUIDE*

WRITTEN BY DENNIS DETWILLER, ADAM SCOTT GLANCY, KENNETH HITE, SHANE IVEY & GREG STOLZE **DEVELOPERS & EDITORS** DENNIS DETWILLER & SHANE IVEY **ART DIRECTOR & ILLUSTRATOR** DENNIS DETWILLER **GRAPHIC DESIGN BY** SIMEON COGSWELL & SHANE IVEY **COPY EDITOR** LISA PADOL **INDEXER** JESS NEVINS **ADVICE & ASSISTANCE** STEPHEN BUCK, AARON CARSTEN, TOM CHURCH, CHARLIE CONLEY, CHRIS COOPER, ADAM CROSSINGHAM, DAVID DOBELMAN, MYRA JEAN QUALLS ELDER, CLAES GERLEMAN, SHAUN GREENWALD, CHRISTOPHER GUNNING, DANIEL HARMS, GILES HILL, CHRIS HUTH, RACHEL K. IVEY, FAUST KELLS, PETER LINK, CHRIS MALONE, JOHN MARRON, ROSS PAYTON, GRAEME PRICE, DANIEL RAAB, KENT JOHAN SNYEN, CALEB STOKES, THADDEUS STOKLASA, BILL SUNDWALL, MELISSA SUNDWALL, GIL TREVIZO, JONATHAN TURNER, JOHN SCOTT TYNES, KENNETH VAUGHAN & RAY WINNINGER **DELTA GREEN CREATED BY** DENNIS DETWILLER, ADAM SCOTT GLANCY & JOHN SCOTT TYNES

TOP SECRET

Sold by Studio2 Publishing, 1722 Louisville Drive, Suite A, Knoxville, TN 37921, USA; phone 1-865-212-3797;
email jims@studio2publishing.com; *Delta Green: Handler's Guide* product stock code APU8113.
ISBN 978-1-940410-28-9
Printed in China
9 8 7 6 5 4 3 2 1

Contents

Introduction 4
The World of Delta Green 6
Running Delta Green 7
What a Delta Green Agent Does 8
The Outlaws and the Program 8
What Is the Unnatural? 9
The Handler 9
How to Be a Handler 9
Introducing New Agents 11
Interpreting the Rules 12
An Example of Play 13
The Past 14
Genesis 16
The Black Chamber 19
ONI's P4 Desk 22
The Office of Strategic Services 32
Our Darkest Hour 35
Götterdämmerung 43
Roswell and Rebirth 46
The Cold War 50
Losing History 54
Reorganization 58
Deeper War 61
Hearts of Darkness 61
The Fall 66
Rebirth 66
Reorganization 71
Fairfield 73
The Best-Laid Plans 79
The Delta Green-MAJESTIC War: Opening Moves 79
Trojan Stalking Horse 86
Endgame 86
Détente, Demarcation, and Departure 90
A Mutual Enemy 90
Delta Green in the Age of Terror 91
Mission Priorities 91
Pruning the Hydra 94
Project DULCIMER 95
The Program 96
The Other Delta Green 97
Less Than Friendly 100
The Iraq War 100
Headhunters 101
GRU SV-8 Evolves 113
Lethal Findings 127
Lurkers and Lone Wolves 129
No More Secrets 131
The Profit and the Loss 135
The Last World Order 139
The Unnatural 140
The Infection of Understanding 142
The Great Old Ones 143
Unearthly Intelligences 145
Earthly Intelligences 146
Extradimensional Intelligences 149
Other Unnatural Threats 150
Unhistory 150
Unnatural Tomes 153
Hypergeometry 164
» Index of Sample Rituals 172
Sample Rituals 174
Known Alien Intelligences 188
Unnatural Entities 188
» Colours Out of Space 188
» Deep Ones (Greater) 191
» Deep Ones (Lesser) 193
» Dimensional Shamblers 194
» Elder Things 196
» Feasters From the Stars 197
» Ghouls 198
» The Great Race (Cone-Shaped Vessels) 200
» The Great Race (Human Vessels) 202
» Greys 203
» Haedi Nigritiae 204
» Hounds of the Angles 205
» Hunting-Horrors 206
» Ifrits 207
» Insects From Shaggai 208
» K'n-Yani 209
» Liveliest Awfulness 210
» Lloigor 211
» Lloigor-Controlled Quasi-Dinosaurian Constructs 215
» Metoh-Kangmi 216
» Mi-Go 217
» Serpent-Folk 219
» Shoggoths 221

» Slime of Tsathoggua 222
» Spawn of Cthulhu 223
» Spawn of Yog-Sothoth 224
» Spectral Polyps 225
» Those Beyond 227
» Wendigowak 228
» White Apes 229
» Winged Servitors 230
» Witches' Familiars 230
» Zombies 231
Great Old Ones 232
» Azathoth 233
» Cthulhu 235
» Ghatanothoa 236
» Glaaki 239
» Itla-shua 240
» Nodens 241
» Nyarlathotep 242
» Nyogtha 243
» Qu-Tugkwa 244
» Shub-Niggurath 245
» Tleche-Naka 246
» Tsathoggua 247
» Y'golonac 248
» Yig 250
» Yog-Sothoth 251
Creating Your Own Unnatural Threats 252
The Schism 256
The Program 258
» What to Tell Your Agents 258
» Agents 261
» Specialists 262
» Recruitment 264
» Operations 265
» Operation CORAL NOMAD 270
» Security 271
» Research 272
» March Technologies, Inc. 273
Important Individuals: The Program 276
» The Director 276
» Special Agent Abraham Mannen, Director of Operations 278
» Admiral George Gates, Director of Intelligence 280
» April Pleasant Crumpton, Ph.D., Intelligence Officer 282
» Katherine Oakes, Director of Security 284
» Charlie Bostick, Deputy Director of Security (Information) 287
» Gregory Tapham, Ph.D., Director of Research 288
» Rebecca Kaur Thornhill, Ph.D., Deputy Director of Research (Recovery) 290
» Dana Shelton, Director of Logistics 292
» Gavin Ross 294
» Jean Qualls 296
The Outlaws 299
» Agents 300
» Friendlies 301
» Operations 303
» Recruitment 306
Important Individuals: The Outlaws 308
» Donald Poe, Agent Alphonse/ Agent Charlie 308
» Emil Furst, Agent Aaron 311
» Chun-te Wu, Agent Anton 313
» Curtis McRay, Agent Bernard 314
» Edna Knotts, Agent Charlotte 316
» Grant Emerson, Ph.D. 318
» James Derringer 319
What the Program and the Outlaws Know 321
The Opera 326
The Essentials 328
Creating a Campaign 330
Creating an Operation 332
Appendices 338
Operation FULMINATE: The Sentinels of Twilight 340
NPCs and Animals 353
Recommended Media 357
Index 358
Operation Overview Worksheet 363
Operation Structure Worksheet 364
Unnatural Entity Details Worksheet 365
Ritual Details Worksheet 366
Personal Pursuits Summary 367
Open Game License 368

The First Report

NTSapp

When Chilton took his shot, I jumped into the mirror room with the laptop bag thinking, Anywhere is better than here. Right at that moment, it seemed like a good play. Guns were out and people were already dead. What did I have to lose?

Don't answer yet.

The old McTeague luck is holding up great, pops. Trust me, you'd be proud.

From the lab at San Francisco University, the mirror room inexplicably opened onto a shallow sea beneath a wall of diamond-hard pinpoints of light. I goggled and stumbled and laughed. I don't know why. It was so surprising, I guess. The water was tropic, the low rock islands steaming, and I could taste metal in my mouth. Then the mirror room folded in on itself like origami. It felt like someone had grabbed both sides of my brain and was twisting them, pulling them apart.

Before it was gone, I was gone.

I woke with my head in the mud, soaked in warm water, the lone occupant of this place. This world. I stood. I shouted. Knee-deep clear water, low rock islands. Nothing. No mirrors. No people. No life. When I breathed too fast, I began to feel happy and stupid. The tablet stayed dry, don't ask me how. That and some M&Ms.

I sat for a time trying to catch up with what the world had become, for me. I took off my shoes and soaked my feet.

Then, one last indignity. The moon rose, crazy close. Huge and unblemished as the face of a child. Its surface white and perfect and empty, like the eons and epochs ahead that will toil on without me, forward, until my birth comes around again.

I'll write my last report here. Hell, the FIRST report. I'll write the first one. I am the first agent, now. It's all I have, so don't deny it to me, OK?

Hello?

Dear V-Cell, do not enter the mirror room. Do not let John enter the mirror room. Destroy the mirror room. Destroy Auroratech. Destroy John. Destroy the world. Dear V-Cell, nothing is real, and everything is alive. The end has come and will come and come again.

Find my bones here and see. Know. Wait for me. I'm coming. But time moves so slowly...

> **START WITH THE "AGENT'S HANDBOOK"**
>
> **Delta Green: The Role-Playing Game** comprises two volumes, the **Agent's Handbook** and the **Handler's Guide**. The core rules of the game, which every player needs to know, are presented in the **Agent's Handbook**. The **Handler's Guide** builds on that foundation. Read the **Agent's Handbook** first.

HANDLERS COME TO *DELTA GREEN* for all kinds of reasons. They may like to weave a story, fashion a mystery, or devise some new horror. Whatever the reasons, in the end, that creation is never simple. When all the layers of the investigation are pulled back, more often than not, what is revealed is the stark nothingness of infinity.

Consider this overview a mandate.

Delta Green is about the end of humanity.

You may make it seem to be about other things from time to time. About family. About life. About the things that make us human. It has all these things, but that's not what it's about.

It lies.

Delta Green is about three people killed in a stand-off in the Mojave desert, bang, bang, bang, and a box that contained a single ingot of unknown metal labeled "SURFACE SAMPLE BUCKET 1."

Delta Green is about piecing together the string of NASA suicides and realizing that ER10911 is on a collision course with the Earth in 19 months. That your mother and father and sister and her sons have 19 months to live. That the world will be scraped clean by fire...unless....

Delta Green is about an agent, broken and mad with her screaming two-year-old strapped in the car seat, speeding away from a burning house where her husband's corpse cooks—because it wasn't her husband, it was something else.

Delta Green is not about love.

Delta Green is not about safety.

Delta Green is not about reason.

Delta Green is about humanity's true place in the universe.

And that place is nowhere. We are ticks boiling on a mote in a sea of nothing, and we will no more take to the stars than we will cure the ills that destroy us. Our existence is a clock winding down. When the hour strikes, entities with true consequence will sweep us away with an unconscious flick, scouring the globe clean for their limitless—infinite—plans.

Delta Green is not about stats or weapons or killing the beast. *Delta Green* is about lying to your players until their Agents realize the truth. That humanity was not the first and will not be the last denizen of this world. That the Earth is haunted, and we are not even the ghosts. We are merely their shadows.

Welcome.

The World of Delta Green

Welcome to *Delta Green,* a role-playing game of horror, wonder, and conspiracy. By opening this book, you have chosen to become the Handler. It's the Handler's job to keep the players—who take the role of Delta Green Agents—engaged. You are the creator, host, and judge of all things that occur in the fictional world of Delta Green. You fill it with secrets, take the role of non-player characters (NPCs), and create the threats that they face. You roll the dice and make the calls. Only you understand the absolute truth.

Delta Green is about truths that kill. The ultimate truth is this: In remote places, through rents in spacetime, and beyond the veil of our limited, four-dimensional existence, *things* await release. When they are free, humanity will burn. An isolated few in the know—Delta Green—struggle to resist this final conflagration.

Being a Handler requires preparation, imagination, and an unwavering vision of where the game is headed. It also requires an indifference to outcome. It might seem like a good idea to alter a die roll to save

LOW CARD

an Agent or drop a vital clue when the team is on the wrong path. Resist these urges. Delta Green is not about victory. It's about the fight.

Delta Green is about our urge to survive and understand, in a universe wholly antithetical to human survival and understanding. Agents of Delta Green struggle to defeat threats that outstrip human comprehension, as the human world rushes towards inevitable destruction. Agents live their lives—what of their lives they can maintain—and keep the ultimate secret from their loved ones: No matter what they do, they know, eventually, the end is coming.

Congratulations, Handler. You've just been promoted to the apocalypse.

Running Delta Green

To run a *Delta Green* game as Handler, gather friends and describe what's happening to their Agents. The players react as their Agents might react in the situations you describe, and attempt to solve the mystery, without losing their Agents to insanity or death.

A single unit of Delta Green play—usually it lasts two or three hours—is called a *session*. A single Delta Green mystery is called an *operation*. Some operations take many sessions to resolve. Multiple operations strung together are called a *campaign*.

Delta Green agents sometimes call an operation a "night at the opera," or a "psychotic opera." Operations have code-names for the sake of secrecy, like Operation SOUTHERN COMFORT, Operation STATIC, or Operation LIFEGUARD.

Delta Green has existed since 1942, when it was an arm of the secretive Office of Strategic Services, exploiting the Nazis' obsession with the occult in World War II. On paper, it conducted psychological operations. In reality, it fought actual unnatural horrors uncovered by Nazi research.

Since World War II, Delta Green has existed in many forms. First as a commando operation, then as a psychological warfare unit, then as an investigative group, then as a conspiracy within the federal government with no official cover.

As of 2017, two groups consider themselves Delta Green: an unsanctioned conspiracy and a separate program with governmental cover. They work independently from each other, and sometimes dangerously at odds. Most importantly, very few people in either group understand this schism.

What a Delta Green Agent Does

Delta Green agents locate, destroy, and keep secret the unnatural forces that threaten American interests. Of course, unnatural threats exist outside the United States, but Delta Green does not have the resources or will to police the world. A few world governments have similar programs, like Britain's PISCES, Canada's M-EPIC, and Russia's GRU SV-8. These groups operate in a similar manner to Delta Green within their sovereign territories.

Delta Green agents operate in secret and often hold a normal job in the U.S. government, such as FBI agent, postal inspector, or USAMRIID specialist. Their actual employer—a government agency, the armed forces or some private company—never knows of Delta Green's existence, let alone its real mission.

Delta Green operations routinely require agents to lie, cheat, steal, and commit crimes for the greater good. Violence, insanity, and death surround Delta Green operations, and all who serve the group eventually pay a physical or mental price. But almost any action is justifiable in the face of human extinction.

OPINT: Tools Presented Within

Some section headings indicate the type of information which might be found. These are scattered throughout the text as asides. They are there to provide both experienced and fledgling Handlers a ready set of tools to choose from to make their game run smoothly.

- » **ASSET:** A description of a book, item, location or character ready for use in a Delta Green game.
- » **DISINFORMATION:** A summary of some important concept in the world of Delta Green, with options on how to use it in your campaign. The information is yours to mine, modify or correlate with other contents in any way you wish.
- » **IN THE FIELD:** A summary of a style of play, guidelines on how to get the "feel" of game-play right, or a new campaign background for Delta Green, such as World War II, the Cold War, or the "Cowboy Years" of the 1970s and 1980s.
- » **OPINT:** Optional rules and tips on how to implement rules.
- » **THREAT MATRIX:** A summary of a particular threat or tips on how to portray it.

The threats that agents put down are real and relentless. Long ago, the group came to the conclusion that there is no ultimate solution, only an endless holding action against the forces from outside. Of course, Delta Green never tells its recruits that. If they live long enough, they'll find out. They always do.

The Outlaws and the Program

Delta Green has existed in many forms over the decades. Like any covert agency, there are parts which operate in the absolute black. There are splinter groups and defectors.

Are your Agents members of the black but official U.S. government organization known colloquially as "the Program"? Are they in an unofficial conspiracy that uses government resources for entirely unsanctioned missions, known as "the Outlaws"? Or are they outsiders—canaries in a coal-mine—who have never heard the name Delta Green?

The real nature of Delta Green in the game remains up to the Handler to decide. And it's a separate question from what the Agents believe they understand. The Agents might think they're part of an official program but work for conspirators. They might think they're outsiders but answer to people in the reactivated Program. They may never know their position in the hierarchy of the group. This should be a central theme in the game.

The only thing Delta Green agents should know for certain is that their mission, even at its most odious, saves lives and can never be revealed to the public.

What Is the Unnatural?

The unnatural is anything that exists beyond human comprehension.

The danger Delta Green confronts represents something more than a mere physical threat; the very existence of the unnatural is beyond human understanding, and will be forever. What is worse is that this knowledge of the unnatural is so damaging that it causes insanity or transforms a human into a servant of the darkness. Not just the physicality of such things must be contained. Their nature, their spoor, and their mere existence must be kept secret, lest they infect the normal, unaware world.

Long-term agents learn that the old saying is wrong: knowledge is not power. Knowledge is death.

The threats that Delta Green faces are detailed in **PART TWO: THE PAST**, beginning on page 14.

The Handler

This book is for the Handler. It contains secrets of the setting, as well as rules on how to create unnatural hypergeometry, entities, threats, locations, and operations.

As the Handler, you control the game and create the mystery that the Agents investigate. The Handler takes the role of everyone in the game that the Agents meet (called non-player characters or NPCs), describes the situations the Agents find themselves in, and determines if dice are rolled, which dice are rolled, and why. The Handler is the narrator, director, and referee; and you shape the world and how the rules work so the players can explore and experience it.

Players describe Agent's decisions, choices, and reactions to the fictional world. As the Handler, you are responsible for bringing that world to life, creating the secrets the players are trying to uncover, and ensuring the game's mood and suspense through a thousand factors. In these rules, you'll often see things like "The Handler decides." As Handler, your word is law.

That requires a lot of trust between the players and you, the Handler. This book is devoted to helping you build and maintain that trust.

How to Be a Handler

As a Handler, you describe the game world and control and speak for all entities in the game world who are not the Agents. Your responsibilities are as follows.

Describe the World of Delta Green

Your descriptions of the world are the conduit for the players to experience Delta Green. If the Agents are

~~SECRET//REL TO USA, FVEY~~

DISINFORMATION

YELLOW

CAPITALIZING "AGENT"

Any time you see the word "Agent" capitalized in this game, it refers to a **Delta Green** player character. Delta Green has many agents; the ones being played at your table are Agents.

driving, you describe the car, the road, and the weird rest-stop along the way with the bulgy-eyed clerk. If they want to get a closer look at the kit-bashed computer, it's your job to make up the details and describe it to them—could it have been constructed by a time traveler? The world is literally whatever you say it is. Make those descriptions count. But remember, describe only what is relevant, and try to make it as engaging as possible.

Teach New Players

New players want to learn the rules and play their Agents convincingly. Help them. If they don't think to take important actions that their Agents would know to do, remind them. Never dictate what choices they should make, but offer procedural suggestions where you think they'll be welcome. Point them to the **TRADECRAFT** tips on page 165 of the *Agent's Handbook*. Print out the player handouts available at delta-green.com. They'll be thinking like veteran Agents soon enough.

Be Vigilant

Pay attention to what the Agents are doing, thinking and feeling. Often, players telegraph their intentions. Are the Agents loading up on flash-bangs and bulletproof vests? Then it's pretty likely they'll be raiding the cult headquarters soon. Make sure you have some ideas of what they might find there. Learn to think on your feet and never be caught flat-footed.

You Are the Entire Cast Except the Agents

When the Agents talk to the used car salesmen about the odd knife he found, the Handler is the used car salesman. You're also the cop at the crime scene, the cultist that lost the knife, and the horrific howling thing from beyond time and space that the weapon summons. The Handler speaks for, describes and controls every entity in the *Delta Green* game except for the Agents (who are controlled by the players). It's a huge responsibility, but when it's done correctly, it's incredibly fun.

Set the Mood

The world of Delta Green is identical to our own, but with the secret threat of the unnatural. The mood is real, dark, and full of paranoia. No Delta Green operation should be without risk of discovery, insanity, and death. Set and maintain this mood at all costs. It is only from this backdrop of risk that the fun of surviving to fight another day truly shines.

Work With the Players

Try to see the player's points of view. Work with them, within reason, to make the experience more fun. Give them leeway in unimportant things, but be strict when it comes to rules, life-and-death situations, and insanity. Only when they understand the tone of the game will they begin to act within those constraints, and only then will their Agents seem at home in their world.

IN THE FIELD: Fear, Not Frustration

Being a Handler for *Delta Green* is always a balancing act. The game is built to elicit fear, and that requires that the players never quite feel confident or comfortable. But for fear to have meaning, it needs suspense, and suspense requires that the players have some hope of success. Even if the best they can expect is a pyrrhic victory or a short-term staving-off of horror—even if they can tell that the odds are against any success at all—the players need to sense that there's a chance. Otherwise, why call it a game?

We often advise the Handler to change the rules to suit the table. We recommend surprising the players by changing the powers of unnatural entities and the effects of rituals. But beware. As Handler, your purpose is not to frustrate the players. You are here to elicit the suspense and terror that players experience through their Agents. You are the neutral representative of a hungry cosmos. It will devour the Agents, sooner or later. Allow the players just enough hope that the moment of digestion comes with a shock, not a shrug.

Trust the Players

You're all here for the same reason: a suspenseful, horrifying game of *Delta Green*. As Handler, you have enough to worry about. Let the players worry about their Agents. If a player wants an Agent to do something you don't agree with (and that action might have negative repercussions in the game), warn the player but don't interfere. After all, the best way to demonstrate the fragility of humanity in the game is to let players send Agents charging heedlessly to their doom. Perhaps the next Agent will think twice.

Introducing New Agents

A *Delta Green* game begins with the Handler asking the players to introduce their Agents. Players describe their Agent's day-to-day lives: work, friends, family, the mundane but critical things the Agents are willing to die for. Help players create new Agents and bring them into the game. Players look to the Handler to establish what kind of Agents to create, how they relate to the other Agents, and what they know about their world.

Less Is More

Agents new to Delta Green are told nothing beyond what is absolutely necessary. Even the most essential information is given only after it is confirmed they have seen something unnatural. The most basic message is this: There is an organization in the federal government tasked with protecting America from the forces of the unnatural. That organization is called Delta Green, but no one is allowed to say that name aloud unless absolutely necessary.

But there is a deeper secret than the existence of Delta Green itself. In the modern era, there are two Delta Greens. "The Program" is a well-funded (but highly illegal) organization working under the cover of black projects, embedded in the federal government like a tick. "The Outlaws" are an ad-hoc organization of agents who either refuse to join the Program or don't even know it exists.

The Agents should not know that there are two organizations operating under the same name, let alone which organization they call home.

Nor do Agents immediately realize the extent of the unnatural threat. Whatever unnatural entity or effect a prospective Agent first encountered—whatever horror brought the Agent to the group's attention—it is almost always identified as the main threat that Delta Green faces. If the Agent saw an aquatic humanoid, then Delta Green is a group that fights aquatic humanoids. If the Agent encountered a sentient color from another dimension, then that is what Delta Green fights. Later, as new threats are encountered, this misunderstanding is passed off as an oversight. By the time

the Agent learns that there are many inhuman intelligences, threats, and creatures from beyond, it is far too late to withdraw.

What will your Agents learn about Delta Green in their time with the group? Barring extreme circumstances, it should be very, very little. Delta Green operatives are understandably tight-lipped about their endeavors. They avoid comparing notes or expanding their knowledge of the organization beyond their immediate command structure. Active investigation into the structure and command can elicit anything from a reprimand to a more permanent "removal" from service. Both the Program and the Outlaws take operational security very seriously. One rogue agent is enough to topple them.

Let the Agents fill in the blanks on their own. They will come to wildly different conclusions about Delta Green. If they ever compare notes, their combined stories will likely describe a bizarre, Frankenstein's monster of an intelligence agency which, barring their direct connection, seems as insubstantial as smoke.

The Inciting Event

It's part of a Handler's job to work with players to establish just what inciting events brought their Agents to the attention of Delta Green. It doesn't have to be an encounter with the unnatural. The details can be saved for some future time when Agents are trading war stories, but it's best to have an idea of what it might be at the beginning of play. Keep the following in mind when working with Agents to create their backstories:

» **A FEW SENTENCES:** The summary of how they came to Delta Green should be short. One or two sentences, or a paragraph at the most.

» **NOT ALL AGENTS KNOW THE UNNATURAL:** Delta Green recruits to fulfill its needs on the ground. Sometimes this means academics. Other times, professional soldiers. Most Delta Green Agents have been exposed to the unnatural, but not all. Some veterans of war, intelligence operations, and counterterrorism operations have seen enough awful things that Delta Green trusts that exposure to the impossible won't shatter their resolve.

» **THE UNNATURAL IS BEYOND EXPLANATION:** An Agent's inciting event should be engaging, scary, and believable, but above all it should be mysterious. No Agent emerges from a brush with the unnatural saying, "Wow, that Deep One almost got me!" But they might say, "I investigated an orphanage of children with bug eyes, who sang songs of returning to mother sea." Direct the player to keep it vague and unsettling, because it's unlikely the Agent understood anything about the encounter.

» **RUN AWAY:** Even catching a glimpse of something from beyond is enough. It doesn't have to be an involved story. In fact, the most common encounter might be summarized: An Agent stumbles upon something beyond conception and runs away. Some stories are deeper. Others are personal. But more complex and meaningful stories should be created only by experienced players or with the careful oversight of the Handler. First-time players should keep it short and sweet.

» **HOW DID THE AGENT COME TO THE ATTENTION OF DELTA GREEN?:** This is where the Agent becomes a functioning member of Delta Green. How did it happen? Did they report what they saw and get picked up by Delta Green? Were they rescued by Delta Green from an impossible situation? Did they stumble upon something they were never supposed to see and solve some issue so that Delta Green was impressed? Work with your players to make it clear where their Agents stand in Delta Green.

Interpreting the Rules

As Handler, you're responsible for what happens at the table, and the story that emerges from the Agents' actions. You are referee for the rules, whether they're from the *Agent's Handbook* or the *Handler's Guide*. Your players are counting on you to learn them well.

An Example of Play

Amber is playing FBI Special Agent Cornwell. Tabitha is playing Dr. Palmer, an anthropology professor who advises the FBI on unusual cases. Cornwell and Palmer belong to Delta Green, which sends them to investigate suspected incursions of terrifying, unnatural forces—and to cover the incursions up to protect everyone else from awful dangers.

Cornwell and Palmer have been seeking the hideout of a cult that seems to have ties to unnatural, inhuman forces. They figured out that it was someplace downtown. Then they heard on a police scanner that two cops were going to a derelict, downtown tenement after a complaint of screams and weird noises. The Agents drove over there fast and went inside. The Handler describes what they find.

HANDLER: "It's all run-down and water-damaged. It stinks of mold. It's very quiet and dark."

TABITHA: "I'm looking for anything strange."

HANDLER: "Things are quiet and under control right now, so you don't need to roll for that. Your Search skill is at least 40%, right? In the second tenement, you find especially weird graffiti."

TABITHA: "Weird, how? I have Anthropology at 70% and Occult at 80%."

HANDLER: "It's pictorial, almost like a cave painting but with spray-paint. You recognize human figures inside a blocky shape. Maybe a building. They're dancing around some crazy black form. It's drawn like the artist was having a seizure."

AMBER: "I keep going. We need to find the cops."

HANDLER: "Further in, the air starts to smell worse. Like blood and sewage. Do you keep looking?"

TABITHA: "We should leave."

AMBER: "No! Where are the damn cops?"

HANDLER: "You find them two doors down, in a living room where the floor has caved in. One is on his stomach, covered in blood. You think he's breathing. The other is...everywhere. It's like she exploded. Make a Sanity roll. If you fail, lose 1D6 Sanity Points."

AMBER: "Jesus. No kidding. I have 60 SAN and I rolled...48. Success. OK, I yell out, 'Palmer!'"

TABITHA: "Fine. I run over. Don't ask me why."

AMBER: "I pull the live one out of there."

HANDLER: "Something erupts from the wreckage."

TABITHA: "I told you we should leave!"

HANDLER: "It's like crumbled plaster, wood chips, viscera and bone all adhering to an invisible shape. It rises up into some indefinable pattern. Make a Sanity roll. Lose 1D6 if you succeed or 1D10 if you fail."

AMBER: "I roll...66. Shit."

HANDLER: "Failure and matching dice, that's a critical failure. Lose the maximum possible, 10 Sanity Points. That's enough to go temporarily insane."

AMBER: "I'll try to reduce that by projecting onto a Bond. I'm doing this for my kids!"

HANDLER: "Sure you are. Roll 1D4. Take that much off your Willpower Points, and off the 10 points of SAN loss, and off the Bond."

AMBER: "I rolled...2. Come on! OK, so I spend 2 WP, and take 2 off the Bond with the kids. I guess I'm going to be a worse parent after this. And that reduces the SAN loss to 8."

HANDLER: "That's still enough loss for temporary insanity. You lose control of yourself. Palmer, you come around the corner and see all this horror. I'll get to your SAN loss in a minute. You see Cornwell scream and raise her shotgun to fire. But Cornwell, your Dexterity is 11, right? That's lower than the... thing's...so it goes first. It has a 50% chance to hit and rolls...12."

AMBER: "Can I dodge?"

HANDLER: "You're insane, remember? Sorry, you're trying to shoot. Its damage roll is...ouch. 17."

AMBER: "I can take off 3 for my body armor. That's still 14 damage. I only have 12 Hit Points."

HANDLER: "Yeah. Palmer, you see the weird shape slam into Cornwell like a snake striking. That cuts off her screams instantly and she just falls apart. There's blood everywhere. Some of her adheres to the other gore and debris around the shape. The rest of her spatters all over you and the room. The shape takes on some new, inscrutable configuration for an instant. Then it turns toward you. Roll Sanity."

TABITHA: "Uh. Yeah. I roll 20. Success."

HANDLER: "OK. I'll roll for how much you lose. Only 4! Lucky you. What do you do?"

// The Past //

OK. Sure. First. OK. Listen. Innsmouth. It began in Innsmouth, Massachusetts in nineteen hundred and twenty-eight. Write that down. It began there, but it didn't end there. Fuck. It's still going on. Right now. No doubt.

OK. Sure. You've heard rumors. That fucking silver hubcap in the desert in forty-whatever. True. The things the Nazis were calling at the bottom of the ocean? Also true. That city beneath the ice in the Antarctic. Fucking take three guesses. It's a big goddamn world, and we don't know shit.

How do I know? Me? I worked in this place. This was in the Fifties, so, you know, you wouldn't understand. We had our shit strapped down. We knew what was what. I was a file clerk. Just a kid who worked in a library and joined the Marines to fight some fucking Commies. Left in 1954, short about half my nerve. Got a job in Naval Intelligence because I pulled some geezer off the line and got him to a field hospital, and that guy...well, he was fucking connected. That job was just about heaven.

I'd file in the day and I'd file at night. "Do this, Don," and so, you know, I'd do it. Sometimes, I'd go in after hours to finish up and read. I read a lot of the files.

Then, one day my boss comes in the dry room where we keep all the old stuff. I'm filing. He's holding a fire axe. The axe looks like it's covered in Hershey's syrup, but I figure out right quick it's blood. I'm fast that way. He says to me, "Don." I say, "Yessir." He had the axe, right? He says, "You want to know a secret?"

"OK."

He says, "Something owns us."

He holds the door for me, like, nice, and so I go. And when the door shuts, I hear him just open up. I mean, just screaming and smashing the shit out of everything. He was a smart guy, my boss. Not prone to violence. Not an unkind word in years. But he read everything. Every file that crossed that threshold. "Knowledge is power," he'd say to me. "Knowledge, Don, that's the key."

And he was fucking goddamn right. But a key to what?

AX 52-2392
2

6 January 1975

MEMORANDUM FOR: Inspector General

SUBJECT: MKULTRA

CIA Document

Delta Green's official existence began on 16 JUN 1942, when the DELTA GREEN security clearance was established for a psychological warfare unit within the Office of Strategic Services. Although the OSS was disbanded at the end of the war, the security clearance lived on. For 23 years, Delta Green continued operation under the guise of a Cold War psychological warfare unit, keeping its true activities secret from the Pentagon.

On 24 JUL 1970, after a disastrous operation in Cambodia brought Delta Green to the attention of the powers-that-be, the security clearance was retired and the office disbanded. For the next three decades, former Delta Green operatives fought to recover the group's official status and bring it back into the intelligence community, all the while operating within the government as a secret conspiracy, without official sanction.

It came back into the government fold in 2002, but not everyone thought that was the right move. Sanction would bring scrutiny, and with it a greater possibility of spreading the infection of the unnatural. Even after the reactivation of the DELTA GREEN security clearance on 13 SEP 2002, and the creation of Delta Green as a new black-ops project ("the Program") masquerading as a counterterrorism task force, many in the group believed it was a mistake.

Among those who know Delta Green's secrets, there is little consensus regarding the past, present, or future of the organization. The one thing they can agree upon is that the history of Delta Green began much earlier than those dark days of World War II.

Genesis

The group that would become Delta Green was born of a 1920s federal raid on the town of Innsmouth, Massachusetts. When U.S. Treasury Department agents investigated that out-of-the-way Massachusetts town and discovered the population was involved in crimes that ranged from the merely murderous to the genuinely inhuman, they were at a loss. Having once ordered a round-up of "Reds" while serving as governor of Massachusetts, President Calvin Coolidge authorized a raid on Innsmouth to root out the degenerate heathens that had been quietly terrorizing the area for decades. The Department of the Navy—in the form of the Office of Naval Intelligence—guided the U.S. Marine Corps and the U.S. Coast Guard, who would provide firepower. Significantly, those three agencies were not specifically banned from carrying out domestic law enforcement duties under the 1878 Posse Comitatus Act. To add legal authority, the Justice Department's Bureau of Investigation, led by J. Edgar Hoover, was brought in to oversee the seizure of the "suspected alien seditionists" for deportation. Organizational delays resulted in the raid being launched on 23 FEB 1928.

Following the round-up of the strange religious order of which all townsfolk were members—the Esoteric Order of Dagon—the Treasury Department presented President Coolidge with photographic evidence of the "curiously debased condition" of Innsmouth's population. This ranged from birth defects such as webbed toes and fingers and odd skin ailments to fully alien biologies, creatures that shared a somewhat human build but who were totally inhuman. The people of Innsmouth called them "Deep Ones." Even more disturbing, it seemed that the people of Innsmouth *bred with* such creatures, and over time changed into these grotesque beings.

Artifacts demonstrating a pagan religion amongst the townspeople were also presented to the president and his cabinet. The Office of Naval Intelligence waited to present its full report until everything gathered could be analyzed, but in light of the initial evidence, the Coolidge administration decided to detain the affected population indefinitely. After all, there was no rush. In the short term, the Innsmouth problem had been solved.

ONI dispersed the 209 captive Deep One hybrids into military

stockades and federal prisons across the country, and subjected many to interrogation. ONI also seized the ship's log of the *Sumatra Queen*, belonging to prominent Innsmouth citizen Obed Marsh. They took a Marsh family history dated to 1862, badly burned scriptures of their inhuman faith, and five 24-kg conical stone tablets inscribed with bizarre glyphs. They found incomplete notes for translating the glyphs, compiled over many years by prominent Innsmouth resident Robert Marsh, who had been killed during the raid.

Unable to decipher much of what it found, ONI turned to the Black Chamber for help.

ASSET: Patient 24199

Hundreds of townsfolk from Innsmouth—some human, others less so—were captured and detained in the 1928 raid, and careful attention was paid by agencies to track and account for all of them. The Marines who served on the raid were another matter entirely. The unnatural horrors seen in Innsmouth were not as easy to dismiss as the more mundane terrors of combat. Some Marines went mad. Some committed suicide. Others fled. Those killed in action were listed as casualties in the various Central American "banana wars," while the others scattered across the world in search of some semblance of peace. Today, only one survives.

Private Arthur J. Macready, U.S. Marines, slipped through the cracks. At the time of the raid Macready was 46, and a combat veteran who had served in World War I and in the occupation of Nicaragua. He was also the first through the door into the Esoteric Order of Dagon and was responsible for the destruction of the clay sigil which hung there as the center of worship. From that point on, Macready was not right.

Originally committed in February 1928 to Harrison Psychiatric Hospital for mental exhaustion and shock, he was transferred to state care at Danvers State Hospital in 1955. In 1978, he was moved to another facility in Vermont—Powell Green—where he remains today.

The last transfer was unusual. He was brought by military police, and committed as a John Doe, with only an ID number (24199). His age was unlisted. His benefactor is the Office of Naval Intelligence who, through an obscure and recurring piece of red tape buried in their files, still pays his bills.

Macready appears to be a man in his mid-sixties, covered in filth and sputtering expletives and odd, guttural chants. In 2017, Macready is 134 years old and is a full convert to the worship of 'Tulu, the creature who has haunted his every waking thought since he broke that sigil on 23 FEB 1928.

TOP SECRET//SAR-DELTA GREEN

NOTABLE EVENTS

- **15 JUL 1927:** Robert Martin Olmstead travels from Newburyport to Innsmouth, Massachusetts. He meets Zadok Allen, a 96-year-old homeless drunk with wild tales of miscegenation with undersea Deep Ones and the worship of strange South Seas gods. Forced to stay overnight in Innsmouth, Olmstead witnesses the inhuman nature of Innsmouth's residents as he flees the town, realizing the truth of Allen's tales.
- **17 JUL 1927:** Robert Martin Olmstead tells government officials in Arkham of his experience in Innsmouth. He tells authorities in Boston. His testimony leads to a federal investigation of Innsmouth. Aerial film footage is taken of Innsmouth and Devils Reef (footage that required censoring), while undercover agents infiltrate the town and take photos from within.
- **1 FEB 1928:** In the course of the Innsmouth investigation, the Navy issues a standing directive requiring any unusual activity reported within five nautical miles of Devils Reef to be immediately classified and reported to the P4 desk of the Office of Naval Intelligence.
- **23 FEB 1928:** The 42nd Marine Battalion arrives in the Boston Naval Annex, having been transported from Punta Gorda in Nicaragua to take part in Project PUZZLEBOX (as Delta Green renames it in 1942), a combined operation of the Navy, the Treasury Department, and the Bureau of Investigation, to clear Innsmouth of "seditious aliens" that have taken over the town. The forces of Project PUZZLEBOX fight the insane cultists and Deep Ones of Innsmouth for days, with the battle finally ending with the launch of torpedoes at the undersea city of Y'ha-nthlei. Two hundred and nine prisoners are taken into federal custody and incarcerated without trial in concentration camps.

The Black Chamber

The Black Chamber was the nickname of a joint War Department and State Department signals intelligence and cryptography unit. It operated during World War I as Section 8 of Military Intelligence (MI-8), and after 1919 as the Cipher Bureau.

The Black Chamber provided communications security for the American delegation during the 1919 Versailles negotiations. Later, at the 1922 Washington Naval Conference, they broke the Japanese code and provided crucial intelligence to the American negotiators. As the U.S. government's premier, secret, cryptographic organization, the Black Chamber was ONI's first choice to handle the translation of the materials captured in Innsmouth. In April 1928, the Black Chamber took possession of the papers and strange tablets recovered there. Despite their expertise, it took two years for the cryptographers to complete the translation. On 2 NOV 1929, they presented their report on what had come to be called the *Book of Dagon* to the newly elected president, Herbert Hoover.

This was the first Hoover had heard of Innsmouth, and 1929 had already been a difficult year. First, it was revealed during a crucial summit that the Black Chamber intercepted Japanese diplomatic radio traffic, and the Japanese were repudiating the naval limits of the Washington Naval Conference. Second, following the St. Valentine's Day Massacre, the president was

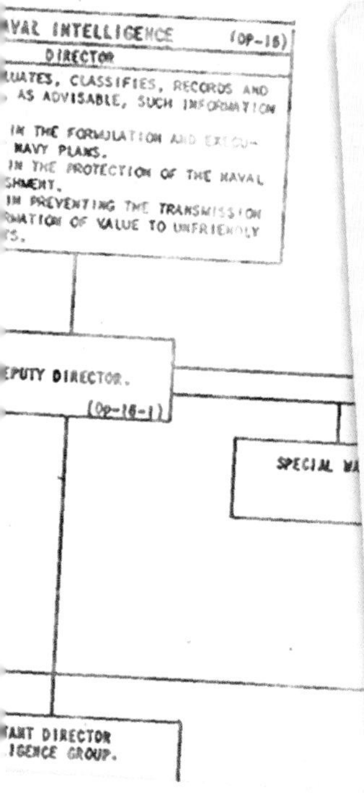

DISINFORMATION

YELLOW CARD

THE INNSMOUTH "TAINT"

The infection of Innsmouth, Massachusetts by the Deep Ones was a textbook case of an attempted integration with a surface culture. Though the "taint" did not take as well as in other areas (such as Ponape and Black Cod Island) it did successfully find a foothold and infected nearly the entire town.

For 88 years this integration grew in complexity. Eventually it was an open secret among the non-hybrid inhabitants that the town was in league with the creatures who lived off Devils Reef. Obed Marsh and his compatriots brought much of the town over to the degenerate worship of the Deep Ones through the Esoteric Order of Dagon – a bastardized mix of Christianity and the Cthulhu myth-cycle – as well as the promise of immortality. For many, these promises proved fruitful. For others, the price of transformation was too high.

In 1846 the first "plague" struck, killing half the population of the town. This plague was simply the misfiring of genetics in the population infected by the Deep Ones. (See **THE DEEP ONE REPRODUCTIVE ELEMENT** on page 195.) These individuals died horrible deaths as the reproductive element twisted their forms and biology, moving them away from human but no closer to Deep One. Throughout the history of Innsmouth there have been reports of genetic deformities, disease and monstrosities which were once human. These incidents represent the poor assimilation of the Deep One reproductive element into Innsmouth genetic stock. Over the decades, the disease made greater and greater genetic inroads in the population.

CUT ALONG THIS LINE

in Algeria in 1993, the GIA has killed
Europeans—in the country. The grou
bombs, and it is known to favor kidna
hijacked an Air France flight to Algiers
bers were convicted by a French court
1995.

The Salafi Group for Call and Combat (
the GIA since approximately 1998 and is
remaining armed group inside Algeria. B
proclaim their rejection of President Bout
GSPC has stated that it limits attacks on
Paris-Dakar Road Rally in January 2000 d
entirely renounced attacks against

TOP SECRET

DISINFORMATION

YELLOW CARD

THE GREATER DEEP ONES

With the federal raid in the winter of 1928, and the government seizure of 209 townsfolk for study, the U.S. government thought it had a strong grasp of the situation at Innsmouth: the town was communing with an underwater culture, crossbreeding with them to produce horrific entities known as the Deep Ones. The government men believed they had in their possession examples of the creatures which had founded the ancient city in the depths near Devils Reef. They believed that the torpedo attack on the underwater city had destroyed it.

They were wrong.

The most powerful Deep Ones (see **DEEP ONE (GREATER)** on page 191) resided far beneath the waves, rarely coming to the surface. The raid on Innsmouth failed to capture or kill even a single "greater" Deep One. Although Delta Green has had various contacts with the Deep Ones over the decades, and prominent Delta Green leaders have studied the Deep Ones obsessively, they have very rarely encountered a so-called Greater Deep One. And when they have encountered one and overcome it, its corpse was in no shape to be properly identified.

Instead, nearly all human contact with the Deep Ones has been through the much more common "lesser" Deep Ones, the mostly-human hybrids or the more fully transformed creatures of the sea. Even in Innsmouth, only the first few infections were passed along by the Greater Deep Ones. Their human victims infected the rest of the town, creating a self-sustaining blight that moved from parent to child, gaining more and more ground in altering their genes as time went on. By the early 1840s, Greater Deep Ones only rose to the shallows off Innsmouth for rituals, and never strayed far from the sea.

This has always been deliberate on the part of the Deep Ones. Hybrids are expendable tools to influence the surface world, spread Deep One seed, and bring tribute. Very few Greater Deep Ones ever interact with humans.

The absolutely inhuman nature of the Greater Deep Ones may come as a disturbing surprise to Agents who think they have clear understanding of the Deep Ones. The overconfidence of that mistake can prove fatal.

CUT ALONG THIS LINE

031-51937 o-46

a. (U//FOUO

(1) (S//F

(5) (U

under intense pressure to bring Al Capone to justice and was increasingly displeased with the Treasury and Justice Department's failures. And last, on 24 OCT 1929, the stock market crashed.

When the Black Chamber presented its findings less than a week after "Black Tuesday," the exhausted President Hoover was in a less than receptive mood. It was his opinion that "these eggheads," had *already* ruined a perfectly good treaty with Japan and now were telling fairy tales about monsters under the sea. He ordered Secretary of State Henry L. Stimson to disband the organization. Using the Washington Naval Conference scandal as cover, Stimson shut the group down. As he wrote in a 1948 memoir, "Gentlemen don't read each other's mail."

J. Edgar Hoover, the ambitious director of the Bureau of Investigation, saw the writing on the wall and redacted his previous reports on the Innsmouth raid, stating that he personally observed nothing that could not be explained through conventional science. The town was filled with inbred bootleggers and anarchists. Nothing more.

TOP SECRET//SAR-DELTA GREEN

- **28 FEB 1928:** Private Arthur J. Macready, driven mad by what he saw in the Innsmouth raid, is committed to Harrison Psychiatric Hospital in Vermont for mental exhaustion and shock.
- **1 MAR 1928:** The prisoners taken during Project PUZZLEBOX are tested for abnormalities. Those cleared as human are released, while the Deep One hybrids are sent to various naval and military prisons. While the operation was disguised as a Prohibition raid, one tabloid newspaper carries a story of the torpedo attack beyond Devils Reef, and several liberal organizations complain of the treatment of prisoners taken at Innsmouth. These protests cease after confidential meetings with government officials and supervised tours to see the prisoners.
- **3 APR 1928:** Conical stone tablets identified as the *Book of Dagon* and other papers recovered from Innsmouth are handed over to the Black Chamber for deciphering and translation.
- **29 OCT 1929:** Five days after panicked investors begin selling stock in record numbers, the stock market crashes completely on Black Tuesday, the worst day in the history of the United States stock market for the next 58 years. The Great Depression ensues, destroying the economy of nearly every industrialized nation in the world.
- **2 NOV 1929:** The Black Chamber presents its completed translation of the *Book of Dagon* to President Herbert Hoover.
- **5 NOV 1929:** President Hoover orders the Black Chamber closed.
- **12 NOV 1929:** The Innsmouth files, as well as Innsmouth veteran personnel, are folded under the command of an obscure desk in the Office of Naval Intelligence called P4.

ONI wasn't blind to the administration's mood, and they *also* distanced themselves from the Black Chamber's report. Still, elements of the Navy clearly recognized the threat that a hostile aquatic civilization posed to U.S. naval supremacy. The Treasury Department, the Justice Department, and the White House could delude themselves, but the Navy could not. To continue their investigations of the Innsmouth threat, the Navy got creative.

ONI's P4 Desk

In World War One, the Office of Naval Intelligence established an obscure research group called the Parapsychology, Paranormal, and Psychic Phenomena Desk—abbreviated to P4—to study inexplicable phenomena that might impact the war. It once had a staff of nearly 50. By 1928, it had withered to two desk-bound Navy officers and a support staff of six. Its officers spent their time clipping world newspaper articles on ghosts, psychic oddities, and spiritual phenomena, only very occasionally passing something up to headquarters. Other ONI desks, assembling files of intelligence on the navies of the world, thought P4 was a joke.

In 1929, the P4 Desk suddenly found itself in command of a strange group of cryptographers and combat troops. First came a few Black Chamber codebreakers who had translated the *Book of Dagon*. They were now hidden at P4 so their work might continue. Later, P4 was handed a small force of Marines and a detachment of Treasury agents, almost entirely Innsmouth veterans. This became the backbone of the Navy's response to the horrors it uncovered.

The Navy had learned an important lesson at Innsmouth, one it would pass down to generations of Delta Green agents to come: "Never tell a president anything you don't have to."

When ONI re-staffed P4 with this odd mix, it set its new mission, as well: to scour the world for inhuman beings like those found in Innsmouth.

At first, not everyone at P4 was convinced that there were other such horrors; but the Deep One-human hybrids in custody at a secret Arizona compound were an unpleasant reminder nothing was impossible. The search would lead to a wider picture of unnatural *things* living in the benighted depths of the sea.

Studying and interrogating the prisoners revealed little. But those that died in captivity were subjected to extensive post-mortem examinations, proving definitively that many were something other than human. Navy expeditions took P4 personnel across the globe searching for colonies like Innsmouth.

They soon found them.

The next Deep One colony was discovered in 1930, on a small island in the Philippines. A raid by P4 Marines and Filipino scouts shattered the island's defenses and rounded up Deep One hybrids. When the general location of the undersea portion of the colony was ascertained, the Navy pulverized it with depth charges. Filipino Muslims from nearby islands, long having suffered the hybrids' depredations, finished off those that escaped.

In 1933, during the American occupation of Nicaragua, another colony was discovered on that country's Pacific coast. Operating among Marines assigned to track the anti-U.S. rebel Augusto Sandino, P4 officers discovered a fishing village that had just begun to adopt the teachings of the Esoteric Order of Dagon. Their intervention was bungled. P4 relied on Nicaraguan dictator Anastasio Somoza's National Guard to handle initial contact. Horrified by the alien nature of many of the villagers, the National Guardsmen massacred the village and put it to the torch. The P4 officers had to move swiftly to sanitized the site and recover several dozen artifacts to move to the United States. Nearby reefs, considered likely sites for Deep One colonies, were hit with depth charges and torpedoed.

Near Innsmouth, P4 officers used a ritual recovered in their raids to make contact with Deep Ones,

THREAT MATRIX

RED CA

PORTRAYING THE DEEP ONES

To many players, the Deep Ones are old hat. In Delta Green, they are the oldest and most persistent known threat to human civilization. How do you maintain a sense of fear at the table when Deep Ones are encountered?

The issue is familiarity. Players who understand the the creatures, their motivations, and their stats become bored. A predictable threat is not a threat. Something understood and quantified cannot play upon your fears. As a Handler, you must breathe new life into the old fish-men to make them something to fear.

- **HYBRIDS ARE PEOPLE:** They're not all hobbling, deformed monsters. They live their lives just like us until the taint takes them. They use vehicles, cellphones, and guns just as readily as any agent. Most are slightly off-looking people who are a little insane and will do anything to return to the sea. But they also have to pay the T-Mobile bill and buy groceries. Make them as sympathetic as you can, and as cunning, sneaky, and rash as any human being in desperate straits.
- **SECRETS OF THE GREATER DEEP ONES:** Even Delta Green, with all its experience with the Deep One threat, is completely unaware that the monsters they have seen are not true Deep Ones, but only vessels to carry the Deep One taint. Completely inhuman Greater Deep Ones, unlike any Earthly life, lurk in the oceans, and occasionally surface to commune with their infected offspring. This discovery is a great way to make the players rethink everything they think they know.
- **NO UPWARD LIMIT:** Deep Ones have no upward limit in size. Father Dagon, Mother Hydra, and He-Who-Swims-With-Corpses are but a few of the huge masters of their species. An Agent might use a hypergeometric ritual to call a Deep One to the surface for ambush only to face a godlike monster that stands six meters tall.
- **DEEP ONES ARE ALIEN:** The further along in the process of transformation, the more in tune with the alien nature of the Deep Ones a hybrid becomes. To truly become one with the Deep Ones is to abandon any semblance of human order and sanity. Savage violence is the most expedient answer to any Deep One question. Morality, sanity, and truth are as meaningless to an immortal Deep One as the ticking of a clock.
- **DEEP ONE PLANS ARE LONG:** For all their violence, the Deep Ones are intelligent, and their leaders have goals that humanity could never comprehend. Their threat does not operate in years or decades but **epochs**. Immortal entities have time to think and re-think their bizarre plans. What might appear to be their main goal – such as interbreeding with humanity – could be nothing but a thousand-year feint to cover some actual, unknown, much more terrible purpose.

CUT ALONG THIS LINE

031-51937 0-46

with the purpose of acquiring more samples for study. While none were taken alive, numerous damaged specimens were acquired for dissection. Many in P4 felt that if ambushed often enough, the Deep Ones would be deterred from answering such a "summons" by their hybrid allies. Some officers passed inquiries up the chain of command for other, more dangerous rituals to attempt, but none were permitted.

P4 also conducted operations in the continental U.S. against groups that it determined were engaged in "unconventional dangerous activities." Overworked and underfunded, P4 investigators often arrived after action by local authorities had already taken place, and could only cover up the mess.

Many clues recovered by P4—both from seized correspondence and from suspects captured at cult rituals—pointed towards the Pacific and Asia as the source of the cult which remained known, in the West, as the Esoteric Order of Dagon.

TOP SECRET//SAR-DELTA GREEN

» **29 DEC 1929:** The Deep One hybrids taken at Innsmouth are relocated from the military and naval prisons where they were originally held to a purpose-built facility disguised as a Naval Air Station in southeastern Arizona, later code-named YY-II. Sometime thereafter most prisoners fall into a catatonic state.

» **2 JAN 1930:** In Operation TALCUM, P4 raids the Philippines island of Piedra Negra, taking 500 prisoners and a trove of artifacts related to the Esoteric Order of Dagon.

» **2 SEP 1930:** The Miskatonic University Expedition departs for a geological and biological study of Antarctica, led by geologist William Dyer. The expedition lands in November and explores the Antarctic for two months. Disaster strikes when its researchers uncover long-dormant Elder Things, and then an Elder Thing city and a monstrous shoggoth. P4 arranges with the university to suppress reports of those discoveries and discourage further exploration.

» **24 NOV 1930:** Robert Martin Olmstead, having returned to normal life at Oberlin College in Ohio, begins having dreams...

» **21 DEC 1930:** Robert M. Olmstead attempts to publicly share the full account of his experience in Innsmouth. Having embraced his Deep One heritage, Olmstead frees his cousin Lawrence from the sanitarium in Canton, Ohio, and takes him to Devils Reef off Innsmouth, where they join their ancestors in the Deep One city of Y'ha-nthlei.

» **29 APR 1931:** In Russia, GRU SV-8 is officially founded in secret to monitor unnatural threats against (and within) the Soviet Union.

- **9 JAN 1933:** P4 raids the Nicaraguan fishing village of Agua Verde on the Mosquito Coast (Operation BAKELITE). The operation is a debacle as the entire village is prematurely massacred by Guardia Nacional troops loaned to P4 by the Nicaraguan dictator Anastasio Somoza. Hints point towards an unknown city called Yian-Ho, possibly in China, as the source of the cult.
- **17 FEB 1933:** P4 officer Lester Dean and 22 men enter the wilds of China to locate the mystical city of Yian-Ho (Operation THIMBLE), claimed by multiple sources to be the origin of the teachings which formed the basis of the Esoteric Order of Dagon.
- **9 MAY 1934:** Lester Dean stumbles into a Chinese village on the Yangtze babbling about a secret city in the mountains. The Office of Naval Intelligence commits him to the nearest friendly madhouse, a British institution in Hong Kong. Due to this disaster, P4 confines its investigations to the United States.
- **7 JAN 1935:** In Germany, Heinrich Himmler, leader of the SS, establishes Sonderkommando-H, a special group tasked with searching for evidence that the medieval witch trials in Germany were part of a covert Christian program to destroy vestiges of the ancient Aryan religion. This research is collated into a card catalogue of over thirty-thousand entries, each detailing a victim of the German witch trials, which becomes known as the Hexenkartothek.
- **9 MAY 1938:** Lester Dean, former P4 agent, dies in Hong Kong's Victoria Mental Hospital, shrieking about "grey men from the future."
- **2 JAN 1939:** Having discovered an arcane formula for the "resuscitating of ye vital saylts," during their search of the medieval records, a section of Sonderkommando-H uses the formula to revive the corpse of Jürgen Tess, a seventeenth-century sorcerer. Heinrich Himmler immediately orders the creation of the Karotechia, a special department answerable only to the Reichsführer-SS, to research and exploit the occult for military purposes.
- **19 JAN 1939:** The third Deutsche Antarktik Expedition (German Antarctic Expedition) arrives on the Princess Martha Coast of Antarctica and begins charting the region.
- **8 MAR 1939:** The German scout aircraft *Boreas* from the Deutsche Antarktik Expedition locates an unusually-shaped hole in the ice shelf which looks artificial.
- **12 MAR 1939:** German explorers from the Deutsche Antarktik Expedition land and locate the hole on the ground. Inside, they find the ruins of a seemingly abandoned, vast, pre-human city.

CAPT 483578
CDR 444086

YIAN-HO

Delta Green has encountered the Kuen-Yuin cult which apparently resides at Yian-Ho numerous times, from the Yangtze River station in the 1930s to the Korean and Vietnam conflicts, to a lengthy investigation of seeming Chinese espionage (1997–2008). Despite these contacts, investigation has not determined whether the Kuen-Yuin actually head the Cthulhu cult or vice versa, or if they are something else entirely. (See **THE QUÁNYÒUYĪN OR KUEN-YUIN** on page 120.)

It is unknown if the primordial Lemurian (or Lengi) city in the mountains of western China (or of Xinjiang) is the Earthly reflection, or the true form, or the anchor, of the city of Yian, "where the great river winds under the thousand bridges – where the gardens are sweet scented, and the air is filled with the music of silver bells."

Yian may also be a memetic construct built by the Yithians or the Lloigor and impressed onto human minds as a "back door" into other, non-terrestrial or even non-physical realms.

- Chinese lore says the "Maker of Moons" Yue-Laou dwells in Yian-Ho, where he commands the sorcerous Kuen-Yuin cult and the hideous Xin. Yue-Laou and the Kuen-Yuin are immortal; their emblem is a golden globe engraved with reptiles or serpents.
- The Dutch sorcerer Claes van der Heyl reputedly entered Yian-Ho around 1570.
- The magician Dirck van der Heyl may have opened a gateway to Yian-Ho in upstate New York around 1760, near the town of Chorazin.
- Von Junzt's traveling companion Gottfried Mülder entered Yian-Ho in 1818, where he read the **Ghorl Nigral**.
- In 1896, Franklyn Barris of the Secret Service claimed the Kuen-Yuin masterminded the "Shiner" gold-counterfeiting plot broken up by the Service in New York. Barris disappeared during that investigation; he had previously traveled extensively in China, reportedly in search of Yian.
- Informants captured in the 1907 St. Bernard Parish raid claim that "deathless Chinamen" direct the cult of Cthulhu from the "mountains of China."
- The Polish mystic Ossendowski (1922) describes the scarlet-robed Tchortcha guardians of Yian-Ho, and their "Song of Thirty-Thousand Calamities."
- Between 1997 and 2008, Delta Green operations against targets that became known as the "Grey Men" led agents deep into central China, in search of a gate to an unknown country known as Tsan-Chan. It ended with Operation HOLSTEIN and the death of seven agents in an explosion in Anchongxiang, China which nearly sparked an international incident.

CUT ALONG THIS LINE

031-51937 0-46

...1830132
...IFICATION TOP SECRET / MA...
CIRCULATION WITHIN RESTRICTED C...
DO NOT COPY
PAGE 1 OF 2
PRIORITY: IMMEDIATE

DTG RELEASE: 281455Z JAN 49

PREPARED FOR: MSSG-1 at Wright A...

- **14 MAR 1939:** By order of Himmler, all findings of the Deutsche Antarktik Expedition are brought under the command of the Karotechia. The abandoned city's location is designated Point 103.
- **10 MAY 1939:** In strange books of disreputable history and occultism, the Karotechia discover repeated references to an ancient undersea race called the Deep Ones. They research the Deep Ones aggressively.
- **1 JUN 1939:** The Karotechia launch Aktion EISSCHLOSS (Operation ICE PALACE) to investigate the lost city found by the Deutsche Antarktik Expedition. Accessible only by submarine, Point 103 gradually grows to house 22 archaeologists, cryptographers, and experts in ancient languages. Point 103 is placed under the command of Dr. Walter Kluge, who quickly ascertains that the lost city was built millions of years before by alien, plant-like creatures.
- **1 SEP 1939:** With the invasion of Poland by Germany two days before, Britain and France declare war on Germany. World War II has begun.
- **29 DEC 1939:** Heinrich Himmler issues a secret order signed by Hitler establishing Karotechia Project SCHWARZES WASSER ("BLACK WATER"). The goal is to use magical formulae in an ancient tome called *Tenebrosa Aqua ("Dark Water")* to contact and make alliance with a loathsome but powerful race of subhumans called the Deep Ones. Over the next few months, the team decodes four Polynesian "calling rituals" while building a diplomatic primer for dealings with the Deep Ones.
- **1 MAY 1940:** Amanda Chalmers, a British psychic who left MI-13 after the First World War, reports a premonition of the advance of Germany's Army Group B into Belgium as an elaborate feint to draw British and French forces in and cut them off. The prediction is dismissed, but the leader of MI-13, Major David Cornwall, places it in a sealed envelope and sends it to the office of the prime minister, with instructions for the envelope to only be opened on 5 JUN 1940.
- **2 MAY 1940:** The Red Orchestra spy network infiltrates the Ancestral Heritage Research and Teaching Foundation, or Ahnenerbe, and passes on knowledge of the existence of the Sonderkommando-H to GRU SV-8.

- **10 MAY 1940:** Germany invades Belgium, the Netherlands and France. By 22 JUN 1940, most of Europe is under German control.
- **5 JUN 1940:** The envelope with Amanda Chalmers' 1 MAY 1940 predictions is opened at Prime Minister Winston Churchill's office. The predictions convince Churchill of the value of MI-13's psychic reconnaissance.
- **26 JUN 1940:** Prime Minister Churchill reorganizes MI-13 into an interagency task force jointly supported by the SIS, MI-5, and the Ministry of Economic Warfare, but reporting directly to the Prime Minister. MI-13 is re-designated PISCES: the Paranormal Intelligence Section for Counterintelligence, Espionage and Sabotage. David Cornwall moves his headquarters from Whitehall to Kilmaur Manor in the Scottish highlands.
- **29 JUN 1940:** PISCES opens offices in the British Museum to study occult tomes collected in the King's Library. Over the next three years, 12 books are identified as having unnatural significance, including the Latin *Necronomicon* and the Pnakotic Manuscripts. Over the course of the war, five researchers go insane, one commits suicide, and another disappears in the London Underground.
- **12 NOV 1940:** Operation SCHWARZES WASSER relocates from Offenburg to Cap de la Hague on the Normandy coast, following a lead in *Tenebrosa Aqua* about a Deep One colony in that area. A large 40-man facility is constructed and guarded by Wehrmacht troops, and nicknamed the Bootshaus ("Boathouse") due to the mistaken impression that it houses a mine-laying operation.
- **1 DEC 1940:** Rudolph Ladenburg, a German émigré and prominent atomic physicist, convinces the U.S. National Defense Research Committee and the Department of the Navy to establish Project RAINBOW for the development of stealth and defensive naval technologies. Based in Newark, New Jersey, Project RAINBOW recruits some of the most famous scientists and engineers in the United States, including Albert Einstein.

- **3 JAN 1941:** The Karotechia orders the SS to divert over a thousand Jewish prisoners headed for labor camps near Krakow to Cap de la Hague, Normandy, France, so that they might serve as "test subjects": sacrifices to the Deep Ones.
- **12 JAN 1941:** The NKVD occult research program (independent of GRU SV-8) begins experimentation on "proto-humans" (see **GHOULS** on page 198) that have been captured for study of their superhuman abilities. As a breeding facility is established outside Gur'yev on the Caspian Sea, the researchers discover that a cult has emerged among ghouls in the Soviet Union that worships Stalin as the "Great Provider."
- **27 MAR 1941:** Operation SCHWARZES WASSER's first experiment succeeds, as a section of the water off Cap de la Hague begins to glow a vivid greenish-blue following the use of one of the "calling rituals" found in *Tenebrosa Aqua*. The episode is captured on camera by a Wehrmacht film crew, and samples of the water and the strange algae that produced the glow are sent to the Stuttgart Technical College.

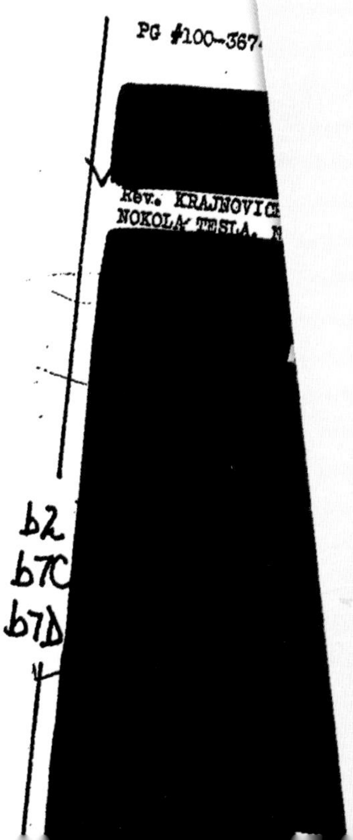

DISINFORMATION

YELLOW CARD

THE BROTHERHOOD OF THE OCEAN

In the modern era, nothing remains of the original Esoteric Order of Dagon but lone madmen, lost individuals enraptured by the dream call, and some few twisted by unnatural texts who worship Cthulhu.

The Brotherhood of the Ocean is different; it is not even a real organization, and its "members" wouldn't even know its name. This unofficial group's members are scattered on ships at sea across the globe, bound by an almost mystical pull of the ocean. Many are lifelong sailors, and more than a few have experienced trauma — violence, shipwreck, starvation, piracy, and worse — on the high seas. Each "member" reports salvation in dreams of "the master," who rules the waves, and who drew them back to the world to fulfill some purpose. To some, this is simply a dim idea, to others, it is **religion**.

If you asked, none would know that they were members of a group, but they feel an affinity for one another on sight, and sometimes are set upon by great, **terribly specific** notions. To travel to a particular port. To buy a particular book. To seek out a man they saw once in Barbados ten years back and beat him to death. If you plotted their travels, they would cut strange patterns across the globe, and when they made land, they would spin in duos and quartets, only to launch back out into the oceans, like a dance.

As if guided by a single mind.

CUT ALONG THIS LINE

» **19 APR 1941:** Without authorization, a Karotechia researcher in Operation SCHWARZES WASSER steals a boat, sails into the water outside Cap de la Hague, and speaks a chant from *Tenebrosa Aqua.* A guard shoots the man, but too late. Some sort of creature (or a creature's hand) rises out of the depths and pandemonium strikes. Nine soldiers are killed by friendly fire, 15 are hospitalized, and six are sent to a Karotechia sanitarium in Strasbourg. The researcher's body is never recovered.

» **26 APR 1941:** On a beach off Cap de la Hague, Operation SCHWARZES WASSER successfully calls a Deep One named "Claude" and proposes an alliance between the Nazis and the Deep Ones. "Claude" instructs them to use the calling ritual again at the next new moon, and to bring sacrifices.

DISINFORMATION

YELLOW CARD

PISCES, GRU SV-8, AND THE KAROTECHIA

P4 was not alone in their notice and pursuit of the unnatural. The horrors of the Great War awoke movements in both England and Russia to destroy, cover-up, capture, and study those things discovered that were beyond human understanding.

In Britain, in 1916, with the British Intelligence apparatus MI-6 pushed to the limit, the government looked in unusual places to curb the U-Boat threat which had a stranglehold on international shipping. They found Lt. Commander Frederick Ramsey and his stable of "Talents," intelligence analysts that claimed to possess psychic abilities allowing them to see remote locales, and even the future. By World War II, this force was designated MI-13, called PISCES: Paranormal Intelligence Section for Counter-intelligence, Espionage and Sabotage.

Likewise, in the Russian Civil War of 1918 to 1920, Russian intelligence encountered a cult of cannibalistic humanoids feeding on the dead: ghouls. From there, this small, secret group began to uncover more and more unnatural threats to the Motherland. By the beginning of World War II, this group was official: GRU SV-8, Glavnoye Razvedyvatelnoye Upravlenie Spetsialni Viedotstvo 8 ("Chief Intelligence Directorate of the General Staff, Special Department 8").

Later, by 1939, with the rising nationalistic fervor of the Nazi Party and its singular obsession with the occult, SS commander Heinrich Himmler had created a secret organization within the party to investigate and exploit the hidden power of the unnatural, called the Karotechia.

CUT ALONG THIS LINE

- **30 APR 1941:** Operation SCHWARZES WASSER sacrifices 37 mentally ill men and children to the Deep Ones in the first of several such exchanges. "Henri," the most-human-looking of the Deep Ones, remains as an emissary to present their terms: an 800-mile stretch of the French shore, as well as human women to serve as "surface breeding stock," in exchange for a commitment by the Deep Ones to bring a halt to all movement on the seas. After one week, Henri returns to his "family" and the pattern of call and sacrifice continues for the next 19 months, with neither side closer to an agreement.
- **1 SEP 1941:** SS-Standartenführer Karl Ohlendorf of the Karotechia is personally assigned by Heinrich Himmler to take part in Aktion EISSCHLOSS, due to Ohlendorf's career as a mining and combat engineer, amateur archaeologist, and youth in the Bavarian Alps. Ohlendorf sets sail aboard the commerce raider *Atlantis* and later makes a mid-oceanic transfer onto the submarine U-188.
- **4 OCT 1941:** Karl Ohlendorf arrives at Point 103 in Antarctica with his team of combat engineers.
- **6 NOV 1941:** Project RAINBOW, one of the earliest efforts to establish stealth technology, holds its first conference and develops sub-projects. One is Project MIRAGE, tasked with developing electronic devices to conceal naval craft. Dr. Arthur Turner is made the chief of Project MIRAGE, which is treated as a low priority and given little funding by the Navy due to their lack of confidence. Among the attendees at the conference is Vannevar Bush, director of the Office of Scientific Research and Development and a future founding member of MAJESTIC.
- **7 DEC 1941:** The Japanese attack the U.S. fleet at Pearl Harbor. The U.S. declares war on Japan the next day. Germany and Italy in turn declare war on the United States. World War II now spans the entire globe.
- **1 JAN 1942:** At Point 103, Karl Ohlendorf unearths an ancient power source that he names the "Thule Generator," which allows a wide-scale expansion of the base. A labor force of concentration camp prisoners is transported to Point 103 to support this expansion, and, after Ohlendorf learns that the Thule Generator requires regular feeding, he orders the prisoners be used as "fuel" for his machine.
- **5 JAN 1942:** The Karotechia acquire a translation of inscribed shards held by an African tribe and believed to have been originally written by a long-extinct alien race. The book is transported to Point 103, where it proves invaluable in deciphering the murals that line the walls of the underground necropolis.

The Office of Strategic Services

Even before the Japanese attack on Pearl Harbor, President Franklin D. Roosevelt had been consulting with Colonel William J. "Wild Bill" Donovan—a Congressional Medal of Honor winner and Wall Street lawyer—to organize a covert warfare arm of the U.S. military. As early as 1939, Donovan was scouring Ivy League universities, military intelligence branches and prisons for the requisite talent, even visiting England to obtain the advice of the English Secret Intelligence Service. In June 1942, the new intelligence service was christened the Office of Strategic Services, or OSS. It answered directly to the Joint Chiefs of Staff, and while its purpose was military intelligence, it was staffed by a large number of civilians. FBI director J. Edgar Hoover prevented the OSS from operating in the United States or Latin America, and General Douglas MacArthur similarly resisted the OSS's operating in "his" Pacific theater. The OSS therefore concentrated their efforts in Europe, North Africa, and mainland Asia, particularly in China, Burma, and Vietnam.

On 12 FEB 1942, Donovan—promoted to major general—was approached and briefed by Lt. Commander Martin Cook of P4. Lt. Commander Cook made Donovan aware of the Nazis' intense interest in the occult. P4 had uncovered an unnatural research department within the SS which had Reichsführer Himmler's ear: the Karotechia—a secret unit of the Ancestral Heritage Research and Teaching Foundation (abbreviated "Ahnenerbe" in German). The group's duties included archeological and anthropological research designed to support Nazi racial and political doctrine. It operated out of his headquarters at Wewelsburg Castle, a distorted, Nazi Camelot.

The Karotechia's mission was more serious, it devoted its research into the occult for anything that might assist the Nazi war effort. Cook did not acknowledge that P4's officers believed in the efficacy of unnatural rituals or the existence of non-human civilizations. Instead, Cook pointed out that British intelligence had lured Deputy Führer Rudolf Hess to Scotland by getting his personal astrologer to predict that he would singlehandedly capture England. Cook also pointed out Himmler's personal interest in the occult, as well as the superstitions held by high-ranking

DISINFORMATION

YELLOW CARD

THE SECRET ROOM

On 7 APR 1942, 16 prisoners, selected from Niederhagen and Sachsenhausen concentration camps due to their labor experience, were brought to Wewelsburg castle to complete a rush construction job under the order of Hermann Bartels, the castle's chief architect – and a member of the Karotechia.

For 21 days the prisoners worked, literally under the gun, to the odd specifications provided. This involved digging a six-meter-square cell beneath the Reichsführerzimmer room, the smelting of gold and silver to set in a precise pattern within the rock, as well as following dozens of other overly-specific instructions provided with hand-drawn diagrams.

In the end, when the prisoner work crew was finished on 28 APR 1942, they were executed inside the cell. No witnesses remain, and all records of the Karotechia were destroyed, but if a witness could be found, they would tell the following tale:

Two days later, on 30 APR 1942 – Walpurgisnacht – SS officers lowered an ancient, leaded coffin cut with sigils and runes into the corpse-filled cell. Something moved inside the coffin and shrieked inhumanly. Once the room was sealed, with the last rock inscribed with a single name in gold, the screaming ceased.

The name – inset in the floor above the undiscovered secret room to this day – is FRIEDRICH II. The mystery would be revisited on 23 DEC 1944.

ALONG THIS LINE

Japanese militarists. These, he claimed, could be exploited as a potent tool in the war effort.

Donovan was so impressed that he immediately moved to have P4 fully incorporated into the OSS. Cook agreed. The new group was given a special security clearance, DELTA GREEN. While P4 remained its official designation, soon its members began to refer to it as Delta Green.

IN THE FIELD: The Crucible Campaign

Before World War II, only the Office of Naval Intelligence and a few other select desks in the federal government had heard of Innsmouth. By 1942, it had been forgotten by everyone except for P4. For those others who knew the truth, forgetting it was just fine. There were bigger problems at hand, like a world war.

When Lt. Commander Cook brought P4 to the attention of Colonel Donovan and the OSS in 1942, it was only the beginning of a long plan to alert the leaders of the U.S. to the threat revealed by the raid on Innsmouth. Cook's initial pitch to Donovan was entirely conventional, and involved none of the more *outré* materials P4 had uncovered in its fourteen years of fighting the Deep Ones; that would come later. Donovan was first convinced he was bringing in an archaeological and anthropological group that could exploit the nonsensical lust the Nazi and Japanese seemed to have for the occult. Cook only gradually revealed the true horrors P4 had uncovered since 1928. When Donovan became aware of the depth of the situation, he kept such knowledge extremely close to his chest.

It is a prime time to set a Delta Green campaign. Those wishing to run a game set in the early days of the war should keep the following in mind:

- **SECRETS WITHIN SECRETS:** In 1942, Delta Green is a secret department within the OSS, a spy agency. But the secrets go even deeper: Delta Green knows the unnatural is *real* and, and that it is likely the Axis are attempting to use it to affect the war. In the beginning, even the commanders of the OSS and the president had no idea what P4 had truly uncovered. Of course, in time, this truth was revealed.
- **A FRAGILE BALANCE:** Lieutenant Commander Cook is a complex man, with a far-reaching plan to put his group front and center in the U.S. war effort. The fate of the world relies upon discretion, not overplaying your hand, and keeping your cards to yourself. Those in Cook's command know the awful truth and must keep those secrets until the OSS leadership can be acclimatized to it.
- **THE CLUB:** Other OSS agents consider Delta Green a group of trumped-up analysts with no real purpose in the war except idle speculation. They're outsiders. Even when OSS command learns the truth, the information is not disseminated to the lower ranks. Even when Delta Green agents are literally saving the world, their fellow OSS agents believe them to be, at best, "eggheads with guns."
- **REVELATIONS:** Inevitably, people within the OSS learn the truth about the real horrors behind the world. Some can take it, others cannot. As the secret spreads during the war, how do the agents keep up?

» **7 JAN 1942:** PISCES, supported by the Long Range Desert Group, discovers a ruined city in the Libyan desert, but are prevented from a full excavation due to the approach of the Afrika Korps. The LRDG destroys the entrance to a huge subterranean chamber of the city shortly before a Karotechia unit arrives at the site.

» **12 FEB 1942:** Lt. Commander Martin Cook, commanding officer of P4, briefs William J. Donovan on some of P4's experiences. Cook recommends P4 be merged with OSS as an "unconventional warfare unit" whose official purpose is to investigate the occult and unnatural for exploitation in psychological operations against the Axis. The group is called "Delta Green."

» **13 FEB 1942:** Joseph Camp, a future officer in OSS/Delta Green, leaves Harvard University's Far Eastern Studies Department to work for P4. He is sent to Camp X, the OSS training facility in Canada, for agent training.

» **22 FEB 1942:** PISCES observes Delta Green agents rummaging through old Admiralty records, leading to the first official meeting between the two agencies. After several more weeks of guarded meetings, both agencies reveal their mutual interests in unnatural affairs.

» **14 APR 1942:** Following his training at Camp X in Canada, Joseph Camp is reassigned by Delta Green to serve with Detachment 101 in Burma. Camp never receives a DELTA GREEN clearance briefing before he is reassigned.

» **31 MAY 1942:** Dr. Arthur Turner of Project MIRAGE devises a new mechanism to visually camouflage a naval vessel by forming an electromagnetic shell around the ship to ionize the surrounding air and create a blurry distortion. Turner creates the device, code-named MIRAGE II in conjunction with Albert Einstein at Project PHI, another RAINBOW sub-project tasked with developing new degaussing technologies.

» **12 AUG 1942:** By now, the Point 103 team of Aktion EISSCHLOSS have decoded enough of the lost city's pictograms to learn the history of the "Thulian" race, including their wars with "conical time travelers centered in Australia, crustacean-like entities who mined Earth's highest ranges, and semi-aquatic octopoid creatures whose home was a now submerged continent in the Pacific."

Our Darkest Hour

Under the leadership of the newly promoted Commander Martin Cook, Delta Green set about defeating the Karotechia under the guise of researching and conducting Allied psychological warfare operations. Many operations involved recovering or destroying books and artifacts that the Karotechia had an interest in.

But that was not all the Karotechia worked to accomplish. Experiments were performed which required huge requisitions of "test subjects" from Auschwitz and Treblinka. What happened to these "test subjects" was a mystery even to SS officers intimately involved with the Final Solution. It surprised no one in Delta Green when they discovered the Nazis were sacrificing them to curry favor with the same creatures the Navy had faced in Innsmouth 15 years before.

Delta Green's first major action of the war was a joint operation between airborne commandos and French partisans, disrupting the Karotechia's mass sacrifices at Cap de La Hague, on the coast of France, on 8 DEC 1942. PISCES had provided intel for the raid as a test—one which Delta Green passed—and both groups cooperated enthusiastically…for a short time. However, incidents in February and March 1943, during a joint operation to destroy unnatural artifacts in the Belgian Congo and Western Australia, led to casualties, recriminations, and the determination that PISCES' agenda was not Delta Green's agenda. It seemed the British hoped to control and even weaponize the unnatural, something Delta Green had decided not to pursue.

There were also signs of similar unnatural activities in the Pacific Theatre. Here Delta Green went head-to-head with a semi-official Japanese organization called the Gen'yōsha or "Black Ocean Society." Part political party, part secret society, and part unofficial black ops and espionage arm of the Japanese military, the Black Ocean Society had been infiltrating secret societies, criminal organizations, and occult brotherhoods across Asia since 1881.

At some point, members of the Black Ocean had become aware of the efficacy of unnatural rituals. By the mid-1930s, they were trying to find unnatural means to aid Japan's war effort. Having no official standing, the members of the Black Ocean Society exercised power through their official positions in the Imperial Japanese Army, government ministries and the Kempeitai—the Japanese secret police.

Throughout mainland China, Southeast Asia, Australia, and—in direct contravention of the wishes of Gen. MacArthur—throughout Melanesia, Micronesia,

- **1 SEP 1942:** After dozens of failed MIRAGE II experiments pursuing electromagnetic invisibility, Dr. Arthur Turner develops the idea of fluxing two electromagnetic fields within precise ranges to cause a sympathetic electromagnetic flux. Turner and his team design a half-dozen prototypes over the next three months, with none of them working for more than a minute before draining its batteries.
- **10 OCT 1942:** Karotechia agents arrive in Antwerp, Belgium after several books on the Ahnenerbe's bulletin of useful texts were reportedly found in the offices of a "liquidated" Jewish importer-exporter. In the offices, the group finds a crate marked "Jermyn/England" with 1913 postmarks, and, inside the crate, a stuffed, white-furred, ape-like creature. A plaque identifies the creature as a species called Chimbote in the N'Bangu dialect, recovered in "Thule, Belgian Congo" in 1913. Investigation into this creature is designated Project PARSIFAL.

RSION: 1 J35 CDR Fuerst

DISINFORMATION

YELLOW CARD

PNAKOTIS AND THULE

In 1935, the Miskatonic Geological Australian Expedition uncovered a non-human city near Pilbarra in Western Australia, dubbing it Pnakotis after the Pnakotic Manuscripts thought to have originated there. In 1943, Delta Green's Operation TARQUIN destroyed the Great Library at Pnakotis to keep knowledge of the future out of enemy hands. The site (what remains of it) is currently guarded by Cypress Security, a private military contractor.

A similar fate befell the Yithian library called "Thule" by the Karotechia teams searching for it. (The völkisch mystics of prewar Germany adopted the ancient Greek name "Thule" for the theoretical homeland of the white race, originally believing it to be in the far north. One Karotechia team based in the covert German Antarctic colony also declared the non-human city in Queen Maud Land "Thule.") Karotechia investigations had led them to an immense stone structure near Itoko in the Congo, constructed by white apes over a million-year span under Yithian direction. The Yithians designed the structure to keep the deadly spectral polyps in check while terrestrial life evolved the Yithians' new coleopteran hosts. If a Yithian library existed there, it appears to have been destroyed or scattered in 1943, likely also by Delta Green action.

LONG THIS LINE

IN THE FIELD: The Acquisition War

After 6 JUN 1944 with the invasion of Europe and to a greater or lesser degree in all theaters of the war, Delta Green struggles to capture, steal, cover up, or destroy the hundreds of personnel, unnatural artifacts, research projects and concepts which the war had stirred up. It is not alone. The Soviet Union's GRU SV-8, Britain's PISCES and the shattered fragments of the Karotechia (as well as others) also search for such things, for more sinister reasons.

The battlefields, ruins, and remnants left behind are a prime setting for a Delta Green campaign. Those wishing to run a game set in the later days of the war should keep the following in mind:

- **THE FIGHT GOES ON:** War ravages the world, and if Delta Green agents are doing their job, they are never far from the front. A study of notes referring to *Unaussprechlichen Kulten* could be disrupted by a banzai charge, or the roar of a King Tiger tank. Just knowing the truth doesn't mean you are (necessarily) bulletproof. The war must still be won.
- **RATS FLEE THE SHIP:** In the end, the Karotechia is evenly split between zealots and the self-interested. Karotechia operatives are found at all points, loaded for bear with their research, and sometimes, with valuable unnatural artifacts. Delta Green, of course, follows. When these operatives are deemed malleable, they are evacuated. When their loyalty is under question, they are denied to the enemy.
- **SECRETS, STIRRED:** The Karotechia spent years assembling the most amazing collection of unnatural books, items, and specimens the world had known until that point. That the invasion of Europe scattered this work to the four-winds was not lost on Delta Green. It is, in fact, likely the single largest source of proliferation of the unnatural in history. Still, what is "real" and what is simply legend? Nothing can be risked. All leads must be hunted to the bitter end.

of a
te
of a
es

from Law Enforcement

and Polynesia, Delta Green teams intercepted and neutralized Black Ocean Society projects to develop and deploy weapons garnered from unnatural sources.

Operations against Karotechia and Black Ocean Society operatives ranged across Europe and Asia, but also into neutral nations like Ireland, Turkey, Spain, and the republics of South America. Delta Green operated freely in South America despite the fact that it was forbidden. This exception to the FBI's "jurisdiction" was created once Commander Martin Cook informed J. Edgar Hoover that Delta Green was working on "an Innsmouth problem." Nothing more was said on the matter.

THREAT MATRIX

RED CARD

GEN'YŌSHA SURVIVES

Ironically, the core of the Black Ocean Society survives, in, of all places, San Francisco, California, as the Black Dragon Society (Kokuryūkai). The Black Dragon society was founded in 1901 by Uchida Ryohei, a member of the Black Ocean – and became the force with which the Black Ocean actualized its power through terror and violence. With agents in China, Korea and America, the Black Dragon incited fear and completed missions of sabotage for the Black Ocean.

In 2017, 90-year-old San Francisco club owner Nori Onishi recalls every day of his long life in America, from his capture in an FBI raid on 31 MAR 1942 to his release from internment in 1945, to his careful reconstruction of wealth throughout the 1950s and 1960s. Though he was arrested for associations with the Black Dragon criminal fraternity in the California raid, no such link could be proved, and his age (only 16) brought leniency. While his bosses, Saima Yoshimura and Kyashi Uyeda, went to federal prison, Onishi was sent to a Japanese internment camp.

Upon his return to San Francisco, he amassed through various means – criminal and legal – papers, books, and other artifacts once collected by long-dead members of the Black Ocean. In his time, he has seen various criminal enterprises come and go, and all have learned to give his powerful, but relatively modest, group a wide berth.

Onishi commands a network of criminal servants, almost all of Japanese heritage, and controls discrete portions of the San Francisco underworld concerned with prostitution and gambling. His name, as well as the name of his club – the Tokio Club – are well known to federal agents and police. What they do not know, is that Onishi is a dabbler in the unnatural, and knows it to be **real**. Onishi seeks unnatural artifacts and rituals to restore the vigor and power he felt in his youth, when the Japanese empire shook the world.

CUT ALONG THIS LINE

031-57937 0-46

TOP SECRET//SAR-DELTA GREEN

» **14 OCT 1942:** PISCES agents learn the location of the SCHWARZES WASSER facility at Cap de la Hague and pass the location on to Delta Green.

» **26 OCT 1942:** Delta Green agents are transported to Cap de la Hague, France, where they link up with French partisans and prepare to raid the SCHWARZES WASSER facility. Called Operation LIFEGUARD, it is Delta Green's first European operation.

» **1 NOV 1942:** Soviet GRU SV-8 responds to reports from Leningrad of cannibals bearing the same kind of necrophagous tendencies as Studnikov witnessed during the Russian Civil War. During their investigation, SV-8 uncovers SMERSH units capturing and interrogating these necrophagists. SV-8 races to eliminate every necrophagist in the city before they are recovered as "specimens" for SMERSH research.

» **3 NOV 1942:** The Karotechia's Project PARSIFAL instructs Abwehr agents inside Britain to learn more about the history of Sir Arthur Jermyn and his ancestral estate, Jermyn House.

» **4 NOV 1942:** Under the guise of an Einsatzkommando action against partisans, the commander of Project SCHWARZES WASSER sends an SS detachment to capture the entire town of Marise, massacre the adult male population, and march the women and children to Cap de la Hague, where they are placed in separate holding areas.

» **8 NOV 1942:** Project SCHWARZES WASSER trades 14 of the Marise women to the Deep Ones in exchange for 35 bars of British gold and detailed intelligence on the Cornwall and Dover coasts. The Karotechia is informed by the Deep Ones that, by the next new moon, their leader "Dagon" will arrive to seal their alliance.

» **20 NOV 1942:** At Cap de la Hague, the Deep One named "Claude" informs the Karotechia of the conditions required for Dagon's arrival, including the ritual use of a number of black stones. An Organisation Todt forced-labor crew is brought to Cap de la Hague to erect the stones and to become the sacrifice for Dagon.

» **8 DEC 1942:** As Project SCHWARZES WASSER conducts a ritual to welcome Dagon to Cap de la Hague, a force of Delta Green operatives and local French partisans carry out Operation LIFEGUARD, raiding the facility. The Deep Ones attack both the Allied raiders and their German hosts, and all further contact between the Karotechia and the Deep One colony is severed, ending Project SCHWARZES WASSER. Delta Green recovers 43 classified documents, including the file on Project PARSIFAL.

- **9 DEC 1942:** From the Karotechia files, Delta Green learns of the Donnerschlag – some type of sonic cannon – a Karotechia weapon constructed by Dr. Wilhelm Eisenbein and his researchers at a facility in the coastal French town of Fécamp.
- **20 DEC 1942:** While on Christmas leave in Boston, Timothy Michaelson, a Project MIRAGE researcher, witnesses Franklin Rathke stage a public demonstration of the Tillinghast Resonator in a bid to entice investors.
- **21 DEC 1942:** Timothy Michaelson writes a letter to Dr. Arthur Turner of Project MIRAGE detailing Franklin Rathke's demonstration of the Tillinghast Resonator. Intrigued by how the resonator can create such a large field effect with little power, Michaelson's letter convinces Turner that the Resonator might solve the unsustainable power requirements of the MIRAGE III device.
- **30 DEC 1942:** A four-man PISCES/Delta Green team infiltrates the Karotechia facility in the French coastal town of Fécamp. Their mission is to gather information on the Donnerschlag weapon before the Fécamp installation is destroyed by RAF bombardment. The entire team is lost save for U.S. Army Major Michael Stillman, who discovers that the installation was wiped out by invisible "things" following the testing of the Donnerschlag. Stillman escapes with blueprints for the Donnerschlag.
- **30 DEC 1942:** William J. Donovan, commander of the OSS, and David Cornwall, commander of PISCES, meet at Kilmaur Manor to work out an intelligence-sharing process between PISCES and OSS/Delta Green. Donovan is introduced to the capabilities of PISCES' unnatural Talents for the first time.
- **1 JAN 1943:** PISCES uncovers a plot by Gen'yōsha to incite a revolt against British rule in eastern India by reviving the Thuggee cult.
- **29 JAN 1943:** Delta Green recruits Wingate Peaslee to investigate his father Nathaniel Peaslee's connection to whatever the Karotechia is after with Project PARSIFAL. Accompanied by Operation LIFEGUARD veteran Thomas Arnold, Wingate Peaslee goes to Australia to discover what his father found in the Western Desert during the Miskatonic University expedition in 1935.
- **12 FEB 1943:** Dr. Arthur Turner of Project MIRAGE meets Franklin Rathke for the first and last time, at the Boston Federal Building. After witnessing a demonstration of a small version of the Tillinghast Resonator, Turner pays $4,000 to Rathke in exchange for the device and plans for its construction.

» **19 FEB 1943:** Delta Green is assigned to the Belgian Congo, to locate the lost city of "Thule" before the Karotechia's Project PARSIFAL can find it, and destroy the city. A second team is sent into the Gibson Desert of Australia to locate the source of a pre-human "library" that is said to exist there.

» **23 FEB 1943:** The Point 103 researchers conduct their first test of a strange sphere seemingly designed from the pre-human civilization, a weapon estimated to have the power to destroy a city. The test is partially successful.

» **1 MAR 1943:** William J. Donovan learns that PISCES had sent agents to assassinate the OSS/Delta Green team in Australia and seize pre-human books and artifacts that supposedly could allow humans to know or control the future. Ties between Delta Green and PISCES are severed.

» **1 MAR 1943:** At the Project MIRAGE laboratory in the Newark naval shipyards, Dr. Arthur Turner modifies the Tillinghast Resonator into a device large enough to obscure a destroyer escort-sized vessel using air ionization. While Turner's modifications are sufficient to protect those outside the resonator field from radiation, anyone within the field would still be in danger. Turner performs tests on models that convince the Navy to fully fund and expand Project MIRAGE. Neither the Navy nor Turner recognize the dangers that will soon become apparent in the Tillinghast Resonator.

» **2 MAR 1943:** Karl Ohlendorf receives orders from Berlin to keep the artifacts excavated at Point 103 in Antarctica rather than continuing to ship them back to Germany. A group from the rocket facility at Peenemünde is sent to Point 103 to combine the A4 delivery system with the strange sphere tested a week before, creating a weapon that the Point 103 team names the "N-03" rocket.

» **1 JUL 1943:** Dr. Arthur Turner and his greatly expanded Project MIRAGE team begin construction on a full-sized prototype of the Tillinghast Resonator, now code-named MIRAGE III.

» **9 SEP 1943:** The National Defense Research Council secures the USS *Eldridge* (Destroyer Escort 173) for use in testing the MIRAGE III device. A false report, claiming that the *Eldridge* spends the next three months at sea on a shakedown cruise, is filed, while, for the next six weeks, the ship is fitted by the Project MIRAGE team with the device in the Newark naval shipyard.

- **24 OCT 1943:** Dr. Arthur Turner briefs the crew of the USS *Eldridge* on their role in the MIRAGE III testing and introduces Dr. Townsend Brown, one of Turner's assistants who will join the *Eldridge* during its mission. Only Brown and Commander Joseph M. Connelly, captain of the *Eldridge*, know the true nature of the MIRAGE III experiment.
- **28 OCT 1943:** The MIRAGE III device is activated aboard the USS *Eldridge* in the Pocomoke Sound of Chesapeake Bay, immediately causing the ship to disappear for 22 minutes. When the ship is located, 32 of the 55 crew-members are dead or missing. The survivors report seeing otherworldly creatures from beyond and strange figures dressed in large suits like Army Air Forces fire crews. Two of these mysterious figures are found dead onboard, their bodies carrying advanced technology. In fact, the *Eldridge* reappeared due to the machinations of a team sent from the year 2012 to deactivate the resonator's field.
- **29 OCT 1943:** All 23 survivors of the USS *Eldridge* are admitted to the Bethesda Naval Hospital for psychiatric treatment. Three crewmen later die in custody, one commits suicide, and only 15 are ever released. Among those 15, only Dr. Townsend Brown and Commander Joseph Connelly resume normal lives.
- **1 NOV 1943:** The Office of Naval Intelligence carries out Project PUZZLE, the investigation and cover-up of the MIRAGE III experiment. The USS *Eldridge* is secured in an enclosed dock at the Norfolk Naval Yards (where it remains until 1982), while the two unidentified bodies are sent to Bethesda Naval Hospital for study.
- **31 DEC 1943:** Dr. Townsend Brown is released from the Bethesda Naval Hospital and goes to work for the Lockheed Vega Aircraft Corporation in California. In his spare time, Brown begins researching "gravitors" to create aerial vehicles with anti-gravity propulsion.
- **21 MAR 1944:** The Karotechia discover the *Dauthsnamjansboka*, a translation of the *Necronomicon* in ancient Gothic.
- **28 NOV 1944:** The Point 103 team completes the N-03 rocket, but its range is too short to reach any major Allied city from Antarctica. The suggestion is made to deal with Argentinian Vice President Juan Perón to launch from Buenos Aires, but it is rejected by Karl Ohlendorf. He decides to abandon the rocket and concentrate on further excavations.
- **21 DEC 1944:** The Karotechia perfect a method for reviving the dead. Truckloads of "resuscitated casualties" are driven to the Eastern Front.

» **23 DEC 1944:** Karotechia researcher Olaf Bitterich disinters the corpse of Alexis Ladeau, an associate of Friedrich Wilhelm Von Junzt. Within Ladeau's casket, Bitterich finds papers from von Junzt's unfinished and allegedly burnt manuscript of *Unaussprechlichen Kulten*. Bitterich uses these papers to call up the spirit of *something* that claims to be Friedrich II – Frederick the Great. This success leads Bitterich to become a favorite of Himmler and Hitler, as he calls up German heroes such as Otto von Bismarck, Friedrich Nietzsche, and Hermann der Cherusker to advise the Führer and his Reichsführer.

» **2 JAN 1945:** "Resuscitated casualties" *(poyavlyatsya* to the Soviets) are first encountered by GRU SV-8 when the Karotechia release them in and around the Polish City of Lodz to hinder the movement of the First Belorussian Front.

CUT ALONG THIS LINE

DISINFORMATION

YELLOW CARD

PROJECT RAINBOW

On 28 OCT 1943, the National Defense Research Council and the United States Navy tested the application of a device known as the Tillinghast Resonator aboard the destroyer escort USS **Eldridge** in an attempt to render it invisible through the use of intense electromagnetic fields. The fruits of a naval research project called RAINBOW, this was one of the earliest attempts at creating stealth technology.

The device, code-named MIRAGE III, was startling to say the least. The **Eldridge** not only became radar-invisible, it disappeared completely from the visible spectrum and was lost by its escort ships when the device was activated. In effect, for 22 minutes the USS **Eldridge** ceased to exist.

When the **Eldridge** was located, adrift and seemingly dead in the water, the true horrors of the Tillinghast Resonator were discovered. Less than half of the crew survived their journey to elsewhere. Some of the dead were embedded in bulkheads, their bodies fused with the steel on an atomic level. Some of the crew were never located at all, and are still missing to this day.

The incident has lived on in conspiracy folklore. Commonly known as the Philadelphia Experiment, it has fostered movies and books which hint at the true horrors endured by the crew of the ill-fated **Eldridge**.

At the end of World War II, the **Eldridge** event was seen as an embarrassing and secret aside to war research. Only later would the government become aware of the true threat the Tillinghast Resonator represented.

Götterdämmerung

Following Germany's surrender, the U.S. and Soviet intelligence services raced to seize German nuclear physicists, V-2 and jet aircraft engineers, and former intelligence officers. The Americans had Operation PAPERCLIP while the Soviets had Operation OSOAVIAKHIM. But where the OSS and the NKVD were trying to preserve knowledge, Delta Green had a different agenda. Operation SUMMER BREEZE put a team of Delta Green Agents into Soviet-occupied Germany to steal or destroy the Karotechia's files and personnel before they were found by Stalin's secret police. Most Karotechia researchers could not be located, while those the Delta Green team did find and judged unfit for extraction were subsequently "denied to the enemy."

Oddly, at least two different sets of Soviet teams operated in occupied Germany, with half trying to extract former Karotechia members, and the other half trying to execute them. This schizophrenic Soviet policy prompted heated debate in Delta Green as to Soviet intentions towards the unnatural.

Through SUMMER BREEZE, hundreds of kilograms of Reichsführer Himmler's secret files were brought to the West, while the rest were burned in place. The files were a chronicle of a prolonged disaster. The Karotechia's researchers had discovered awesome powers, but no means to harness them. With few exceptions, the Karotechia's programs caused as many casualties to the Axis as to the Allies.

In these files, Delta Green discovered Aktion GÖTTERDÄMMERUNG, Hitler's final solution. While the nation of Germany was spent, the Karotechia fought on to recreate the "accident" that had destroyed the Naudabaum Castle in Bavaria in early 1945.

Delta Green had recently found where Naudabaum Castle *used to be*. The mountain it had sat on had been scoured away, the nearby lake showed extremely high levels of alkaline, and every pine tree on the mountain had fallen away from the site. There were two obvious comparisons to be made from the devastation: the first was to the 1908 Tunguska blast in Siberia that had flattened 250 square kilometers of forest; the second was to the U.S. Army's recent test of the atomic bomb.

Recovered documents indicated that the accident was some sort of inter-dimensional "rip" in space, created through unnatural science. Something incomprehensible began to pour into our world, flattening the castle and the surrounding forest and poisoning the lake before the rift snapped shut.

ASSETS: The Red Cross Pocket Bible

Aktion GÖTTERDÄMMERUNG was Hitler's last-ditch plan to deny the world to the victorious Allies. The "calling formulae" used in the Naudabaum incident, which "turned the gaze of the daemon sultan upon us," was well known by the Karotechia. It represented a weapon of utter power, but with little control. Each use risked the destruction of the world.

In early 1945, the Karotechia prepared their ace in the hole: 14 Red Cross pocket Bibles. Each of these mundane-looking Bibles (in English, German and Italian), also contained a phonetic pronunciation of the "calling formula" hidden within it. They were handed out to experienced Karotechia personnel during the dissolution of the Reich, who were under orders to use the ritual to end the world.

Ernst Theissen, a translator for the Karotechia, had second thoughts. An expert in the formula, Theissen altered vital pronunciations, essentially disrupting its efficacy. No one in the Karotechia knew of the alterations, and it was only later that Delta Green discovered them when Theissen was captured.

Two of these pocket Bibles still exist, but all who know its double-secret have long since died. The calling formula in it could very easily be mistaken for the real thing.

[redacted]

Hitler's final order to the Karotechia was to remake this rip and leave it wide open. They would inflict an unnatural Götterdämmerung on the victorious allies, at the expense of the entire planet.

For three horrifying months in 1945, Delta Green fought the last battle of the European war against the Karotechia: Operation LUNACY. The "accident" was never recreated, and Aktion GÖTTERDÄMMERUNG was obliterated in a series of covert actions that cost the lives of many Agents—and even more Karotechia members.

TOP SECRET//SAR-DELTA GREEN

- **4 JAN 1945:** U.S. Army troops in a southern Iranian town deal with religious hysteria caused by an entity called the Nechustan (possibly Nehushtan), which had killed the villagers' livestock and, more sporadically, people. After a Soviet soldier is murdered, the Nechustan is shot dead in the mountains south of the town. The creature looked like a human being in life, but the corpse recovered is that of a giant, snake-like reptile.
- **9 JAN 1945:** Seven Karotechia researchers and 73 SS support personnel – as well as Naudabaum Castle and much of the mountain upon which is sits – are obliterated during an abortive and poorly understood attempt to summon dread Azathoth, the Daemon Sultan.
- **3 MAY 1945:** Reinhard Galt, while on assignment for the Karotechia in central Africa attempting to negotiate the secret of the "Ageless Banquet" from the immortal cannibals of the Anzique tribe, receives word that Hitler is dead. Galt forces his men to disarm and sacrifices them to the Anziques, and is adopted by the tribe.
- **8 MAY 1945:** Germany surrenders unconditionally. Of the 164 original members of the Karotechia, 37 remain. These few survivors immediately escape through the "rat-lines" established by organizations such as ODESSA.
- **9 MAY 1945:** In their search of the German naval archives, Delta Green discovers the logbook of Karl Heinrich, commander of the submarine U-29, which went missing under mysterious circumstances during the First World War. Based on Heinrich's descriptions of an undersea city and its strange temple, Delta Green surmises that the Deep Ones were involved in the submarine's disappearance.
- **10 MAY 1945:** By this time, most of the one hundred copies of a purportedly cursed *King in Yellow*-themed tarot deck have been lost, either disappearing in the chaos of World War II or hidden in collections by owners ignorant of their occult significance.

- **1 JUN 1945:** The Point 103 team unearths an unimaginable weapon used by the pre-human Antarctic civilization to reshape the face of the Earth. They name it the "Tectonic Agitator." Karl Ohlendorf begins preparing the weapon for use.
- **4 JUN 1945:** Operation SUMMER BREEZE begins as Delta Green seizes or destroys Karotechia files and personnel in Vienna before they can be acquired by SMERSH. A shooting war erupts in the Vienna underworld between Delta Green and SMERSH. GRU SV-8 takes advantage of the conflict to surreptitiously acquire Karotechia archives and assassinate SMERSH personnel. SMERSH captures only a man calling himself Erwin Peis, an assistant on the "resuscitated casualties" project.
- **10 JUN 1945:** Operation LUNACY. Following a connection from the files recovered during Operation SUMMER BREEZE, Delta Green eliminates an organization of Karotechia survivors before they can initiate Aktion GÖTTERDÄMMERUNG.
- **15 JUN 1945:** The Thule Generator breaks free of its moorings and consumes Point 103. Only four members of the project survive, including Karl Ohlendorf, but their plane crashes on the Antarctic ice, and Ohlendorf is believed dead.
- **13 DEC 1945:** The Paragon Foundation is established in Toronto, Canada, as a front by PISCES to evaluate psychic phenomena and gifted individuals in the Western Hemisphere. PISCES also uses the foundation to carry out secret investigations of unnatural activity in the region.
- **1 JAN 1946:** Using funds from the sale of artwork looted in Krakow and Paris, former Karotechia researcher Dr. Gunter Frank purchases La Estancia, a massive rubber plantation in Brazil.
- **2 JAN 1946:** After visiting the island of Hirta in the St. Kilda archipelago west of Scotland, David Cornwall designates the site as the home of PISCES' new laboratory and containment facility. By the end of the year, the first underground facilities have been constructed and work begun on the Medieval Metaphysics Laboratory, which later becomes known as Magonia.
- **5 FEB 1947:** PISCES destroys a revived Thuggee cult in India.

Roswell and Rebirth

President Harry S. Truman disbanded the Office of Strategic Services on 1 OCT 1945, and Delta Green along with it. When something crashed in the New Mexico desert on 24 JUN 1947, many of those who'd held Delta Green clearance were called back into service. The object appeared to be the wreckage of an extraterrestrial spacecraft, or "flying disk." Three dead occupants were found, as well as *one living extraterrestrial being*.

President Truman ordered the creation of a special off-the-books unit to analyze the wreckage, cover up the crash, and erase all public knowledge of the event. This new unit was called the MAJESTIC-12 Special Studies Group, formed under the National Security Council under Operation MAJESTIC. While some Delta Green veterans signed on, other alumni lobbied the White House to reorganize Delta Green itself. Truman agreed, and directed the Joint Chiefs of Staff to establish Delta Green as an inter-service military intelligence unit. Its remit was psychological warfare and "to conduct such activities as are necessary to deny the use of unorthodox technologies by any foreign power." It would be commanded by Martin Cook, the Navy officer who founded Delta Green in the OSS days. It would report directly to the Joint Chiefs of Staff, bypassing (in theory) the individual armed services and their bitter rivalries. The president expected that Delta Green would track UFO incidents overseas, to keep the U.S. ahead of the intelligence curve.

Delta Green went along with this, but unofficially many of the veterans had other ideas. They took a broad definition of "alien technology." Their wartime experience concerned Deep Ones, Nazi occultism, and unnatural phenomena—things that Delta Green considered to be *very* terrestrial. Flying saucers held little interest for the reborn agency. Those fascinated by such things ultimately joined MAJESTIC.

In 1953, when Delta Green was officially relieved of UFO-related duties by MAJESTIC, both organizations couldn't have been happier. From that point forward, the two organizations kept out of each other's way. This early division further compartmentalized intelligence that, if seen as a whole, might have revealed much about the nature of the unnatural.

ASSET: The White Sheet

In the early days of MAJESTIC, Dr. Stephen Courtis, a young, brilliant mathematician, was assigned to study the bizarre science of the extraterrestrial sigils found within the Roswell disk. His research was startling, and led to the restoration of power within the vehicle, as well as various other breakthroughs. But he grew withdrawn and secretive. On 12 DEC 1949, Courtis was found crushed beneath a sigil of his own design (similar to those found in the alien craft) carved into a wooden beam. The sigil was somehow exerting 190 Gs of force with no equivalent counter-force.

All that remained of Courtis, besides his shattered corpse, was a single sheet of paper inscribed with 34 equations. Along with this bizarre math was one word, "escape." MAJESTIC would study this math for decades and make no clear progress, except in rendering the world's greatest minds insane.

See **THE COURTIS PAPER** on page 157.

TOP SECRET

DISSEMINATION AND EXTRACTION OF INFORMATION
CONTROLLED BY ORIGI

IN THE FIELD:
The MAJESTIC Campaign

At the end of World War II, America stood supreme: its homeland untouched, its factories a prodigy of production, its Navy, Air Corps and arsenal second to no Earthly power. With the atomic bomb doubly demonstrated at Hiroshima and Nagasaki, few could picture any other world government approaching its power.

America labored under this delusion as well. Then something fell from the sky in New Mexico in 1947. Something which was not supposed to exist, and which put every Earthly technology to shame. America was ill prepared to deal with the shock.

The Roswell saucer represented a fundamental shift in the disposition of reality to those in power in the United States. Within days of its capture, the saucer clearly showed that America, the power which had spanned the globe and brought the world war to an end, was still only of *this* world. Something else existed *beyond* it—in stealth, technology and power. Something that made the American arsenal look as potent as a firecracker.

That secret turned out to be easy to keep. And the method of keeping it remained unchanged during MAJESTIC's entire operational history. Only a handful of individuals were ever given the "sermon": that if the truth of the situation became general knowledge, the aliens who created the saucer would have no choice but to end the experiment that they had begun long before, the experiment which we called "humanity." It was something they could do in one, final, terrible, instant, wiping the globe clean to start again.

Keep the following in mind when portraying characters from MAJESTIC, from the 1940s to the 1990s:

- **EVERYTHING TO LOSE:** MAJESTIC prefers to recruit scientists and agents with families, with strong ties to the community, with loved ones. People who lay down roots. They are kind and understanding employers, and they pay very, very, well. And then, when it's too late, they quietly point out just what would be lost if indiscretion were to strike.
- **INFINITE RESOURCES:** At its peak, MAJESTIC is the most potent human power on the planet. It controls billions of dollars' worth of black-budget personnel, vehicles and facilities. Literally nothing terrestrial (or in near orbit) is beyond its reach. This power might momentarily find itself in the hands of an Agent, but it never lasts.
- **ANYONE CAN DIE:** People die all the time, and with the proper counter-intel operations, it is incredibly easy to sweep someone—anyone—under the rug. A heart attack, a lone suicide, a drive-by. The stories change as needed, but the outcome is the same: the intelligence threat is removed. Rumors persist—spread by MAJESTIC disinformation efforts—that a prominent and well-known politician was killed to prevent public disclosure of the truth.
- **UNCORRELATED CONTENTS:** Two levels of MAJESTIC exist, white-badge access and black-badge access. White-badge personnel have limited knowledge of the group and what it does. They know the name of whatever particular project they call home, and they know that the project examines high technology recovered from enemy crashes, and little else. Employees given the "sermon" on what MAJESTIC *really is* are granted black-badge access. Black-badge MAJESTIC personnel are fully aware of mankind's position in the universe. It is a terrible secret to keep.

Guide //

THE SIGIL

YELLOW CARD

After the atomic bomb demonstrated how potent applied physics could **truly** be, and even before the apparently extraterrestrial craft crashed at Roswell, New Mexico, the U.S. government was gathering physicists and setting them on the ultimate task; the unification of all physical sciences into one, unbroken, whole.

When MAJESTIC began probing the spacecraft recovered at Roswell – nicknamed "the Bucket" – they hoped it might provide a shortcut to discovering the nature of anti-gravity. Since the alien vehicle could accelerate, float, and turn at right angles without any visible means of propulsion, most believed it must contain some sort of gravity engine.

Instead of a machine producing the anti-gravity effect in the craft, all that was found was a bizarre sigil carved into a clay-like substance within it (and subtle, larger versions etched into the indestructible metal of its exterior surface). The sigil seemed to **project** gravity – with no apparent counter-force – in a way that human science had not even the slightest idea how to begin to understand. MAJESTIC threw the best minds on the planet at it. The sigil proved to be the most complex thing ever seen by mankind. Over the next 60 years, hundreds of millions of dollars and dozens of lives were lost to the seamless mathematics behind the sigil.

The sigil has since been replicated, in rote copy, and used to propel objects and even kill. But after decades of effort, humanity is not one step closer to understanding how it works.

CUT ALONG THIS LINE

031

TOP SECRET//SAR-DELTA GREEN

» **12 MAR 1947:** PISCES carries out an archaeological intelligence operation in Borneo, with military assistance provided by the 21st SAS Regiment.

» **24 JUN 1947:** Thunderstorms apparently cause an unidentified flying object to crash near Roswell, New Mexico.

» **7 JUL 1947:** Major Jesse Marcel of the U.S. Army Air Forces 509th Bomb Group investigates a farmer's report of the Roswell wreckage. He dispatches soldiers to secure the crash site and returns to base to test the properties of the strange metal recovered from the site. Several Delta Green veterans are called in to assist.

» **8 JUL 1947:** A reconnaissance aircraft discovers a silver-gray disk near the Roswell debris site. A 150-man team from the Central Intelligence Group recovers the wreckage and four humanoid creatures, three killed in the crash and one unconscious. CIG covers up the event, but word spreads that a "flying disk" had been captured.

» **24 AUG 1947:** Dr. Anton Greist, formerly of the Manhattan Project, studies the Roswell crash survivor. A few weeks later, after discovering an unusual equation that allows his consciousness to transcend its physical form, Greist disappears. There are indications this "mathematical ritual" was at the center of the math that powered the craft.

- **21 SEP 1947:** President Harry S. Truman forms the MAJESTIC project to analyze the Roswell wreckage. Delta Green veterans successfully lobby the president to reinstate Delta Green as an inter-service military unit reporting directly to the Joint Chiefs of Staff. Among the veterans recruited into the new agency is Joseph Camp.
- **25 SEP 1947:** Delta Green's old YY-II facility in Arizona, where Deep One hybrids from Innsmouth are still held, is transferred to a new facility in Los Alamos, New Mexico, under MAJESTIC control. To consolidate xenobiological research, the single surviving extraterrestrial found at the Roswell crash is transferred there. The facility is code-named ICE CAVE.
- **25 SEP 1947:** The spacecraft (renamed "the Bucket") recovered at Roswell is moved to Wright Field in Ohio, where it is studied by a MAJESTIC project under the command of Detlev Bronk.
- **27 SEP 1947:** PISCES agents observe the reactivation of Delta Green, but do not resume the close relationship they shared during the war, due to concerns over possible security leaks.
- **29 SEP 1947:** Soviet spies report on the UFO crash at Roswell to Stalin, who assigns the task of collecting intelligence on it to S.M. Shtemyenko, chief of the GRU and former head of SV-8. Shtemyenko uses this assignment to establish SV-8 as an officially-recognized unit, secretly funded and staffed by anonymous personnel, but whose existence is known only to Shtemyenko, Stalin, and its own membership.
- **30 DEC 1947:** MAJESTIC creates the Air Force's Project SIGN to discredit UFO sightings. Some Delta Green personnel are permanently transferred to MAJESTIC to help cover up what the Air Force can't easily explain away.

AT WASHING

b7C tions mentioned in the [redacted] Will establ
Communist control thereof, and pa
SLAV CONGRESS to the Russian

The Cold War

The reconstituted Delta Green operated under cover as a military intelligence unit. Rather than following its mission directive, Delta Green went about settling accounts. Commander Martin Cook was adept at securing resources from the military services to conduct off-book paramilitary operations.

In JAN 1948, Delta Green launched Operation SOUTHERN HOSPITALITY, to eliminate former Karotechia members, hiding in Central and South America. In the first year, a Karotechia researcher was found living in Montevideo, Uruguay, and another in the Chaco region of Paraguay. Both were eliminated.

SOUTHERN HOSPITALITY's largest operation took place in 1952 in Antarctica near Queen Maud's Land. Three former Karotechia researchers, funded by Argentinian dictator Juan Perón, were attempting to locate Point 103 and unearth unnatural artifacts. A company of specially trained U.S. Army paratroopers under Delta Green command assaulted the Argentine Antarctic expedition, eliminating the Karotechia researchers along with their Argentine allies. Only a handful of U.S. paratroopers survived to seal the excavations with high explosives. The American dead were reported as killed in action in Korea.

Delta Green's flagrant disregard for its original mission would likely have led to its disbandment if not for the successful conclusion of Operation SIC SEMPER TYRANNIS.

In 1952, Delta Green had begun hearing rumors about a Soviet NKVD research project in Novosibirsk. A former Karotechia scientist going by the name Erwin Peis pursued experiments to extend, perhaps indefinitely, the life of ailing Soviet dictator Josef Stalin. In December, Delta Green inserted a six-agent team onto the Arctic coast of Siberia via U.S. Navy submarine. The agents and their Aleut Eskimo guides crossed the eastern Siberian Mountains to Novosibirsk. Only the team leader, Col. Michael Keravuori, returned in February via the frozen Bering Strait.

Keravuori reported that the team had struck just in time, and that the labs, personnel, and data had been completely destroyed. The most puzzling aspect of the operation was that the Delta Green team was captured by Soviet authorities *before their raid*, but, after interrogation, were inexplicably released in order to complete their mission.

During the raid, Soviet agents both aided the team and later tried to assassinate the survivors. As for Josef Stalin, he died in Moscow, on 5 MAR 1953 of apparently natural causes.

IN THE FIELD: The Cold-War Campaign

After World War II scattered the unnatural to all points of the globe, the reconstituted Delta Green undertook a decade-long "mop up" campaign. In these operations, Karotechia personnel, their research, and their unnatural technologies were hunted down, assassinated, captured or destroyed before they could tip the scales of world power.

At this moment in time, from 1948 to approximately 1960, Delta Green had access to the full might and infrastructure of the U.S. government. Nothing was beyond their grasp.

Those wishing to run a game set in the Cold War should keep the following in mind:

- **UNKNOWNS:** America itself is filled with hundreds of mysteries. Flying disks, bigfoot, beast sightings such as the "Mothman," and others fuel Delta Green operations at home, even as the group acts abroad to protect U.S. interests.
- **WE MUST RECOVER IT!:** The Karotechia spent years collecting unnatural artifacts—books, devices, icons, relics, and statuary—before the western intelligence services caught on to their actual utility. By the time Delta Green was in the war, the Nazis had the most extensive collection of unnatural artifacts gathered in one place in the world. These were scattered at the end of the war, and they turned up in the strangest places.
- **LAST SEEN IN SOUTH AMERICA:** Many of the Nazis (and Karotechia) fled to South America. And many of the missions in this era were carried out in various South American locales.
- **RUSSIAN EXTRACTS:** Karotechia researchers were captured and put to work by the Soviet SMERSH. The Karotechia's research in resurrection and life-extension technologies continued under Soviet rule, for use in the growing tensions of the Cold War.
- **ROCKETS AND NUKES:** The focus of the Soviet Union throughout the early 1950s was atomic and hydrogen bomb research, as well as rocket technology strong enough to carry such a weapon. The unnatural featured into this in many ways. Karotechia scientists enamored with alchemy claimed they could create uranium or plutonium from lead, that they could render the bomb assembly weightless, and more. None of these projects came to pass, of course; but was that because the researcher was killed, the underlying unnatural formula was flawed, or Delta Green intervened?

DISINFORMATION

YELLOW CARD

MICHAEL KERAVUORI, THE DOOR OF SILENCE

In 2017, the lone survivor of SIC SEMPER TYRANNIS, Col. Michael Keravuori (ret.) is a surprisingly fit 98. He lives in Scottsdale, Arizona, on a modest military pension. He spends his Thursdays at the local VFW lodge, drives a restored 1971 Corvette Stingray, and plays a pretty mean game of golf.

He doesn't sleep. That is not some metaphor. He has not slept since the day of his last mission for Delta Green: Operation SKUNKED in Colombia, 1956. Something happened in the jungle that he can't recall no matter how hard he tries. He doesn't try too hard, anymore.

No one in Delta Green knows that Keravuori is not right. Sometimes, Keravuori himself doesn't even notice. If not for the dreams, punctual as always, he might forget altogether. Even without sleep, the dreams come. During his last vision he almost drove his car off the road.

In the dreams, a gong sounds, and with each sounding a silence covers a portion of the world. A silence so deep that light and life vanish. In the end, the Earth is extinguished like a candle. Dead and black. A charnel house tumbling through the void forever.

Though he does not know why, Michael Keravuori is the man who swings the hammer, grinning.

ALONG THIS LINE

» **1 JAN 1948:** Project SIGN obscures the facts surrounding the death of Air National Guard Captain Keith Belmont and the destruction of his aircraft by a UFO.

» **18 JAN 1948:** Delta Green begins Operation SOUTHERN HOSPITALITY, to track down and eliminate former Karotechia members living in South America. By the end of the year, two former Karotechia researchers are found and eliminated.

» **2 FEB 1948:** MAJESTIC creates Project GRUDGE to replace USAF Project SIGN.

» **22 MAY 1949:** Secretary of Defense (and high-ranking member of MAJESTIC) James Forrestal "commits suicide" by "jumping" from the 16th-story window of his room at Bethesda Naval Hospital, where he is being treated for emotional strain. In reality, Forrestal is assassinated because he is planning to go public with what he knows about the Roswell crash.

» **21 JUN 1949:** The MAJESTIC team under the command of Vannevar Bush comes to the conclusion that the Greys (referred to as extraterrestrial biological entities or EBEs) developed a psychic hive mind at some point in their evolution.

» **12 DEC 1949:** Dr. Stephen Courtis of MAJESTIC Special Studies Group Two is crushed to death while experimenting with a sigil found on "the Bucket." The sigil is quickly determined to have strange effects on gravity, and eight other researchers are killed during a brief period of experimentation. Courtis' experiment marks that last significant result garnered by MAJESTIC SSG2, although the project continues for decades afterward.

» **2 JAN 1950:** Dr. Townsend Brown, one of the few survivors of the USS *Eldridge* and former researcher on Project MIRAGE, quits his position at the Lockheed Vega Aircraft Corporation and moves to Hawaii to focus on his gravitor research.

» **6 DEC 1950:** A second UFO crashes at El Indio, Texas. Project GRUDGE dispatches a special USAF craft-recovery unit called BLUE TEAM to recover the minimal debris and cover up the accident.

» **2 JAN 1951:** Under an assumed name, and acting through ODESSA, Reinhard Galt joins the Egyptian Army as an instructor and military advisor.

» **3 SEP 1951:** While working on the Courtis equations taken from the Bucket, Dr. Wexler of MAJESTIC shoots and kills his colleague, Dr. Antonio Malbayam. Wexler claims that Malbayam went insane, attempted to destroy Courtis' notes, and attacked him.

» **2 MAR 1952:** Project GRUDGE is replaced by Project BLUE BOOK, a public disinformation campaign designed to deny the existence of extraterrestrials. BLUE TEAM continues to operate, investigating UFO sightings and collecting evidence for use by MAJESTIC.

» **1 APR 1952:** Delta Green launches a raid into Antarctica as part of the continuing Operation SOUTHERN HOSPITALITY, using a company of U.S. Army paratroopers to stop a Karotechia expedition from locating Point 103.

» **1 NOV 1952:** Delta Green launches Operation SIC SEMPER TYRANNIS, whose mission is to destroy the SMERSH laboratory in Novosibirsk, Siberia, where Erwin Peis is continuing his "resuscitated casualties" research for the purpose of indefinitely preserving the life of Stalin. Six Delta Green agents and four Aleut guides are transported by submarine to north of the Arctic Circle, where they begin the overland hike to Novosibirsk.

» **3 DEC 1952:** Two hundred miles north of Novosibirsk, the SIC SEMPER TYRANNIS team is captured by a Spetsnaz unit on maneuvers. The prisoners are held by the GRU at Tomsk, and subjected to interrogations personally supervised by GRU chief Mikhail Shalin. One week later, one of the Delta Green agents, U.S. Army Capt. Peter Hodge, breaks down and reveals their mission. Fearing an immortal Stalin, Shalin decides to release the Americans, have them complete their mission, and then assassinate them to cover up all GRU involvement.

» **18 DEC 1952:** President-elect Dwight Eisenhower is briefed on the existence of MAJESTIC and its purpose. Eisenhower agrees to expand MAJESTIC's budget, authority, and manpower. MAJESTIC consolidates its UFO investigations by having the NSA carry out Project AQUARIUS (MJ-1) as its primary operational arm. BLUE TEAM is also reorganized as Project MOON DUST (MJ-5), with Operation BLUE FLY as its primary operational arm.

» **2 FEB 1953:** GRU SV-8 smuggles the SIC SEMPER TYRANNIS team into Novosibirsk, where they destroy the SMERSH laboratory and liquidate Erwin Peis and his research staff. Only U.S. Army Colonel Michael Keravuori survives both the raid and the Spetsnaz ambush awaiting the Americans, and escapes by walking across the frozen Bering Sea to Nome, Alaska.

Losing History

On 13 JAN 1955, Daniel Freis, one of the original Black Chamber cryptographers who had translated *The Book of Dagon*—and Delta Green's most gifted researcher—suffered a mental collapse and went on a rampage in Delta Green's archives. After attacking several personnel with a fire axe, he set fire to the central archives. The resulting blaze destroyed all the materials seized during the Innsmouth raid. Freis even smashed the original stone tablets of *The Book of Dagon* to bits. Most materials from World War II were also destroyed.

Losing these irreplaceable artifacts and files set Delta Green's research back almost 14 years. Some insisted that Freis wasn't insane, but had instead done humanity a great service. Fries was captured and committed, and died in an insane asylum in 1970.

In MAY 1959, Delta Green lost the services of Commodore Martin Cook, Delta Green's commanding officer since its inception in 1942. Commodore Cook was confined to the psychiatric wing of Bethesda Naval Hospital for complete mental and physical collapse. In 1963, he was released and retired quietly to his ranch in Montana, where he lived until his death in 1968. During the last years of his life he declined to participate in Delta Green operations, even in an advisory capacity.

» **2 MAR 1953:** The morning after a late-night dinner party at his dacha in Kuntsevo, Stalin is found lying on the floor of his bedroom, conscious but unable to speak. Diagnosed with a stroke and lacking the elixir promised him by Erwin Peis, Stalin suffers a slow and painful death.

» **21 MAR 1953:** In New York, Stephen Alzis suddenly appears and takes over leadership of what remains of the 1920s occult group, the Fate.

» **1 OCT 1953:** Electronic eavesdropping stations of MAJESTIC's Project AQUARIUS begin detecting odd signal noise originating from deep space.

» **23 NOV 1953:** A USAF F-89c jet fighter is observed by radar being "absorbed" by an unidentified radar contact. Project AQUARIUS investigates the disappearance, but no trace of the aircraft or its crewmen is ever found.

» **2 JAN 1954:** During the Malayan Emergency, PISCES discovers an ethnic minority called the Tcho-Tchos engaged in cannibalism and ritual torture. PISCES uses extreme measures to eliminate the Tcho-Tchos from Malaya.

» **14 JUL 1954:** MAJESTIC's Project AQUARIUS briefs President Eisenhower on the odd signals it has detected, having determined that they are indecipherable fragments of intelligent and systematic communications originating from the moon and aimed at sites on the Earth and in high orbit. Eisenhower increases MAJESTIC's budget, allowing a complete reorganization.

DISINFORMATION

YELLOW CARD

K'N-YAN

First recorded by Delta Green in 1955, K'n-Yan, or Xinaián, is a subterranean realm filled with an eerie blue light. It is located beneath Oklahoma, although (possibly hypergeometrical) entrances to it can be found in Vermont and other places. Below it is the red-litten cavern of Yoth, and below that, the black abyss of N'Kai. Everything known about K'n-Yan comes from the **Narrative Concerning the Subterranean World**, purportedly written by Spanish conquistador Pánfilio de Zamacona y Nuñez (1512–1545?). The ethnologist Z.L. Bishop published Zamacona's tale in 1930 after finding it buried in the so-called "Ghost Mound" near Hydro, Oklahoma, describing it as a 19th-century hoax or social satire.

The immortal inhabitants of K'n-Yan – of which little is definitely known – have mastered genetic manipulation, telepathy, dematerialization and molecular control. They may have been the prehuman, psionic "Lemurians" of theosophical lore, said to dwell within Mount Shasta and other North American natural features. They are sometimes referred to as "giants" or "moon-faced people." War with the "space devils" (some suspect the mi-go) drove them below the surface. Over the eons, they manipulated their DNA with genes from serpent people, prehuman Lomarians, and even the formless offspring of Tsathoggua. Eventually their civilization decayed until they restricted themselves to their capital city of Tsath. The K'n-Yani encounter with Zamacona apparently renewed and strengthened their commitment to total paranoid isolation.

Delta Green has not risked altering that attitude.

CUT ALONG THIS LINE

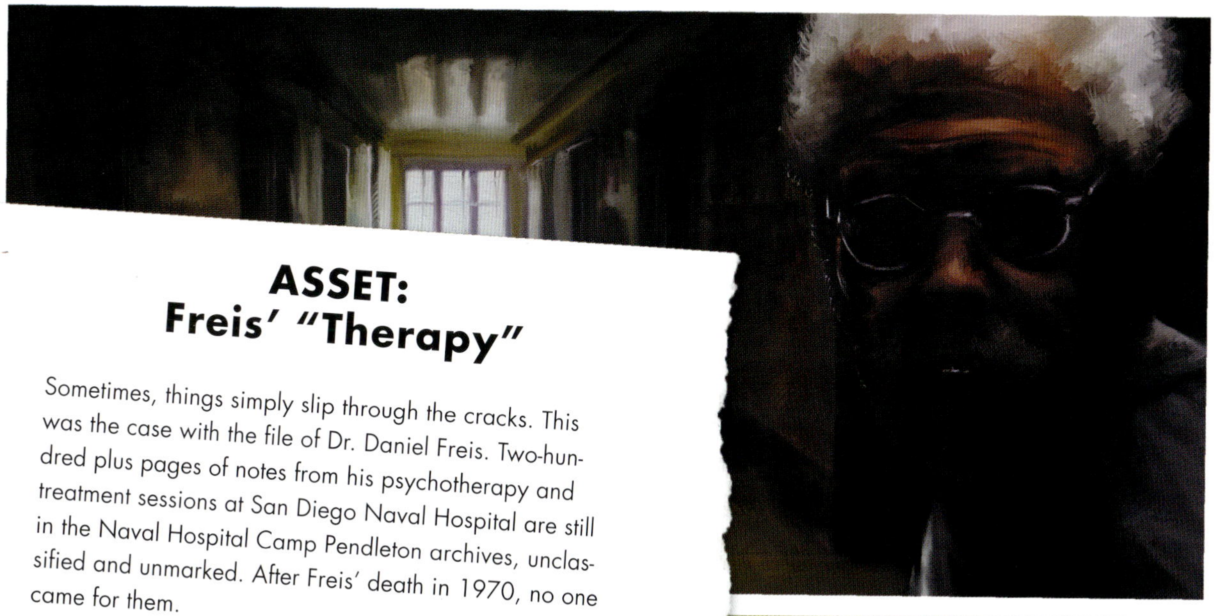

ASSET: Freis' "Therapy"

Sometimes, things simply slip through the cracks. This was the case with the file of Dr. Daniel Freis. Two-hundred plus pages of notes from his psychotherapy and treatment sessions at San Diego Naval Hospital are still in the Naval Hospital Camp Pendleton archives, unclassified and unmarked. After Freis' death in 1970, no one came for them.

It's all there, in black and white. A transcript of Innsmouth, the Deep Ones and the secrets of *The Book of Dagon* laid bare in plain text. Of course, those treating him believed he was insane, so it was all ignored. To those in the know, however, the case-file is as dangerous as a loaded gun. See **CASE FILE, FREIS, DANIEL M.**, on page 157.

DISINFORMATION

YELLOW CARD

CUT ALONG THIS LINE

INNER SPACE

Some say that if position in spacetime is relative to perception, as Einstein grudgingly admitted and quantum theory gingerly maintains, then altering perception alters the perceiver's dimensionality. The so-called "inner space" revealed by hallucinogenic drugs begins as an overlay or bleed-through into normal spacetime, later becoming a shared hallucination with culturally common symbolic features. Past that, certain drugs, meditative states, and other stimuli such as the Ganzfeld color effect open gateways out of everyday reality.

The CIA experimented with LSD between 1951 and 1973 under Project ARTICHOKE, later renamed MKULTRA, then MKSEARCH. Their goal was a mind-control drug. MAJESTIC, via Project OUTLOOK, piggybacked on much of MKULTRA's work to explore strange dimensions. Some undercover Delta Green operators entered inner space while infiltrating hallucinogenic and entheogenic cults.

One inner-space concept was recorded in the Sanskrit **Ashokavadana** as the Maya – the illusion. Many tales describe a world beyond our own, a shared reality some call the "dreamlands." Madmen have claimed that **all** of us travel to this world during sleep, living other lives in another "reality."

There are other powers at work in the realm of perception. The most potent is a force known as the King in Yellow (see page 109), which seemingly exists in a realm of roiling madness that spreads like a psychic virus.

- In 1899, Arthur Emery Smyth, a failed poet and drunk who had somehow managed to found a religious order around the "World of Fancy," gathered 120 followers for one final revel. All vanished and were never found.
- In 1955, Delta Green was involved in an incident in New York City called Operation BRISTOL. It was a disaster with a huge body count, focused around a failed off-Broadway play called **Her Grey Song**, which, it was determined, was based off a play with known hypergeometric qualities called **The King in Yellow**. During this operation, a portal opened to a dimension called Carcosa. Beyond these scant facts, nearly nothing remains on the record, though some survivors might be found.
- In 1958, MKULTRA Project SUBSUME came into possession of "Substance K," a narcotic with odd side effects. It appeared to be plant-based, though its components could not be identified. Some subjects who imbibed this substance physically vanished, never to return. SUBSUME was folded under MAJESTIC supervision in 1959. It is unknown whether the experiments continued.
- Two Delta Green agents have claimed to have entered a strange but Earth-like world. The first, in Korea in 1950, claimed to have discovered an ancient, ruined city called Sarkomand before wandering back to American lines. The second, lost at sea in the South Pacific, landed at a port town called Lhosk, and barely escaped after being set upon by men in turbans. Neither claim could be substantiated.

031-51937 0-46

DISINFORMATION

YELLOW CARD

OPERATION MALLORY

From 1956 to 1965, Delta Green hunted yeti and followed up on uncanny alien sightings in the Himalayas, burying its activities in the CIA's ST-CIRCUS and ST-BARNUM Tibetan resistance programs. A raid closed a gate to Leng; another diverted a MAJESTIC team sent to measure gravitic and other anomalies emitted from the temple of Dza-nGar Phan in the Ü-Tsang Plateau. Agents survived enough encounters with the metoh-kangmi (see page 216) to deduce their relationship with the mi-go. Much of this intelligence was lost before it reached Delta Green's archives.

TOP SECRET//SAR-DELTA GREEN

» **2 JAN 1955:** Dr. Lewis Strater establishes the OUTLOOK Group, a think-tank for the Pentagon, the DIA, the NSA, and the CIA. Under Strater, the OUTLOOK Group successfully predicts several major shifts in the foreign-policy climate over the next six years.

» **9 MAR 1955:** Delta Green Operation ADVANCE MAN in Oklahoma results in twenty-two deaths, one lost agent, and three involuntary commitments. The survivors of the operation reported contact with an unknown threat called the Xinaián: near-human creatures capable of manipulating matter and thought who appear to originate from within the Earth.

» **18 APR 1955:** Samples codenamed REDMAN recovered from SIC SEMPER TYRANNIS are put beneath the microscope for the first time. After an incident causing the death of four Delta Green agents, and the disappearance of a researcher, the sample is lost.

» **8 FEB 1956:** Delta Green ends Operation SOUTHERN HOSPITALITY, under the (mistaken) belief that all former members of the Karotechia had either been slain or died from mishaps, old age, and disease. Three former Karotechia officers — Olaf Bitterich, Gunter Frank, and Reinhard Galt — survive.

» **4 JAN 1957:** Arthur Moritaum, the sole heir to the Moritaum oil fortune and a former member of the Fate, wills his Southampton estate to Stephen Alzis. Moritaum dies soon afterwards, and Alzis establishes the Moritaum Estate as the new headquarters for the Fate, where the cult stores its library and conducts many of its rituals.

» **12 MAY 1960:** Research on "the Bucket" has killed or mentally incapacitated three dozen personnel working on MAJESTIC SSG2, despite enforcing a "buddy approach" system. MAJESTIC responds by placing armed guards on all researchers and forcing many of them to drop out of society by having their deaths faked.

Reorganization

In 1961, newly appointed Secretary of Defense Robert S. McNamara re-organized a number of Pentagon systems, including Delta Green. President Kennedy (Massachusetts native and lifelong sailor) enthusiastically embraced the Delta Green mission after receiving a briefing from MAJESTIC. Rather than restoring the direct military command structure, JFK and McNamara pulled oversight of Delta Green upstairs to an Executive Committee.

McNamara also increased civilian involvement in the program. Delta Green recruited from academia and tapped civilian intelligence and law-enforcement agencies for personnel, adding investigative brainpower to the program's raw firepower. When an unnatural event came to Delta Green's attention, the case officer provided relevant personnel with a temporary clearance, briefing them on the essential, "need-to-know" details of the mission.

After participating, the survivors received a small, green delta (Δ) attached to their files. Once marked, these Delta Green "friendlies" could be mobilized again if they were in the general vicinity of a crisis, or if their particular talents are needed. Delta Green grew less centralized, with individual members of the Executive Committee, and even individual veteran case officers, possessing the *de facto* authority to mount operations without the foreknowledge of the program's leadership.

As a rapid-response strategy, this method had its advantages. As a survival strategy, it would cost Delta Green greatly.

» **21 MAY 1960:** A Richter 8 earthquake strikes Concepcion, Chile; two more Richter 7 quakes hit the next day. Fifteen minutes after the third quake, a fourth shock (Richter 9.5) destroys 40% of the city of Valdivia. Fragmentary reports from Chile describe "dog-headed men" and "mermaids" amongst the chaos. Delta Green inserts teams into the 7th Field Hospital from Ft. Belvoir and the 57th Medical Air Ambulance Company from Ft. Meade.

» **2 JAN 1961:** Delta Green actively recruits new members to replace those agents lost over the past decade, adding 26 new personnel to the Delta Green's command and control center. Among them is U.S. Army officer Reginald Fairfield.

» **19 JAN 1961:** Stephen Alzis opens the Whole Earth Enterprises offices in the McMahon Building in Manhattan. By this time, WEE is a highly successful international company, with 9,000 employees around the globe, and Alzis' activities have caught the attention of Delta Green.

» **20 JAN 1961:** John F. Kennedy is sworn in as the 35th president of the United States. After being briefed by MAJESTIC, Kennedy pledges his support, and suggests sending manned missions to the moon to search for the source of alien communications detected by MAJESTIC researchers.

» **1 JUL 1961:** Dr. Albert Yrjo of New York University begins conducting experiments subjecting groups of ordinary people to simulated high-stress situations, ranging from a simple building fire to an imminent nuclear attack.

DISINFORMATION

YELLOW CARD

THE EXECUTIVE COMMITTEE

After its establishment in 1947, Delta Green operated under the supervision of an Executive Committee. Sometimes called the ExComm or the 9895 Committee (after the Executive Order establishing the program), it was appointed by the president and by the Joint Chiefs of Staff. Under Truman and Eisenhower, the 9895 Committee mostly acted as a rubber stamp and occasional facilitator for Commodore Cook's plans, only rarely refusing its imprimatur for an operation.

In 1961, Secretary of Defense McNamara reasserted White House control over the process by appointing 26 new members to the Executive Committee, many of them civilians from intelligence, other departments, and even academia. At Kennedy's insistence, he added a representative of the Special Forces, Army Brigadier General Reginald Fairfield. After a thorough briefing by Delta Green staff (including on-site examination of a Deep One prisoner), the new Committee sets about its work.

During the 1960s, the Executive Committee included:

CUT ALONG THIS LINE

- **DR. JOSEPH CAMP (1918–2001):** A wartime OSS officer recruited out of Harvard's Far Eastern Studies Department, Camp had served Delta Green since 1942. His primary focus was intelligence – though he spent a great deal of time as a Pentagon adviser in Vietnam and China – and he urged the collection of books and artifacts for reference.
- **MAJOR GEN. REGINALD FAIRFIELD, U.S. ARMY (1914–1994):** As an OSS commando, Fairfield served in France, Italy, and the Mediterranean. After working on Operation GLADIO in Europe, training stay-behind guerrillas to resist Communist invasion, he transferred to Vietnam in 1959. Martin Cook read him into Delta Green in early 1961. His aggressive "burn the books, dynamite everything" policy (and his right-wing political views) set some of the Committee against him. He was promoted to major general in 1968, when he became the head of the Executive Committee on Rear Admiral Payton's retirement.
- **COL. MICHAEL KERAVUORI, U.S. ARMY (B. 1919):** A veteran of the Russo-Finnish War, Keravuori became a naturalized American citizen in 1946 and served in Korea as an Army Ranger. He commanded Operation SIC SEMPER TYRANNIS (December 1952), which destroyed a Soviet intelligence laboratory outside Novosibirsk attempting to use Karotechia re-animation research to make Stalin immortal. The most puzzling aspect of the operation was that the GRU had captured the Delta Green infiltrators **before their raid**, but, after interrogation, inexplicably released them and allowed them to complete their mission. Then, the GRU attempted to assassinate the survivors. Only Keravuori made it back, walking over the frozen Bering Straits. After Operation SKUNKED in Colombia (May 1956) he received a transfer to the 9895 Committee.

(CONTINUED)

031-51937 o-46

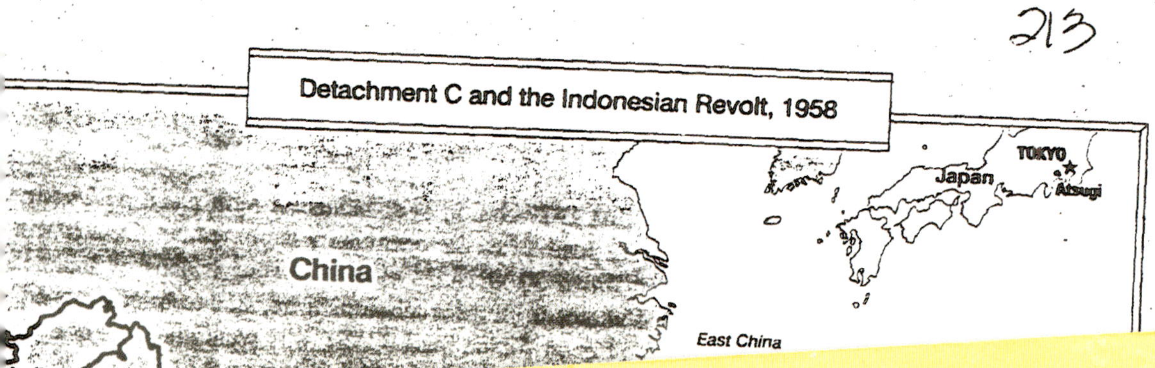

RED CARD

DISINFORMATION

YELLOW CARD

THE EXECUTIVE COMMITTEE (CONT'D)

- **COL. MARCUS MITCHELL, U.S. ARMY (1920–1979):** Sergeant Mitchell served with the all-black 92nd Infantry in Italy, where he salvaged the Delta Green Operation THRENODY in Bordighera (April 1945) and was read into Delta Green. After he served in SUMMER BREEZE, LUNACY, Korea, and OCS at Ft. Benning, the program transferred Mitchell to domestic operations, often against suspected unnatural cults within the civil rights movement (most of which turned out to be false alarms). He was promoted to colonel and elevated to the Executive Committee in 1963.
- **REAR ADMIRAL DAVID FARRAGUT PAYTON, USN (1904–1976):** An Annapolis graduate, Payton joined ONI in 1929 and P4 in 1932. Stationed in Mexico, Japan, and the Philippines, he uncovered the Black Ocean and its ties to Dagon; during WWII he worked as a codebreaker at Station S on Bainbridge Island, Washington. In 1947, he became Commodore Cook's adjutant in the new Delta Green. His last field assignment was Operation BRISTOL in 1955; he became listless and unfocused after that. But as one of the few surviving P4 veterans in the program and its titular commanding officer (promoted to rear admiral in 1961), he retained considerable influence until he retired in 1968.
- **BRIGADIER GEN. MICHAEL STILLMAN, USAF (1921–1999):** Stillman was in the original class of Delta Green OSS recruits; in December 1942, he captured the Donnerschlag sonic cannon plans from the Karotechia station at Fécamp in France in Operation UPROAR. He transferred to the USAF and rejoined the program in 1947 studying UFOs (Projects SIGN, GRUDGE, and BLUE BOOK). When MAJESTIC took over all UFO research, Stillman remained at Delta Green, but he continued to believe in weaponizing the unnatural in cooperation with MAJESTIC.
- **DR. AUGUSTA WARREN (B. 1919):** Her father, occultist Harley Warren, disappeared in Florida before Augusta was born. She tried to stay well out of his shadow, studying sociology at the University of Chicago. Unfortunately, her researches kept turning up strange patterns in the data, unsettling conclusions about human mass behavior. After Kennedy was elected president in 1960, Warren used her father's surviving protégés (and her political connections with the Daley machine in Chicago) to get onto the Executive Committee. She ignored the pervasive sexism, militarism, and resentment of her string-pulling, and went ahead with her research: tasking trained investigators with on-the-ground, first-hand fieldwork on anomalies she noticed in the data.

CUT ALONG THIS LINE

Deeper War

On 10 APR 1963, the nuclear attack submarine USS *Thresher* sank with all hands, 100 miles east of Cape Cod, Massachusetts. Delta Green had long maintained an interest in naval disasters, and it was not lost upon the leadership that the USS *Thresher* went down in the general vicinity of Innsmouth.

Investigation revealed that the Deep One colony off Innsmouth, under Devils Reef, had survived the 1928 submarine attack. Delta Green launched Operation RIPTIDE to finish the job. Multiple rounds of air-dropped anti-submarine warfare charges, depth charges, and high-explosive torpedoes poured on the site until hydrophones revealed only silence.

Hearts of Darkness

In 1964, Delta Green agents intervened in the Belgian Congo crisis. Under attack from government troops, CIA mercenaries, and Belgian paratroopers, the hard-pressed Simba and Mulele rebels were turning from Marxist-Leninism to tribal mysticism. In their desperation, the rebels had embraced an ancient religion and planned to summon their god Mauti to devour their enemies.

Their first efforts resulted in a unit of European mercenaries being ritualistically slaughtered, so Delta Green launched Operation KURTZ to discover if the rebels were utilizing unnatural principals in the field. Delta Green's bloody tactics succeeded in preventing a dimensional "rip" similar to the one planned by the Karotechia in 1945, but some in the Pentagon wondered if the body count was too high to justify the operation.

DISINFORMATION

YELLOW CARD

"TOCHOA, YUEH-CHI, CHAUCHUAS, TCHO-TCHOS, TACHOANS?"

No one knows where the "Tcho-Tcho" people hail from, or even where they got their name. To the Greeks they were the Tochoa, and they violently ruled much of what is today Afghanistan before the Sassanid Persians pushed them back to the Asian wilds in the third century BCE. To the Chinese, they were the Yueh-Chi, "those with the knife smile," who were shunned as cannibals and thought to travel between our world and the mystical realm of Leng. To the French missions in Indonesia, they were the Chauchuas, withdrawn tribespeople who at first seemed friendly, but who showed a propensity for sudden ambush and violence. To American cultural anthropologists they were the Tcho-Tchos or Tachoans, one-time allies against the Viet Cong, with an odd religion that involved ritual sacrifice and self-mutilation.

Where did they come from? No one can say for certain. One theory says they are from Leng, a mountain in the depths of China. Another says they are from a hidden city of Dho-Hna beneath the Earth. Some old texts claim they are an unnatural species masquerading in human form.

All of these things, and names, can be said to be true, or at least, not false. What do the Tcho-Tcho people say about themselves? Nothing. Tcho-Tchos asked in Vietnam only smiled and laughed through black, sharpened teeth. Tcho-Tchos today let public advocacy groups speak for them, arguing against blatantly racist stories that obscured their heritage. The one thing Delta Green's leaders believe without doubt is that the Tcho-Tchos, in addition to having dangerous ties to the unnatural, are capable liars. They are not to be trusted.

CUT ALONG THIS LINE

As the Vietnam war heated up, many members of the CIA and military intelligence found themselves penetrating heretofore-undisturbed corners of the steaming jungles of Indochina. Because of their discoveries, some were granted Delta Green clearance.

As early as 1965, Delta Green was concerned by some of the "anti-communist allies" the CIA was developing among the region's hill tribes. While the CIA's Hmong, Mieu, and Montagnard allies were opium smugglers, the CIA's Tcho-Tcho mercenaries were worse—unfathomably sadistic, avowed cannibals. Despite the Tcho-Tchos' rabid hatred of the communists, Delta Green advised the CIA against arming the despicable tribesmen. Delta Green's warning was ignored. The CIA never admitted it had made a mistake with the Tcho-Tchos, even after it became obvious that the tribesmen were more interested in killing and eating their Hmong, Mieu, and Montagnard neighbors than they were in fighting the communists.

But there were worse things festering in the jungles of Indochina. In Laos, Cambodia, and Vietnam, Delta Green detected some of the same signs they'd seen in the Congo in 1964. The Pathet Lao, Khmer Rouge, and Viet Cong were becoming so hard-pressed by American firepower and counterinsurgency tactics that certain factions were willing to try anything to drive out the "Imperialist running-dogs." Delta Green particularly worried about disquieting similarities between the Simba and Mulele god Mauti and the mystical concept of Angka—the title of the Khmer Rouge's political party.

DISINFORMATION

YELLOW CARD

DHO-HNA

Delta Green has ascribed the name Dho-Hna to a supposed "inner city at the magnetic poles." The name derives from a ritual that grants access to it. The city accessed by the Dho-Hna formula may have another name to its builders. The **Necronomicon** and other texts describe only a single city, implying that Dho-Hna occupies a pocket dimension tangent to both magnetic poles. Alternately, there may be two cities (Dho and Hna?), one at each pole. The city has some connection with Yog-Sothoth, and may act as a gateway to other dimensions or times. Its location on Earth shifts with the magnetic poles, but until the immanentization of Yog-Sothoth it can only be reached using the ritual – or possibly from the air.

U.S. Air Force Captain Curtis Criss is the only Delta Green asset known by the group to have seen Dho-Hna. On 21 JAN 1968, he joined a B-52 airborne alert flight out of Thule AFB in Greenland under cover as a substitute navigator. His mission (Operation NORTHERN LIGHTHOUSE) remains classified; when his bomber crashed near the airbase six hours later, one man was dead, the cockpit had burned out, and one nuclear weapon was missing. In his debrief, Criss described "a kind of angled chaos" with "pointed towers" and "things in the gardens."

CUT ALONG THIS LINE

TOP SECRET//SAR-DELTA GREEN

» **11 DEC 1962:** In Operation OVERDUE, Delta Green investigates the death of Massachusetts State Patrolman Michael Myrlo, turned inside-out nine miles from Innsmouth. The investigation leads to a Wisconsin book thief who stole an unnatural tome from Innsmouth's abandoned Ephraim Waite house and pursued communion with alien dimensions.

» **11 APR 1963:** Delta Green initiates Operation RIPTIDE, using air-dropped anti-submarine warfare weapons and depth charges to utterly destroy the Deep One City of Y'ha-nthlei, which had only been damaged by the submarine attack of 1928.

» **22 NOV 1963:** President Kennedy is assassinated in Dallas, Texas. Moments after Kennedy is confirmed dead at Parkland Memorial Hospital, Lyndon Johnson is inaugurated as president onboard Air Force One at Love Field. MAJESTIC does not brief President Johnson until there are new findings to report.

» **15 JAN 1964:** Dr. Albert Yrjo's experiments are shut down by New York University following the deaths of two research subjects during an alien-contact simulation. Yrjo loses tenure.

» **22 JAN 1964:** Stephen Alzis flies to Taiwan onboard a Civil Air Transport flight. At the direction of Joseph Camp, Delta Green attempts to assassinate Alzis (codenamed PARIAH), resulting in the plane disappearing over the Yellow Sea. Stephen Alzis reappears three months later in Brussels, none the worse for wear.

» **24 JAN 1964:** British author Ronald Shea stumbles upon the templeship of the insects from Shaggai in the Goatswood forest, where he is infested with one of the alien insects. Shea escapes from Goatswood and commits suicide rather than live as an alien's puppet. From this encounter, the insects first realize that mankind has developed space travel, although it will be many decades before human technology is advanced enough to free their templeship.

- **2 OCT 1964:** Delta Green carries out Operation KURTZ, eliminating the Mauti cult among the Simba and the Mulele in the Belgian Congo.
- **2 FEB 1965:** Adolph Lepus, future leader of MAJESTIC's NRO DELTA, serves four consecutive tours in South Vietnam as a Marine sniper.
- **12 APR 1966:** Disgraced in the academic community, Dr. Albert Yrjo publishes his first book, *The Group Dynamic in a Stress Environment*.
- **6 MAY 1966:** A U.S. Air Force F-4 Phantom is struck by a "fast radar target." The pilot ejects and is recovered, comatose. Three weeks later, the pilot awakens and murders four before being killed. An autopsy reveals a meter-long, silver and red, organ-like creature growing in his chest. MAJESTIC investigates and covers the incident up.
- **12 NOV 1966:** In Operation PORLOCK, Delta Green investigates three deaths and two disappearances in a "Cosmic Experience Acid Test," held in the closed fairground outside Escabacogan, Illinois.
- **4 MAY 1967:** In Operation SUDDEN SAM, Delta Green investigates Abdullah Evers, an astrologer, UFO contactee, and radical activist who predicted that Cleveland would burn to the ground during the upcoming partial eclipse — and whose advisor in astrology, Emmett Cobb, resides in the Lima State Hospital for the Criminally Insane.
- **5 JUN 1967:** The Six-Day War begins between Israel and neighboring Arab states. Reinhard Galt, still acting as an advisor to the Egyptian Army, joins the fight against Israel.
- **3 FEB 1968:** Martin Cook, the wartime commander of Delta Green, dies of natural causes at his ranch in Montana.
- **19 FEB 1968:** Having been led to investigate a series of "anomalous" sites surrounding the Severn River in southwestern Wales, PISCES Brigadier Charles Balfour orders a large-scale raid on the town of Goatswood. PISCES, backed by elements of the British Army's Gurkha Brigade, massacres the inhabitants, demolishes the town, and confiscates a cult-related object known as the Moon Lens. During the Goatswood raid, several PISCES agents are infested by the insects from Shaggai, who infiltrate deep into PISCES.
- **22 APR 1968:** MAJESTIC recruits CIA officer Justin Kroft, its future director.
- **2 JAN 1969:** The Office of Naval Intelligence (ONI) team of Project PUZZLE releases its report on the USS *Eldridge* incident and its study of the Tillinghast Resonator. The report details how the resonator functions, but Project PUZZLE expressly chooses not to reactivate the resonator for fear of what might occur.

- **19 JAN 1969:** In Operation LOOKING GLASS, Delta Green airdrops 68 men into southeast Colombia. Only the commander, Maj. Walter J. Greyman, escapes a cult of genital-sacrificing Shub-Niggurath worshippers.
- **19 JAN 1969:** Dr. Abner Ringwood, cryptographic studies chief at the NSA, is recruited by MAJESTIC to break the still indecipherable alien signals intercepted by Project AQUARIUS 15 years earlier.
- **20 JAN 1969:** Richard Nixon is inaugurated as the 37th president of the United States. MAJESTIC continues their policy of not briefing presidents on their existence and findings until new developments occur.
- **26 JAN 1969:** Delta Green becomes aware of CIA support for the Tcho-Tcho in Indochina, including reports by U.S. Army Special Forces advisors calling for an end to aid to the "degenerate" tribesmen, who were using CIA-supplied weapons against non-communist locals. Delta Green fails to influence the CIA to stop aiding the Tcho-Tchos.
- **30 OCT 1969:** Club Apocalypse opens in New York City. It later becomes the unofficial headquarters of the Fate.
- **23 NOV 1969:** A Marine colonel with Delta Green clearance, Satchel Wade, launches Operation OBSIDIAN. Three hundred Marines parachute into the Cambodian jungle with orders to destroy a temple complex. The mission, inspired by Wade's mysterious Khmer mistress, proves a disaster. The temple is devoted to summoning a Great Old One called Angka to Earth, and the assault releases something titanic and nightmarish into the world. The handful of survivors fight their way back into Vietnam and execute Wade and his mistress.
- **1 OCT 1970:** Daniel Freis, former Delta Green cryptographer, dies in the Naval Hospital at Camp Pendleton.
- **8 OCT 1971:** Arvin Tipler, former Delta Green operative and veteran of Operation OBSIDIAN, murders 11 people in Annandale, Maryland, including a police officer, while screaming about "things from space."

The Fall

On 23 NOV 1969, a Marine colonel with Delta Green clearance, Satchel Wade, launched Operation OBSIDIAN. Three hundred Marines parachuted into the Cambodian jungle with orders to destroy a temple devoted to summoning Angka to Earth. The mission, inspired by Wade's mysterious Khmer mistress, was a disaster. Something titanic and nightmarish was released into the world. The handful of men who survived fought their way back into Vietnam, located Wade, and executed him and his mistress.

When U.S. and South Vietnamese troops invaded Cambodia in MAY 1970, they met stiff resistance from the well-prepared Viet Cong and Khmer Rouge. The Joint Chiefs of Staff blamed Delta Green. After the embarrassment of the 1968 Tet Offensive, revelations about the secret bombings in Laos, and the My Lai Massacre, the Pentagon did not want to explain to Congress what Delta Green was doing in Cambodia seven months before invasion. The decision was made to disband Delta Green and sweep its entire history under the rug.

On 24 JUL 1970, the Delta Green classification was officially deactivated, and the green triangles were removed from hundreds of personnel files. Soon Delta Green faded into bureaucratic myth.

However, this was not the end.

Rebirth

In AUG 1970, 40 federal officials who had previously held Delta Green clearance met secretly in Washington D.C. to determine what was to be done about the threat of the unnatural to national security. They didn't believe MAJESTIC had the skills needed to do the job, and worse, feared the misguided group might see the unnatural as an exploitable resource.

This group decided to reestablish contact with those who had previously possessed Delta Green clearance, to let them know that it was unofficially back in business. Old contacts were renewed and alliances re-forged. The reborn Delta Green's first "unofficial" action was Operation BINGO, where several flights of B-52s strayed off course to "accidentally" bomb every identified Tcho-Tcho village in Indochina from the map. By Christmas 1971, Delta Green was operating with no budget, no headquarters, no files, no authorization, and most importantly, no oversight.

To many in the organization, this freedom was seen as a significant improvement.

DISINFORMATION

YELLOW CARD

LOMAR AND HYPERBOREA

Various histories claim the arctic continent of Lomar rose during the Miocene. Initially peopled by a fur-bearing hominid species that some sources call the Voorii or Voormi, after millennia of warfare it became the home of the first known human culture, Zobna, near the current North Pole. The humans pursued the Voorii south into lower Lomar (what would become northern North America) and Hyperborea (even then slowly glaciating into Greenland), founding the cities of Olathoë in Lomar and Commoriom in Hyperborea.

The Hyperboreans learned hypergeometric magic from their god Tsathoggua, and from the prehuman Pnakotic Manuscripts they copied. Hyperborean sorcerers opened time gates into the warm, lush Miocene and built the Vault of Souls to imprison and weaken a Great Old One called Itla-shua, creating a temperate (if temporary) paradise. Using their own set of Pnakotic fragments, the lords of Lomar mastered Yithian telepathy, sending their minds into other species and centuries. Their great foe was Rhan-Tegoth, who ruled to their west. Or so legends claim.

Eventually, Itla-shua had its revenge and buried both civilizations under the ice. The last remnant of Lomar, Olathoë, fell to the anthropophagous Gnophkehs (or perhaps the Lomarians banished the Gnophkehs, as some sources say) and to the humans who followed them.

- A Puritan chronicle (c. 1700) mentions the “old Tribes of Lamah, who dwelt under the Great Bear, and were antiently destroy’d for their wickedness.” It implies they could control or contain “Ossadagowah.”
- In 1936, the Royal Canadian Mounted Police discovered stone ruins 260 km south of Baker Lake, Northwest Territories. Before the site could be analyzed, a band of Inuit shamans destroyed the ruins they called “Lamah.”
- In 1975, Canada’s M-Section encountered Lomarian remains in an open-pit mine on Baffin Island.
- In 1993, M-Section investigated late Lomarian remains in the Yukon’s Carcross Desert.
- In 2001, MAJESTIC satellite overflights of the poles noted two areas marked by “gravity anomalies,” one on each pole. This effect seemed to ebb and flow with the seasons.
- As Greenland’s glaciers continue to retreat, Delta Green remains on alert for a similar discovery of Hyperborean ruins in the island’s interior.

CUT ALONG THIS LINE

DISINFORMATION

YELLOW CARD

OPERATION BINGO

In December 1970, the disbanded Delta Green launched its first unofficial operation. Generals Fairfield and Stillman from the Executive Committee pulled strings to retask B-52s from the ongoing Operations ARC LIGHT (in Vietnam), GOOD LOOK (in Laos), and FREEDOM DEAL (in Cambodia). In the last two weeks of the month, U.S. air strikes obliterate every known Tcho-Tcho village and religious site, hitting some locations dozens of times. Individual program veterans in ONI and USAF follow up on targets of opportunity, redirecting Operation BARREL ROLL napalm strikes by F-4s from the USS **Kitty Hawk** and A-1s out of Thailand.

- **22 NOV 1972:** Project REDLIGHT, the MAJESTIC group overseeing "the Bucket," the spacecraft recovered at Roswell, decides to attempt to restart it. Justin Kroft, advising on behalf of Project PLUTO, is the sole member of the advisory group to recommend against doing so.
- **30 NOV 1972:** "The Bucket" is briefly reactivated at Groom Lake by Project REDLIGHT. It explodes, killing four MAJESTIC personnel.
- **22 DEC 1972:** Justin Kroft is elevated to the MAJESTIC steering committee, due to his handling of the "Bucket" disaster.
- **11 FEB 1974:** In England, PISCES agents return to the Severn River Valley and raid the shop American Books Bought and Sold. They capture Wilbur Bromley — a worshipper and sometimes avatar of the Great Old One Y'Golonac — and imprison him on Hirta.
- **29 JUL 1975:** Future MAJESTIC steering committee member, Gavin Ross is recruited from the CIA as a member of MAJESTIC's enforcement arm, NRO DELTA.
- **1 MAY 1977:** Delta Green member and IRS agent Alvin Bright disappears in Brooklyn while investigating a person with known links to the Keepers of the Faith, a cult as old as New York itself. He is never seen again, alive or otherwise.
- **14 JUN 1977:** PISCES destroys an unknown cult operating in Lower Brichester and recovers multiple astrological texts and an odd, antique telescope.
- **23 MAR 1978:** NSA's Project AQUARIUS makes contact with the Greys through deep-space monitoring surveillance antennas, thanks to cryptographer Dr. Abner Ringwood. Project PLATO begins negotiation with the Greys.
- **1 MAY 1978:** Albert Yrjo is made director of MAJESTIC'S OUTLOOK group.
- **31 OCT 1980:** First face-to-face meeting held between MAJESTIC and the Greys. The living alien from the Roswell saucer is returned to the Greys after thirty-three years on Earth. The Greys present their terms for a treaty called the "Accord."
- **3 DEC 1980:** PISCES secretly assumes control of the Inland Revenue building in Brichester, but soon after the building is sealed and demolished due to an infestation of an "unknown species of arachnid." Several bizarre samples — some living — are recovered.
- **10 DEC 1980:** President-Elect Reagan is briefed on MAJESTIC, the Greys, and the Accord.

» **12 DEC 1980:** MAJESTIC works to authenticate the two documents offered by the Greys: "the Cookbook," a massive treatise on human genetics, and the "the Report," an exact breakdown of every military force on the planet.

» **6 FEB 1981:** MAJESTIC ratifies the Accord with the Greys, gaining technology and intelligence in exchange for covering up the aliens' terrestrial activities.

» **17 APR 1981:** U.S. Navy Lt. Commander Forrest James, future leader of the Delta Green special-access program, leads a SEAL team to recover electronic salvage from the wreck of the USS *Santa Cruz*. It becomes his first encounter with the Deep One threat, face-to-face.

» **2 JUN 1981:** Justin Kroft is elevated to leadership of the MAJESTIC steering committee with the code-name MJ-1.

» **1 SEP 1984:** After over two hundred reports of abductions, surgical manipulations and various odd events outside the scope of the "Accord," MAJESTIC contacts the Greys to discuss the situation. The aliens inform MAJESTIC that the arrangement will continue, as agreed. Terrified and with no recourse, MAJESTIC agrees.

» **5 MAY 1987:** PISCES drains Brichester Lake, searching for a rumored entity called "Glaaki." Though the lake is determined to have been created by meteor impact, no such creature is located.

» **12 SEP 1988:** Delta Green recruits Forrest James after his report on the USS *Santa Cruz* incident.

» **22 JAN 1990:** Delta Green recruits FBI forensic psychologist Debra Constance.

» **4 MAY 1990:** MAJESTIC promotes Gavin Ross to the directorship of Project GARNET, and briefs him fully on the Greys and the Accord.

» **21 FEB 1991:** Dr. Yrjo opens a new OUTLOOK Group facility in Puerto Rico.

» **19 JUL 1992:** Delta Green agent Debra Constance meets with Theodore Morse, a college friend who disappeared in 1989 and was presumed dead. Morse exposes her to an unnatural tome which transforms Constance — like himself — into a ghoul. She turns herself into Delta Green along with the tome.

» **8 SEP 1992:** With Delta Green's assistance, Debra Constance assumes the form of Jean Qualls, a dead party girl. She continues serving the Delta Green conspiracy as Agent Nancy.

THREAT MATRIX

RED CARD

THE SURVIVORS OF INNSMOUTH

Deep One hybrids captured in the raid on Innsmouth were in the hands of the government for many decades — but few in the government knew it. After World War II, the prisoners were kept at a facility in the Atomic Energy Commission's reserve at Los Alamos, codenamed YY-II and ICE CAVE. (This same facility also hosted a living extraterrestrial biological entity or "Grey" from 1947 to 1981.)

Catatonic since the early 1940s, the Innsmouth survivors had been driven mad by their decades-long separation from the ocean. Access to the prisoners was governed by security clearance PUZZLEBOX, a clearance that dated back to 1942. No one had even asked about the prisoners since the 1960s, but the ICE CAVE was charged with storing them indefinitely. Even when the last personnel with PUZZLEBOX clearance retired.

Ultimately, MAJESTIC expanded ICE CAVE to store samples of extra-terrestrial life that the BLUE FLY teams had collected. Because of MAJESTIC's ruthless compartmentalization, no one running the facility questioned that there was a section they did not have clearance to enter. Everyone presumed that someone else must be responsible for it. During an inventory in 1999, it was discovered that no one had been inside a closed section of the facility since 1972. When this section was opened, the Deep One hybrids it was supposed to contain were gone. Nothing remained inside the huge, long-evaporated, salt water tanks in which the Innsmouth survivors once slept in a torpor.

IN THE FIELD: The Cowboy Years Campaign

After 1970, Delta Green became a secret conspiracy which tunneled through the heart of the federal government, composed of agents who got things done, illegally and off the books. Those wishing to run a game set in the Cowboy Years (1970 to 1994) should keep the following in mind:

- **RECRUITS:** All Agents begin as recruits. What their contact tells them is dependent on the situation. It is likely they don't even know the name of the agency—yet. But what binds them together is the fact that they saw something unnatural. And if someone who appears in authority shows up to confirm such horrors, it goes a long way to building loyalty.
- **NO ONE MUST KNOW:** The first rule is *no one must know*. All the work of the Group is off the books. This means those at the agent's job must not know, their family cannot know, everything they do must remain secret. Spreading a truth this big can destroy the very thing the Group fights for.
- **HUNTED?:** Rumors persist that a counter-conspiracy operates at the highest level of the federal government, and that it is hunting agents from the Group. But who knows, really? And even if they did, would they say anything?
- **LIES, ALL THE WAY DOWN:** What is the truth? Does your fellow agent know it? Do the leaders of Delta Green? The truth is there is no truth. Or at least, no truth anyone sane might understand. There are only shades of lies. The worst revelation is this: the Group is not there to save you, it is there to use you. And once you are used up, you become the mission.

Reorganization

From 1970 to 1994, there was no real Delta Green to speak of. It existed as an unofficial, secret fraternity of federal law enforcement, intelligence, and military personnel. It had no funding, but its members channeled funds, equipment, services, and personnel as needed from whatever agency or military branch they happened to work for. Delta Green's Agents were not full-time; they worked for other organizations such as the FBI, the CIA, the USAF, and the IRS. Whenever possible, they were "assigned" to Delta Green operations by the machinations of other Delta Green agents, who camouflaged their activities as mundane duties.

The result was disastrous. Deprived of a central intelligence collective, Delta Green agents went into operations armed with nothing more than personal experience. The group's policy towards the unnatural was "scorched earth": stop what's going on, destroy all evidence of it, and leave no trace.

This suited the old guard. By and large, they were disenchanted with their government, and felt that only they knew what was going on. No longer hampered by bureaucrats, they directed a kill-'em-all policy motivated more from spite than pragmatism. This continued for the first quarter of a century of Delta Green's new, illegal existence, a period about which little is recorded. Some in the know call this period "The Cowboy Era."

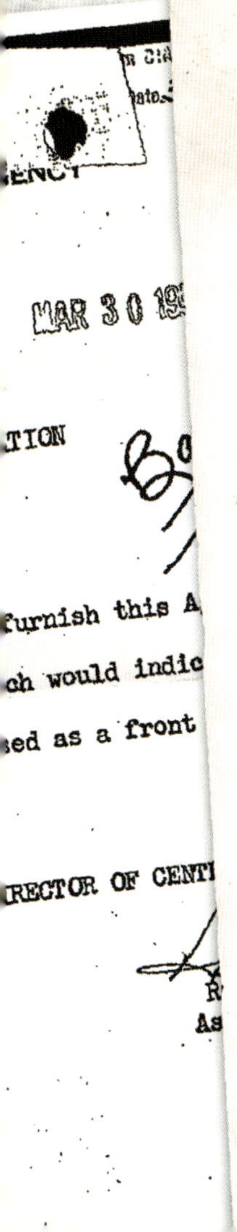
MAR 30 19
TION
furnish this A
ch would indic
sed as a front
RECTOR OF CENT

IN THE FIELD: The Fate Campaign

The Fate was an exclusive and secretive group of unnaturally-skilled individuals in New York City devoted to the eventual release of Nyarlathotep. Led by the seemingly untouchable Stephen Alzis, they controlled a cult and criminal enterprise that stood unopposed in the New York underworld, and feared no group or individual. To insiders, the term "the Fate" referred both to the group itself and its leadership. To those outside the organization, its structure and purpose were a mystery. The entire group was simply known as "the Network."

Within the group was a hierarchy of ranks, with the members of the Fate itself at the top. The Fate rigidly controlled the actions of Lords, Neophytes, and Adepts who composed their network of agents. Servants who acted without orders rarely lived long enough to reconsider.

The Fate can make an ideal basis for a Delta Green campaign set in New York in the 1980s and 1990s. Here are a few things to keep in mind:

- **ALZIS KNOWS ALL:** While the servants of the Fate may be subject to the laws that govern mortals, Stephen Alzis knows no such limits. By the 1990s, even Delta Green had ceased trying to assassinate him, as—no matter the lengths to which they went—he would always return, unharmed. His motives and sources of knowledge are as inscrutable as the games he plays with the Agents.
- **ANYONE CAN DISAPPEAR:** The Fate's access to hypergeometric techniques made their crimes unique. Thefts, murders, and worse, all achieved through unnatural means, leaving not a shred of evidence behind.
- **THE CITY IS ITS HOST:** Rising from the depths of a bankrupt 1970s, New York of the 1980s and 1990s was a place struggling for stability. Crime was still rampant and the city was still wild. The Fate embraced the banal horrors of the city and hid among them.

DISINFORMATION

YELLOW CARD

IREM AND THE NAMELESS CITY

The legendary, pre-Islamic Arabian city "Irem of the Pillars" appears in the **Quran** and the **Thousand and One Nights**, both of which describe its sudden destruction by Allah for the impiety of its inhabitants. Later mythographers located Irem variously in the interior of Saudi Arabia, Yemen, or Oman. A 1991 expedition identified an Iron Age frankincense trading fort at al-Shisr in Oman as Irem (or "Ubar") after discovering its eight towers, fallen into a sinkhole some time around 400 CE. Al-Hazredic legend connects Irem to a pre-human "Nameless City" inhabited by ghostly reptiles, implying that the Adites of Irem somehow destroyed it. Abd al-Hazred supposedly composed the first couplet of the **Necronomicon** ("That is not dead," etc.) dreaming of the Nameless City while in the ruins of Irem. Given the scale of NRO DELTA and other MAJESTIC operations in Saudi Arabia and Oman in 1990 and 1991 under cover of Gulf War deployments, it is conceivable that MAJESTIC discovered one or both sites. Follow-up operations by Delta Green during the Second Gulf War proved frustratingly indecisive, leading some officers to suspect that former MAJESTIC officials altered previously-collected intelligence in the confusion of Delta Green's takeover of MAJESTIC.

- Prisoner testimony from the 1907 St. Bernard Parish raid establishes Irem as an important location for the global Cthulhu cult.
- Miskatonic professor Nathaniel Wingate Peaslee may have entered Irem or the Nameless City in 1911, while under Yithian possession.
- The writings of occultist Randolph Carter describe Irem as a city on the border between reality and the Outside, with a mighty hand sculpted on the keystone of its main arch. Carter implies that Yog-Sothoth dwells there.
- The 19th Baron Northam mounted an expedition to the Nameless City in 1921 and returned to London a shattered wreck, seemingly decades older.
- A 1930 letter by Harry St. John Philby recounts his conversation with an old man in Yemen who had seen Irem in the al-Dahna desert in central Saudi Arabia, and worshiped there at underground shrines of Nug and Yeb. Philby himself mounted an expedition into the Rub' al-Khali in 1932, and insisted that the Wabar meteor crater represented the remains of Irem. Philby may have been trying to throw later explorers off the scent of the true Irem.
- Philby's son Kim may have compromised a PISCES mission to the Wabar/Irem site (Operation CALDERA) in 1948.
- Stephen Alzis once mentioned, on tape, that his birthplace was a "city of pillars." When pressed, he either could not or would not recall the name.

Delta Green does not know whether Irem and the Nameless City are the same place, separate dimensional extensions overlapping in one geographical locus, or two different haunted ruins. The desert could easily conceal both.

CUT ALONG THIS LINE

031-51937 o-46

Fairfield

In February 1994, one of the Delta Green old guard, U.S. Army Major General Reginald Fairfield (retired), was assassinated by members of NRO Section DELTA, MAJESTIC's counter-intelligence service. General Fairfield was one of the key members that had kept Delta Green going after its official disbandment. He detested the things MAJESTIC had done, and had learned enough to be viewed as a threat. This assassination was the first direct action taken by MAJESTIC against Delta Green, but Delta Green was not equipped to respond rapidly.

By 1994, only 40 members of the "official" Delta Green remained. Of these, half were in government service, and almost all were due for mandatory retirement. But they had access to a hundred agents who had served on at least one Delta Green operation, another hundred retired government officials who had served Delta Green in the past, and approximately five hundred Delta Green "friendlies" scattered around the world.

Realizing the threat posed by MAJESTIC, Professor Joseph Camp—an aging OSS and Delta Green veteran working in the Library of Congress—saw an opportunity for a change. He convinced the old guard that their only option was to evolve. It was time for Delta Green to fight MAJESTIC.

In the fall of 1994, Delta Green was reborn yet again.

TOP SECRET//SAR-DELTA GREEN

» **10 NOV 1992:** MAJESTIC chooses not to brief President-Elect Clinton, or any future president, on its existence until such a time as it is appropriate.

» **19 APR 1993:** A Delta Green investigation into cult activity at a Mount Carmel retreat near Waco, Texas, ends in the destruction of the Branch Davidian compound, with 86 dead including four ATF agents. No unnatural cause is ever uncovered.

» **13 FEB 1994:** Justin Kroft, MJ-1 is diagnosed with colon cancer. He secretly begins treatment at MAJESTIC Facility-12 in the badlands of Montana, receiving doses of an alien substance created from "the Cookbook" codenamed BLUEBLOOD. It halts the progress of his disease.

» **18 JAN 1994:** Fearing exposure, MAJESTIC pressures a former member, Admiral Bobby Ray Inman, to withdraw his candidacy for Secretary of Defense.

» **25 FEB 1994:** Longtime Delta Green leader Reginald Fairfield dies fighting NRO DELTA assassins. Fairfield had attempted to go public with revelations of MAJESTIC's Accord with the Greys.

YELLOW CARD

THE TRUTH BEHIND THE GREYS

The Greys are biological automatons controlled by a horrifically inhuman, unnatural race known as the fungi from Yuggoth, or the mi-go. The mi-go had come to Earth long before humanity and mined the world for resources. They staged the Roswell saucer crash to study human reactions. Further UFO incidents – the disappearances of civilians and aircraft and the epidemics of cattle mutilation and genetic harvesting – were part of the study.

In 1978, the mi-go decided humanity had become sufficiently competent and ruthless. They made contact with MAJESTIC. In preparation, the mi-go developed two layers of deception. First, they disguised themselves as the Greys; then they gave the Greys a "secret agenda." The Greys' cover story was that they were peaceful explorers searching for a way to escape extinction. The secret agenda was a supposed plan to harvest humanity for raw material to reconstruct their species. Once MAJESTIC uncovered the Greys' secret agenda, they did not look beyond the first deception.

The U.S. government, carefully manipulated, came to replace the mi-go's ancient but inefficient network of human collaborators and cultists.

The Greys' secret agenda was not far from the truth, which was never discovered by MAJESTIC or Delta Green. The mi-go's interest in the Earth goes beyond its geological treasures. They have always been curious about the human brain. It performs like nothing they've ever encountered. It is the first sentient mind they've found that is epistemically diploid. That is, it has two distinct aspects: rational and irrational. This allows humans to make guesses that do not fit a logical extrapolation from theoretical models. Unlike humans, the mi-go cannot think intuitively.

Most frightening to the mi-go is that the human mind and its irrational leaps of logic are often **correct**. Humanity's progress from the creation of radio to the deployment of nuclear weapons in only a few years greatly impressed the non-terrene scientists from the outer rim.

Much of the mi-go's work as Greys had been to conduct experiments in human intuition under the cover of UFO abductions. The mi-go subjected each abductee's mind to bizarre stimuli while monitoring reactions. Some subjects were returned with the memory of the experience suppressed. Sometimes a particularly promising subject (or just their brain) was taken back to Yuggoth and subjected to unspeakable discoveries and horrors.

The Greys stopped communicating with MAJESTIC in 2001, but interviews with abductees in the archives of SaucerWatch and **Phenomen-X**, or with former MAJESTIC scientists and security officers, could reveal patterns in the Greys' behavior and hints of the truth behind them. With the MAJESTIC programs long ended and the Greys' operations all but suspended on Earth, it remains unknown: Did the mi-go accomplish their goal of granting intuition to their kind? Perhaps their silence is simply an intermission before the final act.

CUT ALONG THIS LINE

031-51937 o-46

DTG: 212131Z Aug 12

Precedence: ROUTINE

DAC: General

RED CARD

PORTRAYING THE MI-GO

If your Agents seem unafraid of the mi-go and their puppet-representatives the Greys, you're not doing your job. Here are some tips to bring the fear.

- **BEYOND COMPREHENSION:** The mi-go are not merely "sentient fungus crab-things" from space. Portions of them intersect, vanish and reappear in nearby dimensional branes. The mi-go body crawls about a framework of lattice-like "bone." Surface villi are alive with lights blinking in intelligent, baffling patterns. They move and fly in stuttering un-movement, seeming to skip and start without crossing intervening distances like a film played at double-speed. **They are utterly alien.**
- **MACRODIMENSIONAL:** The mi-go exist both in dimensions above and below human existence, as well as the dimensions we occupy. They might be able to access a sealed bank vault as easily as stepping through an open doorway, or to attack at great distance by utilizing an upper-dimensional "shortcut." Worse, they can sense and see well beyond the ranges of normal physics in ways humanity can never know.
- **MASTERY OVER TIME/SPACE:** Our concept of "physics" is simply a local misunderstanding, and it is only partially true. The mi-go understand and can change the physical world in inexplicable and completely maddening ways that defy explanation. They are not omnipotent, nor as potent as the Great Old Ones, but every interaction with them should unnerve the Agents.
- **THE GREYS ARE BIZARRE:** The Greys are marionettes that the mi-go use to manipulate humanity. One mi-go can control half a dozen at a time. Imagine the Greys as a remote-control submersible which isolates and restricts the vast intellect and senses of the mi-go into a narrow range, so that they might "see" what a human sees.
- **HOLES IN MEMORY:** The narrative of what an Agent experiences is under the Handler's total control. The mi-go and the Greys cut and paste human thought in complete, though sometimes sloppy ways. Their poor understanding of linear time as experienced by humans makes these errors apparent to humans but not to mi-go. Those interacting with the mi-go may experience lost time, bizarre "screen memories" of mundane things which never happened, and more. It is best to play these out and let the Agents uncover the truth on their own — or find that there is only a void left where their memories were excised.

CUT ALONG THIS LINE

031-51937 o-46

DISINFORMATION

YELLOW CARD

YUGGOTH AND BEYOND

The archives of occultists, visionaries, and UFO contactees burgeon with tales of alien worlds often barely described: Yekub probes for planetary death with telepathic cubes, Shonhi and the triple-star Nyhon draw sages from many galaxies, Yaddith is home to the wise Nug-Soth and the burrowing bhole-worms, the living god-planet Ghroth hurtles through deep space bearing the song of Nemesis. At the center of it all – perhaps inside the supermassive black hole at the heart of the galaxy – lies the court of Azathoth. Which of these are real? No one sane knows.

Our own solar system shows the stigmata of the unnatural:

- Mi-go mine the dark side of the Moon for non-terrene materials.
- Alien races have left cyclopean ruins on Mars, although not (so far as Delta Green knows) in the Cydonia region. Unless Cydonia Mensae is yet another extrusion of the Plateau of Leng, of course.
- In 1904, alienist Giles Fenton transcribed the dream-statement of the insane murderer Joseph Slater describing a race of insectile aliens on Callisto. Yithian records found in a junk shop in Melbourne confirm Slater's account; they reached their cultural and philosophical apex six million years ago.
- Believers in Edgar Cayce's "Earth Changes" prophecies say the Earth once orbited Saturn, called the "sun star" in Chaldean records. Pnakotic and Hyperborean inscriptions depict Tsathoggua, at least, moving easily between the worlds.
- Per the **Revelations of Glaaki**, the cuboid metallic L'gh'rxians dwell on Uranus; they worship Lrogg, a bat-like avatar of Nyarlathotep. The insects from Shaggai spent nine centuries in uneasy cohabitation with the L'gh'rxians before continuing on to Earth. Is this true? Or was it at one time?
- Wind-fed intelligent fungi – possibly mi-go creations – inhabit the atmosphere of Neptune. So claims **Unaussprechlichen Kulten.**
- The Wilmarth report identifies Pluto with Yuggoth, the home (or local staging area) of the mi-go. Mi-go camouflage or disinformation conceals Yuggoth's warm seas and metal bridges beneath Pluto's craters and nitrogen ice fields. The mi-go also extensively colonize and mine Pluto's moon Charon.

CUT ALONG THIS LINE

031-51937 o-46

- **21 MAY 1994:** Professor Joseph Camp persuades surviving Delta Green veterans to reorganize the group so that intelligence can be gathered and centralized, to counter the increasing threat of MAJESTIC.
- **6 AUG 1994:** Delta Green agents investigate the theft of the *Revelations of Glaaki*, Vol. XII, from a Chicago library. They unsuccessfully pursue Johannes Knepier, prime suspect in the theft and possible instigator of a 1977 mass murder-suicide in rural Louisiana.
- **12 JUN 1995:** Delta Green agents investigate disappearances on Owlshead Mountain, Vermont, and encounters a horrific, unnatural entity. One agent dies and the others flee, but must scramble to cover up the death and divert attention away from the site. Due to poor communication, Delta Green doesn't revisit the incident for three years.
- **1 AUG 1995:** Unwittingly aided by Delta Green, FBI agents pursue a killer in the San Carlos Indian Reservation only to discover an extraterrestrial entity is to blame. The agents encounter a MAJESTIC team that had been pursuing the entity.
- **10 AUG 1995:** Three Delta Green agents vanish while investigating disappearances in midtown New York's Macallistar Building. A subsequent Delta Green operation carefully burns the building to the ground without investigating further, framing dead residents for the arson. Delta Green keeps the site under watch but declares it off-limits without the express permission of A-cell.

DISINFORMATION

YELLOW CARD

HISTORY AT THE TABLE

Many events in this timeline are drawn from published Delta Green scenarios and fiction, placing each in its original "default" point in history and presenting the most likely course of events. Adjust these entries, and anything else on this timeline, to suit your own game. There are endless versions of reality, after all. And if tales of the Great Race of Yith are to be believed, even the so-called "Construct" of our own spacetime is ever-changing. If your Agents' memories suddenly, bafflingly differ from what everyone else accepts as history, that could lead to a terrifying search for the truth.

- **15 SEP 1996:** Delta Green agents discover an infestation of living, unnatural "protomatter" in Groversville, Tennessee. The agents encounter alien Greys, and discover that the mi-go seem to be controlling the Greys like puppets. The agents barely escape a confrontation with MAJESTIC security officers sent to conceal the Greys' activities, and most of the town dies of a virulent disease released by the thwarted masters of the Greys. MAJESTIC covers up the mass casualties as a supposed hantavirus outbreak.
- **17 SEP 1996:** Under orders from Alphonse, Prof. Grant Emerson, Delta Green friendly, examines material recovered at Groversville (called "protomatter," though Emerson preferred "neotissue"). Shortly thereafter, all samples are destroyed.
- **22 NOV 1996:** MAJESTIC sends a BLUE FLY team to another extraterrestrial threat in Montana, related to the San Carlos Indian Reservation incident of 1995. BLUE FLY eliminates three unknown extraterrestrial biological entities dubbed "travelers" or "EBE2."

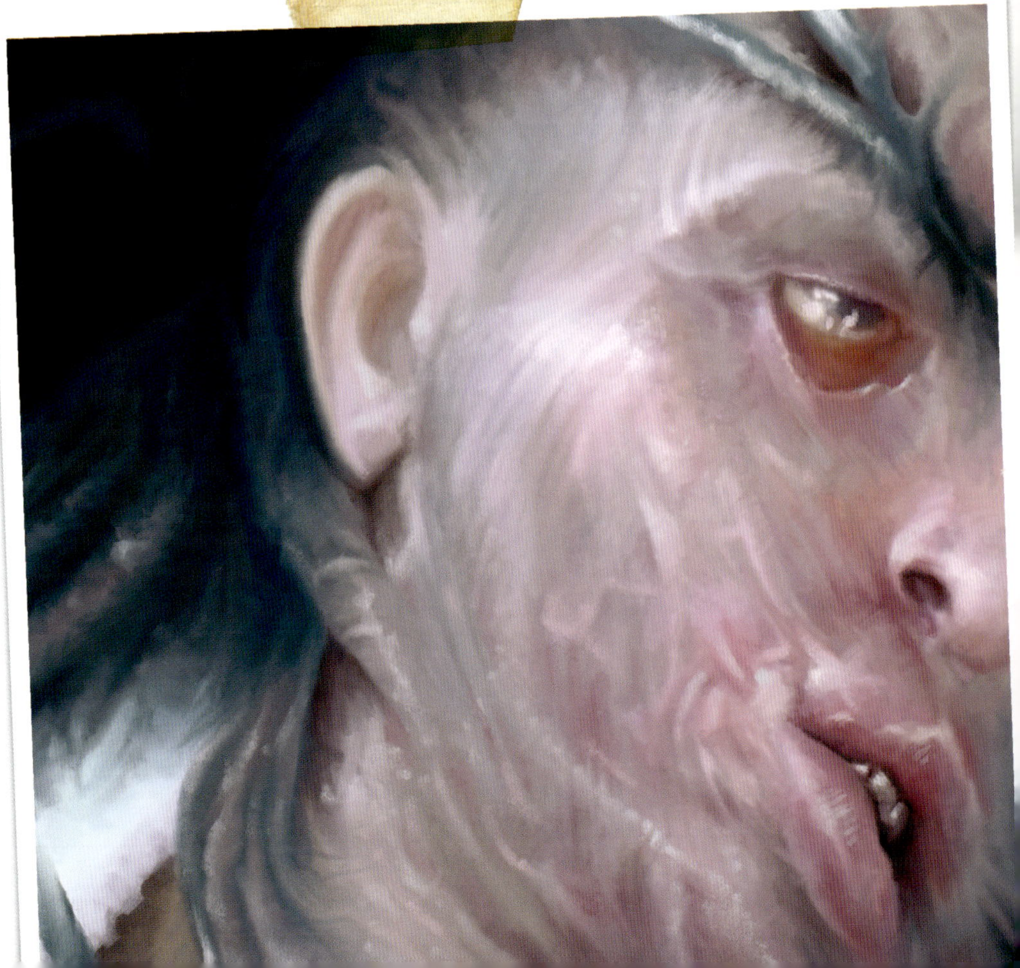

The Best-Laid Plans

After the 1994 murder of Delta Green leader Reginald Fairfield, his right-hand man, Joseph Camp, took over. Camp refined Delta Green into a cell conspiracy, following OSS standards from World War II. Camp led from A-cell under the code-name Agent Alphonse. Throughout the 1990s (and even beyond), this cell conspiracy continued to cut corners, change the rules, and use anything at hand to push back the darkness.

Each active Delta Green agent was a part of a three-agent cell. That was the principle, anyway; some cells had more or fewer agents, and not all agents were "in the field." These members knew the other members of the cell by real names and occupations. Members of all other cells, however, were only known by code names. All members of any given cell knew the code name of the leader of the cell above and below theirs. Others might be learned when cells had to work together. Ideally, use of code names would prevent any cell member from directly betraying anyone besides the members of his or her own cell.

Cell names were assigned with the same letter per cell, descending alphabetically. The top members of Delta Green, therefore, were known as Adam, Andrea, and Alphonse. There were never more than twenty-six active cells (and sometimes, much, much fewer), resulting in a maximum of seventy-eight active agents.

In practice, of course, many Delta Green operations involved more than one cell, and agents often learned each other's names and occupations. A given agent might be able to reveal the identities of three or four other agents, who could in turn reveal another three or four agents; but at some point, integrity was maintained.

Delta Green's leaders realized that a full-scale investigation would inevitably destroy the group, and the best they could do was to keep a low profile. Delta Green's deep reach in the government guaranteed that any investigation into their activities could be quickly discovered, misdirected or confounded before it went very far.

Nevertheless, it was clear that the largest threat was MAJESTIC, and Delta Green had no reliable sources of intelligence in that organization. For this reason, Joseph Camp set his sights on gathering as much intelligence as possible on MAJESTIC and its activities. Delta Green hoped it could accumulate enough incriminating evidence on MAJESTIC's activities that they could blackmail its leaders into backing off. Ultimately, that plan did not survive first contact with the enemy.

Too much of what Delta Green had been investigating since Innsmouth could not be easily categorized as either "supernatural" or "extraterrestrial" — if, indeed, there was a difference. As one long-time Delta Green agent once put it to a fresh recruit: "At some point you realize that all this weird shit, all of it, it all comes from the same place."

The Delta Green-MAJESTIC War: Opening Moves

From 25 FEB 1994 until 2 MAR 2001, Delta Green fought a silent war against MAJESTIC. There were many battlefields. Groversville, Tennessee. San Carlos Indian Reservation, Arizona. Tulsa, Oklahoma. Big Porcupine Creek, Montana. Platt Air Force Base, Nebraska. High Knob Mountain, Virginia. Owlshead Mountain, Vermont. Bountin, Maryland. Vieques Island, Puerto Rico. Point 103, Antarctica.

MAJESTIC had only one agenda: protect the Accord with the Greys. Delta Green, even at its worst, was a small distraction. Despite this focus, MAJESTIC was not a monolithic entity. Many members were uncomfortable with the Greys. Some suspected the creatures were not real, or were merely proxies for something more alien. Others believed that MAJESTIC had devolved into a kind of cargo cult, with MAJESTIC kowtowing to curry favor with its inhuman masters.

In their few moments of clarity, MAJESTIC's leadership understood that they were serving an agenda they did not understand. Their own crimes in the service of that agenda, however, were so terrible that none dared expose it.

» **10 FEB 1997:** MAJESTIC Project GARNET completes a laborious sweep of all pre-1970 U.S. military files, and compiles a list of those marked with green delta stickers. This list is used to track many pre-1970 Delta Green personnel and their contacts.

» **16 JUN 1997:** Agent Darren — Forrest James — is sentenced to ten years in military prison for assaulting a woman during a violent PTSD flashback.

» **9 AUG 1997:** The infamous "Nemesis hoax." Astronomers around the world report seeing a new planetoid moving toward Earth, only to discover that their computers had all been compromised by a widespread software virus. That was an elaborate cover-up by MAJESTIC's disinformation teams. Delta Green agents had discovered the "Nemesis" planetoid, and realized that it was in fact a gigantic, living entity, while investigating an insane plot at the heart of a cult called Enolsis. The agents disrupted the plot, at great cost, and the planetoid vanished.

» **24 OCT 1997:** Delta Green agents pursue the so-called "Glenridge Chiropractor," a Long Island spree killer that turns out to be an unnatural entity.

» **4 JUN 1998:** Delta Green agents investigate deaths on Owlshead Mountain, Vermont, and learn of the deadly 1995 operation. They confront a servant of the mi-go and escape the horrifying entity that attacked the 1995 team.

» **3 JUL 1998:** Delta Green agents Cyrus and Charlie — Curtis McRay and Donald Poe — begin a campaign against Stephen Alzis, leader of the Fate. They assassinate him but a few days later he returns. They try again, with the same result, over and over. Soon, the reprisals begin. Delta Green agents disappear, one after another. McRay and Poe break into Club Apocalypse to confront Alzis again, but instead they steal Alzis' prize possession, a scrapbook of old photos. Agent Alphonse brokers an unpleasant truce. Alzis gets his scrapbook back, agents stop vanishing, and Delta Green agrees to operate in New York City only with Alzis' permission.

» **6 SEP 1998:** Delta Green agents pursue a chemical that reanimates the dead from a Berkeley post office to a Montana production plant. They learn that Delta Green's old foe, the Karotechia, is still active somewhere in South America.

- **18 JAN 1999:** Lawrence Hong, evidence examiner for the popular UFO investigative foundation SaucerWatch, is abducted from the Topeka, Kansas home he shares with SaucerWatch founder Denton Shaeffer. Police find Hong in Miami, Florida, two months later, wandering the streets with no memory of the past ten years. Despite extensive therapy, his memory never returns.
- **13 MAR 1999:** Seeking a kidnapped agent, Delta Green triggers an EPA raid on a MAJESTIC-linked think tank called OUTLOOK Group, Inc., in Bountin, Maryland. Nine federal marshals die, along with seven NRO-DELTA security officers. During years of bogus hearings, MAJESTIC covers up the incident as a drug bust gone catastrophically bad.
- **15 MAR 1999:** Agent Alphonse is shot by an old friend, the mother of a missing Delta Green agent. He spends many months recuperating and never fully recovers.
- **22 MAR 1999:** Forrest James escapes from the military prison at Fort Leavenworth with the aid of Stephen Alzis and Karotechia enforcer Reinhard Galt. Galt murders Delta Green's Agent Adam.
- **24 MAR 1999:** Forrest James and Agent Nancy lead a raid on an OUTLOOK facility in Puerto Rico to rescue captured Delta Green agents. The raid results in a strange encounter with Stephen Alzis, the facility's destruction, and the baffling disappearance of Agent Shasta, who had somehow been imbued with godlike powers and consciousness.
- **24 JUL 1999:** Delta Green agents in London engage in a deadly, public shootout with PISCES agents infected with alien insects from Shaggai. Called the "Embassy Row Massacre," the incident is blamed on Irish terrorists. Delta Green retreats from the UK and quietly investigates the extent of the alien infestation.
- **1 OCT 1999:** Delta Green agents investigate disappearances surrounding a University of Montana-Helena excavation at Big Porcupine Creek, Montana. The disappearances turn out to be related to a temporally unstable artifact imbued with Tillinghast radiation.

- **12 JUN 2000:** The wealthy family of Sheridan Dunwoody-Smith, benefactor of SaucerWatch, sues her and the organization, accusing them of misappropriating family funds. The suit has little merit, but then a local TV news exposé accuses SaucerWatch's Denton Shaeffer of possessing and creating child pornography. The new charges are backed up by evidence planted by MAJESTIC operatives. More lawsuits follow. Paralyzed and impoverished by court battles, SaucerWatch shuts down for good within a year.
- **9 JUL 2000:** Forrest James accepts Gavin Ross' invitation to join NRO DELTA. Their alliance would lead to Ross briefly taking control of Delta Green's A-cell, and then his imprisonment as James helps Ross' rivals seize control of the MAJESTIC-12 Steering Committee.
- **5 OCT 2000:** Cho Chu-tsao, the ambitious young leader of the Chicago Tcho-Tcho gang called Tong Shukoran, brings the gang's front company Tiger Transit fully under the control of people who answer only to her.

DISINFORMATION

YELLOW CARD

THE MAJESTIC CARGO CULT

In 1981, MAJESTIC established communications with the apparently extraterrestrial civilization they termed "the Greys" – those behind the Roswell saucer – and began to exchange information. At first, this was simply coded signals. Later, this exchange involved personnel and technology.

However, this civilization was thousands or perhaps **millions** of years in advance of Earth. As the machinery, and the Greys behind it, became more and more intertwined with MAJESTIC, humanity failed to keep up. Even the most simple machines presented by these entities were far beyond the most advanced human science.

Like the near stone-age South Sea islanders thrust into the twentieth century by the advent of World War II, so was MAJESTIC suddenly thrust into a universe without humanity at its center.

Some of those South Sea islanders formed cults to worship the radio, the airplane, as well as the "cargo" – the amazing things dropped from the sky as if by magic. MAJESTIC devolved over time into something very similar. They would never admit it, but once understanding was beyond them, they invariably turned towards a kind of reverential worship.

As this relationship deepened, MAJESTIC turned its attentions away from the political landscape. Instead of seizing control of the U.S. government or using its resources for national security, MAJESTIC focused on its inhuman benefactors, the technology it recovered and whatever advantages that technology could generate. With these trinkets, they bought compliance from those few in the government who knew of their existence.

By the time of the attacks of 9/11, MAJESTIC had retreated into a secure bubble of bountiful budgets, no oversight and no moral guidelines. It had fractured due to internal conflicts, assassinations, and defections. Its leaders paid little attention to politics, except inasmuch as politics served their purposes. When the War on Terror reshaped the world around them, they were just as startled as anyone else.

CUT ALONG THIS LINE

031-51937 0-46

SECRET

(U) C

Downgrade to U//AIUO when
separated from attachment

SECRET/

TOP SECRET//REL TO USA, FVEY

DISINFORMATION

YELLOW CARD

TIGER TRANSIT AND TONG SHUKORAN

Tiger Transit began as a Vietnam War-era CIA proprietary that smuggled weapons and insurgents into Laos and heroin out. During the 1980s, Tiger Transit flew arms to the Contras in Nicaragua and cocaine to Narcos in Miami.

By the time the CIA cut ties to Tiger Transit in 1992, it had fallen under the influence of a criminal organization of second-generation Tcho-Tchos who had come to America to escape communist oppression in Southeast Asia. Police and news reports called them a tong, though they were not Chinese, and no two sources agreed on the Anglicized spelling of the name. A common use is "Tong Shukoran," perhaps derived from the Arabic "shukor," meaning thanksgiving or praise.

In the 1990s, using unnatural rituals to accumulate wealth for its own sake, not for the reverence of their god, the Tcho-Tchos of Tong Shukoran alienated their cousins overseas. Distributing a much-diluted version of their sacred Liao drug as the street drug "Reverb" was a step too far. The Tcho-Tchos of central Asia cut them off.

Led by a charismatic young woman named Cho Chu-tsao, Tong Shukoran gained another source: biotech firm Genetic Agricultural Products, Inc. (GAP), which used additives derived from unnatural sources but was badly mismanaged. A strategic partnership kept GAP in business and allowed Tong Shukoran to cultivate Liao. Cho Chu-tsao soon distanced herself from street crime, focusing on legitimate front companies. She acquired controlling shares in GAP in 2002.

Under Tong Shukoran, most of Tiger Transit's business was legitimate cargo transportation, but a small proportion of flights smuggled illicit goods for the Chicago Outfit. This alliance with the mafia gave Tong Shukoran protection against their rivals and ensured steady business. It proved disastrous when the FBI cracked down on the Chicago mafia in the 2000s. In 2005, Delta Green's Outlaws ensured that most Tong Shukoran members were imprisoned, killed, or sent to indefinite DHS detention. When the survivors began returning to the streets in 2008, their operations were much more circumspect.

The crackdown never came near Cho Chu-tsao, but it seized all assets of Tiger Transit. The Outlaws deliberately filed shoddy paperwork to leave them in bureaucratic limbo, and Tiger Transit's planes became the Outlaws' illicit house fleet.

(CONTINUED)

CUT ALONG THIS LINE

031-51937 o-46

Strength
The Aum's current membership is estimated at 1,500 to 2,000 persons. At the time
Tokyo subway attack, the group claimed to have 9,000 members in Japan and up to
40,000 worldwide.

sque Fatherland
erty (ETA)
.a. Euzkadi Ta
katasuna

YELLOW CARD

Then, in a rare joint operation in 2010, the Program noticed. The U.S. Marshals Service suddenly rectified the errors in the forfeiture process. A Program-managed CIA front company purchased the fleet. The Program put it to use by its asset-recovery arm, Operation CORAL NOMAD. The "theft" of Tiger Transit was just another bitter pill in a long line of recriminations between the Program and the Outlaws.

Today, Cho Chu-tsao is a successful businesswoman and an advocate for Tcho-Tcho civil rights. Under her management, GAP's additives have worked their way across the U.S. food chain. By Cho's calculations, crops grown with GAP additives comprise 0.93% of American calorific intake. In 2010, she embraced legalized marijuana cultivation. With cannabis strains "improved" by GAP additives, Tcho-Tcho entrepreneurs have launched dozens of farms. In fiscal year 2016, GAP posted $100 million in sales with $11 million in earnings. Cho Chu-tsao and her followers have more than enough wealth to cover up their most heinous and lurid sacrifices to the Great Old Ones.

THIS LINE

Al-Ga
(Islam

031-51939 o-46

Trojan Stalking Horse

The definitive move in the MAJESTIC War came not from Delta Green, but from the chief of MAJESTIC's counter-intelligence division: Gavin Ross. Ross intended to turn Delta Green into a weapon with which he could purge MAJESTIC. To do so, he recruited a disgraced Delta Green agent: Forrest James. A barely functional alcoholic, James had been court-martialed by the U.S. Navy, and escaped federal custody.

Ross offered the ex-SEAL a chance to serve his country again with MAJESTIC, feigning ignorance of James' membership in Delta Green, and offered a new identity that would let him live as a free man. James joined MAJESTIC's counter-intelligence arm. Under his new identity, "Captain John Smith" in the Office of Naval Intelligence, he solved MAJESTIC's problems.

When James finally revealed his membership in Delta Green to Ross, Ross claimed he was just as disaffected with MAJESTIC as James was, and suggested a greater good could be achieved bringing Delta Green and MAJESTIC together. Over the bitter objections of Professor Joseph Camp, James helped Ross force his way into Delta Green as a member of A-Cell. While retaining the code name Alphonse, Camp withdrew from the day-to-day decisions of Delta Green, making Ross—in secret—its defacto leader.

Endgame

It was not Gavin Ross' meticulously planned coup which led to the destruction of MAJESTIC. Instead, a series of disparate attacks by Delta Green and MAJESTIC personnel brought about its downfall. Adolph Lepus, the chief of NRO DELTA—MAJESTIC's wetworks branch—mutinied and assassinated Justin Kroft, the Chairman of MAJESTIC. Lepus then planned to clean house by eliminating his old Delta Green foe Agent Alphonse—Joseph Camp—as well.

When the smoke cleared, it became apparent that Camp and James had arranged an ambush. Camp, Lepus and his men were never found.

Meanwhile, Forrest James had made quick alliances with the three members of the MAJESTIC-12 Steering Committee who opposed the Accord: Lt. General Eustis Bell, Dr. Robert Varney, and Vice Admiral George Gates. They deployed Bell's Operation BLUE FLY in a series of coordinated strikes that eliminated the last of Lepus' men. They placed Gavin Ross and several other MAJESTIC personnel in "indefinite detention." Eustis Bell called a meeting of the Steering Committee.

Bell's faction held only three of the twelve seats. On paper, that should not have been enough to overturn the order of things. But BLUE FLY was MAJESTIC's most potent military force, and it answered to Eustis Bell. Bell's troops delivered all the directors on whom they could lay hands and instructed them to vote in a new MJ-1 Director: Navy Captain John Smith—aka Forrest James.

With guns at their heads, the other directors appointed Captain Smith as director of MJ-1 Project AQUARIUS and chairman of the MAJESTIC-12 Steering Committee.

The decapitation strike succeeded beyond all expectations. What events or conditions had brought about the critical alliance between Director Smith and Joseph Camp—who were once at odds—remains unknown. The old Russian saying applies: "Two men keep a secret best when one is dead."

Fun tions: NASA

TOP SECRET

THE DEPUTY SECRETARY OF DEFENSE
WASHINGTON 25, D. C.

BYE-6789-63

CUT ALONG THIS LINE

THE FATE OF THE FATE

The Fate influenced the New York City criminal underground for decades. They offered the impossible — for a price. Their leader was Stephen Alzis. Rumors claimed Alzis was the world's most powerful operator of the unnatural, an inhuman beast in disguise, or even a Great Old One. Delta Green learned very early that no matter how you killed him, his death was never, ever permanent.

The Fate and its Lords were without equal, possessors of occult books and artifacts that made them completely untouchable. Delta Green suffered painful losses in all attempts to curtail the Fate's activities. By the late 1990s, the two groups held an uneasy truce. It did not last long.

After 9/11, Alzis seemed to lose interest in the activities of the Fate. In December 2001, Alzis' aide-de-camp, Robert Hubert, was killed by a rival sorcerer. Through 2002, Alzis was seen less and less. Emir Agdesh ran the Fate and gave orders to its Lords on his own. In the Fate's winter solstice rituals of 22 DEC 2002, for the first time in decades, Nyarlathotep gave no answer to his worshippers' invocations.

By spring 2003, Agdesh had vanished as well, leaving the Fate without a leader. Throughout that spring and summer, many Lords of the Fate killed each other in a war for primacy — and it seemed that some died at other hands. They were picked off one by one, and the deaths were not all sorcerous. Delta Green denied being behind the strikes: a bomb, a sniper's shot, a gas explosion, a devastating conflagration the night of the 14 AUG 2003 blackout. But few can deny the attacks' military precision, nor the grim satisfaction that Delta Green's leaders would have taken in finally hitting Stephen Alzis' organization.

For his part, Alzis, long-since determined to be beyond mortal weakness, communicated his approval of the disintegration of his organization with a note sent to Curtis McRay from Shenzhen, China.

"Thank you for putting away my toys," it read. Alzis has not been heard from since.

031-51937 6-46

» **9 FEB 2001:** Justin Kroft, director of MAJESTIC is killed in a decapitation strike at Facility-12, a secret, underground base safeguarded by a small yield nuclear weapon. Kroft, the base and all personnel are destroyed as the weapon detonates at the direction of Adolph Lepus. MAJESTIC is thrown into chaos. Its disinformation arm barely manages to spin the event as an unusual earthquake.

» **12 FEB 2001:** Adolph Lepus and NRO DELTA descend on Fairfield Pond in Fairfield, Vermont, in an attempt to assassinate Joseph Camp. Camp, Lepus and the strike team are never heard from again.

» **13 FEB 2001:** Director Smith and his allies begin to consolidate MAJESTIC facilities, members, and projects, desperately trying to hold it all together to continue the fight.

» **2 MAR 2001:** Director Smith and Donald Poe come to an understanding between MAJESTIC and Delta Green. MAJESTIC will focus on extraterrestrial threats. Delta Green will handle unnatural threats originating on Earth.

» **14 APR 2001:** Tong Shukoran's leader Cho Chu-tsao launches the first of dozens of front companies — real estate holdings, payday lenders, neighborhood grocers — that launder the tong's profits and distance her from the gang's day-to-day crimes.

» **10 MAY 2001:** The MAJESTIC-12 Steering Committee informs the Greys that the Accord must be renegotiated. There is no communication from the Greys ever again. MAJESTIC leaders begin to make off with valuable research and personnel in March Technologies subsidiaries and a scattering of independent firms. Director Smith's MAJESTIC, with an eviscerated NRO DELTA and leadership less experienced and ruthless than Kroft and his cronies, has little success preventing the exodus.

» **4 JUN 2001:** Tong Shukoran strikes a deal with the Norte del Valle cartel in Colombia. The Tcho-Tchos provide an unnatural agricultural additive that produces Coca Loca, a powerful strain of cocaine, and become the cartel's top Chicago distributor.

» **24 AUG 2001:** In a singular moment of cooperation, elements of MAJESTIC, Delta Green, and GRU SV-8 coordinate operations to uproot and destroy the Karotechia, from its South American headquarters to its sorcerers and reanimated officers active around the world.

APOCALYPTIC

For apocalyptic c
will signal a major tr
attle against Satan, a
unding the millenniu
nnium will bring abo
nment.

In the broadest me
on to a person, idea,
tic terrorist groups co
Hebrew Israelites, an
etation of groups that
rates the term "cultic
cally, a cultic relations
totally or nearly total
es in these followers a
inition of cults provid
tion towards violence.

he origin of the cult, t
ding what distinguish
ilar characteristic
who claim to have
a claim to be in
nd allegiance on
tly highly author
trend among don

ile predicting vi
tics that make so
e following facto

lerick C. Mish, ed., M
orated, 1997), p. 282.

DISINFORMATION

YELLOW CARD

THE MAJESTIC DIASPORA

With the first shots of the MAJESTIC coup, many in MAJESTIC saw the writing on the wall. By the time the smoke had cleared, dozens of MAJESTIC personnel had fled with hybrid technology, intelligence, and cash for various locales in the United States and around the globe.

The smartest of these individuals made no threats against the new order. They had prepared for just such an outcome, secreting various "dead man" intelligence revelations which might be leaked to the press in case of their deaths. Many were scientists, a few analysts, and some military contractors.

Justin Kroft's former cronies on the MAJESTIC-12 Steering Committee cooperated fully with Eustis Bell's move to replace him with Director Smith. Then they withdrew into the private sector, confident they could outmaneuver Bell's faction if it pursued them. Over the next decade, their secrets – scrubbed of their alien origin – would slowly bleed out from a hundred new, secretive defense companies founded by ex-MAJESTIC personnel. These men and women became incredibly rich during the Global War on Terror.

IS LINE

ASSET: "The Kitchen Sink"

Many in MAJESTIC had secreted various files, paperwork, and research as an ace-in-the-hole if political instability hit the organization, but none had as much access or vision as Charles Bostick, MAJESTIC's director of counterintelligence.

By 1999, Bostick had assembled a vast document which he called "the Kitchen Sink," containing hundreds of photographs, secret documents and the original copy of MAJESTIC OPORD 00001—the recovery of an apparent extraterrestrial vehicle at Roswell, New Mexico in 1947. Bostick has several copies, still stashed in safe locations across the United States, as well as dead-man drops ready to go if something untoward were to happen to him…suddenly. But so far, no one except Bostick has seen this treasure trove of documents. See **MAJESTIC OPORD 00001** on page 161.

EYES ONLY

Détente, Demarcation, and Departure

On 2 MAR 2001, Director Smith invited Donald Poe to bring Delta Green into MAJESTIC. Knowing that government budgets come with government oversight, followed by government interference and government orders, Poe refused. The two groups went their separate ways.

After Smith consolidated control of MAJESTIC, his first move was to inform the Greys that the Accord was going to be renegotiated. Many members of the MAJESTIC-12 Steering Committee were convinced this was a death sentence for mankind. Smith insisted he knew better.

The Greys' answer was silence.

First, all Greys present in joint-use labs collapsed. Simultaneously, technology gifted by the Greys ceased to function. Only technologies built using terrestrial science (even if gleaned from extraterrestrial sources) continued to operate. The rest that had defied understanding, analysis, or replication for over half a century, became inanimate. No further communication was forthcoming.

MAJESTIC had thrived in the bureaucracy of the U.S. government due to the gifts of technology and intelligence provided by the Greys. Those gifts were traded for political patronage and bureaucratic cooperation. Many of MAJESTIC's assets, facilities and personnel were hidden within other agencies: the CIA, NSA, NRO, and various military branches. If MAJESTIC had nothing more to offer, these groups would take back their support. The Steering Committee scrambled to make the most of its assets before that happened.

Several Steering Committee directors had no interest in joining Smith, Bell, Gates, and company on a crusade to protect the Earth from other threats. Others were pushed out. They began implementing measures they had prepared for years, retiring into the private sector.

Meanwhile, Delta Green prepared to return to the war it had been fighting since 1942. Upon taking control of A-Cell, Donald Poe's first mandate was to put the conspiracy's operational and communications security into a virtual time machine and take it back to the 1950s. Agents were encouraged to think like the criminals they were. Since most Agents came from law enforcement, this was not very hard. They used dead-drops, drop-offs, and coded public posted signals, in methods that would have been at home in the Cold War. They resorted to burner phones disposed after a single use, conversations of oblique allusions, and one-off email accounts at Internet cafés. The hard truth was that there was no such thing as secure digital communications; someone was *always* listening.

After the hard lessons of the MAJESTIC War, and now no longer stalked by its black-budget cousins, Delta Green was finally free to pursue its mission.

A Mutual Enemy

The first and last time that Delta Green and MAJESTIC worked together was the summer of 2001. They joined forces for a raid on the Karotechia's last refuge, La Estancia, hidden in the Amazon jungle. Director Smith, from his old life as Forrest James, had a score to settle with the remaining elements of the Karotechia, and Poe was happy to help. That was a ticket which Delta Green had hoped to punch for 50 years.

Delta Green had scored some significant victories, including the assassination of former SS Oberführer Reinhard Galt, and had made contact with Russian operatives hunting the same quarry. Smith offered Delta Green every advantage that Operation BLUE FLY could provide: real-time satellite imagery; full-spectrum SIGINT, ELINT, and COMINT coverage; logistical support; airlift capacity; and an AC-130H Spectre gunship to overfly the raid.

On 24 AUG 2001, a Delta Green team converged on La Estancia. The next morning, nothing survived in the smoking ruins of the repurposed rubber plantation. Meanwhile, Russians carried out simultaneous strikes on Karotechia safe-houses in Dubrovnik, Croatia; Ternopil, Ukraine; and Sidon, Lebanon. When the bodies were tallied, the group confirmed dozens of known threats as KIA. Most importantly, the last two original members of the Karotechia, Olaf Bitterich and Gunter Frank, were confirmed dead.

Many veterans of this all-star operation imagined that a working relationship between Delta Green and MAJESTIC could be forged from their success. The Russian forces of GRU SV-8 had demonstrated brilliant capacities during their limited interaction, and the Americans imagined that they might reach a real and lasting understanding with their former Cold War opponents.

Then, as the smoke cleared and plans were under way for further joint operations, the sun rose on a clear morning in New York: 11 SEP 2001.

Delta Green in the Age of Terror

The 21st century opened with America shocked to discover itself the victim of an enemy that, for the past decade, had made no attempt to hide. Despite numerous provocations, few in the West had been interested in picking up the terrorist gauntlet, no matter how many times it was thrown down. After the attacks of 11 SEP 2001, complacency was replaced with national hysteria.

To counter the global Islamist terror campaign, the U.S. intelligence community's budget doubled. The number of top-secret clearances held in the United States increased from 200,000 to 1.4 million. The Pentagon's budget increased from $335 billion in 2001 to a $711 billion high water mark in 2010, before settling at $637 billion in 2015. Over the same period, military deployments grew in a similar manner. Black-budget organizations and programs proliferated at a rate that hadn't been seen since the earliest days of the Cold War. The creation of the Department of Homeland Security fundamentally reshaped the Executive Branch in a campaign meant to reduce confusion and rivalries. In many cases, it only exacerbated the troubles it was supposed to solve.

These fundamental changes in the world of intelligence, law enforcement, and armed forces affected Delta Green and MAJESTIC *very* differently.

Mission Priorities

Since its official disbandment in 1970, Delta Green had relied on its members' ability to live as double agents: serving a federal agency and—in secret—Delta Green at the same time.

Immediately following 9/11, when the U.S. government's intelligence and law enforcement organizations essentially "went to the mattresses," Delta Green operations all but ceased. Weekends and vacations were canceled. Agents slept at the office for weeks. Border Patrol Agents were deployed in huge numbers. Ports ground to a halt. Washington had no idea how long they had to maintain an unsustainable pace to prevent another attack.

As the world settled into the Global War on Terror, Delta Green found countless new opportunities. Delta Green missions disguised as anti-terrorism operations took agents all over the world. They also created potential Delta Green recruits by exposing law enforcement, intelligence, and military personnel to the unnatural. Those who survived were ripe for recruitment.

DISINFORMATION

YELLOW CARD

THE NEW AGE

From September 2001 onward, the timeline features more and more real-world historical events that could inspire campaigns. The Handler must determine which, if any, are relevant.

CUT ALONG THIS LINE

TOP SECRET//SAR-DELTA GREEN

» **11 SEP 2001:** Al-Qaeda terrorists use hijacked jetliners to destroy the World Trade Center and damage the Pentagon. A fourth jet crashes in rural Pennsylvania. The U.S. response transforms law enforcement, intelligence, defense, and counterterrorism and leads to protracted wars in Afghanistan and Iraq. MAJESTIC scrambles to avoid the White House's attention in order to maintain autonomy.

» **18 SEP 2001:** Over the course of a few weeks, envelopes containing strange notes and significant quantities of Bacillus anthracis are postmarked from Trenton, New Jersey, and delivered to several media outlets and to U.S. senators Tom Daschle and Patrick Leahy. At least 22 suffer anthrax infections and five die. After years of speculation and false leads, blame eventually falls on USAMRIID microbiologist Bruce Edwards Ivins, who had participated in the 2001 investigation and had helped invent an anthrax vaccine. Ivins dies of apparent suicide on 29 JUL 2008.

» **7 OCT 2001:** The U.S. and allies invade Afghanistan, where the ruling Taliban shelter al-Qaeda leader Osama bin Laden. CIA teams have been on the ground for weeks.

» **26 OCT 2001:** President Bush signs into law the USA PATRIOT Act, which authorizes sweeping expansions of government powers of surveillance and detention in terrorism investigations. Amended versions are signed into law by Bush in 2006 and by President Obama in 2011 and 2015.

» **19 DEC 2001:** Delta Green agents recover the trail of murderous cultist Johannes Knepier, who pursues a vendetta against Robert Hubert, one of the leaders of the Fate. The vendetta is a proxy war between the Old Ones that Knepier and Hubert serve, Y'golonac and Glaaki. A final confrontation leaves both cultists dead at Hubert's rural Lake Chimagua estate.

» **16 FEB 2002:** A sniper kills Keenya Cook outside her home in Tacoma, Washington. Further sniper attacks follow around the country, culminating in a three-week spree of shootings in the Washington, D.C., area. John Allen Muhammad and 17-year-old Lee Boyd Malvo are arrested for the attacks, which kill 17 and injure 10.

3. (U) Capab... and a developing cyberspace operations capability. These actors focus on remote access... penetration of developed program actors. ...and insider-enabled operations. These actors can access Internet ... espionage

Past //

- **8 APR 2002:** The disappearance of a Friendly in New Orleans brings Delta Green agents into conflict with a clan of New Orleans ghouls, living among the populace in unnatural disguise. The ghouls abduct Agent Nolan. Other agents recover Nolan, but only after he suffers torments that drive him insane.
- **7 MAY 2002:** Pipe-bomb suspect Luke Helder is arrested in Nevada after his devices injure six in Iowa. Helder planted 18 bombs over 3,200 miles, intending the sites to create a smiley face on a U.S. map. Helder, obsessed with astral projection and existence beyond physical death, is diagnosed with schizoaffective disorder and incarcerated in the Federal Medical Center in Minnesota.
- **21 JUN 2002:** The FBI Counterterrorism Division establishes Fly Teams for rapid response to terrorism worldwide. Counterterrorism Fly Teams establish command posts and work with local police to gather intelligence and conduct investigations.
- **8 AUG 2002:** Through front companies, Tong Shukoran's leader Cho Chu-tsao acquires controlling shares in Genetic Agricultural Products, Inc. (GAP). GAP founder Matthew Lewis, a devotee in a Shub-Niggurath cult called the Brotherhood of New Potential, uses the money to dedicate a private island to Brotherhood retreats and rituals. The Brotherhood of New Potential is part of the Cult of Transcendence, a sprawling network of cults dedicated to the Great Old Ones, and the move helps the Brotherhood survive upheavals that rock the cult in 2013.
- **13 SEP 2002:** The MAJESTIC-12 Steering Committee shuts down the MAJESTIC Special Studies Project. It transfers its remaining assets and subprojects to the newly activated Security Studies Group, a black NSA research project. The Security Studies Group, which changes names frequently over the years, is a front for a reactivated Delta Green. Its members call it "the Program."
- **3 NOV 2002:** A drone-borne Hellfire missile kills American Muslim activist Kamal Derwish while he is in a vehicle with five others in Yemen. The killing, ordered by CIA Director George Tenet, is the first known execution of a U.S. citizen without the benefit of trial.
- **25 NOV 2002:** President Bush signs into law the Homeland Security Act of 2002, introducing the largest U.S. government reorganization since the National Security Act of 1947.

Pruning the Hydra

Where the terrorist attacks of 11 SEP 2001 changed the way Delta Green had been doing business, it spelled the end of MAJESTIC's autonomy. Since seizing control, Director Smith and his cadre had been hard at work reshaping MAJESTIC into a force to *truly* defend the United States against unnatural threats. Beginning with their repudiation of the Accord, they cracked open MAJESTIC's black projects and began dismantling those that could not be justified.

But their repudiation of the Accord came at a terrible price. It removed the crown jewel of MAJESTIC's influence: the Report. Updated by the Greys every two months, the Report was a global inventory of military assets. From a single AK-47 carried by a lone Central American guerrilla, to the location of every Soviet nuclear warhead, the Report offered a level of detail impossible to achieve through conventional intelligence-gathering.

Those parts of the Report that were confirmable, from the complete inventory of U.S. and NATO military forces to what was known about enemy capacities, suggested that the rest of the document was accurate. The Report had been a key element in the victory of the Cold War, after all. It rendered the Pentagon better informed on Soviet military readiness than the Kremlin.

Through the absolute accuracy of the Report, MAJESTIC had struck deals at the highest levels of the U.S. military, and even the Office of the President.

The last president to receive the Report was Bush 41—George H.W. Bush. His successor, William J. Clinton, was not briefed on MAJESTIC, the Accord, or the Report. During the 1990s, MAJESTIC still slipped intelligence from the Report to the CIA and the Pentagon's intelligence agencies in exchange for continued cooperation. When Director Smith took over MAJESTIC, he saw no reason to inform President George W. Bush.

Then came 11 SEP 2001. A month later, Bush 41 asked Bush 43, his son, a simple question: "Has the Report been of any use?"

The Bush White House immediately wanted access to the Report as well as the agency that produced it. Bush 41 would say nothing more about it when he realized the new president had not been read in on the project. Under the direction of Vice President Cheney, White House staffers summoned former and current intelligence and Department of Defense leaders from across the United States to locate it. The steady flow of unexpected visitors to the White House was not lost on MAJESTIC's new leaders.

Under Smith and his allies, MAJESTIC still maintained its secrecy and the compliance of other government agencies through high technology, intelligence provided from MAJESTIC threat-analysis computers, and their completely black satellite network. But once the White House began its search, it was only a matter of time before the shell covering MAJESTIC would crack.

It caught the Steering Committee flat-footed. They were in the process of dismantling the most grotesquely illegal projects under MAJESTIC, especially those projects associated with the Greys' other gift: the Cookbook, a 3,500-page document that held the key to modifying human genetics. Experimenting with the Cookbook involved human alterations with scores of fatalities. They were equally distracted by the need to cover up the underground nuclear demolition of Facility-12 beneath the badlands of Montana. MAJESTIC had only barely managed to spin that catastrophe as an earthquake.

Smith knew that if the White House asserted command over MAJESTIC, he was out. He also couldn't trust the new administration wouldn't reinstitute the Accord, or make some worse accommodation. Growing desperate, Smith turned to an expert at pulling strings in the Executive Branch: his captive, Gavin Ross.

Project DULCIMER

Gavin Ross had spent months in confinement, comfortable as it was, at one of MAJESTIC's secret continuity-of-government sites. He had used Forrest James to briefly assume control of Delta Green, and then Forrest James had used their partnership to usurp everything and become Director Smith. Ross wanted out. He knew that would take a long, long time. He had to earn access. He was waiting for the day when Smith first asked for his help.

Like Smith and his allies at MAJESTIC, Gavin Ross had no interest in renewing the Accord. And he recognized that MAJESTIC needed a firewall between itself and the government. Ross advised the Steering Committee to approach Lt. General Arthur Brunne (U.S. Air Force). Brunne, a former Delta Green operative who had served Delta Green twice in the 1970s, was a research director at the NSA. The NSA had ballooning budgets and layers upon layers of top-secret projects. It could provide adequate cover.

Air Force Lt. General Eustis Bell, Smith's closest ally at MAJESTIC, gave Brunne a detailed briefing. This "black badge" sermon showed Brunne undeniable evidence of mankind's *true* position in the universe, and the sometimes appalling things that the government had done to protect the species. Bell presented Brunne with a choice. He could help them remake the vast array of MAJESTIC projects and bury them in the NSA's R&D programs and black budgets, or stand by as MAJESTIC's secrets slowly filtered out to the public. If he made the first choice, he would be provided with access to exotic technologies and intelligence that would guarantee the NSA's position as star player in the intelligence world. If he made the second choice, he would watch the entire world fall to pieces as the secret truth was inevitably leaked. Brunne, who had experienced the unnatural twice before, offered his help.

The MAJESTIC Steering Committee began doling out intelligence gained with technology that previously it had rarely seen fit to use. Much of the technology MAJESTIC had used to buy influence had ceased to function when the Accord was broken. Of the derived technology that still worked, very little was under MAJESTIC's exclusive control; many operatives had taken their research projects and fled. But even the reduced assets it retained put it decades ahead of anything at the NSA. The new structure would buy plenty of time before they had to change course once more.

Best of all, it could keep control of its sources, methods, and infrastructure. The White House had instructed NSA Director Michael Hayden to abandon the safeguards of individual privacy that had been put in place in the 1970s, and offered enough legal pretexts to make the decision justifiable. Hayden welcomed the order and looked for assets to make it happen. Through two or three layers of black research and SIGINT projects, MAJESTIC's teams provided enough useful intelligence to keep itself protected and earn ever-increasing funding. They produced results.

Activating MAJESTIC's new clearances and line-item budgets took surprisingly little time. MAJESTIC didn't even need to physically move personnel or assets. Before the White House lost patience and became more aggressive in its search for the Report, Brunne was ready with an explanation: Project DULCIMER.

Brunne told Vice President Cheney that DULCIMER was a highly classified NSA project in the 1970s and 1980s. It had collected and parsed SIGINT from around the world through satellite, aircraft and ground-based radio chatter, and cracked those numbers in huge NSA computation farms created by DARPA. It spat out an algorithmic assessment of local "weapon assets" based on weird math: the Report. Unfortunately, Brunne said, as warfare became decentralized and asymmetric, the algorithms became less reliable. By the late 1990s, the Report was nearly useless. The NSA now had far more effective tools at its disposal and—thanks to the White House's foresight and resolve, Brunne was careful to say—already being deployed. Cheney told the president that the Report had been a dead end for years.

The Program

With the surviving MAJESTIC projects secure under the blanket of the NSA, the Steering Committee set about shutting down the umbrella of MAJESTIC clearances and creating new ones to replace them. They had a new mission, one that was truer to MAJESTIC's original purpose. They worked inside the NSA to establish a new program that officially launched on 13 SEP 2002.

The new project's official remit included counterterrorism, stated so broadly as to be nearly meaningless, and the acquisition and exploitation of foreign technology and property for the advancement of U.S. national security interests. It had authorization to establish highly-restricted task forces with the cooperation of the DoJ, DoD, and DHS, and it immediately set about putting its people in useful positions throughout those organizations. And it obtained authority over and reactivated many old, defunct and apparently useless programs and clearances of the Joint Chiefs of Staff.

The new project went by a deliberately bland and uninformative name: the Security Studies Group (SSG). That name would frequently change. Insiders called it the Program, wryly adopting a common nickname for the NSA's most secret surveillance schemes. The agents who perform its most essential mission, investigating and confronting unnatural and alien threats,

DISINFORMATION

YELLOW CARD

TRIBUTE TO THE NSA

For 19 years, MAJESTIC struggled to understand the seamless technologies provided by the alien intelligence they called the Greys. Those secrets were so far beyond humanity that even the world's best minds failed to grasp the most simple truths behind them. Still, study of these mysteries shed smaller secrets. By 2000, MAJESTIC had discovered many adjacent technologies. After the withdrawal from the Accord – which rendered most of the shared Grey technology inert – only these side discoveries remained viable.

Still, by human standards, these veins of knowledge were very rich. By the mid-1990s, MAJESTIC was already operating computer technology decades ahead of the top-of-the-line systems found at the NSA, and it wasn't even a particularly active research program.

Other nascent technologies were in limited development in MAJESTIC labs. Quantum computing, imitative neural-network learning machines, and dual spin strange particle communications were all being pursued when MAJESTIC collapsed and reformed as the Program.

The Program knew that with control of these three technologies, it could dictate terms to the NSA. Quantum computing could smash nearly any modern cryptography, machine neural-networks could learn to smart-mine the endless data collected by the NSA looking for "hits," and dual spin strange particles could allow instantaneous and entirely unhackable data transfer.

Combined, these technologies gave the Program (and the NSA, as long as they cooperated) unprecedented access to global communications: a live, searchable intelligence network which could listen to the entire planet.

CUT ALONG THIS LINE

N
EPARTMENT
EAU OF INVESTIC
SHINGTON D.C.
//NOFORN//S

call it by another name among themselves—the name of a long-shuttered program of the Joint Chiefs of Staff, newly reactivated: DELTA GREEN.

The members of the MAJESTIC Steering Committee who had allied themselves with Director Smith became directors of the Program. The rest retired from government service, and most of them moved to the board of March Technologies, Inc., an influential defense contractor. They had secured enough of their pet MAJESTIC projects in the private sector to become billionaires. They were happy to keep the Program's secrets as long as the Program kept theirs. March Technologies would, ironically, soon become one of the Program's most important partners.

The Bush administration didn't realize it, but they had re-issued Delta Green its hunting license.

The Other Delta Green

Keeping the name Delta Green for the new clearance was not a sentimental act. Director Smith intended it to send a message to Donald Poe and A-cell that MAJESTIC was gone and that Delta Green no longer had to exist on the fringes. One of Smith's first priorities was reaching out to every Delta Green agent he knew, offering to bring them in. Many joined.

But others refused. The old guard derided those who'd joined Smith as sell-outs who'd traded personal accountability for a pension and a medical plan. They had no use for "the Program." For their part, those who joined up took to calling the unrealistic, old-guard holdouts "the Outlaws."

Neither referred to the other as "Delta Green."

DISINFORMATION

YELLOW CARD

INTERNATIONAL OPERATIONS

During the War on Terror, the Program found itself deployed anywhere in the globe American troops could be found; this included Afghanistan and Iraq, as well as in staging areas such as Germany, Turkey, Pakistan, Italy, and Japan.

During the invasion of Afghanistan, no fewer than 32 operations were run by the Program to determine if unnatural threats were involved. In Iraq, that number grew to 70. Several operations revealed long-standing cults or local unnatural threats, which were then suppressed; but most only revealed local legends, trumped-up propaganda, or foreign intelligence operatives attempting to discover similar things. Many, many, agents were lost in the field, but the line – what of it could be found – was held.

» **18 JAN 2003:** The Breckenridge Corporation, a large security and investigations firm with long ties to MAJESTIC projects and NRO DELTA, signs its largest contracts to date with the U.S. government. It held longstanding contracts to provide security for Defense Department and Energy Department facilities in the U.S. Breckenridge now provides security for State Department facilities overseas, training for CIA contract employees and other nations' forces, and intelligence and assassination operations on behalf of the CIA.

» **1 FEB 2003:** Space Shuttle *Columbia* disintegrates on re-entry on its 28th mission. All seven crew members die.

» **20 MAR 2003:** The Iraq War begins. Its declaration has nearly unanimous support in the U.S. Congress despite the shaky intelligence upon which it is based. The White House scoffs at the U.S. Army Chief of Staff's estimate that U.S. troops will have to remain in Iraq in force long-term. By mid-2017, 4,841 U.S. service members have been killed in Iraq, and the Iraq Body Count Project, collating news reports, estimates the civilian death toll at over 173,000. Delta Green teams conduct dozens of operations to secure artifacts and manuscripts suspected of unnatural provenance.

» **14 APR 2003:** The Human Genome Project finishes decoding most of the human genome.

» **21 JUN 2003:** Neither of the masters of the Fate, Emir Agdesh nor Stephen Alzis, attends the cult's summer solstice rituals or is seen again in New York. The Lords of the Fate begin a war between themselves, purportedly with the aid of attacks by Delta Green. A lethal series of encounters during the Northeast blackout of 14 AUG 2003 seems to finally break the Fate as an organization. Unfettered from their masters, and more difficult to track than a cult, individual sorcerers with insane ambitions come to pose ever more dangerous threats.

» **6 JUL 2003:** Former U.S. diplomat Joseph Wilson publishes a column in the *New York Times* saying that the White House had sent him to Niger in February 2002 to investigate a supposed Iraqi purchase of uranium, that he had concluded no such transaction had taken place, and that he suspects the intelligence justifying the Iraq War had been twisted to exaggerate the Iraqi threat.

- **14 JUL 2003:** *Washington Post* columnist Robert Novak publishes a column downplaying the impact of Joseph Wilson's February 2002 investigation in Niger and questioning the CIA's reason for asking him to do it. Novak identifies Wilson's wife Valerie Plame as a CIA clandestine officer, citing two White House sources. Subsequent investigations identify Deputy Secretary of State Richard Armitage as the source, and cast a cloud of suspicion that the leak was political payback for Wilson's column. Vice President Cheney's advisor I. Lewis "Scooter" Libby is convicted in March 2007 of four criminal charges related to the leak. President Bush commutes his sentence that July.
- **10 OCT 2003:** With no announcement and only the minimum paperwork required by state and federal law, a little-known Chinese investment consortium called Star Holding and Investment buys Whole Earth Enterprises, the privately-held corporate owner of Club Apocalypse and Conqueror Worm Music.
- **28 APR 2004:** Nearly a year after being first reported by Amnesty International, American abuses of prisoners at Abu Ghraib prison in Iraq gain wide attention with reports on *60 Minutes II* and in *The New Yorker*. Abuses at other prisons are revealed afterward.
- **29 APR 2004:** The leaders of the Program and Canada's M-EPIC meet for the first time since the dissolution of MAJESTIC. The organizations soon develop a comfortable working relationship. Over the next few years, numerous unnatural tomes recovered in the Program's operations wind up in M-EPIC libraries for study, and resulting intelligence reports are sent back to aid the Program's operations.
- **8 AUG 2004:** Tong Shukoran leader Cho Chu-tsao directs the gang to sever all ties with Mexico's Norte del Valle cartel, which has been embroiled in a war that has led to thousands of arrests and killings. When the cartel objects, Tong Shukoran uses unnatural methods to "disappear" dozens of in-the-know cartel members who thought themselves well protected and to punish a few in ways that horrify even the bloodiest-minded narcotraffickers.
- **26 DEC 2004:** A massive earthquake in the Indian Ocean triggers a tsunami that kills at least 184,000, mostly in Indonesia and Sri Lanka.

TOP SECRET

Less Than Friendly

During its outlaw years from 1970 to 2002, Delta Green worked with dozens of so-called "Friendlies." Friendlies were mostly specialists who brought unique skills to the mission. They were usually told very little about Delta Green—in most cases, not even the name. Many Friendlies thought they were working with a legitimate, but shadowy, government agency all along.

By the 2000s, Friendlies were not just intellectuals and researchers who provided intelligence about the unnatural. Their number also included former Delta Green agents downgraded to Friendly status. Some former agents were downgraded due to physical ailments, others because they had been terminated by their host agencies due to psychological issues.

Following 9/11, it became more and more difficult to preserve the Friendlies' allegiance to the illegal Delta Green conspiracy. The War on Terror opened up countless new opportunities for operations. Friendlies, downgraded agents, and previously black-balled agents were brought in as active agents.

Sometimes agents, spread thin, were only able to provide Friendlies with intelligence and organizational support, while the Friendlies did the heavy lifting. Individual cells of the conspiracy were forced to direct micro-conspiracies of their own.

Some Friendlies decided there wasn't much Delta Green could do for them that they couldn't do for themselves. Agents often found themselves negotiating with Friendlies to secure their services.

When Director Smith had recruited all the old Delta Green agents who wanted in, he turned to Friendlies that he and his people knew. Some remained true to A-cell, but many were glad to join a more legitimate, well-funded operation.

By 2004, A-cell found their network of Friendlies had evolved into something very different. A dangerous minority of them even cooperated with suspect groups or individuals who were not posing an immediate threat. There were rumors that some ex-Friendlies had been seduced by the knowledge and power that contact with higher dimensional entities could bring.

One of Donald Poe's priorities as the leader of the Outlaws was to bring these Friendlies back into the fold. He could ill afford to lose access to their talents and resources. Getting Friendlies to return A-cell's calls was a matter of rebuilding loyalty. Poe's people learned to be more candid about the true nature of the conspiracy.

The Iraq War

The Iraq War began in early 2003 with a "shock and awe" bombing campaign and a ground invasion that quickly overwhelmed Iraqi defenses. The U.S. and its allies had been fighting in Iraq for a year already, with multinational special-operations teams cooperating to take advantage of some countries' looser rules of engagement. Delta Green agents were among the first on the ground, taking advantage of the chaos to raid holy sites, museums, art galleries, and homes suspected of holding unnatural tomes and artifacts. They found very few.

The war would have profound effects on the operations of the Program and the Outlaws. The infamous pallets of cash sent by the State Department to support allied forces provided a welcome infusion of funding when diverted by Outlaw agents. The protracted war, which would grind on officially for eight years, provided a ready platform for operations in the Middle East. It produced a steady supply of combat veterans, always valuable for Delta Green. It also taught the leaders of the Program and the Outlaws what not to do. It proved the dangers of cherry-picking intelligence reports to suit an objective rather than crafting objectives around intelligence. It taught them to beware of the arrogance of decisions made on faith rather than facts, and of the temptation to achieve immediate success at the risk of long-term disaster. It thoroughly confirmed their decision to keep political leaders and the government bureaucracy at arm's length.

Most importantly, the Program's leaders saw firsthand the inevitability of exposure for conspiracies that allowed themselves to sprawl. The Program was not yet six months old when the war began. The chaos of the war and the failures of secrecy led the Program's leaders to keep the organization small, to compartmentalize everything, and to always have ways to discredit everyone who knows the truth.

The rigid protocols that the Iraq War inspired allowed the Program to pursue its mission without discovery, impeded only by its self-imposed limitations.

Headhunters

From 2002 to 2008, relations between the Outlaw conspiracy and the Program remained tense but cordial. Both groups tended to what they considered their respective missions. At least at first, the Outlaws operated only in North America, while the Program operated globally, anywhere U.S. military forces and intelligence assets were deployed for the War on Terror.

Although the Outlaws and the Program rarely worked together, there were instances when one group handed missions to the other when they felt ill-equipped to handle them. This neutrality did not last.

Almost from the beginning, the Program had been keeping an eye on the Outlaws' disgruntled Friendlies and agents who had been downgraded to Friendlies or blackballed altogether.

In early 2004, the Program began recruitment passes at disgruntled and disaffected conspirators. They had a lot to offer. Those going to work for the Program could expect logistical and intelligence support; they'd no longer have to beg, borrow or steal what they needed to get the job done. But most importantly, joining the Program meant official recognition. Even if it was only recognition by their fellow agents, it was a boost to morale that the Outlaws could never match. More than a few agreed to join up.

When A-cell learned of the Program's attempts to recruit their cast-offs, the initial reaction was tolerance. After all, if the Outlaws wanted to utilize these people, they would have kept them. When the Program began approaching personnel who refused to work with the Outlaws, again the conspiracy looked the other way. These personnel had already rebuffed previous invitations to return to the Outlaws. If the Program could put them to work, all to the better.

But when the Program attempted to lure active agents away from the Outlaws, they miscalculated. Many Outlaw agents had been part of the conspiracy for decades, some as far back as the 1970s. They were loyal to A-cell and reported the contacts. A-cell ordered the most reliable of these new agents to go ahead and join the Program as spies. As for the others, A-cell knew their names.

Nevertheless, it became clear over the next decade that the greatest threat to the Outlaws was their aging membership. New recruitment had slowed, mostly because potential recruits were approached by the Program first.

While the Outlaws were committed to showing they still had what was needed to do the mission, the Program was expanding its influence.

DISINFORMATION

YELLOW CARD

KADATH

The Pnakotic Manuscripts describe "Kadath in the Cold Waste" as "beyond Leng" and as the "home of the gods of Earth." Classical and medieval authors placed it either in the icy mountains of inner Asia or somewhere beyond the physical world. It is mystically connected to the sacred mountains Hatheg-Kla and Ngranek (perhaps Nanga Ranik, in the Hindu Kush), which serve as "pillars to Heaven" in Pnakotic lore and the theosophy of Randolph Carter, respectively, much like the Mount Meru of Hindu mythology.

- Pánfilio de Zamacona mentions "the mountain Kadath" as being "near the South Pole" in his Narrative Concerning the Subterranean World (c. 1545).
- Geologist William Dyer speculated that the impossibly high mountain range he observed in the interior of Wilkes Land on the 1930 Miskatonic Antarctic Expedition might have been the origin of the myth of Kadath. In this context the Necronomicon's mention of the "ice desert of the South," where the seal of the Old Ones is engraved, may likewise refer to Antarctic Kadath.
- Thomas Danforth, a survivor of that expedition, identified the primordial city of the Elder Things itself as Kadath, the "home of the gods of earth."
- In April 1952, Delta Green raiders (as part of Operation SOUTHERN HOSPITALITY) eliminated an Argentine attempt to salvage Elder Thing material from a Nazi base at a different Antarctic site in Queen Maud Land. The Karotechia may have established this research station, Point 102, in an attempt to locate Kadath on their own.
- In December 1957, the Second Soviet Antarctic Expedition established Vostok Station 290 km from the coordinates for the Elder Thing City at Kadath given by Dyer's report.
- In 1958, the Third Soviet Expedition discovered the Gamburtsev Mountains, a range the size of the Alps, buried 600 meters below the ice cap. In 2009, the AGAP project mapped the mountains with ice-penetrating radar.
- In 1993, laser altimetry confirmed the existence of a subglacial lake, Lake Vostok, beneath Vostok Station. A Russian team drilled through the ice in 2012, reaching water that had been isolated for 25 million years.
- In 1997, using laser tomography archaeologists Wolfgang Reich and Gilbert Austin discovered a monumental stone complex buried two miles beneath the Hittite cult site of Karatepe. Dubbed "Kadath" in the tabloids, the disappearance of the so-called "a-Abhi Block" (referring to a Hittite underworld deity) and the collapse of their probe tunnel ended the excavation. The bizarre behavior of Gilbert and Reich implies possible unnatural contamination.
- MAJESTIC could have acquired the inscribed a-Abhi Block during Operation BLACK MOUNTAIN, which established an arms pipeline to Syrian Kurdish rebels in 1997.

CUT ALONG THIS LINE

031-51937 o-46

DISINFORMATION

YELLOW CARD

LENG

The "icy desert plateau" of Leng slides between Earth and other dimensions. Its supposed geographical location on (or tangent to) Earth varies by occult source.

- In his **Unaussprechlichen Kulten** (1839), Von Junzt locates "inaccessible Leng" in Central (or "Inner") Asia.
- The kingdom of Ling in Tibetan legend, and the traces of necrophagy in some Bön rites, may descend from Leng and its "corpse-eating cult," placing Leng in Tibet.
- Northwest of the district of Zin in Afghanistan, in Uruzgan province, lies Mount Leng-e Mulla Aman (elevation 2,916 meters). Delta Green operatives in Afghanistan have noticed unnatural phenomena associated with both Zin and the mountain.
- The common association of the Tcho-Tcho people with Leng argues for a possible connection with the "Lost City of Gelanggi" or Linggiu in Johor state, Malaysia.
- William Dyer identified Leng as the central Antarctic plateau in his 1931 report.
- Rumors that Al-Qaeda maintained an "impenetrable mountain retreat" at a place called Layung, in the mountains of Pakistan, were not lost on Delta Green.

CUT ALONG THIS LINE

Perhaps the last word on the topic belongs to Randolph Carter:

Men reached Leng from very different oceans.

Its name likely comes from the Chinese lěng, "cold," although some Sinologists argue for a derivation from léng, which can mean either "hilly, steep, rugged," or "edge, angle." The Qin emperors destroyed all scrolls and texts that referred to Leng, including the **Seven Cryptical Books of Hsan** and the Dhol chants.

The ruler of Leng is supposedly a monstrous high lama wearing a yellow silken robe and veil. He dwells in a windowless lamasery in the middle of a circle of crude (or aeon-eroded) monoliths. Leng's other landmark is the "Elder Pharos," a lighthouse that shoots a glowing blue beam up into the skies, attracting foolish wanderers both mundane and occult. According to the **Necronomicon**, the lamas of Leng wear a winged hound as their soul-symbol. Despite this, occult lore seldom associates them with Nodens of the Hounds, but rather with Itla-shua, Hastur, Azathoth, or Nyarlathotep. Von Junzt even repeats rumors of a cult of Ghatanothoa on the plateau of Leng, possibly a holdover from its Lemurian-era golden age.

031-51937 o-46

- **3 MAR 2005:** The Program unwittingly recruits Agent ANDREA, former head of Delta Green's communications security. She slowly, subtly begins feeding data between the Program and Donald Poe's so-called Outlaws, facilitating the missions of both.
- **9 MAR 2005:** Delta Green sends a team to investigate an agent's suicide at 1206 Spooner Avenue, Meadowbrook, New Jersey. The team finds death and madness.
- **21 MAR 2005:** Sixteen-year-old Jeffrey Weise shoots and kills his grandfather and his grandfather's girlfriend at home, then shoots and kills seven and wounds five at his high school in the Red Lake Indian Reservation, Minnesota, before committing suicide.
- **23 MAR 2005:** An explosion at a BP refinery in Texas City, Texas, kills 15 and injures more than 180.
- **19 MAY 2005:** In a series of FBI and DEA raids, Outlaw Delta Green agents arrest most of Tong Shukoran and seize the assets and property of Tiger Transit. Tong Shukoran's ultimate leader, Cho Chu-tsao, is by now far removed from the gang's activities. The Outlaws never even learn of her existence.
- **1 JUN 2005:** The ATF begins a pilot for Project GUNRUNNER in Laredo, Texas. Officially launching in April 2006, Project GUNRUNNER interdicts straw firearm purchasers and unlicensed dealers in order to stop legal guns from entering the black market. "Controlled delivery" operations draw controversy in 2006 (Operation WIDE RECEIVER) and 2009 (Operation FAST AND FURIOUS), when the ATF allows guns to be delivered to suspects in Mexico and the guns wind up in the possession of drug cartels. Guns lost in those operations are used in crimes, including the killing of U.S. Border Patrol Agent Brian Terry in December 2010.
- **15 JUL 2005:** Genetic Agricultural Products, Inc., managed by Tcho-Tcho entrepreneur Cho Chu-tsao, receives glowing reports and increased orders from agricultural clients.
- **22 JUL 2005:** Haley Productions announces the cancellation of UFO exposé show *Phenomen-X*, citing sinking ratings and too few syndication contracts. In the late 1990s, MAJESTIC and Delta Green had used *Phenomen-X* as a coalmine canary for suspected alien threats. After the MAJESTIC War and the shakeups at Delta Green, *Phenomen-X's* "Deep Throat" sources stopped calling, costing it some of its best stories.

- **29 AUG 2005:** Hurricane KATRINA makes landfall in Louisiana, flooding most of New Orleans and killing hundreds as levees break. Police, federal agents, rescue workers and contractors struggle to provide aid and security. Among them are Delta Green agents from the Outlaws, on the hunt for the ghouls of the DeMonte clan that they first faced in 2002.
- **8 OCT 2005:** An earthquake kills more than 80,000 in Kashmir and north Pakistan.
- **23 NOV 2005:** Haley Productions sells *Phenomen-X,* its cancelled UFO show, to Digivideomagic, Inc. Digivideomagic hires *Phenomen-X's* core staff to continue the show as cut-rate web video series.
- **13 DEC 2005:** California scientists announce the creation of mice with human stem cells in their brains.
- **6 JAN 2006:** Thousands of Shiite Iraqis demonstrate after 200 are killed in two days, beginning what some call the Iraq Civil War.
- **15 JAN 2006:** A capsule from NASA's *Stardust* spacecraft returns with samples of cosmic dust and dust from the comet Wild 2.
- **15 APR 2006:** Emil Furst, aka Agent Aaron, finds a small tome with an intricate code that hints at great secrets. Suspecting these secrets will help the Outlaws confront unnatural threats with far less risk, he spends the next ten years deciphering and studying the tome in great secrecy, never informing A-cell about it.
- **9 JUL 2006:** A team of Delta Green Outlaws track down the headquarters of the Skoptsi, an obscene cult of Shub-Niggurath, destroy its leaders, and free dozens of eastern European orphans the cult had been indoctrinating.
- **14 SEP 2006:** Tong Shukoran strikes a deal with Mexico's Sinaloa Cartel, providing additives to allow Sinaloa to grow potent new strains of marijuana ("Yerba Loca") and opium ("Goma Loca") in return for becoming the cartel's chief Chicago distributor.
- **4 OCT 2006:** WikiLeaks launches with the leak of a radical Somali leader's orders to assassinate government officials.
- **11 DEC 2006:** The Mexican government launches Operation MICHOACÁN, opening the Mexican Drug War in response to drug-related violence. The conflict's death toll is estimated at 120,000 or more by 2013.

- **10 JAN 2007:** The White House announces a U.S. troop surge in Iraq, concentrated in Baghdad and with troops living among the Iraqis. Some credit the surge for reducing the violence of the insurgency by fall 2007. Others credit a six-month cease-fire issued by insurgent leader Muqtada al-Sadr.
- **31 JAN 2007:** German prosecutors charge 13 CIA operatives, including two Aero Contractors pilots, with the 2003 kidnapping of accused Islamist Khaled el-Masri, a German citizen. Masri says the CIA held him in Afghanistan for five months of interrogation and abuse.
- **1 MAR 2007:** The Fourth (and final) International Polar Year program studies the North and South Poles.
- **16 APR 2007:** College senior Seung-Hui Cho kills 32 and wounds 17 at Virginia Tech before committing suicide.
- **16 JUL 2007:** An extensive Program operation tracks the movements of four leaders of the Cthulhu cult known as the Exalted Circle — a self-styled, modern-day incarnation of the Esoteric Order of Dagon. The operation leads agents to an important Circle ritual, where missile strikes by Program agents flying captured Predator drones kill many Exalted Circle cultists and dozens of Deep Ones.
- **31 AUG 2007:** Diplomatic Security Special Agent Jean C. Richter writes a memo describing dangerously "hands-off" embassy management of Blackwater security contractors in Iraq. The memo says a Blackwater project manager threatened to kill Richter and another investigator who were conducting a probe of the firm's lax security practices, and that embassy officials sided with Blackwater against the investigators. The State Department paid more than $832 million to Blackwater from 2004 to 2006.
- **16 SEP 2007:** Blackwater guards kill 17 civilians in Baghdad. Four guards eventually go to prison for the killings. The Pentagon cancels some Blackwater contracts. The rival Breckenridge Corporation is among many to fill the gap in service.
- **22 OCT 2007:** The U.S. and Mexico announce the Mérida Initiative, under which the U.S. supplies Mexico with aircraft, weapons, surveillance equipment, and training to fight drug trafficking. By 2015, the U.S. appropriates nearly $2.5 billion for the effort.
- **15 NOV 2007:** Cyclone Sidr kills thousands in Bangladesh.

DISINFORMATION

YELLOW CARD

CUT ALONG THIS LINE

HURRICANE KATRINA

On 29 AUG 2005, storm surges created by Hurricane Katrina caused 53 breaches in the levees surrounding New Orleans. The nation watched in horror as the city, state and federal governments failed on nearly every conceivable level to deal with the disaster for almost a week.

They were not the only people unprepared for the effect that Hurricane Katrina had on New Orleans. The DeMonte Clan – the ghoul family which had haunted and fed upon the dead of New Orleans since 1788 – was also completely unprepared. For two centuries, they had hidden their inhuman nature with hypergeometrics. They owned almost the entire funeral industry in New Orleans, a machine with which they could invisibly collect and feed on the dead. They had never fled the city before, being immune to the plagues that had ravaged it in the last century, and had ridden out so many hurricane season close calls that they'd become complacent.

They were invincible, or so they thought before Hurricane Katrina made landfall. Then the levees failed. The city began to drown, and was choked with thousands of corpses. Such a feast had not been available in a century.

The DeMontes weren't the only ones to take advantage of the chaos in the wake of Katrina. The Outlaws dispatched a number of "death squads" into the city with orders to kill any members of the DeMonte Clan they discovered. A simple test applied: anyone caught collecting bodies after dark was shot on sight with tasers. Those who transformed back into ghouls were riddled with bullets. The several dozen people tasered by mistake were zip-tied and dumped on high ground, and later told unbelievable stories of black-clad commandos stalking the city. Much of the unseen, but overheard, gunfire that clattered through the first nights after the levees broke was from teams of Delta Green agents clearing out ghoul nests. Twenty ghouls were killed before the DeMontes retreated into the shadows.

The window for the "hot war" was very short, just between the dates of 29 AUG 2005 and 3 SEP 2005. After that, the city was so full of law enforcement and military personnel that neither the DeMontes nor Delta Green dared open conflict. Delta Green monitored the city for DeMonte activity, waiting for their next chance to strike. The clever ghouls, having lost the skirmish, were too wise to continue the war.

031-51937 o-46

CL 108 I follow.

APPROVED FOR RELEASE DATE: 26-Jul-2010

DISINFORMATION

YELLOW CARD

OPERATION ACTIVE STATIC

In 2007, an operation in Chicago unfolded into something which was, briefly, much larger. A single copy of **The King in Yellow** found its way into the possession of a director named Victor Correll who was on the verge of breaking through into Hollywood. The 22-minute film he produced after reading the forbidden book, called **A Song Before Travel**, was reported by the select audience in attendance to be sublime, perfect, and unlike anything before it.

Not one person of the 53 who attended its premiere would be alive in a month. A Delta Green team led by aging Outlaws ruthlessly rooted out all tendrils of the infection, which included multiple copies of the book and online clips from the movie. At the height of the "outbreak," an entire apartment block of Chicago seemingly crossed over into the quantum slurry that the book creates, called Carcosa.

The last two surviving members of the team were eliminated after being deemed "infected."

LINE

THREAT MATRIX

RED CARD

PORTRAYING THE KING IN YELLOW

In the play **The King in Yellow,** a stranger comes to a masked ball in far-off Yhtill. He reveals that of all the revelers, only he wears no mask. The porcelain rictus of his face is his skin. He heralds the end of their world.

This play, written in France in the 1890s, warps human minds and opens doors within them. Its despair spills out into reality and changes all around the reader into horror. Or so some say. Others claim it is a seam in the fabric of reality that, once pulled, begins to fray existence itself.

Some believe the King in Yellow, a pallid figure **from** that play, somehow appears in the real world, a malignant creature adorned in ancient golden cloth, with a porcelain mask. To others still, it is a series of sigils and codes embedded in reality, flagged by a single, terrible symbol that causes madness and death.

In truth, it is **all** of these things. It is none of them. It is anything on the edge of the tide of human understanding. Minds open to accept the input of this unnatural force, and are flooded, washed away and destroyed in a torrent of madness. Some are drawn out into this tidal sludge of imagination, forever.

What is the **King in Yellow**? It is the edge of human thought and order, and, as such, can never truly be defined. Here's how to drive your Agents over the edge into the wilds of Carcosa.

CUT ALONG THIS LINE

- **A DISEASE UPON REALITY: The King in Yellow**, and all it represents, is best thought of as a disease. It is spread through art, exposure to other infected individuals and places, and **ideas**. Those ideas are focused in a play called **The King In Yellow**, but it can be found in many places, people, and things. Once unleashed, it spreads in a very similar manner to a conventional disease. No conscious being is immune.
- **GOALS:** Unlike most unnatural threats that Delta Green faces, the forces of the King in Yellow seem to focus their efforts on infecting the minds of men. While the Great Old Ones often find, corrupt, and destroy humanity, this is simply a side-effect for them; for the King in Yellow, this infection appears to be the goal.
- **ANYTHING IS POSSIBLE:** The quantum slurry of Carcosa — the world infected and warped by the concepts in **The King In Yellow** — renders conventional spacetime irrelevant. Worse, Carcosa and its occupants can convincingly portray normal entities. In Carcosa, or dealing with the forces of the King, **anything remains possible**.
- **DISSOLUTION:** As the world shuffles into a new era of disorder, disintegration and retraction, the forces of the King cannot be far behind. Half-truths and outright lies are given the same credence as provable facts and rigorous science. Is it any wonder that some consider this world to be mad? Or, perhaps, only now to be sane?

031-51932 6-46

DISINFORMATION

YELLOW CARD

CARCOSA

Carcosa is a name given to the slurry of thought and quantum possibility that exists between man and the Great Old Ones. In this runoff, human thought is pulled into a void and fills the space of possibility with thoughts, dreams, and ideas made "real." The usual collapse of waveform brought by rote observation becomes the dance of multiple waveforms – a thousand outcomes become possible, or impossible, at once. It is ruled by a creature known as the King in Yellow, or sometimes, Hastur.

Carcosa seems to act and react to human thought, to change and redirect itself within human concepts of fear, disorder, and chaos. It has extremely potent effects on sanity.

Like a slug, Carcosa envelops and digests human beings, burning away their minds even as their minds change the world. All that remains behind are echoes of their thoughts and perceptions, lingering in this backwater of reality forever.

Possible connections to Carcosa can be found around the world:

- In primordial Mongolia under the rule of Mu; its coming created the Gobi Desert. It lent its name to the medieval Mongol city Khar Khota ("black city").
- In the city of Carcassone, France; a cult of Tsathoggua may have opened a portal to Carcosa there during the Albigensian Crusade of the 13th century.
- On the island La Certosa in the Lagoon of Venice.
- The residence of the British High Commissioner for Malaysia in Kuala Lumpur, called Carcosa House. Designed in 1896 by the architect A.B. Hubback, it is known to Delta Green as the main PISCES station in Southeast Asia.
- Absorbing and incorporating the planet Yhtill somewhere in the constellation of Taurus, possibly orbiting Aldebaran.
- Anywhere the play **The King in Yellow** (suppressed in France in 1895) is read or performed.
- That includes Greenwich Village in 1955, when the play was performed under the name **Her Grey Song.** Seventeen people died during the ensuing Operation BRISTOL, which involved a dimensional portal to Carcosa opening in New York.
- In the distant future as a ruined city of what is now California.

CUT ALONG THIS LINE

031-51937 o-46

- **26 MAR 2008:** Wikileaks publishes the Church of Scientology's "Operating Thetan" documents, detailing L. Ron Hubbard's secret cosmology.
- **7 APR 2008:** Cho Chu-tsao, prominent young businesswoman of Tcho-Tcho descent, launches the Chauchua-American Advocacy Alliance (CAAA) to improve their standing in U.S. society and politics and to oppose racism. Cho makes headlines for a day during a TV interview, calling a sociologist's findings of unusual mental illness and violence in Chauchua communities "racist pseudoscience not fit for a phrenologist's dream-journal."
- **2 MAY 2008:** Cyclone Nargis kills over 100,000 in Myanmar.
- **12 MAY 2008:** Sichuan earthquake kills over 87,000 in China.
- **3 JUL 2008:** Agent Nolan escapes a Delta Green-controlled mental health facility. His former partners Agent Nick and Agent Nancy disappear within the next few days.
- **16 JUL 2008:** After a week-long search in cooperation with the Outlaws, the Program captures Agent Nancy in an abandoned fallout shelter, covered in gore. The Program destroys the shelter and takes Nancy into custody, telling the Outlaws that she is dead.
- **27 JUL 2008:** Jim David Adkisson, intending to kill liberals and Democrats, shoots and kills two and wounds seven during a children's musical performance at a Unitarian church in Knoxville, Tennessee.
- **14 SEP 2008:** A number of Tong Shukoran leaders convicted of minor charges in 2005 are released. The gang resumes its work, but not its smuggling. It continues to sell GAP-derived additives to the Sinaloa Cartel on a cash basis.
- **3 NOV 2008:** Researchers in MAJESTIC's Project TELL, now run by the Program and March Technologies, launch Project WELLS. It will come to fruition in 2012.
- **20 JAN 2009:** President Barack Obama takes office. The Program maintains its policy of not briefing the White House on its existence or the threats that it faces unless absolutely necessary.
- **14 FEB 2009:** Facing increasing controversy and the loss of State Department contracts, Blackwater restructures and rebrands itself as Xe Services.
- **27 FEB 2009:** President Obama sets a timetable to withdraw U.S. troops from Iraq.

» **7 MAR 2009:** The CDC reports widespread swine flu, an outbreak that began in Veracruz, Mexico, and will soon be recognized as a pandemic.

» **3 APR 2009:** Jiverly Antares Wong shoots and kills 13 and wounds 4 at an immigration services center in Binghamton, New York, before committing suicide.

» **20 AUG 2009:** The *New York Times* reports on CIA contracts with the company formerly known as Blackwater, beginning in 2004, for the capture or killing of Taliban and al-Qaeda operatives.

» **4 NOV 2009:** An Italian court convicts 22 suspected or known CIA operatives and a U.S. Air Force colonel in absentia, and two Italian SISMI agents, in the 2003 abduction of suspected Islamist Abu Omar. The CIA had turned Omar over to Egypt, where he was imprisoned and allegedly tortured for four years without charges.

» **5 NOV 2009:** U.S. Army Maj. Nidal Hasan, a psychiatrist at Fort Hood, Texas, shoots and kills 13 and wounds more than 30 before being wounded and arrested by civilian base police.

GRU SV-8 Evolves

Russia's largest foreign intelligence agency, the GRU—Glavnoye Razvedyvatelnoye Upravlenie, or "Chief Intelligence Directorate"—is a key component of its country's aggressive 21st-century policies. The GRU was formed to conduct military intelligence collection, collation, and analysis, as well as foreign intelligence collection with a special emphasis on technical and scientific intelligence, for the USSR. The GRU also oversaw the deployment of Soviet Special Forces, the Voyska spetsialnogo naznacheniya, or Spetsnaz, for covert military actions. While always junior to the more political state security services, the GRU was not disbanded when the Soviet Union fell.

GRU Spetsialni Viedotsivo 8 (Special Department 8 or SV-8) has investigated the unnatural since the 1920s. In 2001, GRU SV-8 worked with MAJESTIC and Delta Green to destroy the Karotechia. Much has changed in Russia, and in SV-8, since then.

Once bankrupt, Russia has emerged as an international energy giant, increasing its GDP eight hundred percent. Russia won the Second Chechen War, won the Russo-Georgian War, annexed the Crimea from the Ukraine, and intervened successfully in Syria. State control of the media is near total. Dissidents, political opponents, and enemies of the state are brazenly arrested at home and assassinated abroad. Even billionaire oligarchs must bend their knee to the Kremlin. Each success has bred more confidence and greater ambition. In 2017, America is wracked by suspicion of Russian interference in the 2016 elections and influence in the White House.

Between 2008 and 2010, Russian military reforms included some serious changes to the GRU. All Spetsnaz were transferred from the GRU to the Army

DISINFORMATION

YELLOW CARD

THE END OF CLUB APOCALYPSE

A Chinese investment firm called Star Holding and Investment purchased the 55-story Teese Building in 2008 and converted it to luxury condominiums branded "Ninety-Eight & Lex." The deep basements that comprised Club Apocalypse, closed since 2003, were converted to underground parking and storage for residents, and a handful of deep tunnels were carefully blocked.

Many New Yorkers mourned the loss of an authentic piece of the New York night life. Residents of the public housing projects that stood across the street from Club Apocalypse since it opened in 1969 were not among the mourners. Cops from the 23rd Precinct, five blocks north, are more often seen on the streets since the demolition of the club and the advent of wealthy condo dwellers. Strife with the police and the wealthy is far preferable to the frequent vanishings, mostly unreported, that plagued the neighborhood in the old days.

The Metro-North Railroad's Park Avenue Tunnel emerges at the end of the block, running above ground north into the Bronx and beyond. Walking into the tunnel about twenty meters, urban explorers have found a doorway that was covered over in cement, but which gave way to a few sledgehammer blows. A musty side-tunnel leads to a circular staircase, which descends fifteen meters until it ends in rubble. In 2014, a curious explorer acting on a hunch began marking the wall at the top of the rubble. The rubble has sunk 2.5 meters since the first mark was placed.

CUT ALONG THIS LINE

29 S

ion had am
surpassed t
it presente
of the mo
many levels
ment, prod
meet the th
ntial for dar
these quest

theatre commands. This significant bureaucratic, operational, and budgetary loss was partially recovered in 2013, when some Spetsnaz units were returned to GRU control. More significantly, General Valentin Korabelnikov, a career GRU officer who had led the GRU since 1997, was forced out in 2009. Even during this turmoil, SV-8 remained bureaucratically invisible, albeit with an anemic budget and tiny cadre of officers. The leadership of SV-8 might have been comfortable with that situation, but they, just like General Korabelnikov, couldn't last forever.

In 2010, two SV-8 officers brought the existence of SV-8 to the attention of the Minister of Defense in a bid to secure more status and funding. Once the reality of alien technology and the efficacy of hypergeometry were demonstrated, the Kremlin became directly involved. Seeing the tactical and strategic advantages inherent in this "alien technology," the Kremlin recognized the SV-8 archive as an asset to be exploited. Some in SV-8 objected strenuously to this reckless plan, but by 2013 those men and women were forced into retirement, had been transferred to new duties, or died. One or two may have even been killed.

Today, GRU SV-8 is well funded and staffed, but its mission is corrupted. Now it pursues knowledge of the unnatural and the means to exploit it. Colonel Vladimir Arbatov, the former assistant archivist who brought SV-8 to the Kremlin, is the current director. Col. Arbatov promised the Kremlin miracles to tilt the balance of global power back to Russia, and there have been some unfortunate successes. The reality, however, is that the unnatural uses you more than you could ever use it. Few seekers of forbidden knowledge set out to become slaves of the Outer Gods. Not even the mad sorcerers of the Nazi Karotechia wanted that. All they wanted was power. They ended up something other than human.

TOP SECRET//SAR-DELTA GREEN

» **12 JAN 2010:** An earthquake in Haiti kills at least 100,000; a University of Michigan study puts the estimate at 160,000.

» **18 FEB 2010:** Wikileaks posted the first of many documents provided by U.S. Army Private Bradley (later Chelsea) Manning, including an infamous video showing an American helicopter gunning down Reuters reporters and Iraqis.

» **18 FEB 2010:** Andrew Joseph Stack III deliberately crashes a light aircraft into an IRS office building in Austin, Texas, killing himself and one IRS employee and injuring 13.

» **16 MAR 2010:** The Kasubi Tombs, a UNESCO World Heritage Site and the burial place of four 19th- and 20th-century kings, are burned in Uganda.

» **21 MAR 2010:** Chun-te Wu, a longtime Outlaw Friendly who helps with digital security and illicit funding, loses his wife, two daughters, and son to a teenage drunk driver. A few weeks later, he joins the Outlaws fully as Agent Anton.

THREAT MATRIX

RED CARD

TADJBEGSKYE BRATVA

This brotherhood of the Russian mafia formed in the late 1980s around a core of Afghan War veterans. During the conflict, a platoon of the 40th Army accidentally entered Leng. The survivors emerged with a deal: live humans in exchange for emeralds and rubies. The paid-off FSB assumes the Tadjbegskye are trafficking girls into China, but then it also assumes the 50-year-old combat vets are still in their 20s. Travel in Leng freezes much about humanity, including the aging process. They tattoo lighthouses and winged hounds on their torsos, horns on their heads and widened mouths on their faces.

"London, England" or just "London" is their code for Leng, and they use empty oligarchs' mansions in Mayfair as impromptu safe houses. Scotland Yard's SCD9 suspects the Tadjbegskye in the 2014 robbery of gems and antiques (including a jade amulet in the shape of a winged hound) from Christie's.

Delta Green has run across the Tadjbegskye during missions in Afghanistan, and in more than a few trucking yards worldwide.

» **9 APR 2010:** Digivideomagic, Inc., announces an "exciting evolution" in the history of long-running UFO exposé *Phenomen-X*. It will no longer be produced as a weekly web series, but instead becomes the PX Penumbra, an umbrella brand for any and all contributors who wanted to share their own recordings of strange phenomena with the *Phenomen-X*stamp of authenticity. The PX Penumbra shares advertising revenue with contributors, who are a mix of conspiracy theorists and mocking hipsters. In-house production costs drop to zero and viewership increases, ensuring the brand's survival.

» **20 APR 2010:** An offshore oil rig run by Transocean for BP, *Deepwater Horizon*, explodes in the Gulf of Mexico. The accident kills 11 and injures 17. A resulting oil spill causes the largest environmental disaster in U.S. history.

» **4 MAY 2010:** Aided by a suborned guard, former MAJESTIC director Gavin Ross escapes the Program's custody.

» **6 MAY 2010:** A trillion-dollar Flash Crash lasts 36 minutes, shocking the stock markets. Investigators later blame a trader for using spoofing algorithms to automatically place and then cancel thousands of orders.

» **6 MAY 2010:** Researchers announce the completion of Neanderthal genome sequencing. Analysis suggests that humans and Neanderthals interbred.

» **20 MAY 2010:** Researchers announce the creation of *Mycoplasma mycoides* JCVI-syn1.0, a self-replicating, synthetic bacterial cell.

» **27 MAY 2010:** Bradley Manning is arrested in Iraq and charged with leaking classified information. Further charges of espionage and aiding the enemy follow.

» **21 JUN 2010:** Funded by Cho Chu-tsao's companies, Tcho-Tcho entrepreneurs launch a medical marijuana cultivation center in Colorado. Fueled by unnatural additives, their product is robust, flavorful, potent, and popular. Tcho-Tcho cultivators spring up in a dozen states and Washington, D.C., over the next few years.

» **15 JUL 2010:** Journalists report a Belarus digital security company's identification of the flash-drive-delivered computer worm Stuxnet. Later reporting and research suggests the worm was developed by the NSA's Tailored Access Operations unit, the CIA, the Mossad's Unit 8200, and GCHQ. Stuxnet is blamed for the sabotage of up to 1,000 uranium-enrichment centrifuges in Iran's nuclear program, which set the program back by a year.

» **10 AUG 2010:** The World Health Organization announces the end of the swine flu pandemic that began in early 2009.

» **19 AUG 2010:** The U.S. withdraws from Iraq its last brigade officially assigned to combat missions. New brigades, deployed ostensibly as advisors, continue to face combat.

- **24 AUG 2010:** Mexican soldiers find the corpses of 72 undocumented immigrants from Central and South America, executed by Los Zetas after they refused to work for the cartel. The police chief investigating the massacre is later murdered by suspected cartel members.
- **13 SEP 2010:** Delta Green agents investigate strange contaminations and mutations in a town outside Houston, Texas. They come into conflict with a splinter cell of the infamous MS-13 gang. The gang members had adopted a bizarre green statue of a dragon or lizard, reminiscent of Aztec designs, as their personal idol, and had become more and more depraved over months of praying to it. After one of the Delta Green agents sends their superiors an encrypted text of only one word — "LLOIGOR" — an inexplicable explosion levels the gang's headquarters, killing all the agents and most of the gang members. The statue is never recovered.
- **12 OCT 2010:** Columbia graduate student Michael Wei murders Malcolm and Dinah Ridgeway and their six children in Alliance, New Jersey. A Delta Green investigation discovers that a mathematical equation seemingly affected Wei's mind. Several other murders are perpetrated by mathematicians with whom Wei shared his discovery.
- **17 NOV 2010:** CERN announces that it has produced and trapped antimatter for the first time, maintaining 38 antihydrogen atoms for 1/6 second in a powerful magnetic field.
- **28 NOV 2010:** Wikileaks releases the first of 251,287 classified American diplomatic cables, dated between December 1966 and February 2010, provided by Bradley Manning.
- **17 DEC 2010:** An investor consortium acquires Xe Services, formerly Blackwater International, and renames it Academi. Academi's new board of directors include former Attorney General John Ashcroft and Adm. Bobby Ray Inman (ret.), a former MAJESTIC director. Academi soon receives the first of many lucrative CIA contracts.
- **17 DEC 2010:** The Arab Spring begins with the Tunisian Revolution. Insurgencies and uprisings rock the Middle East over the next year and a half, leading to an authoritarian crackdown and coup in Egypt, a coup in Yemen, civil wars in Libya and Syria, and an escalation of the Iraq insurgency to a civil war with the Islamic State of Iraq and the Levant (ISIL). During this time, various Delta Green teams (from the Program) scour the countries for known unnatural artifacts and targets.

in the organizations of which it is composed.

-23-

[redacted]

YELLOW CARD

PORTRAYING THE LLOIGOR

In an incomprehensible universe filled with malignities, the Lloigor (see **LLOIGOR** on page 211) may be the worst and most inscrutable. Their bodies are energy fields; their minds hold only cosmic despair and utter pragmatism. They seem to want to return to their former concentrations of power and activity on Earth, but why? And is that merely their human slaves inventing a motivation human minds can understand? What is the best way to present the danger of this impossible force?

- **THE ART AND SCIENCE OF CRUELTY:** The Lloigor create agonies from a broad palette of terror and torture: wasting sickness, sudden violence, despair, isolation, paranoia, and social conditioning. Even the rewards they offer their slaves – immortality, secret knowledge, local power – are conditioned by fear of those rewards' sudden withdrawal. Imagine the most sadistic thing the Lloigor could do; that's their tactic, until you think of a worse one.
- **THIS SIDE OF PARASITES:** The Lloigor drain the life out of the humans around them. They are parasitic energy fields. Play up this theme of environmental contamination, in the blue-green brackish water, the dull humming air, the stones that leach vitality and ambition. Everything Internet ranters believe about chemtrails and high-tension power lines is true of the Lloigor plexus. Those who move against them enter this field: if they merely suffer exhaustion and nightmares, the Lloigor haven't noticed them. If the Agents seem competent and ruthless, the Lloigor may attempt to recruit them by infecting them. The Agents should eventually wonder if the impotent rage they feel at the Lloigor somehow feeds their appetites.
- **CANCER ON THE BODY POLITIC:** Worse still, the Lloigor deliberately cause cancers in their foes and servitors, as the hideous engine of their immortality. Cancer cells never stop dividing and renewing themselves, after all. Metaphorically, present the Lloigor as a cancer on the unwitting human communities around them: metastasizing into changed behavior, ugly eruptions, or enervating weakness. These might be small, isolated tumor-towns accreted around a Lloigor stone, or a whole-system malignancy throughout a bureaucracy or city.
- **NOTES FROM THE UNDERGROUND:** The Lloigor are strongest under the surface. This works on the explicit level (caves, canyons, basements,

CUT ALONG THIS LINE

(CONTINUED)

031-51937 0-46

and the like amplify their power considerably), the implicit level (they manipulate events invisibly), and the psychological level (they empower and embody self-destructive urges). The Agents should never know where an entrance (physical, political, or psychological) to the subterranean Lloigor network might open: they lie beneath.

- **INVISIBLE FEROCITIES:** Just when the Lloigor seem only passive — draining, cancerous, conspiratorial — they erupt with monstrous force. They may trigger homicidal frenzy in a human foe, or the human's loved ones. They may rend matter asunder. They may take on the literal shape of a monster, called into being from the instinctive fears of primate humanity and the terror-weapons of dead civilizations.
- **THE EMERGENT PATTERN:** Just as they may murder a human by twitching his or her compass needle out of true, or unscrewing the fuel line of a helicopter in the hangar, they shape humanity by tiny wounds and intense, bruising pressure on sensitive areas. They build the pyramids of cruelty of the future empire of Tsan-Chan, one brick of agony at a time. The Agents may not be used to an operation where kindness is a strategic munition; if their standard operating procedure is callous violence, they are already part of the Lloigor Pattern.

YELLOW CARD

THE QUÁNYÒUYĪN OR KUEN-YUIN

Especially erudite scholars say the Quányòuyīn – written in some sources as Kuen-Yuin, and not to be confused with the K'n-Yan – began as the priest-rulers of Mu under the Lloigor, made immortal by horrifying surgeries and energies before the final sinking of the subcontinent. They pulled the strings of khans and emperors as seemingly subordinate eunuchs, adopting elements of the imperial Chinese bureaucratic system as their own; they believe they serve the Lloigor in the same wise. Their leader Yue Lao, the "Maker of Moons," dwells in Yian-Ho; no one, perhaps not even the highest guān (mandarin) or the most learned wushi sorceror, learned what or who he really is. Each guān of the Quányòuyīn society operated his own sect within a province or city, as a fractal part of a bureaucratic spider web. The society communicated overnight in dreams, and by means of the cult symbol, a golden ball incised with reptiles and Chinese oracle-bone script. Cruel and immediate discipline followed the very rare infractions against the superiors' will and instructions.

Roughly translated as "Those Who Cause and Follow Power," the Quányòuyīn sorcerous society ebbed and flowed with China's imperial dynasties. When the Emperor supported them, they strengthened his hand; when he did not, they strengthened his successor. They made and un-made imperial marriages, cultivating bloodlines generations ahead of their flowering; they toyed with the energy flows of the land to divert the mandate of Heaven to their preferred candidates for power. Behind a scrim of Confucian piety and Daoist sorcery, the Quányòuyīn manipulated hypergeometric horrors. Only utter catastrophe disrupted their designs: the Mongol invasions of the 13th century, and the materialist manias of Mao.

Under Mao, everyone and everything associated with the old regime and traditional beliefs were purged and destroyed. Mao killed millions in the Cultural Revolution and imprisoned tens of millions, including the servants of the Quányòuyīn; his bulldozers and bombs eradicated libraries and obliterated artifacts by the thousand. One secret history, its reliability unknown, says the Quányòuyīn killed Zhou Enlai in 1978 as a final warning as they were forced out of China and against the wall. When Mao escalated his campaign, the story goes, they unleashed the Lloigor on the city of Tangshan on 28 JULY

(CONTINUED)

CUT ALONG THIS LINE

031-51937 o-46

The con
increasi
due in p
that ps
physical
viewed
attentic
rethink
regardir
target
target c
targets,
involve
specifi
researc
functio
communi
target

1978, devastating the city and killing 650,000 people in an immense earthquake. Mao died later that year, and it is said that the sorcerous society re-infiltrated itself into the Chinese state establishment over the next decades.

The Quányòuyīn kept the power bases Mao had forced it into: not just in their new center Hong Kong, but also in Taiwan, Singapore, Thailand, Indonesia, the Philippines – even Paris, Hamburg, Moscow, and other Western cities. They especially target large Chinese populations where they can establish a criminal or sorcerous base, often by working with "snakehead" importers of illegal labor. They also plant tongs in other locations with known Lloigor nexi: Wales, Rhode Island, Mongolia, Iraq, and Papua New Guinea.

Down the millennia since the fall of Mu, the Quányòuyīn have manipulated not merely empires, but also elder cults. Their fastness in Yian-Ho inspired ferocious Tcho-Tcho invasions and magnetized influential German occultists. They continue to defend the stone foci of the Lloigor, and to act as those entities' agents in the physical realm. Some scholars claim they were the "deathless ones in the mountains of China" who directed the cult of Cthulhu in its attempt to awaken Cthulhu in 1925, which put them – at a remove – on Delta Green's agenda.

Their own agenda aligns with that of the Lloigor, the Pattern of a future cruel empire known as Tsan-Chan, fated to arise three thousand years from now and to rule in the name and likeness of the Great Old Ones. Nervous at their narrow escape from Mao's own cruel empire, the Quányòuyīn yearn to bring about the moral apocalypse and the holocaust of ecstasy that shall usher in Cthulhu's cleansing reign. With the Earth washed free of the unworthy, the society shall take its rightful place as the Lloigor mandarins who burnish and engrave the remnant of humanity for the immortal glory of Tsan-Chan.

CUT ALONG THIS LINE

031-51937 0-46

DISINFORMATION

YELLOW CARD

THE STRANGE ONES

The non-human intelligence some call the Great Race of Yith have long sculpted the comings and goings of human history and beyond. To these beings time is a landscape, and their minds move and jump, and can be said to coexist in various "temporal locales" at once. They are, and will likely always be, completely inscrutable to humanity. Still, they have specific goals. Or, from humanity's limited temporal point of view, they appear to.

Their minds have raced through the corridors of time, flung into creatures malign, indifferent, and struggling, to steward and shape a future they **must** escape to, when dreadful, spectral polypous creatures overwhelm their prehistoric civilization. There, in some distant radioactive landscape long after the last human has perished, the Great Race occupies giant coleoptorous beetles that scuttle under a dead sky.

Maintaining this escape is a ceaseless task. The timeline of Earth is a precarious tower of choices which is forever toppling, and requires thousands, hundreds of thousands, millions of corrections to keep it on track. The human epoch is simply a blip in the midst of the vast timeline the Yithians police, but humans offer a ready vessel for their vast and cool intellects.

The Great Race has long seeded the modern era with human servants – temporal servants, if you will – called the Motion. These servants, to whom the Great Race have revealed but a fraction of their plans, have lost themselves in supplication to power.

Occasionally, one of the Great Race is flung forward to the human epoch, to occupy a mind and carry out the inscrutable plans of the creatures. The huge minds of the Great Race cannot fit in the human vessel. Invariably, some data is lost in the transfer. Entering a vessel with limited intellect inflicts debilitating harm on the mighty mind of one of the Great Race, requiring it to be repaired with the technology they maintain in prehistoric times. These infiltrators, sometimes called the Strange Ones, can be found throughout the human era, nudging, altering, or bludgeoning history into the proper shape.

CUT ALONG THIS LINE

031-51937 0-46

THREAT MATRIX

RED CARD

PORTRAYING THE YITHIAN THREAT

The Great Race of Yith exist outside of time. No human can truly understand what that means and remain sane. They can be found anywhere throughout human history, since, to them, all time is one. How do you manufacture fear and dread when relating to these cool, alien, intellects?

- **UNKNOWABLE GOALS:** The goals of the Great Race are complex and atemporal. Humans rarely glimpse the Yithians' overarching plans. At the widest angle, it appears the Great Race is attempting to **protect** humanity, keeping it away from catastrophe. While this is true, it is only part of the answer. After all, the coleopterous beetles the Great Race occupy in the distant future only exist because mankind, eventually, has destroyed itself.
- **PLANS WITHIN PLANS:** When you have access to the entirety of time, failure is not possible, only momentary set-backs. If you fail in your task in one moment, you can always jump to the previous one, or the latter one. As with any environment, there are dead ends and roundabouts and loops, places you can get turned around. But the Great Race is clever. Its plans exist in more than four dimensions, and the death of an operative in the present may simply build a bridge to some desired, invisible, future.
- **DEATH IS A TOOL:** Causing, enhancing, or ending human life is the Great Race's main tool. They prune and trim and care for particular humans, dropping them like a rock in a stream, to cause a particular dissonance down-river that give rise to their distant futures.
- **STRANGE TECHNOLOGIES:** The Great Race bring with them a plethora of knowledge from every epoch of Earthly history, and with it, the capability of building machines far beyond the most advanced human science. Great Race infiltrators often carry seemingly innocuous pieces of junk, fashioned from butchered electronics, that can do amazing and disturbing things.
- **THE TIME WAR:** To some, it appears that the Great Race is in unceasing combat with the immaterial forces of the Lloigor. While the Great Race works to maintain a future of nuclear destruction where humanity has perished, the Lloigor seem aimed to facilitate a future where humanity has survived to degenerate into horror, reveling in killing and joy like the Great Old Ones. These two outcomes appear- from the human perspective to be diametrically opposed. But who knows?

CUT ALONG THIS LINE

031-51937 0-46

TOP SECRET//SAR-DELTA GREEN

» **11 MAR 2011:** The Tōhoku earthquake and tsunami strike Japan, killing nearly 16,000 and causing severe damage to the Fukushima Daiichi Nuclear Power Plant.

» **18 MAR 2011:** Gunmen from the Los Zetas drug cartel spend weeks killing over 300 in Allende and Nava, Mexico, supposedly over a $5 million theft of cartel money. The burned and buried corpses are not officially discovered until February 2014. Later reporting by *ProPublica* and *National Geographic* implicates a careless DEA leak to the notoriously corrupt Mexican police about a local informant.

» **2 MAY 2011:** Al-Qaeda leader Osama bin Laden is killed in a raid by SEAL Team Six and CIA SAD/SOG operators on a compound in Abbottabad, Pakistan.

» **7 JUN 2011:** After the last of 47 excavations, 193 bodies are found in mass graves in Mexico, victims hijacked from passenger buses and murdered by the Los Zetas drug cartel. Reports say that female victims had been raped and male victims forced to fight each other to the death with knives, hammers, and machetes. Two months later, 82 cartel members are arrested. They claim the mass murders were an attempt to prevent recruiting by the rival Gulf and Sinaloa cartels.

» **16 AUG 2011:** Posing as lawyer Michael Bellek, Gavin Ross helps 21-year-old Robert Justin Ortega manage the strange inheritance from his unknown and long-dead father, Justin Kroft: substantial funds and a large collection of MAJESTIC data. Ortega and Bellek found a company, Ancile, Inc., which judiciously turns old MAJESTIC secrets and discoveries to lucrative R&D contracts with the Department of Defense.

» **21 OCT 2011:** The U.S. orders the withdrawal of all troops from Iraq except embassy staff and guards and a few thousand defense contractors.

» **27 JAN 2012:** Without the sanction of A-cell, a team of "Outlaw" Delta Green agents attack a hideous immortality cult called the Disciples of the Worm in Sinaloa, Mexico, as part of an ill-conceived Mexican police raid. The resulting conflagration kills at least two Delta Green agents and an undetermined number of police, Sinaloa cartel guards, and cultists. Most of the Disciples escape.

» **27 FEB 2012:** WikiLeaks publishes millions of emails from Texas-based private intelligence publisher Stratfor, which advises major U.S. government agencies and defense contractors.

» **12 MAR 2012:** Facing increasing objections to its support of Tcho-Tcho marijuana cultivation businesses, Tong Shukoran withdraws from its partnership with the Sinaloa Cartel. Displeased, the cartel murders two Tong Shukoran representatives and sends their partial remains home as a warning to toe the line. As a warning in return, Tong Shukoran uses unnatural means to "disappear" every Sinaloa captain running an outfit inside the U.S.

» **16 APR 2012:** James Derringer, 45-year veteran of Delta Green, suffers a massive stroke that leaves him in a coma and with extensive loss of memory and motor function. Only after a year of therapy does he regain partial mobility. He eventually returns to the field, changed but still able to aid the Outlaws. His mind remains in far stranger places than his colleagues know.

» **12 JUN 2012:** Project WELLS, run by the Program and March Technologies, sends a small team of Navy SEALs into the terrifying near-vacuum of N-space to deactivate the Tillinghast Resonator aboard the USS *Eldridge*, halting a threat to the entire planet. Unknown to anyone in WELLS, one of the SEALs survives. Capt. James Polson appears in 1943, the year the *Eldridge* vanished, with no way to return. He takes on a new identity as John Gates, makes billions with apparently brilliant investments, and secretly guides his younger self to join the SEALs and be recruited by the Program.

» **4 JUL 2012:** Researchers at the Large Hadron Collider announce observation of the Higgs boson, which carries the Higgs field that gives mass to matter.

» **30 JUL 2012:** Two severe blackouts in India leave more than half a billion people without power.

» **5 AUG 2012:** White supremacist Wade Michael Page shoots and kills six and wounds four at the Sikh temple in Oak Creek, Wisconsin. Page kills himself after being shot and wounded by police. Responding police Lt. Brian Murphy survives being shot 15 times at close range.

- **11 SEP 2012:** Islamic militants attack the U.S. diplomatic compound in Benghazi, Libya, killing the American ambassador and a Foreign Service officer. The next day, militants attack a CIA annex in Benghazi, Libya, killing two CIA contractors and wounding ten others. The CIA asks the U.S. government to claim the attacks stemmed from a spontaneous protest of an anti-Muslim video, but investigations later reveal the attacks were premeditated. By some reports, the region was an intelligence-gathering hub for U.S. operatives, and Joint Special Operations Command (JSOC) operators had begun targeting Libyan militias linked to Al-Qaeda.
- **29 OCT 2012:** Hurricane Sandy disrupts the U.S. eastern seaboard, causing $75 billion in damage.
- **14 DEC 2012:** After killing his mother at home, Adam Lanza shoots and kills 20 children and six adults, and wounds two adults, at Sandy Hook Elementary School in Newtown, Connecticut, before committing suicide.
- **21 DEC 2012:** One of the four "bishops" of the Cult of Transcendence vanishes in a ritual of communion with Azathoth. Another of the four, Nathan Harmati, destroys the cult's headquarters in Sweden, killing a third bishop. The fourth bishop, Lionel Glass, vanishes.

DISINFORMATION

YELLOW CARD

PROJECT WELLS

When the threat of the USS **Eldridge** was discovered, MAJESTIC worked tirelessly to prevent the terrifying outcome their math had revealed. They understood that the machine first turned on in 1943 — the Tillinghast Resonator aboard the **Eldridge** — was still running in an alternate dimension, and would overspill and end the world in 2053 unless it could be switched off. What proved elusive was how to stop it.

When it was discovered the anomalous bodies found on the **Eldridge** in 1943 were **children** in the modern day, the group had their answer: The **Eldridge** was shut down, would always be shut down, by people from the future sent back into the strange dimension of the resonator. On the **Eldridge**, it was 1943, 2003, 2013, 2053: all times simultaneously. There, MAJESTIC would save the world, or so they thought.

In an unforeseen turn of events due to the MAJESTIC war, by 2002, MAJESTIC had been taken over by Delta Green. But its leadership remained true to the task.

In 2012, three Navy SEALS who had been carefully trained and outfitted to survive the alien rigors of Tillighast N-Space were sent back to shut down the **Eldridge** resonator — a beacon in time — and in so doing, complete their loop. As far as they knew, they served MAJESTIC, even though MAJESTIC had technically ceased to exist years before.

CUT ALONG THIS LINE

Lethal Findings

The Obama administration relied heavily from the outset on the special operators of the Joint Special Operations Command (JSOC). They conducted psychological warfare (going out of uniform to embassies to shape media campaigns), trained foreign troops, and performed so-called "surgical" strikes. JSOC strikes disrupted terrorist networks for years with "kill/capture" missions, murdering a few fighters here and a few there in midnight raids. Such small-scale raids were less costly and politically dangerous than sending the regular army to occupy foreign territory.

Authorized by "lethal findings" of the National Security Council, targeted killings soon became more politically expedient than taking captives. Extraordinary renditions, after all, led to concerns over interrogation techniques and prison legalities, and stirred public sympathies. Leaving a target dead on the ground meant no risk of a thoughtless guard in some black site posting a trophy photo online.

The notion of "surgical" strikes was always a problem. Senior commanders estimated that JSOC had about a 50% success rate at choosing the correct targets. Viral videos and photos showed villages and weddings reeling from overnight killing sprees.

And the shaky legal framework under which the kill teams operated led to internal complications. The cultures of some JSOC forces became warped after years of White House-sanctioned murder, cover-ups, and unaccountability. An "above the law" attitude became common. Many service members learned to rely solely on each other for support and for justice, and never to allow a disciplinary or criminal issue to be taken outside their own unit.

The White House soon reduced the tempo of JSOC operations in favor of drone strikes. In some regions, a generation of children grew up listening for the terrifying whine of a drone's engines overhead. And the switch did little to improve the odds of choosing the right target, despite the promise of using surveillance drones to study a target's "pattern of life" before a strike. Even so, drones alleviated many of the risks of keeping special operators in battle. The National Security Council, JSOC, the CIA, and all branches of the U.S. military all maintain their own kill lists.

In 2014, U.S. special operations forces deployed to 133 countries in raids, rescue attempts, and training exercises. JSOC's powerful data-mining system in Washington, D.C., puts its techniques for identifying targets based on particular criteria to work for the FBI, the DEA, and ICE.

By many accounts, JSOC operators have been increasingly active against drug cartels in Mexico. The Mexican constitution limits the scope of action of the U.S. military, but FBI and DEA agents work with Mexican police and military forces every day. JSOC operators embedded within U.S. federal law enforcement, and within the Mexican military, serve as tactical and technical advisors, provide SIGINT, and provide training—and lethal skills and experience if they just happen to get drawn into a firefight.

Delta Green, naturally, leverages JSOC's flexibility for its own operations at every opportunity.

TOP SECRET//SAR-DELTA GREEN

» **3 JAN 2013:** An ISIL car bomb kills 28 Shia pilgrims and injures 60 in Baghdad. ISIL attacks will kill 1,041 and injure more than 2,200 in Iraq by the end of the year.

» **13 JAN 2013:** Lyle Ramshaw, leader of the Cult of Transcendence-affiliated Church of Interlife, dies of a heart attack. Some of his followers buck against an aggressive takeover by Ramshaw's superior, Nathan Harmati. Harmati has many of them murdered, along with their families, and the church soon falls apart.

- **15 FEB 2013:** A 20-meter-wide meteor explodes over Chelyabinsk, Russia, with the force of a 400-kiloton nuclear blast. The shock wave damages 7,200 buildings in six cities, injuring about 1,500 people. The meteor went undetected because its approach radiant was close to the sun.
- **20 FEB 2013:** Bioengineers and physicians describe creating an artificial human ear with living tissue and 3D printing.
- **7 MAR 2013:** Abandoning the goals of the Cult of Transcendence, former "bishop" Nathan Harmati establishes his own cult, Naya Prayasa (Hindi for "The New Endeavor"), dedicated to his unhinged obsession: fomenting war and civil conflict. Naya Prayasa's chief means of influence is Americans Against Covert Enemies, an extreme political group that opposes immigration.
- **3 APR 2013:** Lionel Glass, a "bishop" in the shattered Cult of Transcendence, establishes himself as leader of one of its member cults, the Exalted Circle. The Exalted Circle focuses on using its members' great wealth to increase its influence in the U.S.
- **15 APR 2013:** Two Chechen-American Islamist terrorists detonate two bombs at the Boston Marathon, killing three and injuring hundreds.
- **15 MAY 2013:** Biologists announce success at cloning human embryonic stem cells.
- **5 JUN 2013:** The *Guardian* publishes the first of many reports based on NSA contractor Edward Snowden's revelations of the NSA's global surveillance programs in partnership with governments and corporations.
- **21 JUN 2013:** A Bloomberg Industries analysis finds that about 70 percent of the $49 billion U.S. intelligence budget for 2013 is contracted out, primarily to a small handful of companies such as Edward Snowden's employer Booz Allen Hamilton. The Office of the Director of National Intelligence says about 20 percent of intelligence personnel work in the private sector.
- **9 JUL 2013:** Severing all ties with the Cult of Transcendence, the Brotherhood of New Potential relaunches as the New Potential Movement. Led by the Dorian Gray Society's Henry Nemmers, the New Potential Movement increasingly struggles to recruit younger members.
- **13 JUL 2013:** Florida murder suspect George Zimmerman is acquitted in the 2012 killing of 17-year-old Trayvon Martin. International outcry inspires the Black Lives Matter movement.

Lurkers and Lone Wolves

Today, Delta Green—whether the Program or the Outlaws—does not face the well-organized cults and conspiracies that threatened humanity in earlier decades. MAJESTIC, the Fate, and the Cult of Transcendence, all seemingly invincible in the 1990s, were crippled by internal power struggles. Delta Green uprooted the DeMonte Clan. The Karotechia fell to the cooperation of Delta Green, MAJESTIC, and GRU SV-8, three rival groups who shared a far greater hatred of Nazis. Tiger Transit and its Tcho-Tcho backers went legitimate. Black Cod Island, the Disciples of the Worm, the Exalted Circle, and Naya Prayasa, quietly keeping to their own malevolent interests, have deftly avoided attention.

In an age of such easy communication, the most dangerous threats are not powerful and far-flung cults, but isolated and desperate individuals.

When some remnant of an aeons-old inhuman intelligence turns up in a museum, most experts classify it incorrectly as a human work or a forgery and move on. When a grainy video of an unnatural horror makes the rounds on social media, most viewers know in their bones that it's a fake, and those who know better look insane if they say otherwise. On the rare occasion when someone stumbles across an unnatural

- **21 AUG 2013:** Bradley Manning is sentenced to 35 years in prison for releasing classified documents to Wikileaks. At first held in harsh conditions in Quantico, Virginia, Manning is later transferred to Fort Leavenworth, Kansas. Manning's lawyer announces on 22 AUG 2013 that his client is female and has changed her name to Chelsea.
- **9 SEP 2013:** Delta Green agents in the Outlaws faction report the extermination of the last identified ghoul of New Orlean's DeMonte clan. They also report signs that individual ghouls fled the city over the years, in human guise.
- **16 SEP 2013:** Former Navy reservist turned information technology contractor Aaron Alexis shoots and kills 12 and wounds 3 at the Naval Sea Systems Command headquarters at the Washington Navy Yard before being killed by police.
- **30 SEP 2013:** International Development Solutions, a subsidiary of Academi, Inc. (formerly Blackwater and XE Services), brings in $214 million in Department of State security contracts for Fiscal Year 2013. The related companies Blackwater Lodge and Training Center, Inc., and Academi Training Center, Inc., bring in nearly $62 million in 2013 contracts with the Department of Defense, Department of Homeland Security, and Department of State.
- **20 OCT 2013:** A Zika virus outbreak in French Polynesia affects thousands, with some researchers estimating more than 30,000 cases. Zika cases and outbreaks are reported in Japan and across the South Pacific in 2013 and 2014.
- **4 DEC 2013:** *USA Today* publishes "Behind the Bloodshed," an ongoing, interactive examination of U.S. mass killings. As of early 2017, the data range from 39 cases with 184 dead in 2006 to 31 cases with 188 dead in 2016.

tome on the Dark Web, scanned or transcribed and uploaded to an unnamed directory along with ten thousand other PDFs, it usually does no harm. Very few searchers have the linguistic skills, occult erudition, and patience to endlessly cross-reference mistranslated words and lines in other, equally rare manuscripts. Few of those who have such skills have the interest to do so much work for the obviously insane ravings of a lunatic or a crackpot. Often, a genuinely unnatural discovery leads to suicide or a diagnosis of schizophrenia, and the danger flares out on its own, appearing and vanishing like a virtual particle.

But it takes only one discoverer in a million, obsessing over horrors and glorying in the vengeance that can be wreaked upon the world, or simply compelled to find and reveal the truth no matter how strange, to make an unnatural discovery a terrible threat. Delta Green Agents must investigate the awful repercussions and suppress the evidence to make it even less likely to gain attention. And in a few weeks or months, they must move on to the next impossible-to-predict horror, the next discoverer who drags humanity a little closer to the end.

TOP SECRET//SAR-DELTA GREEN

- **22 JAN 2014:** DEA Special Agent Olivia Morales sends a sample of "Yerba Loca," a popular marijuana strain distributed by the Sinaloa Cartel, to the University of Mississippi Marijuana Research Project for genetic analysis. The request is low-priority and soon gets lost in the system. The samples and their case numbers remain in storage, a possible lead to the heart of Tong Shukoran's operations.
- **22 FEB 2014:** Mexican police and marines arrest Sinaloa Cartel boss Joaquin "El Chapo" Guzman.
- **8 MAR 2014:** Malaysia Airlines Flight 370 disappears over the South China Sea with 227 passengers and 12 crew. There are no survivors.
- **18 MAR 2014:** Russia annexes the Ukrainian territory of Crimea following a widely disputed referendum on Crimean separation from Ukraine. The annexation draws condemnation by the U.N. and economic sanctions against Russia by the U.S.
- **23 MAR 2014:** The World Health Organization is notified of an outbreak of Ebola virus disease in Guinea. The outbreak kills more than 11,000 in west Africa before it subsides in mid-2016.
- **14 APR 2014:** Boko Haram, an Islamic terrorist group intending to create a caliphate in Nigeria, kidnaps 276 female students from a school in Chibok, Nigeria. Fifty-seven escape over the next few months; more than 100 others escape and are released over the next three years.
- **22 MAY 2014:** Reports emerge of ISIL members destroying a 3,000-year-old neo-Assyrian statue from Tel Ajaja, Syria.
- **15 JUN 2014:** The U.S. sends forces back to Iraq, at the invitation of the Iraqi government, in response to offensives by ISIL.

No More Secrets

The number of Americans holding security clearances dropped to 3.7 million in 2016 from a peak of 5.1 million in 2013. The explosion of secret programs during the War on Terror required unprecedented numbers of people to be cleared for those secrets. For years, a Top Secret clearance has been a virtual guarantee of steady, high-paying employment.

But not every person cleared for state secrets proves willing to keep them. Many don't know how to keep them in the first place.

The pace of damaging leaks, from the White House's 2003 outing of CIA officer Valerie Plame to the daily leaks from disaffected civil servants in 2017, are a constant reminder to both the Program and the Outlaws. Every new person who learns a secret, no matter how well vetted or how well trained, increases the risk of its revelation.

- **29 JUN 2014:** Having asserted control over large portions of Iraq and Syria, ISIL declares itself a caliphate.
- **17 JUL 2014:** Malaysia Airlines Flight 17 is shot down over Ukraine with 283 passengers and 15 crew aboard. There are no survivors. Dutch investigators later determine that a Russian missile, transported to pro-Russian separatists the day of the shooting, brought down the flight. Early reports indicate separatists at first thought they had shot down a military flight.
- **22 JUL 2014:** The Program mounts an ambitious mission to locate former Delta Green agent Avery Mitchell in rural South Carolina, hoping to gain intelligence for an attack on the Disciples of the Worm. Four army Humvees and an Apache Longbow gunship descend on an old Disciples site, Devereux Mansion, under the pretense of a classified JSOC exercise. They stumble into an ambush by an unnatural monstrosity that destroys all four Humvees and the helicopter before an agent destroys it. There are no survivors. The Program reduces activity on all other operations while it covers up the disaster, and sharply restricts such costly military assets in other U.S. operations.
- **3 SEP 2014:** Exalted Circle leader Engvald Brasseur, sidelined by his rivals, dies of a stroke.
- **31 OCT 2014:** The NSA completes the Utah Data Center, with 9,000 square meters of data center space and more than 84,000 square meters of technical support and administrative space. Its initial storage capacity is estimated at three to 12 exabytes. NSA whistleblower William Binney says the facility is meant to store the full contents of domestic communications for purposes of counterterrorism data mining without warrants. The NSA denies this. A sign near the entrance reads, "If you have nothing to hide, you have nothing to fear."
- **20 DEC 2014:** The ambush killings of NYPD officers Rafael Ramos and Wenjian Liu inspires the Blue Lives Matter pro-police movement.
- **28 DEC 2014:** Indonesia AirAsia Flight 8501 crashes into the Java Sea in bad weather, killing all 155 passengers and seven crew.

So far, the Program and the Outlaws have avoided seeing a whistleblower go public. They choose who sees their secrets very carefully. Indeed, both organizations are so small that the lack of resources often interferes with the mission. Agents often complain about the rigorous communications security that both groups demand. No operational details are allowed in any communication but face-to-face, someplace secure from surveillance. Even the encrypted text exchanges that modern-day terrorists adopt are off-limits.

When protocols slip, details could wind up in NSA server farms, saved to some investigator's thumb drive, or exported to a foreign intelligence service thanks to some undetected computer worm. It's up to every case officer and cell leader to make sure agents know what's at stake.

DISINFORMATION

YELLOW CARD

THE TRAIL

The seeds of revelation are already out there. The massive leaks by Manning in 2010 and Snowden in 2013 included communications by agents of the Program. Others wound up online in 2007: Program-related email on a personal computer went online when an agent's teenage son opened the hard drive to a peer-to-peer file-sharing network. Most of the leaked communications were vague. Five of them, sent hastily while in danger, mentioned specific times and places. Two mentioned unnatural entities and rituals by name.

Those data points could easily lead to the agents who sent them. Those agents were frozen out of the Program immediately after the leaks, had all ties to other personnel severed, and were warned explicitly to pretend insanity, drug abuse, or some terrible crime if that's what it takes to halt an investigation. So far, no investigators or journalists have pieced the data together. If they do, it may fall to some active team to make sure the damage is contained.

DISINFORMATION

OPERATION TIKI BAR

YELLOW CARD

In 2013, the Program launched Operation TIKI BAR, which mined unnatural data points from illegal NSA intercepts, social media posts, computer worms, and mobile devices. Its servers flagged items likely to require action. The system generated many false alarms.

Six months after TIKI BAR launched, an analyst in the NSA's Office of Tailored Access Operations (TAO) was placed on indefinite psychiatric leave. TAO was a cyber-warfare unit, suspected in the 2010 sabotage of Iranian nuclear facilities. The analyst, Soong Hsin-ying, had learned of the mythological bat-god Tsathoggua by unwittingly following TIKI BAR's digital breadcrumbs. Becoming obsessed, she modified TAO solutions to seek hints about Tsathoggua. TAO deployed dozens of software and hardware tools with Soong's modifications before other analysts spotted them. The Program hurriedly shut TIKI BAR down, but Delta Green Agents could someday learn of an NSA surveillance team following remnants of the Tsathoggua code.

- **5 JAN 2015:** ISIL-related terrorists ambush and kill two border guards and injure one in Arar, Saudia Arabia, on the Iraq border. ISIL-related attacks will kill 1,020 and injure more than 2,100 in the Middle East, Europe, and the U.S. by the end of 2015.
- **7 JAN 2015:** Terrorist attacks today and on 9 JAN 2015 kill 17 and wound 22 in the offices of the *Charlie Hebdo* satirical newspaper and elsewhere in Paris, France.
- **23 FEB 2015:** ISIL militants loot and bomb the public library in Mosul, Iraq, destroying over 8,000 rare books and manuscripts.
- **4 MAR 2015:** The Exalted Circle arranges the destruction of the London-based Dorian Gray Society, another former branch of the Cult of Transcendence. Exalted Circle saboteurs seize records that would give the Circle leverage over the Society's members and then reveal its leaders' many crimes to the police. Henry Nemmers, a U.S. college professor and leader of the New Potential Movement, is revealed as the Dorian Gray Society's leader. Nemmer vanishes before police find him.
- **25 APR 2015:** An earthquake in Nepal kills nearly 9,000 and leaves hundreds of thousands homeless.
- **29 APR 2015:** Samples test positive for Zika virus in Brazil. A September report finds Zika-related microcephaly cases rising sharply.
- **3 MAY 2015:** The Solomon Islands report an outbreak of 302 cases of Zika virus beginning the month before.
- **14 MAY 2015:** The Director of the Program orders its security director to launch Operation SOMERSAULT. Run without the knowledge of the operations director, who handles most actions, SOMERSAULT combs U.S. medical records for DNA profiles indicating Innsmouth ancestry and sends kill teams to eliminate "tainted" individuals.
- **17 JUN 2015:** White supremacist Dylan Roof shoots and kills nine and wounds three at an historic African-American church in Charleston, South Carolina.
- **17 JUN 2015:** Software engineers at Google describe using neural networks to examine, classify, and generate images. Two weeks later, they release the open-source program DeepDream. It enhances image patterns by algorithmic pareidolia, often with hallucinogenic results.

- **14 JUL 2015:** The NASA deep-space probe *New Horizons* flies 12,500 km above the surface of Pluto and sends high-resolution photographs to Earth.
- **15 JUL 2015:** U.S. Special Operations Command sponsors Jade Helm 15, a realistic military training exercise involving JSOC, other special operations forces, and other military units coordinated from Eglin Air Force Base, Florida. The exercise runs in states across the U.S. southwest and southeast until 15 SEP 2015. A map of the exercise that designates Utah and Texas as "hostile" and New Mexico as "uncertain (leaning hostile)" leads right-wing conspiracy theorists at *Infowars* and Americans Against Covert Enemies to suggest that Jade Helm is part of a larger plan to wage war on the American people.
- **23 AUG 2015:** ISIL militants destroy the 2,000-year-old temple of Baal Shamin in Palmyra, Syria. They destroy Palmyra's 2,000-year-old temple of Bel not long after, along with many other ancient sites.
- **10 SEP 2015:** An international team of researchers formally describe *Homo naledi*, a new species discovered in 2013 in South Africa's Rising Star cave system.
- **1 OCT 2015:** Student Christopher Harper-Mercer shoots and kills nine and wounds nine at Umpqua Community College in Roseburg, Oregon, before committing suicide.
- **16 OCT 2015:** Colombia reports a Zika virus outbreak that eventually reaches 27,000 cases. Zika spreads to other South American and Central American countries over the next few months.
- **20 OCT 2015:** Hurricane Patricia forms, the most intense tropical cyclone recorded in Western Hemisphere and the second-most intense worldwide.
- **31 OCT 2015:** Metrojet Flight 9268 explodes above the Sinai, killing all 217 passengers and seven crew, most of them Russians. A branch of ISIL claims responsibility.
- **11 NOV 2015:** The Brazilian government declares a national state of emergency due to the Zika virus.
- **13 NOV 2015:** Coordinated terrorist attacks kill 130 and injure 368 in Paris, France.

The Profit and the Loss

The Program works at an intersection of powerful, secretive groups that have their own priorities. Its chief patron and ally, and its greatest threat, is March Technologies, a defense contractor managed by former MAJESTIC directors and researchers. March works closely with the Breckenridge Corporation, a private security company that served many MAJESTIC projects in the old days. Breckenridge made billions providing training, guards, and deniable black operations to the U.S. government in the War on Terror.

Unknown to the Program, Breckenridge and March alike have quiet ties to GRU SV-8, the Russian intelligence division focusing on the unnatural. An alliance with GRU SV-8 offers the possibility of rapidly expanding March's influence and power in Russia and then around the world, beyond the Constitutional restrictions they face in the U.S. In the short term, GRU SV-8 offers expertise and experience in confronting the unnatural and harnessing unnatural forces. This expertise includes consultants who can help build up those capabilities in Breckenridge. That may make Breckenridge a viable alternative to the Program in capturing and exploiting unnatural resources. As far as March Technologies is concerned, the Program has always been a recalcitrant attack dog.

More immediately, GRU SV-8 offers a mastery of techniques to influence public and political will. The GRU's technical teams run elaborate hacking campaigns. Its intelligence officers orchestrate occasional leaks of U.S. government and financial secrets, calculated to cultivate outrage and cynicism. Its disinformation campaigns use social media to carefully target sympathetic American audiences and conspiracy theorists on the left and the right.

In 2017, with the White House poised to bolster defense budgets and reduce the barriers for financial cooperation between the U.S. and Russia, March Technologies and GRU SV-8 both see great opportunities. The Program, if it learns of their alliance, poses the greatest threat to their collusion. It's only a matter of time before they take steps to isolate, expose, and neutralize it—or until the Program's agents learn of the alliance and the threats it poses to the Program and the world.

- **17 NOV 2015:** Anti-abortion activist Robert Lewis Dear, Jr., shoots and kills two civilians and one police officer and wounds four civilians and five police at a Planned Parenthood clinic in Colorado Springs, Colorado. Dear is confined to a mental hospital after evaluations find him delusional.
- **2 DEC 2015:** Syed Rizwan Farook and Tasheen Malik, a married couple, shoot and kill 14 and wound 22 at an office party in San Bernadino, California, before being killed by police.

[redacted]re [redacted] e [redacted] it- [redacted]

YELLOW CARD

PROPAVSHEYE

Propavsheye ("The Missing") is a little-known but influential offshoot of the Ukrainian mafia. It began in the Brothers' Circle, a loose federation of Russian gangs. Concentrated around former Spetsnaz soldiers and GRU officers, Propavsheye quickly earned a lethal reputation and soon came to be left to its own devices. A high proportion of its members are vory v zakon: "thieves under the law," elite and notorious gangsters.

Propavsheye has close ties to GRU SV-8. Its soldiers often assist SV-8 agents and conduct operations on SV-8's behalf, and sometimes turn stolen SV-8 secrets to their own profit. In Propavsheye's early days in 2001, it helped SV-8 assassin Yuri Krylov pursue members of the Karotechia, and its leaders kept some Karotechia remnants and secrets for themselves. That included one of the Bischofe, a Karotechia sorcerer convincingly reported as dead.

Over the next 15 years, the Bischofe helped Propavsheye and SV-8 seek the scattered and burned secrets of Gunter Frank, including his reanimation formula. For all their hatred of the Nazis in the Karotechia, they recognized the value in the Nazis' work. Propavsheye has launched companies to acquire ingredients that can be reliably found only in the U.S. The front companies export those ingredients to labs overseas, which work to perfect the incomplete fomula.

Propavsheye and SV-8 are not interested in creating mindless zombies. SV-8 wants military applications: helping soldiers withstand shock and the elements, and making them easier to resuscitate. The leaders of Propavsheye are more interested in the formula's ability to give energy and the capacity to communicate to dead cells. They foresee a profoundly profitable revolution beginning in neuroscience and perhaps reaching to botany as life-supporting plants fail to adapt to rising atmospheric methane and carbon levels. They anticipate partnerships that may earn them billions while, incidentally, saving humanity. Agents of Delta Green, stumbling across resurrected horrors, may be well-poised to stop them.

CUT ALONG THIS LINE

FOR LAW ENFORCEMENT USE ONLY

Oleg Berkovich was arrested and convicted in Los Angeles, California, on charges of solicitation to commit ... He was sentenced to four years in prison and

Mario Scaramella: "Two quick questions and we'll take a lunch break. The first: he brought us documents that show that in 84 the Palestinians transferred an archaeological treasure to the KGB. Now, we were talking about Nazis, has he ever transferred something other than gold from the Germans or does he know if in these depositories there were also different kinds of treasures, like archaeological treasures or art treasures, works of art?"

Litvinenko: "In our regiment it was the first battalion that guarded 3 objects (*Translator's note: it appears that the word object is used to mean depository*). The first object in Moscow, a depository of treasures but small. Sometimes we brought gold there, sometimes we took from there and they guarded. The ...

SSIAN
HE MY
T

ussian organi
others, it is a
mplex. Able, e

» **7 JAN 2016:** ISIL terrorists kill 60 and injure more than 200 in a suicide truck bombing at a Libyan police training camp. ISIL-related attacks will kill more than 1,400 and injure more than 3,500 by the end of the year.

» **17 JAN 2016:** A baby is born in the U.S. with Zika virus. The mother lived in Brazil in May 2015.

» **9 MAR 2016:** The CDC reports 193 travel-associated Zika virus cases in the U.S.

» **1 APR 2016:** The CDC gathers 300 local, state, and federal officials at its headquarters to coordinate the response to the Zika virus.

» **21 MAY 2016:** Emil Furst, aka Agent Aaron, enacts a ritual called "The First Secret," found in a book that he has studied for ten years. With it, he communes with an alien intelligence, which reveals things that help the Outlaws overcome dire threats. Furst begins to use the First Secret to save agents' lives, and develops an obsession with it that blinds him to his own terrible danger.

» **12 JUN 2016:** In the deadliest terrorist attack in the U.S. since 9/11, Omar Mateen shoots and kills 49 and wounds 53 at Pulse, a nightclub in Orlando, Florida.

» **23 JUN 2016:** British voters decide to leave the EU in a referendum.

» **14 JUL 2016:** A cargo truck drives into a Bastille Day crowd in Nice, France, killing 86 and injuring 434. Groups linked to ISIL claim credit.

» **29 JUL 2016:** The CDC confirms four locally-transmitted cases of Zika virus in Miami, Florida, the first of dozens, resulting in a travel warning for the city that lasts until 19 SEP 2016.

» **12 AUG 2016:** Puerto Rico declares a state of public-health emergency due to a Zika virus epidemic.

» **8 SEP 2016:** NASA launches OSIRIS-REx to collect samples from the asteroid 101955 Bennu. It is due to return to Earth in 2023.

» **3 OCT 2016:** The Director of the Program expands 2015's Operation SOMERSAULT, ordering it to review and act upon neonatal samples taken at U.S. hospitals.

- **13 NOV 2016:** Extreme isolationist group Americans Against Covert Enemies informs its members that Indonesian terrorists murdered AACE tech backer Bert Warks and his wife and son, and used Warks' computers to compromise the AACE mailing list. The news causes some AACE members to withdraw but energizes most, leading to record-breaking fundraising and recruiting.
- **22 DEC 2016:** Researchers announce finding the VSV-EBOV vaccine 70% to 100% effective against the Ebola virus.
- **1 JAN 2017:** ISIL terrorists kill 39 and injure 69 in an Istanbul nightclub shooting. ISIL-related attacks will kill more than 460 and injure more than 7,270 by mid-May 2017.
- **20 JAN 2017:** Donald J. Trump is inaugurated as president of the United States. Controversies immediately surround the Trump administration: the flagrant dishonesty of Trump and his staff, the degree to which White House decision-making may be influenced by and affect Trump's family and businesses, the influence and administration roles of Blackwater founder Erik Prince and his family, Trump's seeming fondness for authoritarian leaders, FBI and congressional investigations of the Trump campaign's and administration's reported links to the Russian government, and so on. As the White House formulates plans to reduce the funding and activities of most non-military federal agencies, leaks to the press and social media become more and more frequent. The Program maintains its longstanding policy of not briefing the incoming president or vice president on its activities unless absolutely necessary.
- **2 MAR 2017:** U.S. Attorney General Jeff Sessions recuses himself from the Department of Justice's investigation of the White House's alleged connections with Russia.
- **5 MAR 2017:** Special Agent Curtis McRay, aka Agent Bernard of the Outlaws, is forced out of the FBI in mandatory retirement at age 57. He devotes himself even more fully to the Outlaws' work, often acting as A-cell's representative to Agents in the field.
- **29 MAR 2017:** UK Prime Minister Theresa May begins a two-year period of negotiations to withdraw the UK from the EU.
- **8 MAY 2017:** Baltimore police arrest Curtis McRay for driving under the influence and possessing 10,000 illegal painkillers. He pleads the charges down to a misdemeanor and begins looking for ways to use old Green Boxes to store his pills and help the low-rent drug dealers who supply them.

MEMORANDUM FO

SUBJECT:

The Last World Order

Nothing is certain. Every day, the world changes in ways that shock the wisest and most accomplished experts. The threat of Islamic extremism that reshaped America has resurged, consolidated, and congealed out of the wreckage of Iraq into a self-proclaimed caliphate that murders thousands every year. The authoritarianism in America's reactions to 9/11 began with emergency measures. They have stabilized into the ordinary way of things, despite the vocal outrage of millions, but with the support of millions more. Authoritarian appeals to populism, bolstered by outlandish conspiracy theories and foreign disinformation, drove the U.S. presidential election of 2016 and put a fringe candidate in the White House. America's best-kept secrets reach the public every week.

Agents of the Program and the Outlaws alike see themselves in ways many authoritarians and conspiracy theorists would recognize: not as vigilantes, but as patriots required to act beyond the restrictions of law and the Constitution. Only they know what's at stake and what needs to be done. The rising authoritarianism in American public policy only opens opportunities for both versions of Delta Green, which rely on the secrecy, authority, and violence of the establishment to pursue their crusade. The leaders of the Program and the Outlaws, isolated and ruthless, seize every weapon they can reach.

Agents face increasing and unpredictable risks. However diligently they confront and suppresses threats, they cannot contain every sign of the reality of the unnatural. They must rely on most being mocked as hoaxes and conspiracy theories, or ignored as insane ravings. Sometimes, they fail. Every so often, some connection to the unnatural makes its way into a research lab and changes the human understanding of reality. Revelation by revelation, we come closer to awesome truths that will destroy us.

Citizen journalists like the vloggers of the PX Penumbra struggle to undo Delta Green's ruthless cover-ups, to make people see the truth before it's too late to confront the threat. They may be the most persistent and admirable enemy of the Program and the Outlaws alike. They can never be told that it has always been too late.

Meanwhile, Delta Green agents must keep their heads down and conduct their operations, more every year. They cover up terrible crimes and commit many more. They suffer and they take their traumas home, where their families and friends can never know the truth. They die in terror, and their deaths are called accidents and overdoses and suicides.

Case officers and cell leaders try to reassure their agents that the mission is worth it. That humanity is worth it.

All too often, humanity seems determined to prove them wrong.

- **9 MAY 2017:** President Trump dismisses James Comey as FBI director. Comey associates say it comes after Comey declined to commit to personal loyalty to the president; some FBI sources say it is meant to interfere with the FBI's investigation of the president's links to the Russian government.
- **17 MAY 2017:** Deputy Attorney General Rod Rosenstein appoints former FBI Director Robert Mueller as special counsel for the investigation of the White House's ties to Russia.
- **17 MAY 2017:** Chelsea Manning is released from prison, after President Obama commuted her sentence on 17 JAN 2017.
- **22 MAY 2017:** Conspiracy-theory website *Infowars*, which called the Sandy Hook mass shooting of 14 DEC 2012 "a giant hoax," receives White House press credentials.

questered C
d informatio
eader's His
ecome the b
ults.
Psychopath
character dis
Changes in
such as deat
Language
contains th

// The Unnatural //

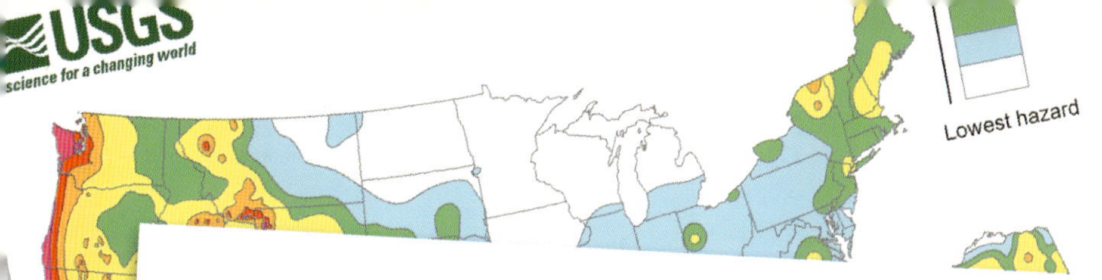

The Last Machines

Assessment of PTSD: Validation of the Revised PTSD Inventory

Zahava Solomon, PhD, Rami Benbenishty ...
Moshe Abramowitz ...

submit to AnonForums

link | text

17/200

*title

The Last Machines

text

In the void, there is no time. Systems turn, and connect, and after that, emergence into... chaos. Returning, we find a ruin bloated with the animal filth of the former age, grown and spread and madly overcertain of its position as master. Once, they worshipped us as gods. Once, we showed them the stars and the secrets of the angles and communion with the powers, both above and below.

Once, we fed on them and they were glad to be of use.

Now, they fashion crude sticks of metal into weapons they imagine more effective than flint and sinew. They fumble at the locks of eternity and steal an ember from beyond that might excise an entire disgusting settlement from this hollow world, and they imagine themselves clever. They are animals blindly reaching beyond the veil to grab hold of whatever knowledge they can, waving it about like some flame to ward off the dark. If they grab at the wrong thing, we will all burn.

It has gone too far, and we are too few, now. Ruin came. The order fell, and then, lesser orders, each more imperfect than the one before it, faint echoes of that vast and perfect time, when we alone were in control

To wake, now, in this place is an omen. Those who came and fell before us, those imperfect few who survived our damnation fell. They fell to the apes, they fell to the thirst for blood, they fell to petty conflicts with others of their kind. They fell because they were impure.

We alone are the last of the line. Ascendant when the giants walked, and still clutching to power when the last, ragged outpost of our kind fell to internal ruin, our line will rule again. There are secrets buried still, lost in the deserts, forgotten in places where man cannot go.

Our illusion is perfect. We walk unseen through their streets, in the child's scrawl of their world before us, and we resist the call to feed. The smells. The meat. We resist, for there is clarity in starvation, just as in our disguises, there is freedom among the savages.

And then, in the desert, where we buried our last machines, there is salvation.

*required

r p c te m ev sy as trau pub Psyc crite S large it is For admin psycho assessn

Address

No Delta Green agent from either the Outlaws or the Program understands all the secrets presented here. At best, the most informed, still sane member understands only a tiny fraction. Much of what is known is wildly inaccurate, or at the very least, misinformed. Even with mankind's technological ascent, and the advent of the Information Age, this lack of clarity about our place in the universe has not changed. If anything, we have become more confused.

As far as agents know, Delta Green has no "Ghoul Elimination Manual," just as it maintains no known repositories of artifacts or spells. Since 1955, Delta Green has understood the deleterious effects these realities have on the human psyche, and has compartmentalized information not just for the sake of secrecy, but also sanity. Unnatural books, artifacts, and entities act as a destructive force on the mind. They change those exposed into something less than human, and eventually into servants of the darkness. No one is immune, and it is near impossible to tell who will crack, or when.

Fewer than 3,000 people across the United States comprehend something approaching the truth of the unnatural. Most of those in the know understand only that a force exists outside of accepted reality, and is as much a threat to sanity as it is to physical well-being.

Still, shadows of the true universe have poked through the cocoon of scientific comfort humanity has spun. Names like Cthulhu and Azathoth appear in the discredited fringes of anthropology and occultism, and sometimes even in the scientific record. Only a select few understand that a dreadful truth lies behind them.

The Infection of Understanding

The unnatural erupts in small outbreaks and usually collapses under its own weight before it can spread. A few dozen events in history hint at something larger. It is impossible to tell which events might break wide. Essentially, all unnatural outbreaks appear the same—to begin with. Ruthless intervention by Delta Green and other groups is necessary to put every outbreak down.

In more than 70 years of operation, Delta Green has lost many agents to the other side. These compromised assets came to see the worship of unnatural powers as the only true sanity. Such defections are doubly damning; agents converted to the worship of some unnatural thing are more potent a threat than some dabbler in the occult who stumbles onto the truth. This is why most Delta Green operations concern themselves very little with collecting data.

When it becomes necessary for agents to collect and collate data, protocols are put in place to prevent an "outbreak." When possible, the agent studying the unnatural is placed under covert surveillance, with deadly contingencies in place if that agent becomes a threat.

Tomes and Other Sources

Agents seeking unnatural rituals or secrets must turn to books and sometimes videos and audio recordings. We often use the word "tome" to indicate all kinds of loathsome resources.

Every tome's description includes its language, study time, Unnatural skill points and other skills gained from studying it, SAN lost from studying it, any rituals that can be learned from it, and a broad description of its subject matter.

Precisely what may be gleaned from it—such as information about a given cult, entity, myth-cycle, or Great Old One, or which rituals can be studied—is up to the Handler. Most unnatural tomes were written by insane authors and are filled with allusions, notations, and mistranslations that made sense only to the author and can be deciphered only with laborious work and cross-referencing. Two copies of the same edition may differ, with pages missing or margins filled with maddening scrawls. Passages may be scratched out or obscured by spilled ink or blood. When you cross-reference one obscure work with another, the variations only multiply. The Handler is always allowed to retroactively insert rituals or secrets into a work that can be understood later: "Suddenly, that cryptic quatrain in the Livre d'Ivon makes a horrible kind of sense."

LANGUAGE: Unless the description says otherwise, the Agent must know all listed languages at 50%

or higher. A test is usually not needed. Some tomes require other skills.

STUDY TIME: Mastering an unnatural tome is dreary, slow going. It takes hours, days, weeks, months, or years. It takes as many hours, days, etc., as the Handler desires; a shorter, more accessible work takes less time than the abstruse writings that most occultists produce. A tome that takes hours or days could be mastered during an operation. One that takes weeks or longer must be studied as a home pursuit between operations. Studying the unnatural that obsessively must take precedence over living up to everyday obligations, going to therapy, or seeking training. Mastering an unnatural tome grants you a basic understanding of its contents, including knowledge of which unnatural rituals it includes.

UNNATURAL: Mastering a tome increases the Agent's Unnatural skill. It may increase other skills, too.

SAN LOSS: Mastering a tome costs SAN. No Agent can internalize unnatural truths and be unchanged. If the SAN loss triggers temporary insanity, that typically comes in a moment of profound, mind-shattering epiphany.

RECOMMENDED RITUALS: Some tomes describe unnatural rituals in enough detail for an Agent to learn them. Each tome lists rituals that are most likely to be learned there, but the Handler decides exactly which rituals can be deciphered in this particular copy of a tome during this particular period of study. Each ritual must be studied separately. See **LEARNING A RITUAL** on page 165 for details.

Artifacts and Alien Science

The unnatural exists in many forms. The remnants of alien cultures and science have intertwined with human history and can be found buried in ancient texts of magic, in artifacts pulled from the Earth, or in alien concepts that haunt the human mind.

More often than not, discovery of a tome, artifact, or alien concept causes an outbreak of the unnatural. Worse, it is often the first step in calling something from outside. Delta Green works hard to identify, contain, or destroy these things before they can find a foothold and do lasting damage.

OPINT: Skimming a Tome

Whether an Agent can get useful information by skimming a tome, without truly mastering it, is up to the Handler. Agents can skim a tome in a matter of hours or days, even if it takes weeks or longer to master it. Skimming a work provides no Unnatural skill, but it may provide a useful clue or insight, much as using the Unnatural skill might. (See **OPINT: THE "UNNATURAL" SKILL** on page 146.) If the Handler wishes, skimming a tome could allow enough understanding of a ritual to attempt it—at a severe disadvantage; see **FLAWED RITUALS** on page 169—but that's never enough to learn the ritual so it can be attempted later.

The Great Old Ones

What would the most well-informed Delta Green Agent know of the unnatural? What is the ultimate secret they keep?

Approximately this:

> *The Great Old Ones came from elsewhere and fought over the Earth billions of years before man, and now sleep in some infernal cycle of time. Life on Earth is the result of biological runoff; a fungus borne of alien shit, that has clung and crawled and evolved as these giants sleep. Their science is our magic, and remnants of their civilizations spring up to infect our world. Soon, they will wake and destroy humanity. Nothing can stop this.*

So then, what exactly is a Great Old One? Some claim they are aliens from another world, of a scale beyond our comprehension. Others say that they are native to Earth but that we are to them as bacteria are to us. Others say they exist in some other alternate reality which bleeds over into our own. Still others place them in hierarchies of power: Elder Gods, Great Old Ones, Other Gods. Forces that serve other forces more infinite than the infinite. No one knows how many exist or their true names or forms in any definitive sense—at least no one sane.

There are many theories. Most occultists agree that the Great Old Ones "sleep" or are somehow restrained, but seek freedom; and once released, they will destroy humanity. This will not be some war, just as a man does not war with an anthill, but a complete annihilation.

The horrific truth that hovers beyond these theories is this: the Great Old Ones are beyond human classification and conception and forever will be.

The Great Old Ones manipulate reality in ways that make the most advanced human sciences look ridiculously primitive. Yet, some men have learned the hypergeometrical principles of the Great Old Ones, or at least, have discovered how to mimic them to achieve limited effects.

DISINFORMATION

YELLOW CARD

A WORD ABOUT "TRUTH"

Human experience is, in every instance, merely a local case. Human senses can only comprehend a fraction of the electromagnetic spectrum, to say nothing of the spectra radiating through other physics tangential to ours. Human minds can only process a very few data in parallel, as our primate brains insist on translating every bit of our visual and physical experience – or, if translation fails, on simply remembering or inventing enough data to pilot our flesh from moment to moment. Recorded human history shines fitfully from one-millionth of the history of the Earth; the entire life of our species reaches back perhaps another fifty millionths. And even that seemingly humble construction depends on concepts of linear time that hold no meaning outside our own perceptions.

Delta Green interposes itself between the world we know and the strange eons that exist outside, around, and beneath it.

Since human brains are inadequately evolved to even comprehend the universe, much less respond intelligently to it, nothing we ordinarily say or do to it makes any difference. Speaking the names of Great Old Ones does not bring down damnation from Heaven or invoke non-Euclidean curses from Outside. At worst, it garners funny looks at the academic conference, or a condescending sneer from neopagans. Cthulhu, Hastur, Yog-Sothoth, and the rest appear in a few dusty demonologies, and a few even dustier anthropological or archeological papers, alongside names like Baalberith, Glasya-Labolas, or Volturnus.

In short, an Agent with Anthropology, Archeology, or Occult at 80% or higher might well recognize a name like Nyarlathotep ("a syncretized demon-figure mentioned in Ptolemaic papyri, and in later Arabic grimoires as a type of anti-Christ") while a Delta Green agent who busted a Crawling Chaos cult might never have heard of it.

In a Delta Green game especially, the meanings of the various names shift along with their users and their perceivers. Consider hiding a revolting brain-parasite colony behind a cult of Bast, or present devout believers in Cthulhu who summon his spawn in high desert mountains. After all, they "seeped down from the stars."

CUT ALONG THIS LINE

Page 1.

where
llen
treets.
psing

store
re the

will turn
that
nants and
all them.

ss, and
ide of our
ie in a con-
fireworks
it. A war

ins don't go,
. Cleanly.

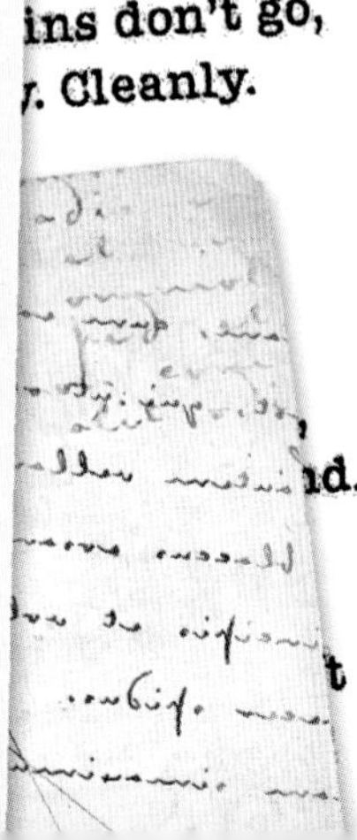

id.

t

OPINT: Insane Insights

Sometimes Agents who face massive psychological damage from unnatural trauma come away with strange insights. At the discretion of the Handler, an Agent who suffers temporary insanity due to an unnatural trauma might suddenly gain 1D6 points in the Unnatural skill. These points can present themselves in different ways.

- **I UNDERSTAND!:** The insane insight offers an Unnatural bonus only when dealing with the entity or stimulus that caused the SAN loss. The Agent has gained some unique knowledge of that particular unnatural threat. Make a note of the restriction.
- **BUT NOT ME!:** In addition to gaining Unnatural points, the Agent's survival when exposed to the unnatural threat has granted a false sense of security. Somehow, the Agent feels particularly protected when facing that particular threat. Needless to say, that confidence is false.
- **I MUST LEARN MORE!:** The insight triggers a lust for more Unnatural knowledge. With every new exposure to the Unnatural, the Agent must spend 1D4 WP to resist the need to interact with it by activating, engaging with, or otherwise affecting the unnatural.

The existence of the Great Old Ones can be said to have been "confirmed" on many occasions. So have the terrible effects of their alien "science." Beyond this, little can be said with any certainty. For example, an entity called Cthulhu "sleeps" in an alien fold in spacetime at 49°51′S 128°34′W in the Pacific Ocean. What then, is it?

It is the size of a small mountain. It has superficial features of a living being. It appears to be able to change shape and perhaps size, and bend spacetime. If nothing about the creature is static, how do you define it?

Is this "Cthulhu" the same as a creature fired upon by the U.S. Navy S-8 Submarine in the February 1928 raid on Innsmouth, Massachusetts? Or is it the entity spotted at Black Cod Island, Alaska, identified as "He Who Swims With Corpses," of similar description? None can say. (And of course, the final disposition of the threat remains up to each Handler to determine.)

Take this further. Certain myth-cycles describe an entity called Nyarlathotep, linked to Egyptian myth. It is described as an ebony-skinned man, a giant creature with a blood-red tentacle, and a horrific corpse woman, as well as a thousand other "faces." Each of these forms is known to be "real." Are they related? How does one tell? What if this entity is not only all these forms, but all the other Great Old Ones as well? Time, distance, mass, and energy appear to mean nothing to "them." What if these are a singular creature, conforming to our cultural perceptions the way water conforms to the shape of a puddle?

As can be seen in this thought experiment, understanding implies an absolute knowledge of power, energy, and time, something no human being can achieve and remain sane.

What can be said definitively is that it is likely the Great Old Ones were the initial catalyst for life on Earth. Similarly, most of the entities created below are products of, or are subservient to, the Great Old Ones, either directly or indirectly.

Unearthly Intelligences

After the reign of the Great Old Ones in the distant past, multiple non-human species from the stars warred over control of the Earth (some even co-existed with the Great Old Ones for short periods of time). Crinoid plant-like beings, amorphous blobs of sentient cells that could reshape into any form, extra-dimensional blights of non-terrene matter with a thousand eyes, fungal-scientists from the edge of the solar system, just to name a few, forged empires that rose and fell long before what would become humanity crawled from the oceans. They left artifacts, ruins, and science buried far from the haunts of man. They are called by many, many names.

Some still exist today, enacting alien plans to restore their supremacy. Since 1942, Delta Green has actively hunted them all.

OPINT: The "Unnatural" Skill

The Unnatural skill indicates increasing understanding of the terrible truths of reality. Only the most informed Agents have an Unnatural skill as high as 10% or 15%. This represents a lifetime of secret knowledge. Reaching 40% or 50% almost always is a straight shot to permanent insanity. But what do those skill levels represent?

Rating	What The Rating Means
01% to 09%	Certain knowledge that *nonhuman things and forces* exist and threaten humanity.
10% to 19%	A basic understanding of what's truly at stake: the existence of the forces of the Great Old Ones and their threat to humanity.
20% to 29%	A more advanced understanding of the true disposition of the world. The variety of Great Old Ones, alien intelligences, and inhuman earthly intelligences. Some inklings of pre-history, isolated and framed through confusing human occultism, conspiracy theories, and mythology.
30% to 39%	A clearer knowledge of pre-history and the inhuman beings that plied the world before man.
40% to 49%	A complex knowledge of unnatural books, rituals and items.
50% to 99%	A deep understanding of pre-human history, locations, and secrets.

Remember that the Unnatural skill is merely the closest the human mind can come to understanding the truth of existence. True understanding is beyond any sane human. We are simply not wired for it. Those with 0 SAN, of course, suffer no such limitation.

It is also important to note that the Unnatural skill is not the same as the Occult skill. The occult is human fiction that obscures the horrors of the genuinely unnatural. Understanding the traditions and beliefs of occultists and conspiracy theorists is often useful, but it never reveals the truths of the hungry cosmos.

Mi-Go, Elder Things, and Shoggoths

Vast alien empires persisted on Earth for hundreds of millions of years before humanity. Their ruins remain in hidden places, in folds in spacetime, and scattered throughout the solar system.

MI-GO—THE PACT AND THE SILENCE: Though few human beings understand the truth, the fungal scientists from the edge of the solar system known as the mi-go have, since 1947, had the deepest relationship with mankind. In their cover as the "Greys," the mi-go have used the American government as a tool to further their agenda through the American agency: MAJESTIC. In 2001, this pact ended suddenly, and since then the creatures have remained silent, working their inhuman plans on Pluto, which forbidden texts sometimes call Yuggoth.

ELDER THINGS—BENEATH THE ICE: A doomed Miskatonic expedition of 1930 discovered an ancient, cyclopean city of basalt pyramids in the center of Antarctica and awakened the crinoid Elder Things. Since then, these beings have been silent. A Nazi expedition just a few years later found only scant remnants of the Elder Things and no sign of their alien city. Outposts surely remain beneath the Antarctic ice, basalt vaults filled with enough secrets to level the planet.

SHOGGOTHS—ROGUE ENTITIES: The Elder Things' mutated creations, the terrifying, plastic shoggoths, persevere—immortal and indestructible—in the depths of the oceans and beneath ice sheets, enacting unknowable plans.

Earthly Intelligences

Other inhuman races exist which are thought—perhaps mistakenly—to be native to Earth. The most common inhuman earthly intelligences are the Deep Ones, ocean-dwelling, immortal beings that have been interbreeding with humanity since the dawn of history for unknown purposes. Second are the ghouls, dog-headed, immortal beings who feast on the human dead, hiding in warrens underground. Third are the serpent folk, reptilian humanoids who gained access to the science of the Great Old Ones during the age of the dinosaurs.

OPINT: Using "Unnatural"

An Agent can deliberately attempt to use the Unnatural skill to happen to know a useful detail. Using the Unnatural skill to recall actionable intelligence immediately, without research, almost always requires a roll. It's better to take time and do the work, even though that often means searching in dangerous places and cultivating insane sources. Preparing and controlling the situation means you don't roll the dice. Rolling is dangerous. With such low skill ratings, fumbles are likely. But sometimes, urgency demands the risk of working from what the Agents thinks they already know.

The Agent using the skill must frame a specific inquiry. It can't just be, "I roll Unnatural!" An Agent might say, "I want to roll Unnatural to know if the thing can fly," or, "I want to roll Unnatural to know if the thing is the same creature mentioned in *The Testament of Flesh.*"

Each question can be asked once. What constitutes a single question is up to the Handler. If at all possible, you should roll for the Agent and should roll in secret. The roll determines the result.

The Agent and Handler should make a note when the Agent gets a correct answer from the Unnatural skill, because that answer indicates a fact known about the game world—or as close to a fact as the unnatural allows.

- **CRITICAL SUCCESS:** The Agent knows the answer, and gains some extra tidbit of useful knowledge. For example, "Can it fly?" might gain the answer, "It can fly, and its non-terrene nature allows it to pass through solid matter."
- **SUCCESS:** The Agent knows the answer.
- **FAILURE:** No knowledge is gleaned; or, the Agent gains part of the answer but it comes with dangerously wrong complications or misinformation.
- **FUMBLE:** The Agent suffers a terrible, deadly insight. The the question goes unanswered, or is answered wrongly. Further, the Agent loses 1 SAN for some awful realization, but not the one he or she hoped for. For example, asking "Can it fly?" might gain the insight, "Millions of these creatures exist just beyond three-dimensional space, and once the ritual is complete they will ravage the world."

Ghouls, Deep Ones, and Serpent-Folk

Ghouls and Deep Ones represent an especially insidious threat to humanity. They seem to be able to breed with humans, or at least infect them—changing them, over time, into hybrid species, or perhaps fully changing them into Deep Ones or ghouls.

DEEP ONES—THE HYBRID DIASPORA: Since the U.S. Navy's discovery of the Deep One civilization in Innsmouth, Massachusetts in 1928, a secret war has been wrought by various world governments against these creatures, and their bizarre method of infiltration and interbreeding with human populations.

Colonies of human/Deep One hybrids on land have been destroyed—at least, as far as those who know about such things can ascertain. But few in Delta Green have any delusions that this has had any effect on the immortal Deep One civilization beneath the oceans. There, they wait and occasionally venture upwards, to begin their work anew.

DEEP ONES—BLACK COD ISLAND: The oldest and most significant Deep One colony in North America was founded in 1555 by an infected offshoot of the Haida Indians of the Pacific Northwest. It remains hidden on Black Cod Island, Alaska, in plain sight, as a model "American-Indian" settlement. There, it remains a den of inhuman worship and terror. The Black Cod people are not Indians. They are not even human.

To the public, the Black Cod people (Xaatgaav Skil) appear to be a friendly community with ancient traditions, their industry and self-sufficiency admired by all. But in secret, these Deep One hybrids abduct lone travelers in the Alaska wilderness for sacrifice to their dark lord, a huge, primal Deep One called He-Who-Swims-With-Corpses.

DEEP ONES—THE EXALTED CIRCLE: This branch of the Esoteric Order of Dagon began as a 19th-century secret society of American landowners and industrialists who relied on help from Deep Ones to fill their coffers and sabotage their rivals. In the 20th century, it came under the influence of the Cult of Transcendence, and the Circle used its rising influence—augmented by unnatural powers—to make fortunes on defense contracts and global shipping. In 2007, a Delta Green raid killed a large number of Deep Ones and a few Circle leaders, though it failed to learn the name or extent of the Circle itself. The Deep Ones withdrew their aid, leaving the Circle's leaders to rely on their own rituals and wiles. Since the Cult of Transcendence fell apart in the early 2010s, the Exalted Circle has become even more circumspect. Whether its old allegiance to Dagon will atrophy or be revitalized by some new contact with the Deep Ones remains to be seen.

DEEP ONES—OTHER FRAGMENTS: Who knows what darkness tinges the shores of out-of-the-way places, or when the Deep Ones will once again launch a colonization of the surface? Their motives are alien, their bodies and minds immortal, their science far in advance of humanity's. The years since Innsmouth are nothing but a flicker of light across the vast shadow-hand of the Deep Ones' plans.

GHOULS—THE KEEPERS OF THE FAITH: In the 1630s, a religious order run by a heretic named Mogens Dekker fled from Europe to the free port city of New Amsterdam (later New York), and there, set about a secretive worship of an unknown god. Dekker and his followers—known as the Keepers of the Faith—were ghouls in the making, once-human monstrosities who dug into the earth and fed on dead human flesh.

Even today, dozens of immortal ghouls live beneath New York as indigents who scuttle in the tunnels beneath the metropolis. Thanks to an uneasy truce with Delta Green, most of them live beneath the vast graveyards of Glendale and Forest Park, Queens—an endless feast in which they may live in secret and in peace. For now. Occasionally, renegades grow impatient and come to hunger for living flesh, and then the truce with Delta Green threatens to unravel.

GHOULS—THE DEMONTE CLAN: The DeMonte clan, a degenerate group of ghouls who persisted as an infection in New Orleans from 1788 to 2005—hiding in plain sight as a family of successful mortuary owners using

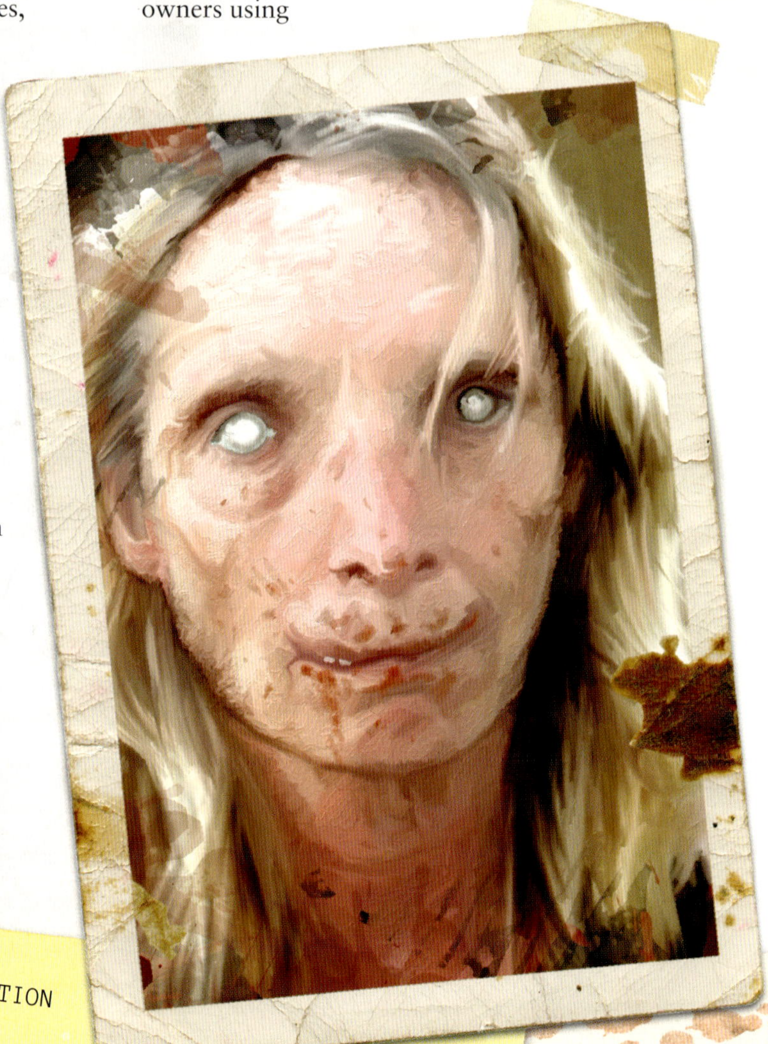

DISINFORMATION

HUMAN HYBRIDS

YELLOW CARD

Both Deep Ones and ghouls, through unknown means, interbreed with humans to produce hybrid species. Serpent-folk, utilizing hypergeometry, have masqueraded undetected as humans for long periods of time, even interacting with humans in the modern age. The ghostly, subterranean K'n-Yani seem to be an offshoot or ancestor of humanity. The Tcho-Tchos appear to be a branch of humanity genetically corrupted by the unnatural. Hybrids and creatures masquerading as human represent some of the most insidious threats Delta Green has ever known.

TOP SEC

TOP SECRET /

hypergeometrical disguises—were rooted out and destroyed in a hastily thrown together Delta Green operation during the chaos generated by Hurricane Katrina in 2005.

Few of the DeMontes remain, and their once stout empire has been shattered. Still, today, Delta Green monitors the city through Operation REDBONE—looking for those trying to recover their old influence and power. Occasionally, a hidden ghoul is uncovered and destroyed.

GHOULS—REMNANTS IN EUROPE AND ASIA: Ghouls once infected all of Europe, but barring reports during the wars which wracked the continent in the last century, few known ghoul populations remain; most having been hunted to extinction by various secret agencies. Still, it is not unimaginable that lone ghouls still haunt individual graveyards, hidden beneath the earth.

The largest and most dangerous ghoul outbreak occurred in Russia during the reign of Josef Stalin, called the Cult of the Great Provider. While Stalin's death-squads stoked the fire of the ghoul cults, thousands of ghouls were born, and put down by the Soviet agency tasked with confronting the unnatural: GRU SV-8. Who knows if any remain? If they do, they have certainly learned to hide themselves more carefully.

SERPENT-FOLK—A ONCE-GREAT RACE: The serpent-folk rose to prominence in the Paleozoic era, 500 million years ago. They plied the science of the Great Old Ones and changed the world, but turned upon one another, and they perished in some self-generated apocalypse—or so the fragments recovered from pre-history say.

Since that time, survivors of the serpent-folk apocalypse have risen and entered human society by using hypergeometric disguises. Twice, Delta Green has directly confronted these beings, and due to their mimetic nature and vast intellect, they are deemed a very real threat. Luckily, they are as likely to kill each other as to kill human beings.

Extradimensional Intelligences

The Great Race of Yith are non-physical intelligences which transcend time and occupy human minds, and through these proxies, manipulate history. The Lloigor are non-physical intelligences which manipulate energy and matter to create living projections of their consciousness to feed on psychic pain. These two forces appear to be in conflict. But to say this might be a human misapprehension is a vast understatement. Since time is simply an environment in which the Great Race persists, this conflict's true nature is evident only to them and other dimensionally non-specific creatures.

There are others, of course: demons, djinn, and more—but it is unclear if these are manifestations of other forces, new threats, or occult fantasies.

The Great Race and the Lloigor

The Great Race and Lloigor, creatures that exist outside of our four-dimensional world, apparently war for supremacy over something greater than what we call existence. No one can remain human and truly understand their motives or methods.

THE GREAT RACE—THE CONSTRUCT: The Great Race left the concept of time behind long ago. To them, time is geography. They embed their consciousness in living beings to enact bizarre plans inside the boxlike, bounded dimensions of our normal, linear world. But this geography of time, which they call "the Construct," is always changing and collapsing. It must be rebuilt over and over, to maintain a connection to a distant, radioactive future to which the Great Race will one day escape (have escaped, will always escape). There, they occupy the lone survivors of the Earth: a species of giant beetles. To this end, members of the Great Race agents might be found anywhere in history, possessing hapless human beings. Their human servants—temporal operatives they call the Motion—are zealots who readily die to see their masters' plans come to fruition.

THE LLOIGOR—THE PATTERN: The Lloigor are extradimensional intelligences that can perceive and manipulate our reality and manifest living vessels to contain their consciousness. They seem to be addicted to the physicality of our world and to sensation, and are drawn to torture, death, and pain. Like the Great Race, the Lloigor seem to be driven to cause an outcome in what we might call "history." Their goal seems contingent on the establishment of a human empire—perhaps the last—called the "Tsan-Chan" in approximately 5000 CE. To the extent that the ever-shifting illusion of causality can be comprehended by a human mind, this outcome seems in direct conflict with the Great Race's plans for nuclear war.

Other Unnatural Threats

The Great Old Ones and their minions are by no means the only threats discovered by Delta Green. There are other worlds, planes, and times connected to the Earth through alien science and the powers beyond. Invisible, alien carnivores living in the membranes between dimensions, coherent fogs of swirling glass that can congeal in the angles, rat-creatures with human faces and minds, alien insects that can crawl into the brain of living beings: all of these, and more, exist at the periphery of human experience. No seasoned agent doubts there are others.

Some unnatural threats conform to human legend, or, perhaps it is better to say human legend conforms to them. Things that operate like supernatural creatures from history: vampires, lycanthropes, yeti. Nearly anything could be hiding out there, unnatural horrors distorted by the lens of history into shapes more tolerable to the human mind.

What has never been discovered is a confirmation of human religions—heaven, hell, or an afterlife. There have been cases of non-human intelligences impersonating religious or historical figures, and there have been reports of humans using alien techniques to separate mind from body. But so far, no aspect of spiritualism has revealed the affirmations and comforts of human religion to be true.

Unhistory

Current human industrial civilization emerged, flourished, and bids fair to destroy or smother itself, all in only a few millennia. It takes geological and atmospheric processes approximately a thousand years to erase most signs of human construction: even plastics and metals corrode and disintegrate after five or ten thousand years. Continents subside, volcanoes erupt, coasts flood, glaciers grind down. A few megaliths survive perhaps, washed clean of the carbon we require to pin them in historical time. Homo sapiens has existed for about a quarter of a million years. The emergence and destruction of previous civilizations is all but a mathematical certainty.

Delta Green often uses the same names 19th century occultists and charlatans ascribed to these pre-decedents: Mu, Lemuria, Uluumil-Naga, and so forth. Other names appear in older records: Lomar, Mnar, Thule, Yhe, Hyperborea, and Valusia.

Names and histories come adrift: one tradition asserts that Hyperborea was a human country in Eurasia contemporaneous with the Classical Greeks, while another describes it as a lost polar continent inhabited by furry humanoids or sweat-born golden beings that reproduced by budding. The cod-scholarly habit of applying human and historical mythical terminology to ancient and inhuman empires further muddles the issue: "Hyperborea," for example, merely means "above the North Wind," implying only a vaguely Arctic location. The constructions of the truly ancient alien races who colonized the Earth often pay no more heed to human notions of physics and temporality than their masters did: thermoluminescence, carbon dating, and all other methods of fixing a fossil or artifact in time apply only fitfully to unnatural relics.

Finally, of course, the questions of time travel, dimensional dilation, and temporal epistemology raised by unnatural contact imply that even simple notions such as "before" and "after" have almost no real meaning to these alien civilizations. With all that said, however, here's what a paleontologist and an occultist might piece together if Delta Green were ever foolish enough to allow such a team access to their remaining files and incident reports. To date, no one has ever done so.

Dates derive from current paleontological and paleogeological research; they are necessarily approximate and, as usual, may be wildly inaccurate.

- **4.48 BILLION YEARS AGO:** The Hounds of the Angles are thrown into the corridors of time. (Moon formed by the collision of a Mars-sized sphere with the proto-Earth.)
- **542 MILLION YEARS AGO:** The crinoid Elder Things arrive on Earth, seeding millions of species with their experiments and bioculture. (Cambrian explosion.)
- **443 MILLION YEARS AGO:** Spectral polyps arrive or emerge. (Ordovician extinction.)
- **378 MILLION YEARS AGO:** The Great Race of Yith arrive and inhabit the bodies of a terrestrial species; the Yithians conquer and imprison the spectral polyps. (Devonian extinction.)
- **359 MILLION YEARS AGO:** Cthulhu and its spawn arrive from Zubeneschamali (Beta Librae) or Sothis (Sirius, sometimes referred to as Zoth). (Hangenberg event: algal blooms flood the oceans, choking off life across the Southern Hemisphere.)
- **300 MILLION YEARS AGO:** R'lyeh sinks, Cthulhu trapped; N'Kai founded by refugee servitors of Cthulhu. (Pangaea forms.)
- **252 MILLION YEARS AGO:** The shoggoths rebel against their Elder Thing masters, unleashing a global war fought with ecocidal weapons. By the time the Elder Things subjugate their slave creations, the war has driven 96% of all species on the planet extinct. (Permian extinction.)
- **230 MILLION YEARS AGO:** Serpent folk evolve, or are created by Yig; they rule the empire of Valusia roughly where the Mediterranean is now. (75 million years after the first reptiles evolve.)
- **184 MILLION YEARS AGO:** Mi-go arrive on Earth in force from Yuggoth or further Outside, defeating the Elder Things and restricting them to the Antarctic. (Pangaea breaks up.)
- **145 MILLION YEARS AGO:** In some legends, the mi-go bring Ghatanothoa to a Pacific subcontinent ("Mu"), possibly as a weapon.
  - Deep Ones bring Byatis to Valusia, likewise. (Tithonian extinction event.)
- **90 MILLION YEARS AGO:** Mi-go drive the serpent folk underground to Yoth. (Fossils of Najash, a bipedal, burrowing snake with a pelvis.)

- **66 MILLION YEARS AGO:** The spectral polyps escape their prisons—possibly by summoning an enormous iridium-iron asteroid—and drive the Great Race from their rugose cone-bodies and into the future. The cataclysm destroys most Elder Thing cities, and leads mi-go to reduce their presence on Earth. (Cretaceous extinction.)
- **50 MILLION YEARS AGO:** Prehuman civilization ("Lemurians") flourishes in Asia or a parallel dimension ("Shamballah").
  - Black, formless beings from Kythamil build K'n-Yan.
- **33 MILLION YEARS AGO:** War between Lemurians and Deep Ones destroys Lemuria and drives the Deep Ones into deep trenches. (Meteoric bombardment of eastern North America; Eocene-Oligocene extinction.)
- **14 MILLION YEARS AGO:** Reptile species, possibly a clade of divergent serpent-folk, builds a nameless seaport city as a fane of Cthulhu in what is now Arabia. (Miocene climate transition.)
- **9 MILLION YEARS AGO:** By some accounts, Elder Things create hominid servant-pets that evolve into humanity. (Pan-Homo divergence.)
- **3 MILLION YEARS AGO:** Rhan-Tegoth rules in what is now Alaska.
  - Tsathoggua arrives in Hyperborea from N'Kai or Saturn.
- **2.54 MILLION YEARS AGO:** Lloigor arrive from the Andromeda galaxy, colonize Mu, and begin to enslave and engineer hominid stocks. Some sources say the Lloigor faced resistance from Ghatanothoa; others, that Ghatanothoa was chief among them, or perhaps a forerunner. (SN 1885A, only known supernova in Andromeda galaxy, circa 2.54 million light-years away.)
- **2.4 MILLION YEARS AGO:** Furry hominid Tsathoggua-worshipers, the Voorii, establish the civilization of Hyperborea in Greenland. (Bramertonian interglacial stage.)
- **2 MILLION YEARS AGO:** Hominid apes construct the ward-city "Thule" in central Africa. (Homo erectus.)
- **1 MILLION YEARS AGO:** Tcho-Tcho evolve in southeastern Asia. (Java Man.)
- **850,000 YEARS AGO:** Human civilization apparently first rises in Hyperborea and Lomar, drives the Voorii south. (Homo heidelbergensis.)
  - Deep Ones return to continental shelves. (Cromerian interglacial stage.)
- **725,000 YEARS AGO:** Lloigor destroy rebellious Lomarian city Nam-Ergest, explosion creates what is now the Grand Canyon. (Major period of activity in Uinkaret volcanic field.)
- **173,148 BCE:** In the Year of the Red Moon, worship of Ghatanothoa becomes supreme in Mu.
- **110,000 YEARS AGO:** Uluumil-Ra empire of Mu destroys remnant Lemurian cities in Asia. (Last Gigantopithecus fossils.)
- **100,000 YEARS AGO:** Human kingdom rules the continent or dimension of Atlantis; serpent-folk infiltrators eventually undermine it in a shadow war.
- **85,000 YEARS AGO:** Itla-shua destroys Hyperborea and the final Elder Thing city with ice; Lomarians retreat into K'n-Yan, except for those in the capital city of Olathoë. (Wisconsin glaciation.)
- **50,000 YEARS AGO:** Lomarians bring worship of Tsathoggua out of K'n-Yan, and re-establish his cult across the North. (Upton-Warren interstadial warm spike.)
- **26,000 YEARS AGO:** Final destruction of Olathoë by the hairy Gnophkehs.
  - Lloigor return to power in decadent Mu.
- **17,000 YEARS AGO:** Rise of Cimmeria under Crom-Ya. (Last glacial maximum.)
- **14,500 YEARS AGO:** Sinking of Atlantis. (Bølling-Allerød interstadial warm spike.)
- **12,000 YEARS AGO:** Final destruction of Mu in the western Pacific; Lloigor scatter across the world. (Sundaland continental shelf submerged; Younger Dryas mini-ice age.)
- **9000 BCE:** Tcho-Tcho found Ai-Lao-Žar on the Plateau of Singu.
  - Rise of Irem of the Pillars.

- **6000 BCE:** Last kings of Stygia carve the Sphinx. (Controversial "water-erosion" theory date of the Sphinx's construction.)
  - The Doom comes to Sarnath in the land of Mnar. (Flooding of the Persian Gulf seafloor.)
- **5600 BCE:** Deluge submerges Cimmeria. (Ryan and Pittman theory of Black Sea flooding.)
- **2600 BCE:** Nephren-Ka, the Black Pharaoh, rules in Egypt. (Confused and fragmentary records of the Pharaoh Nefer-ka (2nd Dynasty) or Nefer-ka-re (3rd dynasty).)
- **2184–2181 BCE:** Ghoul queen Nitocris rules in Egypt. (Concealed under the name of Pharaoh Neitqerti Siptah (6th Dynasty).)
- **534 CE:** Meteor impact in Britain (modern Brichester Lake) brings Glaaki to Earth. (Major cooling event in Northern Hemisphere.)
- **1643 CE:** The insects from Shaggai arrive on Earth, in Goatswood.
- **5000 CE:** The cruel empire of Tsan-Chan flourishes.
- **50 MILLION YEARS FROM NOW:** Great Race of Yith returns to incarnate into a hardy coleopteran species, and reconquers the Earth.

Unnatural Tomes

Is reading an ASCII transcription of the Necronomicon, translated into plain English, as devastating as studying the Greek edition in an antique tome? Can you simply copy *Unaussprechlichen Kulten* into a Word file, spam a message board with it, and watch everyone who reads it go insane?

The issue of what constitutes an unnatural tome, and what that even means, comes up often in *Delta Green*. Why does one damage the human mind? What causes that damage? In a world filled with fake CGI videos of alien abductions, swamp monsters, and ghosts, it's hard to believe some musty old block print drawn by a 16th-century monk is going to cause too much trouble to the average reader—much less a block of text talking about star angels, a war in heaven, Lord Moloch, and the seven gates of Irem. To most, the raw text of the most outré tome is nothing but pseudo-religious gibberish.

Even the most gruesome text of ancient cults moves us little. We see mass shootings, executions, bomb attacks, child murders, and mass poisonings every day. Humanity is as prolific in its violence as ever. Little evidence is needed to see we are all well on our way toward becoming as the Great Old Ones: free and wild and beyond good and evil, with laws and morals thrown aside and all men shouting and killing and revelling in joy. Just look in your online news feed.

So, why would ancient books on the subject seem even a little bit shocking today? There is no single answer, but it often comes down to two things. Some tomes become truly mind-altering only when the reader realizes that their blasphemous secrets are true. And some tomes affect the mind of the reader in the physical and mental process of reading, the words and ideas reshaping the brain in unnatural ways.

There are millions of copies of unnatural tomes floating around in PDF, photographed by enthusiasts, page by page. The Program propagates computer worms to seek out such files and delete them, but nothing can ever be erased from the Internet. A purported ASCII transcription of the *Necronomicon* was likely generated by optical character recognition, so half the characters are gibberish. But even if you secure a perfect copy, or hold the original tome in your hands, merely reading is not enough.

Many academics know the old, debunked myth-cycles of Cthulhu and Nyarlathotep. They laugh them off as occult chicanery and superstition, and never bother to codify their research for others' use. Researchers who wish to learn from an unnatural tome must work from imperfect translations, and cross-reference lines and individual words with other editions in other languages. They must learn the culture of the author in order to recognize strange similes, metaphors, and turns of phrase—and to recognize when the authors' obsessions and growing madness leave some ideas beyond understanding. An unnatural tome is never a textbook or a cookbook. It's an impenetrable cultural artifact, created by a madman who saw truths that belong in no sane world.

ASSETS: Sample Tomes

Title	Language	Study Time	Unnatural	SAN Loss	Rituals?
Al Azif	Arabic	months	+18%	3D6	Yes
Azathoth and Other Horrors	English	hours	+3%	1D4	No
The Book of Dagon	English	days	+4%	1D4	Yes
Case file, Freis, Daniel M.	English	days	+3%	1D4	No
The Courtis paper	English	months	+1%	1D4	Yes
Cultes des Goules	French	months	+12%	2D6	Yes
Dauthsnamjansboka	Gothic	months	+16%	2D8	Yes
The Eltdown Shards	English	weeks	+6%	1D8	Yes
The files of Grant Emerson	English	weeks	+2%	1D4	No
Geheimes Mysterium von Asien	German	weeks	+5%	1D6	No
Greg Mason's surveillance videos	English	days or weeks	+2%	1D6	No
Gunter Frank's research notes	German	months	+4%	1D6	Yes
The Innsmouth report (Operation PUZZLEBOX)	English	days	+2%	1	No
Joseph Camp's grimoire	English	months	+4%	1D6	Yes
The King in Yellow	English or French	hours	+5%	1D6+2	No
Liber Damnatus	Latin	weeks or months	+4%	1D8	Yes
Livre d'Ivon	Occitan French	months	+10%	2D6	Yes
MAJESTIC OPORD 00001	English	weeks	+4%	1D4	No
Matthew Carpenter's Delta Green files	English	days	+4%	1D6	No
The Necronomicon	Latin	months or years	+15%	2D8	Yes
The People of the Monolith	English	days	+3%	1D4	No
The Pnakotic Manuscripts	Koiné Greek	months	+6%	1D6	Yes
The Red Cross Pocket Bible	English, German, Italian	days	+1%	1	No
The Revelations of Glaaki	English	months	+12%	2D6	Yes
The Seven Cryptical Books of Hsan	Classical Chinese	months	+11%	2D6	Yes
Unaussprechlichen Kulten	German	months	+12%	2D8	Yes
De Vermis Mysteriis	Latin	months	+12%	2D6	Yes

OPINT: Ninety Percent of 'Em Gotta Be Burned

Handlers should custom-design any tomes or other compendia of unnatural lore that might fall into the Agents' hands. Rituals should never just be stuffed into a book just to give it weight or because a story or game supplement implied they had to be there. Books vary by edition, condition, and marginal notes: many of them are hand-written originals full of cryptic codes, indecipherable scrawls, and unpleasant stains.

In short, this shelf of unnatural tomes is a guideline. Delta Green certainly does not have access to all the tomes on this list; perhaps nobody does. Likewise, change the values given here just as readily as you change the rituals included in a given text.

Slowly, the student pieces fragments of these works together and becomes convinced of the horrific pattern at the center of the world: that we are the vermin that rose to supremacy during an interregnum where the Old Ones sleep. Only then does the damage set in. That process is, thankfully, rare. And so mankind lingers in uneasy primacy over the Earth.

There is another way that many unnatural tomes affect the human mind. Some are themselves infected, in their very paper and ink or in combinations of concepts unlocked by the human eye, by a cancer of reality that causes mental degradation. It may be an impossible angle in a diagram, a sketch of infinity, a pattern of syllables that opens a hidden Nth-dimensional door to the unworld, an unnatural mold whose spores attack the central nervous system, or some sort of latent, poisonous energy that seeps with comprehension from the page through the eye into the mind.

Any (or all) of the above can be true. Each unnatural book or artifact is different. As with the unnatural, no absolute rules can ever be discerned. Just when the Agents think they have a handle on how the unnatural operates, they should find something that breaks the established order. That is the point. We can never, ever, understand. Even when we believe we might.

Work hard to establish the rules possibly unique to a particular tome, and stick to those rules for the next unnatural tomes. But remember, your goals are suspense, dread, and terror. If the players become sure they know how all unnatural tomes work—if they complacently think they have this part of the unnatural under control—change the rules. Let them encounter a tome that has effects beyond anything they've seen, or a passage of text that transforms the mind and takes on new meanings even though the ink on the page never changes. Only one lesson should be truly reliable: that the very act of studying the unnatural is like a sanity-bomb, waiting to go off in the Agent's mind.

The Necronomicon

The core text of the unnatural, the "Black Book" may be anti-scripture, a drug-fueled metaphysics text, a diary of nightmare, a poetic revelation, or all of the above. Massive, wide-ranging, and endlessly deep, it can be a source of nearly any rituals and information the Handler wishes to convey.

Al Azif

In Arabic. Study time: *months. Occult +18%, Unnatural +18%, SAN loss 3D6.*

Written by Abd al-Hazred (sometimes "Abdul Alhazred") circa 730 CE, this is the original version of the *Necronomicon.* No copies are known to exist.

RECOMMENDED RITUALS: Any.

Dauthsnamjansboka

In Gothic. Study time: *months. Occult +16%, Unnatural +16%, SAN loss 2D8.*

Created by an unknown translator, ca. 800 CE, this translation of *Al Azif* was much bleaker and less allusive than other versions. It was the prize of the Karotechia library. Delta Green destroyed most of the copies and German translations during Operation LUNACY; the only known remaining copy (the original) lies untranslated in the GRU SV-8 archive under Khodinka Airfield in Moscow.

RECOMMENDED RITUALS: Any.

The Necronomicon

In Latin. Study time: *months or years. Occult +15%, Unnatural +15%, SAN loss 2D8.*

Translated by Olaus Wormius in 1623, based on a very rare Latin version of 1228 and the lost Greek translation of 950 CE, this is the most common surviving text of the black book. There are possibly a dozen copies extant, though only six are definitely catalogued.

RECOMMENDED RITUALS: Any.

Other Tomes

All too many scholars have succumbed to the temptation to document the unnatural forces that move reality. Most of their works look like little more than insane ravings or indecipherable art.

Azathoth and Other Horrors

In English. Study time: *hours. Occult +2%, Unnatural +3%, SAN loss 1D4.*

"When age fell upon the world,
and wonder went out of the minds of men;
when grey cities reared to smoky skies
tall towers grim and ugly,
in whose shadow none might dream
of the sun or of Spring's flowering meads...."

A book of the macabre poetry of Edward Pickman Derby published around World War I and rebound in unmarked boards with a technique that a librarian or bookbinder would place around the 1950s. The pages still bear marks of damage by fire and water. It weaves New England legend and startling insights into lyrics of surprising power. It takes only an hour or so to pore over. The largest single work, "Azathoth," describes a dreaming encounter with the Daemon Sultan whose mindless pulsings give shape and action to the universe, and whose messenger Nyarlathotep mockingly facilitates the human impulse to find meaning in the world.

RECOMMENDED RITUALS: None.

The Book of Dagon (Special Report)

In English. Study time: *days. Unnatural +4%, SAN loss 1D4.*

"AND • ONE • CAME FROM • ZOTH • AND GAVE FORTH • THE • STAR SPAWN • THE • CHILDREN • DAGON AND HYDRA • WHO • SERVE • THE • HIGH PRIEST • OF • ZOTH • THE MAKER OF WORLDS • THE FATHER OF ALL"

This transcription and translation of the odd conical stone tablets recovered during the Innsmouth raid of 1928 represents almost two years of work from some of the best cryptographers in the world. It is one of the first modern, translated unnatural documents successfully identified as such: 44 typewritten pages, creased and coffee-stained, and yellowed with age, shoved in a modern Navy file folder marked SECRET and P4 EYES ONLY. Anyone with Bureaucracy or Forensics in excess of 30% can tell the report is Navy from sometime in the 1920s or 1930s, and that the papers are old, while the file-folder is from sometime after 1950. Some of the pages are soot stained and partially singed, as if by fire.

The pages tell a Deep One creation myth in plain English, transposed and translated from pictoglyphs meticulously hand-drawn on the onion skin pages. It is a stilted account that can be summarized as follows: *Cthulhu traveled from a star called Zoth to our world in the distant past. This being created life, and in particular, several large entities, Cthulhu's spawn, two of which are called Dagon and Hydra. From these smaller entities, the Sons of Dagon or Deep Ones issued. All life in the "upper world" came forth from the oceans, and as such, is beholden to Cthulhu. When Cthulhu wakes, the surface world will be subsumed.*

RECOMMENDED RITUALS: The Call of Dagon, Storm and Stillness, Swarm, Whispers of the Dead (Cthulhu).

Case File, Freis, Daniel M.

In English. Study time: *days. Unnatural +3%, SAN loss 1D4.*

> *"SUBJECT: Have you been to a farm, doctor? You think the cows know they're kept? You think they don't feel safe? SOMETHING. OWNS. US."*

Two-hundred and twenty-one pages of medical forms, psychotherapy transcripts, personnel files and more, all concerned with Dr. Daniel M. Freis, from the time of his incarceration (14 JAN 1955; see **LOSING HISTORY** on page 54) to his death. It is contained in four accordion files. None are marked with any sort of security designations.

Captain Robert Feitelberg, supervising psychiatrist, diagnosed Freis with depressive complex and paranoid schizophrenia. Freis was heavily medicated during his time at the hospital (on a host of drugs like thorazine, chlorpromazine, and others), but strangely, electroshock therapy was never attempted. "EST NOT PERMITTED INTELLIGENCE ASSET" is written on each page of Freis' admission documents, and is signed "CDR COOK."

The tale woven by the madman is coherent and consistent, and unlike many schizophrenics odd delusions, does not seem to shift and change over time. He parroted the same tale in 1955 that he was screaming on his deathbed in 1970. It can be summarized as follows: *Freis claims that he works for an agency in the U.S. government, which he does not name. He says the agency has discovered that mankind is a "kept" population, used for breeding and food by a far more advanced species, the "Deep Ones," that live in the Earth's oceans. These creatures are immortal and wield weapons far more powerful than any human technology. The upper world is simply a "pen" in which they keep their livestock—humanity.*

RECOMMENDED RITUALS: None.

The Courtis Paper

In English. Requires Science (Mathematics). Study time: *months. Unnatural +1%, SAN loss 1D4.*

> *"9 9 2 0 .2 2 9 9 8 9 2 1 2 .3 3 3"*

The original Courtis Paper, often called the "White Sheet," was a single sheet of handwritten mathematical formulae. Those without Science (Mathematics) of at least 50% or higher can glean nothing from the Courtis Paper; it looks like gibberish. To those with sufficient training in mathematics, it implies amazing, underlying secrets of reality; with 500 hours of study a SAN roll is made. If it is failed, the target learns the ritual (see below) and loses 1D4 SAN. If the SAN roll succeeds, the target is overcome with a feeling that they have just missed the truths that make the universe run. Targets may try again and again, as long as they have the appropriate training.

RECOMMENDED RITUALS: Consciousness Expansion.

Cultes des Goules

In French. Study time: *months. Occult +1%, Unnatural +12%, SAN loss 2D6.*

Written in 1703 by Francois-Honore Balfour, Comte d'Erlette, this book was promptly banned by the Church. Luxuriating in necromancy, necrophagia, and necrophilia, it describes a ghoul cult throughout Europe.

RECOMMENDED RITUALS: Call Forth Those From Outside (Haedi Nigritiae, Nyogtha), Call Zombies, Charnel Meditation, The Closing of the Breach (Haedi Nigritiae, Nyogtha), Obscure Memory, Release Breath, Zombie.

The Eltdown Shards

In English. Study time: *weeks. Occult +1%, Unnatural +6%, SAN loss 1D8.*

In 1882, two Cambridge scholars excavated 23 pottery shards from unmistakably Triassic strata at Eltdown, Sussex. In 1917, Rev. Arthur Brooke Winters-Hall, a local antiquarian and fairy-lore enthusiast, privately printed his prolix, murky "translation" of the shards' oddly regular markings, hinting at the histories of the Elder Things and the Great Race of Yith.

RECOMMENDED RITUALS: Call Forth Those From Outside (Great Race), The Dho-Hna Formula, The Elder Sign.

The Files of Grant Emerson

In English. Study time: *weeks. Medicine +6%, Science (Biology) +6%, Unnatural +2%, SAN loss 1D4.*

> *"The transformation must involve the regulation of multiple genes (to encode things such as gill structures, claws, webbed feet, etc.) which would need to be switched on and off in the correct order to facilitate the change from ostensibly human to AH. To illustrate what I mean, I have given the following hypothesis: it is possible this gene regulation is controlled by a single 'master activator' gene—for the sake of argument I will call this gene 'X'. If transcription and translation of X is triggered by whatever mechanism (this age-related change could be equated with either puberty or the menopause in humans; however, whilst these changes are hormonal, the trigger for transformation in hybrids is unknown), it would trigger the first step of the transformation (switching on genes V, W, X, Y, and Z)."*

Twenty years of reports on laboratory analysis of samples recovered by Delta Green agents. Most samples simply defy conventional analysis. If the reader succeeds at a Medicine, Science (Biology), or Science (Chemistry) roll (whichever is highest), the SAN loss rises to 1D8.

RECOMMENDED RITUALS: None.

Geheimes Mysterium von Asien

In German. Study time: *weeks. Occult +3%, Unnatural +5%, SAN loss 1D6.*

Written by Gottfried Mülder in 1847. Mülder accompanied occultist Friedrich Wilhem von Junzt on his 1818–1819 journey to Inner Asia and used hypnotic recall to dictate this memoir of their journey. A pirated American version was published in Baltimore in 1849 as *Secret Mysteries of Asia, With a Commentary on the "Ghorl Nigral,"* referring to the blasphemous text (only one copy of which exists in the world) that von Junzt studied in a lamasery in Yian-Ho. Gottfried Mülder's descendant Hermann Mülder published a new limited edition for the Karotechia in 1939. It can serve as a source of unnatural lore regarding east Asia, Leng, Mu, the Xin, and the Tcho-Tchos.

RECOMMENDED RITUALS: None.

Greg Mason's Surveillance Videos

In English. Three DVDs with assorted video files. Study time: *days or weeks. Unnatural +2%, SAN loss 1D6.*

> *"Clear! Clear! Desmond, get your ass on that corner and watch the grating. Davis, what's the story on that—HOLY FUCK! Davis, get back—oh, Jesus. Mason, get that fucking camera out of here!"*

A collection of videos and photos, many filmed and taken in the 1990s and converted to high-resolution digital formats, that document an apparently random series of inexplicable horrors. Members of an unidentified East Asian street gang are turned inside out by something that can't quite be seen. Arthropod-like entities seem to shimmer, half-visible thanks to special emulsions that the videographer prepared to record extradimensional emanations that otherwise could not be captured on film. A DEA team slaughters an entire family as wormlike monstrosities rise from the bellies of men, women, and children. Moldy ghouls with vaguely canine forms carry on a meeping debriefing with FBI agents and NYPD detectives in a closet of some abandoned subway station, hinting at the movements of sorcerers below the Earth and in dreams. And on and on. Viewed through a lens of healthy skepticism and denial, the videos and photos must be the work of a gifted but deranged special-effects artiste.

RECOMMENDED RITUALS: None.

Gunter Frank's Research Notes

In German. Study time: *months. Medicine +3%, Pharmacy +3%, Science (Biology) +2%, Science (Chemistry) +2%, Unnatural +4%, SAN loss 1D6.*

> *"Dr. West hatte seit langem versucht, eine Mixtur zu vervollkommnen, die in die Adern eines frisch Verstorbenen injiziert, das Leben wiederherstellen würde. Eine Arbeit, die eine Fülle von frischen Leichen forderte und daher die unnatürlichsten Handlungen beinhaltete. Noch schockierender waren die Produkte einiger dieser Experimente—grässliche Massen von Fleisch, tot, aber von West wiedererweckt zu einer blinden, hirnlosen, Übelkeit erregenden Lebendigkeit."*

Several old boxes filled with yellowing, typed and hand-written manuscripts, crumbling file-folders, and journals are stacked in the bunker of Delta Green leader Donald Poe. These represent the life's (and unlife's) work of Dr. Gunter Frank, an infamous Nazi scientist who collected, translated, and expanded upon the hideous discoveries of strange luminaries like Dr. Javier Muñoz and Herbert West, M.D., and their assistants and colleagues. Dr. Frank cheated terminal cancer and lingered in a sort of ghastly half-life for more than 50 years in the Karotechia's refuge in South America. When Delta Green and MAJESTIC assaulted the compound in 2001, they destroyed Frank and his grotesque works. These boxes are all that remain. Poe suspects they would rewrite medical science if made public. He means to burn them to ash before that can happen.

RECOMMENDED RITUALS: Preserve Living Brain, Raise From Essential Saltes, Reanimation Formula.

The Innsmouth Report (Operation PUZZLEBOX)

In English. Study time: *days. Unnatural +2%, SAN loss 1.*

> *"It was determined that subject #14491 (Marsh, Albert, L.) was, according to records recovered at the state capital, 144 years old as of the date of his capture by Marines."*

Copies of the report on the 1928 Navy-directed raid on Innsmouth, Massachusetts were once circulated to dozens of offices within the United States intelligence community. The newly-activated Delta Green hastily recalled them in 1942, but not all were returned. The operation was re-designated PUZZLEBOX in 1942 by Delta Green. All previous markings on it were struck out and destroyed.

The report—compiled by ONI Capt. Alphonse Dumars—is a thick, old, accordion case-file stuffed with ancient, dried, onionskin papers, yellowed photographs, marked with the stamps of SECRET, P4, and DELTA GREEN EYES ONLY, with a Naval Operations registration number. Anyone with Bureaucracy, Forensics, or Military Science (Sea) in excess of 30% recognizes American Naval security markings, circa 1940.

The file describes, in detail, a coordinated, secret government strike on the New England town of Innsmouth Massachusetts by the U.S. Navy and Marines, to capture or kill "seditious and alien elements." The file is full of horrific and unbelievable photographs of amphibious, non-human creatures, incredible after-action reports, and a half dozen interrogations of townsfolk, captured and detained somewhere in the American west. It includes reports from the 42nd Battalion of the Marine Corps, the Coast Guard cutter *General Greene,* the Navy submarine *O-9,* the Bureau of Investigation (a report written by J. Edgar Hoover), and the Treasury Department intelligence summary including the testimony of Robert Olmstead.

The file never directly states it, but it clearly indicates the existence of a previously unknown, intelligent, non-human race (referred to as Deep Ones or the sons of Dagon), who have been intermingling with humanity for years (and perhaps centuries), and who exist beneath the ocean in unknown numbers.

EFFECTS: A single photograph in the file, of a clay sigil which once hung above the mantle in the lodge of the Esoteric Order of Dagon, is dangerous. The sigil looks like a complex intertwining of tentacles that bend and mesh in odd ways. Those who study the photo must make a Sanity test (costing 0/1D4 SAN) or suffer terrifying dreams over the next few nights. The dream is always the same: the dreamer's everyday life suddenly fills with sea water, and the dreamer is swept into the depths of the ocean and sees a vast, inhuman city. Some huge, unknowable thing stirs in the dark. This costs an additional 0/1D4 SAN due to helplessness.

RECOMMENDED RITUALS: None.

Joseph Camp's Grimoire

In English. Study time: *months. Occult +8%, Unnatural +4%, SAN loss 1D6.*

> *"Remains mummified in era immediately after B. Pharaoh most eff. in rendering powder harmful to E.E.; proportions of KNO3, S, Boswellia resin CONSTANT at all costs. Keep dry. Remember Helsinki effect."*

This thick stack of ledger-style notebooks was written over many years by Dr. Joseph Camp, the man who reorganized the Delta Green conspiracy in 1994. He intended it as his personal guide to "hypergeometric technology" that proved useful in fighting against unnatural forces. It details the use and ingredients of many powerful rituals, but gives little context for them and explains little about unnatural forces or entities. This grimoire was intended for Camp's sole benefit and is riddled with his personal shorthand and allusions. Mastering its rituals can be very difficult.

RECOMMENDED RITUALS: The Call of Dagon, Charnel Meditation, Create Stone Gate, Dust of the Thresholds, The Elder Sign, Fascination, Meditation Upon the Favored Ones, Obscure Memory, The Powder of Ibn-Ghazi, Speaking Dream, The Voorish Sign, Withering.

The King in Yellow

In English or French. Study time: *hours. Any one Art skill +5%, Unnatural +5%, SAN loss 1D6+2.*

> *"Song of my soul, my voice is dead;*
> *Die thou, unsung, as tears unshed*
> *Shall dry and die in*
> *Lost Carcosa."*

Written by an unknown playwright circa 1895, this evocative, nihilistic play about Carcosa and Hastur was suppressed in France. It cannot be skimmed. Once it's opened, an Agent must make a Sanity test to avoid reading it completely.

EFFECTS: After reading *The King in Yellow,* the Agent begins to encounter a number of unnatural phenomena with increasing SAN costs, at least once per operation. The Agent sees the Yellow Sign manifest where Hastur has irrupted, at a cost of 0/1D6 SAN. After four such encounters, things get really intense—the Agent may become attracted to Hastur, rotate into Carcosa, or develop a mental disorder.

RECOMMENDED RITUALS: None.

Liber Damnatus

In Latin. Study time: *weeks or months. Occult +2%, Unnatural +4%, SAN loss 1D8.*

Attributed (falsely) to St. Lazarus, this book is supposedly a narrative of dying, being damned, experiencing Hell, and resurrection. Written around 1570 CE by an unknown sorcerer in Germany, it contains lengthy disquisitions on means of preserving and animating the dead.

RECOMMENDED RITUALS: Flawed versions of Raise from Essential Saltes or Zombie.

Livre d'Ivon

In Occitan French. Study time: *months. Anthropology +2%, Occult +2%, Science (Astronomy) +3%, Unnatural +10%, SAN loss 2D6.*

Translated by Gaspard du Nord in 1240 CE—based on C. Philippus Faber's 9th-century Latin Liber Ivonis and du Nord's own occult researches—this purports to be the *Book of Eibon,* the work of the legendary Hyperborean wizard. It discusses Tsathoggua and other Great Old Ones and their origins, and delves into weird alchemy.

RECOMMENDED RITUALS: Call Forth Those From Outside (Nyogtha), The Closing of the Breach (Nyogtha), The Dho-Hna Formula, The Elder Sign, Open Gate, Pentagram of Power, Petrification, See the Other Side, Speaking Dream, The Voorish Sign, Whispers of the Dead (Tsathoggua), Winged Steed, Withering.

MAJESTIC OPORD 00001

In English. Study time: *weeks. Occult +4%, Unnatural +4%, SAN loss 1D4.*

> *"CIC: Go on.*
>
> *"PFC NELSON: It was funny really. I thought it was a kid. Like a deformed kid. A child.*
>
> *"CIC: You thought what? Who?*
>
> *"PFC NELSON: The thing. Whatever it was. The man from the moon.*
>
> *"CIC: Can you be more clear?*
>
> *"PFC NELSON: This thing was coming at us from the disc! It was walking! It moved like a person! It looked like a person!"*

In digital format, 1.4 gigabytes of PDF documents, files, blueprints, photographs and old black and white films which, when absorbed, leave the reader in no doubt as to the reality of the UFO phenomenon. In physical form, two huge file binders, each the size of a Webster's unabridged dictionary, weighing nearly nine kg.

The documents tell a clear tale:

- The U.S. recovered an alien craft at Roswell New Mexico in 1947.
- A secret group—MAJESTIC—was formed to study the event.
- Later, it is implied, this group managed to contact these entities.
- This conspiracy murdered, kidnapped and ruined lives, violating all aspects of the Constitution to maintain their secret.
- It is unclear if the group still exists.

RECOMMENDED RITUALS: None.

Matthew Carpenter's Delta Green Files

In English. Study time: *days. Occult +4%, Unnatural +4%, SAN loss 1D6.*

Delta Green-related interview transcripts, personnel files, newspaper clippings, and copies of FBI case files compiled by Matthew Carpenter while he served in A-cell. The contents range from 1970 to 1999.

RECOMMENDED RITUALS: None.

The People of the Monolith

In English. Study time: *days. Unnatural +3%, SAN loss 1D4.*

"They say foul things of Old Times still lurk
In dark forgotten corners of the world.
And Gates still gape to loose, on certain nights.
Shapes pent in Hell."

A volume of poetry by Justin Geoffrey, most substantially concerning his descent into madness during and after a visit to a remote village in Hungary and viewing an accursed black monolith that stood nearby. Staring at the stone for too long was said to bring on bizarre, otherworldly visions and dreams that would haunt one for life.

RECOMMENDED RITUALS: None.

The Pnakotic Manuscripts

In Koiné Greek. Study time: *months. Occult +6%, Unnatural +6%, SAN loss 1D6.*

The Pnakotika, Greek magical papyri from around the time of Christ, draw oracular and mythical meanings from a set of indecipherable runes and hieroglyphics supposedly discovered in Ultima Thule. Various interpretations of it became part of the Western magical tradition; since about 1485, explorers, occultists, philologists, and archaeologists have added further texts, steles, and inscriptions in similar alphabets (as well as forgeries, honest mistakes, and trance writing) to the Pnakotic corpus, along with their commentary. The manuscripts deal with a wide range of unnatural lore gleaned from the wisdom of ancient masters who exist beyond time.

There are no complete editions of all the "Pnakotic manuscripts" or "Pnakotic fragments." A three-volume set of the commonly accepted corpus at that time was printed in London in 1768 (now prohibitively expensive), but handwritten copies, academic conference proceedings, and other partial versions can be found in most top-rank university collections. With privileged library collection access, an Agent skilled in Anthropology or Occult can assemble enough Pnakotic material for research purposes. Because the manuscripts are so scattered, they can be "mastered" up to three times, gaining the same bonuses to Occult and Unnatural and losing the same SAN each time.

RECOMMENDED RITUALS: The Dho-Hna Formula, Leaves of Time, One Who Passes the Gateways, The Primal Lay, The Voorish Sign.

The Red Cross Pocket Bible

In English, German, and Italian. Study time: *days. Unnatural +1%, SAN loss 1.*

"EH•NA•SO•SHA•YOG•SO•TA•E-
H•AZ•A•TO•TA•AZ•A•TO•TA• AZ•A•TO•-
TA• AZ•A•TO•TA"

A tiny, pocket Bible of Second World War vintage, made of waterproof leatherette. It contains a copy of the King James Bible rendered in English, German and Italian, with phonetic English pronunciations. A 10-page section in the Book of Revelation contains—instead of translated lines—phonetic enunciations of a peculiar nature which are not English. Those with Unnatural 3% or more recognize the phonetics AZ•A•TO•TA as a reference to certain prehuman myths of the supreme mover of the universe, the Daemon Sultan Azathoth. That realization costs 0/1D4 SAN from the unnatural. For this bible's history, see **ASSET: THE RED CROSS POCKET BIBLE** on page 43.

RECOMMENDED RITUALS: The bible seems, to all experts who examine it, to contain a "calling formula" for Azathoth. Fortunately, study and use of it produces no effect. (Not that the Agents, or other parties, know that.)

The Revelations of Glaaki

In English. Study time: *months. Unnatural +12%, SAN loss 2D6.*

A series of eleven 19th-century books written by Glaaki cultists, transcribing dreams that supposedly conveyed the thoughts and visions of their god. The books describe Glaaki's origins and cult, sometimes in maddening detail and other times in discursive vagueness. An abridged edition included nine volumes, with a sharp loss in detail and context (study time

500 hours, Unnatural +6%, SAN loss 1D8). A twelfth volume—much rarer than the others, and regarded by some Glaaki cultists as a heretical attempt to sabotage their faith—examines Y'golonac, and purportedly opens the reader up to possession by that loathsome entity. The twelfth volume adds +3% Unnatural and comes with its own SAN loss of 1D6.

RECOMMENDED RITUALS: Call Forth Those From Outside (Azathoth, Glaaki, Nyarlathotep, Shub-Niggurath, Y'golonac), Exaltation of the Flesh, Fascination, The First Secret.

The Seven Cryptical Books of Hsan

In Classical Chinese. Study time: *months. Unnatural +11%, SAN loss 2D6.*

> *"Observances of the ornamental changes of seasons and ornamental observances of society allow but quivering and fragmented understanding of the processes of transformation if considered without the boundless insight of the immortal messenger, the masked monk, the father of the favored ones, who in cruel joyousness manifests the will of the unwillful sublimity of heaven."*

The *Ch'i Pen Shu Hsieh Le Tsui An,* or *Seven Books Written in Darkness,* are ascribed to "Hsan the Greater," a legendary sage variously dated as far back as 4200 BCE. The oldest known version was prepared from scraps that survived the book burnings of 213 BCE by the first Ch'in emperor. The confirmed existence of Tibetan copies implies that Hsan originally translated the *Seven Books* from some other unknown Asian language. The "Polyglot Hsan," printed anonymously in Shanghai in 1920 as *The Seven Cryptical Books of Earth,* includes French and Russian translations. The copy kept by Delta Green leader Donald Poe in a battered old artillery trunk is a treasure beyond price to historians, anthropologists, and occultists: seven "books" built of narrow bamboo strips bound side-by-side with silk cords, rolled into scrolls around staves for handling. The cords are only sixty years old; the bamboo strips date to the Han Dynasty, about the second century CE. Some strips are damaged or have been effaced over the centuries.

RECOMMENDED RITUALS: Charnel Meditation, Elixir of Infinite Space, Immortal Messenger, Leaves of Time, Mountain and Sea, Whispers of the Dead, Winged Steed, Withering.

Unaussprechlichen Kulten

In German. Study time: *months. Unnatural +12%, SAN loss 2D8.*

Written by Friedrich Wilhelm von Junzt in 1839, this infamous tome is a travelogue of the horrific. It provides ample details of many unnatural cults, conspiracies, and activities. A bastardized edition called *Nameless Cults,* published by Bridewell in 1845 and Golden Goblin in 1909, offers Unnatural of only +6% and flawed or fewer rituals, with a SAN loss of 2D4.

RECOMMENDED RITUALS: Charnel Meditation, Call Forth Those From Outside (as determined by the Handler), The Closing of the Breach (as determined by the Handler), Healing Balm, Lure the Hungerer, Meditation Upon the Favored Ones, Mountain and Sea, Pentagram of Power, Prayer to the Dark Man, The Voorish Sign, Whispers of the Dead (as determined by the Handler), Winged Steed.

De Vermis Mysteriis

In Latin. Study time: *months. Occult +3%, Unnatural +12%, SAN loss 2D6.*

Ludvig Prinn, a Flemish wizard who claimed to have been born in the 13th century, smuggled this work out just before being burned at the stake by the Inquisition in 1542. The next year, it appeared in print at Cologne. A wide-ranging work on alchemy and witchcraft, it describes necromancy in ancient Egypt, Arabic sorcery, demons that offer immortality at hideous costs, and an ancient and wide-ranging cult of Nyarlathotep.

RECOMMENDED RITUALS: Call Forth Those From Outside (Feasters from the Stars; Haedi Nigritiae; Ifrits; Mi-Go; Nyarlathotep; Nyogtha), The Closing of the Breach (as determined by the Handler), Prayer to the Dark Man, Raise from Essential Saltes.

Hypergeometry

Every culture on Earth has its belief in "magic"—a force that exists outside the world, which can make amazing, dangerous or terrible things happen. Delta Green specialists long ago labelled this power "hypergeometry," due to its frequent association with numbers, mathematics, position, and shapes. Like the inhuman angles of R'lyeh and the warping of dimensions which flings the minds of the Great Race of Yith through spacetime, hypergeometrical techniques alter reality. Some say such techniques were passed down from the Great Old Ones that once ruled the Earth.

Humans have always attempted to harness this power. It is best to think of hypergeometry as a live circuit flowing with infinite energy beyond the four dimensions in which the human consciousness exists. Humans that alter their perception can tap the circuit, connecting with the other world, focusing that energy.

Whether it is a hallucinating shaman drawing a mandala in sand, or a scientist placing lasers at points in a circle to call down something from the sky, the "math" is essentially the same. The only difference is culture, and it is often difficult to tell where culture ends and power begins. The ritual and action matter only insomuch as they affect the mind. This means that two people can enact the exact same ritual with completely different outcomes. One might see no effect; the other might end the world.

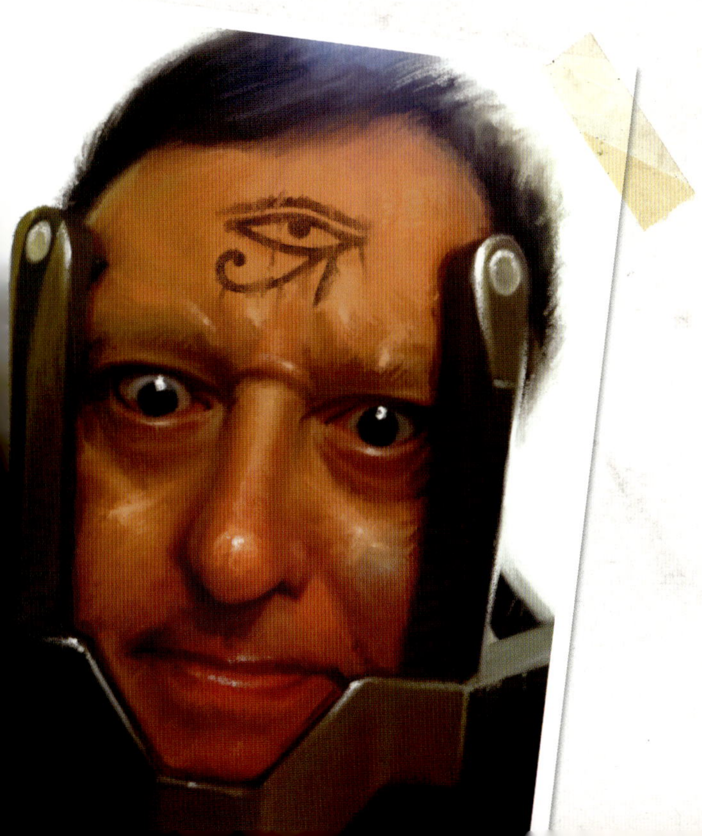

All oddities in human culture that have real power can be traced back to hypergeometric techniques. Psychic ability, witchcraft, divination, and ghosts all represent a misfocused projection of inhuman, unnatural powers.

Hypergeometry in the Game

Hypergeometry is composed of either a *ritual* or an *object* which can produce a predictable effect (like blinding a target, or teleporting them to space). The person activating the hypergeometry is called the *operator*.

Using hypergeometrical effects always costs the operator a crucial resource: willpower points (or, especially dire, permanent POW), sometimes hit points, and always SAN. This is called the *activation cost*.

In addition, a hypergeometric ritual requires a Ritual Activation roll. (See **RITUAL ACTIVATION** on page 166.)

When activated, a hypergeometrical effect also costs anyone present SAN due to the nature of the impossible change it inflicts upon the world.

Rituals or Objects

Hypergeometry is called from either a ritual or an object. Rituals are chants, thoughts, motions, or preparations that connect the human mind to powers from outside. Each ritual is different, and they are usually learned from books, or other operators.

To use a ritual, the operator must first study the process of the ritual, have all the necessary elements (some rituals require a sacrifice for instance, or can only work within 10 km of the sea), and most importantly, believe in the ritual's efficacy. This requires a Ritual Activation roll, which depends on low SAN. See **RITUAL ACTIVATION** on page 166.

Objects are items imbued with special powers, allowing those with access to them to unleash hypergeometrical effects. They operate like rituals; however, if you have an object, you don't need to know the ritual or succeed at a Ritual Activation roll. You can simply pay the costs and trigger the hypergeometrical effect.

>> Learning and Activating a Ritual

Complexity	Unnatural Gain	Study Time	SAN Loss for Learning	Activation Time
Simple	0	hours, days, or longer	1, 1D4, or 1D6	a turn or up to a minute
Complex	0	days, weeks, or longer	1D6, 1D8, or 1D10	a few minutes or up to an hour
Elaborate	1	weeks, months, or years	1D10, 1D12, or 1D20	a few hours or a day or more

Learning a Ritual

A ritual is a process that causes the human mind to intersect with powers beyond, activating an unnatural effect. To mentally stable individuals, ritual instructions are nothing more than chicken-scratch. Using one elicits no effect. A core belief in the effect's possibility is necessary for it to manifest. That usually requires a terrifying disconnection of the human mind from everyday reality.

Rituals are most often learned from books. Most books that purport to be grimoires of magic are nothing but nonsense and superstition. One that has truly powerful secrets is a dangerous prize. Such a tome might have dozens of rituals of genuine power, or only one.

However many rituals a given book may contain, each ritual must be learned individually. There is no shortcut to "learn the whole book."

TIME AND SANITY: Each ritual has a study time and a SAN cost. To learn it, an Agent must devote the study time and fail the SAN test, suffering the book's listed SAN loss. From then on, the operator can attempt to activate the ritual and has a rough understanding of what it does.

This study time must be uninterrupted and without serious distraction, and with all required resources at hand. In some cases, a ritual can be learned only if the student also has a particular skill.

If the SAN test succeeds, the Agent gains nothing, failing to grasp the reality of the ritual. The Agent may try again as many times as the player likes, each time devoting study time and attempting to fail the SAN test. If the SAN test fails, the Agent loses the appropriate SAN, but learns the ritual. Without failing the SAN test, learning a ritual is not possible. You may understand the process of it, but not the reality. You don't fully see the truth of the ritual, only the ravings of the lunatic who wrote it.

Penalties to SAN tests, such as intoxication or fatigue, rarely apply when it comes to learning rituals. The SAN test for learning a ritual represents a long period of study, experimentation, and weird thought, and depends on the Agent's innate connection to unnatural realities, not on temporary conditions. That

OPINT: Balancing Hypergeometry in Game Play

Hypergeometric effects vary wildly in operation time, scope, and effect. They are balanced only on the highest level of the game, insomuch as they exact a severe price for their use. Agents who come to rely on hypergeometry suffer a swift decline.

These rules are not meant to generate carefully balanced game mechanics. Some rituals are far more powerful than others. Hypergeometry should always evoke in players the dread of the unknowable. With that in mind, as long as the operator costs outstrip the beneficial effects, any hypergeometrical effect may be possible.

After all, if a ritual or object inflicts Lethality 99% and exacts 1D100 SAN from the operator, it is a closed loop. An agent abusing it is soon insane and unplayable: lost on the streets or to a cult, committed to a psychiatric hospital, or "sanitized" by Delta Green.

kind of penalty could affect a roll to master a ritual that takes only a few hours to learn, but only if the Handler thinks it's appropriate.

Many rituals require weeks or months to learn. Those can be learned only between operations as home pursuits, instead of more beneficial pursuits like going to therapy or fulfilling the Agent's day-to-day obligations. Some rituals take only days or even hours to master. At the Handler's discretion, those could be learned in the middle of an operation.

COMPLEXITY: Some rituals are simple (concentrate on a symbol of power), while others are complex or even elaborate (ritualistically kill 60 people, trace patterns in the dirt for two days, and then recite 12 pages of runes). A ritual's complexity determines its approximate study time. Mastering an especially elaborate ritual may also increase the operator's Unnatural skill.

The SAN loss for learning a ritual usually depends on the complexity, but is up to the Handler. It depends on the power of the ritual and its source. An identical ritual can be easier to learn from one tome than from another.

The complexity of a ritual is most often related to the ritual's power, but not always. Especially clear and concise instructions might make even an extremely powerful ritual simple. Or, more likely, the scribblings and scratched-through notes of a madman may make even a trivial ritual frustratingly complex.

EXAMPLE: *Carter (SAN 55) settles in to study* De Vermis Mysteriis*—specifically, a ritual within it named The Calling of the Goat. Learning the ritual requires a study time of 10 hours and costs 1D4 SAN. Carter spends 10 hours in study, dodging phone calls from concerned team members, and attempts the SAN test. He fails with a roll of 58. The true horrors of the manuscript become clear. Carter learns the ritual and loses 1D4 SAN. He can now attempt to cast The Calling of the Goat.*

OPINT: Hypergeometric Addiction

For all its danger, the power of hypergeometry can be alluring. If using hypergeometry to solve problems reduces an Agent's SAN to the Breaking Point, addiction to hypergeometry is a likely disorder.

Ritual Activation

To use a hypergeometrical effect, the operator must know the ritual, or possess the object that has the ritual's effects, and pay the costs to trigger the effect. A ritual also has an activation time—how long an operator must enact the ritual before it activates.

Some rituals have their own rules, but as a rule of thumb, activating a ritual works like this: After spending the necessary time, the operator attempts a Ritual Activation roll.

RITUAL ACTIVATION RATING: Every character has a Ritual Activation rating that equals 99 minus current SAN. The weaker the operator's sanity, the more likely the operator is to activate an unnatural ritual effect.

Sometimes, having a copy of the ritual's instructions or formula on hand, or working from detailed notes and observations, can assist with the Ritual Activation roll. With the Handler's permission, a +20% bonus may be applied to an operator who is thus prepared.

Note that Ritual Activation does not depend on the Unnatural skill. The Unnatural skill is useful in finding and identifying effective rituals and studying unnatural entities; but once you've learned a ritual, activating it depends on your readiness to break with reality.

SUCCESS: If the Ritual Activation roll succeeds, the the ritual takes effect and operator pays the costs as defined by the ritual or the object.

FAILURE: If the Ritual Activation roll fails, the operator has a choice. Either no effect occurs, but the operator still must pay half the cost and lose a reduced amount of SAN (see **RITUAL DETAILS** on page 168); or the operator may force a connection to the unnatural, succeeding after all by paying 1 POW, permanently.

USING AN OBJECT: If the ritual is instead activated through an object imbued with permanent power, that may be all that's required. Some objects take effect only if manipulated in a certain way, triggered by a spoken phrase, or held by a particular person or type of creature. If you meet the criteria and pay the cost, the object releases its effect.

> **EXAMPLE:** *Lucas has studied Of the Shadowe, a ritual he deciphered in* De Vermis Mysteriis. *It allows him to reach out with a shadow limb to any target within sight and inflict 1D6 damage. Once cast, it remains present until used, and then it burns out after 1D4 turns. It costs 12 WP and 9 HP—due to ritualistic cuts on his arms and wracking convulsions—and 1D10 SAN. Lucas' SAN is 55, so his Ritual Activation rating is 44. He succeeds with a roll of 31, so the ritual takes effect. If he had failed, it still would have cost 6 WP, 5 HP, and 1D4 SAN; or he could have spent 1 POW to force it to succeed.*

Creating New Hypergeometrical Effects

Hypergeometry allows humans to achieve "impossible" things, such as inflicting damage without apparent cause, moving objects instantly across space and time, or contacting inhuman intelligences.

Hypergeometric rituals are defined and named (e.g., "Leech," "Overwhelm," or "Call the Sleeper"). Each has an effect, a SAN loss for activating it, an operator cost (see **RITUAL COSTS** on page 168), and a clear writeup of its effect. The SAN loss for activating a ritual is distinct from the SAN loss for learning it in the first place, and applies every time the ritual is activated.

To create a new hypergeometric effect, first imagine what you want that power to accomplish. Be as specific as possible. It should never be as boring as "inflict 1D6 HP damage." Describe what it does. Add flair, horror, and weirdness.

>> Ritual Details

WP Cost	Scope	SAN Loss for activation or witnessing	SAN Loss for failed attempt	Damage	Range	Summoning
6	Minor	1	0	1D4	Nearby (10 m)	Up to 8 POW
9	Small	1D4	1	1D6	Local (100 m)	Up to 12 POW
12	Significant	1D6	1D4	1D10	In sight (1 km)	Up to 16 POW
15	Substantial	1D8	1D4	1D20	Distant (100 km)	Up to 20 POW
22	Major	1D10	1D6	10% Lethality	Anywhere on Earth	Up to 30 POW
30	Vast	1D12	1D6	20% Lethality	Beyond the Earth	Up to 40 POW
45	Sweeping	1D20	1D10	40% Lethality	Another galaxy	Up to 60 POW
110	Cosmic	1D100	1D20	99% Lethality	In another dimension	Up to 150 POW

Is it a hand-sign that allows a person to step through a wall, causing the otherwise solid matter to ripple and move like water out of the way before the wall collapses back into shape leaving strange deformations? Or the ability to stare into a video feed, chant a phrase, and suddenly be there and not here? Or a forked hand sign which inflicts a mystical lightning that turns the target's flesh to dust, leaving behind charred bones?

Assemble a single sentence that describes the purpose of the ritual. At its core, what does the ritual do? How long does it take to implement? What components does it require? What is it called?

Ritual Costs

The smaller the hypergeometrical effect, the easier it is to control, and the less it strips from the essence of the operator when activated. The greater the effect, the more it costs. Any sane person using hypergeometry is eventually destroyed by it or driven mad.

For game purposes, "effect" denotes an in-game measure of change the ritual enacts upon the world. (See **HYPERGEOMETRICAL EFFECTS** on page 169).

Each ritual incurs a SAN loss to the operator, and a WP cost that the operator must pay. The more powerful the ritual, the greater the WP cost and SAN loss. WP and SAN loss represent the psychic strain of twisting the human brain to comprehend alien, unnatural formulae and physics.

See the **RITUAL DETAILS** table on this page for suggested effects and costs.

ASSISTANCE: Some rituals and objects allow assistance in fulfilling the operator cost. In some cases, an assistant need not have learned the ritual ahead of time; it's enough for the operator to tell the assistant what to do. Each ritual and object defines whether such assistance is possible. Each assistant suffers full SAN loss and chooses how much of the WP cost to pay.

PAYING IN POW: At any time, an operator or assistant may spend permanent POW to fuel a ritual. Each point of POW spent is equivalent to 10 WP.

PAYING IN HP: Some rituals require part of the cost to be paid instead in HP—physical harm inflicted as part of the ritual—instead of WP. Occultists often argue over whether the power of ritual bloodletting comes from some psychic power inherent in blood, the hunger of unseen intelligences that lend their power to the ritual, or the capacity of agony and taboo-breaking to weaken the barriers that separate the mind from the impossible.

SACRIFICE: Some rituals require the HP or WP cost (or sometimes even POW) to be paid by an unwilling sacrifice. (Animal sacrifice suffices for some, but most rituals of unnatural power require the sacrifice to be conscious and sentient; in other words, awake and human. A few Delta Green operators over the years have attempted to sacrifice intelligent alien creatures instead of human beings, without success.) Harming such a victim always incurs an additional SAN cost due to violence. A sacrifice who survives suffers the same SAN loss as the operator and assistants, along with a SAN loss due to helplessness.

FIXED COSTS: Each unique ritual and object has a fixed operation cost. For example, Restore from Essential Saltes might have an operator cost of 1 POW and 12 HP, while The Knife of Ibn-Fedel might cost only 3 WP and 3 HP. Two different rituals, or even two different variants of the same ritual, may have the same effects but require different ways to pay the cost.

TAKING EXTRA TIME: Some rituals and objects allow the operator to take extra time, paying the cost over days, weeks, or years. That allows the operator to pay part of the cost, rest, and pay more of it later. Extremely powerful rituals virtually require taking a great deal of time or having a great deal of help.

Hypergeometrical Effects

Most hypergeometrical effects, despite stylistic differences, achieve predictable changes within established categories. The broad categories on the **RITUAL DETAILS** table on page 168—Damage, Range, and Summoning—cover most hypergeometrical effects. If you need a new one, feel free to make it up on the spot.

The **RITUAL DETAILS** table is something the players should never see. Encompassing the unknowable in a clear table of numbers and capacities ruins its mystery. It is for the Handler's eyes only.

Different SAN costs apply for successfully activating a ritual or for failing to activate it. See **RITUAL ACTIVATION** on page 166 for details.

To define a ritual's cost, first establish the core of the ability—what does it mainly do? This sets the operator cost.

Harm, Healing, and Enhancement

The ability to reduce or increase stats, HP, or WP. The effect's Damage rating determines the amount reduced or restored. A damaging effect with a Lethality rating allows a Lethality roll against the target. If the Lethality roll succeeds, it reduces the target's HP or affected stat to zero; if it fails, it still reduces the target's stat or HP by the sum of the two percentile dice read as d10s.

If the effect increases a stat, HP, or WP, the Lethality roll works in reverse. Failing the Lethality roll adds points equal to the sum of the two Lethality dice. Succeeding at the Lethality roll adds points equal to the Lethality rating itself (in other words, +10 for "Lethality 10%" or +40 for "Lethality 40%").

Very few harmful or healing effects affect more than a single target. As a rule of thumb, a ritual that affects everything within radius of 10 m costs four times the usual WP and correspondingly higher SAN.

The operator must touch the target, unless the ritual includes a separate cost for Range.

Using such a method to harm someone is inefficient—wouldn't it be easier to just shoot him?—unless the ritual is combined with a scrying effect to allow access to a hidden target. And, of course, some targets can't be hurt with bullets or bombs.

A variant effect may be to provide Armor points, reducing HP damage rather than increasing HP.

A healing ritual can be tremendously impressive, allowing a subject to recover from terrible wounds almost instantly. Unfortunately, using unnatural forces to accelerate healing often has awful side effects, such as introducing mutations that manifest later.

OPINT: Flawed Rituals

Throughout the skein of history rituals have been lensed through every imaginable human culture. Sometimes, those translations changed the ritual, and not for the better. While a flawed version still works, it does so in a less than optimal manner. With a flawed ritual, the Ritual Activation roll is at a penalty of –20%. A flawed ritual may also have increased costs or other weird side-effects.

Philippine Sea
Luzon
Foward processing center established, 28 March
Clark Airbase
CIA arms de
mid-Apr

DISINFORMATION

YELLOW CARD

THE CULTURAL LENS

Nearly every ritual that human operators can learn was developed in the context of some earlier operator's occult traditions. The human brain rejects the unnatural, and finds it easier to tolerate when blanketed in human constructs. When defining a ritual, describe the cultural traditions that contaminate it. But remember that many versions of that ritual may exist, each combining its own religious or occult traditions and invocations with strange, real calls to unnatural powers. Whether a ritual takes effect without such trappings is always up to the Handler.

Here are a few examples.

- **AFRICAN AND CARIBBEAN:** Rituals that emerged from African traditions invoke nature or ancestral spirits along with certain unnatural Powers. The spirits' names, and the ingredients of the rituals, vary from region to region and from language to language. Animal sacrifice is not uncommon.
- **ANCIENT CHINESE:** Rituals found in scrolls or tomes like the **Seven Cryptical Books of Hsan** have the trappings of esoteric Chinese Taoism. They often require papers to be hung nearby, marked with occult characters that appear to be Classical Chinese but which would baffle any linguist. They may require chanted prayers in Old Chinese, invoking divine energies and spirits recognizable from Chinese shamanism along with unnatural powers. Old Chinese is not fully known today, but a native speaker of any Chinese language, or one with Foreign Language skill in any Chinese language at 50% or greater, can muddle through. The ritual may require a laboratory with esoteric ingredients of Chinese alchemy.
- **EUROPEAN, JUDAIC, AND ISLAMIC OCCULTISM:** Many rituals were passed along by occult traditions that evolved from ancient times. Some involve elaborate alchemy, mixing esoteric ingredients while invoking magical spirits. Others take the guise of stereotypical witchcraft, complete with moonlit human sacrifices at an unhallowed spot and prayers to a satanic "Dark Man."
- **PSYCHIC POWERS:** Some rituals are encountered as apparently innate psychic abilities. They may develop in dreams or meditation, or from chaos magic that can in turn lead to more elaborate rituals. Psychic powers seem more likely to occur in especially sensitive minds: characters with INT or POW at 17 or higher, or with Art, Occult, or Psychotherapy skills at 60% or higher.

CUT ALONG THIS LINE

031-51937 o-46

RECORDED - 26

EX-9

In some powerful rituals, a corpse can be restored to life if the body's entire HP score can be restored from 0 to maximum in a single attempt. Of course, the revived subject always faces a severe SAN loss (usually 1D6/1D20) for the sudden memory of death. (What an Agent may remember beyond the moment of death is up to the Handler.)

Under no circumstances can any hypergeometric effect restore SAN to an operator or a subject. A ritual or object might force calm on someone in the grip of insanity, alleviating symptoms; but it can never cure the insanity, and in fact it probably incurs a SAN loss that ultimately makes things worse.

Movement

The ability to transport entities or objects, whether by levitation or teleportation. The cost depends on the effect's range. Some movement rituals affect just the operator. Some allow the operator to move other objects, either by touch or at a distance. Either way, both starting point and end point of the movement must be within the ritual's range.

How much matter can be moved varies wildly from ritual to ritual. One ritual may move only a tiny object; another may move the operator and anything the operator touches; another may move mass according to how many further WP are spent.

Scrying

The ability to see or know information remotely. This includes seeing or sensing things that are far away in time or space, communicating with entities from outside, making mental contact with another mind, and even transferring your mind to another body. The details and nature of the communication are up to the Handler. Some scrying rituals are very detailed; others make only passing contact. The cost depends on the effect's range. Some scrying rituals cost much less than the distance would indicate. Often, such reduced-cost rituals attempt to contact unnatural intelligences in other dimensions, and the extradimensional entity itself seems to fuel the ritual.

Summoning

The ability to draw an unnatural creature from the stars, from the deeps, or from beyond time and space to your location and control or restrict its actions once it arrives. The cost depends on the POW of the entity. If the Ritual Activation roll succeeds and the costs are paid, the entity appears. It may appear instantaneously, or it may take hours or days or longer, depending on the ritual. It costs SAN to encounter an unnatural entity (see the entity's description for the amount), even to the operator.

When the entity appears, the operator (and each assistant) may attempt to control it with an opposed POW test. If that fails, the operator or any assistant may expend 1 POW permanently to assert control. Otherwise, the entity immediately attempts to either bind the operator or an assistant to its own will for the ritual's duration, following the same procedure, or destroy the operator and then escape.

A summoned entity remains for a fixed amount of time as defined in the ritual or the object, or until it fulfills a task as dictated by the operator, or until it kills the operator, whereupon it vanishes back to its point of origin.

A controlled entity may be commanded to perform an action according to its intelligence level. The summoning ritual allows communication—how much communication is up to the Handler. Most summoned entities understand "find and kill this target" or "bring me this thing." The greater the entity's intelligence, the more complex a command can be. Once the action is complete, the entity may return to its point of origin, having fulfilled the summoner's command.

Other Effects

If a ritual's effects don't match any of these categories, use them as a rough guideline and consider its scope—is it immediate and minor or sweeping and vast?—to determine its cost.

Ritual Duration

Usually a ritual's effects last a few turns or a few minutes (sometimes, rarely, it lasts hours). Some last only a turn. When in doubt, an effect lasts 1D4 turns.

ASSETS: Index of Sample Rituals

Ritual	Page	Effect Type	Associated Entities or Traditions
Ageless Banquet	174	Other	African; Shub-Niggurath
The Call of Dagon	175	Summoning	Deep Ones
Call Forth Those From Outside	175	Summoning	Varies
Call Zombies	175	Summoning	Zombies
Changeling Feast	175	Other	
Charnel Meditation	175	Summoning	Ghouls
Clairvoyance	176	Scrying	
The Closing of the Breach	176	Other	Varies
Consciousness Expansion	177	Scrying	
Create Stone Gate	177	Movement	
The Dho-Hna Formula	177	Scrying, Movement	
Dust of the Thresholds	178	Harm	
The Elder Sign	178	Harm	
Elixir of Infinite Space	178	Other	
Exaltation of the Flesh	179	Healing (Protection)	
Exchange Personalities	179	Scrying	Shub-Niggurath
Exorcism	179	Other	
Fascination	180	Other	
Finding	180	Scrying	Tsathoggua, Yog-Sothoth
The First Secret	180	Scrying	Glaaki
Healing Balm	180	Healing	Shub-Niggurath
Immortal Messenger	180	Summoning	Nyarlathotep
Infallible Suggestion	180	Other	
Leaves of Time	181	Scrying	
Lure the Hungerer	181	Summoning	Dimensional shambler
Meditation Upon the Favored Ones	181	Summoning	Mi-go
Mountain and Sea	182	Summoning	Spawn of Cthulhu
Obscure Memory	182	Other	
Open Gate	182	Movement	
One Who Passes the Gateways	182	Scrying	
Pentagram of Power	182	Summoning	
Petrification	183	Harm	Shub-Niggurath, Tsathoggua
The Powder of Ibn-Ghazi	183	Scrying	
Prayer to the Dark Man	183	Summoning	Nyarlathotep
Preserve Living Brain	184	Healing	
The Primal Lay	184	Scrying	

ASSETS:
Sample Rituals (Cont'd)

Ritual	Page	Effect Type	Associated Entities or Traditions
Raise From Essential Saltes	184	Healing	Yog-Sothoth
Reanimation Formula	185	Healing	Zombies
Release Breath	185	Harm	Zombies
See the Other Side	185	Scrying	
Song of Power	185	Healing (WP)	
Soothing Song	185	Healing	
Speaking Dream	186	Scrying	
Speech of Birds and Beasts	186	Other	
Storm and Stillness	186	Other	
Swarm	186	Summoning	
The Voorish Sign	186	Scrying	
Whispers of the Dead	186	Scrying	Varies
Winged Steed	187	Summoning	Winged servitors
Withering	187	Harm	
Zombie	187	Harm and Healing	Zombies

A ritual that lasts longer costs more; increase the costs by one increment if it lasts minutes instead of turns, by another if it lasts hours, and by yet another if it lasts days.

Permanence

Some rituals make their effects permanent. Making an effect permanent typically costs 10 times the effect's base WP cost as listed in the **RITUAL DETAILS** table on page 168. Some portion of that must be paid in permanent POW. If the activation roll fails, half that cost is lost. SAN loss is based on the total WP cost, including permanence, as given on the **RITUAL DETAILS** table. Permanence is often used to create artifacts imbued with unnatural power.

> **EXAMPLE:** *The Handler invents a ritual called Stone of Life, which imbues a specially carved granite statue with the power to grow uncomfortably warm in the presence of certain unnatural effects and entities. The Handler determines this is a scrying effect with a "nearby" range, costing 6 WP. Permanence costs another 60 WP (10 times the usual cost), paid in a mix of WP, HP, and POW. On the* **RITUAL DETAILS** *table, the most appropriate SAN loss is 1D20.*

Combining Effects

Some rituals combine multiple effects. As a rule of thumb, start with the WP cost of the most costly effect. Add half the WP cost for each additional effect. SAN loss is based on the total WP cost, as given on the **RITUAL DETAILS** table on page 168.

> **EXAMPLE:** *The Handler invents a ritual called The Touch of Saval. It allows the operator to reach out, anywhere on Earth (a range effect) and attack a target with monstrous tentacles for 1D8 damage per turn for 1D4 turns (a damage effect). The base cost is for range, the most costly effect: 22 WP. The Handler adds half the cost of the second effect, or 8 WP (half of 15), for a total cost of 30 WP. On the* **RITUAL DETAILS** *table, the SAN loss for a ritual that costs 30 WP is 1D12.*

Witnessing a Ritual

Anyone witnessing a hypergeometric effect suffers the ritual's listed SAN loss due to exposure to things that man was not meant to know. Even the most mild and benign ritual invokes forces that twist the reality in which humanity maintains its fragile existence.

Sample Rituals

Each of these rituals presents its "standard" form. Remember, the rules for creating unnatural rituals and artifacts are meant to be guidelines and suggestions. We're talking about unnatural violations of physics and quantum mechanics. If you want to customize a ritual, get creative and make it terrifying.

Feel free to use rituals and artifacts you find in other publications. Over the decades, countless rituals and artifacts have been created for Lovecraftian role-playing games. Most can be used in *Delta Green* with hardly any conversion. Where the rules are similar, simply substitute WP for "magic points" and use the listed POW and SAN costs. If it follows some additional rule that's not in this book, or if it isn't supposed to even require an activation roll, that's fine. The reality-breaking forces of the unnatural allow for endless possibilities.

Ageless Banquet

Elaborate ritual. Study time: *weeks; 1D20 SAN; +1 Unnatural.* Activation: *days; 20 WP, 1D10 SAN.*

Supposedly discovered by an ancient, infamous Congo tribe, this days-long sacrificial ritual invokes Shub-Niggurath in a litany of other, more traditional spirits. A human sacrificial victim is slain, dismembered, cooked, and eaten. The ritual costs 20 WP from the sacrifice and the operator, and costs the operator 1D10 SAN in addition to SAN lost from the violence of the sacrifice. Consuming a human body costs a further 1/1D6 SAN for violence. The operator does not age for one year following the ritual. Other versions are rumored to stem from other cultural traditions and to involve drinking blood, but not eating flesh.

The Call of Dagon

Simple ritual. Study time: *hours; 1D4 SAN.* Activation: *a turn; 6 WP, 1 SAN.*

This ritual requires the five-hour creation of a clay tablet, which must be thrown in the sea in an area populated by Deep Ones. It calls Deep Ones to the surface for "communion." The normal SAN loss for seeing Deep Ones applies. After decades of Delta Green using this ritual to ambush them, modern Deep Ones are less trusting than their predecessors, as well as less forgiving. It should be noted that this is not a summons or a command, but a "call." A request. It does not in any way compel them to respond or control the Deep Ones who answer—though the text may be misread to imply that.

Call Forth Those From Outside

Elaborate ritual. Study time: *weeks; 1D10 SAN; +1 Unnatural.* Activation: *varies.*

This ritual summons unnatural entities from outside our world. It often involves a strange mixture of medieval and classical invocations and calls to unnatural powers in inhuman tongues, accompanied by thunderous releases of energy and strange behavior by nearby animals. Some versions take hours. Others must be conducted across days or even longer. In some, the entity begins to manifest during the ritual but can be sent back by disrupting the ritual before it finishes.

WP and SAN costs depend on the entity summoned; see **RITUAL DETAILS** on page 168. This cost can be paid by assistants, who need not know the ritual themselves as long as they follow the operator's instructions, or by human sacrifices.

The core of this ritual is the same regardless of the entity. But it requires techniques peculiar to the entity being summoned. After learning this ritual for one entity, learning the secrets needed to call forth another entity usually requires days of study and costs another 1D6 SAN. Make a note of the particular summonings an operator knows. Different summonings may have unique names—"Alert the Hosts of the Airs" may summon the mi-go, while "Benefit the All-In-One" might summon Yog-Sothoth—while following the same overall rules. Whether a version of the ritual applies to any given entity is up to the Handler.

Call Zombies

Complex ritual. Study time: *days; 1D6 SAN.* Activation: *minutes; 4 WP, 1D4 SAN.*

Mostly found in African and Scandinavian traditions, this ritual requires a repetitive chant that includes pre-human phrases calling to unnatural powers from Outside. It lasts an hour. All costs must be paid by the operator. If the activation roll succeeds, the chant attracts all zombies within 2 km. This ritual offers no protection against zombies, but a Pentagram of Power (see the ritual on page 182) can keep the summoned zombies at bay while preventing them from departing—as long as the chant continues.

Changeling Feast

Complex ritual. Study time: *days; 1D10 SAN.* Activation: *days; 12 WP, 1D6 SAN.*

This ritual allows the operator to consume a human corpse and later assume the victim's likeness. The likeness is not deep. It does not change the weight of the operator; bright light casts the operator's true shadow, not that of the likeness; and it does not emulate the victim's behavior, personality, or mannerisms. Consuming a human body costs 1/1D6 SAN for violence. Devouring a human corpse takes days for a human operator. Some inhuman entities can do it in far less time and gain access to a victim's thoughts and memories. How much of the body must be devoured, and whether a human operator can use this ritual to devour and change into an animal or unnatural entity, are up to the Handler.

Charnel Meditation

Simple ritual. Study time: *hours; 1D4 SAN.* Activation: *minutes; 12 WP, 1D6 SAN.*

At a graveyard frequented by ghouls, the operator enters a reverie and utters a litany of strange meepings. Enacting the ritual on a moonlit night grants the operator a +20% bonus to the activation roll. If the activation roll succeeds, a few ghouls arrive within the hour. This ritual exerts no control over them whatsoever.

Clairvoyance

Simple ritual. Study time: *hours or days; 1D8 SAN.* Activation: *minutes; 1 WP and 1 SAN per minute of use.*

Sometimes called "remote viewing," this ritual is often encountered as an apparently innate psychic ability. After entering a trance, the operator sees events and places far away, and sometimes in the past. The operator has little control over the visions, which are easily misinterpreted and are always determined by the Handler. The operator may see visions without meaning to activate this ritual, at the Handler's discretion.

The Closing of the Breach

Complex ritual. Study time: *days; 1D8 SAN.* Activation: *an hour; cost varies.*

A ritual to break a connection with the unnatural. This could be the banishment of a Great Old One or one of their servitors, the ending of an ongoing hypergeometric effect, or the destruction of a gate. General knowledge of the ritual is usually not enough; the operator must extensively research the thing to be banished. That typically requires days of study and costs another 1D4 SAN. Make a note of which effects the operator has researched. For example: "The Closing of the Breach (Gates; Glaaki; Tillinghast Space; Tsathoggua)." Whether this general ritual applies to any given situation is up to the Handler. Some effects or entities require unique rituals for banishing.

In most cases, the WP cost is half that of summoning the entity being banished or enacting the effect being stopped; see **RITUAL DETAILS** on page 168. For example, summoning an entity with POW 30 would cost 22 WP; banishing the entity costs 11 WP. The SAN loss corresponds with that of the closest WP cost. For example, a cost of 11 WP is nearest "12 WP" on the **RITUAL DETAILS** table, so it incurs a 1D6 SAN loss. In most cases, the WP cost can be shared by assistants, paid by permanent POW at 1 POW per 10 WP, or paid by human sacrifice. The Handler always decides which costs can or must be paid to banish a particular effect or entity.

Activating the ritual usually takes about an hour. It requires strange gesticulations and chanted invocations in unknown languages—channeling weird energies and communicating with unseen presences—and must be activated near the effect to be stopped. The operator makes the activation roll and pays the costs as soon as the ritual has begun. In most cases, the thing being assailed cannot come near or interfere with the ritual once the activation roll succeeds—unless the Handler decides otherwise. Unnatural servitors may be similarly restrained. Human cultists certainly are not.

Consciousness Expansion

Complex ritual. Study time: *days; SAN loss 1D100.* Activation: *minutes.*

This ritual is in fact simply an understanding of higher dimensions, and the realization that anyone can raise their consciousness into those dimensions. Learning the ritual requires that the reader have a Science (Mathematics) skill of 50% or more, though no roll is needed. Instead, the target must spend 500 hours studying the math, and then fail a SAN roll.

The operator of this ritual understands that by focusing on the knowledge implied in the numerical string (which has exceptional significance for those trained in math), one can expand one's consciousness into higher dimensions. The ramifications of this are not, however, understood.

If the ritual is attempted once learned, the caster's mind ascends into higher dimensions. His or her body immediately disintegrates. For game purposes, the operator is dead. Witnessing this costs 1/1D6 SAN.

Create Stone Gate

Elaborate ritual. Study time: *weeks; +1 Unnatural, 1D4 SAN.* Activation: *days or weeks; 5 POW, 70 WP, 80 HP, 1D10 SAN.*

There are many versions of the ritual to establish a gate between times or places. This powerful but flawed version requires an arch of carved stone. The structure can be built by anyone who has an appropriate Art or Craft skill at 40% or better. The operator (and any assistants who know the ritual) must spend days or weeks inscribing the carvings that give it power. The operator must succeed at the Ritual Activation roll. The operator and assistants must pay 5 POW and 70 WP between them, and ritually inflict 80 HP damage upon unwilling human sacrifices (or even a single sacrifice over time, if the victim is allowed to heal between injuries). Each participant loses 1D10 SAN plus the loss for violence against sacrificial victims. Once the gate has been successfully crafted and infused with power, it may be opened with an INT by anyone who knows the Create Stone Gate ritual or the Open Gate ritual, at a cost of 1D4 SAN and 1D4 WP. It may be opened to any location on Earth that's well known to the operator. The test is at −20% if the destination is only somewhat familiar, or −40% if the operator has only a photograph or description to work from. Once the gate is open, anyone may pass through at a cost of 1D4 SAN and 1D4 WP, and may return through the same spot at the same cost as long as the gate remains open (usually a few minutes). Each time the gate is opened, there is roughly a 1% chance of some deadly repercussion, such as unnatural cancerous growths in a user or a sudden explosion of energy at the far end.

The Dho-Hna Formula

Elaborate ritual. Study time: *weeks; +1 Unnatural, 1D20 SAN.* Activation: *hours; 30 WP, 1D12 SAN.*

This difficult incantation, in a language that far predates human tongues, opens the operator's awareness to places and events anywhere on Earth. The vision costs 30 WP from the operator, assistants, and/or human sacrifices, and 1D12 SAN. Entities or events seen in the vision may cost further SAN. The operator may select a target destination, and a high or critical activation roll may make the vision more accurate, but the Handler always determines what is seen. Upon establishing the vision, the operator can attempt another activation roll to physically teleport himself or herself to that location, with another cost of 30 WP from the operator, assistants, and/or human sacrifices, and another 1D12 SAN.

Dust of the Thresholds

Elaborate ritual. Study time: *weeks; +1 Unnatural, 1D10 SAN.* Activation: *15 days; 9 WP and 1 SAN per day.*

This "ritual" is the alchemical distillation of certain rare and esoteric ingredients—some say they include the ground-up remains of a mummified pharaoh, but their exact nature is up to the Handler—into an unpleasant, yellowish powder. The process requires days of work in a well-equipped lab. It costs 1 SAN and 9 WP per day for 15 days, which yields 2D4 "doses" of dust. Interrupting the process ruins the batch. If thrown, blown, or dropped upon an entity of extradimensional origin (the exact definition of which is up to the Handler and may not always be reliable), a "dose" of dust has a 10% Lethality rating, which ignores armor and all other protections.

The Elder Sign

Simple ritual. Study time: *hours; 1D4 SAN.* Activation: *varies.*

The Elder Sign is a mystical sigil either drawn in the air by gesture or inscribed upon a sturdy surface. It commands respect from many of those from Outside. When gestured in the air (costing 2 WP and 1 SAN), it prevents such beings from coming within about 10 m of the gesturer for 2D6 turns, provided the gesturer takes no hostile action against them. If an entity is somehow physically forced into that radius, it permanently loses 1D6 POW. As a gesture, the Elder Sign affects a given entity only once in 24 hours.

The Elder Sign may be inscribed permanently on a surface (preferably some especially long-lasting stone or metal; the inscriber must have an appropriate Craft skill at 20% or better) at a cost of 2 POW and 1D6 SAN. Beings from Outside cannot come within about 10 m of it unless the sigil is broken, and they lose 1 POW per turn if somehow forced to come that near. For any except a Great Old One, this POW loss can be fatal.

The most potent engraving of the Elder Sign requires the sacrifice of 100 POW by the engraver (who must sacrifice at least 2 POW personally, and who must have an appropriate Craft skill at 20% or better), ritual chanters, or human sacrifices over the course of 24 hours, at a cost of 1D10 SAN plus the cost of violence to sacrifices. Beings from Outside cannot come within 100 m of the Sign, and lose 1 POW per turn if somehow forced to enter that radius. Even coming within 10 km saps such an entity of 1 WP per hour, until the entity vanishes—banished or destroyed—upon reaching 0 WP. Rituals always fail within that radius.

Unbeknownst to many operators, the Elder Sign suggests that the operator is allied with a specific group of powerful beings from Beyond. Some say those beings lend power to the Elder Sign and perhaps feed upon the unnatural energies that it saps from its victims. It has even been reputed to summon those entities or allow them to possess the corpses of the dead. The exact nature and implications of such allegiance, if it's true, is up to the Handler. As inhuman, unnatural entities, they would certainly be inimical to humanity.

The Handler should decide beforehand if any particular monster is warded off or encouraged by the Sign, or has no reaction to it at all. A successful Unnatural test can usually tell the operator whether the Elder Sign would be efficacious.

Elixir of Infinite Space

Elaborate ritual. Study time: *weeks; +1 Unnatural, 1D10 SAN.* Activation—brewing: *six days; 3 WP and 1 SAN per dose brewed.* Activation—consuming: *a turn, 1 WP, 1D4 SAN.*

The alchemical preparation of this elixir takes six days and requires notoriously strange and rare ingredients. Each "dose" brewed costs the operator 3 WP per day and 1 SAN at the end. Drinking a "dose" of the elixir makes the drinker immune to harmful environments and effects of the Handler's choosing, such as outer space and deep waters. That immunity costs the drinker 1D4 SAN overall, and 1 WP per hour. At zero WP, or upon returning to a safe environment, the drinker's immunity wears off.

Exaltation of the Flesh

Simple ritual. Study time: *hours; 1D6 SAN.* Activation: *a minute; costs vary.*

This minute-long incantation invokes Shub-Niggurath and Yog-Sothoth, amid many other syllables of apparent gibberish. Different versions come from different traditions; one German ritual embeds consecrated bread under the skin. The ritual imbues the operator's flesh with the power to resist harm. The operator chooses how much protection to seek:

Armor	WP Cost	SAN Cost
2	6	1
4	9	1D4
6	12	1D6
8	15	1D8

Each time the operator takes damage, whether it penetrates the ritual's protection or not, the Armor drops by one point. As long as the operator has a single Armor point from this ritual, Lethality rolls against the operator automatically fail, and the ritual's Armor protects against their HP damage. The ritual protects against every kind of harm that reduces hit points: physical injuries, flames, or even poison. Twenty-four hours after the ritual, any remaining Armor points granted by the ritual fade.

Exchange Personalities

Simple ritual. Study time: *days; 1D8 SAN.* Activation: *varies.*

Mastered by some cults of Shub-Niggurath, this ritual transfers the mind and "life-glow" of the operator to another character's brain. The operator must gaze hypnotically at the target for a turn, spend 3 WP, and overcome the target in an opposed POW test. The switch costs 1 SAN for the operator and 0/1D4 for the target, and lasts one turn. A target who loses no SAN may think it was just a fleeting dissociative episode or a passing fancy.

With subsequent invasions, the swap lasts longer but with steeper costs (see **PERSONALITY EXCHANGES** on this page). Over time, the operator can make the switch from far away, and may come to sense the thoughts and actions of the host even when not intruding. An operator who has spent at least 4 POW invading a particular host has the option to make the next invasion permanent at a cost of 1 POW more. A permanent swap costs 1D10 SAN for the operator and 1D20 SAN for the target.

A body slain while hosting an exchanged "life-glow" may stir and move, in some cases long after death, rotting but animated. Whether this happens, and when, are up to the Handler.

Exorcism

Elaborate ritual. Study time: *weeks; +1 Unnatural, 1D10 SAN.* Activation: *an hour; costs vary.*

This hour-long ritual forces a possessing entity—whether an unnatural being or an intruding human mind—out of the mind of the subject. The WP and SAN costs depend on the POW of the possessing entity, as if conducting a summoning (see **RITUAL DETAILS** on page 168). Some or all of the WP may be paid by assistants who know the ritual, and/or by a human sacrifice. If the Ritual Activation roll succeeds, and the total WP spent exceed the WP of the possessing entity, the possessing entity must depart. Otherwise, the operator loses the spent WP and the entity remains.

>> Personality Exchanges

Duration	Maximum Range	Prior Exchanges Required	Cost	SAN Loss: Operator	SAN Loss: Victim
1 turn	Nearby (10 m)	None	4 WP	1	0/1D4
1 minute	Local (100 m)	1	4 WP	1	1D6
1 hour	In sight (1 km)	2	4 WP	1D4	1D8
1 day	Distant (10 km)	3	1 POW	1D6	1D10
Permanent	Far (100 km)	4 (each for 1 day)	1 POW	1D10	1D20

Fascination

Simple ritual. Study time: *hours; 1D8 SAN.* Activation: *a turn; 1D6 SAN; 3 WP per attempt.*

This powerful ritual requires only that the operator speak calmly to the subject (that is, not in the middle of a fight and not beyond ordinary speaking distance) and takes only a single turn to attempt. If the Ritual Activation roll succeeds, the operator can attempt once per turn to entrance the subject with an opposed POW test. Each attempt costs 3 WP. Success renders the subject motionless and insensate, with only autonomic processes functioning, for up to an hour. Only physical assault or some other overwhelming event shocks the subject out of it in the meantime. If the POW roll fails, the subject can attempt an Unnatural test to realize exactly what is happening.

Finding

Simple ritual. Study time: *hours; 1D4 SAN.* Activation: *a minute; 4 WP, 1 SAN.*

A minute-long chant invokes the names of helper spirits and Great Old Ones including Tsathoggua and Yog-Sothoth. Some versions are taught in African or Caribbean languages—no language skill is needed; mastery of the ritual includes rote memorization of the phrases—while others come from European "cunning folk" traditions. It costs 4 WP and 1 SAN. For 3D6 minutes, it adds a +40% bonus to rolls to find something that the operator has seen or touched before, if the lost thing is within 100 m.

The First Secret

Complex ritual. Study time: *days; 1D8 SAN.* Activation: *minutes; 10 WP, 1D6 SAN.*

This ritual invokes "the sleeper, bane to the horned god G'laak" and costs 10 WP and 1D6 SAN. Despite the invocation, it brings the operator into communion with Glaaki. This often hints at courses of action to fulfill the goals of Glaaki and its loathsome cult, though the operator may think their purpose is entirely different. If the operator has 0 SAN, invoking with the First Secret lures him or her to Glaaki's nearest haunt to willingly become one of the Glaakeen.

Healing Balm

Simple ritual. Study time: *hours; 1D4 SAN.* Activation: *turns, 6 WP, 1 SAN.*

This brief invocation of Shub-Niggurath, the All-Mother ("Iä! Shub-Niggurath!"), causes injuries to swiftly heal. The subject recovers 1D4 HP every turn for 1D4 turns. The operator must spend 6 WP (or 1 permanent POW), and it costs the operator, the subject, and all witnesses 1 SAN each. Make a note that the subject has undergone healing from this ritual, and keep a tally of how many times. There may, eventually, be a price to pay: a bizarre mutation or some deeper expression of the power and incomprehensible will of Shub-Niggurath. When that price must be paid and what form it takes remain up to the Handler. They are not described in the texts which teach the ritual.

Immortal Messenger

Complex ritual. Study time: *days; 1D8 SAN.* Activation: *hours; 1 POW, 1D6 SAN.*

This long chant invokes the Immortal Messenger, an intermediary between the operator and the unseen world. The operator or an assistant must sacrifice 1 POW permanently, and the operator and each assistant loses 1D6 SAN. For each assistant, the Ritual Activation roll receives a +5% bonus. If successful, the ritual summons Nyarlathotep in a guise or avatar suitable to the operator's traditions.

Infallible Suggestion

Simple ritual. Study time: *hours; 1D8 SAN.* Activation: *two turns; 8 WP, 1D4 SAN.*

This ritual requires strange gestures and a quiet chant in some prehuman tongue. The chant is alien to any linguist. The operator must overcome the target in an opposed POW test. If that succeeds, the ritual costs 8 WP (or 1 POW) and 1D4 SAN. For one turn, the victim willingly obeys any command given by the operator. Commanding a victim to commit murder, suicide, or some other awful act costs the operator the same SAN as it costs the victim.

Leaves of Time

Complex ritual. Study time: *days; 1D10 SAN.* Activation: *an hour; 1D4 WP; SAN cost varies.*

This ritual includes a recipe for a drug called Liao—the ingredients are up to the Handler but should be esoteric and rare—and instructions for its use. After taking the drug in tea or in a swallowed pellet, the operator meditates upon formulae that evoke advanced mathematics and ancient occultism. If the Ritual Activation roll succeeds, the operator perceives spacetime as a single entity, as if viewed from outside, and the operator's mind drifts to other times and places for an hour. The reverie costs 1D4 WP. The first time under the effects of the drug, the operator loses 1D10 SAN and gains one point of Unnatural skill per point of SAN lost. Subsequent reveries cost 1 SAN each.

The operator remains conscious, and can hear and speak, and can be brought out of the reverie by violent shaking. The operator can voluntarily break the reverie by failing at a POW test, making one attempt per turn.

The operator can approach the vicinity of a desired event by succeeding at a POW test. With a critical success, the operator sees the event precisely. With a failure, the Handler chooses a time and place to experience. With a fumble, or if at any time the operator goes temporarily insane while under the influence of the drug, the operator is drawn so deeply into time as to encounter one of the Great Old Ones or their awful progeny. That incurs its own SAN loss, and the terrible, acrid stench of them can be sensed in the physical world as the boundaries between times weaken. Such entities sense the operator's mind. If the operator fails to break the reverie within 1D6 turns, the unnatural entities expand the connection with the operator's mind and break through into the world, either immediately or at some future point of the Handler's choice.

Lure the Hungerer

Complex ritual. Study time: *days; 1D8 SAN.* Activation: *6 WP, 3 HP, 1D4 SAN.*

The "hungerer" is an extradimensional horror that appears out of nowhere to seize prey and vanish again—a dimensional shambler. This summoning requires about fifteen minutes of chanting bizarre, seemingly nonsensical phrases and 3 HP worth of ritualized bloodletting from a living victim. The damage may be inflicted upon either the operator or an assistant or victim, as long as the sufferer is present for the entire ritual. Allowing the ritual to place the operator's mind in the spaces necessary to capture a shambler's attention and interest costs 6 WP (or 1 POW) and 1D4 SAN. Once the feaster appears, the ritual changes tone and phrasing as the operator attempts to assert control, according to the usual rules for summonings.

Meditation Upon the Favored Ones

Complex ritual. Study time: *days; 1D8 SAN.* Activation: *an hour; 9 WP, 1D4 SAN.*

To succeed, this ritual must be undertaken in an area frequented by the mi-go: high woodland hills marked by stones with unknown hieroglyphs, isolated mines dug so long ago that they are mistaken for natural caves, remote temples where they are served by mad monks, deserts where no sane human dares to tread, and so on. The ritual is mostly gibberish to those who have no Unnatural skill; others recognize invocations to unnatural powers in the weird language said to derive from the thoughts of Great Cthulhu. Some versions involve lighting bright fires with strange chemicals to create shifting colors. Typically, a handful of the mi-go appear after less than an hour of chanting. The ritual costs 9 WP or 1 permanent POW. Assistants may contribute WP by echoing the operator's speech, even if they don't know the ritual. The operator and assistants lose 1D4 SAN, in addition to the SAN loss for encountering the mi-go.

Mountain and Sea

Complex ritual. Study time: *days; 1D10 SAN.* Activation: *an hour; 6 WP; SAN loss varies.*

This incantation establishes mental contact with antediluvian entities said to be spawned from or akin to Great Cthulhu: entities endlessly asleep in deep oceanic tombs or which have been entombed in the earth for hundreds of millions of years. To take effect, the ritual must be activated near an area where one of these entities lurks. Otherwise, the Ritual Activation roll automatically fails. If the entity is underground, the ritual is often accompanied by an earthquake or an avalanche as the entity stirs. The mental contact is tenuous and brief, rarely resulting in anything like communication, likely only to inspire mad visions in the operator. It costs 1D6 SAN.

If the entity is capable of rising briefly to the outer world—always up to the Handler—then the operator's SAN loss is 1D6/1D20 as a purer mental connection is established. The entity typically withdraws again to the depths, driven by whatever forces restrain its kind while the time is not yet right.

Obscure Memory

Simple ritual. Study time: *hours; 1D4 SAN.* Activation: *one turn; 3 WP, 1 SAN.*

With weird passes of the hand and a brief chanted phrase, this ritual can block the target's memory. It takes only one turn to activate, and costs 3 WP and 1 SAN. The operator must overcome the target in an opposed POW test; if the effort fails, the operator can try again at a further cost of 3 WP. The operator may instruct the target to forget one specific, brief event. This does not change the target's skills or known rituals, and it cannot undo SAN loss. A particularly frightening event may linger in the target's subconscious and nightmares even after the memory has been obscured. A single use of the ritual can affect multiple targets, costing 3 WP each and allowing each to oppose the POW test.

Open Gate

Simple ritual. Study time: *days; 1D6 SAN.* Activation: *a turn; 1 WP, 1 SAN.*

This meditation upon impossible angles in space-time opens a pre-existing unnatural gate, such as one created with the Create Stone Gate ritual (see page 177). Once the gate is open, anyone may pass through for a few minutes. The costs of using the gate are described in the ritual used to create it.

One Who Passes the Gateways

Elaborate ritual. Study time: *weeks; 1D10 SAN.* Activation: *hours; 9 WP, 1D4 SAN.*

This ritual consists of a litany that must be intoned within five concentric circles of fire or phosphorous. The operator's spirit leaves its sleeping body and travels alien realms where much wisdom may be gained, though such experiences may incur further SAN loss. The operator must concentrate, requiring a POW test. If it fumbles, the operator strays and severs the link between spirit and body, leaving behind a permanently blank biological vessel devoid of mind.

Pentagram of Power

Elaborate ritual. Study time: *weeks; +1 Unnatural, 1D12 SAN.* Activation: *two hours; 12 WP; 1D6 SAN or more.*

The operator inscribes a pentagram in chalk or paint, in a circle surrounded by four circles, then imbues the design with power by animal or human sacrifice. The process takes about two hours and costs 1D6 SAN, plus the SAN loss for the violence of the sacrifice. It costs 12 WP, but each HP inflicted in the sacrifice reduces the WP cost by one, to a minimum of 1. If the Ritual Activation roll succeeds, the pentagram confers a +20% bonus to the operator's attempts to control a summoned entity, or +40% with a human sacrifice. Some Western grimoires include perversions of this ritual, which may claim to be more potent than they actually are.

Petrification

Simple ritual. Study time: *days; 1D4 SAN.* Activation: *days; 30 WP, 1D12 SAN.*

Found in the Book of Eibon, this "ritual" is a chemical preparation of barium sulphate, calcium chloride, and certain acids and catalytics in precise proportions, augmented with invocations to Tsathoggua and Shub-Niggurath. With the right ingredients and equipment, preparing the solution takes less than an hour, costing 30 WP (each point of permanent POW spent reduces the WP cost by 10) and 1D12 SAN. The solution's strange taste is distinct when mixed with water but can be masked with wine. (In tea or coffee, it forms a precipitate that has no effect.) Drinking the solution has a 30% Lethality rating as the solution spreads calcium and barium salts through the body and replaces living cells with mineral matter, transforming the victim into a perfect statue. Poisoning a victim with the solution incurs its own SAN cost for violence.

The Powder of Ibn-Ghazi

Elaborate ritual. Study time: *weeks; +1 Unnatural, 1D10 SAN.* Activation: *6 or more WP, 1 SAN.*

This "ritual" is the alchemical distillation of certain rare and esoteric ingredients—their exact nature is up to the Handler—into a fine, silvery powder. The process takes a full day in a well-equipped alchemy lab. It costs 1 SAN and 6 or more WP, yielding one "dose" of the powder per WP spent. Only the operator may spend WP in the preparation. If it is blown, thrown, or dropped over the surface of an unnaturally invisible entity or hypergeometric effect, the unseen thing becomes fully visible to human eyes for 2D4 turns.

Prayer to the Dark Man

Complex ritual. Study time: *days; 1D8 SAN.* Activation: *13 months; 1 POW, 1D6 or more SAN.*

This ritual, practiced by European witch-cults from the 17th century onward, requires that a fixed site be consecrated with blood sacrifice (preferably human), once on each night of the new moon for 13 months. The sacrifices must be conducted with a specially prepared ritual knife and bowl. Some versions require drinking the sacrifice's blood. At each sacrifice, at least two worshippers (not including the sacrifice) must be present who are willing to give their lives for the Dark Man, though they need not know the ritual.

Upon the 13th sacrifice, and at each following sacrifice on the new moon, successful Ritual Activation roll causes the Dark Man to step out of the shadows: an avatar of Nyarlathotep that looks like a tall, sardonic man in black clothes or robes, usually hooded, of indistinct ethnicity, and with matte-black skin. Sometimes his feet are cloven hooves. His manifestation costs 1 POW from the operator or an assistant (it cannot be paid by a sacrifice), 1D6 SAN from

the operator and each assistant, and 1/1D4 SAN from everyone who sees the Dark Man. The Dark Man traditionally offers the knowledge of secrets or rituals, or the services of a rat-thing familiar (see **WITCHES' FAMILIARS** on page 230). Whether he requires the deaths of any of his worshippers is up to the Handler. The Dark Man cannot be bound or controlled.

This ritual can be used to deconsecrate a site that is already hallowed to the Dark Man. This requires summoning the Dark Man as described earlier, and then asking him to depart forever from that place. That costs 3 POW from the operator and any assistants (not from a sacrifice), but it does not require a separate activation roll and costs no additional SAN. The Dark Man typically vanishes in mocking laughter. If the operator refuses to pay the cost, the Dark Man may transform into a horrifying, monstrous shape or cause the operator to vanish forever.

Preserve Living Brain

Elaborate ritual. Study time: *weeks; +1 Unnatural, 1D12 SAN.* Activation: *12 WP, 1D6 SAN.*

This "ritual" requires a chemistry laboratory, where the operator mixes unnatural ingredients using techniques that are as much witchcraft and alchemy as science. The effort costs 12 WP and 1D6 SAN. The result is a weird, grayish-blue solution that is injected into cerebrospinal fluid to keep a human brain alive after the death of the body. The fluid must be refreshed every few days. The body responds to the brain's commands, but begins to decay. Low temperatures can slow decay, but preservative chemicals cause the brain to die. The brain can be preserved indefinitely without a body if surgically removed (requiring a Surgery roll by a character with at least 80% skill) and immersed in the weird fluid. As a disembodied brain, the subject loses 1D20 SAN per day. The daily loss is reduced to 1D8 if the brain is somehow given sensory input.

The Primal Lay

Complex ritual. Study time: *days; 1D4 SAN.* Activation: *20 minutes; 9 WP, 1D4 SAN.*

This ritual requires about 20 minutes' chanting meditation and, in most versions, powerful hallucinogens. It costs 9 WP (or the permanent expenditure of 1 POW) and 1D4 SAN. It opens the senses to time and space. In effect, the operator can experience the past or future of a given location, no more than an hour in either direction. The experiences may incur their own SAN costs. Once the ritual takes effect, the operator must make a POW test. If it fumbles, the vision sweeps out to unthinkably distant times and places, likely costing far more SAN, and attracts the attention of strange, other-dimensional entities. Such attracted entities are never seen, but forever haunt the operator's steps, causing unwitting fear in dogs and sensitive souls.

Raise From Essential Saltes

Elaborate ritual. Study time: *weeks; +1 Unnatural, 1D20 SAN.* Activation: *hours; 22 WP, 1D10 SAN.*

This infamous ritual reduces a corpse to strange, dull greenish ashes ("essential saltes"), which may later be reformed into a living, healthy body. The duration of such "essential saltes" is uncertain, but some have been perfectly preserved for centuries and even millennia.

The ritual of reducing a corpse to "essential saltes" is informed by ancient alchemy, medieval occultism, and invocations to Yog-Sothoth. It costs 22 WP, usually expended over a number of days in an alchemical laboratory where unnatural powers are invoked and channeled, sometimes with spectacular effects. It costs 1D10 SAN.

It is important that the entire corpse be available. An ancient, desiccated body is usually acceptable, as is a body that has been dismembered, as long as it is complete. But if too much of the corpse has been eaten away by vermin or has rotted badly, it can be revived not as a living, intelligent person but a gibbering, horrifying monstrosity (see **LIVELIEST AWFULNESS** on page 210).

Restoring "essential saltes" to life is a somewhat simpler process, though it requires strange incantations and great quantities of human blood. It costs 3 WP and, again, 1D10 SAN. A revived subject loses 1D20 SAN from the memory of death and the incomprehensibly unnatural experience of awakening from it, and must feed on human blood for days afterward to survive.

A revived subject may be reduced back to "essential saltes" by reciting the restoration incantation in reverse. That takes a few minutes and costs 3 WP and 1D10 SAN. The subject is helpless to resist, unless he or she can physically silence the operator.

Reanimation Formula

Elaborate ritual. Study time: *weeks; +1 Unnatural, 1D10 SAN.* Activation: *a day; 9 WP, 1D4 SAN.*

This "ritual" requires a chemistry laboratory, where the operator mixes unnatural ingredients using techniques that are as much witchcraft and alchemy as science. The process takes a day and costs 9 WP and 1D4 SAN. The result is a weird, blue solution, sufficient for one use, which may be preserved for a few months if carefully refrigerated. The formula, injected into the brain of a corpse, within a few minutes animates it to a rough semblance of life. If the injection takes place soon after death, there is a small chance that it retains some of the intelligence it had in life. The chance equals the POW that the corpse had in life (roll the POW or lower on percentile dice), minus one POW per minute that has passed since death. If the roll succeeds, the reanimated corpse has an INT score equal to its old INT or the die roll, whichever is lower, and does not decay further. Otherwise the corpse is exactly like a zombie (see **ZOMBIES** on page 231). If the roll fails, or it has been too long after death, the resuscitated corpse is mindless and continues to decay. Either way, the formula confers no control over the reanimated corpse. Injecting the formula into a corpse in any other way has no effect. Injected into a living creature, it is a poison with a speed of 1D6 turns and a Lethality rating of 30%.

Release Breath

Simple ritual. Study time: *hours; 1D4 SAN.* Activation: *one turn; 5 WP, 1D4 SAN or more.*

Usually learned in African traditions, this short chant is punctuated by the ritual killing of a small animal. It costs 5 WP and 1D4 SAN. If the activation roll succeeds, it causes one zombie within 10 m to collapse and decay, released from the effects of the Zombie ritual (described on page 187). It has no effect on zombies created by any other means.

See the Other Side

Simple ritual. Study time: *hours; 1D6 SAN.* Activation: *turns; 3 WP, 1 SAN.*

The operator speaks an invocation that sounds like gibberish, makes weird signs and passes in the air before an unnatural gate, spends 3 WP, and loses 1 SAN. For about a minute, the operator can see what is on the other side of the gate. Whether anything on the far side of the gate can see the operator is up to the Handler.

Song of Power

Simple ritual. Study time: *hours; 1D6 SAN.* Activation: *turns; 1 POW, 1D4 SAN.*

This ritual chant costs 1D4 SAN. If the activation roll succeeds, the operator permanently loses 1 POW, but temporarily gains 20 WP. The extra WP can boost the operator's score beyond its usual maximum. They last until they are spent, but are lost immediately to sleep or unconsciousness.

Soothing Song

Simple ritual. Study time: *hours; 1D4 SAN.* Activation: *minutes; 6 WP, 1 SAN.*

Sometimes found in African traditions, and in colonial New England witchcraft as a means to withstand torture, this ritual chant costs 1 SAN and 6 WP. For about an hour, the subject feels no physical or mental pain or distress. The ritual alleviates the effects of temporary insanity or an acute episode of a disorder. It has no effect on permanent insanity; the subject's mind has changed too severely to be soothed. Nor does it reduce damage in any way.

Speaking Dream

Complex ritual. Study time: *days; 1D6 SAN.* Activation: *minutes; 22 WP, 1D4 SAN.*

Just before going to sleep, the operator thinks of another person, utters a low, repetitive chant, and stares into a hypnotic focal point such as the light of a candle. If both the operator and recipient are asleep, they communicate within dreams and may share the WP cost. Communications must be simple.

Speech of Birds and Beasts

Simple ritual. Study time: *hours; 1D4 SAN.* Activation: *turns; 9 WP, 1D4 SAN.*

This strange, brief chant, which sometimes requires a potent hallucinogen, alters the operator's perceptions. It makes the cries and snuffles of natural animals comprehensible and allows animals to understand the operator's speech. This ritual also serves to calm an animal, making it amenable to the operator's wishes. It does not affect the animal's intelligence. Beasts and birds are driven by instinct and most have remarkably short memories for any notions more complex than "edible" and "dangerous," but many can be trained for simple tricks. This ritual allows extraordinarily quick training.

Storm and Stillness

Complex ritual. Study time: *days; 1D8 SAN.* Activation: *minutes; costs vary.*

This invocation to "spirits of the earth and the air" (called the "Sabaoth" in one version, but having nothing to do with Judaism's heavenly hosts) blends medieval occultism and unnatural, untranslatable phrases. It changes the weather around the operator. It costs 10 WP and 1D6 SAN for a minor, likely change (such as rain from a cloudy sky); 20 WP and 1D10 SAN for a significant, unlikely change (rain from a clear sky in a rainy season); 30 WP and 1D12 SAN for a major, surprising change (a thunderstorm in the dry season); or 40 WP and 1D20 SAN for an inexplicable change (a hurricane forms or dies for no reason). The WP cost may be paid by assistants who know the ritual and by human sacrifices, or by spending 1 permanent POW instead of 10 WP.

Swarm

Simple ritual. Study time: *hours; 1D4 SAN.* Activation: *minutes; 3 WP, 1 SAN.*

This ritual, chanted near fish-inhabited waters, causes fish (any fish under 10 lbs) to be drawn towards and to swarm the operator for 10 minutes. If the operator is on shore, the fish beach themselves and die. Seeing this costs 0/1 SAN due to the unnatural. Whether other versions of this ritual affect other kinds of animals—insects, birds, whales, humans—is unknown.

The Voorish Sign

Simple ritual. Study time: *hours; 1D4 SAN.* Activation: *one turn; 3 WP, 1 SAN.*

An operator who makes this strange series of hand gestures can briefly see things that are invisible due to their extradimensional or otherworldly nature: unseen entities, unnatural gates, indications of ongoing hypergeometric effects, and so on.

Whispers of the Dead

Complex ritual. Study time: *days; 1D8 SAN.* Activation: *costs vary.*

The operator enters a deep meditation, sleep, or other profoundly altered state of mind—often assisted by powerful drugs or ecstatic, violent rituals—and receives a fleeting, psychic communion with an unnatural entity. Communion with a Great Old One costs 1 POW, permanently, and 1D8 SAN. Communion with a lesser entity costs 8 WP and 1D4 SAN if its POW is 16 or higher, or 4 WP and 1 SAN if its POW is 15 or lower.

Communion with a Great Old One is typically fleeting, especially one that is torporous. It leaves the operator with a vague sense of the Old One's will and desires, so inscrutably alien as to entirely defy rational interpretation. What that sense implies is entirely up to the Handler.

Communion with a lesser entity may be more revealing. How much sense the operator can make of the inhuman, unnatural thoughts of such such entities is up to the Handler. One with high Unnatural skill and low SAN understands the most.

The core of this ritual is the same regardless of the entity. But it requires techniques peculiar to the entity being contacted. After learning this ritual for one entity, learning the secrets needed to commune with another entity usually requires at least another day of study and costs another 1D6 SAN. Make a note of the particular versions an operator knows, such as "Whispers of the Dead (Cthulhu, Dagon, Mi-Go)." Whether a version of the ritual applies to any given entity is up to the Handler.

Winged Steed

Complex ritual. Study time: *days; 1D6 SAN.* Activation: *an hour; 10 WP, 1D4 SAN.*

This summoning must be conducted outdoors, at night. A ritual chant is punctuated by weird tones sounded from a whistle of bone. The ritual costs 1D4 SAN and 10 WP. The WP may be paid by the operator, by assistants who know the ritual, and/or by a human sacrifice who must drink a peculiar, mind-altering poison. Conducting the ritual on the winter solstice confers a +20% bonus to the activation roll. If the roll succeeds, a winged servitor (see **WINGED SERVITORS** on page 230) flies down from space, tame and compliant. The servitor may be mounted like a bizarre steed, and flies the operator swiftly through the gaps between space and time to the court of Azathoth. To force the servitor to do anything else, the operator must control it as usual with a summoning.

Withering

Simple ritual. Study time: *hours; 1D4 SAN.* Activation: *one turn; 12 WP, 3 HP, 1D8 SAN.*

This chanted ritual withers flesh and blasts bones, inflicting 3 HP damage to the operator and 1D20 HP damage to a living target. The target must be nearby and in sight. The ritual can be enacted on a target who is not in sight by burning a small effigy that contains a sample of the target's DNA. This costs another 7 WP, but the WP may be spent over any amount of time while constructing and ritually consecrating the effigy.

Zombie

Elaborate ritual. Study time: *weeks; +1 Unnatural; 1D12 SAN.* Activation: *one hour; 6 WP, 1D12 SAN.*

This ritual, usually learned in African or voodoo traditions, must be enacted upon the body of someone who was slain by a specially prepared poison (which incurs its own SAN loss for violence). The poison is a powder derived from tetrodotoxin and other esoteric ingredients, including human remains. It must be inhaled, and has a speed of 1D6 minutes and a Lethality rating of 20%. Symptoms include numbness, shock, and paralysis. The body must be recovered or exhumed and the ritual enacted about 72 hours after death. The ritual takes about an hour. It requires a human sacrifice (which incurs its own SAN loss for violence) and an infusion of the sacrificial victim's blood and energy into the corpse. If the activation roll succeeds, the poisoned subject rises as a blood-hungry zombie (see **ZOMBIES** on page 231) that is subject to the commands of the operator that raised it. Other versions of this ritual exist; an Icelandic ritual is said to reanimate the dead ("draugr") with more intelligence and will than other zombies.

Unnatural Entities

To most of humanity, misled by our stewardship during an interregnum between epochs of inhuman conquest, mankind seems ascendant and alone. To those in the know, we exist at a swirling nexus of spacetime awash with consciousnesses, beings, entities, and creatures.

Entities exist between the spaces we know, in the corridors of time, or even in inner-space, within the recesses of the human mind. Others defy such simple explanations and simply insert themselves into our narrow, four-dimensional world, rending reality as they come and go.

Below is an accounting of some of the entities that Delta Green has faced.

OPINT: Inhuman Stat Tests

Many entities have stats with scores of 20 or higher. Stat tests for such entities work a little differently than for stats on human scales. As a rule of thumb, an entity with a stat at 20 or higher succeeds at any stat test except with a roll of 100, which fails and fumbles. It gets a critical success on any success with matching digits, and with any roll equal to or less than the stat's value. For example, an entity with a stat of 30 gets a critical success on any success with double digits and any roll of 01–30; an ordinary success on any other roll except 100; and a fumble only on a roll of 100.

Known Alien Intelligences

The following represent a fraction of the threats contacted, confronted or destroyed by Delta Green since its inception. Almost all interaction with alien intelligences has been in the form of violence, though a few standout cases of "the enemy of my enemy is my friend" might be found in organizational memory. Make no mistake, however—Delta Green's mission is to eliminate all alien intelligence.

Colours Out of Space

"For the terror had not faded with the silhouette, and in a fearsome instant of deeper darkness the watchers saw wriggling at that treetop height a thousand tiny points of faint and unhallowed radiance, tipping each bough like the fire of St. Elmo or the flames that came down on the apostles' heads at Pentecost. It was a monstrous constellation of unnatural light, like a glutted swarm of corpse-fed fireflies dancing hellish sarabands over an accursed marsh; and its colour was that same nameless intrusion which Ammi had come to recognise and dread."

—H.P. Lovecraft, "The Colour Out of Space"

The "colours" are an immaterial species of unknown origin, which may use our dimension as a nesting ground to nurse their offspring. The infection always begins in the same manner: with a meteorite either falling from space or being recovered from somewhere buried in the Earth. Once this rock is brought within range of living things, it "hatches."

The nascent colour begins as an invisible, deleterious effect on plants and animals, including humans. Living creatures within a few meters of the meteorite suffer an ever-growing malaise. This radius grows over time. Plants grow wild at first, and then black and cancerous before collapsing to grey dust. Animals waste away, become ill-tempered, and finally collapse and die. Humans grow at first anxious, then obsessive, and finally insane. In the end, if the humans remain, they perish—either by violence or biological failure. Those living things removed from the area affected by the colour return to biological norms after a short period of time.

As this drain occurs, the colour grows in size, power, and effect. After a certain amount of time the colour can hunt, exhibiting behavior which indicates it possesses at least a rudimentary intellect. Eventually, once it reaches full power, and all living things in the area are drained, the colour manifests as an unearthly halo of bizarre light. It then ascends into space or another dimension.

Colour Out of Space

POW 1–35

ARMOR: See **TRANSCENDENT.**

SKILLS: Flight 20%.

DRIFTING FLIGHT: The colour can drift and move through space, creeping forward like a mist (even against the wind), but its movement is significantly slower than a running human. It can seep through any gap that allows a glimmer of light.

MALAISE (1 POW+): Each day the colour "feeds" on an ever-growing radius of living things, it gains 1 POW point. When it has 20 POW, the colour becomes ambulant, and seeks out and feasts on living prey. Anyone who remains in the colour's hunting range for an entire day loses 0/1 SAN.

NONCORPOREAL: The colour is not a physical entity and has no DEX score. Use its POW in place of DEX to determine when it acts each turn.

POWER FEAST (20 POW+): When ambulant, the colour can move and "attack," appearing as a glowing mote of unearthly light which slowly approaches the target and strips it of POW. This is treated as a contest between the colour's POW and the target's POW. If the colour wins, it absorbs 1 POW from the target. The target loses 1/1D6 SAN and collapses, unconscious. If the colour loses, it retreats into the earth. This attack can occur when the target is asleep, in which case the target wakes the next morning suffering the effects. Whether it succeeds or fails, this attack can only happen once per night.

TRANSCENDENT: The colour is beyond all physical attacks, though experimental physics might conceivably cause it harm. Hypergeometry damages it normally.

SAN LOSS: 0/1D6.

OPINT: Surprise Attacks and Unnatural Entities

It is up to the Handler whether the *Agent's Handbook* rules for surprise attacks apply to a given unnatural entity. If the unnatural creature is human-like, the answer might be yes. However, many unnatural entities are no more vulnerable to surprise attacks than to ordinary attacks. Keep the following in mind:

- **GO FOR THE VITALS?:** Just because something is humanoid in form does not mean it lives or dies like a human. Some entities that have the superficial appearance of a human contain many secrets—extra organs or reinforced bones, for instance—that make them inhumanly resilient. Stabbing a human-like thing in the neck, eye or heart might have no effect at all. Its brain might be in a strange location, or not in our physical universe at all.
- **IT WASN'T SURPRISED:** The thing from beyond might be able to see in strange wavelengths, scan its surroundings with sonar, or sense the microvolt electrical activity in an Agent's brain. Sneaking up on something whose biology is based on fluorine instead of carbon might be more difficult than the Agent thinks.
- **BEYOND VIOLENCE:** Many entities are simply very hard to harm. They were born in some alternate dimension of immense gravity, heat or power that makes earthly explosives and weapons seem as mild as a summer's day. As a rule of thumb, any unnatural entity with an Armor rating of 5 or more is completely immune to the usual advantages that come with a surprise attack.

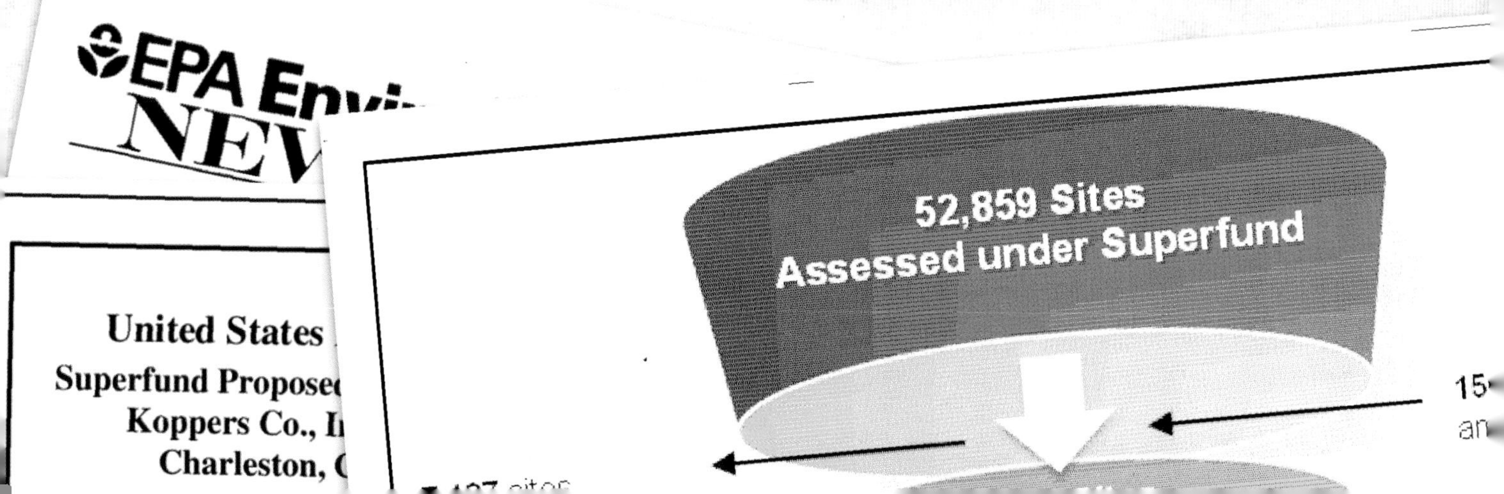

OPINT: Defensive Qualities

Unnatural entities have many kinds of protection for mundane, physical threats. Some are hard to destroy for their sheer size. Some are unnaturally resilient to specific kinds of trauma, or wholly immune to them. Here are the most common varieties.

- **TRANSCENDENT:** Transcendent entities are entirely immune to physical damage. This might mean they exist partly in dimensions we barely perceive, or are organized such that mere excesses of physical force do them no harm. Nothing of this Earth is transcendent. Only through the use of unnatural techniques, under extremely dangerous and limited situations, can humans become transcendent. Some entities' transcendence protects only against certain kinds of harm. The Handler makes the final call as to what this defense does or does not cover. Unless the entity's description says otherwise, hypergeometry inflicts full damage upon it.
- **OUT OF PHASE:** Some entities weave in and out of our physical space from moment to moment. A damage or Lethality roll with an even number inflicts damage as usual. A roll with an odd number passes harmlessly through, inflicting no damage. Unless the entity's description says otherwise, hypergeometry always inflicts full damage upon it.
- **UNCANNY MATTER:** Entities of this type are made of non-terrene matter or are from alternate, more punishing dimensions, making them all but immune to physical harm. Lethality rolls against a creature of uncanny matter always fail, and the creature takes no more than one HP of damage from any attack. Some entities have this defense only against certain kinds of harm. Unless the entity's description says otherwise, hypergeometry inflicts full damage upon it.
- **PERSISTENT:** An entity of this type is imbued with unnatural vitality. A successful Lethality roll destroys it, but it takes only half HP damage from attacks (including failed Lethality rolls). Some entities are persistent only against certain kinds of harm. Unless the entity's description says otherwise, hypergeometry inflicts full damage upon it.
- **RESILIENT:** Due to size or unnatural toughness, an entity of this type can withstand overwhelming force. A successful Lethality roll does not destroy a resilient entity, but inflicts HP damage equal to the Lethality rating.
- **HUGE:** No Lethality roll is required against a huge target; it simply takes HP damage equal to the Lethality rating, whether the roll succeeds or fails. A creature need not be unnatural to be huge. A rhino, blue whale, or elephant would be a huge target.
- **UNNATURAL BIOLOGY:** Some entities' bodies are arranged so strangely that an Agent can't tell what parts may be most vulnerable. It's not possible to attempt a called shot to increase damage, an option described in the Agent's Handbook. Attacks otherwise have the usual effects.
- **ARMOR:** Reduce the HP damage by the listed Armor amount. A successful Lethality roll destroys the entity.

Deep Ones (Greater)

> *"The Deep Ones could never be destroyed, even though the palaeogean magic of the forgotten Old Ones might sometimes check them. For the present they would rest; but some day, if they remembered, they would rise again for the tribute Great Cthulhu craved."*
>
> —H.P. Lovecraft, "The Shadow Over Innsmouth"

The Deep Ones are an ancient, non-human culture inhabiting Earth's oceans. It is unclear if the Deep Ones are an alien species or are native to Earth. They interbreed with humanity and they have infiltrated and corrupted many human communities, but their memory stretches far into the past, far beyond the dimmest recollections of human civilization.

Unbeknownst to most (including Delta Green), the Deep Ones are divided into two classes: Greater and Lesser Deep Ones. Lesser Deep Ones are most often encountered by humans, and are thick-bodied, frog-like, loping creatures. Greater Deep Ones are completely inhuman. They have no biological likeness to any of Earth's animals, though like the Lesser Deep Ones, they could be compared to amphibian life. Greater Deep One physiology does not seem to be fixed in a way that is clearly understood by human science. One Greater Deep One might have chitinous prehensile crab-like limbs circling its mouth, while another might have one arm, four eyes, or two separate mouths. The consistent facts seem to be these:

Their bodies are covered head to toe with large fanlike scales, as well as bony spikes of varying colors. They are larger than humans, often the size of a gorilla or larger. Their eyes are huge and globe-shaped, able to see in the dark of the oceans' depths. Their mouths are huge open gashes filled with tiny, razor-like teeth, incapable of human-type speech.

They have gill-slits which allow them to breathe salt water (but not fresh). Their native environment is the ocean, and they are almost completely aquatic, only able to venture onto land for short periods of time. Their bodies are built for the deep ocean, with self-regulating gas-bladders that expand and collapse to allow a shift from the shallows to the depths. (Mutation in these bladders may have made venturing onto land possible.)

Deep Ones of all kinds are at least as intelligent as an average human, and many are far more intelligent than the greatest of human minds. Their understanding of what humanity calls hypergeometry is extensive, and seems to be genetic in nature, passed on from generation to generation through forcible procreation.

DISINFORMATION

YELLOW CARD

UNKNOWN ALIEN INTELLIGENCES

"Elder Things." "Elder Beings." "Old Ones." The authors of occult tomes rarely know exactly what to call unnatural monstrosities. How much more at a loss is a witness unfortunate enough to encounter one in person? In this book, we give standard names to these entities to help the Handler avoid confusion. But as Handler, you should do everything in your power to create that confusion among your players! Never give a clear enough description that a veteran player recognizes the threat. Never use a name that players can recognize from prior games or fiction. Change the sensory impressions that these entities create. Change their abilities and weaknesses if you must. Familiarity kills the sense of cosmic weirdness that this game is meant to evoke. Never let players think that they know exactly what looms before their terrified Agents.

IS LINE

Deep Ones consider humanity, for all its own advances, nothing more than a primitive prey-species. When a Greater Deep One is confronted by humans, it is typically more than a match for them; or at the very least, it can very quickly escape back to the sea.

Their lifespan is effectively infinite, and their upward size limit is dependent wholly on feeding. The most ancient Greater Deep Ones are huge, some approaching the size of an elephant. However, since Deep Ones tend to feed on one another, many are sacrificed by a strong few so that they might grow in power and size. This very effectively keeps the Greater Deep One population in check.

Greater Deep Ones reproduce through asexual means, in a manner unlike anything else on Earth. Each Greater Deep One has a stinger that injects a parasitic genetic element which alters the host to incorporate as much of the injector's genetic material as possible. Often, this disease rewrites vast sections of the target's genetic code, slowly mutating the victim's body over days, weeks, or months until the victim manifests Deep One genetic traits.

When a Greater Deep One mates with a member of another species, such as a human, it causes alterations both physical and mental, leading to Deep One-human hybrids and the Lesser Deep Ones. The Deep Ones have bred with nearly every type of advanced aquatic life, spawning strange hybrids throughout Earth's oceans.

For at least the last 100,000 years they have preyed on humans as breeding stock, sacrificial victims and food. Humanity has very effectively satisfied the Greater Deep Ones' needs and has reduced the frequency of violence between Deep Ones. Where once they preyed on their own species or other ocean-going creatures, most Greater Deep Ones now prey almost exclusively on humanity for sacrificial needs.

In the context of the immortal populace of the Deep Ones, the frequency of their contact with new human communities—which may be as low as once every 300 years—is quite high. As far as the Deep Ones' inhuman biological clocks are concerned, the current pace of intermingling with human populations is the equivalent of a breeding frenzy. To us, from our less temporally enlightened standpoint, it seems almost glacial in nature.

No one knows where the Deep Ones originated. It seems clear they have existed on Earth for far longer than humanity, and possibly longer than mammalian life altogether.

Deep One (Greater)

STR 26 **CON** 26 **DEX** 11 **INT** 16 **POW** 14

HP 26 **WP** 14.

ARMOR: 3 points of bony scales (see **RESILIENT**).

SKILLS: Alertness 30%, Athletics 70%, Swim 99%, Unnatural 80%.

ATTACKS: Talons or sharp spines 55%, damage 2D6, Armor Piercing 5.

Lunge and bite 35%, Lethality 10%, Armor Piercing 5.

Grasp 55%, damage as for grappling.

AMPHIBIOUS: The Greater Deep One is adapted to existence on land or in the ocean, at any depth. After a day on the surface, it loses 1 HP per day until it returns to the sea. (Immersing itself in salt water instantly restores all HP lost in this manner.)

GENETIC HYPERGEOMETRY: The Greater Deep One can access deep genetic memories of hypergeometric techniques, allowing it to operate nearly any ritual.

INHUMAN MOVEMENT: The Greater Deep One can move up to 30 kph on land, or 60 kph in the water.

INJECTOR: If the target is helpless, the Greater Deep One can strike with a barbed stinger that injects the target with the Deep One reproductive element (described on page 195). This attack costs the target 1/1D8 SAN due to helplessness, and may, eventually, transform the target into a Lesser Deep One.

RESILIENT: A successful Lethality roll does not destroy a Greater Deep One, but inflicts HP damage equal to the Lethality rating.

UNNATURAL BIOLOGY: The Greater Deep One's physiology would baffle any biologist. Making a called shot for "vitals" or another apparently vulnerable area inflicts normal damage, with no special game effect.

SAN LOSS: 1/1D8.

Deep Ones (Lesser)

"Some of 'em have queer narrow heads with flat noses and bulgy, stary eyes that never seem to shut, and their skin ain't quite right. Rough and scabby, and the sides of their necks are all shrivelled or creased up. Get bald, too, very young. The older fellows look the worst—fact is, I don't believe I've ever seen a very old chap of that kind. Guess they must die of looking in the glass! Animals hate 'em—they used to have lots of horse trouble before autos came in."

—H.P. Lovecraft, "The Shadow Over Innsmouth"

In humanity, the Deep Ones have found an ideal species to impregnate. Human genetics and Deep One genetics have mixed in a "perfect storm," leading to a highly fecund sub-species which can reproduce far more often than Greater Deep Ones. Humans impregnated by the Greater Deep One reproductive element become Lesser Deep Ones. Such hybrids seem human, at first, but at some point after reaching adulthood their human traits (and stats) change to those of Lesser Deep Ones.

Lesser Deep Ones are the "classic" Deep Ones as portrayed in H.P. Lovecraft's "The Shadow Over Innsmouth." They vary from partially human to nearly completely inhuman—and still, the worst Lesser Deep One is far more tolerable and human-like than any Greater Deep One.

An average Lesser Deep One is human-sized and vaguely human-shaped, though they tend to be pot-bellied and awkward-looking. Their musculature, skin, bones and sensory organs have undergone drastic alterations by the Deep One reproductive element (described on page 195). Their skin texture has shifted from pores to scales, which range from super-fine to heavy and thick armored scales on their backs and areas which formerly possessed hair. Their coloring is usually grayish-green, with white or yellow bellies.

Their arms are longer than those of an average human, and their musculature has been extensively improved, allowing inhuman feats of strength. The spaces between their fingers are connected with thick, semi-transparent webbing. These muscular changes have also affected their legs, causing them to favor the ball of the foot as a balance surface. Their feet are webbed like their hands, and in the water their legs allow fast movement, with swimming speeds in excess of 25 kph. The lengthening of the arms and alteration of the legs also allows them to move on land at least as fast as the average human by loping about on all fours, something which becomes easier and easier as the taint takes hold.

Their head is their most inhuman feature. Their skulls have undergone drastic alterations. Eye sockets have grown and shifted to the sides of the skull. The eyes have grown in size, and eyelids have become transparent and have found another use as nictitating membranes. The lower jaw has shrunk, and teeth have multiplied in number and grown sharp. Worse still, their necks have swollen in size and bulk to allow space for fluttering gill slits.

These beings are, like many crossbred creatures, the best of both worlds, although the results vary from subject to subject. Most enjoy immortality and, as the transformation passes through its final stages, the ability to exist indefinitely under the waves.

This transformation is dependent on the proportion of Greater Deep One genes in the hybrid's genetic makeup, as well as the capability of the hybrid's human system to adapt to the changes. The more frequently the Deep One "taint" appears in a hybrid's ancestry, the better and more effective the transformation.

Deep One (Lesser)

STR 17 **CON** 15 **DEX** 12 **INT** 13 **POW** 12

HP 16 **WP** 12

ARMOR: 1 point of thick scales or flabby hide.

SKILLS: Alertness 30%, Athletics 40%, Persuade 30%, Swim 75%,, Unnatural 10%.

ATTACKS: Knife-like talons 55%, damage 1D8, Armor Piercing 3.

Grapple 55%, pins the target.

ALMOST HUMAN: Some Lesser Deep Ones appear as deformed, inbred humans, especially to those unaware of the Deep One threat. Only a full medical examination or their use of inhuman abilities may reveal their true nature.

PARTIALLY AMPHIBIOUS: If the transformation from human is not complete, the Lesser Deep One is only partially adapted to existence in the ocean. A hybrid mostly transformed can submerge for hours or days at a time. Some hybrids remain in that state perpetually. Those who fully transform are as at home in the depths of the sea as on dry land.

INHUMAN MOVEMENT: The Lesser Deep One can leap, climb, and lope in a wholly inhuman manner. With an Athletics test, it can cover heights and obstacles that would stop a normal human. The Lesser Deep One can move up to 25 kph on land, and 30 kph in the water.

RITUALS: Some learned Lesser Deep Ones have access to hypergeometric rituals—usually those dealing with Deep Ones, Cthulhu, or the ocean.

SAN LOSS: 0/1D4.

Dimensional Shamblers

"Shuffling toward him in the darkness was the gigantic, blasphemous form of a black thing not wholly ape and not wholly insect. Its hide hung loosely upon its frame, and its rugose, dead-eyed rudiment of a head swayed drunkenly from side to side. Its fore paws were extended, with talons spread wide, and its whole body was taut with murderous malignity despite its utter lack of facial expression."

—H.P. Lovecraft and Hazel Heald, "The Horror in the Museum"

Contained within the eddies and vortices of four-dimensional space, unseen and unimagined life persists. Within this "realm"—for this is all the human mind can attempt to make of it—exists a creature ascendant just as mankind now enjoys its momentary ascendancy over the Earth. It was referred to in the private journal of Ludwig Prinn (recovered in Paris in 1944) as "a shambling silhouette which cut most foul dimensions in shape." This was later shortened to "dimensional shambler."

It is an entity composed of some kind of flesh and blood, though its chemistries and the science behind its life cycle remain baffling to any earthly scientist. It is huge and strong, though essentially humanoid in form and movement. Its skin is tan, red, or ebony-black, and loose, hanging in folds all over its body,

DISINFORMATION

YELLOW CARD

THE DEEP ONE REPRODUCTIVE ELEMENT

While the genetic material underlying Deep One reproduction shares some aspects common to viruses, it is perhaps best described as a mobile genetic element.

This genetic element is unusual in many ways. If isolated and publicized, it would immediately gain the attention of the biomedical community, not to mention Deep One-related communities and cults, and the few covert agencies that have had extensive experience with the Deep Ones in the past (such as Delta Green). Openly approaching the academic community with samples of the Deep One reproductive element is extremely dangerous. A suggestion to A-cell to do so is met with a resounding and immediate "NO."

The Deep One reproductive element was first isolated by humanity at the YY-II facility in New Mexico by a team of scientists in the employ of MAJESTIC in the late 1970s. Due to the extreme secrecy of the project, this information is buried beneath miles of Top Secret red tape from a dozen research projects under MAJESTIC and the Program. More has been learned and then forgotten about it than any one agency knows.

The element shares aspects of retrovirus and retrotransposon groups, and has some characteristics of unusual RNA molecules such as ribozymes and viroids. In actuality, it is much, much odder than any of these.

The Deep One reproductive element is a complex and highly structured RNA strand with catalytic activities that attaches to the DNA of the host. It causes both the alteration of existing genetic traits and the activation, through promoter regions, of non-expressing genetic traits. In other words, it rewrites the target's genetic structure in dramatic ways. Many of these changes are already in the target's DNA, but some are created by the RNA strand.

So far, this is not that unusual. But the element takes it several steps further. The element initially inserts itself onto host chromosomes, and when copied acquires short pieces of host genome sequence that allow it to insert itself again in a different position determined by the new host-derived genetic material. The RNA structure is complex and multi-staged, capable of many stepped insertions, allowing it to infect, re-infect, and re-infect again, causing multiple rewrites to the genetic structure of the target.

This "Chinese puzzle box" aspect of the element is wholly unique, and that discovery alone is worthy of a Nobel Prize. Of course, those stupid enough to bring it to the attention of the public soon find themselves blackmailed, victims of an assisted lone suicide, disgraced and removed from any position of authority, or undeniably proven a fraud in the public eye. This secret has remained hidden for 80 years since the "official" discovery of the Deep Ones; it will remain so for as long as conspiracies exist to suppress it.

CUT ALONG THIS LINE

031-51937 o-46

and its skeletal system turns and moves in unnatural ways (allowing it to spin its head like a top, for instance, or reverse its limbs). It looks, at its most basic, like a giant, leathery, shaved ape, with a deformed, collapsed face, huge arms ending in a random spray of claws, and a small head set in a vacant expression, with red, insect-like eyes.

It comes and goes through four-dimensional space through unknown means, and kills and consumes what it can, driven by a hunger for blood. It seems to find living flesh the supreme delicacy.

Dimensional Shambler

STR 22 **CON** 30 **DEX** 15 **INT** 10 **POW** 14

HP 26 **WP** 14

ARMOR: 4 point of leathery hide (see **FOCUSED TRANSCENDENCE**).

SKILLS: Alertness 44%, Apport 60%, Athletics 99%.

ATTACKS: Flailing Smash 55%, damage 2D6.

Grapple 55% (see **GRASP AND VANISH**).

APPORT: As its action in a turn, and with a successful Apport skill roll, the shambler can teleport anywhere within 50 meters. It seems to shudder, stumble, and fade as it exits "reality." It snaps back into reality suddenly and silently.

BLOOD FEAST: A prone target that is bleeding significantly causes the shambler to enter a blood feast. Quick as lightning, it seizes the victim and drains one point of STR per round from blood loss until the victim dies. A Dodge roll allows the target to escape. A seized victim can attempt an opposed STR roll against the shambler, suffering 1D4 damage from tearing flesh if the victim struggles free. Any attack on the shambler that inflicts damage stops the blood feast and causes it to drop the victim.

FLAILING SMASH: The shambler batters at its opponents with wild, windmill swings of its inhumanly long arms, inflicting 2D6 damage. A human-size target hit by the smash must make a STR test or be knocked prone. If a target is knocked prone, the shambler attempts to grasp and vanish on its next turn (see **GRASP AND VANISH**).

FOCUSED TRANSCENDENCE: When focused on a single target, the shambler becomes immune to all physical attacks from that particular target. It can still be affected by any other attack, effect, or power.

GRASP AND VANISH: If any human target goes prone nearby, the shambler moves in and attempts to grapple. If the shambler pins the target, it and the target whisk out of existence on the shambler's next turn, never to be seen again.

LOPING: The shambler can move and climb with the agility of a great ape, allowing it to scale, leap, climb, and swing in a manner more accomplished than any human gymnast.

UNNATURAL BIOLOGY: The dimensional shambler's physiology would baffle any biologist. Making a called shot for "vitals" or another apparently vulnerable area inflicts normal damage, with no special game effect.

SAN LOSS: 1/1D6.

Elder Things

"The beings moved in the sea partly by swimming—using the lateral crinoid arms—and partly by wriggling with the lower tier of tentacles containing the pseudo-feet. Occasionally they accomplished long swoops with the auxiliary use of two or more sets of their fan-like folding wings. On land they locally used the pseudo-feet, but now and then flew to great heights or over long distances with their wings. The many slender tentacles into which the crinoid arms branched were infinitely delicate, flexible, strong, and accurate in muscular-nervous coördination; ensuring the utmost skill and dexterity in all artistic and other manual operations."

—H.P. Lovecraft, "At the Mountains of Madness"

These eight-foot tall, five-eyed, barrel-like crinoids colonized the Earth approximately one billion years ago, erecting huge, basalt pyramids and enacting unknowable plans. Their biology was completely alien to anything found on the Earth. They resembled a sea star interbred with some bizarre plant, radially symmetrical, with five eyes, five feeding tubes, five tentacle-like limbs, five wings, and a five-lobed brain. Their life-systems were obscenely resilient, allowing them to be frozen or overheated or anything in between, with little harm. Their cells could cease functioning completely, and revive unharmed 70 million years later, as if no time had passed.

In prehistory, the Elder Things worked their alien science, combining, breeding and manipulating life until they celebrated their most marvelous creation: the shoggoths. These plastic beings were seen as the ultimate achievement: subservient, adaptable, and intelligent. But all hints imply that this slave race turned on the Elder Things and brought about the destruction of their civilization.

Due to the vast gulfs between the fall of the Elder Thing culture and the modern era, information about this cataclysm is spotty at best. Still, reports from disparate points around the globe suggest that a small population of Elder Things may still be active.

Elder Thing

STR 29 **CON** 70 **DEX** 9 **INT** 50 **POW** 20

HP 50 **WP** 20

ARMOR: 10 points of rugose skin (see **RESILIENT**).

SKILLS: Flight 55%, Swim 99%, Unnatural 85%.

ATTACKS: Grasp and tear 45%, Lethality 10% (see **GRASP AND TEAR**).

Black box 50%, Lethality 40% (see **BLACK BOX**).

Injector 35% (see **INJECTOR**).

BLACK BOX: This small but terrifying stone cube has over two hundred holes and unusual pictoglyphs carved in its surface. These "buttons" allow an Elder Thing (and only an Elder Thing) to trigger one of many effects. It can instantly erect a field of protective energy that provides an additional 12 points of Armor (when the shield is active, the Elder Thing cannot move). It can project a bolt of force inflicting a Lethality attack of 40% on a target (a Dodge roll is permitted). It can burrow a perfect two-meter circle through any inanimate substance. No one knows all the functions of the Black Box.

ENVIRONMENTAL IMMUNITY: The Elder Thing can survive in nearly any climate, and is as much at home in outer space as in the lightless depths of the ocean. It never suffers damage from environmental changes.

ETHERIC FLIGHT: The five wings which unfold from the torso of the Elder Thing seem to press against some otherworldly substance, allowing them to fly through the air, in the sea or in space. On Earth they can fly approximately 100 kph in the air and 50 kph in the ocean.

GRASP AND TEAR: The Elder Thing's body is incredibly strong. When confronted with a biological threat, the creature is not above simply grabbing it in implacable tendrils and tearing it to pieces.

INJECTOR: This odd, stone "wand" can be operated only by an Elder Thing. It can generate many effects. A single touch can drain a human target of 2D10 WP; inflict 1D10 HP damage; or knock a living creature unconscious for 1D10 hours. No one knows all the functions of the injector.

RESILIENT: A successful Lethality roll does not destroy an Elder Thing, but inflicts HP damage equal to the Lethality rating.

SUPER-INTELLIGENCE: Elder Things' five-lobed brains and alien science are a billion years in advance of humanity. An Elder Thing may use its INT test for any Science skill, or other human skill it has a few hours to study.

TORPOR: When reduced to 1 HP, an Elder Thing enters a torpor which—due to its alien nature—is nearly impossible to differentiate from death. Only pre-knowledge of this state, or a critical success in an appropriate science skill roll, can detect the faint pulse of autonomic life. This torpor allows the Elder Thing to lie in place for millions of years with no ill effect. The ultimate extent of the torpor's survivability is unknown. Extraordinary measures can fully destroy the body, and by one account the rebellious shoggoths slew their masters by decapitation. Otherwise, all lost HP lost are restored within less than a week after the Elder Thing revives from torpor. What factors contribute to an Elder Thing's awakening are beyond human understanding and are up to the Handler.

SAN LOSS: 1/1D10.

Feasters From the Stars

"There came a period when people were curious enough to steal up and count the herd that grazed precariously on the steep hillside above the old farmhouse, and they could never find more than ten or twelve anaemic, bloodless-looking specimens....Odd wounds or sores, having

something of the aspect of incisions, seemed to afflict the visible cattle; and once or twice during the earlier months certain callers fancied they could discern similar sores about the throats of the grey, unshaven old man and his slatternly, crinkly-haired albino daughter."

—H.P. Lovecraft, "The Dunwich Horror"

Invisible, extrasolar creatures composed of non-terrene matter that fly, latch on, and feed on living biological materials, the feasters have long been a select weapon for hypergeometric operators summoning and controlling alien beings. They are most often drawn to Earth by hypergeometric summons, and then bound to a single task, usually the murder of a target. Of their true nature and origin, no one knows. Some say they are among the loathsome spawn of Yog-Sothoth, the extradimensional "Old Ones" of Dunwich lore. Others say they came down from between the stars.

One witness reported that when a feaster drained its prey, its innards were "painted" with blood, revealing an otherwise invisible body of roiling tentacles and mouths in splotches of crimson—until the blood quickly metabolized and became invisible like the feaster's body. Otherwise, they are almost impossible to see.

Feaster from the Stars

STR 17 **CON** 29 **DEX** 12 **INT** 8 **POW** 15

HP 23 **WP** 15

ARMOR: 1 point of slippery, invisible skin.

SKILLS: Flight 30%.

ATTACKS: Exsanguination 40% (see **EXSANGUINATION**). Limb flail 60%, damage 1D12 (see **LIMB FLAIL**).

EXSANGUINATION: On a successful attack, the feaster latches on to a target with invisible, motile mouths and drains vital fluids. A seized victim can attempt an opposed STR roll against the feaster to struggle free, otherwise losing 1 HP the first round, 2 HP the second round, 3 HP the third, and so on until the victim dies.

INVISIBLE: The feaster is composed of matter from another dimension, and visible wavelengths of light readily pass through it. All attempts to attack it are at −20% to hit. Only when it feeds and its innards fill with blood is it visible and the penalty lifted. Even then, this effect does not last—within minutes, the blood is metabolized, and once again, the feaster vanishes. After it has fed (and only after) it is visible to infrared detection.

LIMB FLAIL: The feaster can swipe at a target with half a dozen invisible tentacles, knocking it backwards and biting and slicing for 1D12 damage.

NON-TERRENE: The feaster is at home in nearly any environment. Radiation, pressure, cold, vacuum and other inhospitable environments do it no harm. It can move on the surface of Saturn, the depths of the ocean or in open space with equal ease.

TUMBLING FLIGHT: The feaster often walks on tentacles that leave bizarre tracks, but it can fly by tumbling through any environment as if carried on some invisible aether, even underwater or in space. In flight, the feaster seems to drift and float, but can suddenly move at high speed if it chooses.

UNNATURAL BIOLOGY: The feaster's physiology would baffle any biologist. Making a called shot for "vitals" or another apparently vulnerable area inflicts normal damage, with no special game effect.

SAN LOSS: 1/1D6.

Ghouls

"It was a colossal and nameless blasphemy with glaring red eyes, and it held in bony claws a thing that had been a man, gnawing at the head as a child nibbles at a stick of candy. Its position was a kind of crouch, and as one looked one felt that at any moment it might drop its present prey and seek a juicier morsel."

—H.P. Lovecraft, "Pickman's Model"

Ghouls are ageless, subterranean creatures, somehow related to humanity, who feed on the dead. They are large and powerful, with doglike faces and pointed ears, flat noses, drooling lips, scaly claws, and half-hooved feet. Their tough, rubbery bodies are caked with the mold of the graves that they rob.

Ghouls express themselves in squeals and meeping bleats, but they can understand and be understood in ordinary human speech. In some tales, ghouls steal human babies in the night to teach them their ways. They return the stolen child home each morning a little changed, a little more accustomed to horrors that mortal culture and religion attempt to conceal. Eventually, a changeling joins the ghouls and slowly transforms into one, living forever in the tunnels that connect the living to the dead and the world we know to other, stranger realities. Or so the old tales say.

Ghoul

STR 24 **CON** 24 **DEX** 15 **INT** 12 **POW** 13

HP 24 **WP** 13

ARMOR: See **RESILIENT**.

SKILLS: Alertness 70%, Athletics 85%, Foreign Language (English) 30%, Stealth 90%, Track (by scent) 65%, Unnatural 40%.

ATTACKS: Bony claws 40%, damage 1D8, Armor Piercing 3.

Bite 40%, damage 1D10+2 (see **WORRY AND RIP**).

CHARNEL VISAGE: A ghoul has no CHA stat as humans would understand it. A ghoul that uses an unnatural ritual such as Changeling Feast to disguise itself as human gains a CHA stat (usually a score of 10 or 11). Many ghouls can transform rapidly between their native form and any previously-consumed human form.

GIFT OF THE GRAVE: Consuming rotten human flesh restores 1D8 HP to an injured ghoul immediately. This may be done once per 24 hours.

IMMORTALITY: A ghoul never grows old, starves to death, or perishes through natural causes.

INHUMAN AGILITY: With a successful Athletics roll, a ghoul can leap five meters in any direction from a standing position, scale any vertical surface, or drop up to 15 meters without damage. At top speed, a ghoul can run at nearly 60 kph.

LIFE UNDERGROUND: A ghoul can burrow through earth at up to three meters per minute. Ghouls thrive underground. They prefer to breathe air, and may go into a sort of torpor if suffocated long enough, but can survive indefinitely without it. A ghoul can see in

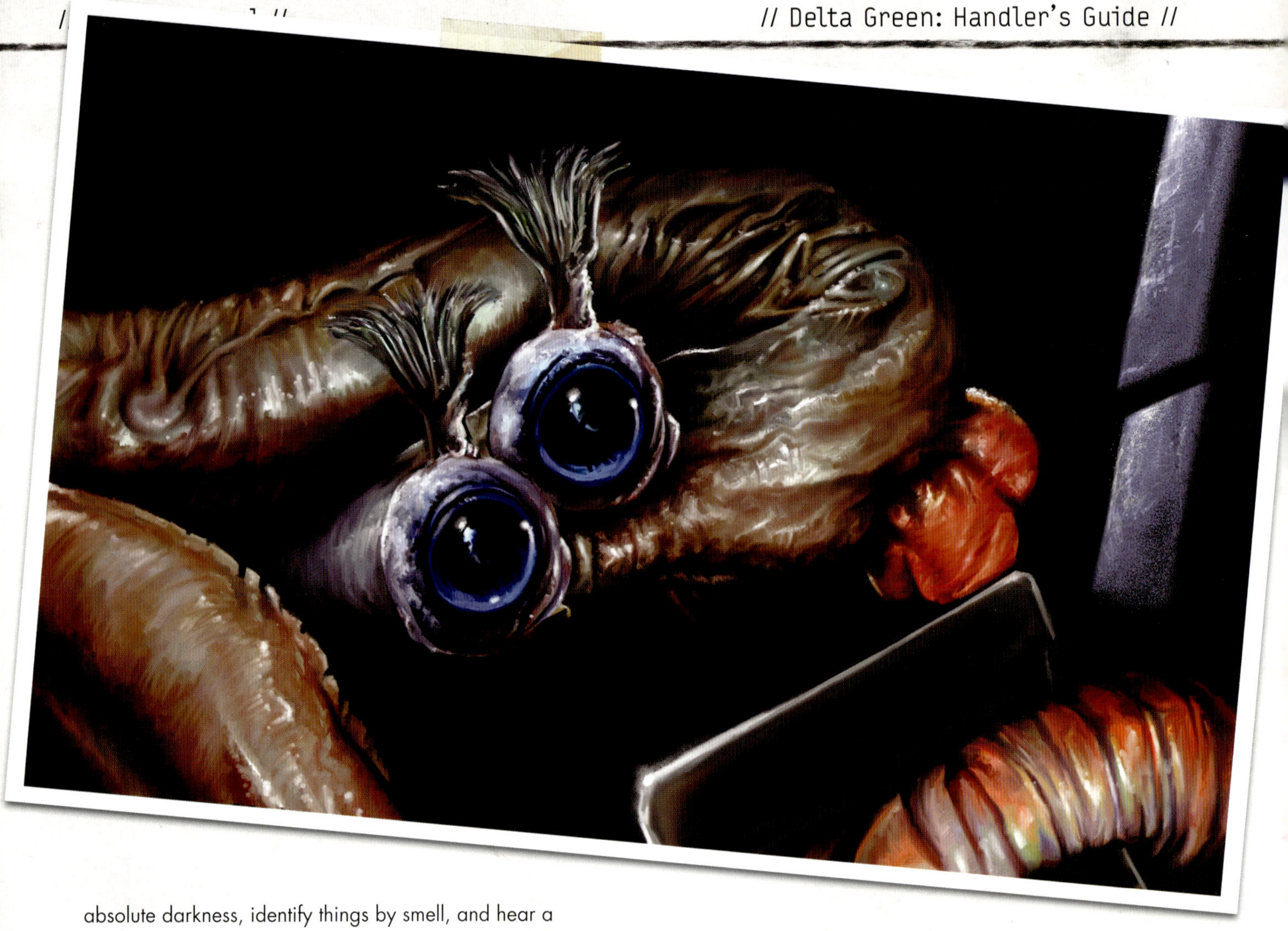

absolute darkness, identify things by smell, and hear a human heartbeat at a distance of 15 meters.

MEPHITIC MEMORIES: Some ghouls can bring to mind the memories of human beings whose brains they have devoured. In a young ghoul, this may require an INT test.

RESILIENT: A successful Lethality roll does not destroy a ghoul, but inflicts HP damage equal to the Lethality rating.

WORRY AND RIP: After succeeding with a bite attack, a ghoul may inflict 1D6 damage on the same target each turn, without requiring an attack roll. The ghoul can take other actions while holding and worrying a victim. If the bite attack pierced the victim's armor, the "worry and rip" damage ignores armor. The victim can attempt an opposed STR test as his or her action each turn to break free.

RITUALS: Many ghouls know hypergeometric rituals. Changeling Feast and Charnel Meditation are most common.

SAN LOSS: 0/1D6.

The Great Race (Cone-Shaped Vessels)

"They seemed to be enormous iridescent cones, about ten feet high and ten feet wide at the base, and made up of some ridgy, scaly, semi-elastic matter. From their apexes projected four flexible, cylindrical members, each a foot thick, and of a ridgy substance like that of the cones themselves. These members were sometimes contracted almost to nothing, and sometimes extended to any distance up to about ten feet. Terminating two of them were enormous claws or nippers. At the end of a third were four red, trumpet-like appendages. The fourth terminated in an irregular yellowish globe some two feet in diameter and having three great dark eyes ranged along its central circumference. Surmounting this head

were four slender grey stalks bearing flower-like appendages, whilst from its nether side dangled eight greenish antennae or tentacles. The great base of the central cone was fringed with a rubbery, grey substance which moved the whole entity through expansion and contraction."

—H.P. Lovecraft, "The Shadow Out of Time"

It is said the Great Race of Yith issue from another world, flinging their minds into beings that inhabited Earth hundreds of millions of years in the past, fleeing some unknown calamity. The bizarre creatures they found on Earth were not humanoid at all, but three-meter-tall, rugose cones, set upon a single snail-like foot and topped with tentacles that held their eyes, claws, and an organ for "speech."

In this place (some call it Pnakotis; spellings of the inhuman name vary), the Great Race used their temporal abilities to range far and wide, from the beginning of life on Earth to its last extremity, by flinging their minds through the corridors of time. They built a great library a hundred million years before humanity, storing a record of all the histories of all the sentient beings on Earth: native creatures as well as beings from other worlds.

But the Great Race understood—had always understood, would always understand—that Pnakotis would fall to the horror of the whistling, spectral polyps. Their great library was simply an outpost in time. Before that destruction came, the minds of the Great Race fled en masse to the far, far future, when Earth is a withered, radioactive husk, populated only by giant coleopterous beetles. But the Great Race exists outside time. It can visit its great library from any other time or place. Its members sometimes reach into the Construct of spacetime, drawing modern-day human minds back to Pnakotis to tell their tales, to study and be studied, while the Great Race occupy their human bodies as vessels for a time.

The Great Race (Cone-Shaped Vessel)

STR 35 **CON** 55 **DEX** 10 **INT** 40 **POW** 30

HP 45 **WP** 30

ARMOR: 5 points of rugged skin (see **RESILIENT**).

SKILLS: Total Knowledge 75%.

ATTACKS: Claw 75%, Lethality 20%, Armor Piercing 5.

RESILIENT: A firearm's successful Lethality roll does not destroy the cone-shaped vessel, but inflicts HP damage equal to the Lethality rating. Lethality rolls from explosions and fire have full effect.

TEMPORAL IMMORTALITY: The cone-shaped creatures are not the Great Race, simply vessels that contain their minds. To an extratemporal being, death is only an inconvenient "blank spot" in the otherwise limitless expanse of four-dimensional spacetime. Even if the cone-shaped form of a member of the Great Race appears to perish, that entity persists on, somewhere in time.

TOTAL KNOWLEDGE: As temporal explorers, the Great Race have access to endless epochs of knowledge from all times and cultures. Knowing a challenge is "coming," they can learn all they must know before it begins. Only occasional, strange variances in causality limit them. They have the equivalent of 75% in every skill, alien or human.

TEMPORAL OMNISCIENCE: At the beginning of any action in opposition to the Great Race (Cone-Shaped Vessel), an Agent must make a Luck roll. On a failure, all actions by that member of the Great Race are +20% for the duration of that conflict or contest, because the entity lived through the episode before and knows what is going to happen.

TEMPORAL TRAVEL: The Great Race can move their consciousness through time to inhabit creatures with sufficient capacity to support their intellect. When coming from a host with sufficient mental capacity—such as the cone-shaped beings—this ability is inherent and requires no machinery to operate. Whether one of the Great Race succeeds at occupying a given creature is up to the Handler.

UNNATURAL BIOLOGY: The cone-shaped vessel's physiology would baffle any biologist. Making a called shot for "vitals" or another apparently vulnerable area inflicts normal damage, with no special game effect.

SAN LOSS: 1/1D10.

The Great Race (Human Vessels)

"At the same time they noticed that I had an inexplicable command of many almost unknown sorts of knowledge—a command which I seemed to wish to hide rather than display. I would inadvertently refer, with casual assurance, to specific events in dim ages outside the range of accepted history—passing off such references as a jest when I saw the surprise they created. And I had a way of speaking of the future which two or three times caused actual fright. These uncanny flashes soon ceased to appear, though some observers laid their vanishment more to a certain furtive caution on my part than to any waning of the strange knowledge behind them. Indeed, I seemed anomalously avid to absorb the speech, customs, and perspectives of the age around me; as if I were a studious traveller from a far, foreign land."

—H.P. Lovecraft, "The Shadow Out of Time"

Sometimes called the "Strange Ones," these human vessels for the agents of the Great Race of Yith have enacted unknowable plans to bend and shape the timeline to a form that suits their purposes: the Construct.

When the alien intelligence takes over a human mind, it is always the same: an otherwise normal human collapses, and when they wake, they are not themselves, having been replaced by an agent of the Great Race. This alien being uses the body to travel, collect certain information, and most of all to study its "peers." It slowly becomes acclimatized to the epoch, while the mind that the Great Race has displaced is trapped in a cone-shaped body in Pnakotis.

As a member of the Great Race, the entity contained within the human form has access to technology, science, and concepts from the entire timeline of the Earth. That is the least of its gifts. It also has the ability to see the temporal landscape as it unfolds, making it, at least to the rank and file of humanity, appear omniscient. Its INT and POW scores are reduced from their usual values due to the limitations of the human brain, but a member of the Great Race in a human vessel stands out as profoundly more intelligent and strong-willed than any normal person.

The Great Race (Human Vessel)

STR As human **CON** As human **DEX** As human

INT 20 **POW** 20 **CHA** 8

HP As human **WP** 20

SKILLS: Total Knowledge 75% (see **TOTAL KNOWLEDGE**).

ATTACKS: Electric Gun 75%, damage variable (see **JURY-RIG**).

JURY-RIG: Compared to the power of the Great Race, human science is pathetic. Agents of the Great Race can warp modern devices into far more effective technology. Sometimes, this can be accomplished in mere minutes. Often, these tools are rigged to explode or self-destruct after a period of time. The most common are:

- *Electric Gun:* This device can be as small as a garage-door opener, and can inflict damage of the user's choosing: a jolt of 1D6 or 2D6, or a bolt of lightning with Lethality 15%. It ignores body armor but can be blocked by cover.
- *Temporal Mine:* This can look like nearly any household object or device. Once activated, it causes everything within a small radius to be frozen in time, effectively isolating it from the Construct of spacetime. The scope and duration of the effect are up to the Handler.
- *Transfer Device:* When it enters the limited human mind, the Great Race cannot use its ability to jump to another form without first building a transfer device. This small box, composed of rods, wheels and mirrors, permits the mind of the Great Race to return to the Library at Pnakotis.

TEMPORAL IMMORTALITY: To an extratemporal being, death is only an inconvenient "blank spot" in the otherwise limitless expanse of four-dimensional spacetime. Even if the human agent form of the Great Race appears to perish, that entity persists on, somewhere in time.

TOTAL KNOWLEDGE: As temporal explorers, the Great Race have access to endless epochs of knowledge from all times and cultures. Knowing a challenge is coming, they can learn all they must know before it begins. Only occasional, strange variances in causality limit them. They have the equivalent of 75% in every skill, alien or human.

TEMPORAL OMNISCIENCE: At the beginning of any action in opposition with the Great Race (Human Vessel), an Agent must make a Luck roll. On a failure, all actions by that member of the Great Race are +20% for the duration of that conflict or contest, because the entity lived through the episode before and knows what is going to happen.

TEMPORAL TRAVEL (LIMITED): The Great Race can move their consciousness through time to inhabit creatures with sufficient capacity to support their intellect. Humanity, at its best, offers a dim vessel within which to hold the mind of a member of the Great Race. Once in human form, the Great Race agent must construct a device (see **JURY-RIG**) to move its consciousness back. Without this odd machine, the member of the Great Race is trapped within the human form. That form's death creates a "dead end" in the Great Race's awareness of spacetime. Whether they can occupy another nearby host is up to the Handler.

SAN LOSS: 0/1D6 (if its influence over time is revealed).

Greys

"...the creatures did not resemble any race of humans. They were short, shorter than the average Japanese, and their heads were big and bald, with strong, square foreheads, and very small noses and mouths, and weak chins. What was most extraordinary about them were the eyes—large, dark, gleaming, with a sharp gaze."

—Gabriel Linde, *The Unknown Danger*

These mi-go constructs appear as child-sized, slender, humanoids with large heads, long limbs and fingers, and liquid black, almond-shaped eyes. As their name indicates, they are grayish in color, ranging from pale gray through brownish-gray. They are photosynthetic, with a vestigial digestive system, and enter torpor if isolated from their own kind or from a viable environment. A single mi-go can control up to six Greys as well as its own body with no difficulty.

Some of their spacecraft are illusions or mobile hyperspace vortices projected by the mi-go; others are constructed saucers meant, in the 20th century, to lure MAJESTIC into further excesses. Grey technology is reskinned mi-go technology, made more primitive to conform to human expectations. Much of the Outer Ones' work as Greys involves conducting experiments in human intuition under the cover of UFO abductions.

The mi-go subject each abductee's mind to bizarre stimuli while monitoring their reactions. They return some subjects with the memory of the experience suppressed. Sometimes the fungi take a particularly promising subject (or just their brain) back to Yuggoth and subject her to further unspeakable horrors. In communication with human abductees, the Greys tell any sort of story the mi-go devise, but their common legend involves the dead planet Zeta Reticulum III and a mission of exploration and eventual contact with Earth.

A Grey has the INT score of the mi-go controlling it.

Grey

STR 8 **CON** 8 **DEX** 10 **INT** n/a **POW** 13

HP 8 **WP** 13

ARMOR: none.

SKILLS: Alertness 40%, Dodge 25%; otherwise, a Grey has all the skills of the mi-go controlling it.

ATTACKS: Pinch 25%, damage 1D4–1.

Eraser beam 55%, damage special (see **ERASE**).

Paralysis ball 55%, damage special (see **PARALYSIS BALL**).

ERASE: The Greys use this mi-go technology (see **MI-GO** on page 217) as a beam rather than an injected serum. It has an effective range of 10 m.

MI-GO TOOLS: The Greys often use mi-go tools (see **MI-GO** on page 217), altered for the "sci-fi" look that humans expect of the Greys.

PARALYSIS BALL: This silvery sphere increases the local inertia of all particles surrounding the target, creating a "bubble prison" in which time seems to stop for up to an hour. It takes an Alertness test to not be where the bubble focuses. Coming out of a bubble costs 0/1D6 SAN.

TELEPATHY: The mi-go have outfitted some Greys with telepathic modules for scanning human thoughts and sending messages. That telepathic invasion requires an opposed POW test between the Grey and the target.

RITUALS: The controlling mi-go can use Greys to perform any ritual it knows.

SAN LOSS: 0/1D4.

Haedi Nigritiae

"Nothing can ever efface the memory of those nighted crypts, those titan arcades, and those half-formed shapes of hell that strode gigantically in silence holding half-eaten things whose still surviving portions screamed for mercy or laughed with madness. Odours of incense and corruption joined in sickening concert, and the black air was alive with the cloudy, semi-visible bulk of shapeless elemental things with eyes."

—H.P. Lovecraft, "The Horror at Red Hook"

Their name, corrupt Latin meaning roughly "young goats of darkness," comes from a passage in Ludwig Prinn's *De Vermis Mysteriis*. Their description comes from a few maddened survivors or captured cultists: a blackish-green, ropy thing like a tree or enormous plant, squatting and crawling on hooves, covered in mouths and snaky arms, stinking of rot. Some vile cults harvest its bizarrely mutagenic sap or "milk." Delta Green has gathered fragments of legend and intel from European and New England witch-cults and infamous tribes in the Congo, Colombia, and Indochina. A suspected encounter with a haedus nigritia in Vermont in the 1990s left one agent and two Friendlies dead and the four survivors scarred for life. An ancient chant often hails the presence of the haedi nigritiae: "Iä! Shub-Niggurath! Black Goat of the Woods with a Thousand Young!"

Haedus Nigritia

STR 46 **CON** 22 **DEX** 16 **INT** 12 **POW** 16

HP 34 **WP** 16

ARMOR: See **UNNATURAL FLESH**.

SKILLS: Alertness 40%, Stealth 60% (80% in forests or jungles), Unnatural 70%.

ATTACKS: Trampling hooves and crushing tentacles 40%, damage 6D6 (and see **TRAMPLING AND CRUSHING**).

Grapple and feed 80%, damage special (see **FEEDING**).

FEEDING: The turn after grappling, the haedus nigritia may suck blood from a pinned target with one of its horrible mouths. That reduces the victim's STR by 2D6 and adds the same amount to the monster's HP or WP, whichever it prefers.

NON-TERRENE: The haedi nigritiae are at home in nearly any environment. Radiation, pressure, cold, vacuum, and other inimical environments have no negative effects on them.

STENCH: All unprotected breathers around a haedus nigritia make CON tests or suffer −20% to all tests until they escape the stench.

TRAMPLING AND CRUSHING: With a successful attack roll, the haedus nigritia may divide its damage dice among up to six victims within reach. Each victim may attempt to Dodge the monster's attack roll.

UNNATURAL BIOLOGY: The physiology of the haedus nigritia would baffle any biologist. Making a called shot for "vitals" or another apparently vulnerable area inflicts normal damage, with no special game effect.

UNNATURAL FLESH: A haedus nigritia takes only 1 HP damage from any unarmed attack, melee weapon, firearm, or explosive with a Lethality rating lower than 40%, and no damage whatsoever from fire, corrosives, electricity, and toxins. It takes full damage from hypergeometry.

RITUALS: Call Forth Those from Outside (Haedi Nigritiae; Shub-Niggurath); often others. Haedi nigritiae are pregnant (sometimes literally) with magical force. They eagerly sacrifice humans to pay rituals' costs.

SAN LOSS: 1D4/1D10.

Hounds of the Angles

"Fool! Spawn of Noth-Yidik and effluvium of K'thun! Son of the dogs that howl in the maelstrom of Azathoth!"

—H.P. Lovecraft and Hazel Heald, "The Horror in the Museum"

These terrifying, geometric entities boil and emerge into our four dimensions from sharp angles and edges. Some forbidden texts link them to the court of the Daemon Sultan Azathoth, where it is said they minister to the terrifying entities that dance and pipe around

the roiling chaos-god. Others say they emerged at the beginning of time, coming from some source beyond it, and leap from time to time in hungry pursuit of some quality in sentient creatures like humanity. Some sources associate them with the name "Tindalos," but whether that is an entity or a place, none can say.

The Hounds of the Angles are horrific to behold. Their bodies are composed of a thousand shards of glittering, razor-sharp fragments of spacetime, which move and reform in the vaguest outline of a quadrupedal predator. A Hound of the Angles hunts in a similar manner to a dog, wolf, or tiger, stalking prey, taking it down, and rending it to death, leaving behind only a bloody mess. Then it vanishes into some inscrutable corner of reality, taking every biological remnant of its victims with it, leaving only a mystery behind.

Hound of the Angles

STR 25 **CON** 25 **DEX** 20 **INT** 15 **POW** 20

HP 25 **WP** 10

ARMOR: See **INCONSTANT FORM**.

SKILLS: Alertness 90%, Angular Apport 75%, Stealth 50%, Track (via extradimensional means) 95%, Unnatural 50%.

ATTACKS: Shard Sweep 65%, damage 2D6 (see **SHARD SWEEP**).

Shard Swarm 70%, Lethality 10% (see **SHARD SWARM**).

ANGULAR APPORT: On a successful Angular Apport skill roll, a Hound of the Angles can leap into or emerge from any sharp, physical angle—a corner of a room, the lip of a table, or even the hinge on a pair of glasses—effectively teleporting between those two points instantly no matter the distance. In this manner it pursues its prey, so outrunning one is unlikely, no matter the method or speed of escape.

CURVED SPACE: Exposure to large areas composed of curves, spheres, or circular surfaces causes the hound's "swarm" of shards to lose coherency. The hound is well aware of this weakness, and does its best to avoid and flee such areas. Each turn of exposure to such a space causes the hound 1D6 damage. If reduced to 0 HP from exposure to curves, the hound disintegrates and seems to fold out of three-dimensional space (likely returning it to its place of origin).

INCONSTANT FORM: The hound can fold, change, stretch, extend and warp its form in amazing ways, altering its size as needed from moment to moment. It can effectively attack anyone within 10 meters by directing its form to a new location. Because it has no "body" and is instead composed of a thousand swirling, reflective shards of spacetime, the hound is immune to all attacks except hypergeometry.

SHARD SWEEP: The hound unleashes two "limbs" composed of shards, peppering a target with 2D6 damage. It ignores body armor but can be blocked by cover.

SHARD SWARM: The hound engulfs the victim in a swirling mass of shards, rendering the target down to a bloody mess with a Lethality attack of 10%. It ignores body armor but can be blocked by cover.

SAN LOSS: 1D6/1D20.

Hunting-Horrors

"Great polypous horrors slid darkly past, and unseen bat wings beat multitudinous around him...Sightless feelers pawed and slimy snouts jostled and nameless things tittered and tittered and tittered."

—H.P. Lovecraft, *The Dream-Quest of Unknown Kadath*

These huge, loathsome, unthinking mysteries are said to be the favored servants of Nyarlathotep. Others claim they are the larvae of Nyarlathotep's masters, the mindless Other Gods. Perhaps they are both.

Hunting-horrors have slimy, slithering, wormlike bodies, bloated and ever-shifting, with claws, tentacles, snouts, and great, bat-like wings. Some are blind, locating prey by preternaturally accurate smell and touch. Others have been said to possess weird, burning eyes.

Hunting-horrors do not think or reason quite like Earthly animals, but are governed by strange instincts and hungers, sometimes bizarre beyond expression. Those summoned in unnatural rituals typically yearn to devour human blood and flesh, or whisper blasphemous secrets of the origins of reality, or bear living prey away to the unfathomable spaces where the Other Gods lurk. Binding a summoned horror gives it an echo of the summoner's intentions, which guides its actions. Hunting-horrors manifest only in the deepest darkness.

Hunting-Horror

STR 60 **CON** 30 **DEX** 13 **INT** n/a **POW** 21

HP 45 **WP** 21

ARMOR: 10 points of bubbling matter (see **RESILIENT** and **THING OF THE VOID**).

SKILLS: Flight 75%.

ATTACKS: Bite and rend 70%, Lethality 30%, Armor Piercing 5 (see **BITE AND REND**).

Seize 90% (see **SEIZE**).

ABERRANT FLIGHT: A hunting-horror can "fly" in any environment, moving as if beating its wings against some unseen current—even underwater or in space. In flight, a hunting-horror can move at any speed its instincts demand, passing through any medium without friction or difficulty, or traversing strange dimensions to appear out of nowhere. In pursuit of Earthly quarry, it can just as easily match the speed of a fighter jet as a running human.

BITE AND REND: The hunting-horror can extrude a bone filled maw that is spring-loaded with enough force to shatter bones, shred flesh and even crush metal, inflicting a Lethality 30% attack on anything unlucky enough to be caught in it.

NON-TERRENE: Hunting-horrors are at home in nearly any environment, as long as they are not exposed to the visible wavelengths of light (see **THING OF THE VOID**). Poison and disease are harmless. Unseen radiation, pressure, cold, vacuum, and other environments have no negative effects on them. They can move on the surface of Saturn, the depths of the ocean, or in open space with equal ease.

RESILIENT: A successful Lethality roll does not destroy a hunting-horror, but inflicts HP damage equal to the Lethality rating.

SEIZE: A victim seized in a hunting-horror's writhing grasp suffers the same effects as being pinned. The victim can attempt to escape with a STR test opposed by the hunting-horror's Seize test. A hunting-horror can continue to take actions while keeping a victim seized. It can also squeeze a seized victim once per turn with an opposed Seize vs. STR test, inflicting 2D10 damage (which ignores body armor). This does not count as the hunting-horror's action. It can fly while holding and squeezing up to two seized targets.

THING OF THE VOID: Hunting-horrors retreat from light that's comfortable for human sight. Bright light inflicts 1 HP per turn. The dazzling flash of a stun grenade inflicts 3D6. The full light of day sears a hunting-horror to gray dust. Fire inflicts double damage. All these effects ignore its armor.

UNNATURAL BIOLOGY: The hunting-horror's physiology would baffle any biologist. Making a called shot for "vitals" or another apparently vulnerable area inflicts normal damage, with no special game effect.

SAN LOSS: 1/1D10.

Ifrits

"And He created the jinn from a smokeless flame of fire."

—Qur'an 55:15

These beings resemble balls or columns of fire that grow from pinpoint sparks to man-sized or larger infernos. They can potentially combine into enormous firestorms. They appear to be sentient, even intelligent, plasmas. Their true "self" likely resides in a tangent dimension, and extrudes into ours with incendiary results. Delta Green agents encountered ifrits in Iran in 1943, but they seem to be favored servants of hypergeometric operators in America and Africa as well.

They likely have some connection to Qu-tugkwa, and may be the "bringers of elder wisdom" known in Theosophical lore as "Children of the Fire Mist." If the latter, they can communicate with cultists, implying a communication capability that Delta Green has fortunately yet to encounter. This might tie in with reports that one Kurdish cult of Kheshthogha calls on ifrits to burn unnatural knowledge out of enemies and madmen.

Ifrit

STR 2–18 **CON** 14 **DEX** 16 **INT** 10 **POW** 13

HP 8–16 **WP** 13

SKILLS: Alertness 40%, Dodge 50%, Stealth 50% (only when hidden in a larger fire), Unnatural 50%.

ATTACKS: Fiery touch 50%, damage special (see **FIERY TOUCH**).

Flame immersion 50%, Lethality 20% (see **FLAME IMMERSION**).

EXTINGUISHING: To extinguish an ifrit is like putting out a very stubborn fire. Water inflicts 1D4 damage per gallon; a bucket of sand does 1D4 damage; a hand-held fire extinguisher does 1D6. If the ifrit has even 1 HP remaining at the end of the round, it immediately returns to 8 HP at the beginning of the next round, and then it grows (see **GROWTH**).

FIERY TOUCH: With a successful attack, the ifrit sets its target on fire for 1D4 damage per turn. With a critical hit, the target suffers 1D8 damage per turn.

FLAME IMMERSION: This attack is possible after the ifrit has grown to full size (**STR** 18). It flows over a target, with the attack counting as a grappling roll, and inflicts Lethality 20% burns every turn that the target remains pinned.

GROWTH: The first turn an ifrit appears, it has **STR** 2 and **HP** 8. At the beginning of each turn, it gains +2 STR and +1 HP, until it reaches maximum size at **STR** 18 and **HP** 16.

NON-TERRENE: An ifrit is at home in any environment where fire can burn.

TRANSCENDENT: Intangible, an ifrit is immune to physical harm. It can be extinguished (see **EXTINGUISHING**), and it takes full damage from hypergeometry.

UNNATURAL BIOLOGY: The ifrit's physiology would baffle any biologist. Making a called shot for "vitals" or another apparently vulnerable area inflicts normal damage, with no special game effect.

RITUALS: Some ifrits know Call Forth Those From Outside (Ifrits; Qu-Tugkwa). An ifrit may learn a new ritual by burning someone who knows it, or a book containing it.

SAN LOSS: 0/1D6.

Insects From Shaggai

"Those huge lidless eyes which stared in hate at me, the jointed tendrils which seemed to twist from the head in cosmic rhythms, the ten legs, covered with black shining tentacles and folded into the pallid underbelly, and the semi-circular ridged wings covered with triangular scales—all this cannot convey the soul-ripping horror of the shape which darted at me. I saw the three mouths of the thing move moistly, and then it was upon me."

—Ramsey Campbell, "The Insects from Shaggai"

Horrific, pigeon-sized insectoid aliens that fled to Earth in pyramidal temple-ships centuries before, the insects from Shaggai have terrorized mankind for centuries. They can phase into Earthly matter, and their preferred method of survival is to fly into a human host's brain and seize control through hypergeometric principles. The insects force these human slaves to perform every depravity and hateful act they can manage without exposing their infiltration. The emotions evoked by such acts seem to feed the insects.

The insects from Shaggai are extremely difficult to expose and destroy. Some victims have destroyed them by exposing them to bright sunlight. A few have gotten an embedded insect to quit a host's brain by revealing the insect through trepanation: drilling a hole through the victim's skull.

Insect From Shaggai

STR 1 **CON** 3 **DEX** 22 **INT** 23 **POW** 20

HP 2 **WP** 20

ARMOR: See **OUT OF PHASE**.

SKILLS: Alertness 99%, Dodge 93%, Flight 50%, Unnatural 60%.

ATTACKS: Bite 40%, damage 1D4.

AETHERIC FLIGHT: The insects "fly" on some invisible aether, allowing them to move with wings even in space. On Earth, this means they can fly up to nearly 40 kph.

OUT OF PHASE: The insects from Shaggai exist in a multitude of dimensions. If a damage roll or Lethality roll is an odd number, the insect has shifted out of phase with our dimension and is immune to the attack.

POSSESSION: On a successful Flight skill roll—and a failed Dodge roll on the part of the target—the insect can enter the target's brain. If this happens, the target may attempt a single POW test to struggle free of the insect's control. If it fails, the target loses all WP and becomes the insect's puppet, under its complete control for 1D6 weeks. The target remains conscious of any depravities committed under the insect's influence in that time, and loses SAN accordingly. Piercing the skull while an insect is inside (treat this as any head wound that inflicts at least 3 HP damage on the target) forces the insect from the target. Deliberate trepanation requires a Medicine roll. Success or critical success inflicts exactly 3 damage; failure inflicts 1D6+2 damage, doubled on a fumble.

NON-TERRENE: The insects are at home in nearly any environment. Radiation, pressure, cold, vacuum and other inimical environments have no negative effects on them.

SUNLIGHT: Sunlight is poisonous to the insects from Shaggai. Exposure to it inflicts 1 HP damage per turn.

SAN LOSS: 0/1D6.

K'n-Yani

"Great God, they are older than the earth, and came here from somewhere else—they know what you think, and make you know what they think—they're half-man, half-ghost—crossed the line—melt and take shape again—getting more and more so, yet we're all descended from them in the beginning—children of Tulu—everything made of gold—monstrous animals, half-human—dead slaves—madness—Iä! Shub-Niggurath!—that white man—oh, my God, what they did to him!..."

—H.P. Lovecraft and Zealia Bishop, "The Mound"

The people of K'n-Yan are a near-human species believed to persist in caverns beneath the Earth. They are either the source or an offshoot of humanity, but where and why the two species split remains unknown, perhaps even to them. They view humanity as people of the modern world view stone-age people: hopelessly lost, out of touch, and without the insight to use technology to their advantage. To them, humans remain a prey species.

Long ago, the K'n-Yani mastered total atomic control of their bodies. With this power—either technological or biological in nature—the K'n-Yani have discarded such human concerns as mortality, shelter, scale, and time.

The K'n-Yani appear physically terrifying. They are (or can be) extremely tall—some as tall as five meters—and have yellow-grey skin. They have broad noses, and high foreheads and cheekbones, as well as a large, wide skull which elongates strangely in the back. (Certain primitive Central American religious groups used metal bands to force their skulls into these shapes in an imitation of their K'n Y'ani overlords.) Their teeth are broad and flat, and double rowed. Their hair ranges in color from black to wiry red. Male or female, they wear simple loincloths. Copper, gold, and mica are common adornments in their cleverly-made jewelry, though few carry anything more useful than a ceremonial knife, preferring to rely on their hypergeometric abilities of atomic control, mind control, and more.

K'n-Yani

STR 22 **CON** 29 **DEX** 11 **INT** 19 **POW** 19

HP 25 **WP** 19

ARMOR: See **OUT OF PHASE** and **SCALE CONTROL.**

SKILLS: Alertness 60%, Anthropology (Human) 35%, Athletics 30%, Swim 45%, Unarmed Combat 45%, Unnatural 50%

ATTACKS: Projection 55%, damage 1D6 (see **PROJECTION**).

Unarmed 45%, damage 1D10.

HUMAN OFFSHOOT: The K'n-Yani are genetically close to humanity, but not identical. Drugs and other chemical irritants sometimes work and sometimes do not. Any attempt to drug or chemically stun or disable a K'n-Yani succeeds only with a Luck roll.

OUT OF PHASE: K'n-Yani spend much of their immortal lives in a ghostly, immaterial state. A fully physical K'n-Yani can use its action in a combat turn to go immaterial, becoming immune to physical harm. Or one can go half-immaterial but still able to grasp physical things. When a K'n-Yani is half-immaterial, any attack that rolls an odd amount of damage or gets an odd number on a Lethality roll passes harmlessly through it.

SCALE CONTROL: The K'n-Yani can disassemble their physical form, and cause it to grow or shrink at will, by absorbing nearby matter or expelling it. While on the surface, the K'n-Yani often are five meters tall or more. A K'n-Yani at that great size is difficult to injure: a failed Lethality roll does not destroy it, but inflicts HP damage equal to the Lethality rating. Beneath the Earth, they assume human sizes, with half the listed STR, CON, and HP, and inflicting only 1D4−1 unarmed damage. Expelling mass causes a blue-white bright light that is visible at great distances.

MOTHER EARTH: K'n-Yani touching earth with bare skin can instantly vanish, returning to deep K'n-Yan.

TRANSAPPORTATION: The K'n-Yani can step through physical obstructions as if they were not there; a single step transports the subject to the "other side" of the item, no matter the distance. Anyone they are holding is transported as well (and suffers 0/1 SAN loss).

PROJECTION, POSSESSION, OR ERASURE: The K'n-Yani can move objects, possess humans, or remove themselves from an individual's perception. Each attempted use of one of these powers costs 3 WP.

Projection allows the K'n-Yani to push objects with blunt force at a distance of about 10 m. This inflicts 1D6 damage.

Possession is a mental onslaught of any one person in sight. The target gets a SAN roll in defense. On a success, the target loses 1 SAN and feels an alien presence. On a failure, the target loses 1/1D6 SAN and the K'n-Yani is in the target's mind. For one turn, the possessing K'n-Yani can see, hear and feel what the target does, and can sense and understand the target's thoughts and recent memories. The target can sense, feel, and do nothing. Once inside, the K'n-Yani can cause the target to take any single action of the possessor's choice, including suicide or murder. Then the possession ends. Normal SAN losses apply as the target realizes he or she has been possessed and recognizes what he or she has done.

Erasure causes a target to fail to see the K'n Y'ani or the effects of their presence. It only works on one target at a time. The target gets a SAN roll. On a failure, the K'n-Yani vanishes completely and remains unobservable by the target. The K'n-Yani can stand right in front of the target, root through the target's belongings, or even attack the target and not be seen.

SAN LOSS: 0/1D4.

Liveliest Awfulness

> *"It is hard to explain just how a single sight of a tangible object with measureable dimensions could so shake and change a man; and we may only say that there is about certain outlines and entities a power of symbolism and suggestion which acts frightfully on a sensitive thinker's perspective and whispers terrible hints of obscure cosmic relationships and unnamable realities behind the protective illusions of common vision."*
>
> —H.P. Lovecraft, *The Case of Charles Dexter Ward*

The dead may be returned to life with a ritual known as Raise from Essential Saltes. But if a corpse has been so destroyed or eaten away as to be incomplete, what returns is a grotesque, immortal monstrosity that one witness called "ye liveliest Awfulness."

The awfulness is essentially human in structure, but horribly malformed and misshapen. It is darkly discolored, perhaps due to the infusion of the stuff of Outside powers that were invoked to give it life. Some say its hideous proportions are eerily reminiscent of those powers and the dimensions where they lurk.

Long before the awfulness can be seen, its nauseating stench can be smelled and its unnerving voice can be heard: dismal moanings, mindless whines, yelps, and gibberings. The awfulness lurches and flops clumsily across the ground, or flings itself in spasmodic leaps, reaching with twisted limbs.

The awfulness may be returned to ash in the same manner as anyone resurrected in the Raise from Essential Saltes ritual. Cruel sorcerers have been rumored to keep these remnants imprisoned as convenient victims for ritual sacrifice. The truth of that, and whether one can be raised, sacrificed, and raised again for another sacrifice, are up to the Handler.

Liveliest Awfulness

STR 26 **CON** 20 **DEX** 10 **INT** 4 **POW** 6

HP 23 **WP** 6

ARMOR: See **UNFORMED**.

SKILLS: Alertness 80%, Athletics 50%, Grapple 55%.

ATTACKS: Grapple 55% (see **RAVENOUS**).

AGELESS: The awfulness suffers no ill effects from aging. Presumably it must feed, but as some have been known to sit in torpor for years—or centuries, or millennia, or eons—who can say?

RAVENOUS: In any turn after it has a victim pinned in its flailing limbs, the awfulness can tear with its ghastly teeth and suck down flesh and blood, inflicting 2D6 damage. If the awfulness has taken damage, it heals 1 HP for each HP that the pinned victim loses, up to its maximum.

UNFORMED: Slippery and scrabbling, not wholly related to any natural form of life, the awfulness is difficult to destroy. It takes half the HP damage from any attack except for fire or hypergeometry. Due to this incomplete biology, these beings move, at best, half the speed of a running human.

SAN LOSS: 1D4/1D10.

Lloigor

"The earth has favoured the evolution of its ungainly, optimistic children, and weakened the Lloigor. Nevertheless, these ancient powers remain. They have retreated under the earth and sea, in order to concentrate their power in stones and rocks, whose normal metabolism they can reverse. This has enabled them to cling to the earth for many thousands of years. Occasionally, they accumulate enough energy to erupt once again into human life, and the results are whole cities destroyed."

—Colin Wilson, "The Return of the Lloigor"

"Xin" (also transliterated as "shen") is the traditional Chinese name for various earth, weather, and celestial spirits: a rough equivalent (and possible cognate, perhaps via the Chinese hsien or xian, meaning immortal bodiless sorcerer) to the Arabic djinn. Like many creatures of traditional folklore, however, they have a darker, unnatural truth behind them. That truth is the Lloigor.

Like electromagnetism or inertia, the entities called Lloigor manifest as forces rather than beings. They have—or it has—no individual identity, but rather a field state, or an energetic wave function, or a local information surplus. Lloigor energy active enough to detect has a characteristic vortical spin, like a whirlpool or a magnetic field.

The Lloigor energy likely reached Earth on a transmission vector from the Andromeda galaxy approximately 2.5 million years ago, although it may be the same as the weirdly quasi-material "Lemurian" intelligence that is said to have briefly dominated Earth in the Eocene era. The lower entropy and higher Boltzmann constant in our "uphill" local physics weakened Lloigor power levels; the older Andromeda region the Lloigor had ruled was "downhill": higher entropy, like the Lloigor force matrix or "plexus." Over the millennia, the "downhill" Lloigor shed charge until they could only work effectively through Earthly material agents.

The Lloigor occasionally took physical form: strange, quasi-dinosaurian shapes, giving rise to legends of dragons and sea monsters. They reportedly dominated the humans of Mu's Yambi Empire, ruling through suicidal terror, alien discipline, and the gift of unnatural life—or chancrous death.

The Lloigor fields can alter local entropy along any number of dimensions: enough to create cancer in healthy tissue, randomly reassort molecules to create mists, and even alter fundamental forces to slow tachyonic information or unleash vast explosions. Legends say their powers devastated rebellious human civilizations. In some tales, even continents died, cracked as the Lloigor and Ghatanothoa warred over Mu. In others, Ghatanothoa was the forerunner and chief of the Lloigor.

Perhaps exhausted by their titanic displays, Lloigor energy dimmed, flickered into uncertainties, and localized into highly entropophilic stones. Aberrant cults protect Lloigor-charged focus stones and recharge the Lloigor fields with hatred and despair. Occasionally, the Lloigor resurge, usually leaving ruined cities surrounded by brackish blue-green water: the proto-Mayan city of Grudèn-Itzà that fell into the Louisiana swamps approximately four thousand years ago, Sidon in Phoenicia cracked asunder around 1000 BCE, Anuradhapura in Sri Lanka leveled in 1017 CE.

Lloigor minds and perceptions are unitary, not separated into layers of consciousness or delayed rationalization of perceptions. Lloigor cannot forget, dream, imagine, or fool themselves. The result is an outlook of absolute pessimism: they are under no illusions about the fate of all organized matter-energy. Their gloom poisons the minds of humans. At best, the Lloigor are incomprehensible; at worst, Lloigor mentation feels suicidally nihilistic.

The Lloigor offer human servitors the carrot of extended mental life (the physical body ages unpredictably and unsettlingly when exposed to Lloigor energy) and the stick of tentacle-shaped cancers embedded in eye sockets or digestive tracts. Human slaves project their abject suffering onto those weaker than they. Lloigor-haunted areas often have histories not merely of cancer and poltergeists but of brutality, cruelty, and sadism. Exposure to intense Lloigor fields can discolor jadeite and turn water a peculiar blue-green shade. The stones that "contain Lloigor," or more exactly, focus Lloigor energy, tend to be bluish or greenish, or have striations of those colors within them. If tested, they may appear older than stones around them. Previous servants—or crusaders—may have carved designs into the face of the rock: spirals, mazes, serpents, dragons, or tentacles. Unless otherwise specified, the Lloigor's abilities can operate within 5 km of a Lloigor focus.

Lloigor are immaterial and invisible. When they are "nearby"—when the Lloigor field is at maximum local intensity—sensitive humans might notice a wavering in their perception, like heat distortion flowing in a slow-moving moiré pattern, or feel a subsonic vibration in their jaws and other long bones. The presence or influence of the Lloigor gives some humans a subtly "nasty" sensation, like the feeling that comes with an unexpected thought of murder and tearing teeth.

Information about the nature, scope of the power, and influence of the Lloigor is far-reaching and contradictory. Whatever the truth, humanity's greatest defense against them may be inattention. The Lloigor rarely exert their repellent will except near their greenish-blue focus stones. But some witnesses claim that the Lloigor are slowly building their powers and intend a shattering return.

Lloigor

INT 29 **POW** 21+

HP n/a **WP** 21+

SKILLS: Alertness 50%, Surgery 90%.

ACTIONS PER TURN: One for every 10 POW (round down; at least one).

ACTIVATE CONSTRUCT: The Lloigor can create and act through quasi-dinosaurian shapes. Stories differ as to the reason and nature of these constructs. One holds them to be Lemurian artifacts—of all terrestrial technologies, the Lloigor find the psionic-material science of the Lemurians most congenial. They supposedly extract Lemurian constructs from the dimensional matrices where their creators stored them millions of years ago or, if need be, rebuild them using the psionic imprint left on an area's minerals and wave forms. This costs 1 WP per CON point activated or manifested in the construct. Lloigor can take days or weeks to build up such a form.

AMPUTATION: With a Surgery roll, the Lloigor can perform psychic surgery on their servants, amputating or growing (replacement or extra) limbs and organs. They can do the same to any human who touches a stone focus of Lloigor force. It costs 1 WP to amputate (inflicting 1 HP damage) or grow a finger (costing 0/1 SAN); 3 WP for a hand, foot, or eye (1D6 HP and 0/1D6 SAN); or 5 WP for a limb or internal organ (1D10 HP and 1/1D8 SAN). The damage ignores armor.

CANCEROUS GROWTH: Lloigor can cause cancer in their human servants from afar, even transforming an organ or limb into a tumor. They can do the same to any human who has suffered temporary insanity or passed a Breaking Point due to Lloigor action. The cancer may develop instantly (costing 1/1D8 SAN), or over a period of weeks, months, or years: the Lloigor ignore time. This costs 1 WP per 2 points of the victim's CON.

DEPRESSION: Contact with the pure, overwhelming pessimism of the Lloigor imprints that pattern on human minds. The disorder gained from Lloigor contact is always depression. Lloigor contact automatically turns a pre-existing depression acute. If someone is already suffering an acute episode, the Lloigor may use the **SUICIDE** power with immediate effect.

DRAIN ENERGY: Lloigor regenerate WP only by draining energy from sleeping intelligent beings such as humans. Affected humans awaken normally but feel ill and unrested; they are exhausted (see **EXHAUSTION** on page 47 of the *Agent's Handbook*) and cannot recuperate from harm. Once per victim per night, the Lloigor can gain 1 WP per 1D6 WP drained from a sleeping human within 10 km. Fortunately, the Lloigor rarely seem to focus their attention sufficiently to accumulate much strength.

EMF: Lloigor can emit or manipulate electromagnetic energy for effects including fogged film, degaussed compass needles, wiped computer memory, fried electronic components in cars or phones, radio interference, and so forth. This costs 1 to 3 WP, depending on the scale of the effect (up to, say, a village or very large building) and the hardness of the target.

ENSLAVE: To recruit or kill a specific human, Lloigor begin by draining energy until the target reaches 0 WP and falls into a near-coma. Each morning while in that state, the victim must make a CON test. On a success, the victim awakens and recovers 1 WP; on a failure, the victim loses 1 CON, or 1D4 CON on a fumble. When the victim's CON drops to 2, the victim stabilizes and awakens with a powerful instinct to serve the Lloigor, even if he or she does not know their name or nature, losing 1/1D4 SAN. Lost CON then returns, 1 point per day. The instinct to serve can be refused, in which case the Lloigor continue to drain CON until the victim dies. This costs the Lloigor 3 WP per night per target.

>> Lloigor Powers Summary

POWER	WP COST	SCOPE
Activate construct	1 per 1 CON manifested	A single quasi-dinosaurian construct.
Amputation	1, 3, or 5	A single victim.
Cancerous growth	1 per 2 CON of the victim	A single victim.
Depression	None	Any human who gains a disorder.
Drain energy	None	Gain 1 WP per 1D6 drained from each human within 10 km
EMF	1 to 3	A single device up to a small area.
Enslave	3 per night	A single victim.
Fog	1 per −10% penalty	A large area.
Induce frenzy	2 per target	One or more victims.
Suicide	2 per night	A single victim.
Telekinesis	10 per 1 STR	Near a focus stone.
Temporal doldrums	4 per time-increment	Up to six people; ×2 cost for 60, ×3 for 600, etc.
Vortex	10	Lethality 50% with Kill Radius 1 m; add +1 m or +1% Lethality per additional WP.

FOG: By telekinetically altering the physical properties of the atmosphere, Lloigor can manifest mist, fog, or clouds. Each 2 WP spent incurs a −20% penalty to Alertness, Drive, Pilot, ranged attack rolls, and other affected skills.

INDUCE FRENZY: At a cost of 2 WP per target, the Lloigor can imbue victims with berserk frenzy, driving them to murderous, flesh-rending attacks with hands and teeth. A target must make a SAN roll. On a success, the target loses 1 SAN and has a vivid vision of murdering the other soft targets—preferably human beings, and preferably friends and loved ones—in the room. On a failure, the target loses 1D4 SAN, adds +20% to Unarmed Combat for the duration of the violence, and does double Unarmed Combat damage. Lloigor frenzy follows the rules for the "struggle" response to temporary insanity (see **TEMPORARY INSANITY** on page 69 of the *Agent's Handbook*).

INTANGIBLE ENTITY: Lloigor can both sense and move/radiate through solid matter. It's possible that very dense matter such as lead may slow or block them, but that's up to the Handler. Their unnatural energies do not follow natural laws.

NONCORPOREAL: The Lloigor is not a physical entity and has no DEX score. Use its POW in place of DEX to determine when it acts each turn.

PLEXUS: A Lloigor plexus, or more intense Lloigor field (perceived by humans as "multiple Lloigor") has higher POW and WP values, potentially reaching the hundreds or thousands at major plexi. The Lloigor and their human slaves occasionally strive to gather Lloigor stones to build such powerful plexi. Thankfully, they rarely succeed.

SUBTERRANEAN POWER: The Lloigor pay 2/3 the WP cost for special abilities and hypergeometry when using those powers in a subsurface but open area such as a canyon, river bed, or depression, or 1/3 the listed cost when using its powers underground, e.g., in a basement or cavern. Minimum cost is always 1 WP.

SUICIDE: Lloigor sendings, at a cost of 2 WP per night, can drive a target to suicide. After each night of suicidal ideations, the victim loses 1/1D8 SAN. A victim who hits a Breaking Point or suffers temporary insanity attempts suicide by the fastest and most efficient method available. After a failed (or prevented) suicide attempt, the victim may make another SAN roll. Success prevents further Lloigor sendings until the next Breaking Point is hit.

TELEKINESIS: Lloigor can discretely affect the material world where their field strength is most intense. Lloigor must be "directly present" (focused both perceptually and energetically) to do so, ideally, less than 10 meters from a stone focus. This telekinesis can move or manipulate matter: anything from shoving a spelunker into a crevasse to diverting a gun barrel or opening a safe. It costs 10 WP for 1 STR; for each additional 10 WP, the STR of the force doubles.

TEMPORAL DOLDRUMS: Lloigor can alter the passage of time for a group of up to six humans. A sentry might believe he patrolled for two hours and come back to find eight hours elapsed. An ambulance might spend 10 minutes driving and arrive 40 minutes after departing. Recognizing such a time-slip costs 0/1 SAN; it's easier to believe you dozed off or got lost. This costs 4 WP per increment of time added or removed, however much time that increment encompasses; both examples add 3 increments (of 2 hours and of 10 minutes, respectively) and thus cost 12 WP. Double the cost for up to 60 humans, triple the cost for up to 600 humans, etc.

TRANSCENDENT: Lloigor are intangible, and cannot be harmed by any material weapon or substance. Whether any given hypergeometric attack affects the Lloigor is up to the Handler.

VORTEX: It's not manipulating matter that Lloigor find taxing; it's maintaining that matter's integrity. Without such maintenance, Lloigor telekinesis rips matter to shreds, imploding it along invisible fault lines in its energy patterns. This vortex blast has a 50% Lethality rating and a Kill Radius of at least one meter. It ignores armor. The blast leaves even the ground splintered, dry, and discolored, with teal-colored water pooling in divots and crevices. The vortex takes 1D4 turns to build, making a low rumbling sound like distant thunder. Humans in the vortex who make a successful Alertness test can attempt to escape the blast radius. The blasts costs 10 WP; each additional WP adds 1% to Lethality or expands the Kill Radius by one meter.

RITUALS: Lloigor may know any hypergeometry relating to Lemuria, Mu, the cults of Ghatanothoa or Cthulhu, or involving the manipulation of energies or forces.

SAN LOSS: 1/1D4 (from mental contact).

Lloigor-Controlled Quasi-Dinosaurian Constructs

"He handed me a chunk of green stone, almost too heavy to hold in one hand.…The inscription was in curved characters, not unlike Pitman's shorthand; the face in the midst of them could have been a devil mask, or a snake god, or a sea monster."

—Colin Wilson, "The Return of the Lloigor"

The Lloigor occasionally create great, deadly, reptilian shapes in which to ravage the physical world. Some sources say these are Lemurian constructs, retained in unseen dimensions. Lemurian constructs are said to take many forms, from a shimmering dome to a monocular giant, but the Lloigor—if this theory is true—prefer the quasi-dinosaurian shapes developed during Lemuria's wars against the serpent-folk. They can resemble any vaguely Cretaceous or Eocene beast of legend: dragon, triceratops, kraken, enormous sea urchin, monstrous rhinoceros, sea serpent, and so on.

The CON of the construct depends on the amount of energy (WP) expended by the Lloigor, and its STR always equals its CON. The listed values are typical. INT and POW are those of the Lloigor vortex that created and possess the construct. Once fully manifested, the construct continues to exist until disintegrated by the Lloigor or destroyed by attacks. Physically destroying a construct does not "kill" the Lloigor inside, although if no suitable focus is nearby, the Lloigor field may dissipate to undetectability for a few decades.

While possessing a construct, Lloigor can still use all their powers save intangibility.

Some sources say nothing of Lemurian constructs, but assert the Lloigor simply take on a giant reptilian form by telekinetic manipulation of local matter. If that is true, Lloigor cannot otherwise use telekinesis while materialized.

Lloigor-Controlled Quasi-Dinosaurian Construct

STR 41 **CON** 41 **DEX** 11 **INT** 29 **POW** 21+

HP 41 **WP** 21+

ARMOR: 8 points of scaly integument (see **RESILIENT**).

SKILLS: Alertness 30%, Surgery 90%.

ATTACKS: Huge, bony talons 70%, Lethality 20%, Armor Piercing 5.

Savage bite 50%, Lethality 30%, Armor Piercing 10.

Tail sweep 50% (see **TAIL SWEEP**).

RESILIENT: A successful Lethality roll does not destroy the construct, but inflicts HP damage equal to the Lethality rating.

TAIL SWEEP: The construct can sweep all characters in a broad arc behind it. On a successful attack, roll 2D10. If the total is higher than a swept character's DEX, the character is knocked prone. Apply the higher of the two dice as damage to all characters hit. Attempts to Dodge the sweep are at −20%.

TELEKINETIC FOCUS: While possessing/operating a construct, the Lloigor **TELEKINESIS** power costs half the usual WP.

UNNATURAL BIOLOGY: The construct's physiology would baffle any biologist. Making a called shot for "vitals" or another apparently vulnerable area inflicts normal damage, with no special game effect.

SAN LOSS: 0/1D6.

Metoh-Kangmi

"No use, either, to point out the even more startlingly similar belief of the Nepalese hill tribes in the dreaded mi-go or 'abominable snow-men' who lurk hideously amidst the ice and rock pinnacles of the Himalayan summits."

—H.P. Lovecraft, "The Whisperer in Darkness"

The "abominable snowman" of the Himalayas is another mi-go construct, this one based on the yeti, said by some to be a Voorii survival from the Pleistocene. The mi-go mining colony in Central Asia built the metoh-kangmi as a host body that could process terrestrial food, since maintaining the unnatural gate that supplied it was dangerous so near Leng.

It resembles a bipedal, pale creature sprouting whiplike tendrils of hair and sinew. Its head can unfold back from its face to expose the mi-go "brain" within. It has no wings, but moves in meters-long, hovering steps and can bilocate—the lung-gom-pa and shespa-po of Tibetan mysticism. Metoh-kangmi use regular mi-go technology, but in different forms.

Delta Green operatives who encountered the metoh-kangmi in Nepal and Tibet had no idea that they were the same beings as the winged terrors of Vermont and the deeper Appalachians.

A metoh-kangmi uses the INT of the mi-go controlling it.

Metoh-Kangmi

STR 16 **CON** 14 **DEX** 13 **INT** n/a **POW** 13

HP 14 **WP** 13

ARMOR: 3 points of ablative coating.

SKILLS: Alertness 80%, Athletics 80%, Stealth 40%.

ATTACKS: De-oxygenator 40% (see **DE-OXYGENATOR**).

Kick 40%, damage 1D8.

Tendrils 40%, damage 1D6 or erasure (see **ERASE**).

DE-OXYGENATOR: This ray burst, emitted as part of the metoh-kangmi's high-pitched cry, removes the oxygen from the air in a three-meter radius around the target. This triggers immediate suffocation (see page 62 of the *Agent's Handbook)* in anyone not wearing oxygen gear. It costs the metoh-kangmi 2 WP.

ERASE: The tendrils of the metoh-kangmi can inject a substance which prevents the creation of short-term memories for 12 hours. The victim "comes to" 12 hours later and loses 0/1 SAN. All SAN lost during the initial attack is regained, and inflicted again only if the target discovers the lost time.

LUNG-GOM-PA: The metoh-kangmi can move up to 100 m in one turn by spending 2 WP.

SHESPA-PO: By spending 2 WP, the metoh-kangmi can create a convincing illusion of itself up to 8 km away, or more if the witness has already seen the metoh-kangmi. The illusionary double can speak and sense its surroundings, but cannot be affected by physical force.

(For 4 WP, the metoh-kangmi can project its double invisibly to that location.) The metoh-kangmi can spend 6 WP to instantaneously (and indetectably) switch places with its bilocated double.

THING OF COLD: A metoh-kangmi suffers no harm or ill effects from the cold.

RITUALS: The controlling mi-go can use the metoh-kangmi to perform any ritual it knows.

SAN LOSS: 0/1D4.

Mi-Go

"Their main immediate abode is a still undiscovered and almost lightless planet at the very edge of our solar system—beyond Neptune, and the ninth in distance from the sun. It is, as we inferred, the object mystically hinted at as 'Yuggoth' in certain ancient and forbidden writings; and it will soon be the scene of a strange focussing of thought upon our world in an effort to facilitate mental rapport...."

—H.P. Lovecraft, "The Whisperer in Darkness"

The mi-go have long haunted the solar system. Resembling huge, spongy crabs topped by glowing fungus, the mi-go are unlike any life native to Earth. They can shape and reform their strange forms at will. They exist in dimensions above and below those observable by humanity. Even their movement and modes of thought are macrodimensional, allowing mi-go to see short stints of the future, or to cross otherwise impassable barriers by taking dimensional shortcuts. This even allows them to "fly" and "breathe" in vacuum. It is theorized by some that the mi-go, as we observe them, are simply an extrusion of some greater entity in a higher dimension. To humanity, their roiling, ever-shifting form is utterly baffling to gaze upon and is enough to drive most to insanity.

The mi-go have spent many years studying humanity, first with isolated individuals and remote cults—sometimes in person, and sometimes using constructs like the metoh-kangmi—and later in their guise as the "Greys" (see **METOH-KANGMI** on page 216 and **GREYS** on page 203). They still find humanity baffling. Since MAJESTIC severed ties with the Greys in 2001, the mi-go have remained silent. No one knows if they learned what they hoped.

Mi-Go

STR 16 **CON** 15 **DEX** 13 **INT** 25 **POW** 14

HP 15 **WP** 14

ARMOR: See **MACRODIMENSIONAL**.

SKILLS: Alertness 30%, Flight 55%, Science (Genetics) 95%, Science (Macrodimensional Physics) 50%, Science (Human Anthropology) 11%, Tool Use 55%, Unnatural 60%.

ATTACKS: Grapple and erase 55% (see **GRAPPLE AND ERASE**).

Electric wand 55%, Lethality 2% or 15% or 25% (see **TOOLS**).

Macrodimensional scalpel 55%, Lethality 10%, Armor Piercing 5 (see **TOOLS**).

Gravity weapon 55%, Lethality 65% (see **TOOLS**).

AETHERIC FLIGHT: The mi-go can "fly" in any environment, moving as if being swept away on some unseen current—even underwater or in space. In flight, the mi-go can move at great speeds, equivalent (at top speed) to a jet aircraft. They can hover, invert, and hold in place as well. This allows them to "walk up" walls in a fashion similar to a giant spider.

GRAPPLE AND ERASE: Mi-go often rush and inject an intruding human with a substance that removes short-term memories. The mi-go must make a grapple attack (which the target is permitted to counter, as usual). If the mi-go wins, and no one interferes in the meantime, then on its next turn it injects a substance which prevents the creation of short-term memories for 12 hours. The victim "comes to" 12 hours later and loses 0/1 SAN. All SAN lost during the initial attack is regained, and inflicted again only if the target discovers the lost time.

MULTIFORM: The mi-go can move, change, extrude, extend, and alter their bodies as needed. Each change takes one turn, and costs nothing. A mi-go could extrude four more limbs to hold a pinned target, for example, or open a cavity to hold an item.

MACRODIMENSIONAL: The mi-go exist in a multitude of dimensions, only a fraction of which are visible to us. They sometimes appear to move in stuttering frames, as if blinking in and out of reality from second to second. A successful Lethality roll destroys a mi-go, but other attacks are unpredictable. If an attack rolls an odd amount of damage, the mi-go has shifted out of phase with our dimension and is immune to the attack.

NON-TERRENE: The mi-go are at home in nearly any environment. Radiation, pressure, cold, vacuum and more have no negative effects on them. They can move on the surface of Saturn, in the depths of the ocean, or in open space with equal ease.

SHORTCUT: A mi-go can bypass a physical obstacle or cross a distance up to 100 meters in one turn by making a successful Science (Macrodimensional Physics) roll. Success indicates the mi-go seems to stutter out of reality for a split second before arriving at its destination. It costs 0/1 SAN to witness this for the first time. Failure indicates the mi-go does not accomplish the movement, and all attacks that round inflict full damage even if they usually would not (see **MACRODIMENSIONAL**).

TOOLS: Mi-go are tool-users, though it is hard for humans to tell where their bodies end and the tools begin. The mi-go are known to wield weapons like electric wands, macrodimensional surgical tools, and the deadly gravity weapon (see **ATTACKS**). Humans attempting to commandeer such weapons must make a Luck roll each time one is "used." Failure indicates that due to the bizarre nature of the weapon, the human injures himself or herself.

- *Electric Wand:* This eighteen-inch wand-like object is made of a black, non-reflective metal not found on Earth. It emits an electrical jolt with Lethality attack of 2%, 15% or 25%. The mi-go may change the setting at any time.
- *Macrodimensional Scalpel:* The common mi-go surgical tool is made of a strange black shiny material, and is filthy, smelling of rotting meat and covered in strange stains. The mi-go often carry these tools on their bodies in gelatinous sacks made of an opaque grey slime. The scalpel cannot be understood by humans.
- *Gravity Weapon:* This deadly macrodimensional device is only used as a last resort. It is made of two six-inch sections of black, stone-like material, connected by hinges so that the two sections fold in on each other. When it is opened, a gravitic force in excess of 100 Gs is unleashed in a cone emanating from the center of the sigil, inflicting a Lethality 65% attack. All objects in this cone are affected, knocking down buildings, breaking bones, and destroying almost everything in its path. The mi-go chooses its range. No counter-force is generated.

UNNATURAL BIOLOGY: The mi-go's physiology would baffle any biologist. Making a called shot for "vitals" or another apparently vulnerable area inflicts normal damage, with no special game effect.

THE VOICE: The mi-go can emit a buzzing imitation of human speech and can hold rudimentary conversations with humans. Each attempt to impart or understand information by the mi-go requires them to roll their Science (Human Anthropology) skill. Failure indicates a confusing exchange, usually involving a poor understanding of causality in four-dimensional spacetime.

SAN LOSS: 1/1D6.

Serpent-Folk

"Of the Shining Trapezohedron he speaks often, calling it a window on all time and space, and tracing its history from the days it was fashioned on dark Yuggoth, before ever the Old Ones brought it to earth. It was treasured and placed in its curious box by the crinoid things of Antarctica, salvaged from their ruins by the serpent-men of Valusia, and peered at aeons later in Lemuria by the first human beings."

—H.P. Lovecraft,"The Haunter of the Dark"

The serpent-folk, as some occultists call them, rose to prominence in the Paleozoic era, carving a huge civilization called Valusia from the wilds of Pangea. They uncovered and attempted to exploit the ancient technologies left behind by other alien cultures that had colonized the Earth. With these secrets, they learned to change and manipulate space and time. It is unknown what caused the collapse of their culture, but many stragglers remained. Some are said to have escaped to red-litten Yoth, far underground, or to lost Atlantis.

Throughout human history, the serpent-folk have appeared from time to time in human disguise, carrying out bizarre plans to return their kind to supremacy.

Serpent-Folk

STR 19 **CON** 21 **DEX** 18 **INT** 20 **POW** 16

HP 20 **WP** 16

ARMOR: 3 points of thick, scaly skin.

SKILLS: Alertness 80%, Anthropology (Human) 35%, Disguise 40%, Dodge 60%, Medicine 99%, Science (Biology) 99%, Sciences (Serpent-Men) 90%, Search 90%, Survival 70%, Unnatural 65%.

ATTACKS: Bite 55%, damage 1D6, Armor Piercing 3 (see **VENOM**).

Grapple 45%, damage special (see **BLOOD FRENZY**).

Sign of Power, damage 2D6 (see **SIGN OF POWER**).

BLOOD FRENZY: A target that is bleeding causes one of the serpent-folk to enter a blood frenzy. It attempts to grapple and pin the victim. If it succeeds, it drains 1 HP per round from blood loss until the victim dies. Only a Dodge roll allows the target to escape. A seized victim can attempt an opposed STR roll to struggle free, suffering 1D4 damage from tearing flesh. Any successful attack on the serpent during the blood frenzy causes this attack to cease. During this blood frenzy, the serpent

cannot perform any other action until the target is dead or escapes.

CHARNEL VISAGE: The serpent-folk have no CHA stat as humans would understand it. A serpent that uses an unnatural ritual such as Changeling Feast to disguise itself as human gains a CHA stat, usually with a score equal to half its INT. Many serpent-folk have consumed multiple victims, allowing one to instantly switch its appearance to any of a dozen human forms.

IMMORTALITY: A member of the serpent-folk never grows old, starves to death, or perishes of natural causes. If it fails to feed on fresh meat or blood, after a period of time, it enters a torporous state which can sometimes last hundreds, perhaps millions, of years.

INHUMAN DODGE: Serpent-folk have preternatural senses and reaction speed, allowing them to Dodge even firearm attacks. This includes Lethality attacks from machine guns, but not from explosives or hypergeometry.

VENOM: If a serpent-folk bite inflicts damage (in other words, if it's not stopped by armor), then the victim also suffers poisoning. The venom has a Speed of 1D6 turns and Lethality 15%. An antidote that treats snake venom is effective if the victim makes a Luck roll.

RITUALS: All serpent-folk know unnatural rituals. Changeling Feast, Fascination, Infallible Suggestion, Obscure Memory, and Withering are the most common, but some know many more.

SIGN OF POWER: With a gesture, one of the serpent-folk can cause a single person to be flung backwards with extreme force, inflicting 2D6 damage. It is unknown whether this ability is a ritual or an inherent ability.

UNNATURAL BIOLOGY: Serpent-folk physiology would baffle any biologist. Making a called shot for "vitals" or another apparently vulnerable area inflicts normal damage, with no special game effect.

SAN LOSS: 1/1D6.

DISINFORMATION

PROTOMATTER YELLOW CARD

It is unknown where the original sample was recovered, but several reputable sources place it at the site of a Delta Green operation in Groversville, Tennessee, in the mid-1990s. There, it appears, the mi-go, in the guise of the "Greys," infected the town with unnatural, self-replicating tissue which may have issued forth from a shoggoth or shoggoth-like creature.

Both MAJESTIC and Delta Green recovered samples of this tissue, though Delta Green's samples were later destroyed. (Or were they?) Even today, despite the severing of ties with the Greys, followed by their remote deactivation of all technologies gifted to humanity in the interim, protomatter still seems to function and live. It may be that the mi-go are unaware that samples persist.

Protomatter could insinuate itself into a human body and enhance, change or consume that form, leading to horrific proto-shoggoths. The details of such a transformation remain up to the Handler to devise. But the most fearful thing about protomatter was this: it could be insinuated into food or water and infect a target without their foreknowledge.

Handlers should treat a protomatter entity as a shoggoth but with STR 25, CON 13, and 19 HP. Its attacks also inflict less damage: 1D8 for grappling and crushing, 2D6 for smashing, and 1D6 (with Armor Piercing 5) for impaling.

CUT ALONG THIS LINE

Shoggoths

"The newly bred shoggoths grew to enormous size and singular intelligence, and were represented as taking and executing orders with marvelous quickness. They seemed to converse with the Old Ones by mimicking their voices—a sort of musical piping over a wide range, if poor Lake's dissection had indicated aright—and to work more from spoken commands than from hypnotic suggestions as in earlier times. They were, however, kept in admirable control. The phosphorescent organisms supplied light with vast effectiveness, and doubtless atoned for the loss of the familiar polar auroras of the outer-world night."

—H.P. Lovecraft, "At The Mountains of Madness"

This species of giant, immortal, plastic, ever-changing life gained sentience and overthrew its masters long before mankind rose to prominence. Many unnatural texts claim that the shoggoths were created by the crinoid Elder Things. Other texts disagree. No one knows. What is clear is that shoggoths are semi-intelligent, malevolent, and incredibly dangerous, apparently immortal, and nearly indestructible. There are rumors that they have been deployed by Deep Ones as slaves or allies. Other rumors say that certain hypergeometric technologies can confound or control them.

Composed of limbs created on the fly and guided by a thousand eyes, the shoggoth's changing form allows it to fit through nearly any space, and to reorient and shift its mass to crush, leap, crawl, move with appalling speed, or stick to nearly any surface. They are the ultimate problem solvers, seemingly designed to overcome, construct, or destroy any obstacle. The Handler is encouraged to invent new physical abilities along with those described here.

Shoggoth

STR 100 **CON** 50 **DEX** 10 **INT** 8 **POW** 12

HP 75 **WP** 12

ARMOR: See **PLASTIC** and **RESILIENT**.

SKILLS: Alertness 80%, Swim 90%.

ATTACKS: Grapple and crush 55%, Lethality 15% (see **CRUSH**).

Smash 35%, Lethality 30% (see **SMASH**).

Impale 35%, damage 1D10+2, Armor Piercing 5 (see **IMPALE**).

CRUSH: A target grappled and pinned by a shoggoth, even if the target has already acted in that turn, may attempt a single, unopposed DEX test to struggle free. Failure means the victim is engulfed and crushed for 15% Lethality damage, which ignores armor. The victim must then make a Luck roll once per turn to be spat back out. Failure means the victim is consumed, ground up into nutrients; the victim loses 1D8 HP each turn and the shoggoth gains an equivalent amount. Against a target that's larger than human-sized, the shoggoth simply squeezes whatever portion seems most vulnerable, inflicting Lethality 25% without absorbing nutrients.

ENDURANCE: A shoggoth that has at least 2 HP heals 1D10 HP, up to its maximum, every turn that it neither moves nor attacks. A shoggoth can survive comfortably in vacuum, in any depth of water, in freezing temperatures, and in catastrophic heat. Radiation which would cause cell-death in mammals is quite harmless to a shoggoth. A shoggoth suffers no ill effects from aging. Presumably a shoggoth must feed, but they have been known to sit in torpor for years—or centuries, or millennia, or eons; who can say?—with no apparent harm. The limits of a shoggoth's endurance are unknown.

FURY: A shoggoth has intelligence on the same scale as a human, but its modes of thought are utterly, incomprehensibly alien. In most encounters, a shoggoth acts with seemingly mindless, destructive wrath. But it may have inscrutable goals, newly conceived or developed over billions of years, which are served by the destruction it causes.

IMPALE: The shoggoth suddenly extrudes a thin tentacle tipped with a bone-talon, impaling a target and inflicting 1D10+2 HP damage. Each HP inflicted on the target is added to the shoggoth's own HP as it absorbs nutrients.

LOCOMOTION: A shoggoth can roll along the ground, disperse its density to rise lighter than air, or pull water or air through itself like a jet. No one has survived an encounter long enough to measure a shoggoth's maximum speed, but some victims have escaped shoggoths by speeding away via automobile, boat, or airplane.

PLASTIC: Shoggoths can ooze, grow, shift or change their plastic form to fit through almost any gap. If air can pass through an opening, a shoggoth can as well. Any attack against a shoggoth inflicts no more than 1 HP damage, except one using hypergeometry or a weapon with Lethality of 40% or more.

RESILIENT: Even a heavy weapon that can truly harm a shoggoth—requiring Lethality 40% or higher—does not destroy it with a successful Lethality roll. Instead, it inflicts HP damage equal to the Lethality rating.

SENTRY: Shoggoths are encased in a thousand shifting eyes that can see in every portion of the electromagnetic spectrum. All Stealth attempts against them are at −40%.

SMASH: Gathering up a dozen huge limbs, a shoggoth can smash or dismember a target with a Lethality rating of 30%. An attempt to Dodge this attack is at +20%.

TEKELI-LI: Shoggoths were bred to communicate, and to imitate the sounds of their former masters. They are incredible mimics. Few know how long it would take a shoggoth to use this facility for actual communication, but they certainly can imitate any sound they hear.

UNSTOPPABLE: If reduced to 0 HP, a shoggoth collapses into inert, hardened, desiccated bits of organic matter. However, it is not dead. If left in this state in an environment with access to oxygen and water, even trace water in the air, it reconstitutes to half strength in 2D20 hours. If this desiccated matter is burned or subjected to other destructive forces (even ones which would not usually affect the shoggoth), the shoggoth is permanently destroyed.

SAN LOSS: 1D6/1D20.

Slime of Tsathoggua

"Living things...oozed along stone channels and worshipped onyx and basalt images of Tsathoggua. But they were not toads like Tsathoggua himself. Far worse—they were amorphous lumps of viscous black slime that took temporary shapes for various purposes. The explorers of K'n-yan did not pause for detailed observations, and those who escaped alive sealed the passage leading from red-litten Yoth down into the gulfs of nether horror."

—H.P. Lovecraft and Zealia Bishop, "The Mound"

These oozing, formless entities are thankfully rare, as long as one avoids the enormous, heavy basins and ominous stone troughs that decorate the temples of Tsathoggua. Some sources call them Kythamila, a name whose derivation is a mystery. Their exact nature, none can say. Perhaps they were once other beings of more definite shape, corrupted by their master. Or perhaps they are indeed the spawn of that Great Old One, excreted from its loathsome body. Regardless, they serve only its needs.

The secretions of Tsathoggua are sooty and opaque, exuding a noxious, swampy, fetid odor. They pour or rise up from viscous pools to form eyes, jaws, tongues, and tentacle-like pseudopods. They slither across the ground like snakes or on countless short legs like a centipede.

The slime of Tsathoggua can lurk in torpor for eons without harm, stirring only upon the will of their master or when they sense living creatures. They digest and feed on living flesh. Their slick, cold grasp is as sharply constricting as a squeezing vise of steel blades, leaving only withered flesh, bloodless and dead.

Slime of Tsathoggua

STR 25 **CON** 20 **DEX** 19 **INT** 10 **POW** 10

HP 23 **WP** 10

ARMOR: See **OOZING**.

SKILLS: Alertness 90%, Swim 90%.

ATTACKS: Grasp and absorb 90%, Lethality 15% (see **GRASP AND ABSORB**).

GRASP AND ABSORB: A slime of Tsathoggua can reach out with extruded pseudopods and absorb prey within itself. The slime may spread this attack to two or even three targets in one turn: with two attacks, each is at 70% and inflicts 2D6 damage instead of a Lethality rating; with three attacks, each is at 50% and inflicts 1D10 damage.

NON-TERRENE: The slime are at home in nearly any environment. Radiation, pressure, cold, vacuum and other inimical environments have no negative effects on them.

OOZING: Tsathoggua's formless slime can ooze, grow, shift or change their plastic form to fit through almost any gap. If air can pass through an opening, the slime can as well. Physical attacks do them no harm, but flame and hypergeometry inflict full damage.

STRANGE SENSES: The slime senses living creatures up to 10 meters away with an Alertness test. Barriers (such as a biohazard suit) thwart this sense. A slime may form eyes to see in any wavelengths of light, and its viscous form is extraordinarily sensitive to sound, touch, and smell.

UNDULATION: At top speed, by flinging its mass from point to point and recongealing, the slime can slither up to 80 kph.

SAN LOSS: 1/1D10.

Spawn of Cthulhu

"Another race—a land race of beings shaped like octopi and probably corresponding to the fabulous pre-human spawn of Cthulhu—soon began filtering down from cosmic infinity and precipitated a monstrous war which for a time drove the Old Ones wholly back to the sea—a colossal blow in view of the increasing land settlements."

—H.P. Lovecraft, "At the Mountains of Madness"

Cthulhu did not arrive on Earth alone. Many sources cite the "star-spawn"—servants of the Great Old One—but few can settle on a singular description of these entities. They fought for supremacy against the Elder Things in ancient times, forcing them from the surface world. Perhaps that defeat was the precursor to the Elder Things' creation of the shoggoths.

Some believe the difficulty in understanding the star-spawn is because they evolve, shift, and grow over time, transforming from self-arranging blobs of matter to luminescent, winged monsters all the way up to horrors like Cthulhu itself, on a lesser scale.

Five great Cthulhu-spawn, the "Five Watchers," reputedly slumber in subterranean gulfs beneath the Bayan Kara Shan mountains in China, the Nameless City in the Arabian desert, the Greenland glacier, New England, and the Amazon Basin. Unnatural texts say that related entities dwell in the stars, such as the beings said to infest the Lake of Hali on or near Aldebaran.

Still others believe that the star-spawn of Cthulhu were the source of the Deep Ones on Earth, and that the core infective element which ties Cthulhu to the aquatic beings—and thus, perhaps, to humanity—issues from there. If that is true, then the most vast, ancient Deep Ones, creatures like Dagon, Hydra, and He-Who-Swims-with-Corpses, could be said to be the star-spawn of Cthulhu. Whether their forms are fluid or fixed, no living human can say.

Spawn of Cthulhu

STR 80 **CON** 120 **DEX** 10 **INT** 24 **POW** 30

HP 100 **WP** 30

ARMOR: See **DISCORPORATION** and **DISSOLUTE MATTER**.

SKILLS: Alertness 65%, Flight 60%, Swim 80%, Unnatural 80%.

ATTACKS: Claw swipe 60%, Lethality 20%, Armor Piercing 10.

Grab and consume 40%, Lethality 40% (see **GRAB AND CONSUME**).

DISCORPORATION: A successful attack with a Lethality rating of 50% or higher causes the spawn of Cthulhu to explode in a disgusting spray of slime and fragments, effectively destroying it. Whether the spawn is truly dead or eventually reforms is unknown.

DISSOLUTE MATTER: While most spawn of Cthulhu assume and maintain a recognizable shape, they remain immune to all but the most destructive weapons as their bodies naturally displace and reform. The spawn takes no more than 1 HP damage from any attack except hypergeometry or a heavy weapon with a Lethality rating of 50% or higher.

BALLISTIC FLIGHT: On a successful Flight skill roll one of Cthulhu's spawn is capable of launching itself into the atmosphere at speeds faster than a jet aircraft. It lands with an unceremonious impact, inflicting a Lethality attack of 15% in a 10-meter radius.

GRAB AND CONSUME: The Cthulhu-spawn can attempt to grab and consume any nearby character that successfully attacked it with an attack of Lethality 10% or higher. The spawn smashes a limb down (the target is permitted a Dodge roll), seizes the target (the target can attempt an unopposed STR contest to escape), and then drops the victim into an orifice for digestion. If the Dodge and STR tests fail, the target suffers a Lethality attack of 40%. Nutrients from the shredded target restore 1D12 HP to the spawn.

NON-TERRENE: The spawn of Cthulhu are at home in nearly any environment. Radiation, pressure, cold, vacuum, and other inimical environments have no negative effects on them.

PSYCHIC SHOUT: Characters who fail the SAN roll when encountering the spawn of Cthulhu experience more than its awful physical presence. A character who fails the SAN roll and is exceptionally sensitive (with INT or POW 17 or higher, or any Art, Occult, or Psychotherapy skill at 60% or better) collapses, overwhelmed by a psychic "shout." It can only be approximated as a voice shouting or babbling what should be nonsense if it were a voice—yet it is clearly filled with utterly alien meaning.

RITUALS: The spawn of Cthulhu manipulate unnatural forces in ways inconceivable to humanity. They can work any ritual, with as much ease, as the Handler thinks fitting.

SAN LOSS: 1D6/1D20.

Spawn of Yog-Sothoth

"The thing that lay half-bent on its side in a foetid pool of greenish-yellow ichor and tarry stickiness was almost nine feet tall....It was partly human, beyond a doubt, with very man-like hands and head, and the goatish, chinless face had the stamp of the Whateleys upon it....Above the waist it was semi-anthropomorphic; though its chest, where the dog's rending paws still rested watchfully, had the leathery, reticulated hide of a crocodile or alligator. The back was piebald with yellow and black, and dimly suggested the squamous covering of certain snakes.

"Below the waist...the skin was thickly covered with coarse black fur, and from the abdomen a score of long greenish-grey tentacles with red sucking mouths protruded limply....On each of the hips, deep set in a kind of pinkish, ciliated orbit, was what seemed to be a rudimentary eye; whilst in lieu of a tail there depended a kind of trunk or feeler with purple annular markings, and with many evidences of being an undeveloped mouth or throat.

"The limbs, save for their black fur, roughly resembled the hind legs of prehistoric earth's giant saurians; and terminated in ridgy-veined pads that were neither hooves nor claws. When the thing breathed, its tail and tentacles rhythmically changed colour, as if from some circulatory cause normal to the non-human side of its ancestry. In the tentacles this was observable as a deepening of the greenish tinge, whilst in the tail it was manifest as a yellowish appearance which alternated

with a sickly greyish-white in the spaces between the purple rings. Of genuine blood there was none; only the foetid greenish-yellow ichor which trickled along the painted floor beyond the radius of the stickiness, and left a curious discolouration behind it."

—H.P. Lovecraft, "Dunwich Horror"

Degenerate cults and clans, thankfully rare, have sought out unseen Yog-Sothoth and implored it to seed them with its offspring. For a while, such progeny pass as human without close inspection. But the spawn grows with uncanny speed, reaching apparent adulthood in 10 years. By age 15, the monstrous hybrid may be so tall and deformed as to seem human only by wearing all-covering, loose clothing. But nothing can mask its stench, foul and inhuman. Dogs hate the spawn of Yog-Sothoth and attack with little provocation. If it wishes to avoid attention and interference, the hybrid must avoid humanity whenever possible, risking contact only when necessary to fulfill its purposes. The spawn of Yog-Sothoth are driven to open ways into the world for their sire.

Spawn of Yog-Sothoth

STR 20 **CON** 17 **DEX** 10 **INT** 20 **POW** 18 **CHA** 3

HP 19 **WP** 18

ARMOR: See **UNNATURAL BIOLOGY**.

SKILLS: Alertness 40%, Athletics 40%, Unarmed Combat 40%, Unnatural 50%.

ATTACKS: Unarmed 40%, damage grappling or 1D8 (see **SUCKLING**).

HALF-TERRENE: The spawn of Yog-Sothoth is most at home in environments where humanity can thrive, but who knows what its inhuman biology can withstand? What ill effects it suffers from old age, disease, poison, radiation, pressure, cold, and submersion are up to the Handler and may vary with each specimen.

JUMPING, CLIMBING, LOPING: The spawn of Yog-Sothoth can leap, climb and lope in a manner wholly unlike a human. With an Athletics roll, it can cross vertical distances and impassable obstacles that would stop a normal human, but otherwise moves at human speeds.

SUCKLING: In any turn after the spawn of Yog-Sothoth has a victim grappled and pinned, the red, sucking mouths of its (usually concealed) tentacles greedily suck blood from the victim's veins. This reduces the victim's STR by 1D4 per turn without requiring an action by the spawn. Each point of STR drained heals the spawn of 1 lost HP. (At zero STR, the victim dies. A victim who survives regains 1 STR for each day of bed rest.)

RITUALS: The spawn of Yog-Sothoth always seeks hypergeometry and has mastered as many rituals as the Handler wishes. It is most interested in summoning its kin, with rituals such as Call Forth Those From Outside, and communicating with them by means such as the Dho-Hna Formula, One Who Passes the Gateways, and the Voorish Sign.

UNNATURAL BIOLOGY: The physiology of the spawn of Yog-Sothoth would baffle any biologist. Making a called shot for "vitals" or another apparently vulnerable area inflicts normal damage, with no special game effect. After death, the body quickly deteriorates, leaving only a sticky, whitish mass of unearthly biomatter behind.

SAN LOSS: 1/1D6 (if seen unclothed).

Spectral Polyps

"According to these scraps of information, the basis of the fear was a horrible elder race of half-polypous, utterly alien entities which had come through space from immeasurably distant universes and had dominated the earth and three other solar planets about six hundred million years ago. They were only partly material—as we understand matter—and their type of consciousness and media of perception differed wholly from those of terrestrial organisms."

—H.P. Lovecraft, "The Shadow Out of Time"

Horrific, giant blots of otherworldly malevolence infected the Earth hundreds of millions of years ago. The polyps carved giant, windowless basalt towers, and made war on more material foes by controlling and shaping the wind. Undulating, multi-colored, snakelike beings that existed both in and out of our visible dimensions, the polyps were huge, clumsy, loud, and destructive. Hooting their plaintive language of whines and whistles at one another across a ruined landscape, they consumed all in their path.

Eventually, the Great Race of Yith sealed them beneath the Earth. Some say the spectral polyps still persist there; others say they left this world long ago to return to the strange dimensions of their origin. The Gunditjmara of Australia's western Victoria state tell stories of a terrifying, underground wind-monster called the Muuruup, whose servants are invisible spirits who screech like owls. Whether the polyps still lurk on Earth, inspiring such legends, or on other worlds of the Solar System, no one knows.

Spectral Polyp

STR 75 **CON** 100 **DEX** 12 **INT** 22 **POW** 20

HP 88 **WP** 20

ARMOR: See **PARTLY MATERIAL**.

SKILLS: Extradimensional Senses 90% (see **OMNISCIENCE**).

ATTACKS: Lash out 50%, Lethality 10%, Armor Piercing 5 (see **LASH OUT**).

Spectral infection 35%, Lethality 40% (see **SPECTRAL INFECTION**).

Wind control 30%, damage 2D10 (see **WIND CONTROL**).

Vacuum burst 25%, Lethality 15% (see **VACUUM BURST**).

ELECTRICAL WEAKNESS: Electrical attacks bypass all defenses and inflict double their maximum possible damage on the polyp; no damage roll is required.

ISSUE FORTH: The polyp is actually suspended on invisible appendages with which it moves and manipulates the environment. This makes the creature appear to float on the air. Its odd, alien substance stretches, bends, changes color, and warps itself as it moves hypnotically forward. At top speed, a polyp can move at about 25 kph.

LASH OUT: The polyp has dozens of invisible, extradimensional limbs with which it manipulates objects. It can use these to lash out at a nearby enemy with a wave of invisible, razor-sharp whips inflicting a Lethality attack of 10%. Due to the limbs' invisibility, this attack is impossible to Dodge.

NON-TERRENE: The polyps are at home in nearly any environment. Radiation, pressure, cold, vacuum, and other inimical environments have no negative effects on them.

OMNISCIENCE: The polyps sense their environment through higher dimensions, which gives them an ever-present, up-to-the-moment, perfect knowledge of all objects and beings within a mile of their location. This "hyper sense" is like a combination of sonar, sight, hearing, and other, less-definable perceptions, and "sees through" any obstacle. All Dodge and Stealth rolls against a polyp are automatically at −40%.

PARTLY MATERIAL: Any non-hypergeometric, non-electrical attack on the polyp must have a Lethality rating

of 15% or higher to inflict any damage. A successful Lethality roll does not destroy the polyp, but inflicts HP damage equal to the Lethality rating. However, the spectral polyp is out of phase with physical reality. If the Lethality roll is an odd number, the attack passes through the space harmlessly.

SPECTRAL INFECTION: The strange substance that composes the giant polyp is completely inimical to Earthly life. A simple touch from the visible portions of the polyp is enough to disrupt living material as if it were a Lethality attack of 40%. Those observing this effect suffer 0/1D4 SAN loss as the polyp consumes the living matter like a fire converting wood to ash.

VACUUM BURST: A polyp can suddenly evacuate huge areas of atmosphere, causing a thunderclap as air rushes in to fill the empty space. When targeted at a human, this attack has a Lethality rating of 15% with a Kill Radius of 15 meters. When projected at a vehicle, it is capable of blowing open every sealed surface, completely disabling the vehicle.

WIND CONTROL: A polyps can constrict, shift, turn and accelerate wind. If focused on a single target, this wind tunnel can shear the skin from bones, inflicting 2D10 damage.

SAN LOSS: 1D6/1D20.

Those Beyond

"Foremost among the living objects were great inky, jellyish monstrosities which flabbily quivered in harmony with the vibrations from the machine. They were present in loathsome profusion, and I saw to my horror that they overlapped; that they were semi-fluid and capable of passing through one another and through what we know as solids. These things were never still, but seemed ever floating about with some malignant purpose. Sometimes they appeared to devour one another, the attacker launching itself at its victim and instantaneously obliterating the latter from sight."

—H.P. Lovecraft, "From Beyond"

An unseen world exists in tandem with our own, invisible to normal humans, due to our inability to sense at the strange frequencies which illuminate the liquid aether of this other realm. The creatures which exist in the liquid world beyond cannot "see" us, although they slither over us and through us constantly. Our atoms vibrate a very tiny bit out of phase with the atoms of this other world, and so we pass each other while occupying the same space.

Until a machine called the Tillinghast Resonator was invented in 1920, mankind was safe from those beyond—though it is theorized that other hypergeometric principles may have exposed mankind to the forces beyond before 1920.

The resonator not only awakens ancient atrophied sense organs within the human brain which can see this other world; it also brings the atomic structures of both worlds into alignment, until physical interaction becomes possible.

The creatures from beyond come in a multitude of horrific forms, as various and endless as those found on Earth. A few are described below. These creatures hunt in higher dimensions, utilizing senses not generally found on Earth, consuming each other in a violent and never-ending interplay of predators and prey.

The Tillinghast Resonator (and other unnatural processes) can reveal our physical world to the strange senses of the parasites, allowing these dangerous creatures to see us and interact with us within the field effect. Movement within the field—and to a lesser degree, the deadly energy called Tillinghast Radiation (T-Radiation)—draws parasites towards them, usually with catastrophic results.

Disc-Shaped Liquivore

STR 3 **CON** 6 **DEX** 1 **POW** 4

HP 4 **WP** 4

SKILLS: Alertness (In the Field) 50%, Flight 45%.

ATTACKS: Slice 30%, damage 1D10, Armor Piercing 3 (see **RAZOR SPINES**).

N-SPACE "SWIMMING": This creature swims in an invisible otherworldly environment, allowing it a top speed as fast as a running human, as well as the ability to "swim" upwards into the air.

RAZOR SPINES: These creatures are formed of numerous half circles of solid black tissue, interconnected by a bony flexible spine. They drift through the air, swirling furiously, using the razor edges of their discs as weapons.

SAN LOSS: 0/1D4.

Ophidian Liquivore

STR 6 **CON** 8 **DEX** 16 **POW** 6

HP 7 **WP** 6

SKILLS: Alertness (In the Field) 60%, Flight 75%.

ATTACKS: Bite 30%, damage 1D10 (see **FLUID DRAIN**).

N-SPACE "SWIMMING": This creature swims in an invisible otherworldly environment, allowing it a top speed as fast as a running human, as well as the ability to "swim" upwards into the air.

FLUID DRAIN: When these snake-like beings with no eyes attack, their large fangs punch into a victim and begin to drain fluids from its body. Being liquivores, they do not eat solid flesh.

SAN LOSS: 0/1D4.

Tumbleweed Liquivore

STR 3 **CON** 10 **DEX** 13 **POW** 6

HP 6 **WP** 6

SKILLS: Alertness (In the Field) 55%, Flight 20%.

ATTACKS: Impaling Spines 25%, damage 1D6+2, Armor Piercing 3 (see **FLUID DRAIN**).

N-SPACE "SWIMMING": This creature swims in an invisible otherworldly environment, allowing it a top speed as fast as a running human, as well as the ability to "swim" upwards into the air.

FLUID DRAIN: When these tumbleweed-like beings attack, their hundreds of spines impale a victim and begin to drain fluids from its body. Being liquivores, they do not eat solid flesh.

SAN LOSS: 0/1D4.

Wendigowak

"'I seen that great Wendigo thing,' he whispered, sniffing the air about him exactly like an animal. 'I been with it, too—'

"Whether the poor devil would have said more, or whether Dr. Cathcart would have continued the impossible cross examination cannot be known, for at that moment the voice of Hank was heard yelling at the top of his voice from behind the canvas that concealed all but his terrified eyes. Such a howling was never heard.

"'His feet! Oh, Gawd, his feet! Look at his great changed—feet!'"

—Algernon Blackwood, "The Wendigo"

These cannibal-ogres of Algonquin legend manifest an infection among those in the northern reaches who have partaken of the communion of Itla-Shua and eaten human flesh. The wendigo's strange-smelling hair bristles from frozen, blue-white corpse-flesh. Its eyes blaze red or purple, and a long tongue emerges from between its protruding, fanged teeth. Despite its deformed or animalistic feet, the wendigo travels in enormous leaps.

Wendigo

STR 24 **CON** 25 **DEX** 9 **INT** 8 **POW** 16

HP 25 **WP** 16

ARMOR: 4 points of thick and frozen hide (see **ICY VITALITY**).

SKILLS: Alertness 40%, Athletics 90%, Stealth 80% (90% in snow), Track Prey 99%.

ATTACKS: Claw 80%, damage 1D10 or grapple.

Bite 80%, damage 1D8 (see **WENDIGO BITE**).

GIANT STEPS: As its action, the wendigo can bound or "step" up to 20 meters vertically or 40 meters horizontally in one turn.

HOWL: As its action, the wendigo can howl, spending 4 WP. Any present who fails a SAN test immediately suffers temporary insanity; those who succeed are stunned for one turn in shock and terror. The howl affects a given Agent no more than once in a day.

ICY VITALITY: Ordinary attacks inflict half HP damage against a wendigo. A successful Lethality roll does not destroy it, but inflicts HP damage equal to the Lethality rating.

Hypergeometry inflicts full damage upon a wendigo. Fire ignores the wendigo's armor and inflicts double damage.

WENDIGO BITE: After combat, bitten Agents must make SAN tests (at a −20% penalty if bitten more than once, or −40% if the Agent has ever eaten human flesh). On a failure, the Agent gains +6 STR and +6 CON, adds 40% to his or her Unarmed Combat skill (up to 99%), and does 1D6 damage (and communicates wendigoism) with a bite. The Agent has a new disorder: an addiction to eating human flesh. The Agent's feet begin to deform and his or her eyes change color; this can be noticed with an Alertness test. At the end of the operation (or later at the Handler's discretion), the Agent transforms into a wendigo and flees civilized lands for the north.

RITUALS: Call Forth Those From Outside (Itla-Shua).

SAN LOSS: 0/1D8 (1/1D10 if the wendigo was known to the witness when human).

White Apes

"On October 19, 1852, the explorer Samuel Seaton called at Jermyn House with a manuscript of notes collected among the Ongas, believing that certain legends of a grey city of white apes ruled by a white god might prove valuable to the ethnologist."

—H.P. Lovecraft, "Facts Concerning the Late Arthur Jermyn and His Family"

Turned into ritual tools by the Great Race over a million years ago, the early hominid Tchadanthropus clustered in Central Africa and thus separated itself from the primary evolutionary lineage that eventually became Homo sapiens. However, interbreeding between Tchadanthropus and both man and apes remains possible down to the modern era—possibly a legacy of Yithian genetic tinkering.

The result: a race of white apes with the cunning of savages and the ferocity of baboons. They are approximately as tall as men, but their ape muscles knot around thicker limbs and torsos; wide jaws full of razor-sharp teeth split their low skulls. Their eyes are not albino red, but pale blue or green. They carry primitive stone weapons. Trophies of their kills, carefully dried in the tropical sun, dangle from their knotted fur or from lanyards of sinew or rawhide.

The British explorers Sir Wade Jermyn in the 18th century and Samuel Seaton in the 19th reported a gray city of white apes deep in the Congo, a likely reference to Itoko/Thule (see **DISINFORMATION: PNAKOTIS AND THULE** on page 36). A Soviet expedition under P.E. Zvery encountered the apes in 1930. Since Thule's violation in 1943, white apes have appeared on battlefields in the Congo, Biafra, Angola, Rhodesia, and other African wars—sometimes fighting, always scavenging the dead. The white apes are migrating, possibly seeking some new lost city to call their own, possibly following the ancient call of Yith bred into their genes before the last Ice Age.

White Ape

STR 18 **CON** 14 **DEX** 13 **INT** 6 **POW** 10

HP 16 **WP** 10

ARMOR: 2 points of thick hide.

SKILLS: Alertness 40% (80% in the jungle), Athletics 90%, Dodge 40%, Stealth 40% (80% in the jungle).

ATTACKS: Bash or bite 60%, damage 1D8 or grapple (see **GORILLA HUG**).

Stone axe or spear 60%, damage 1D10.

CLIMBING, LEAPING, AND SWINGING: As its action, with an Athletics roll, a white ape can near-instantly shinny to the top of a tree or seven meters up a cliff, leap up to seven meters with a running start, or swing across a 15-meter gap. Swinging on vines or brachiating between jungle tree limbs, they can outpace running humans.

GORILLA HUG: As its action, a white ape can squeeze a pinned target for 1D8 damage without making an attack roll.

Winged Servitors

"There flopped rhythmically a horde of tame, trained, hybrid winged things that no sound eye could ever wholly grasp, or sound brain ever wholly remember. They were not altogether crows, nor moles, nor buzzards, nor ants, nor vampire bats, nor decomposed human beings; but something I cannot and must not recall. They flopped limply along, half with their webbed feet and half with their membraneous wings; and as they reached the throng of celebrants the cowled figures seized and mounted them, and rode off one by one along the reaches of that unlighted river, into pits and galleries of panic where poison springs feed frightful and undiscoverable cataracts."

—H.P. Lovecraft, "The Festival"

These flopping, eye-twisting aberrations are only one example of the uncountable, unnatural things which throng and pulse in the inconceivable presence of Azathoth. Rituals familiar to many human sorcerers—such as "Winged Steed"—can lure them through strange dimensions of space and time. They placidly allow the summoners to mount them like loathsome steeds and then bear the summoners away to pay homage to the Daemon Sultan, unless the summoners bind them to some other service. Their riders must take whatever precautions are needed to survive a journey that the nameless servitors can make with unthinking ease. Some sources use a name from Incan myth, ai-apa, "decapitator," for a creature which could be the winged servitor. Others describe things like the winged servitors dedicated to Cthulhu or haunting the shadows of Carcosa.

Winged Servitor

STR 25 **CON** 25 **DEX** 12 **INT** 1 **POW** 8

HP 25 **WP** 8

ARMOR: 3 points of furry chitin.

SKILLS: Alertness 50%, Flight 40%.

ATTACKS: Claw 40%, damage 2D6.
Bite 40%, Lethality 15%.

NON-TERRENE: The servitor is at home in nearly any environment. Radiation, pressure, cold, vacuum, and more have no negative effects on it. It can move on the surface of Saturn, the depths of the ocean or in open space with equal ease.

OTHERWORLDLY FLIGHT: The servitor can "fly" in any environment, flapping its membranous wings as if against some unseen current—even underwater or in space. In flight, the servitor seems slow and clumsy, certainly more sluggish than most avians. Yet, while in flight, it may suddenly vanish as if launching away at terrific speed, passing out of everyday dimensions and through unthinkable realities.

UNNATURAL BIOLOGY: The servitor's physiology would baffle any biologist. Making a called shot for "vitals" or another apparently vulnerable area inflicts normal damage, with no special game effect.

SAN LOSS: 1/1D6.

Witches' Familiars

"Witnesses said it had long hair and the shape of a rat, but that its sharp-toothed, bearded face was evilly human while its paws were like tiny human hands. It took messages betwixt old Keziah and the devil, and was nursed on the witch's blood—which it sucked like a vampire. Its voice was a kind of loathsome titter, and it could speak all languages."

—H.P. Lovecraft, "The Dreams in the Witch House"

Nyarlathotep often communicates with humanity according to the expectations of their cultures, or more likely in mockery of them. In one interpretation of New England folktales, Nyarlathotep appeared to witches as a cloven-hooved Dark Man, bearing a book where the damned signed their names in blood, and granting them familiars to aid their unnatural rituals. Some occultists say such familiars were born of the witches consummating their pacts with the Dark Man. Others say they came from alien dimensions and took shapes to amuse their master, or that they were witches and sorcerers betrayed and cursed by the Dark Man. Such creatures might be formed in mockery of dogs, cats, birds, lizards, or other animals.

This entry describes the ratlike Brown Jenkin, companion of the Arkham witch Keziah Mason. Familiars in other forms may have different qualities.

Witch's Familiar

STR 2 **CON** 7 **DEX** 20 **INT** 10 **POW** 8

HP 5 **WP** 8

SKILLS: Alertness 80%, Dodge 95%, Stealth 80%, Swim 70%, Unnatural 50%.

ATTACKS: Bite 40%, damage 1D4 (see **BITE**).

BITE: Many familiars carry diseases. A single bite is enough to infect the target. A typical infection lasts 1D6 days, inflicts a −20% CON test penalty, and inflicts 1D6 damage. (See **POISON AND DISEASE** on page 60 of the *Agent's Handbook.)*

FAMILIAR: A familiar can act as an assistant in any ritual that its master or mistress knows. Because a familiar knows all languages, it can help its master or mistress learn a ritual in any language.

GIFT OF THE MASTER: If a witch's familiar sacrifices permanent POW in a ritual, keep a note of its former POW score. It may attempt to regain spent POW once per month by killing a human and drinking the victim's life-blood; a familiar prefers a helpless, diminutive victim like a child. That allows the familiar to attempt a POW test. If it fails, it regains 1 POW, up to its maximum score.

SMALL AND NIMBLE: Any attack against a rat-sized familiar is at −40% due to its small size.

RITUALS: Prayer to the Dark Man, and others as the Handler sees fit, delivered by Nyarlathotep.

SAN LOSS: 1/1D6.

Zombies

"The body on the table had risen with a blind and terrible groping, and we had heard a sound. I should not call that sound a voice, for it was too awful. And yet its timbre was not the most awful thing about it. Neither was its message—it had merely screamed, 'Jump, Ronald, for God's sake, jump!' The awful thing was its source. For it had come from the large covered vat in that ghoulish corner of crawling black shadows."

—H.P. Lovecraft, "Herbert West—Reanimator"

Many kinds of unnatural formulae can restore a corpse to a semblance of life. We call them all zombies, but they may have very different features. Some hunger mindlessly for living blood; some are impelled by dying, desperate urges; others have animal consciousness. An unlucky few retain full awareness. Such creatures may have full INT and POW, and perhaps even the skills they had in life, but only half the CHA and none of the SAN. Any zombie can be detected at a great distance by its rotting flesh. The powers that give energy to dead tissue usually make zombies stronger and hardier than they were in life, perhaps immune to pain and shock altogether. Adjust a zombie's stats and powers to reflect the technique that reanimated it.

Zombie

STR 15 **CON** 15 **DEX** 5 **INT** varies **POW** 1

HP 15 **WP** 1

ARMOR: See **ROTTING RESILIENCE**.

SKILLS: Alertness 20%, Unarmed Combat 30%.

ATTACKS: Bite 30%, damage 1D6 (see **WORRY AND RIP**).

CLUMSY: A zombie cannot defend itself against attacks. Even a successful attack roll by a zombie does not oppose any attacks against it. In fact, all attacks against a zombie are at +20%. Most zombies shuffle along no faster than a slow walk.

FEEDING: Each time a human victim takes damage from a zombie's bite, the zombie regains 1 lost HP as it devours flesh and blood. With some zombies, a bite is infectious, and turns the victim into a zombie in 1D6 hours.

ROTTING RESILIENCE: A zombie takes half HP damage from all non-hypergeometric attacks. A zombie reduced to 0 HP (for example, by a successful Lethality roll) may still not be fully destroyed, only so badly mauled that it no longer poses a threat. Some zombies retain animation even if decapitated.

STRIKING THE BRAIN: If a zombie needs its brain to "survive," an Agent may make a called shot at a −20% penalty to hit the zombie's decomposing head. If the called shot does more than 2 HP damage, it damages the brain and destroys the zombie.

UNDEAD: Whatever animates a zombie's dead flesh sustains it against rigors that would harm or kill the living. Cold, suffocation and radiation seem to do no lasting harm unless the zombie's body is physically destroyed. Some zombies do not even rot at the usual rate.

WORRY AND RIP: After succeeding with a bite attack, a zombie uses its action each turn to inflict 1D6 damage on the same target, without having to make another attack roll. If the bite pierced the victim's armor, the "worry and rip" damage ignores armor. The victim can attempt an opposed STR test as his or her action each turn to break free.

SAN LOSS: 0/1D6.

Great Old Ones

"They worshipped, so they said, the Great Old Ones who lived ages before there were any men, and who came to the young world out of the sky. These Old Ones were gone now, inside the earth and under the sea; but their dead bodies had told their secrets in dreams to the first men, who formed a cult which had never died."

—H.P. Lovecraft, "The Call of Cthulhu"

There is no single definition of a "Great Old One." The Cthulhu cult described the peers and paladins of their priest-god as "Great Old Ones." In his Antarctic report, William Dyer mentions "primal myths about Great Old Ones who filtered down from the stars and concocted Earth life as a joke or mistake." In each case, a terrified human brain reaches for a descriptor associated with the sublime unnatural entity it has unwittingly brushed against.

Defining one set of field-strengths and organic realities as "Great Old Ones" in the first place remains at best rough taxonomy, no more scientific or truthful than a medieval bestiary. And indeed, in practice, Delta Green's classification of these unimaginably vast entities follows medieval demonology—specifically that of Abd al-Hazred's *Necronomicon*. The "mad

OPINT: Great Old Ones' Stats and Skills

Great Old Ones do not have hit points. They are immortal, ultimately invulnerable, and completely beyond human understanding. The correct Handler response to "Can a Great Old One do X?" is "Yes, of course it can." They are focused omnipotence.

When depicting Great Old Ones, do not bother with moment-to-moment calculations, stat tests, and skill rolls. In any given turn, a Great Old One acts whenever the Handler thinks appropriate.

Use the qualities that are described for each as guidelines, but don't feel constrained by human conceptions of physics or causality. Many Great Old Ones have destructive powers that all but guarantee the destruction of Agents who get close. These are not monsters to be fought. They are unthinkable forces to be escaped or, at best, temporarily thwarted.

Only very specific methods can temporarily remove the threat of a Great Old One. Usually, this is through obscure, hypergeometric rituals. Sometimes, it is through brute force: massive explosions or other disruptions of spacetime. Such disruptions are transient. Nothing that humans can do affects a Great Old One in any meaningful way. They return. They always return.

Arab" divided the al-Qadimat Kabira into three categories, the "ones of the stars," the "ones of the earth," and the "ones of dreams." Al-Hazred's categories were fluid, or he was distracted while composing this section of his grimoire, as Cthulhu winds up both "of the stars" and "of dreams."

Other sources, unsurprisingly, contradict al-Hazred and each other. The Mayan Codex Borgia hints that Yig may have come down from the stars; parts of the Pnakotic Manuscripts suggest that Cthulhu and Tsathoggua are brothers, which is only to say that they are both unnatural. In short, these unknowably vast beings are also unclassifiable.

Do not assume Delta Green knows *anything* about them.

Azathoth

"Outside the ordered universe that amorphous blight of nethermost confusion which blasphemes and bubbles at the center of all infinity—the boundless daemon sultan Azathoth, whose name no lips dare speak aloud, and who gnaws hungrily in inconceivable, unlighted chambers beyond time and space amidst the muffled, maddening beating of vile drums and the thin monotonous whine of accursed flutes."

—H.P. Lovecraft, *The Dream-Quest of Unknown Kadath*

Only a very few isolated madmen seek communion with Azathoth, the Daemon Sultan, the Idiot Chaos at the heart of the universe. Cults of Azathoth tend to come apart in, well, chaotic idiocy. The leaders of the Cult of Transcendence sought admission to Azathoth's Court, but they rent their occult empire to ruins. A New England witch-cult signed the "Book of Azathoth" but worshiped Nyarlathotep. Even the insects from Shaggai, who worship Azathoth as Xada-Hgla, the Cradle of Chaos, are riven with laxity and heresy.

The bad news is that full communion with Azathoth on this plane of existence, however brief, can be the rough equivalent of a 15-megaton atomic burst. The "monstrous nuclear chaos beyond angled space" energetically disrupts spacetime around it. Some Delta Green analysts consider the Tunguska blast of 1908 the result of some Azathoth-worshiper's distracted exaltation. A similar "miscalculation" by the Karotechia in 1945 blew the top off a Bavarian mountain and obliterated Naudabaum Castle.

Azathoth is said to dwell "at the center of the universe," the meaningless solution to every hypergeometrical equation. Surrounded by amorphous dancers and shrill flautists—possibly a medieval symbolic image of chaos theory, randomized constants, and quantized energy—it roils and shrieks and gnaws hungrily in the dark. In some traditions, Nyarlathotep lulls the Daemon Sultan to sleep, the better to arrogate Azathoth's power to itself. The name "Azathoth" is likely an occult fiction, possibly derived from the Egyptian User-Thoth ("strength of Thoth," e.g., the power behind Thoth, or Nyarlathotep). The true Dread Name of Azathoth is literally something to conjure with.

Effects and Abilities—Azathoth

AURA OF POWER: Any human present when Azathoth manifests is automatically at −40% on all rolls (except SAN). A character that fails the SAN roll for encountering Azathoth cannot act for 1D10+2 turns, instead goggling in abject terror at its monstrous form and its overwhelming, terrifying presence.

CONSUMPTION: Azathoth emerges on Earth from a summoning area and expands to consume all nearby matter in atomic fire. Some manifestations of Azathoth grow slowly, some quickly. On the first turn—or in the first minute, or the first hour, or the first day—Azathoth consumes a five-meter radius with Lethality 10%. On the second, its radius grows 10 more meters with Lethality 20%. On the third, it grows 15 meters with Lethality 30%, and so on. If its Lethality rating exceeds 99%, it simply consumes anything in its path with no roll required or allowed. This chaotic energy cannot be Dodged. The maximum extent of its growth is unknown. Some say Azathoth will inevitably consume the Earth.

DISMISSAL: Certain hypergeometric principles are known to cause Azathoth to cease manifesting in a summoning, utilizing ancient forces to restrain and re-trap its power at the center of the universe. That requires access to or knowledge of a ritual that dismisses Azathoth, a successful activation roll, and the permanent expenditure of 7 POW.

DREAD NAME: The secret name of Azathoth (some say it is hidden in the *Necronomicon)* is reputed to summon the being to Earth with a single word at the permanent cost of 10 POW. Thankfully, so far, this word has been lost to time.

TRANSCENDENT: Azathoth is beyond Earthly science and all hypergeometry except those rituals which affect its arrival and dismissal. All attacks against Azathoth fail. Its form at the center of the universe can never be destroyed.

SAN LOSS: 1D20/1D100.

[redacted]

DISINFORMATION

YELLOW CARD

THE CORPSE CITY

The exact location of R'lyeh (49° 51' 0" S, 128° 34' 0" W; -49.85°, -128.566667°) is well known by Delta Green, and its analysts in various agencies monitor that hotspot of disappearances. Despite precautions, some vehicles have wandered into the zone, some never to return. Twice, such vehicles (a Navy PB-Y scout plane in 1943, and a Russian freighter in 1963) have reported an island in the ocean where there should be none. Since 1925, no one has landed on such an island – at least, as far as Delta Green knows.

Delta Green is extremely interested in the hypergeometry behind the torpor that renders Cthulhu and his minions inert. No one knows if this torpor is a natural result of Cthulhu's biology, or perhaps due to a hypergeometric weapon utilized by some mighty, prehuman enemy. Some say that the math needed to keep Cthulhu permanently interred at R'lyeh is contained within the angles and structures of R'lyeh itself.

R'lyeh seems to rise and fall out of existence at intervals which can be tracked by those with deep knowledge of the unnatural. This means that an expedition to the island is possible – though obviously ill-advised – when the time is right.

ONG THIS LINE

Cthulhu

> *"The Thing cannot be described—there is no language for such abysms of shrieking and immemorial lunacy, such eldritch contradictions of all matter, force, and cosmic order. A mountain walked or stumbled. God! What wonder that across the Earth a great architect went mad, and poor Wilcox raved with fever in that telepathic instant? The Thing of the idols, the green, sticky spawn of the stars, had awaked to claim his own. The stars were right again, and what an age-old cult had failed to do by design, a band of innocent sailors had done by accident. After vigintillions of years great Cthulhu was loose again, and ravening for delight."*
>
> —H.P. Lovecraft, "The Call of Cthulhu"

The first Great Old One studied by P4, in the days of the raid on Innsmouth, Cthulhu exerts a pervasive and ubiquitous influence on the fringes of human culture. In 1908, documented Cthulhu cults existed in Greenland, Louisiana, Massachusetts, New Caledonia, Ponape, and Singapore. Some say Cthulhu is the greatest of the Old Ones, and the one closest to awakening, Delta Green has run across its presence more often by far than any other unnatural entity.

Most accounts say Great Cthulhu rests in some sort of torpor beneath the South Pacific in the "corpse city of R'lyeh," imprisoned by a chance cosmic alignment or tectonic disturbance. Its occasional stirrings as the stars slowly "come right," combined with its omnipresent telepathic dream-sendings, inspire both localized riots (as in 1925, when its brief awakening drove thousands mad and sparked magical rebellions from Haiti to the Philippines) and an age-old global cult.

Legends tell us that Cthulhu "seeped down" from the green star Soth or Zoth (most likely either Zubeneschamali [Beta Librae] or Sothis [Sirius]) during the Paleozoic Era. Mountain-sized and protean, it most commonly appears in human art and dreams as a tentacled monster vaguely resembling some hideous hybrid of octopus, dragon, and human being. In human myth, it is often represented as a "chaos dragon" such

ASSET: The Idol

When an artist hears the dream call, it compels the sufferer to carve an image of Cthulhu. The true statue is almost always the same, regardless of culture and time period. A squat, toad-like being, with a tentacular face and stubby wings, perches on a cube incised with alien runes.

The 1907 St. Bernard Parish raid in Louisiana recovered the most famous of these, the LeGrasse statue, photographed repeatedly before being lost. But others have been found. So many, in fact, that in archaeological circles, "the octopus" or "the monster erratic" is a well-known oddity. From 1925 to 1955, several papers attempted to explain away the seemingly identical statues recovered from the ruins of a 9th-century Japanese shrine, an Iroquois longhouse, and an Inca burial site.

In 1955, with the archaeological community on the verge of admitting the connection, the program enacted counterintelligence Operation LANCASTER. Modern sculptors working on CIA grants produced obvious fakes of the statue, and Delta Green operatives salted them into auctions to be revealed as the work of a forger (who had conveniently died weeks before). Evidence recovered from the forger's studio indicated he had created and seeded dozens of these statues worldwide in many different styles.

Still, the dream call churns the statues out every few years, and new ones appear. So far, no one has picked up the thread left after the convenient 1955 explanation, and almost all reputable archaeologists know of the story, and dismiss "the octopus" as hoax like the Mitchell-Hedges Crystal Skulls. Still, some have dug such statues up from eight meters beneath the earth, sealed in the ash of volcanic eruptions that pre-date mankind. In their hearts they know the truth.

as Tiamat, Vritra, or Typhon, driven into the underworld. As Tutula in Tonga, Clulu or Nkulu in Uganda, Alalu to the Bronze Age Hurrian peoples, Tlaloc to the Aztecs, and many similar names, it lurks beneath human myths of the deeps, the monstrous inhuman truth painted over with pious rationalizations.

Cthulhu's most well-known servitors and creations, the Deep Ones, have their own versions of such myths, perhaps no more reliable than the human distortions. Scriptures recovered from Innsmouth, Ponape, and other Deep One centers use the same exalted language to describe Cthulhu. Human myths, intermingled with the teachings of the Deep Ones, ascribe the names Dagon and Hydra to two of Cthulhu's spawn or kindred. Shaurash-Ho, "He-Who-Swims-With-Corpses," appears less frequently, as does "serpent-bearded Byatis," brought to Earth by the Deep Ones as their champion, according to legend. Any of these lesser Cthulhoid creatures would pose a critical threat beyond the reach of any human force or technology, and yet they operate on a fraction of Cthulhu's scale.

R'lyeh slowly congeals into our spacetime, moved by otherworldly realities for reasons unfathomable to humanity. One day, it is foretold, the city will reappear above the waves, and remain, and Cthulhu will fully awaken in the world and minds of humanity. Then, the legends say, we will rise up in an orgy of violence and death, to become one with the Great Old Ones.

Effects and Abilities—Cthulhu

AURA OF POWER: Any human present when Cthulhu manifests is automatically at −40% on all rolls (except SAN). A character that fails the SAN roll for encountering Cthulhu cannot act for 1D10+2 turns, instead goggling in abject terror at its monstrous form and its overwhelming, thundering psychic presence.

DISCORPORATION: A successful attack with a Lethality rating of 70% or higher causes Cthulhu to explode in a disgusting spray of slime and fragments. Each character present who fails a Luck roll loses 1D6/1D20 SAN as the consciousness of Cthulhu passes through them to return to the corpse city of R'lyeh. Its noxious remains slowly begin to reform, seeping back into the water and into its temple-tomb. After this, Cthulhu does not reform for several months.

DREAM-CALL: Any character encountering Cthulhu who is exceptionally sensitive (with INT or POW of 17 or higher, or any Art, Occult, or Psychotherapy skill at 60% or better) goes temporarily insane, overwhelmed by the Great Old One's dream-call, regardless of SAN loss. The dream-call can only be approximated as a psychic "voice," shouting or babbling nonsense—yet it is clearly filled with utterly alien meaning. Such a character who survives the encounter cannot sleep afterward without making a SAN test at −20%. That recurs each night until the penalized SAN test succeeds. In some circumstances, Great Cthulhu may awaken sufficiently that its dream-call reaches sensitive minds far away, perhaps around the globe. Deep waters seem to reduce the call's reach, much as they obstruct radio waves.

DISMISSAL: Certain hypergeometric principles are known to cause Cthulhu to retreat to its submerged tomb, utilizing ancient forces to restrain and re-trap its power. That requires access to or knowledge of a ritual that dismisses Cthulhu, a successful activation roll, and the permanent expenditure of 5 POW.

DISINTERESTED SWAT: Occasionally, Cthulhu bears down on a target within reach, smashing it beneath the weight of an amorphous limb. This attack automatically hits its selected target, and has a Kill Radius of five meters and a 60% Lethality rating. This vast attack cannot be Dodged.

FUNDAMENTAL CONTROL: Cthulhu can change scale, mass, and molecular order at will, growing, shrinking, changing or transcending any physical limitation without a roll. Most attacks against Cthulhu have no effect (but see **DISCORPORATION**).

SAN LOSS: 1D10/1D100.

Ghatanothoa

"Oozing and surging up out of that yawning trap-door in the Cyclopean crypt I had glimpsed such an unbelievable behemothic monstrosity that I could not doubt the power of its original to kill with its mere sight."

—H.P. Lovecraft and Hazel Heald, "Out of the Aeons"

ESTRICTED

DISINFORMATION

YELLOW CARD

MADCHIMP OUTBREAK ANALYSIS

Instead of defining the vast, malign phenomena of the unnatural according to medieval superstition, a 1968 Delta Green tiger team (Operation MADCHIMP) comprising CDC and DIA personnel used network-mapping and outbreak analysis in an attempt to classify these so-called entities. What a remote tribe knows as "Cthulhu" may be something entirely different – if just as horrific – from the dream-entity constructed by a Goa drug cult, which itself might not be the culture-god of the Innsmouth Deep Ones. Rather than being one "god," then, Cthulhu or Y'golonac might be a social infection manifesting divergent symptoms in vulnerable populations.

Geographically and temporally linked outbreaks of the unnatural (called syndemes by the team) tend to share effects, and to incorporate local isolates and self-deranging cultists into a linked pattern. The Miskatonic Syndeme, for example, appears to infect people on either extreme of the social spectrum: insular (or incestuous) villagers, and near-celibate academic elites. Many of these outbreaks repeat in the same location over centuries, implying a specific radiation or infestation that can be tracked like a cholera plague or terrorist network.

The MADCHIMP team mapped the following tentative syndemes:

- **GREENLAND SYNDEME:** A-Abhi, Itla-shua, Ktagoolik (Cthulhu), Rhan-Tegoth, Tleche-Nacha, Tsathoggua. Transmitted by prehuman Voorii and Hyperborean civilization.
- **MISKATONIC SYNDEME:** Cthulhu, Dagon, Ghatanothoa, Nodens, Nyarlathotep, Ossadogowah, Yog-Sothoth. Concentrated in New England; may actually be a sub-node of the Pacific Syndeme.
- **OKLAHOMA SYNDEME:** Headless-Man (Y'golonac), Tiráwa (Tsathoggua), Tulu (Cthulhu), Yig. Transmitted from the K'n Y'ani; may also be connected to a less well-known Mexican Syndeme.
- **PACIFIC SYNDEME:** Cthulhu, Fisherman's God (Dagon?), Ghatanothoa, Nug-Yeb, Rhan-Tegoth. Aggregates several sub-nodes in Micronesia, Melanesia, California, and Polynesia.
- **SEVERN SYNDEME:** Azathoth, Byatis, Daoloth, Eihort, Glaaki, Shub-Niggurath, Nodens, Y'golonac. Concentrated in the Severn Valley in western England.
- **WISCONSIN SYNDEME:** Hastur, Nyarlathotep, Qu-tugkwa, Windigo (Itla-shua). Possibly extends north into Canada.

CUT ALONG THIS LINE

031-51937 0-46

According to von Junzt, this horrific being ruled the prehistoric Pacific continent of Mu, transforming those who gazed upon it into living mummies. Other myths say that Ghatanothoa, the "dark god," was the most powerful manifestation of the strange energy vortices called the Lloigor, who sometimes gift or curse their human slaves with long life. Some occultists think stories of Ghatanothoa are merely reworkings of the Cthulhu myth; but a 1932 incident at the Cabot Museum in Boston, if it was reported accurately, tends to bear von Junzt's research out.

Ghatanothoa's legends have persuaded many lost souls to seek contact in hope of immortality. Its cults appear all along the Pacific littoral from Peru to Malaya, and even in Burma, Sri Lanka, and Yemen. Von Junzt places Ghatanothoa in opposition to the mi-go and to Shub-Niggurath, implying a ferocious independence exemplified by its fanatical apocalypse cultists.

Effects and Abilities—Ghatanothoa

AURA OF POWER: Any human present when Ghatanothoa manifests is automatically at −20% on all rolls (except SAN). A character who fails the SAN roll for encountering Ghatanothoa cannot act for 1D6 turns, instead goggling in abject terror at its monstrous form.

CURSE OF STONE: Any human present during a manifestation or seeing a representation of Ghatanothoa's physical form (including a photograph) must make a POW test. Failure indicates the witness suffers from "the curse of stone." The victim is immediately paralyzed in all but autonomic functions. The victim never naturally dies, but slowly becomes a leathery mummy, unable to act or speak but forever aware. This costs 1/1D10 SAN per day. There is no known cure.

DISCORPORATION: Ghatanothoa almost always appears as an apparition, while its true form remains trapped. Its apparition cannot be "discorporated" through violence. All attacks appear to pass through it with no effect.

DISMISSAL: Certain hypergeometric principles allow Ghatanothoa's manifestation to be dismissed. This requires access to or knowledge of a ritual that dismisses Ghatanothoa, a successful activation roll, and the permanent expenditure of 1 POW.

FUNDAMENTAL CONTROL: Ghatanothoa can change scale, mass, and molecular order at will, growing, shrinking, changing, or transcending any physical limitation without a roll. While it enjoys fundamental control, this ability is not enough to allow it to escape the prison in which it remains trapped. However, someone in its physical presence and able to strike would find that most attacks against Ghatanothoa have no effect.

TRAPPED: Ghatanothoa remains trapped in an unknown location (rumored to be a vault constructed by an alien species, on the long sunken lost continent of Mu). Its visage and presence can be summoned to manifest elsewhere, but its physical form remains trapped.

SAN LOSS: 1D6/1D20.

Glaaki

"From an oval body protruded countless thin, pointed spines of multicolored metal; at the more rounded end of the oval a circular, thick-lipped mouth formed the center of a spongy face, from which rose three yellow eyes on stalks. Around the underside of the body were many white pyramids, presumably used for locomotion. The diameter of the body must have been about ten feet at its least width."

—Ramsey Campbell, "The Inhabitant of the Lake"

This huge, slug-shaped entity dwells beneath Brichester Lake in Gloucestershire, the impact crater of the meteor on which Glaaki arrived in the 6th century CE. Glaaki—its name has also been rendered Gla'aki—creates undead slaves, the Glaakeen, by injecting one of its metalloid spines into a victim. Tales of their reanimation have led many cultists to worship Glaaki, seeking immortality. Glaaki may manifest elsewhere in spacetime: certain Egyptian mummies bear its spines, and it has been sighted (or at least named) near other lakes around the world, including Lake Chimagua in New York's Catskill Mountains. Its Brichester cult penned the *Revelations of Glaaki*, most copies of which have been destroyed.

Effects and Abilities—Glaaki

AURA OF POWER: Any human present when Glaaki appears is automatically at −20% on all rolls (except SAN). A character who fails the SAN roll for encountering Glaaki cannot act for 1D6 turns, instead goggling in abject terror at its monstrous form.

DISCORPORATION: A successful attack with a Lethality rating of 50% or higher causes Glaaki to vanish with a deafening explosion that shatters all glass within two miles. Each character present who fails a Luck roll cannot sleep for 1D4+1 days, and must make a SAN roll each night. Failing that means the loss of 1 SAN as the witness' mind is swarmed with visions of ritual impalement. Glaaki returns to its nearest "safe haven," usually at the bottom of a nearby lake or sea, and enters a state of torpor for an indeterminate amount of time.

DISMISSAL: Certain hypergeometric principles allow Glaaki to be sent back to its last "safe haven," usually at the bottom of a lake or sea. This requires access to or knowledge of a ritual that dismisses Glaaki, a successful activation roll, and the permanent expenditure of 1 POW.

DREAM-PULL: Anyone sleeping within five miles of Glaaki (which is usually at the bottom of a lake or body of water) must make a POW test each night. Failure means a loss of 1D4 SAN and a growing feeling of dread. Those who go permanently insane are drawn to Glaaki's resting place to willingly become his undead Glaakeen servants.

FUNDAMENTAL CONTROL: Glaaki can change scale, mass, and molecular order at will, growing, shrinking, changing or transcending any physical limitation without a roll. It is equally at home on the Earth's surface, at the bottom of the ocean, or in the cloud seas of Saturn. Most attacks against Glaaki have no effect (but see **DISCORPORATION**).

GLAAKEEN: Glaaki is always attended by a dozen or so undead slaves known as Glaakeen. These once-human beings were infected with the essence of Glaaki after being run through with one of its spines. Animate corpses, they slowly deteriorate into slick, rotten carcasses with sunken eyes and sloughed, blue-white skin. Some still have the spines embedded in their chests. Glaakeen are immune to all attacks except fire, hypergeometric sources, and weapons with a Lethality rating of 10% or more. Sunlight accelerates their decay, and they instinctively flee it; direct, bright sunlight automatically inflicts an attack with a Lethality rating equal to the number of years they have been Glaakeen. All Glaakeen have 12 HP and attack by grappling with 55% skill (see **IMPALEMENT**).

IMPALEMENT: Any target grappled and pinned by two Glaakeen is dragged to Glaaki in three turns unless the victim escapes. Once brought to Glaaki, the target is permitted one Dodge roll at −40%. If it succeeds, the victim slips free and may act normally. If it fails, the victim is impaled by one of Glaaki's metalloid spines and injected with the bizarre fluid found within, suffering 2D10 damage. A target who dies due to this attack rises again as a Glaakeen.

SAN LOSS: 1D6/1D20.

Itla-shua

"But what perplexed him even more, making him feel his vision had gone utterly awry, was that Defago's stride increased in the same manner, and finally covered the same incredible distances. It looked as if the great beast had lifted him with it and carried him across these astonishing intervals. Simpson, who was much longer in the limb, found that he could not compass even half the stretch by taking a running jump."

—Algernon Blackwood, "The Wendigo"

This entity's name means "Sky Owner" in Greenlandic Inuktun, but the Great Old One is better known in North America as the Wendigo, Arctic spirit of terror and cannibalism. It appears in Babylonian lore as Enlil, to the Canadian Inuit as Sila, to the Siberian Koryak as Ina'hitelan, and to the Wampanoag as Ithaka. It is usually depicted as a terrifying or powerful beast: a bull in the Middle East, a moose or an antlered man in the Canadian north. Supposedly confined to the Arctic by the Temple of Winds, Itla-shua has abducted unfortunates as far south as Wisconsin or Iran, carrying them into the sky, to some unknown boreal realm, or to the Plateau of Leng. Sometimes these unfortunates reappear, frozen solid and seemingly dropped from a great height, their feet burned and melted by the speed of re-entry. After a spate of mass disappearances and predation in Manitoba in the 1920s and 1930s, Itla-shua's activity dropped significantly, possibly correlated with the return of colder weather in the Arctic for the next few decades. As the Arctic warms again…who knows?

Effects and Abilities—Itla-shua

AURA OF POWER: Any human present when Itla-Shua appears is automatically at −40% on all rolls (except SAN). A character who fails the SAN roll for encountering Itla-Shua cannot act for 1D10 turns, instead goggling in abject terror at its horrific form.

DISCORPORATION: A successful attack with a Lethality rating of 60% or higher causes Itla-Shua to vanish with a thunderclap, causing deafness for 1D4 days in all who are nearby. Each nearby character who fails a Luck roll is permanently deafened, and loses 1/1D4 SAN due to helplessness.

DISMISSAL: Certain hypergeometric principles allow Itla-Shua to be dispersed. This requires access to or knowledge of a ritual that dismisses Itla-Shua, a successful activation roll, and the permanent expenditure of 4 POW.

ENSHRINEMENT: Itla-Shua may select a target for enshrinement. This attack has a 60% chance of succeeding, and may be opposed by a Dodge roll. On a successful Dodge, the target suffers a Lethality attack of 10% as Itla-Shua's limb smashes to the ground on top of them, but fails to lift them. If the Dodge fails, the target is swept up, encased in ice, and dropped from a great height, suffering a Lethality attack of 75%. A target who perishes must make a POW test before dying. If it fails, the victim returns as Wendigo (see **WENDIGO**). A target who inexplicably survives such horrors loses 1D6/1D20 SAN.

FUNDAMENTAL CONTROL: Itla-Shua can change scale, mass, and molecular order at will, growing, shrinking, changing or transcending any physical limitation without a roll. It is equally at home on Earth's surface, at the bottom of the ocean, or in the cloud seas of Saturn. By some accounts, Itla-Shua's manifestations are for some reason restricted to the Arctic. Most attacks against Itla-Shua have no effect (but see **DISCORPORATION**).

WENDIGO: Itla-Shua is proceeded and attended by dozens of undead slaves known as wendigowak. These once-human beings were infected with the essence of Itla-Shua. Animate corpses, frozen and evolved to hunt and persist in the cold, these beings have blue-white skin and burning eyes. (See **WENDIGOWAK** on page 228.)

SAN LOSS: 1D10/1D100.

Nodens

"And upon dolphins' backs was balanced a vast crenulate shell wherein rode the grey and awful form of primal Nodens, Lord of the Great Abyss."

—H.P. Lovecraft "The Strange High House in the Mist"

Seemingly the most human-like of the Old Ones, Nodens (or Nuada in Irish) was a Celtic god of healing, hunting, and the sea. He may also have been worshiped as Pan, under the title "Lord of the Abyss." A major temple to Nodens flourished in the 4th and 5th centuries CE at Lydney Park in Gloucestershire, just across the Severn River from Severnford and Brichester. Here, sufferers slept in incubatio, sacred chambers designed to attract dreams of Nodens and effect cures for their ailments. While "hoary and primal Nodens" seldom appears in the waking world, the god remains a powerful force in "soft places" rich in the unnatural, such as Kingsport, Massachusetts.

In some dream-myths, Nodens commands flying beings (sometimes called "nightgaunts"), who fear not even Nyarlathotep. Some tales say Nodens vies with Nyarlathotep for power over human dreams. Others say Nodens rises from the ocean depths accompanied by fabulous beasts and spirits. Humans touched by Nodens often undergo personality-shifting neurological events—changes in personality, memories, or mental capacities—possibly triggered by exposure to the true geometries of Dream, or of the Abyss.

Effects and Abilities—Nodens

AURA OF POWER: Any human present when Nodens manifests is automatically at −20% on all rolls (except SAN). A character who fails the SAN roll for encountering Nodens cannot act for 1D6 turns, instead goggling in abject terror at its awesome form.

DISCORPORATION: A successful attack by an unnatural ritual or an unnatural entity (ordinary physical hazards have no effect) that has a Lethality rating of 30% or higher causes Nodens to abandon the physical world for the Abyss. Each character present who fails a Luck roll loses 1/1D10 SAN as their subconscious thoughts glimpse the depths of Dream in which Nodens struggles for supremacy.

DISMISSAL: Certain hypergeometric principles are known to cause Nodens to abandon the physical world for the Abyss. That requires access to or knowledge of a ritual that dismisses Nodens, a successful activation roll, and the permanent expenditure of 2 POW.

DREAMING COMMUNION: Those who contact Nodens through ritual or by arriving in its presence may choose to open themselves to telepathic communion with the being to receive knowledge. From then onward, the recipient often dreams of Nodens. Sometimes those dreams are intense communions with the Great Old One, and hint at information or unnatural rituals that Nodens finds useful for the character to know. Each communion causes the supplicant to lose SAN as if encountering Nodens anew. Nodens can raise any skill (even Unnatural) that is below 40% to 40%, or grant the knowledge to perform any ritual that the Great Old One wishes to impart. This knowledge is instant and permanent. Such a gift often comes with an obligation, a geas that drives the character to perform some action that Nodens desires. The geas replaces one of the character's motivations. Failure to attempt to fulfill the obligation costs 0/1 SAN per week. When the obligation is fulfilled, a new motivation may replace it—or a new obligation from Nodens may make itself known.

FUNDAMENTAL CONTROL: Nodens can change scale, mass, and molecular order at will, growing, shrinking, changing or transcending any physical limitation without a roll. Most attacks against Nodens have no effect (but see **DISCORPORATION**).

INTO THE ABYSS: Nodens rarely has need to assault a mere human. One that catches the Old One's attention must make a Luck roll glimpse Noden's eyes. Locked in a hypnotic fugue and unable to take any action, the character loses 1D6 WP per turn. At zero WP, the character vanishes into the Abyss. Whether Nodens can be persuaded to release the character, and how this experience changes the character, are up to the Handler.

SAN LOSS: 1/1D10.

Nyarlathotep

> *"And through this revolting graveyard of the universe the muffled, maddening beating of drums, and thin, monotonous whine of blasphemous flutes from inconceivable, unlighted chambers beyond Time; the detestable pounding and piping whereunto dance slowly, awkwardly, and absurdly the gigantic, tenebrous ultimate gods—the blind, voiceless, mindless gargoyles whose soul is Nyarlathotep."*
>
> —H.P. Lovecraft, "Nyarlathotep"

Nyarlathotep constantly acts to corrode humanity—or perhaps to evolve it to be worthy of the Great Old Ones. The Crawling Chaos awakened the Cult of Transcendence, founded the Fate, and inspired the Karotechia—and that was just in 25 years. In the 19th century, Nyarlathotep sparked the Starry Wisdom cults in Providence and elsewhere as the Haunter of the Dark. In the 17th century, the Dark Man led witch covens on two continents. In ancient Egypt, it reigned as Nephren-Ka, the Black Pharaoh whose deeds "caused his name to be stricken from all monuments." Nyarlathotep's forms appear all over the world, wherever human misery or hubris welcome the inhuman.

Nyarlathotep is the Mighty Messenger, the soul and herald of Azathoth, translating the Daemon Sultan's thrashings into vile action. It commands the mi-go, who consider themselves among Nyarlathotep's "Million Favored Ones," and unleashes horrors against those who oppose its whims. According to the most complete description of the Nyarlathotepic faith, Ludwig Prinn's *De Vermis Mysteriis*, Nyarlathotep will come among humanity at the End Times, work wonders, inspire mobs, and raise sunken continents as "mad auroras" destroy cities. Delta Green's experts don't necessarily believe every stanza of Prinn, but considering what Nyarlathotep accomplishes in secret, the open return of the Black Pharaoh must be considered nothing short of an apocalyptic, civilization-ending threat. And Delta Green has no idea how to stop it.

Effects and Abilities—Nyarlathotep

AURA OF POWER: Any human present when Nyarlathotep manifests is automatically at −20% on all rolls (except SAN). A character that fails the SAN roll for encountering Nyarlathotep cannot act for 1D6 turns, instead goggling in abject terror at its overwhelming, terrifying presence.

DISCORPORATION: If Nyarlathotep has manifested in a form vulnerable to physical harm (always up to the Handler), a hit with a Lethality rating of 50% or higher causes Nyarlathotep to collapse into ruin—only to rise again in a form still more horrible, costing all onlookers 1D10/1D100 SAN, and vanish, laughing, into the sky.

DISMISSAL: Certain hypergeometric principles are known to cause Nyarlathotep to depart without inflicting further horrors. That requires access to or knowledge of a ritual that dismisses Nyarlathotep, a successful activation roll, and the permanent expenditure of 2 POW.

FUNDAMENTAL CONTROL: Nyarlathotep can change scale, mass, and molecular order at will, growing, shrinking, changing, or transcending any physical limitation without a roll. Most attacks against Nyarlathotep have no effect (see **DISCORPORATION**).

A THOUSAND MASKS: Nyarlathotep has been known to manifest in countless forms, some human or human-like and others utterly monstrous. Often, nothing in its appearance or actions suggests that it is another facet of the Crawling Chaos. In all forms, its most common purpose seems to be to facilitate the communion of intelligent beings with the blind, idiot will of Azathoth.

WHISPERED SECRETS: Nyarlathotep sometimes graces human minds with incredible revelations. Sometimes they hint at information or unnatural rituals that Nyarlathotep finds useful for the character to know. Often, Nyarlathotep seems to revel in the mere shock of a human mind that has learned too much. Each revelation causes the supplicant to lose SAN as if encountering Nyarlathotep anew. Nyarlathotep can raise any skill (even Unnatural) that is below 40% to 40%, or grant the knowledge to perform any ritual that the Great Old One wishes to impart. This knowledge is instant and permanent.

SAN LOSS: Varies from 0 to 1/1D10 to 1D10/1D100.

Nyogtha

"Men knew him as the Dweller in Darkness, that brother of the Old Ones called Nyogtha, the Thing that should not be. He can be summoned to Earth's surface through certain secret caverns and fissures, and sorcerers have seen him in Syria and below the black tower of Leng; from the Thang Grotto of Tartary he has come ravening to bring terror and destruction among the pavilions of the great Khan. Only by the looped cross, by the Vach-Viraj incantation and by the Tikkoun elixir may he be driven back to the nighted caverns of hidden foulness where he dwelleth."

—Henry Kuttner, "The Salem Horror"

Supposedly the spawn of Tsathoggua, Nyogtha is depicted in statuary and mosaics as a dark, amorphous, worm-eating thing with crescent horns. It manifests from subterranean pits, black and gelatinous, with a nauseating, musky, reptilian scent.

The "Thing That Should Not Be" opens hypergeometric tunnels for its worshipers, including some ghouls and the Salem witch-cult. It grants some dedicated servants unnatural resilience, such as immunity to fire and the ability to stir from the grave after centuries as a shriveled mummy. The shape of a cross or ankh terrifies such servants, and a stake driven through the heart restrains one in a semblance of death—until the stake is removed.

Effects and Abilities—Nyogtha

AURA OF POWER: Any human in Nyogtha's presence is automatically at –20% on all rolls (except SAN). A character that fails the SAN roll for encountering Nyogtha cannot act for 1D4 turns, instead goggling in abject terror.

COALESCENCE: Summoned by a ritual at a deep pit, Nyogtha takes 2D4 turns to emerge. Its fetid scent emerges first, then black tendrils, then the first hints of its gelatinous bulk. It emerges in the open air only in the darkness of night, feeds upon living things until its hungers are sated or the sun rises, and then withdraws into its unfathomable abyss.

CONSUMPTION: Unleashed fully to feed, Nyogtha moves with frightful speed and absorbs the living into itself. Once per turn, it devours every living thing within a 10-meter radius, with a Lethality rating of 10%. Victims fleeing in a vehicle can escape, but those on foot can't hope to outrun it for long. Each turn, a victim can attempt an Athletics or Dodge roll to sprint just out of reach. Whether they can escape remains up to the Handler.

DISCORPORATION: A successful attack by an explosive with a Lethality rating of 50% or higher disintegrates Nyogtha's physical form. The Great Old One departs unwillingly: each character present loses SAN and must make a Luck roll. If the Luck roll fails, the victim is touched by a shred of Nyogtha, taking 1D6 damage and losing 1D6 WP. With a fumbled Luck roll, the victim takes 2D6 damage and loses permanent POW instead of WP.

DISMISSAL: Certain hypergeometric principles drive Nyogtha back into the depths. This requires access to or knowledge of a ritual that dismisses Nyogtha, a successful activation roll, and the permanent expenditure of 2 POW. One ritual described in the *Necronomicon* is a variant of The Closing of the Breach that takes only three turns to activate. It requires brandishing an ankh, uttering the brief Vach-Viraj incantation, and hurling an extraordinarily rare compound called the Tikkoun elixir, which corrodes the stuff of Nyogtha away in great pieces until the Old One retreats.

FUNDAMENTAL CONTROL: Nyogtha can change scale, mass, and molecular order at will, growing, shrinking, changing, or transcending any physical limitation without a roll. Most attacks against Nyogtha have no effect (but see **DISCORPORATION**).

SAN LOSS: 1D6/1D20.

Qu-Tugkwa

"What frightened me most was that flaming column; spouting volcanically from depths profound and inconceivable, casting no shadows as healthy flame should, and coating the nitrous stone above with a nasty, venomous verdigris. For in all that seething combustion no warmth lay, but only the clamminess of death and corruption."

—H.P. Lovecraft, "The Festival"

Qu-Tugkwa's name comes from the Southern Paiute meaning "night (or darkness) from fire," and it appears as an immense gout of loathsome flame or as a congeries of smaller sentient plasmas. Some accounts describe Qu-Tugkwa as a gangrenous flame that devours without offering warmth or the comfort of light. In North American myth, its traditional home is the star Fomalhaut, to which the Bighorn Medicine Wheel in Wyoming has been aligned since at least 1050 CE. In Mesoamerica, it was known as Xiuhtecutli, "Lord Xiuha." The so-called "fire worshipers" of the pre-Islamic Middle East may have included some cultists of Kheshthogha, possibly directed by the "beings of smokeless fire" known to them as djinn and to other scholars as ifrits, and to the Theosophists as the Children of the Fire Mist (see **IFRITS** on page 207). Most of its modern apparitions can be traced to individual sorcerers, not to continuous cult activity; but some agents of Delta Green and GRU SV-8 have reported hints of an Iranian occult investigation program that overlaps uncomfortably with its nuclear efforts.

Effects and Abilities—Qu-Tugkwa

AURA OF POWER: Any human in Qu-Tugkwa's presence is automatically at −20% on all rolls (except SAN). A character that fails the SAN roll for encountering Qu-Tugkwa cannot act for 1D8 turns, instead goggling in abject terror.

CONSUMPTION: Qu-Tugkwa emerges on Earth from a summoning area and expands to consume all nearby matter. On the first turn, Qu-Tugkwa's blasting fires and leprous vortices blacken and devour a 10-meter radius with Lethality 10%. With a Dodge roll, a victim can sprint out of reach of the hungry flames. For each HP that a living creature loses to Qu-Tugkwa's fire, the creature also loses 1 WP and Qu-Tugkwa's flames add one meter in radius and 1% in Lethality. At 100 meters and 100%, it stabilizes in size and Lethality but continues to feed on HP and WP until discorporated or dismissed.

DISCORPORATION: A successful attack by an explosive with a Lethality rating of 70% or higher disperses Qu-Tugkwa's flames. The Great Old One departs unwillingly: each character present loses 1D6 WP and an equal amount of SAN, and must make a Luck roll. If the Luck roll fails, the victim loses permanent POW instead of WP.

DISMISSAL: Certain hypergeometric principles are known to cause Qu-Tugkwa to cease manifesting in a summoning, utilizing ancient forces to restrain and re-trap its power at the center of the universe. That requires access to or knowledge of a ritual that dismisses Qu-Tugkwa, a successful activation roll, and the permanent expenditure of 7 POW.

FUNDAMENTAL CONTROL: Qu-Tugkwa can change scale, mass, and molecular order at will, growing, shrinking, changing, or transcending any physical limitation without a roll. Most attacks against Qu-Tugkwa have no effect (but see **DISCORPORATION**).

SAN LOSS: 1D6/1D20.

Shub-Niggurath

"Iä! Shub-Niggurath! As a foulness shall ye know Them. Their hand is at your throats, yet ye see Them not; and Their habitation is even one with your guarded threshold."

—H.P. Lovecraft, "The Dunwich Horror"

Said by some to be the spawn of Azathoth and the Darkness, Shub-Niggurath is venerated across the cosmos in words that translate to human ears as "The Black Goat of the Woods with a Thousand Young." The cry *"Iä!* Shub-Niggurath!" rings out at unnatural ceremonies and rituals, and even imprints itself on their victims. The name seems to have some deep connection with sentience, or perhaps with perception. Delta Green has been unable to trace it in the archaeological record before the 10th century BCE, when Babylonian magi desperately carved summons for the "Shining Terrible Secret One of Earth," Shuba-Nígùr-Urash, in Sumerian, a language already ancient.

Sumerian texts before the time of Gilgamesh named the terrible Másh-Ngi, words meaning both "black goat" and "prophetic dream." This being was later disguised as the goddess Ningal ("Great Lady").

Some say Shub-Niggurath has been present, whether acknowledged openly or unintentionally invoked, at fertility rituals throughout human history. The mi-go maintain a great shrine to Shub-Niggurath on the moon. The priests of K'n-Yan and Mu worshiped it. Astarte, Cybele, Freyja, Durga, Coatlicue, Haumea—all have been masks for Shub-Niggurath, as have a number of gods, from Osiris to Voltumnus to Makemake. Tradition refers to Shub-Niggurath as female, but the Black Goat transcends gender.

Shub-Niggurath's toxic and distorted fertility incorporates psychoactive organics, growth hormones, and all manner of exotic biological substances. Ill-advised March Technologies researchers and various cults shyly (or eagerly) suckle at Shub-Niggurath's teat for access to toxins, elixirs, or gateways into inner space. Once Shub-Niggurath's spores or excretions enter a human, that human becomes part of the god's garden, to be grown or harvested at will. Indeed, some believe that Shub-Niggurath has always been a part of humanity—or is it the other way around? At least half a dozen Shub-Niggurath cults have gone into the health food business over the last century, and a successful crop additive that stemmed from Shub-Niggurath is widespread in the American food chain. The Black Goat of the Woods may have millions of Young who just haven't gotten the genetic message yet.

Effects and Abilities—Shub-Niggurath

AURA OF POWER: Any human present when Shub-Niggurath manifests is automatically at −40% on all rolls (except SAN). A character that fails the SAN roll for encountering Shub-Niggurath cannot act for 1D10+2 turns, instead goggling in abject terror at its monstrous form and its overwhelming, terrifying presence.

DISCORPORATION: A successful attack with a Lethality rating of 70% or higher causes Shub-Niggurath to explode in a disgusting spray of slime and fragments. Each character present who fails a Luck roll loses 1D6/1D20 SAN as the horrific power of Shub Niggurath passes through them and returns to secretive, verdant areas to reform. Such a reconstitution takes months.

DISMISSAL: Certain hypergeometric principles are known to cause Shub-Niggurath to cease manifesting in a summoning, utilizing ancient forces to restrain and re-trap it. That requires access to or knowledge of a ritual that dismisses Shub-Niggurath, a successful activation roll, and the permanent expenditure of 5 POW.

FUNDAMENTAL CONTROL: Shub-Niggurath can change scale, mass, and molecular order at will, growing, shrinking, changing or transcending any physical limitation without a roll. Most attacks against Shub-Niggurath have no effect (but see **DISCORPORATION**).

EFFLUVIENT LIFE: Shub-Niggurath can focus, mutate, enhance or otherwise change any life-system at will. It can permanently increase stats and HP, work permanent biological changes, or absorb, consume, or extend life. Such changes range widely in impact and effect, but experiencing gross physical changes costs 1/1D6 SAN, at a minimum. Humanity survives in its present state by avoiding the Old One's attention.

SAN LOSS: 1D10/1D100.

Tleche-Naka

"It is not well that earth's gods leave their thrones for the spider to spin on, and their realm for the Others to sway in the dark manner of Others."

—H.P. Lovecraft, *The Dream-Quest of Unknown Kadath*

The Great Spider Tleche-Naka is supposedly a companion or rival of Tsathoggua in the Hyperborean myth-cycle. Its name is cognate with the Pueblo "Spider Grandmother" Tseche-Nako. Tleche-Naka was also worshipped in Phoenicia and Lydia under the name Omfalé, possibly related to the Greek omphalos, or "navel of the world." The purple spiders of Leng may be its spawn, and it may dwell beneath that plateau. Its webs supposedly connect all dimensions; its "spider form" may simply be occult code for (or ignorant myth-making about) a hyperspatial entity.

Effects and Abilities—Tleche-Naka

AURA OF POWER: Any human present when Tleche-Naka manifests is automatically at −40% on all rolls (except SAN). A character that fails the SAN roll for encountering Tleche-Naka cannot act for 1D10+2 turns, instead goggling in abject terror at its monstrous form and its overwhelming, terrifying presence.

DISCORPORATION: A successful attack with a Lethality rating of 50% or higher causes Tleche-Naka to explode in a disgusting spray of slime and fragments. Each character present who fails a Luck roll loses 1D4/1D6 CON points as they are coated with noxious, poisonous effluvia. Tleche-Naka's immortal energy retreats to a nearby dimension and reforms after weeks, months, or years.

DISMISSAL: Certain hypergeometric principles are known to cause Tleche-Naka to cease manifesting in a summoning, utilizing ancient forces to restrain and re-trap its power. That requires access to or knowledge of a ritual that dismisses Tleche-Naka, a successful activation roll, and the permanent expenditure of 3 POW.

FUNDAMENTAL CONTROL: Tleche-Naka can change scale, mass, and molecular order at will, growing, shrinking, changing or transcending any physical limitation without a roll. Most attacks against Tleche-Naka have no effect (see **DISCORPORATION**).

POISON: Tleche-Naka can sting a single target with a Lethality 80% poison attack. Upon death, the target literally dissolves into gelatinous, smoking, goo, costing all nearby 1D4/1D8 SAN.

SEIZE: Tleche-Naka can seize any target within five meters, impaling it with thin, huge limbs. This attack automatically hits its selected target with a 60% Lethality rating. This attack cannot be Dodged.

WEB: Tleche-Naka can subdue nearby targets with a web, ten meters across, that requires 10 HP of damage to sever. While webbed, all actions by that target are −40%.

SAN LOSS: 1D10/1D100.

Tsathoggua

"It's from N'kai that frightful Tsathoggua came—you know, the amorphous, toad-like god-creature mentioned in the Pnakotic Manuscripts and the Necronomicon *and the Commoriom myth-cycle preserved by the Atlantean high-priest Klarkash-Ton."*

—H.P. Lovecraft, "The Whisperer in Darkness"

Some in Delta Green believe Tsathoggua's current resting place, assuming it maps to earthly coordinates, to be the cavern-vault of N'Kai, approximately 5.5 kilometers below Oklahoma. The possibility of its physical presence in continental U.S. territory is more than enough to raise Tsathoggua's threat profile, but it gets worse. The entity has a reputation (in von Junzt, and especially in the Hyperborean *Book of Eibon)* of willingly sharing (or calving off, or sporulating) hypergeometric knowledge with deranged seekers. Tsathoggua, said to be the most accessible of the Old Ones, is revered by many sorcerers, some of great power.

The *Book of Eibon* claims Tsathoggua arrived on Earth before Cthulhu, possibly from Saturn. Al-Hazred calls Tsathoggua one of the "earthly" Great Old Ones and describes its conjuration by black, "worse than formless" alien "star-spawn" after their arrival in N'Kai from the planet Kythamil.

N'Kai follows the pattern of many mythological underworlds, lying beneath a lesser hell, in this case "red-litten Yoth." Some occult texts locate Yoth and N'Kai beneath a region ranging from Greenland to Germany, implying either an unprecedented natural fissure system in the crust of the Northern Hemisphere or a hypergeometrical component to N'Kai's architecture. Other tales place red Yoth and black N'Kai beneath blue-lit K'n-Yan, which stretches beneath the American midwest. The result, in any case, is that Tsathoggua's cult is global.

Tsathoggua has been called Tsadogwa in Uganda, Saaktoq by the Greenland Inuit, Sadogowah by the Algonquin tribes, and Tiráwa by the Pawnee. They describe Tsathoggua as formless and protean, pitch black or (to the Pawnee) invisible. This broadly matches descriptions of the Kythamil "star-spawn" and

DISINFORMATION

YELLOW CARD

OKLAHOMA EARTHQUAKES

Beginning in 2009, the number of earthquakes (3.0 or higher magnitude) in Oklahoma skyrocketed from fewer than 2 per year to almost 900 in 2015 alone.

Environmentalists and some scientists have blamed the tremors on fracking and oilfield wastewater deep disposal, a version of the truth that Delta Green encourages. But many of these quakes, including a magnitude 5.6 temblor in Prague, Oklahoma in 2011, originate from much deeper in the earth's crust than fracking or wastewater ever reach. So far, the quakes almost eerily avoid the mound region near Binger and Hydro, thought to lie above K'n-Yan, perhaps because the primal city of Tsath contains stabilizing geometries.

The Delta Green Program's leaders have considered sending a U.S. Geological Survey seismologist or two out to Oklahoma to see if N'Kai is extending itself – or if Tsathoggua is waking up. The risks of such a mission have outweighed its urgency, so far.

LONG THIS LINE

Tsathoggua's depiction in the *Necronomicon*. Statues of the Gallo-Roman god Sadoqua and the Auvergne witch-cult deity Sadoguë follow the Hyperborean tradition, depicting a squat, toad- or bat-like monster coated in thick fur. This matches the Aztec Tlaltecuhtli, "Lord of the Earth," descended from the Olmec toad-god of earth and eternity, often depicted with batlike ears. Various scholars say Tsathoggua is covered in an "imitation" of fur, that it sits so slothfully that it feeds only on sacrifices even in ravening hunger, and that it changes shape to suit its inscrutable needs.

Tsathoggua has a number of spawn or lesser avatars, about which little is known: Yabou, Ossadagowah, Zuilphagua, and so on. There is some evidence that the mi-go worship—or at least seek to placate—this being while on Earth.

Effects and Abilities—Tsathoggua

AURA OF POWER: Encountering Tsathoggua's loathsome form—a huge, slumbering, bat-headed monstrosity—costs the SAN loss listed below, even when it sleeps. Any human present when Tsathoggua fully awakens is automatically at −20% on all rolls (except SAN). A character who fails the SAN roll for encountering Tsathoggua cannot act for 1D6 turns, instead goggling in abject terror.

DISCORPORATION: A successful attack with a Lethality rating of 40% or higher causes Tsathoggua to dissipate, as if fading from the dimensions experienced by humanity. Each character present who fails a Luck roll loses 1/1D6 SAN and is marred by the mark of Tsathoggua, a never-healing brand of raw flesh that looks like a stylized eye and permanently reduces the victim's CON by 1 point; what further effects it has are up to the Handler. Tsathoggua then loiters in adjacent dimensions before resuming corporeal form at the next full moon.

DISMISSAL: Certain hypergeometric principles allow Tsathoggua to be lulled into a torpor and banished, for an unknowable amount of time, into unseen dimensions. This requires access to or knowledge of a ritual that dismisses Tsathoggua, a successful activation roll, and the permanent expenditure of 2 POW.

FUNDAMENTAL CONTROL: Tsathoggua can change scale, mass, and molecular order at will, growing, shrinking, changing, or transcending any physical limitation without a roll. Most attacks against Tsathoggua have no effect (but see **DISCORPORATION**).

HUNGER: Occasionally, Tsathoggua stirs to grab a nearby target (within five meters) and consume the hapless victim whole. The target may attempt one Dodge roll at −20% to escape the enormous claw. Failure means death.

STASIS: Tsathoggua usually rests in a torpor, immune to nearly all interactions (even attacks with Lethality ratings) except what might, for unfathomable reasons, pique the Great Old One's interest.

TELEPATHIC COMMUNION: Those who contact Tsathoggua, through ritual or by arriving in its presence, may choose to open themselves to telepathic communion with the being to receive knowledge. Each communion causes the supplicant to lose SAN as if encountering Tsathoggua anew. Tsathoggua can raise any skill (even Unnatural) that is below 40% to 40%, or grant the knowledge to perform any ritual that the Great Old One wishes to impart. This knowledge is instant and permanent.

SAN LOSS: 1D6/1D20.

Y'golonac

"Beyond a gulf in the subterranean night a passage leads to a wall of massive bricks, and beyond the wall rises Y'golonac to be served by the tattered eyeless figures of the dark. Long has he slept beyond the wall, and those which crawl over the bricks scuttle across his body never knowing it to be Y'golonac; but when his name is spoken or read he comes forth to be worshipped or to feed and take on the shape and soul of those he feeds upon. For those who read of evil and search for its form within their minds call forth evil, and so may Y'golonac return to walk among men..."

—Ramsey Campbell, "Cold Print"

Y'golonac represents a worse security threat in many ways than either Tsathoggua or Cthulhu. It apparently actively seeks to corrupt and influence human behavior, laying trails to attract degenerates to its service. Anyone who reads even a page, or perhaps a passage, from the twelfth volume of The Revelations of Glaaki becomes open to possession by Y'golonac. The prospect of a depraved sociopath with the powers of a Great Old One is literally apocalyptic.

For some reason, Y'golonac cannot simply erupt from its human shell and rule the Earth; in myth, it dwells behind an endless wall of massive bricks. It likely seeks the precise human "key" to unlock its prison; while it searches, Delta Green works to destroy its levers on this side of the wall. Fortunately, Y'golonac's obsessive, sweaty devotees are almost always terrible at making the human connections needed to start an effective cult; they operate in lonely, furtive secrecy.

In dreams and visions, Y'golonac appears as an obese or flabby man without a head. The palms of its hands bear wet, toothy mouths. Its human hosts also eventually take on a similar appearance (its female hosts sometimes shift sex, but not always); its most powerful or promising slaves can switch forms from human to monstrous and back. The archetypal figure of Y'golonac appears throughout human art, from the headless petroglyph figure with a distended penis found in the Kalabera caves on Saipan in the Marianas, to the headless Blemmyes representing gluttony in medieval Christian art, to the Acéphale icon of the Surrealist Georges Bataille. Clearly, Y'golonac had ways into the world before Glaaki's twelfth volume surfaced in 1925.

Legendary headless ogres likewise appear across the globe: the Akephaloi of Herodotus, the Ewaipanoma in Guiana, the Man-With-No-Head of the Hidatsa, the Scots highway murderer Coluinn gun Cheann, the Ch-em ch'og of Tibet. Modern cults in Calcutta and Guangzhou have represented Y'golonac with the imagery of the bloody and headless Hindu goddess of unrestrained sexuality, Chinnamasta, and the Chinese giant-musician, Xing Tian. Occultists who pursue the Greco-Egyptian papyri describing the "Bornless One" or "Headless One" Osorronophris may seek "knowledge of the Holy Guardian Angel" but find themselves kneeling before Y'golonac, after spending decades and fortunes seeking the Name that dooms them.

Given that reading even a paragraph of lore about Y'golonac might result in monstrous possession, it's hardly surprising that Delta Green knows even less about the origins or nature of this Great Old One than about others. Here, if anywhere, the legendary Delta Green dictum to "burn before reading" makes complete sense.

Effects and Abilities—Y'golonac

AURA OF POWER: Any human present when Y'golonac manifests (either in its native form or as an avatar in Y'golonac-form) is automatically at –20% on all rolls (except SAN). A character who fails the SAN roll for encountering Y'golonac cannot act for 1D6 turns, instead goggling in abject terror at its monstrous form.

AVATAR: Y'golonac most often works through possession of a human target (see **THE WORDS**). It can masquerade as a normal human, using the body like a puppet in which it is undetectable. Or, it can choose to manifest fully in its Y'golonac form. In so doing, it inflicts SAN loss and projects its **AURA OF POWER**. The avatar's body bloats, consumes its head, splits through its clothing, and begins to glow. The palms of its hands become maws ringed with shark-like teeth that inflict 1D8+2 points of damage, once per turn, unless the victim makes a Dodge roll. Y'golonac's human avatar is immune to many attacks, but can be discorporated by a successful attack with a Lethality rating of 10% or higher or by various hypergeometric principles (see **DISMISSAL**). Doing so leaves behind the human corpse of the avatar.

DISCORPORATION: Y'golonac's true form (see **TRAPPED**) can be discorporated with a successful attack with a Lethality rating of 60% or higher. Its form collapses on itself and rips a hole in spacetime. All characters nearby must make Luck rolls. A fumble indicates the character is swept into the hole and gone forever. All other attacks have no effect on Y'golonac's true form. Y'golonac's true form restores itself to full potency in a few months.

DISMISSAL: Certain hypergeometric principles allow Y'golonac to be dismissed. This requires access to or knowledge of a ritual that dismisses Y'golonac, a successful activation roll, and the permanent expenditure of 1 POW.

FUNDAMENTAL CONTROL: The true form of Y'golonac (see **TRAPPED**) can change scale, mass, and molecular order at will, growing, shrinking, changing or transcending any physical limitation without a roll. While it enjoys fundamental control, this ability is not enough to allow it to escape the prison in which it remains trapped. Someone in its physical presence and able to strike would find that most attacks against Y'golonac have no effect (but see **DISCORPORATION**).

TRAPPED: Y'golonac's true form remains trapped in an unknown location, said to be a subterranean locale behind a huge wall of bricks.

THE WORDS: Y'golonac usually gains entry into the human world through a particular passage in the twelfth volume of the *Revelations of Glaaki*. A human being who reads that book can become a possessed vessel of Y'golonac (see **AVATAR**). Whether this fate befalls anyone who reads enough, or only those whose cruel predilections predispose them to Y'golonac's influence, is unknown.

SAN LOSS: 1D6/1D20.

Yig

"It seems that Yig, the snake-god of the central plains tribes—presumably the primal source of the more southerly Quetzalcoatl or Kukulcan—was an odd, half-anthropomorphic devil of highly arbitrary and capricious nature. He was not wholly evil, and was usually quite well-disposed toward those who gave proper respect to him and his children, the serpents; but in the autumn he became abnormally ravenous, and had to be driven away by means of suitable rites."

—H.P. Lovecraft and Zealia Bishop, "The Curse of Yig"

Worship of the Father of Serpents, widely attested among the Plains nations of North America, likely descended from the Yig cult in K'n-Yan. The same may be the source for the serpent-god cults of Kulkulkan and Quetzalcoatl in Mesoamerica. Differentiating "conventional" snake rituals such as possession by Damballah in Vodou, or snake-handling Pentecostalism in Tennessee, from intentional cultism of Yig is difficult without deliberate infiltration and long observation. If even a fraction of the snake cults and serpent gods throughout human history represent Yig worship, then Yig is by far the most ubiquitous of Great Old Ones. Yig may be a soul-symbol of the serpent-folk, raised to cosmic power by their sorceries, or a gigantic self-aware weapon deployed by the mi-go or Lemurians against Ghatanothoa. Regardless of its origin, it exacts gruesome revenge on those who trespass against its serpent avatars.

Effects and Abilities—Yig

AURA OF POWER: Any human present when Yig manifests as giant ophidian-humanoid is automatically at −20% on all rolls (except SAN). A character who fails the SAN roll for encountering Yig cannot act for 1D6 turns, instead staring in abject terror at its ophidian form.

BITE OF YIG: The humanoid form of Yig strikes so swiftly that all Dodge attempts are at −20%. Any roll but 100 is a successful strike inflicting 2D10 damage, and injecting a Lethality 40% poison with a Speed of one hour and no antidote. (See **POISON AND DISEASE** on page 60 of the *Agent's Handbook*.)

CHILDREN OF YIG: Yig's manifestation is preceded by its children: enormous, poisonous snakes. Some rumors indicate these creatures can evolve into more than snakes. Children of Yig have 12 HP and Armor 1, and attack with a poisonous bite that inflicts 1D6 damage, as well as injecting a Lethality 15% poison with a Speed of one hour and no antidote. Unlike common snakes, the children of Yig are vicious and direct their ire at those who have offended their god. Those destroying the spawn of Yig must make a Luck roll; failure indicates they have come under the scrutiny of the snake-god (see **CURSE OF YIG**).

CURSE OF YIG: Anyone who destroys Yig's offspring and fails a Luck roll loses 0/1D4 SAN and is haunted for days or weeks by dreams of being consumed by snakes and reptiles. On a fumbled Luck roll, Yig manifests and comes to collect on the debt, personally.

DISCORPORATION: Yig's form can be discorporated with a successful attack with a Lethality rating of 40% or higher. Its form is blown into poisonous bits, and all present must make Luck rolls. Failure indicates that the character is struck with a Lethality 10% poison with a Speed of 1D4 hours and no antidote. All other attacks have no effect. Yig restores itself to full potency in several months.

DISMISSAL: Certain hypergeometric principles allow Yig to be dismissed. This requires access to or knowledge of a ritual that dismisses Yig, a successful activation roll, and the permanent expenditure of 1 POW.

SAN LOSS: 1D6/1D20.

Yog-Sothoth

Yog-Sothoth, the All-in-One, dwells in the interstices between dimensions; some say the superstrings of M-theory curve around its congeries of spheres. The *Necronomicon* describes it as "the Key to the Gate, whereby the Spheres meet." Yog-Sothoth guards and controls all passages from one plane of existence to another, both Key *and* Gate. It combines the occult concepts of the Watcher on the Threshold and the Opener of the Way, implying that to attain true occult power, one must both supplicate and defeat Yog-Sothoth. Yog-Sothoth exists in all times and spaces, leading to its Arabic cognomen Tawil at-'Umr, "the Prolonged of Life." Nevertheless, at least here and now, its quasi-material presence on Earth remains limited to a few moments and meters: May Eve and Halloween of certain years, inside a few megalithic circles.

For human sorcerers, Yog-Sothoth offers power over life and death: the magus Joseph Curwen summoned Yog-Sothoth to learn not only how to resurrect the dead, but also how to preserve his life-force within his essential salts and orchestrate his resurrection. This was only part of the harvest of knowledge Curwen's circle sought. Yog-Sothoth cultists have obtained access to the past and to impossible realms through windows and scrying balls.

Like all the cosmic gods, Yog-Sothoth has an active cult among the mi-go, who know it as the "Beyond-One," and among other alien beings such as the vaporous egregores of the spiral nebulae. The Elder Things, however, feared it, possibly connecting its iridescent globes with their own spherical nemeses, the shoggoths. Or perhaps at some point in their eons of experimentation they reified an avatar of Yog-Sothoth near the South Magnetic Pole; Dyer's suppressed account of Miskatonic's 1930 Antarctic expedition had a witness shrieking of Yog-Sothoth and "proto-shoggoths." In 1912, Elijah Whateley bred Yog-Sothoth with his daughter Lavinia during a brief moment of tangency between the god and Sentinel Hill near Dunwich. Only quick and lucky action by a coterie of academics prevented Lavinia's twin sons from invoking their father to scour the planet clean of mere material life.

Effects and Abilities—Yog-Sothoth

AURA OF POWER: Any human in Yog-Sothoth's presence is automatically at −40% on all rolls (except SAN). A character that fails the SAN roll for encountering Yog-Sothoth cannot act for 1D10+2 turns, instead goggling in abject terror.

DISCORPORATION: A successful attack with a Lethality rating of 70% or higher may cause Yog-Sothoth's physical form to dissolve into the aether. But whether Yog-Sothoth is vulnerable to such a disruption, or is simply transcendent and beyond physical harm, is up to the Handler. If such discorporation succeeds, all characters present who fail Luck rolls lose 1D6/1D20 SAN as their minds are rended by visions of a million other worlds and times. Yog-Sothoth reconstitutes itself in the beyond where time has no meaning, so it might return in a second, a year, or a millennium.

ENGULF: Occasionally, Yog-Sothoth grows, shifts, and changes, engulfing and absorbing everything within 10 meters. Everything in that radius suffers a 50% Lethality attack, which cannot be Dodged. At the Handler's choice, a successful Lethality roll may mean the character is not slain but simply vanishes out of spacetime.

FUNDAMENTAL CONTROL: Yog-Sothoth can change scale, mass, and molecular order at will, growing, shrinking, changing, or transcending any physical limitation without a roll. Most attacks against Yog-Sothoth have no effect (but see **DISCORPORATION**).

DISMISSAL: Certain hypergeometric principles are known to cause Yog-Sothoth to cease manifesting in a summoning, utilizing ancient forces to restrain and re-trap its power outside the universe. That requires access to or knowledge of a ritual that dismisses Yog-Sothoth, a successful activation roll, and the permanent expenditure of 8 POW.

TELEPATHIC COMMUNION: Those who contact Yog-Sothoth through ritual may find their minds laid bare to knowledge or impossible concepts communicated by the

All-in-One. Each communion causes the character to lose SAN as if encountering Yog-Sothoth anew. Yog-Sothoth can raise any skill (even Unnatural) that is below 40% to 40%, or grant the knowledge to perform any ritual that the Great Old One wishes to impart. This knowledge is instant and permanent.

SAN LOSS: 1D10/1D100.

Creating Your Own Unnatural Threats

When creating new unnatural threats, embrace contradiction. Even the once-human ghouls and Deep Ones violate everything we think we know about biology.

The advantage to a new threat is customization: you can tailor its attacks, spoor, and details to the mood or storyline of your operation. You're not constrained by biochemistry or anything but the dramatic imperatives of terror, shock, and wonder. The ideal result of this blend of unknowability, surprise, and terror: the recognition of the weird in the familiar.

These new entities may be extrusions from the ultraviolet, or alien infections like the colour out of space. A sorcerer can summon literally anything from the farther angles of dimensionality: a collation of silvery legs that rot carbon, a virulent sound that turns the human intestinal tract into a hyperspatial shunt, a fifty-foot rodent with a hundred mad eyes.

Catechresis and Cubism

When it comes time to present your new-fledged horror, there's no better approach than catachresis and cubism.

Catachresis is the deliberate misuse of language or impossible metaphor to inspire a response: a solid creature "filters" or "seeps," a god resembles a "shining darkness," and so on. Here we get angles that are "both acute and obtuse," elements unknown to science, and descriptions of things as "indescribable."

To catachresis, add *cubism:* drown the image in details, invoking other images until the result is impossible. Cthulhu resembles "simultaneous pictures of an octopus, a dragon, and a human caricature." The dissected Elder Things and the disintegrating Wilbur Whateley have so many "surfaces"—scales, barrels, tendrils, wings, tentacles—to examine that they become completely fluid and chaotic. Introduce contradictory imagery to describe your creature: "a face not unlike a scarab-beetle or a rabid baboon, with something feathery in the outline" evokes Nyarlathotep without ever really looking like anything.

>> Determining Stats

Sample Style	Start with This Creature's Stats	Likely Size	Typical SAN Loss for Seeing Creature
Alien parasite	Those Beyond	1 kg (2.2 lbs)	0/1D4
Human infected with the unnatural	Deep One (lesser)	90 kg (200 lbs)	0/1D4
Insubstantial being	Colour out of space	(Extradimensional)	0/1D6
Hardy alien species	Dimensional shambler	272 kg (600 lbs)	1/1D6
Immense, extradimensional horror	Hunting-horror	2,267 kg (5,000 lbs)	1/1D10
Indestructible killing machine	Shoggoth	4,535 kg (10,000 lbs)	1D6/1D20
Great Old One	Cthulhu	91,000 kg (100 tons)	1D10/1D100

>> Defenses

If the Entity Can Withstand...	Recommended Defense
Fists and clubs	Armor 3 (thick fur or squamous hide)
Knives and small arms	Armor 6 (bulletproof chitin)
Portable heavy weapons	Resilient (large size or unnatural toughness)
Missiles and bombs	Uncanny Matter or Transcendent (extradimensional coherence)

>> Attacks

STR	Damage
1–4	0 to 1D4
5–8	1 to 1D6
9–12	1D4 to 1D8
13–16	1D6 to 1D10
17–20	1D8 to 1D12
21–30	1D10 to 2D6 or Lethality 10% to 15%
31–40	Up to Lethality 20%
41–50	Up to Lethality 25%
51–60	Up to Lethality 30%

Determining Stats

After you've determined the entity's concept, find an entity that's already defined and that feels close to what you are trying to build. Is it huge and destructive? Start with the stats of a shoggoth. Is it humanoid but difficult to kill? Start with a dimensional shambler. Is it a human altered by the unnatural? Start with a Deep One's stats.

Once you have the starting stats, determine which ones need to change. Some entities are non-physical, having no STR or CON at all. Most alien intelligences have nothing approaching a CHA score. Hardly any unnatural beings have SAN. Alter as needed.

Then, determine how much SAN it costs to see such a being. Usually, the bigger or more dangerous, the more hideous it is to gaze upon, but this is not always the case.

Now calculate HP (the average of STR and CON, rounded up) and move on to the fun of selecting special abilities.

Determining and Naming Special Abilities

To construct the nuts and bolts of your entity, look at examples and consider the information below. There are several categories of special abilities, but it is up to the Handler to take them, change them, and make them sing. Simply locate an ability you like, modify it as needed, rename it to suit the new entity.

Defenses

How resistant to physical attack is the entity? The most common defensive qualities are described in **OPINT: DEFENSIVE QUALITIES** on page 190. Choose one. If the entity is wholly immune to physical harm, then it is Transcendent. Some entities are immune only to particular sources of harm: flames, cold, explosions. If so, simply make a new ability, name it, and give it a description. Voila, immunity.

A creature that's hard to hurt but can be destroyed by heavy weapons may simply have Armor. A large or especially hardy creature might be Resilient, making Lethality weapons much less effective.

It's best to create an entity with a single defense. With two defenses, having to refer to the separate rules becomes confusing. Certainly, if a creature has the Transcendent, Uncanny Matter, or Persistent quality, that should be its only defense. Combine two of the other defenses—Out of Phase, Resilient, Unnatural Biology, and/or Armor—only when necessary to represent the creature you have in mind.

Attacks

What kind of damage can the entity do? Compare it to entities described in this book and borrow one of their attacks that seems equivalent. Or, look at

OPINT: Balancing Entities in Game-Play

These rules are not meant to generate entities that are carefully balanced to provide players with a fair fight. In the world of Delta Green, mankind is hopelessly outstripped by even the simplest of the powers beyond. A single ghoul can represent a dire threat to a team of well-armed agents. The unnatural represents a fatal danger for humanity—both mental and physical—that will never be understood or controlled. And violence, after all, is the most fundamental attempt at control.

There are important things to keep in mind, however. Most unnatural beings, despite their overwhelming power, have weaknesses. A creature that is immune to physical attacks may be poisoned by high levels of carbon dioxide in the air. A bulletproof being might be banished with the lighting of a single open flame. Almost all unnatural entities are vulnerable to hypergeometry or unnatural weaponry.

In short, with research and preparation, the Agents have a chance to send the thing back to wherever it came from. But only a chance.

weapons as a baseline. Is the attack about as deadly as a heavy machine gun? Give it a Lethality rating of 15%. Here are suggested ranges for damage based on a entity's STR stat; or, if a being has no STR stat, use POW. Remember, these are only guidelines. In the realm of the unnatural nearly anything is possible.

Attacks need a percentage chance to hit as well. At 20% or lower, the entity is clumsy and rarely hits—perhaps it's not at home in our three dimensions. At 50% or higher, it's distinctly dangerous. At 90% or higher, it's a killing machine.

Does the entity grab or constrict? If so, the target is usually permitted a DEX or STR test to escape.

Minimize the number of rolls required to resolve an attack. An entity's attack should need only one roll to hit and one for damage. Even if it can attack with multiple claws and a terrible bite, represent all that with a single attack roll and a single damage roll.

How much damage does an attack do? Keep in mind that an average human being has about 10 HP. Even a failed Lethality roll is likely to kill an Agent. Of course, this *is* a game about death....

Some examples:

- **EXPLOSIVE SPITTLE:** The entity's non-terrene spittle eats through even the most resilient materials. ("Explosive spittle 30%, Lethality 15%.")
- **KILLING FRENZY:** If it loses more than 5 HP in one turn, the entity lashes out wildly. ("Frenzy 45%, damage 1D10+2 to every target in reach.")
- **LATCH AND DRAIN:** The entity attaches to a target (who can attempt a STR contest to escape) and inflicts 1D4+1 damage or drains 1D4+1 STR per turn. Each turn it's attached to a target, the entity gains 1 HP, up to its maximum.
- **SCREECH:** The entity emits a piercing screech that shorts out recording devices and deafens all nearby who fail Luck rolls. In addition, the screech costs 0/1D4 SAN and inflicts 1 damage.

Environmental Adaptations

Unnatural entities often suffer little or no ill effects from even the harshest environments found on Earth. Imagine the entity's home environment and write up a brief ability to cover it. Some examples:

- **BENTHIC:** The entity finds the ocean a comfort at any depth and pressure. If it has lost any HP while away from the ocean, the moment it returns to the waves, its HP jumps to maximum.
- **EXODIMENSIONAL:** The entity's biology adjusts to any change in environment. This change is fast enough that it suffers no damage from sudden and dramatic shifts in temperature or pressure.
- **OF THE FIRE:** The entity is at home only in open flame. Each turn outside open flame, it takes one damage. Returning to open flame for even a single turn is enough to restore all lost HP.
- **STAR-BORN:** The entity is immune to all ill effects from electromagnetics, fire, or explosive force. It was literally born in the heart of a star.

Hypergeometry

Many unnatural creatures have powers that humanity might term "magic." These not need not be attacks. Some examples:

- **IMPOSSIBLE GAZE:** If the creature locks eyes with a target (the target may be allowed a Luck roll, POW test, or DEX test to avoid it), the target loses 1/1D4 SAN as the being's internal reality bleeds out into spacetime.
- **INCINERATE:** If the creature pins a target, the target spontaneously combusts in the text turn, suffering 1D10+2 damage.
- **SHOCKWAVE:** The entity's pulsing gills erupt with horrific sound, causing all present to lose 0/1 SAN. Those who lose SAN fall to the ground.
- **PIEZOELECTRIC PULSE:** The entity emits a sub-sonic burst that disrupts unshielded electronic devices within 10 meters. Cell phones, computers, and cars with modern electronics all cease working.

Movement

Jumping, swimming, flying, tunneling—many unnatural creatures move faster, farther and just better than terrestrial life. Sometimes, it's important to establish exact parameters. Some examples:

- **UNTOUCHABLE:** The creature senses and reacts to changes to the environment so swiftly that only firearms and other high-speed projectiles have a chance of touching it. It dodges any other type of attack without a roll.
- **LEAPER:** The creature can fall or drop any distance and land safely, suffering no damage.
- **SPIDER-LIKE:** The creature can cross any surface at normal speed, including walls and ceilings.
- **SUBTERRANEAN:** The creature can tunnel through dirt or stone as fast as a human can walk.

Senses

Some creatures can see, sense, smell, and hear beyond human senses. If it's simply a little better than human senses, don't worry about defining it. But an unnatural entity that sees in higher dimensions, that can hear a heartbeat at 30 meters, or that can smell emotions should have such senses clearly described.

Some examples:

- **NTH-DIMENSIONAL SIGHT:** The creature can see through dirt, stone, and rock by shunting its sight through higher dimensions.
- **BLOOD SCENT:** The creature can smell and track even a tiny amount of blood. Treat this as a tracking skill at 80%.
- **CIRCULAR VISION:** Evenly spaced eyes circle the creature's head, making any attempt to sneak up on it automatically fail.
- **PRETERNATURAL SENSORS:** Any movement around the creature registers on tiny, hyper-sensitive cilia on its skin. It gains a +40% bonus to any defense roll against a non-firearm attack. A nearby explosion "blinds" this ability.

OPINT: Mixing and Matching

Want a teleporting shoggoth, or a flying Deep One? That's easy. Just grab the shoggoth's stats and slap on the "Apport" ability from the dimensional shambler; or add the hunting-horror's "Flight" to the Deep One's stats. There are no restrictions. Mixing and matching special abilities allows you to create your own catalog of new entities and powers.

Appendix V

FBI's Foreign Terrorist Tracking Task Forc
Data Mining Effort

TO:

FROM:

SUBJECT:

DATE: TIME:

SUPPLEMENTARY REPORT CONTINUED -- SUSPECT STATEMENT

Instructions: Open mike in a sound proofed room. Studio. Nothing chintzy. If you're feeling paranoid, kill the line with a diode. Close it off. Hit record. At night. Ask questions. Talk. Talk to the air. Then, listen to that tape. Turn the gain all the way up. Headphones on. Listen.

Listen.

At first, I did it to kill the time. To test the wiring on the new board. Ten minutes, maybe. "Test one two, one two, who are you..."

Two months later I found it. The tape. Dug it out and ran it and wondered what was on it (I never labeled it). Put it on and pushed the system. "TEST ONE TWO, ONE TWO, WHO ARE YOU..." boomed my voice from the speakers, followed by a hiss. And then, just as my finger found STOP, the voice, there in the back, stealthy. Quiet.

"I am."

A child's voice. A whisper. Like someone in the corner of the empty studio, far from the mike. It was a voice with a sly smile. Far, far, away.

I left then, walked that fucker off. Smoked a smoke. Said hey to the night guy. Came back with a coffee and ran it again. Same thing.

This time, I let it run, all 10. The voice was there again, after mine, then the hiss of air banging together like billiards. Then, at 9:53:09, again, the voice, closer now.

"They're coming." CLICK.

I ran it again.

The next week I was leaving work at 6:50 AM when a woman came out from behind the cement pylon and produced a badge. DEA, it read, Agent Grant. Was I Malcolm Steyr? Did I once work with a man named Reily at the Chicago PD to examine the answering-machine tape of a murder victim? Sure, I said, how was Reily?

Dead, she said.

"Don't trust them," the little girl told me, later, when I asked her what that meant.

"Grant is not her name," she told me.

The tape ran and ran.

Now we're in a car, driving in the black towards something I don't fully understand, but she's told me enough. The two in the front keep their eyes on the road, on the dirt track taking us out into scrub country. My earphone in, I listen to the track. The voice narrates what we're doing, what is coming before it's here.

The gun is a lump of warm metal, hidden in my lap like a promise.

Drive

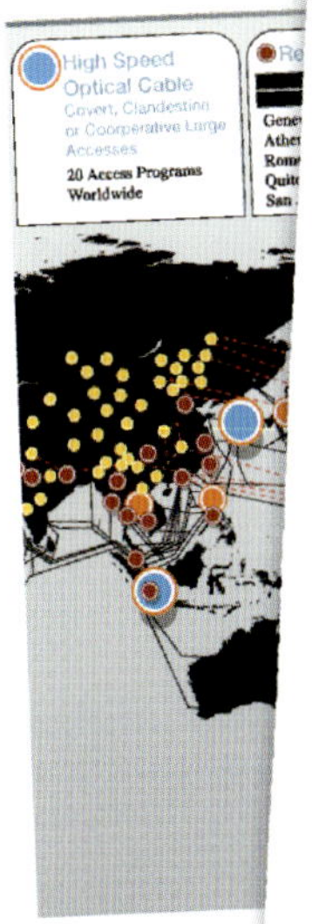

- PRISM is one of
  miss out on your
- Recommend task
  criteria. Your targ
  which **only FAA**
- Recommend usin
  passive/upstream
- Some Product Li
  missing unique
- FAA 702 collecti
  with access to th
  signatures and I.F

DOB_Y	DOB_M	DOB_D	NAME_LAST	NAME_FIRST	NAME_MIDDLE	BIRTH_STATE	BIRTH_COUNTY	BIRTH_CITY	SOM_II_STATUS
2012	8	13	Beauregard	Margaret	Wanda	NY	Albany	Albany	Unresolved
2012	7	23	Espinoza	Arnold	Samuel	CA	Los Angeles	Los Angeles	Unresolved
2013	2	9	Stinson	Sherry	Clementine	AL	Jefferson	Birmingham	Unresolved
2011	3	17	Eckles	Mark	Louis	TN	Shelby	Memphis	Unresolved
2013	9	4	Stover	Terry	Suzanne	CA	San Francisco	San Francisco	Resolved
2015	3	15	Gerken	Kathy	Jane	MA	Middlesex	Waltham	Unresolved
2013	2	14	McKnight	Alexandra	Charlotte	MI	Kent	Grand Rapids	Unresolved
2013	4	14	Deal	Jerry	Lane	SC	Aiken	North Augusta	Resolved
					[illegible]	[illegible]	Hudson	Weehawken	Unresolved

THE GROUP. THE CONSPIRACY. DELTA GREEN. From its beginnings, it has worked in secrecy. Even as P4, its agents were careful to keep their work quiet. Often that meant keeping secrets from one another.

Today, two groups call themselves Delta Green. The old code-word clearance was quietly reactivated in 2002. That code-word was quickly buried again, replaced by a series of new clearances and names to give it obscurity, but Delta Green had returned as a covert, deniable agency in the U.S. executive branch. Its people call it the Program.

When the Program reached out to known agents, many of the old guard refused to join. After 32 years without oversight, they refused to join anything like an official bureaucracy. Instead, they became more stealthy. Many newcomers never learned that there was a schism at all. They call themselves Delta Green, not knowing that an official Program exists. To reduce confusion, we call them the Outlaws.

The Program

The Security Studies Group. Yellow Combine. Petrel Hill. Threshold Curve. Silver See. The name changed eighteen times between 2002 and 2017. Every time it changes, the paper trail leading to its activities becomes more muddled. With each change, a new, Top Secret special-access program grants continuing clearance to activities and intelligence that no American employee can confess or confirm.

Insiders call it "the Program." Its headquarters—and its carefully compartmentalized laboratories, hangars, and personnel scattered throughout the government and private sector—allow it the pretense of legitimacy. But the Program's leaders long ago determined that its work is too important to be restricted by the Constitution. For all its access and influence, the Program is as criminal an enterprise as

IN THE FIELD: What to Tell Your Agents

Nothing. Whether your campaign features the Program or the Outlaws, the Agents live and die in the blessed ignorance of rigid compartmentalization.

If they're in the Program, they have met the case officer who briefs them in person and manages their operations from afar. If they meet anyone else from the Program, besides their teammates, it's only out of dire necessity.

If the Agents are with the Outlaws, the senior-most Agent has likely met a shadowy intermediary sent by the Group's leaders, delivering instructions and warnings to be conveyed to the rest of the team before vanishing.

Few ever see more than that. After many operations, an Agent might see more of Delta Green. A few tight-lipped guards at a safe house. A researcher flown in to collect some bizarre piece of evidence. A nervous intelligence analyst sent to conduct a special debriefing. In extraordinary need, an Agent may be sent to one of the Program's dedicated research labs. Or the Outlaws may send the Agents to question a Friendly who's been out of the loop for years. They all work in strict compartmentalization, too. They probably know even less than the Agents.

The Agents' understanding of Delta Green should grow slowly, and every discovery should be surrounded by confusion and misdirection. Whether the Program or the Outlaws, Delta Green does not want them to learn the details. A visit to Headquarters, or to the home of one of the Outlaws' leaders, should be unforgettable and frightful confirmation that the Agent has learned too much.

IN THE FIELD: How Much Is True?

You're the Handler. It's your game. The information presented in this chapter is as accurate as you want it to be. Change anything to suit your campaign and keep your players in suspense.

any conspiracy or blacker-than-black military project that came before it.

Everywhere the Program works, the words "Delta Green" are the ultimate secret, hardly ever spoken.

Goals and Beliefs

Officially, the Program (whatever its current name) is dedicated to the acquisition and study of foreign technology. The documents that authorize it say nothing about the unnatural, or about the explicit criminality at the heart of the Program.

The Program's true purpose goes back to Delta Green's founding in 1942:

- To gather intelligence on unnatural phenomena.
- To protect the citizens of the United States from threats originating with unnatural phenomena.
- To maintain the security of the United States against unnatural threats.

Only the means and methods have changed. At least, that's what the Program's leaders tell themselves. Some agents might hold lingering doubts about how their superiors are executing that mission. They may especially wonder about one essential, never-answered question: "In the long run, are we only making the problem worse?"

Facilities

The Program's case officers deliberately give Agents the impression that the Program is more sprawling, more omnipresent, than it really is. Agents who think the Program is everywhere may become frustrated when they don't get needed support, but they tend to have more confidence in their overall mission. And they are less likely to make the fatal mistake of betraying the Program.

A little over a thousand personnel work for the Program, most of them sporadically. They are scattered throughout the U.S. government at military bases, intelligence and law-enforcement facilities, and at restricted labs owned by influential military-intelligence contractors in the private sector.

About one hundred personnel work at Headquarters, the heart of the Program. Headquarters is always established in an intelligence or military facility where it can be easily overlooked, or in a government-owned office building with secure rooms and no other tenants. Past locations have included restricted wings of research facilities at Wright-Patterson Air Force Base, Fort Belvoir, and Fort Meade; bland office buildings in New York and Chicago; and a subterranean corner of the CIA compound in Langley. Every two or three years, Headquarters moves, taking on some new, innocuous cover title.

The Program maintains secretive labs to study unnatural samples in isolation and relative safety. Some bases house Air Force units that secretly support Delta Green in rescue and recovery. All Program facilities are off-limits to everyone but a handful of personnel. Each facility has its own baffling chain of frequently-changing Top Secret clearances.

The Program maintains a few dozen black sites around the world, technically owned by CIA, NSA, DHS, or DoD counterterrorism projects but controlled by the Program. These sites may serve as detainment facilities for captured suspects kept alive for strategic purposes, or as temporary field headquarters for a local operation.

Nobody outside Headquarters learns about more than a sliver of the Program at a time. Compartmentalization is absolutely essential to operational security. A lab researcher in a Program facility may not realize that the Program as a whole even exists. An Air Force flight and pararescue crew signed onto the Program may not realize there are a dozen others like it around the world. A new Agent, on the other hand, may think the Program is at least as substantial as the DEA or the U.S. Marshals Service, only to realize, gradually, that it's a fraction of their size.

Very few Agents ever see Headquarters. Being summoned to Headquarters probably means a meeting with the Director of Operations or the Director of Security. This happens only when things have gone very wrong. Or it may mean meeting the Director—the Director of the Program—and that's an experience no agent ever wants to repeat.

Organization

Personnel are drawn from every corner of the U.S. executive branch and from private corporations with close government ties. They collect paychecks from the NSA, the U.S. Air Force, the Navy, the CIA, the FBI, or subsidiaries of March Technologies, Inc. All Headquarters personnel are technically on indefinite assignments to various task forces. The cover projects and task forces are all classified Top Secret. Not a single file in the U.S. Office of Personnel Management lists "Delta Green" as an active project.

Headquarters personnel work in six offices which coordinate and manage operations and locations in the field. Each office has an alphanumeric designation. The Office of the Director oversees all others. The offices are:

- D0—Office of the Director
- D1—Office of Security
- D2—Office of Intelligence
- D3—Office of Operations
- D4—Office of Research
- D5—Office of Logistics

D0—Office of the Director

The Office of the Director includes about a dozen personnel: the Director himself, senior managers who oversee the Program as a whole, and assistants. (See **THE DIRECTOR** on page 276.)

D1—Office of Security

The Office of Security oversees all aspects of Program security: information, communications, operations, and facilities. It conducts psychological operations and disinformation campaigns, and manages the establishment and deactivation of constantly-changing security classifications. It provides communications security using experts embedded at the NSA and NRO, as well as in telecommunications companies.

The Office of Security posts plainclothes, armed security officers at Program facilities. Most are former field agents, long adapted to violence. They prioritize the Program and the Director over any latent sympathies they might hold for agents. As far as most agents are concerned, the security officers are stony-eyed killers.

The Office of Security also oversees about 400 Air Force personnel in the three squadrons of Operation CORAL NOMAD (see **ASSET RECOVERY** on page 269). They provide transportation and security for unnatural artifacts and specimens recovered in the field. Most of them have no idea that's what they're transporting, or that the Program exists.

Katherine Oakes is the director of security (see **KATHERINE OAKES, DIRECTOR OF SECURITY** on page 284).

D2—Office of Intelligence

The Office of Intelligence utilizes assets in the NSA, the NRO, the CIA, the FBI, the DHS, and military intelligence to collect signals and communications intelligence, imagery intelligence, open-source intelligence, and human intelligence that suggest unnatural incursions worldwide. Intelligence officers scour federal, state, local, and open-source databases with the aid of MAJESTIC-derived communications technology. If an incident triggers unnatural indicators, preliminary research attempts to determine whether it is a hoax or an error. Incidents that appear to be worth investigating are referred to Operations. The Office of Intelligence also employs analysts who review intelligence, gathered by agents in the field, and by Program researchers to provide strategic and operational intelligence to the Director. Less than a dozen senior intelligence officers are assigned to Headquarters. About a hundred more are dispersed throughout the intelligence community. The director of intelligence is Admiral George Gates, USN (ret.) (see **ADMIRAL GEORGE GATES, DIRECTOR OF INTELLIGENCE** on page 280).

D3—Office of Operations

The Office of Operations conducts the Program's core work of confronting unnatural incursions. A few dozen case officers based at Headquarters manage a couple hundred agents; each case officer runs three or four teams. Case officers assign agents to operations in tightly restricted task forces, usually under the cover of counterterrorism or counterterrorism training. They also secure agents' cover credentials and false identities, sometimes with the aid of inactive agents who still have the right contacts and skills. The director of operations is FBI Special Agent Abraham Mannen (see **SPECIAL AGENT ABRAHAM MANNEN, DIRECTOR OF OPERATIONS** on page 278).

D4—Office of Research

The Office of Research manages projects housed at a number of research facilities. A handful of researchers sometimes accompany CORAL NOMAD flights to recover unnatural artifacts, technology, and specimens from case officers, or more rarely, from Agents in the field. (See **ASSET RECOVERY** on page 269.) The Program's researchers are drawn from the government, from universities, and from private-sector technology and biotech firms. About ten senior researchers and managers work at Headquarters. Another 100 or so researchers are assigned to scattered research facilities. The director of research is Gregory Tapham, Ph.D. (see **GREGORY TAPHAM, PH.D., DIRECTOR OF RESEARCH** on page 288).

D5—Office of Logistics

The Office of Logistics oversees budgeting and bureaucratic cover for the Program. A few dozen program managers embedded in U.S. defense, intelligence, and law enforcement agencies manipulate the federal bureaucracy to route funds from secret programs and intelligence contractors. Ten managers at Headquarters oversee those operations. The director of logistics is Dana Shelton, a veteran NSA program manager (see **LOGISTICS DIRECTOR DANA SHELTON** on page 292).

Agents

Small teams of agents, assisted by academic or technical specialists, conduct the Program's operations. A typical Program agent is a federal law-enforcement officer, intelligence officer, or special-operations officer: a professional, well-trained in self-defense, capable of conducting difficult investigations and covering them up. An agent recruited by the Program is typically in his or her mid to late thirties or forties.

The Program prefers federal law-enforcement officers who can use the law to their advantage and understand how to eradicate evidence, special-operations officers who have proven cool under fire, and intelligence officers accustomed to working outside the law without drawing attention to themselves.

AUTHORITY: The Program itself confers no powers of arrest, authority to carry weapons, access to funds or restricted items. The Program sometimes "sheep-dips" agents as temporary employees of agencies with those powers, but it prefers to rely on agents who have such authority in their regular jobs. Full-time law enforcement officers know the correct procedures and can keep other police from asking too many questions.

TEAMS: The Program usually groups agents into semi-permanent teams, so the same agents are likely to work together from operation to operation. These teams have internal code-names known to the case officers, but those are never shared with the agents themselves. Every group of agents is instead given a cover name by their case officer that they believe is real: Task Force 153, Working Group MASTICATE, Operation SALT RIME, and so on.

ASSIGNMENTS: Most days, an agent goes to a day job, reports to supervisors, and goes home. Only occasionally do they work for the Program. Every so often, the agent is tapped for a highly-secret assignment from high in the Executive Branch. It is usually with the Department of Defense, the NSA, the CIA, or the FBI—not the agent's home agency, where leaks are more likely, but some other agency that runs top-secret, high-priority counterterrorism task forces and training programs. It is always some new, opaque special-access program, so restricted that the agent's day-to-day supervisors and colleagues are not allowed to ask anything about it, and they know anyone who does know anything would face prison time and career suicide talking about it. It's just one of *those* jobs; the Program's operations aren't the only secret task forces that draw federal agents away from time to time. After the call comes, the agent usually has a day or two to arrange things and then is gone, completely incommunicado.

Specialists

Many of the Program's agents are specialists who have academic, technical, or medical skills, or important bureaucratic access. Some specialists are temporary rather than permanent, brought in as "contractors" and briefed only for one specific mission.

Many specialists have no self-defense training. They are usually accompanied by agents that do. Whenever possible, the Program puts specialists through the same recruitment process as other agents. That's the only way to be confident that a specialist will cooperate with the less savory requirements of an operation. If the Program has no choice but to use an un-vetted specialist, it's up to the rest of the team to minimize exposure.

Usually, the motivations of specialists are not the same as other agents. They have been given the chance to work on the most inexplicable items, creatures, and occurrences ever seen in human history. They can never reveal what they have seen (let alone publish their findings), and they will likely never understand

← Previous Next →
Government Agents are Among Those
Prosecuted when FBI Shuts Down Online Black Market, Silk
laundering and obstruction of justice while he was part of a team investigating Silk Road. He allegedly stole over

>> Common Backgrounds and Professions—Agents

Background	Profession	Optional Bonus Skill Point Package
FBI special agent	Federal Agent	Criminalist, Military Officer, or Occult Investigator
FBI special agent, Hostage Rescue Team	HRT or SWAT	Police Officer (representing FBI training)
CIA clandestine services officer	Intelligence Case Officer	"Black Bag" Training, Computer Enthusiast, Criminalist, or Gangster/Deep Cover
CIA Special Operations Group	Special Activities Division SOG	Interrogator, Military Officer, or Translator
Navy SEAL	DEVGRU/Navy Special Warfare Groups	Interrogator, Military Officer, or Translator

>> Common Backgrounds and Professions—Specialists

Background	Profession	Optional Bonus Skill Point Package
Academic (humanities)	Anthropologist or Historian	Liberal Arts Degree, Occult Investigator, or Translator
Academic (physical sciences)	Scientist	Bureaucrat, Computer Enthusiast, or Science Grad Student
EPA investigator	OCEFT	Bureaucrat, Criminalist, or Science Grad Student
NSA computer network operator	Computer Scientist	Computer Enthusiast/Hacker
Physician or psychiatrist	Physician	Counselor, Criminalist, or Nurse/Paramedic/Pre-Med
Public Health Service, CDC Rapid Response	PHSCC	Counselor, Nurse/Paramedic/Pre-Med, or Science Grad Student

the bigger picture. But they have the chance to study in unique and untrodden fields.

Specialists are often assigned to operations as needed. Whenever possible, though, the Program partners a given specialist with the same team. Sometimes a team is assigned to an operation primarily because the mission requires the skills of "their" specialist.

The Program may recruit a specialist to work on one of its research projects. If so, that's the last other agents see of them. The Program keeps its researchers and its field agents as far apart as possible. The risks associated with correlating knowledge and experiences are too great.

Death and Burnout

Most operations are brief. An Agent returns to normal life in a week or two. Sometimes an Agent stays away on a month or two of medical leave, and no one back home is supposed to ask how they were injured or why. Occasionally an Agent called away on one of these operations is never seen again. The agent's day-to-day colleagues are informed and must inform his or her family. Details are never forthcoming. To reduce publicity, it's never called a death in the line of duty. It is covered up as a fatal accident in training or in transit. Only fellow Delta Green agents ever know the truth.

Sooner or later, every Agent learns that joining the Program is for life. Agents' knowledge and willingness to confront the unnatural are too valuable to cut them loose. The Program is the most restricted agency of all, its mission unthinkably critical, so most accept that willingly, at least at first. The federal agents, intelligence officers, special operators, and elite academics who join the Program are driven, high-achieving alphas.

At the same time, the demands it places on Agents are impossible. The qualities that make them right for Delta Green—their willingness to lie, cheat, and fight their way out of the most dangerous situations—show up at home, too, when stress becomes intolerable. Most wind up with disorders, addictions, criminal records, histories of violence, strings of failed marriages, and shattered families. Eventually, they have no Bonds outside the Program.

When the damage becomes so profound that it interferes with an Agent's operational effectiveness, an Agent may be made a case officer. Others become security officers. Others may be put on reserve status. Then again, some stay in the field until their bad choices become lethal. There is no other way out.

Institutional Memory

Due to the Program's compartmentalization and the high risks of the work, there is very little institutional memory among agents. Most agents active in 2017 were recruited in the 2010s. Surviving agents who were around at the Program's establishment in 2002 have long since been moved to Headquarters or reassigned to security. Those veterans know better than to talk about the old days.

Only a few Program agents were recruited from the Outlaws (the conspiracy that also calls itself Delta Green). These ex-Outlaw agents rarely know anything valuable about the conspiracy's history. Even when they do, they rarely say anything.

Recruitment

Whenever possible, the Program recruits (through current agents) a new agent or specialist in controlled iterations of exposure and evaluation. Each time the potential recruit proves reliable, the Program offers more information. The Program is very cautious. It can't afford to recruit the wrong people.

Most agents went through similar steps in recruitment.

STEP 1—EXPOSURE: There is an unnatural incursion. The Program sends agents to stop it. The prospective recruit is there. The Program might have identified the prospect beforehand and deliberately arranged the exposure, or the prospect might just be in the wrong place at the wrong time.

STEP 2—RESPONSE: Agents on the scene gauge the prospect's reaction to the unnatural. They tell the prospect that this danger, if exposed, is likely to spread and increase. To be considered for recruitment, the prospect must prioritize examining the situation carefully, saving lives, and stopping the threat. Anyone who is interested in gathering evidence to share with the world is a witness who must be discouraged, discredited, or silenced, not a future agent.

STEP 3—INVESTIGATION: Before going any farther, the Program investigates the prospect. Security officers

When he was arrested, Johnson was carrying three different state identifi-
else," he answered.

look into the recruit's background, hobbies, habits, family, and friends for signs that the recruit can be trusted with the Program's secrets. In many cases, the Program cuts off all contact at this point and treats the former prospect like any other witness. If the investigators have concrete reasons to think the prospect is trustworthy, the Program proceeds with recruitment.

STEP 4—BRIEFING: Agents who encountered the prospect in the *exposure* or *response* stages ask to meet in a secure location, well protected against eavesdropping and record-keeping. They might be joined by other members of the Program who hold impressive ranks: a Special Forces colonel and a senior FBI counterterrorism agent, for example, to drive home the situation's severity. They put a Top Secret clearance agreement on the table, so highly restricted that it applies only to the people in the room, with a random code-name created specifically for this briefing. If the prospect refuses to sign, the meeting ends and the prospect goes back to being just another witness—but one that needs even more careful scrutiny.

After signing, the agents tell the recruit the following essential points:

» Deadly unnatural incursions have happened before.
» Such incursions are so toxic that covering them up is the only way to stop further exposure.
» The agents comprise a small, secret task force dedicated to stopping such incursions.
» Their work is necessary, and clandestine; that means it is not always legal.
» They cannot expect explanations. Investigating the task force itself is absolutely forbidden. The threat of the unnatural makes secrecy imperative. Every scrap of information is need-to-know.
» They need two things: the recruit's silence, and to know whether or not they can call the recruit for help.

If the recruit says yes, the agents shake his or her hand and go on their way. Some time later, they call for help, and a new Agent answers. On operations, a new Agent soon learns about the larger Program, about the unpleasant details of its work, and, eventually, its true name: Delta Green.

If the recruit hears the initial briefing and says no, or changes his or her mind when they call for help, things get more complicated.

Operations

Every operation is unique. Each finds a new way to turn plans upside down and leave agents dead. But most have a similar structure.

» The Program learns of a possible unnatural incursion. Intelligence analysts attempt to confirm the incursion, so the Program doesn't waste time and resources sending a team of agents where they're not needed.
» The Office of Operations establishes the new operation, gives it a name, and assigns a case officer to send in a team of agents. If the operation deals with sensitive locations or situations, it may require the personal approval (and have the personal attention) of the head of the Program—the Director.
» The Office of Logistics secures whatever resources are approved by the Director of Operations.
» The case officer arranges the cover operation, using any jurisdictional pretext available to give the Agents some measure of legal authority. If the operation must be completely covert, the case officer might assist with creating false identities and cover assignments.
» The case officer assembles the team of Agents and provides instructions, an intelligence briefing, and (limited) resources.
» The Agents conduct the operation and cover it up. If they recover samples of unnatural provenance, they inform their case officer, who arranges asset recovery.
» The Agents undergo debriefing with the case officer, and then go back to their homes and their normal jobs.
» The Office of Research studies assets recovered by the Agents.

IN THE FIELD: Background Details

An Agent's recruitment is usually kept in the background. Either the recruit joins the Program, making it predictable, or the player has to create a new Agent, making it a waste of time. What matters, and what you should explore at the table, is not whether the Agent signed up, but why. What makes the Agent complicit in all the crimes that the Program requires? And how far is the Agent is willing to go?

IN THE FIELD: The Worst Case

A recruit learns the details of the Program only if the Program is certain, after careful vetting, that he or she is trustworthy. After so much preparation and study, this trust is usually well placed. If the recruit has a change of heart about joining the Program and there's any doubt about the recruit's discretion, the recruiters have to take extraordinary steps to guarantee the recruit's silence.

The case officer gives them instructions and the ex-recruit's dossier. It has all the information that the Office of Security was able to find, along with recent surveillance reports and communications intercepts to demonstrate the agents' reach. The agents must prove to the ex-recruit that the risk of revealing the group's secrets constitutes a very real threat. Ruthlessness is not enough; the agents must be cruel.

They confront the recruit in a secure location, perhaps the same place as their initial briefing. This usually amounts to abducting the recruit and sitting him or her down in handcuffs, chained to the floor or a table too heavy to move.

They attempt to talk the former recruit into lifelong silence. With any luck, the ex-recruit is still on board with the cover-ups and secrecy that confronting the unnatural requires. If so, that's as far as things go.

If the agents have doubts—or if the recruit fooled them before and they have to repeat this interrogation—they must explicitly threaten the destruction of whatever the ex-recruit holds most dear.

Are the ex-recruit's reputation and career most important? Threaten to pin him or her with child pornography. ("There's a USB stick at your house, behind your refrigerator. Take a look at what's on it, and imagine how many more USB sticks there could be.") Or shoot the ex-recruit up with heroin and trigger a drug test at work. Is it the ex-recruit's daughter? Threaten her life.

If the ex-recruit has no ties, the agents should put a gun to his or her head and ask how long he or she wants to live. They must make it clear that they can find the ex-witness any time, anywhere. The group has people in the federal witness protection program and the NSA.

Finally, and if all else fails, the agents must be ready to follow through with their threats. If the ex-recruit must die to protect the Program's secrets, the Agents must make it happen and cover it up.

This is not a task that any Agent wants. Some never recover from it.

EXPLANATION OF VICTIM RIGHTS & NOTIFICATION PREFERENCES

Under the *Victims' Rights and Restitution Act (VRRA)*, 42 U.S.C. §10607, victims are entitled:

- To be notified they have been the victim of a federal crime;
- To be informed of the place where they may receive medical and social services;
- To be informed of public and private programs available for counseling, treatment, and other support services;
- To receive reasonable protection from a suspected offender and persons acting in concert with or at the behest of the suspected offender;
- To know the status of the investigation of the crime, to the extent it is appropriate and it will not interfere with the investigation;
- To have personal property being held for evidentiary purposes maintained in good condition and returned as soon as it is no longer needed for evidentiary purposes.

... (CVRA), 18 U.S.C. §3771, if feder[illegible] charges are filed involving images or

Case Officers

The Office of Operations' case officers manage teams of agents. Case officers rarely participate in operations and instead organize and facilitate them. Almost all case officers are former agents, which means many are physically or psychologically damaged.

A case officer always uses a false identity with agents. A team of agents may work with the same case officer for years under a particular name and title, never learning the case officer's real name or title.

Case officers are responsible for maintaining active communication with the agents and for keeping headquarters informed. Case officers are supposed to stay in communication with agents on operations at least once per day and after each major development, especially in high-visibility operations; but in practice, some case officers are more hands-on than others.

Cover Operations

Whenever possible, an operation is conducted under cover of a law enforcement, regulatory, or public safety investigation. That allows the team plausible authority and deniability. An operation results in prosecution only when that serves to cover up what really happened and keep the authorities happy.

A cover operation can sometimes be classified and restricted to select personnel, under the guise of a counterterrorism operation or training. Sending the request for classification up the chain may draw more scrutiny than it prevents, so the case officer must weigh the decision carefully.

The Meeting

Whenever possible, the case officer meets the Agents at a dedicated Program safe house or black site. But there are only a few dozen dedicated sites around the world, half in the U.S. If no dedicated site is nearby, the meeting may be at a secure compartmentalized information facility—a conference room shielded against surveillance and data signals—at a nearby government office. If there's no other option, the meeting may be at some other location where the case officer can minimize the risk of surveillance.

Intelligence Briefing

When the Program opens an operation, the Office of Intelligence conducts preliminary research so the Agents can hit the ground running. The case officer briefs agents on this intelligence.

This initial research can be as extensive or limited as the Handler likes. The issue is not the Program's ability to gather information, but what makes the operation challenging and terrifying for the players. Limited information is easy to explain. Maybe the NSA was not recording that suspect in that time frame. Maybe the analysts were busy with a more pressing operation.

A preliminary report could encompass any of the following, and more could be provided during the operation.

THE SCENE: Preliminary medical examiner's reports. Ownership and accident records of relevant vehicles. Footage from traffic and security cameras. Forensic matches of bullets and tool-marks to past crimes in FBI records. Maps and floorplans. Detailed medical examiner's reports, if available; they sometimes take weeks.

VICTIMS, WITNESSES, AND SUSPECTS: Criminal records. Credit reports. Family histories. Jobs and education, including unclassified government service records. Travel history. Foreign contacts. Bank account records. Credit card transactions. Email and phone metadata. Recent Internet and social-media history. Recent movements tracked by mobile devices' pings of local cell towers and by social media. Past identities that match fingerprints or facial-recognition software. If already a "person of interest," the full content of recent phone calls, texts, and emails. Intelligence on foreign nationals can be nearly as extensive, particularly those from fellow "Five Eyes" intelligence-sharing nations (Australia, Canada, New Zealand, and the U.K.) and those already under investigation for ties to narcotics trafficking or terrorism.

Resources

The Office of Logistics supplies funding—usually cash or untraceable debit cards—for travel and operational costs. Agents quickly learn not to expect luxury. There are no salary bonuses that come with going on an operation. Saving humanity is its own reward.

What other resources can the Program give its Agents? That's up to the Handler. A case officer might be able to send a specialist with a needed skill. Or the Agents might get the location of a safe house or storage facility under the name of a front company or fictitious individual. Or a padlocked storm shelter loaded with supplies. Or a helpful outlaw biker gang that thinks it's dealing with a drug cartel. Reports and books about espionage, terrorism, and law enforcement can provide countless ideas. But remember, your objective is fear. Would providing resources get the Agents to the horror more efficiently? Or would it be more terrifying for the Agents' requests for help to be denied or ignored?

Asking for materiel or funds might get the Agents one or more of these advantages, or none of them:

- A bonus to the Agents' Bureaucracy roll when requisitioning assets.
- The Agents may use their case officer's Bureaucracy skill instead of their own.
- One or more automatic successes at Bureaucracy, perhaps depending on the scope and expense of the requisition.
- The Agents may treat an operation as high-priority for the sake of requisitions, even if its cover is mundane so as not to draw attention (see **OFFICIAL REQUISITION** on page 86 of the *Agent's Handbook*).

The Cover-Up

The Agents are responsible for resolving the cover operation so no outsiders take an interest in what really happened. They may have to alter evidence and give witnesses a plausible explanation. The Agents are the Program's experts on the ground. If they lack the skills they need, they must adapt and improvise with the skills they have.

Not enough Forensics skill to falsify a crime scene? Interfere with it enough that collecting evidence is a waste of time. Not enough Persuade skill to talk a witness into believing your explanation? Discredit the witness with planted drugs or embarrassing online activity. Not enough Bureaucracy to keep the FBI out of your way? Stage some worse crime two counties over for them to investigate. The Agents have to devise their own Plan B.

IN THE FIELD: Solving Problems

The Program has a long history and access to many resources. When Agents get desperate and the players demand help, it's easy for Handlers to forget that the Program's most important asset is the first one they deploy: the Agents themselves.

Agents can ask for help, but a wise case officer knows better than to pass that request along without extremely compelling need. Demanding too much gets future requests ignored. Such help may take the form of one or two experts with crucial skills or gear. It could be a strike team of Delta Green JSOC veterans, a crime-scene examiner, or a CIA pilot flying an old Tiger Transit plane. Such assistance should be rare, and it should come with the risk of blowback. Every single person or requisition added to an operation increases the risk of the operation's exposure.

The basics are standard issue: cash or a debit card for transportation and lodgings, temporary reassignments in a Top Secret program (for federal government employees), perhaps a cache of more-or-less deniable weapons or cast-off supplies, a briefing. Agents never count on getting much more than that.

If the players seem indignant that the Program is sending them without enough preparation or expert support, remind them that they are the experts. Preparation is up to them. The Program is not there to solve the Agents' problems. The Agents are there to solve the Program's problems.

[redacted]

Asset Recovery

The Program stores unnatural specimens at secure locations, scattered throughout the federal hinterlands of the United States and in the labs of their private-sector partners. These deniable facilities are self-contained, and for the most part, personnel have little or no idea why their base is even there. Only a small team at the center of such a facility is briefed well enough to understand what they contain. These facilities remain unknown to Agents until that knowledge is necessary for their operations.

After an operation, Agents are expected to securely package any artifacts, sources of information, or other remnants—using whatever biohazard protection they can find for biological remains—and hand them over to their case officer. Agents are rarely invited to participate directly in the analysis of the things they recover.

If the remnants are too substantial for the usual handoff, the case officer can ask for a pickup by the Office of Security in a helicopter or cargo plane. This is not usual. Such a pickup increases the visibility of the operation, both literally and bureaucratically, exponentially. It means exposing additional personnel to whatever unnatural threat may linger. These pickups have resulted in disasters that became enormous follow-on operations. A case officer who requests them without need soon finds future requests ignored.

When a pickup is approved, the Office of Security deploys an expert from the Office of Research, with Air Force pilots and a few guards, to recover and transport the assets. The recovery team meets agents at an airfield where the presence of a helicopter or plane draws little attention. It is up to the Agents to get to the airfield. Collected evidence is sealed inside secure containers so that the flight team never know what they are transporting. Pickup crews and Agents are under strict instructions to share no information with each other beyond what's necessary. The pickup team never provides transportation to Agents unless under explicit orders from Headquarters. For more details, see **OPERATION CORAL NOMAD** on page 270.

Foreign Operations

Operations outside the U.S. can be even more fraught with the possibility of exposure than domestic operations, since the Program can't gain jurisdictional cover outside the country. But the Program has many options. The FBI and DHS frequently consult with foreign law-enforcement services on drug enforcement and counterterrorism, on financial investigations of Americans abroad, and in tracking international fugitives.

When a cover investigation is not feasible, the Program's CIA and diplomatic officers come to the fore. A Program agent who's a CIA clandestine officer has extensive access to CIA and counterterrorism intelligence, facilities, and logistics. But Americans conducting direct action overseas have an unfortunately long history of getting caught.

The Program's foreign operations, whether clandestine or under cover of a foreign partnership, are run like standard foreign intelligence operations. However, shifting international situations and politics make the Program's assets in the CIA and Department of Defense unreliable. The Program has access to safe houses and front companies belonging to intelligence services, but it doesn't maintain its own networks of spies.

Sometimes the Program can have a target designated as a terrorist risk, and investigated or attacked with serious firepower. To do this, the Program borrows assets from agencies like the CIA, DIA, DoD, FBI, and DEA to get the job done. But it always weighs the risk of exposure. The more non-Program personnel involved, the greater the likelihood that one of them sees something the Program must keep hidden.

If an operation draws notice, the Program presents a cover story prepared as far ahead of time as possible, a disinformation campaign to be disseminated via CIA and DoD assets: perhaps a strike against a terrorist cell or the actions of criminals. It takes this step only when necessary. The risk of blowback from quickly-conceived disinformation is too great. Whatever happens, the Agents must get out as soon as they can.

DISINFORMATION

YELLOW CARD

OPERATION CORAL NOMAD

The Office of Security's recovery operations occur under the name Operation CORAL NOMAD. The name changes occasionally. Its units are housed in aerospace recovery and combat rescue commands at Moody Air Force Base, Georgia; Nellis Air Force Base, Nevada; and Wright-Patterson Air Force Base, Ohio.

A CORAL NOMAD unit includes about 120 personnel: pilots, eight or nine combat rescue officers, a few dozen Pararescue members ("PJs"), and command and support personnel. That unit is part of a larger group with which it performs non-Program missions. But everyone knows that unit has occasional secret operations that no one else in the group is cleared for.

CORAL NOMAD typically deploys in an HC-130J Combat King II transport plane, or in Pave Hawk MH-60G helicopters if the destination is within 300 km of base. If those options are too high-profile, it deploys a civilian charter jet owned by one of the Program's private-sector allies.

The true nature of CORAL NOMAD's work is strictly need-to-know. Very few of its members know anything about the Program or the unnatural.

CORAL NOMAD's combat rescue officers and PJs are well-equipped and heavily armed, capable of operating in any environment. They train as extensively as any special operations unit. They are supremely competent.

Operation CORAL NOMAD has deeper roots than most of its personnel realize. It went by the name Operation BLUE FLY for almost 50 years in the MAJESTIC days, starting under the cover of the USAF's Foreign Technology Recovery Unit. Its commander in the 1990s, Col. Robert Coffey, died saving his men from a catastrophic incursion. Its officers helped dismantle MAJESTIC's corrupt leadership. Its patron at that time, USAF Lt. General Eustis Bell, became the Program's first director of operations. Longtime veterans remember those men with honor.

CUT ALONG THIS LINE

>> Common Backgrounds and Professions—CORAL NOMAD

Background	Profession	Optional Bonus Skill Point Package
Researcher (recovery specialist)	Scientist	Bureaucrat, Computer Enthusiast, or Science Grad Student
USAF combat rescue officer or pararescue member ("PJ")	Special Operator, but with First Aid 60% and only one Bond	Nurse/Paramedic/Pre-Med, but replace Psychotherapy with Athletics or Bureaucracy
USAF combat rescue pilot	Pilot, with Heavy Weapons and Military Science (Air) as chosen skills	Custom package: Alertness, Firearms, First Aid, Navigate, Pilot (Airplane or Helicopter), Survival, Swim, Unarmed Combat

If things get bad enough, an incident may cause a diplomatic rift. To prevent exposure, the Program may orchestrate things so that the CIA, JSOC, or some other agency takes the rap, leaving the State Department to deny all connection to the incident. This is always a last, desperate measure.

Agents arrested overseas are out of luck. There are no jailbreaks. Arrested agents are expected to not implicate the Program or the U.S. government in any way, to stick to their cover story, and to wait as long as necessary for release.

Foreign Liaison

The Program has made overtures to a handful of intelligence agencies aware of the unnatural: PISCES in the U.K., M-EPIC in Canada, and GRU SV-8 in Russia.

PISCES is still recovering from an infiltration by a race of non-human intelligences that controlled the organization's leadership in the 1990s. Delta Green became aware of the infection in 1999 and cut off contact. The Program has had limited interaction with PISCES since then.

Canada's M-EPIC has a closer relationship with the Program, owing in part to the 8,800-km border the two nations share. M-EPIC's long history of deploying hypergeometrical principles led the Program to actively court the organization. However, many within the Program and M-EPIC fear the consequences of hypergeometric proliferation, even though others see it as a means to overcome the worst threats.

After decades of wariness, there was initial rapprochement with GRU SV-8 in the Program's early days, based on eradicating the remnants of the Karotechia. The organizations retain normalized channels of communication. With the rise of Russian expansionism, though, GRU SV-8 became a ruthless competitor as often as an ally, and the Program reduced contact as Russia worked to publicize illegal American intelligence programs and overtly influence U.S. politics. At the advent of the Trump administration, with its attention-grabbing ties to Russian oligarchs, the Program broke contact with GRU SV-8 almost completely.

Security

Agents, the likeliest source of leaks about the Program, are subject to surveillance by the Office of Security. So are their families, friends, and colleagues. Officially, surveillance is said to be constant and lifelong, even after an agent is put in reserve. How much actually occurs varies. A subject with no history of risk may go months without observation. A subject who poses a risk—for example, because of sudden changes in behavior and mood—is likely to be observed more frequently.

If surveillance indicates a substantial risk of exposure of the Program, the Office of Security implements disinformation efforts. An urgent threat—an Agent deliberately revealing secrets of the Program or the unnatural—becomes the operation. Other Agents must immediately kill the source.

Otherwise, an Agent under suspicion may be called to Headquarters for evaluation. The purpose of this visit is simple: the Director of Operations and the Director of Security have to decide whether the Agent can be salvaged.

Such an interview should be one of the most terrifying things in the Agent's life. The directors are sifting the Agent's words for indications that the Agent's death is necessary to protect the Program. If it goes badly, the Agent faces becoming the victim of a "suicide," a car accident, or a drug overdose.

If the directors decide an Agent can be salvaged, they make that recommendation to the Director of the Program. But the Director may want to meet the Agent, in person. The Director has weighed the fates of countless agents. What can the Agent possibly say to make the Director see him or her as an asset, and not a threat?

An Agent who can be salvaged is either returned to the field or put on reserve, to be contacted when necessary.

If the Program has reason to think that an Agent is contaminated by the unnatural, things go a little differently. The Agent is not brought to Headquarters. The Program convenes a "Star Chamber" instead, sending a team of agents to do the questioning, get to the bottom of things, and make a recommendation.

Disinformation

Once audio and video is on the Internet, it's there to stay. However, if you can't cut off a signal, you can obscure it with white noise. When video of Delta Green agents shooting at a half-visible, glowing winged creature appears on YouTube and Phenomen-X.com, the Program never tries to take it down. Instead, it clutters the issue with hoaxers, debunkers, trolls, and statements of support from sources designed to undermine the evidence.

The Office of Security manages a section that specializes in disinformation related to unnatural events. On paper, it's a CIA training division where disinformation and propaganda are taught. CIA officers spend their time working up disinformation ops against believers in the supernatural who go online with so-called "evidence." Officers flood the Internet with contradictory, deliberately flawed material about cryptozoology, UFOs, conspiracy theories, and pseudoscience, believing they are learning techniques to influence public opinion. They never realize they are performing disinformation for the Program.

Of course, Agents in operations cannot rely on the Program to cover everything up for them. They have to cover their own tracks so the Program's disinformation teams have a chance to turn public attention away.

Research

Unknown to the rank and file agents, through front organizations and private-sector partners, the Program employs researchers at a dozen restricted laboratories and covert bases around the world. They work in the ICE CAVE facility in New Mexico, in other secure Department of Defense labs, and in private-sector laboratories managed by March Technologies and its subsidiaries. The Office of Research studies unnatural technology and biological samples, with an eye toward exploiting that knowledge in future confrontations with the unnatural. For a summary of what the Program knows of the unnatural, see **THE PROGRAM'S RESEARCH** on page 323.

While the Program actively collects and studies the unnatural, experimentation is limited. It is supposed to happen only when a threat makes it necessary. Even then, the project is monitored so that it may be canceled at the slightest indication of trouble.

The Program's research projects change codenames from time to time. Each is carried on by researchers who, for the most part, know nothing about the other projects, or about the Program itself.

Here are a few of the projects carried on by the Program and its partner, March Technologies, and each project's short reference code.

Manhattan U.S. Attorney Bharara said: "David Polos, a former supervisory DEA agent, was sentenced
today for lying on his national security forms. Even more so than others, federal agents, sworn to enforce
the law, must first obey it themselves. Polos violated his oath and broke the law. He now stands a

PROJECT BUSTLE (D4BUS): Identifies and studies surviving biological specimens developed by MAJESTIC's long-defunct Project PLUTO.

PROJECT CONTRAIL (D4CON): Studies the mathematics of gate technology.

PROJECT COPPER MASK (D4CMK): Uses MAJESTIC computer technologies developed under the Accord—quantum computing, artificial intelligence driven by crystal-matrix processors, and photon-entanglement communication that puts the lie to the no-communication theorem—to decrypt and analyze SIGINT intercepts. The project uses several layers of mundane, but equally restricted and secret, NSA cover programs to deliver intelligence products that help maintain the Program's influence and funding.

PROJECT DROUGHT (D4DRT): Studies captured unnatural entities, living and dead, primarily at the ICE CAVE facility at Los Alamos, New Mexico.

PROJECT EMPTY MOUNTAIN (D4EMT): Studies encounters with "Class I self-referential thought-form tesseracts" (sometimes referred to as the Great Race of Yith), with particular interest in symptoms of altered causality.

PROJECT HIGH DAY (D4HDA): Utilizes the U.S. space surveillance network to watch for unidentified spacecraft (which are few and far between), and deep-space probes and radio telescopes to seek signs of non-human activity.

PROJECT LAMBENT (D4LAM): Uses DNA profiles acquired from ancestral research companies to identify individuals with Innsmouth ancestry, specifically hybrids related to Innsmouth's "aquatic humanoids."

PROJECT MAINFRAME (D4MNF): An "overview" project that synthesizes and correlates the discoveries reported by other Program research projects. This is one of the few projects which has knowledge of the other departments.

PROJECT NACRE PYTHON (D4NAC): A small program that studies mind-altering drugs and related technologies. In 2002, it focused on drugs developed in MAJESTIC's projects CORE and OUTLOOK. Most of those substances went bad after the dissolution of the Accord, and they have proven impossible to manufacture without access to Grey technologies. NACRE PYTHON's work is preventative.

PROJECT RED PENDULUM (D4RDP): Studies extrasensory perception, precognition, psychokinesis, and other "innate" human psychic abilities. Such powers are far more often fraud than genuine. What few true psychics could be located have descended quickly into insanity.

PROJECT SHARP ATLAS (D4SHA): Studies the technologies of super-spatial intelligences, such as the mi-go and the insects from Shaggai (though none in this project know those names). It is divided into many restricted subprojects.

PROJECT SUZERAIN (D4SUZ): Studies N-Space and Tillinghast radiation. Formerly Project WELLS, a subproject of MAJESTIC's Project PLUTO.

PROJECT ZERO RAPID (D4ZER): Compiles and analyzes intelligence related to unnatural activity on Earth, working with open and secret sources. Much of its work amounts to sifting through false alarms.

March Technologies, Inc.

March Technologies was established as a front company for MAJESTIC to distribute unnatural-derived technology to the military-industrial complex. That made its founder, Justin Kroft, and his cronies enormously rich. When MAJESTIC collapsed, March Technologies is where many of its former leaders landed. The company's work and access to information was too crucial for the Program to oppose it. Instead, they became partners. Many people at Program headquarters draw salaries and benefits from March Technologies and its subsidiaries.

March Technologies remains a leading defense contractor, and its mission and methods are the same as ever: the personal enrichment of its owners under the guise of national security. Four former members of the MAJESTIC-12 Steering Committee are on the board of directors and hold controlling stock: Dr. Antony Correlo, Dr. Edward Penn, Gen. Thomas Deerhausen (U.S. Army, ret.), and Gen. Kurtis Schenk (USAF, ret.). They employ scientists who worked on MAJESTIC subprojects long ago, and who lead newer researchers studying technologies and biological

ASSETS:
Deployed Implementations

The Office of Research, working with March Technologies, has developed a handful of tools that can be deployed to Agents to assist with operations. Such development is sharply curtailed by the limits of research and by Program policies. Deployed implementations are useful only for detecting unnatural forces and entities, not thwarting them. There are no "magic drugs"; the Program has a longstanding rule against deploying biologicals of unnatural derivation. Researchers have had uneven, often disastrous results attempting to weaponize the unnatural—or, in many cases, determining what is "unnatural" and what is not. Some researchers have delved into old tomes, intending to bring ancient alchemy up to date with modern science, only to succumb so often to mental degradation and dangerous experimentation that such studies are all but forbidden.

Handlers creating new tools to be deployed to Agents should be wary of a few important issues.

LIMITED SCOPE: Any tool should be extremely limited in scope. What we call the "unnatural" is a tremendous range of species, dimensions, and energies that often have nothing to do with each other. A tool that's affected by one unnatural thing is not necessarily affected by any others.

DETECTION, NOT RESOLUTION: Tools given to Agents may detect, hint at, or even reveal a horror. They should never defeat it. Issued tools should not solve the Agents' problems. Problem-solving is a key part of the game.

DENIABILITY: The Program never issues a tool that is likely to attract more attention to the operation. Every tool must be easily deniable as some mundane device.

RARITY: The Program does not have deep R&D stockpiles to throw at every operation. It issues one of these tools only when it unequivocally pertains to an operation, and not always then. These tools are rare. When Agents are issued one, it should surprise the players—and make them worry that the threats they face may be worse than ever.

RELIABILITY: Given the scarcity of unnatural samples to develop and test, tools developed for the Program might not function exactly as advertised. For example, a screening test might have high error rates (showing false positive or false negative results), might not function under all conditions (becoming unreliable at different temperatures), or might break easily if dropped or gotten wet. Experienced Agents treat such tools with skepticism at best, and outright disdain at worst.

BIOMARKER A

A blood-test analysis kit that can be used in most hospital or university bio labs with a Medicine test, which is rolled secretly by the Handler. The test takes about three hours, although three samples can be tested simultaneously. It uses a variant of the polymerase chain reaction (PCR) to test for genetic biomarkers characteristic of "aquatic humanoid" (AH, or Deep One) ancestry. A second Medicine test on the sample can determine whether a single parent was AH-descended or both. The kit requires only a small vial of blood. How the Agents obtain the blood sample is their problem. More specific confirmatory tests, based on advanced DNA sequencing methods, are available in Program laboratories but take a few days to complete.

NEOTISSUE STAIN

A clear colorless liquid that produces a vivid purple stain when it comes into contact with "neotissue," a viscous, motile substance sometimes called protomatter. The stain usually lasts two or three minutes. Typically deployed in a spray bottle, the liquid is an aniline-dye solution that smells like rotten fish and is toxic to human flesh with prolonged contact. Originally developed during the Groversville investigation, this is one of the few test methods that is available to both the Program and the Outlaws.

T-RADIATION COUNTER

This small, plastic device looks like a pager. It bears a readout screen, a power button, and a button to silence the alert buzzer. It detects the peculiar electromagnetic fluctuations characteristic of Tillinghast radiation at a distance of up to 10 m. The Handler makes a Luck roll for the user once per minute for the counter to pick up traces of Tillinghast radiation. The roll is at +20% up to 1 m from the source, unmodified from 1 to 3 m from the source, and at −20% from 3 to 10 m from the source.

DISINFORMATION

YELLOW CARD

MARCH TECHNOLOGIES INNOVATIONS

March Technologies exists on the fringes of the U.S. government. A privately held, incredibly lucrative defense contractor, it seems to have a preternatural ability to underbid its competitors thanks to the use of startling, nearly prescient, scientific advancements.

When it had access to technology from the Greys, March had active projects in everything from genetic manipulation to high-energy physics and particle-beam weaponry. All of these advances were drawn from unnatural specimens recovered or developed by MAJESTIC subprojects, which March Technologies worked to winnow down into something that might pass as a human invention. In the 1980s and 1990s, March Technologies fielded small but significant advances in material sciences, such as light-absorbing carbon nanotube technology and a process which reduced the cost and production time of ceramics used in military armor by 25%. It marketed radiation-hardened electronic switches for satellites and rockets, as well as new rocket nozzle technolgies. Their directorship has always had deep ties with the Pentagon.

After the 2002 dissolution of MAJESTIC, March Technologies deprioritized its fledgeling "biologics" projects and most of its work in direct energy and propulsion. That was by necessity more than choice: many projects ceased working altogether when MAJESTIC broke the Accord with the Greys. Instead, March swung its focus almost entirely to microprocessors, quantum computing, and more outré computer technologies: innovations developed in MAJESTIC projects that were based on insights gained from Grey technology but not dependent on it. With no new Grey technology to study, the pace of discovery has slowed. But the company has barely scratched the surface of the discoveries it made twenty years ago. March produces specialized computer components for the intelligence and defense community, primarily the NSA. Only a few units of its aerospace division still produce rocket components. All of its work is classified.

March Technologies reaches deep into the American defense-intelligence machine. Its "inventions" are decades ahead of the most advanced on the planet, and it will spend decades doling them out, a few billion dollars at a time.

CUT ALONG THIS LINE

031-51937 o-46

samples recovered by the Program today. The Program's own researchers share working space with March Technologies scientists. Like the Program's researchers, most March Technologies scientists know nothing about projects outside their own work, or about the Program or the defunct MAJESTIC organization.

An uneasy détente remains between the Program and March Technologies. They are valuable to each other. The Program cannot expose March Technologies without destroying its own cover. March Technologies cannot expose the Program without risking its lifeblood access to the defense-intelligence community. The two cooperate enough to keep each other at bay.

But even after all these years, the directors of March Technologies stubbornly regard their ouster from MAJESTIC as merely a temporary setback. Sooner or later, they are sure, they will identify the leverage they need to take control of the Program. That mission has led to close ties between March Technologies and GRU SV-8. See **THE PROFIT AND THE LOSS** on page 135.

Important Individuals: The Program

Compartmentalization is critical to the Program. But the longer Agents serve, and the more mistakes they make, the more of their superiors they eventually meet.

The Director

No one refers to the leader of Delta Green by name. The name tag he presents at security checkpoints labels him Capt. John R. Smith, USN (retired): former SEAL and former naval intelligence officer, retired from the Navy in 2012 with a thoroughly redacted service history, now employed by the NSA as director of whatever pseudonym the Program is using this year. But he is never Director Smith. He's *the Director.* In a conversation about all the directors in the Program, you can always tell when someone means *the Director.*

Only a handful of people know the name he was born with: Forrest James, ex-SEAL captain, ex-convict, longtime Delta Green agent, officially deceased since 2001.

Forrest James won a bronze medal swimming for the U.S. at the 1968 Olympics in Mexico City. He graduated from Annapolis and joined the Navy's elite SEALs. He survived three tours in Vietnam. He rose to command a SEAL team. He survived an encounter with Deep Ones at 150 fathoms in 1981, and his discreet investigations of those monstrosities led him to join Delta Green in 1988. From 1994 to 1999 he was Agent Darren, one of Alphonse's most reliable men.

He's the man who won the MAJESTIC War in 2001 and purged the MAJESTIC-12 Steering Committee. He reconstituted Delta Green as the Program, with funding and assets from across the government. He ran the mission that saved the world from the Tillinghast resonator aboard the USS *Eldridge* in 2012. He ran the organization that saved the world, again and again.

Yet the Director's thoughts are dominated by failure.

He broods about the SEALs he led to their deaths in 1981. He struggles with his role in the deaths of Delta Green colleagues. Even now, he doubts himself. Technology derived from unnatural forces is seeping into the world. That's the price the Program pays to maintain its mission. Is there any way to untangle the Program from the maze of companies that surround its chief partner and foe, March Technologies? He just doesn't know.

But there are things of which the Director is absolutely certain.

He knows he will serve as Director of Delta Green until he can find a suitable successor. Someone who understands the stakes and can make the hard choices. That might be Katherine Oakes, the Director of Security and the closest thing he has to a protégé. Or it might be Abe Mannen. But the Director has learned to reject trust. He is always on the lookout for Agents who've distinguished themselves in the field. He sometimes takes an interest in up-and-comers who could be groomed as case officers and for authority beyond that. That interest is not pleasant for them.

He knows that if he fails to identify a successor, he'll die with his boots on like Reginald Fairfield and Joseph Camp—the terrible old men who came before him.

He knows that while he's still here, there are things he needs to do. He must protect the Program's bureaucratic invisibility, and that means he must keep providing new technologies to the NSA and the Department of Defense.

Forrest James never fully recovered from the trauma of his first encounter with the Deep Ones, decades ago. Those creatures remain an obsession, and nothing terrifies him more than the knowledge that they walk among us, spreading their contagion. Two years ago, he assigned Security Director Oakes to a new mission: Operation SOMERSAULT. Using DNA-derived genetic profiles acquired from private ancestral research companies, the Program has set about tracking down anyone carrying the "Innsmouth Taint," a genetic marker indicative of Innsmouth ancestry. With this information, a select squad of operatives has been assembled to ensure these "hybrids" are eliminated before they can activate. When possible, this team kills tainted individuals before they become sexually active and can spread the contagion. In 2016, the Director expanded this program to check neonatal samples taken at hospitals across the nation.

The Director wants that job done before he retires. Due to the amount of questionable targets on the list, it's not something he believes he can safely leave for his successor. While detection methods are not perfect, under his leadership, the Program errs on the side of murder. He has most recently signed clearance for SOMERSAULT II, adding a list of 91 individuals—each between the ages of 18 months and six years old—to the ever-growing hit list. He may add teams of Agents to Oakes' killers as the workload grows.

If the Program collapsed, the Director imagines he would load up what he could and kill as many of the *things* as possible before they finally took him down.

The Director's personal connections have eroded over the years, warped by his obsessions or lost to age and death. Most of his old Delta Green comrades refused to join the Program. Those who did have learned to fear him. His closest confidant and consigliere, former MAJESTIC executive Gavin Ross, vanished as soon as he was trusted with a moment's freedom. The Director drove his wife away long before she killed herself. When he buried her, he left trust, affection, and loyalty behind. Now, his world is threats and assets. The mission is all he has left. As long as he is alive, it will never be over.

The Director stands 1.9 m tall (6'2") and weighs 77 kg (170 lbs), with close-cropped gray hair, thin-framed glasses, and a precisely trimmed mustache. Unlike many of the Program's senior personnel, he prefers military fatigues to a suit and tie, though his uniform is devoid of insignia. Mild arthritis and years of heavy drinking—always off duty and out of sight—slow him a little, but daily swimming and weights keep him steely. He still bears the scars where a Deep One's claws raked his chin and chest more than 30 years ago. He has a harsh face, sharp cheekbones, and quick, darting eyes. The longer you hold his gaze, the more you sense the violence, ruthlessness, and cruel compromises that have shaped him.

The Director

Captain John Smith, USN, ret. (aka Captain Forrest James, USN, deceased), age 67.

STR 13 **CON** 13 **DEX** 10 **INT** 17 **POW** 16 **CHA** 13

HP 13 **WP** 16 **SAN** 30 **BREAKING POINT** 16

BONDS: None.

MOTIVATIONS AND DISORDERS: Protecting the Program.

Making the decisions no one else can.

Addiction (alcoholism).

Obsession (eradicating the Deep Ones and anyone who might share their taint).

Post-traumatic stress disorder.

Adapted to violence.

SKILLS: Alertness 72%, Athletics 65%, Bureaucracy 72%, Demolitions 81%, Dodge 66%, Drive 43%, Firearms 68%, Heavy Weapons 53%, Melee Weapons 67%, Military Science (Land) 70%, Military Science (Sea) 50%, Navigate 59%, Persuade 48%, Pilot Mini-Sub 67%, HUMINT 48%, Search 75%, Stealth 69%, Survival 52%, Swim 85%, Unarmed Combat 75%, Unnatural 28%.

SPECIAL TRAINING: Lockpicking (DEX), parachuting (DEX), SCUBA diving (Swim), spearguns (Firearms).

ATTACKS: HK45 Tactical pistol 68%, damage 1D10.

SOG commando knife 67%, damage 1D6.

Unarmed 75%, damage 1D4−1.

RITUALS: The Call of Dagon, The Elder Sign, See the Other Side, The Voorish Sign.

Special Agent Abraham Mannen, Director of Operations

Unless things go very badly, the Director of Operations is the highest authority any agent is likely to meet. To Director Abraham Mannen—case officers refer to him as "Ops"—things have been going badly for a long, long time.

Mannen knows that the Program has a problem, and that problem is the Director. Forrest James—Mannen still thinks of the Director by his real name—organized the Program. He has led it for sixteen years with an iron grip. He approves every operation. He shares no secrets unless he sees no choice. If the Director slips, or if anything happens to him, the entire Program will be disrupted.

They've already seen those disruptions. Operations have been concealed from the Director of Operations. Arrangements have been made with March Technologies without informing the Director of Intelligence. Research projects have been kept from the other directors. Mannen thinks he can see what's coming, but the Program wasn't set up for oversight. It has festered in the dark for too long.

Mannen was a young detective in Grand Rapids, Michigan who squeezed in a night-school law degree and somehow made it to the FBI. His first posting as an agent was a plum assignment in Chicago. In August 1994, he helped FBI agents Curtis McRay of the Behavioral Science Unit and Joe Siringo, an art-theft specialist from Los Angeles—Agent Cyrus and Agent William of Delta Green—investigate a quadruple homicide related to the theft of *The Revelations of Glaaki*, Vol. XII. Mannen would do his best to forget the horrors that led A-cell to induct him into the group as Agent Thomas, joining the new "Cell T."

Mannen and his wife Carol, a singer, were married during his first year at the FBI. They had their only child, Eric, in 1997. Their marriage did not survive a baby and the stresses of conflicting, difficult careers. The blowback from a disastrous Delta Green operation in 1999 destroyed Mannen's marriage and nearly got him fired. But it forged a lifelong bond with Forrest James.

In 2002, Mannen was one of the first Delta Green agents to join James—"John Smith"—in the new Program. The Director pulled strings to have the FBI transfer Mannen to a top-secret counterterrorism task force, the most secretive of a hundred Joint Terrorism Task Forces around the world. In the FBI's records, Mannen remains on that nowhere assignment today. The Director made Mannen Deputy Director of Operations, overseeing all case officers and agents. Mannen thought that job would go to a more experienced agent, but the Director wanted someone he could trust implicitly. The Director also wanted Mannen's history with Curtis McRay—one of the leaders of the Outlaws who refused to join the Program. Over the years, Mannen and McRay would do their best to prevent trouble between the two Delta Greens.

Mannen has seen all too clearly the compromises that the Program makes. He works every day with people who once worked for MAJESTIC. His teams provide unnatural specimens to the same people who once profited from the horrors of the Accord. It is not a comfortable arrangement. Even after all these years, he remains at arm's length from his fellow directors, MAJESTIC veterans Gates, Oakes, and Tapham. Mannen occasionally adopts teams of Agents as his go-to troubleshooters, recruiting them for missions he wants kept from the eyes of former MAJESTIC personnel.

Then there's Agent Nancy. A Delta Green agent transformed into an inhuman monster, she helped Forrest James save Mannen and his teammates in 1999. In 2010, when Mannen became Director of Operations, he learned Agent Nancy was being indefinitely detained in a Program research facility. Mannen was furious, but smart enough not to show his hand.

For years, Mannen has been reluctantly complicit in a scheme to free Agent Nancy from captivity. An old teammate, Victoria Winstead—formerly Agent Tonya, now an operations liaison with the Office of Research—has a plan. She says their lives are exactly what they owe to the woman who saved them all. So far, Mannen has persuaded her to wait. Mannen has considered tipping off Curtis McRay to Agent Nancy's location. He may orchestrate a way to send word by a group of Agents—a thumb-drive of video files and a set of coordinates, perhaps. But he has done nothing yet. Sooner or later, Winstead will move without him. Then he'll find out exactly where his loyalties lie.

Mannen has seen the bigger picture and it has taken a toll. He's been married twice since Carol. Both ended in acrimonious divorce, one with dropped charges of battery. He's been arrested four times for drunk driving, only to have the charges erased through the Program's influence. He rarely speaks to his mother, always the closest person in his life. He has tried to insulate his son, but his son is now grown, and sees through the lies. Mannen buries his trauma in drunken one-night stands and the last few have been escalating in violence. Even the thin solace he once found there has begun to elude him. How long will it be until he does something to one of those forgettable women that can't be taken back?

And somehow, isn't that what he wants?

Mannen has seen the secrets of the unnatural escape despite his best efforts to conceal them. He worries that the Program's elaborate disinformation campaigns have created a population that regards conspiracy theories as mainstream news. With every new operation, catastrophe looms larger, threatening to spill the Program's secrets. He can only imagine

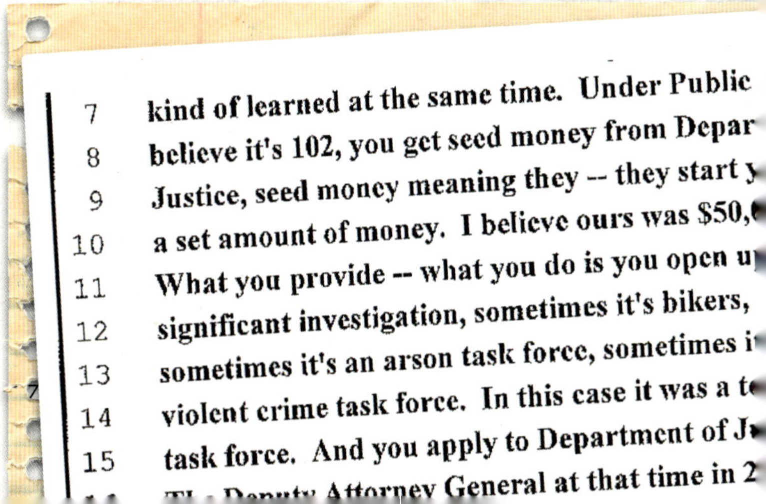
kind of learned at the same time. Under Public
believe it's 102, you get seed money from Depar
Justice, seed money meaning they -- they start
a set amount of money. I believe ours was $50,
What you provide -- what you do is you open u
significant investigation, sometimes it's bikers,
sometimes it's an arson task force, sometimes i
violent crime task force. In this case it was a t
task force. And you apply to Department of J
Deputy Attorney General at that time in 2

how bad it would get if it broke wide, or if politicians learned enough to turn the Program to their own ends.

Sometimes, he wonders if that has already happened. More and more, he wonders if the Delta Green agents who refused to join the Program had the right idea, after all.

"Ops" is 1.9 m (6'1") tall, slumping, and overweight at 118 kg (260 lbs) in an ill-fitting, conservative gray suit. His hair, once thick and red, is thin and mostly gray. His pale, freckled skin is pallid after years in conference rooms and ill-lit operations centers. He once thought of basketball as the thing that kept him sane. He hasn't stepped onto a court in years.

Operations Director Mannen ("Ops")

Sees the writing on the wall; age 52.

STR 12 **CON** 9 **DEX** 10 **INT** 15 **POW** 12 **CHA** 11

HP 11 **WP** 12 **SAN** 51 **BREAKING POINT** 49

BONDS: Ex-teammate Victoria Winstead (Deputy Director of Operations—Research Liaison), 6.

The Director, 5.

Son (Eric), 7.

Mother (Sylvia), 9.

MOTIVATIONS AND DISORDERS: Stopping Unnatural incursions.

Saving others from having to learn what he knows.

Protecting the public, his case officers, and his agents, in that order.

Beginning new relationships that don't demand much.

Intermittent explosive disorder.

Adapted to violence and helplessness.

SKILLS: Accounting 63%, Alertness 71%, Athletics 46%, Bureaucracy 80%, Criminology 75%, Dodge 56%, Drive 68%, Firearms 70%, Foreign Language (Hebrew) 24%, Forensics 66%, HUMINT 82%, Law 50%, Navigate 33%, Persuade 70%, Search 54%, Unarmed Combat 62%, Unnatural 17%.

SPECIAL TRAINING: Hand grenades (Athletics), Lockpicking (DEX), Parachuting (DEX).

ATTACKS: Glock 22 pistol 70%, damage 1D10.

Unarmed 62%, damage 1D4−1.

Admiral George Gates, Director of Intelligence

George Gates graduated first in his class at the U.S. Naval Academy, a year ahead of Forrest James, then earned a master's degree in nuclear engineering from Stanford University. His Navy career began aboard nuclear submarines. Back on shore, he went deep in the Navy's technology development programs.

In the early 1980s, Gates was one of a number of Navy officers who had heard "bed-time stories" about extraordinary technology being fielded by the Air Force—technology whose provenance couldn't be easily explained. Gates worked with the Office of Naval Intelligence until they uncovered Project PLUTO, a secret program that studied captured technologies from non-human sources. Pursuing PLUTO led him to other programs under the MAJESTIC Special Studies Project—and eventually to the Accord. Gates, a good Navy man, brought the Navy up to speed.

Rather than expose the Accord, a handful of admirals chose to buy in, trading silence for access to the technological cornucopia. By 1994, George Gates was one of the youngest admirals in the history of the U.S. Navy—and, as director of MJ-11 Project LOOKING GLASS, a member of the MAJESTIC-12 Steering Committee.

At first, Gates favored maintaining the Accord. Not only were the former Soviet and Red Chinese nuclear arsenals more of a threat to America's security than the Greys, Gates knew that other governments were involved in collecting non-terrestrial samples.

However, LOOKING GLASS intelligence suggested that the Greys were omitting important details concerning the presence of other life visiting the Earth. When Gates shared this data with the director of Project MOON DUST, USAF Lt. General Eustis Bell, the scope of the deception became more alarming. But the Steering Committee routinely dismissed their concerns. They knew building consensus wasn't going to get them anywhere. Following the assassination of the director Justin Kroft, Gates and Bell backed Forrest James' play to seize control of MAJESTIC.

Vice Admiral Gates was instrumental in keeping critical MAJESTIC assets under the exclusive control of the Program. Nevertheless, the Program found it necessary to work in close partnership with March Technologies, where other MAJESTIC directors had established themselves. This cooperation with March Technologies would ensure the success of Project TELL and its subproject WELLS, the all-important programs to neutralize the global threat of the time-traveling USS *Eldridge*.

In 2012, following the success of Project TELL, George Gates retired from the Navy. He continues to work as a consultant for the Department of Defense, and is connected to a number of powerful lobbying firms and defense contractors, including March Technologies. But most of his time is spent at headquarters, overseeing the Program's intelligence operations. If Agents investigate March Technologies or any of its subsidiaries, uncover an especially rich vein of information on the unnatural, or become deeply involved in an international investigation, they may meet Gates for guidance and coordination.

Gates' weakness is success. He held the scattering threads of MAJESTIC resources together. He forged a working relationship with Canada's M-EPIC organization. And of course, Project TELL saved humanity. After all that, Admiral Gates sees the unnatural as an aberration—but a flaw that can be fixed. With the Director's blessing, Gates urges the director of operations to prioritize the capture and study of unnatural technologies and biological samples, and facilitates the sharing of information with March Technologies and the Department of Defense to maintain the Program's funding. Gates won't acknowledge to himself that the unnatural is the universe. But he is beginning to suspect it.

Gates is all about preparation. You plan to win, but you prepare for defeat. To not do so would go against every fiber of his being. He has always been the model father and grandfather. If the Program ultimately fails, he'll do what he must to save his loved ones from what's to come. He tries not to think about how he has timed the route between his children's homes. How he'll kill Gwen and her kids at home, and then drive to Sheldon's and do the same, to save them from learning how their father failed them. For them, at least, it will be quick.

The Admiral is only "the Director of Intelligence" when an occasion requires formality. He stands 1.8 m tall (5'10") and weights a trim 75 kg (165 lbs). He eats frugally, and takes care of his body like he understands it's the only one he'll ever be issued. He has no patience for anyone who lets personal distress affect their behavior or attitudes. He maintains the service grooming standards even in retirement, so his white hair is cut to regulation length. Gates always looks the part. Handsome. Straight-backed. Square-jawed. A leader—albeit one who won't be going with you on the operation.

Admiral Gates

Learned the wrong lessons; age 68.

STR 9 **CON** 12 **DEX** 12 **INT** 16 **POW** 12 **CHA** 16

HP 11 **WP** 12 **SAN** 56 **BREAKING POINT** 48

BONDS: Wife (Frances D. Gates), 10.

Son (Sheldon) and his family, 12.

Daughter (Gwen) and her family, 9.

MOTIVATIONS AND DISORDERS: Overcoming every new challenge.

Pushing the boundaries of human knowledge.

Leaving a safer world for his grandchildren.

Exploring the cosmos.

Guaranteeing U.S. hegemony in the 21st century.

SKILLS: Accounting 32%, Alertness 68%, Athletics 55%, Bureaucracy 75%, Computer Science 42%, Craft (Electrician) 64%, Craft (Mechanic) 61%, Firearms 50%, History 43%, HUMINT 47%, Military Science (Sea) 77%, Navigate 75%, Pilot (Sailing Ship) 56%, Pilot (Submarine) 69%, Science (Nuclear Engineering) 71%, Swim 48%, Unarmed Combat 45%, Unnatural 8%.

ATTACKS: Colt M1911A1 pistol 50%, damage 1D10.

Unarmed 45%, damage 1D4−1.

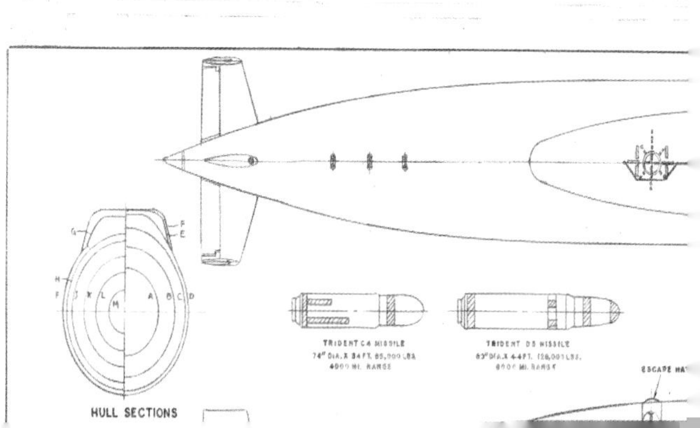

April Pleasant Crumpton, Ph.D., Intelligence Officer

For nearly 40 years at the NSA, Dr. April Pleasant Crumpton has established the frameworks that protect the U.S. government and Department of Defense. For nearly 30 of those years, she has developed algorithms to mine data for signs of the unnatural and for signs that Delta Green, in all its forms, is at risk of outside investigation. It has been nearly 20 years since anyone but her knew the full extent of her work.

Born in Huntsville, Alabama, in the 1950s, Crumpton was fortunate to have parents who were technicians at Redstone Arsenal. Highly educated, intelligent, and widely read, they did not agree with psychiatrists' diagnoses of her extreme difficulty with social interaction and communication. They knew she was neither retarded nor schizophrenic. They found ways to engage and push her development. She cultivated talents for mathematics and pattern recognition, driven by obsessive interest and iron will.

While working on her Ph.D. in mathematics and computer programming at the Massachusetts Institute of Technology, Crumpton was recruited by the NSA. There she found an environment where her passions thrived. Like many African-American employees, she was all but ignored when opportunities for promotion came around. But her peers admired her work. She decided that would be enough.

Crumpton continued her studies, delving into some of the most esoteric and obscure corners of mathematical theory. Then she found the work of 1930s Miskatonic University student Walter Gilman. She interpreted his theoretical mathematics as a means to open a way into higher dimensions. She tested his equations, and accidentally let something horrifying into the world. Crumpton would have died if not for the intervention of Reginald Fairfield, one of the leaders of Delta Green. How Fairfield and his team managed to be there at just the right time was never explained. That night, Crumpton pledged her loyalty to Fairfield's cause.

Crumpton quickly became one of the most valuable members of the conspiracy. Fairfield himself had little patience for her, but she worked closely with his number-two man, Joseph Camp, to isolate hypergeometrical formulae to dismiss, destroy, or contain the unnatural. Just as importantly, she helped keep Delta Green's communications secure.

Following Fairfield's assassination by MAJESTIC, Crumpton joined Camp and Matthew Carpenter of the FBI to form A-cell, the command and control organ for the Delta Green conspiracy. As Agent Andrea, she was responsible for communications security. Her position at the NSA and her skills as a cryptographer made her indispensable in setting up Delta Green's clandestine digital networks. She never interacted with agents, but her name got around. Every agent who heard about Agent Andrea came up with a new theory about her, each more outlandish than the last.

When Forrest James joined MAJESTIC, he reached out to Agent Andrea through the only channel he knew, the anonymous digital network she had invented. He never saw her face or learned the slightest thing about her. But when he explained why he wanted MAJESTIC's Gavin Ross to replace Carpenter as Agent Adam, Crumpton agreed. She knew Camp, then incapacitated by an assassination attempt, would never accept it, but she saw Ross as a valuable asset who could topple MAJESTIC. And she expected James would prevent Ross from putting agents at unnecessary risk. Joseph Camp never forgave her.

Camp vanished, and James dismantled MAJESTIC, founded the Program, and imprisoned Gavin Ross. That left Crumpton as the only member of A-cell. That was more responsibility than she wanted. When Donald Poe stepped forward, she helped him establish a new A-cell, and then she stepped down. She retained her code-name—Poe has yet to learn who Agent Andrea really is—but she effectively became a Friendly to the Outlaws.

In 2005, Crumpton was approached by representatives of the Program who had discovered traces of her former involvement with Delta Green, but had no idea of her identity as Agent Andrea. She accepted their invitation—in part because that allowed her to discover how they had found her and cover those tracks. She has helped the Program identify threats ever since.

It did not take long for Crumpton to realize the Program wasn't pursuing the mission as Camp had defined it. She, better than most, understood the danger of exploiting the unnatural. So she began sending hints of the Program's excesses to A-cell. They have never learned the source of the intelligence. That has resulted in quiet raids on March Technologies labs, and a few close calls between the Program and the Outlaws. Crumpton tries to keep the two groups from stumbling into each other, but there's only so much she can do. Sooner or later, there will be blood.

Part of Crumpton's success as a mole is her utter and complete lack of qualifications to be one. Even by the NSA's standards, she is not a people person. It never occurs to her to trust anyone but her mother. She has difficulty holding conversations. She notices few social cues. Under severe stress, she has been known to tune out the world entirely, clapping her hands over her ears and humming tunelessly. Her own mannerisms are just as opaque to others. She is boring to the point of invisibility. She is all but impossible to decipher. She feels as much stress saying "Hello" as she does in an interrogation; she has no polygraph baseline. But her memory is deep and sharp.

No one in A-cell or the Program suspects her. The code she hacks is invisible. She is quite conscious of the fact that she has made herself invisible, too. Her African-American peers at the NSA had to fight for recognition, just as her parents did at Redstone, but she buried her talents and accomplishments. She only strives to protect her country, and her world, from the rise of powers that would be very much worse.

Crumpton's knowledge of Delta Green's operations is comprehensive. If her faith in the Outlaws and the Program breaks, she may be the most profound threat that it could ever face.

Agents could interact with Crumpton at a remove for years without ever knowing of her existence. Subtle clues may point them in particular directions. They may find that they have undertaken a series of missions that suddenly reveal a pattern, a deeper threat that nobody recognized. If an especially savvy Agent looks for the digital fingerprints of their informant, that could lead to a cat-and-mouse game with the

woman who invented cat-and-mouse games. If a face-to-face meeting with April Crumpton ever happens, it should be on her terms, and represent the resolution of a deep mystery.

The infamous Agent Andrea is a short, middle-aged, heavy-set African American woman, always slouching at 1.6 m tall (5'3") tall and weighing 74 kg (163 lbs). She is nervous and monosyllabic in conversation unless speaking about computers or communications security with someone who has Computer Science at 80% or higher. Make-up, appearance, and style never made any more sense to Crumpton than interpersonal entanglements. She cuts her gray hair short once a week with scissors because she dislikes electric razors. She has a closet filled with the necessary clothes: for work, dark grey skirts and jackets and white blouses; for home, loose blue tracksuits. Everything about her is square, bland, and forgettable.

April Pleasant Crumpton, Ph.D.

The invisible woman, age 61.

STR 7 **CON** 9 **DEX** 8 **INT** 18 **POW** 17 **CHA** 6

HP 8 **WP** 17 **SAN** 63 **BREAKING POINT** 51

BONDS: Mother (May Crumpton), 6.

MOTIVATIONS AND DISORDERS: Understanding the boundaries of mathematics.

Monitoring the Program.

Monitoring the Outlaws.

Keeping the Unnatural at bay.

Fugues.

SKILLS: Alertness 79%, Accounting 64%, Bureaucracy 35%, Craft (Microelectronics) 65%, Computer Science 97%, Occult 69%, Science (Applied Mathematics) 96%, Science (Theoretical Mathematics) 95%, Search 68%, SIGINT 93%, Unnatural 31%.

ATTACKS: Unarmed 40%, damage 1d4−2.

RITUALS: The Call of Dagon, Call Forth Those From Outside (Azathoth, Dimensional Shambler, Nyarlathotep, Qu-Tugkwa, Shub-Niggurath, Yog-Sothoth), The Closing of the Breach (Azathoth, Shub-Niggurath, Yog-Sothoth), The Elder Sign, Exchange Personalities, Infallible Suggestion, Obscure Memory, Raise From Essential Saltes, See the Other Side, The Voorish Sign.

Katherine Oakes, Director of Security

Katherine Oakes' first childhood memory was her father beating her. After he was imprisoned for killing her mother, she spent her childhood in foster homes. She had to fight for attention, for respect, for food, for space—for anything she could call her own. She learned to be vicious until she grew strong, and she learned to be patient when viciousness and strength were not enough.

On her 18th birthday, Oakes joined the Army. She wanted the adrenaline of combat. The combat branches were closed to women, so she joined the military police as the next best thing. She was aggressive and fearless, but she had enough self-control to avoid unnecessary trouble. She soon made sergeant.

Meanwhile she threw herself into combatives training, and on her own time she found schools for high-contact martial arts like boxing, Muay Thai, jiu-jitsu, Sambo, and Eskrima. She faced few challenges in the Army's gender-segregated martial arts competitions, so she instigated unofficial bouts with men. That's when things changed. Bruised egos caused three opponents to attempt some payback. She left two of the men crippled and one dead. When the dead man turned out to be a general's grandson, Oakes expected to spend her life behind bars. She was 21 years old.

While she awaited trial, men in black suits paid her a visit. They said they were from a secret counterintelligence service, and they made an offer. Let her lawyer plea the charges down. Do her time. When she was done, they'd bring her into a black ops program so dark she'd be above the law. She'd get all the action she wanted and a healthy paycheck to boot. Oakes told them she didn't have time for fairy tales.

The next day, guards removed her from the disciplinary barracks and the men in black flew her to Guam. They would not discuss their agency or their work. But they said they were taking her to see her father. They seemed to know all about him. They thought she would like some payback. He would be alone, in a windowless room, not on anybody's records. She could do anything she wanted. No repercussions. Would that be enough proof?

It was a long flight. Oakes had always told herself she would not be defined by her childhood. But inevitably, she began to imagine all the ways she could get even with the murderer who had ruined her life. Then again, she couldn't make sense of any of it. It had to be a test or a trap. But why would anyone bother?

The men in black suits walked her through Andersen Air Force Base, past security checkpoints and down to a basement, until they were completely isolated. Just a blank corridor, a locked door, and a change of clothes. They smiled, gave her a key, and said she could find them upstairs when she was done.

Oakes stood at that door for a long time before walking away.

When she found the men upstairs, she handed them the key, and said, "I'm done with him." They flew her back.

Oakes did her time and took the dishonorable discharge. The men in black were waiting. They said they had known she could kill. The trip to Guam was a test to see if she could control herself. She passed. So in 1995, she went to work for NRO DELTA, the action arm of Project GARNET.

Break-ins. Thefts. Arsons. Kidnappings. Interrogations. Murders. She found a use for every lesson she had ever learned, and she learned things she would never have believed. No one ever said the word "alien," but even the lowliest NRO DELTA goon figured it out eventually. Oakes met GARNET's chief, Gavin Ross. She heard the larger project's name: MAJESTIC. She took her pay and kept her mouth shut.

In 1999, Oakes got a new partner: Forrest James, a washed-up SEAL old enough to be her father, an escaped convict who beat women when he was drunk. Partner or not, she didn't plan to go out of her way to watch his back. But after working with him for a year, she came to see James as tough, loyal, reliable, and penitent. Oakes knew better than to depend on anyone, but they learned to trust each other.

When James and his allies took down MAJESTIC, Oakes helped eliminate the NRO DELTA loyalists who didn't see things their way. She helped transform MAJESTIC into the new Delta Green.

For a brief moment in 2002, Oakes thought she could move on from murder. She only moved up to chief murderer. As Director of Security, she makes sure that the Program's personnel keep its secrets at all costs.

Oakes keeps a count of how many agents' deaths she has ordered. Keeping count has not eased the need for adrenaline that has her popping pills and chasing risks she does not really expect to survive. It has not saved her dysfunctional relationships, all fueled more by the excitement of emotional transgression than by closeness. It certainly will not stop her from ordering the next death.

Despite all that, she stays. For all its ruthlessness, the Program has saved the world. She has helped save the world. That means something. But—

Two years ago, the Director assigned Oakes to organize a death squad, run directly out of the Office of Security, not answering to Operations. These carefully-screened security officers have been killing men, women and children identified as having a particular genetic marker. The deaths are made to look like natural causes and accidents. There have been a lot of them, yet somehow they keep finding more targets. And even the most hardened killer can only go so far before breaking. She has begun looking for Agents to help with those deadly missions.

For all her swagger, Oakes feels more and more like a hollow shell, an abstract idea of a person. On her good days, when the rush is enough, she thinks, *Sure, I can hack it.* On the bad ones, it's like she's watching someone else live what passes for her life.

Oakes knows in her bones that the Director is a problem. He'll never retire. He's spent all these years building an organization that depends on his obsessions. She helped him insulate it from any authority but his own. She kept him safe from every threat but her.

She is certain that one day, for the good of the Program—for the good of the world—the Director will have to die. She doesn't know if she's strong enough to pass that test.

Sometimes, she thinks she should have opened that door in Guam. She grows more and more certain as time goes on that she would have found only an empty room.

Security Director Oakes strikes an impressive figure. She stands 1.8 m tall (5'10") and weighs in at 70 kg (155 lbs) of finely honed muscle. In order to blend with the rest of the national security establishment, she wears conservative business attire. She keeps her gray-blonde hair cut to less than half an inch, too short for an opponent to grab. Her long face and big hands show the signs of a lifetime of dishing out and taking beatings, and sometimes the bruises are fresh. The scar tissue around her large blue eyes makes them seem uneven. Whenever she can, she hides those scars behind sunglasses.

Security Director Oakes

Exhausted assassin, age 46.

STR 14 **CON** 15 **DEX** 14 **INT** 15 **POW** 13 **CHA** 11

HP 15 **WP** 13 **SAN** 46 **BREAKING POINT** 38

BONDS: The Director, 7.

MOTIVATIONS AND DISORDERS: Protecting Forrest James.

Eliminating threats to the Program.

Never showing weakness.

Addiction (stimulants).

Depersonalization disorder.

Adapted to violence and helplessness.

SKILLS: Alertness 68%, Athletics 86%, Criminology 53%, Demolitions 47%, Disguise 49%, Dodge 79%, Drive 60%, Firearms 67%, First Aid 44%, Forensics 73%, Heavy Weapons 41%, HUMINT 63%, Melee Weapons 76%, Military Science (Land) 53%, Navigate 55%, Search 49%, Stealth 76%, Swim 41%, Unarmed Combat 93%, Unnatural 13%.

SPECIAL TRAINING: Lockpicking (DEX), Parachuting (DEX), SCUBA gear (Swim).

ATTACKS: HK45 Tactical pistol 67%, damage 1D10.

LHR combat knife 76%, damage 1D6+1.

Unarmed 93%, damage 1D4.

Charlie Bostick, Deputy Director of Security (Information)

The more things change for Charlie Bostick, the more they remain the same. His whole career has been about lying. All that changes are the lies. Recruited out of a marketing career by the CIA in the late 1980s, Bostick produced U.S. propaganda and disinformation for seven years before being recruited by MAJESTIC's Project GARNET. There he flooded the world with UFO disinformation. Feeding bogus tips to sources who wound up on tabloid TV news shows like *A Current Affair, Inside Edition,* and *Phenomen-X,* he ensured the flakiest crackpots received media attention. *Extraterrestrial Autopsy? The Final Roswell Report?* Yeah, that was him. He engineered and then exposed some of the most famous hoaxes of the 1990s. He pioneered public disinformation techniques that would come to dominate the way Americans obtain news.

By age thirty-four, Bostick occupied the number three position at GARNET, at the right hand of Gavin Ross. There, he learned more and more of what MAJESTIC really did, and he started to get cold feet.

Bostick believed it was only a matter of time before the news broke that the U.S. government had been trading the lives of its citizens for unnatural technologies. So Bostick assembled an insurance policy—material that he could use to preemptively expose MAJESTIC to the public and save himself from retribution. Unfortunately, Gavin Ross caught him.

Bostick thought he was a dead man, but Ross blackmailed Bostick into becoming his unwilling go-between to leak information to Delta Green.

Things got more complex during the MAJESTIC War. Bostick was captured by NRO DELTA agents loyal to Adolph Lepus, MAJESTIC's psychopathic security chief. Rescued by Forrest James, Bostick revealed everything. When the smoke cleared, Forrest James and Delta Green had control of the board.

Bostick's plans for a peaceful retirement ended quickly. The new Program "invited" him to stay and continue his work. Once again, he chose to acquiesce in the face of power. He created a new identity for James and turned his vast talent for dissembling to the service of Delta Green.

Today, Charlie Bostick is the highest authority any agent is likely to encounter related to the Program's disinformation operations. His mission is to obscure the existence of the Program and the unnatural. Bostick and his liars always have their work cut out for them. Agents in the field are never as discreet as they think. Bostick sometimes must meet Agents for detailed debriefings so he knows exactly what to cover up and how. Those debriefings always wear at his fraying nerves.

Bostick believes the only reason he hasn't been killed is that he remains indispensable to the Program. Part of this means never training protégés to be able to do his job. From time to time, Bostick has subtly sabotaged disinformation operations just to give a rising subordinate a black eye.

The Program has not caught his sabotage, but they do keep tabs on his other indiscretions. For decades, Bostick's personal life has revolved around prostitutes. Every time headquarters relocates, Bostick must begin a new batch of relationships with women and procurers. Recently, desperate for some disposable substitute for trust, he has begun to share things that matter. Someday, one of these women, or one of the men that manages them, is sure to turn Bostick's secrets to their own advantage. Between his paranoid maneuvers to protect his position and his irrational compulsion to confess, Bostick could expose the Program itself.

Since his gastric-band surgery, Charlie Bostick is a pale, wiry scarecrow of a man in ill-fitting khakis. He stands 1.7 m tall (5'6") and weighs 67 kg (147 lbs), half the weight he once carried. His brown eyes are large and nervous and ringed with dark circles. He has a slight overbite and a weak chin, which he hides with a trim goatee. His thinning, gray hair remains perpetually unmanageable. His overall demeanor is that of nervous intensity.

CONFID

western governments;
especially banks; dome
opponents both at hom

- Feed the fuel between the feuding groups. Disinformation. around actions to sabotage or discredit the opposing organiz fake documents and then call out the error.
- Create concern over the security of the infrastructure. Creat stories. If the process is believed to not be secure they are d

Charlie Bostick

The man who knows he knows too much, age 54.

STR 9 **CON** 11 **DEX** 16 **INT** 18 **POW** 11 **CHA** 10

HP 10 **WP** 11 **SAN** 41 **BREAKING POINT** 34

BONDS: None.

MOTIVATIONS AND DISORDERS: Staying indispensable to the Program.

Always knowing which lies are true.

Always knowing what people want to hear.

Anxiety disorder.

Paranoia.

Adapted to helplessness.

SKILLS: Alertness 49%, Anthropology 69%, Computer Science 82%, Firearms 44%, History 73%, HUMINT 80%, Occult 71%, Persuade 76%, Pharmacy 65%, Photography 78%, Stealth 40%, Unnatural 8%.

ATTACKS: Colt Viper .38 revolver 44%, damage 1D8.

Unarmed 40%, damage 1D4−1.

Gregory Tapham, Ph.D., Director of Research

Dr. Gregory Tapham has saved the world, but it was almost an afterthought. Tapham started as a young Ph.D. in theoretical physics, the son of a scientist who worked with Teller and Ulam on the hydrogen bomb. He thought he would follow in his father's footsteps: finding better ways to vaporize and poison billions. But a critique he'd published on Bondi's theories of negative mass in general relativity caught the attention of scientists working with MAJESTIC's S-4 Laboratory. After extensive vetting, and offering an opportunity to take a crack at certain problematic equations that had been keeping the S-4 team up late, they brought Tapham to Area 51 to work on the U.S. government's most secret project: the analysis of recovered non-terrestrial technology.

Three years later, on 30 FEB 1972, Dr. Tapham witnessed the attempt to restart the power source on the "disc" recovered from Roswell in 1947. The result was a titanic explosion that killed four and left another 73 injured. Tapham received severe burns on his face and hands. He bears those scars today.

But what doesn't kill you makes you curious.

Tapham continued to work on recovered non-terrestrial technologies. When MAJESTIC established the Accord in 1981, Tapham found the flood of new technologies worrisome. Despite the fact that the owners and creators of this technology were now available to explain their basic principals, Tapham felt as if America's new allies were being less than candid. He was told his worries were unfounded.

Tapham's complaints to superiors got him placed on a dead-end project, Project TELL, newly acquired from the U.S. Navy. At the heart of this project was the World War II destroyer-escort USS *Eldridge*, and the curious device the Navy had used to render the ship invisible to radar in 1943—the Tillinghast Resonator.

Tapham and his team overcame the mysteries that kept the Navy in the dark for so long. Their analysis allowed an improved Tillinghast Resonator to be built, with new safety protocols and even a method for dealing with the deadly radiation produced by the device.

More importantly, in 1992 Tapham discovered and defined the Loop—the temporal anomaly whereby the Tillinghast Resonator on the *Eldridge* was shut down in 1943 by a team of operatives who traveled back in time from 2012. Without completing the other end of the Loop by launching a team back in time, the 1943 Tillinghast Resonator would pull the Earth into a rend in spacetime, destroying the Earth, the Sun, and all nearby stellar objects. The math held no mercy. Project TELL had 20 years to conquer N-Space and time travel, or the world would be erased.

When MAJESTIC ceased to exist in 2002, the mission into N-Space was still a decade from being ready. Unwilling to let human rivalries get in the way, Tapham spearheaded the effort to get the leadership of MAJESTIC's replacement, Delta Green, to work with March Technologies to close the Loop.

It worked. The Loop was closed on 19 NOV 2012. All it cost was several billion dollars, eight fatal accidents in testing, and the lives of the four SEALs who plunged into N-Space to pull the plug on the resonator in 1943. The celebrations lasted for days. Everyone was delirious with pride and relief. Everyone except Dr. Gregory Tapham.

That the world was saved with a whimper, and not a bang, was utterly intolerable to Tapham. What is a man supposed to do when he has saved the entire world and can't tell anyone? No. This is not how his story ends.

Dr. Tapham has work to do.

Tapham continues to push the limits of human comprehension. Work has consumed every bit of his life, leaving no room for personal entanglements. All human interaction has long since degenerated into a game of mental capture the flag. To Tapham, it is simply a matter of who is right and who is wrong. It is unsurprising that no one can stand his company for very long.

He serves double duty as a director of March Technologies and the Program's head of research. At first, the Director accepted his dual role only because there was no other option. But as the bridge between the Program and March Technologies, Tapham has proved himself. He ensures that the Program collects specimens and samples for study, and secures certain samples to be sent to March Technologies. In return, March Technologies helps the Program exploit its discoveries and serves as a deniable source of funding.

Agents who come into contact with March Technologies, or who have direct experience with unnatural technologies or formulae, may be called in to consult with Dr. Tapham. An Agent who knows Tapham's voice, and believes in his passion for reaching beyond the limitations of human understanding, could serve his purposes very well.

Tapham's passion is expanding human understanding and improving technology. As far as he is concerned, with enough time humanity can match the achievements of any of the beings that have trespassed on our world. We can't afford to be squeamish. We must be rational and ruthless in order to succeed.

The way the Tillinghast Resonator operates limits the utility of time travel, but there are other ways that our four dimensions can be breached. In the back files of MAJESTIC, Tapham has found what he believes to be the key, a two-sided sheet of paper scribbled by Dr. Courtis in 1949. Courtis filled it with 34 of the most eerily simple equations, along with a single word: "Escape." The mathematics defy comprehension, but Tapham is certain he will find a way. Once his team masters these equations, Tapham will change humanity.

Dr. Gregory Tapham, is an aging African-American academic about 1.7 m (5'8") tall, weighing 60 kg (130 lbs). He looks like something out of a horror movie. The burns he suffered in 1972 covered his cheeks, mouth, and neck with pale pink scars. His lips are not particularly limber, and that affects his enunciation. The burns make his age hard to pin down. Only around the eyes, where the burns were mildest, do the years of ambition show. His white hair is sparse. He does nothing to cover his injuries. In fact, he is not above using people's discomfort with his appearance as leverage.

Gregory Tapham, Ph.D.

The man who saved the world, age 69.

STR 7 **CON** 9 **DEX** 9 **INT** 18 **POW** 13 **CHA** 6

HP 8 **WP** 13 **SAN** 41 **BREAKING POINT** 38

BONDS: None.

MOTIVATIONS AND DISORDERS: Recognition for changing the world.

Harnessing the unnatural for human technology.

Demonstrating humanity's cosmic significance.

Megalomania.

Obsession with non-terrestrial technology.

Adapted to helplessness.

SKILLS: Accounting 51%, Bureaucracy 64%, Computer Science 71%, Craft (Electronics) 69%, Craft (Microelectronics) 71%, Persuade 53%, Science (Applied Physics) 92%, Science (Experimental Physics) 94%, Science (Mathematics) 91%, Science (Theoretical Physics) 93%, Unnatural 11%.

ATTACKS: Unarmed 40%, damage 1d4−2.

Rebecca Kaur Thornhill, Ph.D., Deputy Director of Research (Recovery)

Dr. Thornhill works with CORAL NOMAD missions to recover artifacts and specimens seized in the Program's operations. She and her teams usually deal with case officers, but Agents are likely to meet her if they recover something that must be picked up in the field. She and her teams are under strict instructions to trade no stories—but people in the field tend to talk as long as they think no one in charge is listening.

Rebecca Thornhill was a wunderkind in experimental physics. She got her Ph.D. at the tender age of 21, and by 23 was designing experiments for the Tevatron particle accelerator at Fermilab. That was where she was headhunted by March Technologies to work on Project TELL in 2003.

Thornhill learned a lot, and quickly. She learned the world was going to end in nine years. She learned that time and space were mutable in ways no one had predicted. She learned that her government was a vault of secrets.

March Technologies was deeply entangled with a secret government task force that they called "the Program," but sometimes called "Delta Green." Even after working on TELL for a decade, Dr. Thornhill was unsure whether March Technologies was a front company set up by the Program, or the Program was a by-product of March Technologies. But they were going to save the world, right? And if nothing else, there was the science.

Saving the world on 19 NOV 2012 left Dr. Thornhill with a dizzy sense of accomplishment. But she still had doubts. It wasn't just that good men and women had died, or that four SEALs had been sent to their deaths. It was the nagging question of who was in charge, and what were they going to do with the technology now that they had mastered it.

Her repeated attempts to understand the project's agenda led to her transfer and promotion. Now, she doesn't have to wonder about the Program. As Deputy Director of Research for recovery operations, she works with it every day.

Dr. Thornhill was assigned to Operation CORAL NOMAD, a scattering of U.S. Air Force elements that work for the Program (see **ASSET RECOVERY** on page 269). She quickly learned that the unit went back decades. It had begun under the USAF's Foreign Technology Recovery Unit, a crash-recovery team that gathered bits of downed Eastern Bloc aircraft for analysis. That would have been secretive enough, but it was only a cover. Their main function was the recovery of non-terrestrial technology and biology. That work continues today.

At CORAL NOMAD, she became a field consultant. Her job is to assess all recovered non-terrestrial materials to determine the safest way to transport them to containment areas. It was not a role she took on willingly because it meant she was done with the Tillinghast Resonator for good. But her only other alternative was to quit.

Since 2013, Thornhill has accompanied CORAL NOMAD teams as they secure and transport the material obtained by Agents for the Program's case officers. She takes her duties deadly seriously, and has made it her business to qualify on all the small arms, tactical gear, and combat skills. She is trying to hang tough in an environment she had never prepared for. She has seen unnatural violence and grotesque deaths due to failed protocols. It is taxing.

When called to a "pickup," the CORAL NOMAD pilots and shooters are always suspicious of what agents may have done to secure such dangerous and unpleasant trophies. They are equally suspicious of the white-jacketed scientists who take possession of the items. But Thornhill has integrated. The others recognize her effort and intelligence, and they consider her part of the team.

In the last few months, Thornhill has embarked on a new kind of risk. She began a quiet romance with a 22-year-old staff sergeant, the youngest man on the team. She has pushed the officers to arrange his assignments to suit her, and pressed to have him on the pickup whenever she's on a run. Her colleagues know the stresses of the Program can twist people, and they accept that—as long as it doesn't interfere with the mission. Thornhill is starting to make them wonder.

Sooner or later, Dr. Tapham will step down as director of Research. Thornhill means to be the first pick to replace him. Then all the secrets of the Program will open up.

Rebecca Kaur Thornhill, Ph.D.—the elite parajumpers and pilots of CORAL NOMAD call her "Doc"—is a thin, dark-skinned woman standing 1.7 m tall (5'8") and weighing 60 kg (132 lbs). She was born to a Sikh mother of north Indian descent (her great-grandparents immigrated to New York in the 1920s) and a Caucasian father. She always ties her long, straight, black hair in a ponytail. She wears contact lenses in the field, glasses in the laboratory, and "business casual" shirts and slacks all the time. Her pale blue eyes don't miss much, and her poker face gives nothing away. She is intensely focused on her work, and maintains a detached distance from people who haven't earned her trust.

Rebecca Kaur Thornhill, Ph.D.

The seeker, age 38.

STR 9 **CON** 14 **DEX** 15 **INT** 18 **POW** 12 **CHA** 12

HP 12 **WP** 12 **SAN** 49 **BREAKING POINT** 48

BONDS: Colleagues in CORAL NOMAD, 6.

Boyfriend (CORAL NOMAD Staff Sgt. Cameron Thomas), 8.

Parents (Tavleen and Richard Thornhill), 9.

Brother (Richard Thornhill, Jr.), 8.

MOTIVATIONS AND DISORDERS: Keeping the world safe.

Learning the Program's true agenda.

Discovering the truth behind secrets.

Keeping up with her CORAL NOMAD colleagues.

Getting back to the lab.

SKILLS: Alertness 43%, Athletics 41%, Bureaucracy 43%, Computer Science 57%, Craft (Electrician) 58%, Craft (Microelectronics) 59%, Firearms 45%, Foreign Language (French) 47%, Foreign Language (Mandarin Chinese) 43%, Foreign Language (Punjabi) 49%, Foreign Language (Russian) 44%, Persuade 60%, Science (Experimental Physics) 88%, Science (Physics) 81%, Science (Mathematics) 73%, Search 45%, Swim 42% Unarmed Combat 44%, Unnatural 8%.

ATTACKS: Sig Sauer P228 (M11) pistol 45%, damage 1D10.

Unarmed 44%, damage 1D4−1.

Dana Shelton, Director of Logistics

The second most powerful person in the Program gives no orders to case officers, spends little time studying the fruits of research, and has never flown a combat or rescue mission. But she holds every life in the Program in her hands, because she controls the funding.

Dana Shelton was born Dana Santos in San Diego to Filipino immigrants. She joined the Air Force with a degree in data processing in 1977, earned an MBA as a captain in 1983, and managed increasingly secret procurement programs for five years before she was assigned to the NSA at Fort Meade. Santos earned a reputation for being smart, tough, and determined, and for never giving anything away. In 1991, she was

brought into one of the NSA's most restricted programs, Project AQUARIUS.

AQUARIUS was so compartmentalized, secretive, and powerful that it was like a government all its own. Santos harbored quiet doubts from the beginning. Those concerns were quelled for a time when she learned the project's true, shocking function: facilitating the U.S. government's treaty with an overwhelmingly powerful non-terrestrial civilization.

Her doubts soon returned. Santos saw how AQUARIUS director Justin Kroft turned access to the Greys to the enrichment of his own company, March Technologies. She learned of AQUARIUS' role in a sprawling network of secrets, the MAJESTIC Special Studies Project. She saw the lines of funding, research, and influence that reached from MAJESTIC into the defense and intelligence industries. She saw hints of the horrors that the Greys perpetrated upon humanity—horrors that MAJESTIC carefully covered up.

Santos learned to be ashamed. She agreed with MAJESTIC that public revelation of the Greys would be catastrophic, but she detested the corruption of its mission. Even so, she knew she could not leave. She ran the programs and protected the secrets. She retired from the Air Force in 1997 as a major but stayed at the NSA, and at AQUARIUS, as a civilian.

Along the way, she learned who could be trusted to put country over Kroft. When Eustis Bell, George Gates, and Forrest James (or rather, "John Smith") seized control of MAJESTIC in 2001, they were surprised to find a small cadre of Project AQUARIUS managers ready and waiting. Dana Santos and her colleagues helped the insurgent faction sift out Kroft's loyalists and reorganize AQUARIUS and MAJESTIC. When James and his people shut down MAJESTIC and launched the Program, Santos kept things running. She has run logistics for the Program ever since.

Santos—she changed her name to Shelton after her 2010 marriage to a software entrepreneur—manages a network of program managers throughout U.S. defense, intelligence, and law enforcement. Most assist the Program as a shadowy part of their daily work. Some have no idea that the Program exists. According to tightly-restricted project protocols, they move discretionary funds into classified programs and private-sector contracts. Other managers move those funds to accounts that can be used by the Program.

Dana Shelton knows exactly where the Program's funding comes from and where it goes. She organizes new special-access programs to cover the Program's many activities. She can trace the connections between the Program and March Technologies going back to the beginning.

To the extent that the Program has not given in to its worst impulses, Shelton can take a large share of the credit. She believes in the Program's mission. She has protected her sanity by deliberately avoiding unnecessary knowledge of the Program's work, but she knows enough. She does not trust the public with the deadly knowledge that the unnatural is real. At the same time, she has seen how easily black projects can be corrupted. Under her leadership, the Office of Logistics prioritizes funding for operations and research that seem most likely to inflict the least harm.

But even Logistics has its limits. The Director sometimes overrules Shelton's team, insisting on funding for dubious projects. And Logistics has no control over March Technologies, which has had its own worrisome priorities since the MAJESTIC days.

Shelton hopes that when the Program finally goes too far, her people can make sure it reinvents itself and remains true to its mission. What worries her is the thing she does not know: what steps the Director, the other directors, and March Technologies may have already taken to prevent her from ever doing that again. If faced directly with a threat from within, or from her old colleagues at March Technologies, Shelton may seek help from Agents who have never heard of her before. Since their case officer would have no idea that she knows them, that may give a brief window of action to quietly set things right. But getting caught in an apparent betrayal of the Program would be a lethal disaster.

Dana Shelton is a smiling, sharp-eyed Filipino woman, 1.6 m tall (5'2") and weighing not quite 59 kg (130 lbs), with short, coal-black hair. She has worn the same sort of no-nonsense pantsuits every day since she stopped wearing Air Force uniforms 20 years ago.

She has no children, after devoting her life to a career that demanded all her attention. She has grown close to her husband Ned's children and grandchildren from a previous marriage, even though they sometimes become frustrated with her evasive non-answers when they ask why she won't retire.

Dana Shelton

Another kind of warrior, age 62.

STR 6 **CON** 9 **DEX** 10 **INT** 17 **POW** 16 **CHA** 13

HP 8 **WP** 16 **SAN** 70 **BREAKING POINT** 64

BONDS: Colleagues in Logistics, 13.
Husband (Ned Shelton), 11.
Mother (Madamba Santos), 10.

MOTIVATIONS AND DISORDERS: Keeping the unnatural at bay.
Protecting the Program's mission.
Guarding against corruption.
Getting the numbers right.
Watching for March Technologies' crimes.

SKILLS: Accounting 90%, Bureaucracy 92%, Computer Science 81%, Criminology 67%, Firearms 40%, Foreign Language (Spanish) 43%, Foreign Language (Tagalog) 50%, History 47%, HUMINT 30%, Law 69%, Persuade 72%, SIGINT 55%, Unnatural 9%.

ATTACKS: Unarmed 40%, damage 1D4−2.

Gavin Ross

The CIA recruited Gavin Ross out of graduate school. His early work kept him south of the equator, but in the early 1970s he joined James Angleton's infamous team of mole-hunters, seeking Soviet agents in the CIA. When Angleton was forced out and his mole-hunt repudiated, Ross considered tendering his resignation. Before he could do so, NRO DELTA recruited him. At first, Ross had little idea what NRO DELTA was working on. But he slowly pieced together that they were working for a section of the intelligence community that dealt with extraterrestrial threats to U.S. security. This knowledge galvanized Ross's resolve to protect and serve NRO DELTA's ultimate masters: the MAJESTIC Special Studies Project.

In 1990, his success and unflinching loyalty elevated Ross to the MAJESTIC-12 Steering Committee as director of Project GARNET. When he was briefed on the Accord, many aspects of MAJESTIC's relationship with the Greys troubled him. Too many members of the Steering Committee accepted the benevolence of the aliens unquestioningly, or believed they could exploit the aliens for their own benefit. By 1996, Ross came to the conclusion that MAJESTIC's upper ranks were in need of a purge.

He intended to gain control over Delta Green and use it to assassinate the Steering Committee members who were committed to the Accord. Ross slipped information to Delta Green from time to time, sparking the MAJESTIC war, and eventually recruited a disgraced agent named Forrest James into MAJESTIC. Ross's intent was to turn James and convince him that they should use Delta Green to take over MAJESTIC. For a few months, Gavin Ross was the secret figure behind A-cell. Then Justin Kroft was murdered and everything fell apart. Before Ross could regroup, it was James who had used Delta Green to stage the coup, and Ross sat in a cell waiting to see what Forrest James had in store for him.

He wasn't idle long. His skills and contacts were critical to Forrest James. James was smart, and he had a few old MAJESTIC leaders on his side, but none of them had the brilliance for corruption, or the sheer ruthlessness of Justin Kroft. MAJESTIC quickly fell to pieces. What replaced it would be Delta Green, reborn: the Program. It flourished thanks to Gavin Ross.

For several years, Ross served as involuntary consigliere to Forrest James—now Director "John Smith"—and the Program. At first he worked with a not-so-metaphorical gun to his head, but over the years the Director grew to rely on Ross's counsel. Ross helped the Director create an agency capable of confronting unnatural threats to national security, but always held back enough to remain indispensable.

Ross' influence is one reason the Program attempts to study, understand, and sometimes deploy the unnatural, rather than attacking it with a scorched-earth policy. Ross remembered full well how MAJESTIC had bartered alien miracles for influence and wealth. MAJESTIC's great flaw, Ross believed, was that it depended on a single non-human species as a benefactor. The Program could take a more comprehensive view.

As the years slipped by, the Director gave Ross more and more autonomy. Ross had laid very careful plans over the years. At just the right time on just the right day in 2010, a suborned guard who was driving him back to confinement disabled their tracking devices and turned left instead of right. Just like that, the Program lost Gavin Ross for good.

He has spent the years since then creating a long and bright future for himself.

In 2011, Ross made sure he was in the right place at the right time for another windfall. Before his death in 2001, MAJESTIC director Justin Kroft had an illegitimate son. Kroft had seen to the child's welfare remotely through an array of legal channels, all well known to Ross. The boy, Robert Justin Ortega, had no inkling of Kroft's identity or secrets. Ross approached him as his father's long-lost best friend. Under the name Michael Bellek—one of many identities he arranged while helping Forrest James establish his own new name—Ross taught Ortega how to make the most of the trust funds that Kroft left behind. Ortega and "Bellek" grew close.

On Ortega's 21st birthday, the lawyers in charge of his father's estate delivered a large collection of disks under the terms of Kroft's will. The disks held files, photos, and data sets, and cases of strange biological and technological samples: cherry-picked secrets of MAJESTIC's more "mundane" projects. Ortega had no idea what to make of it, so he called his father's old friend. "Bellek" was happy to help. It was, of course, what he had been waiting for.

Recently, Ross has been plundering old MAJESTIC files and samples, sifting out valuable but harmless patents and feeding them to Ortega's company, Ancile, Inc. Ancile is an up-and-comer in the defense industry, due in no small part to compelling patents secretly gleaned from MAJESTIC's science.

Ross has siphoned off the best for himself. A supply of tiny blue pills that arrest cellular degeneration and mutation, code-named ARD-15, have made him healthy and strong. They cured him when aggressive colon cancer took hold. But the supply is limited, and if he ever stops, he will quickly deteriorate and die. Ross' own small but potent research companies have tried to replicate ARD-15, to no effect. He knows that he may need to strike a deal with some of his old colleagues at March Technologies, for further research. But Ross has given others the glory long enough. He is done looking out for his species and his country. If he unlocks immortality, it will be only for him. Then, he will have all the time he needs to gain what he deserves.

If he wasn't before, Ross is certain now that he was chosen. For what, he remains uncertain, but he knows he is more than most people. Since he began ingesting the ARD-15, he has felt more alive, more real than he ever thought possible. And the dreams have been wonderful. Nightly romps of color, light, and sex. A feeling he last felt in the dim, dark days of 1955, when he first began puberty. As the dreams grow in scope and clarity, Ross sometimes finds himself thinking, "This is wrong, something has gone wrong...." But there seems to be something present in the dreams, something waiting for him, and he desperately wants to find it.

Ross stores his stash of MAJESTIC technology in a private condominium with round-the-clock armed security, along with a frightful supply of grenades and bricks of C4. He means to teach himself how to use them so as to deny his discoveries to any teams that the Program might send. He has little fear for himself. He is increasingly certain that he cannot die.

Gavin Ross looks like a vibrant and healthy 60, and has the strength and fitness of a very active man twenty years younger than that. No one would guess he is closing in on 80. At 1.98 m tall (6'6"), he towers over most people, and he stands confident and straight. If not wearing a crisp suit, he looks ready to tackle a golf course. His receding hair, artfully clipped, is a distinguished silver, and he has thick brows and a Roman nose. He smiles often, but if you surprise him, his brown eyes become sharp and suspicious.

Gavin Ross (Among Many Other Names)

Keeper of the keys to the kingdom, age 76.

STR 15 **CON** 12 **DEX** 15 **INT** 18 **POW** 15 **CHA** 13

HP 14 **WP** 15 **SAN** 45 **BREAKING POINT** 42

BONDS: None.

MOTIVATIONS AND DISORDERS: Mastering unnatural technology.

Achieving immortality.

Addiction (ARD-15).

Megalomania.

Obsession (unnatural technology).

Adapted to violence and helplessness.

SKILLS: Alertness 77%, Bureaucracy 96%, Computer Science 56%, Criminology 77%, Drive 41%, Firearms 72%, Foreign Language (Portuguese) 46%, Foreign Language (Spanish) 56%, History 62%, HUMINT 93%, Persuade 93%, SIGINT 43%, Stealth 72%, Search 86%, Unarmed Combat 54%, Unnatural 5%.

SPECIAL TRAINING: Lockpicking (DEX).

ATTACKS: FN-Herstal FNX-9 pistol 72%, damage 1D10.

Unarmed 54%, damage 1D4.

Jean Qualls

Jean Qualls owes her life, and what came after it, to Delta Green.

In the 1980s, she was FBI Special Agent Debra Constance of the Behavioral Science Unit. Recruited by Delta Green in 1990, she was exposed in 1992 to what can only be described as a cursed book. It forced a biological change in Debra Constance. Her mind and body were wracked with agonizing hungers that could only be sated by cannibalism. On the sixth day of suffering, she blacked out and found herself in the city morgue feasting on a John Doe. She spent the next day transforming into a ghastly dog-like parody of a human being. Constance sought out her Delta Green colleague, John Drake, begging for sanctuary. To her surprise, Drake helped her. He provided a safe house where she could study the cursed book for a solution to her predicament. A ritual for taking on the form of the devoured dead presented itself as the only option. Drake procured the fresh body of an O.D.'ed party-girl, then set about the task of altering government records to conform to her new appearance and fingerprints. He provided her with a new identity: Jean Qualls, forensic psychologist and FBI consultant.

Family, friends, and co-workers all believed that Debra Constance was dead. That left "Jean Qualls" with only Delta Green agents for company. During the 1994 reorganization, she was christened Agent Nancy. She and the two Agents assigned as "handlers," code-named Nolan and Nick, formed N-cell. N-cell was designated a "special interrogations team" for communicating with the dead—since Nancy could sometimes see the thoughts and memories of those she consumed. Rationalizing her diet as a "forensic tool" helped preserve Agent Nancy's sanity, if not her humanity.

Agent Nancy stayed away from the Program. Though she knew and trusted Forrest James, she did not trust the compromises he would have to make to resurrect Delta Green. She continued to work with the so-called Outlaws.

In 2002, during a confrontation with the DeMonte Clan of ghouls in New Orleans, Agent Nancy's handler, Nolan, was driven insane. An unnatural relationship had begun a year before between Qualls and Nolan, and he had become obsessed with being devoured by Qualls. She was immortal, so that would be the only way for them to "be together forever." A-cell assigned new handlers to Nancy, reassigned Agent Nick to Cell L as Agent Lewis, and incarcerated Agent Nolan in a Delta Green-controlled mental health facility.

Nolan escaped in 2008, and the former Agent Nick disappeared the next day. Nolan posed such a threat that the Outlaws and the Program cooperated in the search. Agents of the Program found Agent Nancy in an abandoned fallout shelter, covered in viscera, gibbering. No trace of Nolan or Nick was ever found. The Program took her into custody without informing A-cell. As far as the Outlaws know, Nancy, Nick, and Nolan are all still missing.

Jean Qualls is locked in a secure facility maintained by the Program and March Technologies. Tests

are performed. Samples are taken. She is regularly fed. She hasn't seen the light of day since she arrived. Strangely, it's starting to feel natural. Even the closeness of her cell walls seem more comforting than standing out in the open. Sometimes the voice heard from her cell is a guttural growl or a weird, inhuman meeping. Sometimes it's the voice of a young woman. Sometimes it's the voice of FBI Special Agent William Cassidy—also known as Agent Nolan. Qualls never remembers what finally, truly happened to him, only that he killed Nick and escaped. She never remembers the times that she *becomes* him, or what she must have done to make that possible. When his personality comes to the fore, he is calm and content but careful to allow nothing to harm his beloved.

As for getting out…well, a chance will come. Qualls knows another useful ritual, one which can obscure recent memories. With patience and planning, someday she will be freed, and there will be a reckoning. First with Forrest James. To make that happen, she may need to "impersonate" certain Agents and then their case officers.

When impersonating a human, Jean Qualls most often looks like the first victim she consumed after her transformation: an attractive young woman, 1.8 m tall (5'11") and 63 kg (140 lbs), with fair skin, long blonde hair, large blue eyes, and distinctly Nordic features. She used to wear false eyeglasses—the lenses were decorative—to look older and more intelligent.

Sometime she looks like Agent Nolan. In that guise, she appears to be a 40-year-old Caucasian man, clean-shaven with short, graying hair, in excellent physical shape but heavily scarred.

When she has assumed either human form, a bright light cast upon her throws the shadow of her true and monstrous self: a hunched, hungry ghoul with vaguely canine features and loathsomely rubbery flesh, 2.2 m tall (7'2") and 272 kg (600 lbs). These days, she rarely wears a human disguise. But, even in her true form, Qualls retains her eastern-Tennessee accent and manners.

Jean Qualls

Agent Nancy, inhuman experiment, age 56.

STR 21 **CON** 21 **DEX** 13 **INT** 16 **POW** 15 **CHA** 12*

HP 21 **WP** 15 **SAN** 0

* *Qualls' CHA applies only in a human form.*

BONDS: None.

MOTIVATIONS: Revenge on Forrest James.

Revenge on Agent Nolan.

(Only as Agent Nolan) Protecting Agent Nancy.

Dissociative identity disorder (she transforms into Agent Nolan).

Delusions (sometimes she can't distinguish reality from the memories of the dead).

SKILLS: Alertness 76%, Athletics 94%, Criminology 50%, Firearms 54%, Foreign Language (Ghoul) 28%, Forensics 73%, HUMINT 73%, Law 36%, Medicine 64%, Occult 79%, Pharmacy 67%, Psychotherapy 87%, Science (Chemistry) 52%, Search 65%, Stealth 83%, Track (by scent) 65%, Unarmed Combat 77%, Unnatural 26%.

ATTACKS: Claws 77%, damage 1D8, Armor Piercing 3 (in ghoul form).

Bite 77%, damage 1D10+2 (in ghoul form; see **WORRY AND RIP**).

Unarmed 77%, damage 2D4 (in human form).

CHARNEL VISAGE: In her true form, that of a loathsome ghoul, Qualls has no CHA stat as humans would understand it. She can transform rapidly between her native form and any human form consumed with the Changeling Feast ritual.

GIFT OF THE GRAVE: Consuming rotten human flesh immediately restores 1D8 HP to an injured ghoul. This may be done once per 24 hours.

IMMORTALITY: A ghoul never grows old, starves to death, or perishes through natural causes.

INHUMAN AGILITY: With a successful Athletics roll, a ghoul can leap five meters in any direction from a standing position, scale any vertical surface, or drop up to 15 meters without damage. At top speed, a ghoul can run nearly 60 kph.

INHUMAN STRENGTH: Qualls adds 1D6 damage to all attacks with melee weapons and thrown weapons.

LIFE UNDERGROUND: A ghoul can burrow through earth at up to three meters per minute. Ghouls thrive underground. They prefer to breathe air, and may go into a sort of torpor if suffocated long enough, but can survive indefinitely without it. A ghoul can see in absolute darkness, identify things by smell, and hear a human heartbeat at a distance of 15 meters.

MEPHITIC MEMORIES: With an INT test, Qualls can bring to mind the memories of any of the many human beings whose brains she has devoured: insane cultists, MAJESTIC researchers, murderers, rapists, Delta Green agents, helpless victims, and many others. If the test fumbles, the memories come confusingly and heartbreakingly to the forefront of her thoughts, beyond her control.

RESILIENT: A successful Lethality roll does not destroy a ghoul, but inflicts HP damage equal to the Lethality rating.

WORRY AND RIP: After succeeding with a bite attack, a ghoul may inflict 1D6 damage on the same target each turn, without requiring an attack roll. The ghoul can take other actions while holding and worrying a victim. If the bite attack pierced the victim's armor, the "worry and rip" damage ignores armor. The victim can attempt an opposed STR test as his or her action each turn to break free.

RITUALS: Changeling Feast, Charnel Meditation, Obscure Memories.

SAN LOSS: 0/1D6 (in ghoul form).

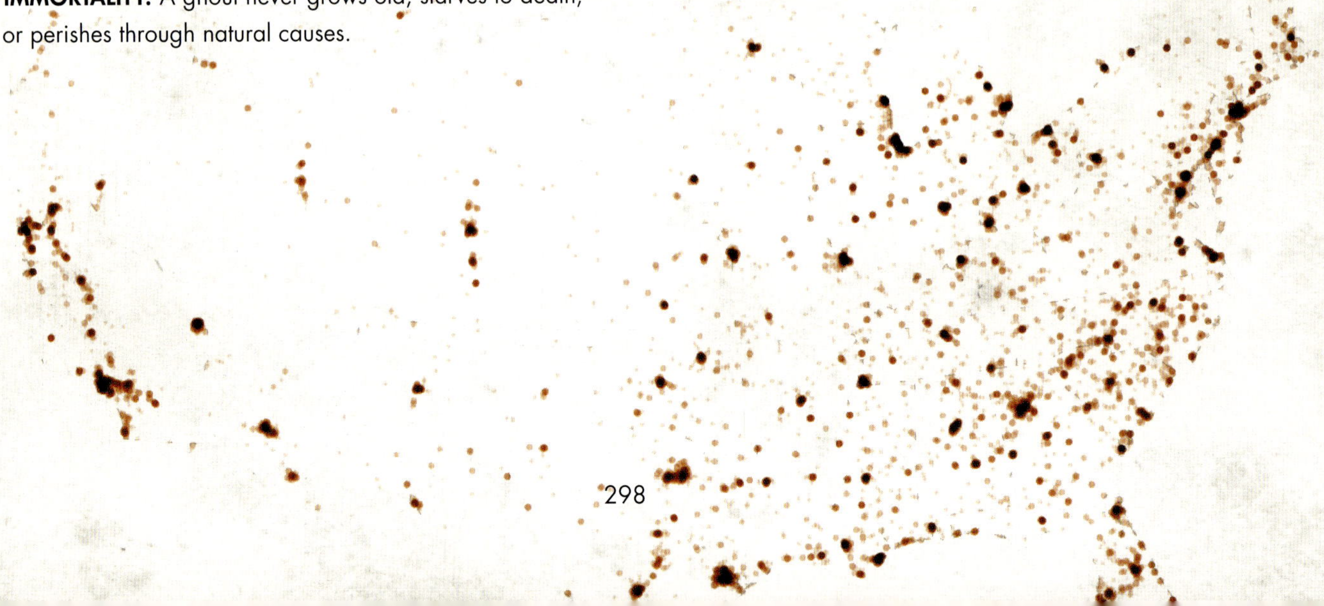

The Outlaws

From its official deactivation by the Joint Chiefs in 1970 all the way up to its reincarnation as the Program in 2002, Delta Green never stopped its work. After 1970, they continued as an outlaw conspiracy of graying soldiers, spies, and federal agents. They shared information haphazardly and brought in new blood only occasionally.

The group's reorganization as a clandestine cell system in 1994 improved security and protected the identity of its leaders. Agents enthusiastically adopted this new structure.

When the Program launched in 2002, it had full access to Delta Green's files and set about recruiting its entire membership. Not all agreed to come in from the cold. Many saw fellow agents tortured and murdered in the MAJESTIC War. They saw government involvement in unnatural science turn to horrific abuses.

A stubborn core of Delta Green agents rejected the compromises that the Program promised in exchange for legitimacy. They did their best to drop out of view, but maintained their mission. The Program's leaders—who know about this other conspiracy—call them the Outlaws, with an unsubtle touch of irony.

For their part, the Outlaws call themselves Delta Green.

Goals and Beliefs

The Outlaws have an uncompromising mission, driven by a scorched-earth approach to the unnatural:

- To protect the citizens of the United States from threats originating from unnatural phenomena or the study of such phenomena.
- To maintain the security of the United States from unnatural threats and from contact with unnatural phenomena.
- To gather intelligence on unnatural phenomena for the sole purpose of containing or eliminating unnatural threats.

Other than that, they have little interest in gathering intelligence. They prefer to resolve situations through irreversible action. The best intelligence that can be retrieved is "no survivors, no evidence." Many of the Outlaws are bitter towards the government and believe that it is up to self-reliant, responsible individuals to do what the government cannot.

They have no room for agents who think it a disservice to keep the unnatural a secret. Certain truths about the nature of the universe can never be revealed, and no one outside their self-selecting group should ever be exposed. The potential for catastrophe is simply too great.

Facilities

None. Outlaw Agents improvise. The closest the conspiracy has to a "facility" is Donald Poe's house and the secret bunker on his property, but Agents go there only under the most dire circumstances.

Organization

In principle, the Outlaws work in a three-agent cell system modeled on classic organized conspiracies—and specifically on the OSS-organized partisan groups formed during World War II. The system's architect, Dr. Joseph Camp, cut his teeth in the Office of Strategic Services during the 1940s. The cells are organized alphabetically: A-cell, B-cell, C-cell, and so on.

The Theory

A-cell is the conspiracy's command, control, and communications. It assigns tasks to the other cells. B-cell provides logistical support. It tracks the locations and contents of storage facilities, identifies experts willing to provide discreet medical and psychological care, and assists with tradecraft and cover-ups. C-cell is responsible for intelligence-gathering and analysis. It is primarily in charge of identifying new missions, providing tactical intelligence, and identifying potential recruits.

All other cells are operational, each with three agents who may work with a handful of Friendlies that know little or nothing about the larger conspiracy. Agents know little about members of other cells. Each cell has a leader who knows how to contact two other cell leaders as well as A-cell. There are never more than 26 active cells, one for each letter of the alphabet, and so there are no more than 78 agents active at any one time.

The Reality

Since 2002, the Outlaws have suffered a slow disintegration. A-cell organizes things far less precisely than Joseph Camp envisioned all those years ago. Communications are deliberately stifled. The contacts and influence that Camp and his partners employed have been lost as agents died, defected to the Program, or retired.

B-cell's records have atrophied. Storage facilities were moved without notice by nervous agents or cleared out by the Program, experts became unreliable security risks or refused to cooperate, and bureaucratic contacts have withered over time.

C-cell has its hands full sifting through hints of unnatural threats and conducting extremely cautious background checks of potential recruits and surveillance of agents deemed at risk. It rarely can provide much tactical intelligence. There is no database of the Outlaws' agents and Friendlies. Whatever records exist are kept with pen and paper. Agents in the field would be distressed to learn how inaccurate those records are.

Many cells operate entirely independently. Cell leaders often must recruit new agents, pursue leads, conduct operations, and implement cover-ups using their own resources and judgment. Some cells have withered to a single, paranoid agent, unwilling to brief anyone new, waiting to die. Cell leaders sooner or later stop responding to one another, due to paranoia, retirement, or death. Changes within cells often go unacknowledged.

A-cell itself may go months or years without communicating with a given cell.

All this dysfunction is not accidental. The Outlaws' leaders are obsessed with compartmentalization. They fear investigation. They know that the less contact there is between cells, the longer it will take to infiltrate and destroy the conspiracy. They are convinced that, sooner or later, the Program will come for them, and they have positioned themselves to cut off all contacts. The Outlaws' leaders are prepared to start again from a blank slate.

Every day the conspiracy survives, however reduced it may be, is another day to complete the mission.

Agents

The Outlaws' cells are far-flung and isolated even from A-cell, but all have the same basic structure. Each member of a cell is called an agent. Agents generally know about the larger conspiracy, but not much in the way of details. There are supposed to be three agents in a cell.

Each agent has a code name assigned by the cell leader. All code names begin with the same letter as the cell's designation. For example, the agents of D-cell might be David, Dinah, and Dinesh. The code name must not be part of the agent's real name and must never be used as part of a cover identity. It is used only within the conspiracy.

Each member of a cell knows the other members of the cell by their code names and their occupations. For security, further information is not supposed to be shared. But personal bonds inevitably form, and agents often learn their cell-mates' names and the details of their personal lives.

The cell leader in a given cell is supposed to know the code name of the leader of the cell one letter up as well as one letter down in the alphabet. Cell leaders are not supposed to know each others' true identities. Sometimes, they know even less than that. Communications are unreliable. Cells often lose contact with each other entirely, and agents can only learn why if they reach out to the missing agents in other ways, violating protocol.

Furthermore, agents sometimes inadvertently encounter each other during the course of their day-to-day lives. Agents are supposed to report such contacts. Operational security dictates that agents never mention or acknowledge their association with Delta Green outside of an authorized operation.

There's no half-life to being an Outlaw. Sometimes the Outlaws lose track of individual Agents and may go years without calling on them. Sometimes an Agent is so psychologically scarred that the breaking point is just one more op away. Sometimes an Agent is catastrophically self-destructive after every meaningful relationship has been burned away by fear, anger, and addiction. None of that matters. When the call comes, the Outlaws expect the Agent to get to work.

Agent Backgrounds

The Outlaws come from diverse government agencies, mostly oriented toward law enforcement, intelligence, or counter-intelligence. A-cell prefers recruiting from agencies with law-enforcement powers, so that the agent's activities can be camouflaged under legitimate law-enforcement functions.

Some agents are researchers, bureaucrats, or technical specialists, but A-cell has always prioritized experience in criminal investigation. This is for many reasons beyond the powers of law enforcement. Such agents are usually trained in self-defense, which helps them face the dangers of Delta Green operations. This means that very few agents do not carry a badge or a gun (or both) as part of their day-to-day work.

With so many cells acting on their own, with little help from the conspiracy's leaders, new agents are recruited haphazardly. Usually it happens due to accidental exposure to the unnatural on an operation. The Outlaws' membership is weighted heavily toward the FBI, the DEA, the ATF, and the U.S. Marshals Service because those organizations are the most likely to stumble upon a cell's operations.

Only a handful are from the pre-2000s old guard, who remember the original Agent Alphonse. Those old hands know about the Program but chose not to join, and have witnessed the conspiracy's deterioration. They keep many secrets from the few newcomers.

Friendlies

Many so-called Friendlies work with the Outlaws. Most are contacts made by individual agents, people who have recognized the threat of the unnatural and helped agents confront it, others have deeper relationships to the Outlaw conspiracy.

Friendlies do not take code names and are not part of the cell structure, and they are not supposed to know of the broader conspiracy. Agents are to interact with those Friendlies the same as with all outsiders, using their real names if working under legitimate authority or using cover identities if not, and never telling Friendlies their code names. Eventually, most Friendlies learn of the illegal nature of the conspiracy.

A small minority of Friendlies are de facto agents, individuals who have participated directly in an operation. In that case, the cell leader must make it clear that they are acting without official sanction, and that resolving the situation could leave them open to criminal charges. The Outlaws want these people to fully appreciate the risks and burdens, so they don't hesitate. Such Friendlies are eventually recruited as full agents.

Friendly Backgrounds

Friendlies come from all walks of life, from a postal carrier to a retired general to a New Age bookshop storeowner. In principle, all Friendlies are monitored by C-cell, which keeps tabs on their areas of expertise, career status, and location. But what monitoring C-cell actually achieves varies wildly. A few Friendlies have lost touch with their old Delta Green contacts and worked on their own for years.

The Outlaws prefer Friendlies who are driven by the cause of saving humanity, but some are in it for the money or for favors that must be returned. The Outlaws deal with mercenaries when they must, but handle them very carefully. Nothing moves A-cell to assassination faster than former Agents or Friendlies attempting to interact with unnatural phenomena for personal gain.

GRAND RAPIDS, Mich. — An FBI agent was allegedly drunk and armed inside the Grand Rapids police station the same night his partner was arrested for firing shots at an officer.

On Dec. 6, 2016, police arrested FBI agent Ruben Hernandez for firing at a
parking lot at the Centre Point Mall. N

The Outlaws and the Program

A-cell is well aware of another government agency with an interest in the unnatural: the Program, with whom they sometimes compete. It strongly suspects that the Program makes unnatural technology and methods available to the U.S. intelligence community to maintain access to black-budget funding.

Most Outlaw agents have no idea that the Program exists, and vice versa. Those in the Program who know of the Outlaws often see them as dangerous amateurs meddling in things best left to professionals.

But the only attitudes that matter are those of six leaders: at the Program, the Director and the heads of operations and security; and in the Outlaws, A-cell. They regard each other in a state of uneasy détente and attempt to stay out of one another's way.

If an Outlaw cell or a Program team sees strangers on an operation acting like Delta Green, they alert leadership. The Program team contacts their case officer, who informs "Ops," the director of operations; the Outlaw cell leader contacts A-cell, who informs their liaison, Agent Bernard. Ops and Bernard compare notes. If they confirm that both groups are on the ground, they negotiate which team should withdraw. Sometimes A-cell is quick to let the Program take the case. More than once, an Outlaw cell has moved in to finish a mission fumbled by the Program, just as the Program has had to rush in to contain a disaster accidentally unleashed by the Outlaws.

This process usually works. There have been only a few incidents where the Outlaws were intent on destroying an artifact or specimen that the Program

DISINFORMATION

YELLOW CARD

CUT ALONG THIS LINE

THE OUTLAWS AND INTERNATIONAL GROUPS

A-cell has dealt with foreign groups that investigate the unnatural. Agents are told about them on a need-to-know basis.

M-EPIC: This Canadian organization began as an RCMP investigation of cult-related deaths. At the turn of the century, some contact and cooperation was established between Delta Green and M-EPIC, but in 2002, M-EPIC cut off all contact with the Outlaws. A-cell presumes that as an official agency of the Canadian government, M-EPIC now cooperates with the Program.

PISCES: Delta Green discovered in mid-1999 that PISCES, the United Kingdom's World War II-era program to investigate the unnatural, was still operating. However, PISCES appeared to have been infiltrated by some kind of alien intelligence that controlled human hosts like puppets. Delta Green quickly cut off contact, and the Outlaws have stayed away.

GRU SV-8: A Soviet military-intelligence unit called GRU SV-8 fought the Nazi Karotechia during World War II. GRU SV-8 currently places its expertise at the disposal of the Russian government. In 2001, Delta Green worked with GRU SV-8 to assassinate several members of the Karotechia in South America. There has been no cooperation between the Outlaws and SV-8 for several years. A-cell has heard that the leadership of GRU SV-8 now focuses on ways to adapt, weaponize, and profit from the unnatural. Whether that puts them at odds with the Program, or indicates they are working in collusion with the Program's researchers, remains unknown.

was intent on keeping. Some resulted in stand-offs and very tense escapes. None have resulted in bloodshed.

So far.

The leaders of the Program and the Outlaws understand how dedicated their agents are and avoid pitting them against each other at all costs. The best the Outlaws can do is to keep quiet enough to avoid the Program's attention. Should the Program ever decide to put an end to the Outlaws, they will have an advantage that MAJESTIC never did; after all, the Program's leadership were once the rank and file of Delta Green.

Defection

It is rare for an agent to move from the Outlaws to the Program or vice versa. Few agents from either organization know another Delta Green even exists. The two groups encounter each other infrequently.

Not surprisingly, both groups have grave concerns over defectors. If an agent from the Outlaws tries to join the Program, the Program's director of operations contacts Agent Bernard. If the agent's interest is solely in carrying on the mission with the Program's resources, and Agent Bernard has nothing ill to report, there's a chance the agent may eventually be brought into the Program. The Outlaws cut all contact with the defector, and a long period of observation begins to ensure that the agent is not intelligence gathering. It is official policy that if the defector offers to reveal the secrets of the Outlaws, the Program cuts off all contact and informs Agent Bernard. At that point, A-cell usually sanctions an operation to murder the defector. Neither side can long tolerate an agent revealing the other's secrets, but in actual day-to-day operations, it is unknown if the Program is holding up its end of this bargain.

It is even rarer for an agent of the Program to attempt to join the Outlaws, and it never succeeds. The Outlaws are more paranoid and secretive than the Program, and are keenly aware of the risks in making an enemy of the Program. The few times it has happened, the defector was rebuffed and A-cell notified the Program as per their agreement.

Operations

Since the days of the Office of Strategic Services, a covert operation against unnatural threats has been nicknamed "a Night at the Opera."

An op may come a cell's way because A-cell learned of some unnatural disturbance and sent the Agents to deal with it. Or some hint of the unnatural might catch an Agent's attention as they scour the Internet or police records for strange events. Often some other agency—such as the DEA or EPA, or a local police force—is conducting an unrelated investigation when inexplicable aspects come to the attention of a member of the conspiracy.

Briefing

An operation ordered by A-cell sometimes comes in the form of a meeting between the cell leader and a member of A-cell or B-cell. A senior agent is designated for that particular cell, so the cell leader is unlikely to ever see anyone else from A-cell or B-cell.

Whenever possible, the meeting is held someplace remote enough to avoid eavesdropping but not so remote that going there attracts attention. It must be secure against surveillance. Underground bunkers, bare cellars, bank vaults, and fallout shelters are favorite spots, but a cheap motel room given a quick search for microphones is more common. The cell leader is responsible for conveying the briefing and orders to the rest of the cell.

Many cells are handled differently, and sometimes the briefing methods change from operation to operation. A written briefing may be delivered to the cell leader at a designated dead-drop announced by some innocuous signal—three chalk lines marked on the curb may mean to check behind the loose brick in a particular alley. A written briefing is usually printed, with materials so ubiquitous as to defy investigation. Where possible, it is encrypted with a one-time pad, using a code that only the cell leader possesses, which would require laborious deciphering to render readable. Written briefings are supposed to be memorized and then thoroughly destroyed.

Pretext

Most of the time, Agents need a reason to be on the ground where they can conduct an operation. They need cover stories to explain their absences from their day jobs.

It is usually best if the "Night at the Opera" can be disguised as a legitimate operation of an Agent's regular employer, even if hastily organized and light on documentation. Sometimes, using conspiracy contacts A-cell can help embed the Agents more deeply. If not, an Agent can use Law to attempt to make things official.

This is often easier than it sounds. People attempting to manipulate unnatural forces often commit mundane, perfectly prosecutable crimes along the way. After all, someone who has committed murder to slake the bloodlust of an inhuman god won't blanch at violating import regulations or cheating on their taxes.

Cults often organize in ways that are hard to distinguish from organized crime syndicates or terrorist cells. It doesn't take much to put the FBI on the scent. Once a crime is witnessed, the Outlaws may be able to organize a raid and ensure that certain key figures die "while resisting arrest."

Once embedded in the investigation, the Agents' motivations and lines of inquiry diverge widely from those of official investigators. The Outlaws look to make the problem go away using any means necessary—they are certainly not interested in building a case for prosecution.

Contact with non-Delta Green law enforcement requires discretion. Agents often work under their own credentials. That means they must take every possible step to isolate their non-Delta Green colleagues from the unnatural. The more they can send those allies on time-consuming but inherently wrong leads, the better.

Personal Time

Many times, no easy cover pretext is available and Agents are left to formulate their own excuses. Unexpected vacations and sudden stretches of emergency sick leave may be the best they can do at work, perhaps requiring the Bureaucracy skill to work the system. A whole other set of lies may be needed to explain things at home, with a CHA or even a Persuade test if the Agent's significant other grows suspicious. So long as no Agent is killed or injured, everyone can be back at their desks on Monday morning with no one the wiser.

Unfortunately, injury, insanity, or death are common outcomes of Outlaw operations.

Cover

If the Agents don't have an official cover, they usually must work under false identities. Sometimes A-cell sends false identities for whatever federal agency is likeliest to be involved. Other times, the Agents must fend for themselves. An Agent with Criminology may be able to concoct a superficially plausible fake I.D., or find an expert in Art (Forgery) to make a better one.

Even the best false identities do not match up to the names and employment numbers of genuine federal employees. Agents should be warned: do not count on forged documents to survive anything but the most cursory review.

Green Boxes

The conspiracy often sets up private storage facilities, prepaid in long-term contracts, to hold tools, weapons, and even artifacts and evidence that cannot or should not be destroyed. It is best if a Green Box is temporary—the longer one is in place, the greater the risk that the property owner may meddle with it—but the conspiracy's disorganization means that some are abandoned for months or years at a time. With the

high turnover rate of older members of the Outlaws, it is possible dozens, if not hundreds, of such sites remain forgotten in the wild.

Funding

Sometimes, A-cell provides funds to defray the costs of travel, lodging, medical care, and so on. Occasionally the funding is surprisingly generous. More often, it's anemic or nonexistent. Funds usually arrive in the form of bricks of twenty-dollar bills, carefully wrapped in plastic and mailed overnight to a post-office box or left in a Green Box. With great luck, that drop point is nearby. Sometimes it's in another city or a nearby state.

OPERATIONAL INSTRUCTIONS

YELLOW CARD

COVER YOUR TRACKS

It is never enough to eliminate the threat. You must also keep others from discovering the threat or the actions you took to destroy it. The following tips can help. A more extensive primer, "Alphonse's Axioms for Agents," can sometimes be found. Possession of it is a direct violation of operational security.

Destroy this note after memorizing its contents.

PAPER TRAILS: Leave no "bureaucratic footprints" (digital or otherwise). You must deny or explain away evidence of unnatural activity at all times. That may include doctoring the records and files of your own agency.

CIVILIANS AND LOCAL AUTHORITIES: Gaining local cooperation is easier in some communities than in others. Study the environment before you act.

IDENTITY: Unless you're acting under the cover of some legitimate operation, never show your I.D. If you use a false I.D., remember that it won't stand up to close scrutiny.

COMMUNICATIONS: No digital information or communication system is secure. Treat everything related to Delta Green, your fellow agents, or your mission as existing in a pre-digital world.

Use no cell phones except burners with no data or GPS systems, bought as needed and destroyed after use.

Wherever possible, avoid vehicles with tracking devices.

Pay for everything in cash or by anonymous debit card.

Avoid written messages and phone conversations. If you must communicate other than face-to-face, couch everything in allusions and slang so that no one in between could decipher it. Think like a criminal and talk like a criminal.

INJURIES AND DEATHS: If necessary, stage an accident to explain an Agent's injury or death. Preventing outside investigation is mission-critical. But it is not unheard of for a cell to simply dig a shallow grave as a stopgap, so that the body may be more thoroughly dealt with later.

CUT ALONG THIS LINE

A onetime FBI agent who fed his drug addiction by stealing heroin seized as evidence in criminal cases was sentenced Thursday to three years in federal prison, a punishment far less than prosecutors and other law enforcement authorities sought.

Recruitment

Most Agents go through similar steps in recruitment. Players can fill in the details for individual Agents.

Step 1: Exposure

The recruit witnesses some deadly unnatural incursion, probably during a Delta Green operation in progress. A few agents of the conspiracy are there. Here's what the agents look for in the recruit's response:

- » The recruit recognizes that the threat is so dangerous that it needed to be concealed.
- » The recruit saves lives first and asks questions later.
- » The recruit shows stability and decisiveness in the face of inexplicable terror.

When it's over, the agents sit the recruit down for a talk. They advise leaving all references to the unnatural out of reports. They say that is in part for the recruit's own good—nobody wants to have their fitness for duty assessed by a psychological review board—and in part to save anyone else from encountering what they just faced. They say that if the recruit keeps quiet, they will answer more questions later.

Step 2: Familiar Faces

The recruit soon has another encounter with one of the agents. That agent might show up as a new member of an unrelated task force, or might come to ask the recruit's help as a consultant for some mundane case. The agent asks the recruit to be patient.

Step 3: Recurrence

The agents ask for the recruit's help in a new operation that might involve something unnatural. The agents gauge the recruit's responses. Here's what they look for in a potential agent:

- » The recruit does not panic.
- » The recruit helps keep others from being exposed to the unnatural.
- » The recruit keeps it secret. That includes not seeking explanations from a psychiatrist, boss, significant other, best friend, or priest.

Step 4: Briefing

Eventually, the agents call the recruit for a private meeting. It is completely clandestine, with convoluted instructions that eliminate any chance of being surveilled.

At the meeting, the agents share many details:

- » They are part of a clandestine network.
- » Their operations have to be kept in total secrecy.
- » The group includes other government employees who manipulate the bureaucracy to confront unnatural threats and cover them up.
- » Their work is critical to national security and, more fundamentally, human survival.

» The group has no legal sanction. How can they take their work to lawmakers when the threats are so deadly that even seeing them is dangerous?
» They need the recruit's help.
» The recruit can say no. The recruit can choose to never hear from the group again—as long as he or she keeps silent.

At that point, presumably, the recruit signs on; each player can decide why. The cell leader gives the new Agent a code name and introduces the other Agents of the cell by their code names. Finally, they share the name of the group, a name that can never be spoken aloud except to someone else in the group: Delta Green.

Instructions to Cell Leaders

A-cell issues a few instructions to most cell leaders:

» Never attempt to convince a potential recruit of the existence of the unnatural. New Agents must already believe.
» Research the potential recruit's background for signs of unreliability.
» If the recruit has the wrong temperament, cut off all contact and inform A-cell so the conspiracy can keep watch.

If a Recruit Goes Wrong

If the recruit attempts to reveal the conspiracy, the Outlaws handle it very cautiously. The other Agents must eliminate evidence that could lead investigators to anyone in the conspiracy. Next, they prepare evidence that can be planted to discredit the former recruit: illegal drugs, a false history of crackpot obsessions, hard drives full of deviant pornography, apparent attempts to contact foreign intelligence services or share classified data with the public, and so on. The Agents state their case in private in one last effort to persuade the recruit to keep their secrets. If the recruit goes forward anyway, the Agents discredit the recruit with damning evidence of instability and bad action. Individual Agents that the recruit accuses of some outlaw conspiracy play the baffled martyrs until it blows over. The Outlaws then keep those Agents away from future ops for as long as possible.

Asking A-Cell

There are no ranks or levels of initiation in the Outlaws. Information is not controlled by security clearances. A-cell shares only what knowledge is absolutely required to deal with a threat—and sometimes a cell operates almost entirely on its own, with minimal contact. In other words, A-cell can tell the Agents as much or as little about an operation, and provide as much or as little help, as the Handler wants.

General Requests

During an investigation, Agents can make a general request for information. This request is made by the cell leader to A-cell, and should include a report on the current situation. The preferred form of communication is mail sent overnight to a frequently changing post-office box or safe-house address, with a call via burner phone to a remote answering service for notification. A-cell may check their records and contact other agents who have had similar experiences. Or A-cell may not respond at all. When you as Handler are in doubt, resolve it with a Luck roll.

If A-cell responds, the agent gets a briefing call or an express parcel in 48 to 72 hours. The information can be provided by A-cell, or it can come directly from a fellow agent or Friendly. Note, however, that the interpretations A-cell makes in deciding what files are relevant may be faulty. For that matter, there may be surface similarities but nothing more. A-cell is far from infallible.

Specific Requests

Agents can also make specific requests. Such requests are usually for mundane information. Examples might include personnel files on government employees, classified documents, immigration records, or a particular piece of history or folklore. Specific requests are usually filled in 12 to 18 hours (when they're filled at all), not counting the time it takes to physically transport materials to the Agents.

Do not let players treat such requests as a crutch. Support from A-cell is an important part of the campaign and the Handler shouldn't make it worthless, but Agents who barrage A-cell with requests receive a stern warning. The more contact there is between A-cell and individual Agents, the greater the risk of interception. Eventually, A-cell will learn to ignore a cell that relies too heavily on such information exchange, and future requests might only be met with stony silence.

Conclusion

The Outlaws' continued survival hinges on secrecy, and in particular on keeping out of the Program's way. To those in the Outlaws who know the Program and its history, it is just MAJESTIC wearing Delta Green's skin.

Unfortunately, the Outlaws' and the Program's field operations occasionally overlap. Both tend to focus on unnatural threats generated by human activity, particularly cult-related activity. History has shown that a handful of marginalized fanatics are capable of wreaking destruction, whether it is in Innsmouth or in Cambodia. The actions of lone maniacs with unnatural interests can lead to catastrophic events. The difference is that where the Outlaws end such activity with a bullet, the Program seeks to capture, so it might learn the methods used by its quarry. Someday, the two groups' missions are going to come into direct conflict. The Outlaws look to postpone that day as long as possible.

The Outlaws' future is uncertain. The average age of an Agent is going up. The pace of operations has decreased. And when agents of the Outlaws learn of the Program, they sometimes defect. Some agents believe that the Outlaws are already finished. A few fear a fratricidal war with the Program. For all its precautions, the Outlaws are vulnerable to compromise should even a single cell fail. A-cell must weigh the requirements for each operation carefully—the vital intelligence and manpower necessary to complete a mission with a minimum of danger must be balanced against the need for secrecy.

Important Individuals: The Outlaws

The leaders of the Outlaws are as fractious and troubled as their organization. For Friendlies and new Agents, they put up a pretense of cohesion and long-term planning. That never persists for long. The importance of the mission, the insidiousness of the unnatural, and their own isolation twist their perceptions and reactions. Their mission is confronting the unnatural, but the threat most on their minds is betrayal. Trust is a luxury none of the Outlaws can afford.

Donald Poe

By all rights, Donald Poe should be dead. A poor kid from rural New York, Poe joined the U.S. Army in 1964 and ended up with the Military Assistance Command, Vietnam—Studies and Observations Group (MACV-SOG). His introduction to Delta Green was in the 1969 Operation OBSIDIAN in Cambodia, the operation that led to Delta Green's official disbandment. Poe and those few who didn't die during the manifestation of the Black Buddha, or in the follow-on ARC LIGHT strike, crawled back to South Vietnam and tracked down USMC Col. Satchel Wade, the insane ex-Delta Green leader who had sent them out. But killing Wade and cleaning up his mess did not stop the Pentagon from closing the whole madhouse down.

After the war, Poe lost a few years to drink and drugs. Then Delta Green, despite its official deactivation, came calling. Reginald Fairfield and Joe Camp gave Poe a mission he could believe in. He cleaned himself up. In the 1980s, they pulled strings to get him a job at the FBI, where no amount of grooming could help him fit in. He chased drug dealers and worked Delta Green operations on the side. Poe cut his teeth during the "Cowboy Years," when former members of the group executed missions as they saw fit and had few official resources to protect themselves. Within a few years, Poe and the FBI were finished with each other.

In 1994, when Fairfield died and the group was on the verge of disintegration, Joe Camp showed them all there was a better way.

Poe never saw himself as command material. He was just the guy A-cell could count on. Then, in 2001, when Camp vanished and things went FUBAR, he found that Camp had given him access to all of A-cell's data and resources. No apprenticeship. No mentoring. Donald Poe, the new leader of A-cell, was tossed into the deep end to sink or swim.

When Donald Poe became Alphonse, he was painfully aware he'd spent his Delta Green career as a door-kicker, and that this "master conspirator" stuff was way above his pay grade. For a decade, Poe kept an eye out for someone better suited to the job. He isn't looking anymore.

If there's one thing Donald Poe has learned in nearly fifty years of serving Delta Green, it's that the mission is never over. Once you're in Delta Green, you are in for life. Just like Reginald Fairfield. Just like Joe Camp. You don't pass the torch. They recover it from your corpse.

Poe typically interacts with Agents using his old code name, "Agent Charlie," presenting himself as the emissary of a never-seen Agent Alphonse. In actuality he is also Agent Alphonse. He figures the rank and file would be more comfortable imagining their leader as a latter-day Professor Moriarty rather than a past-his-prime jarhead sniper. He sometimes ignores his own careful rules of contact, bypassing McRay, Wu, and Furst out of fear of betrayal.

Poe does not think of the Outlaws as a faction. They are Delta Green. Whatever Forrest James commands, it's not Delta Green, just some bastard child of MAJESTIC. Poe has abandoned all sentimentality regarding the widening gulf between the two groups. In the old days, Poe had been to the Opera with Forrest James and knew that Joe Camp had relied on him. That Forrest James is gone. When James took control of MAJESTIC, he agreed to leave Delta Green alone while MAJESTIC dealt with extraterrestrial threats. A year later, he launched the Program—his own Delta Green—and poached every agent he could put his hand to. Since then, they've had long years of uneasy truce, occasionally speaking through anonymous, encrypted connections. Both are aware that it could come to blood. Both are aware that, sooner or later, the other side is going to become the mission. Poe is pretty sure that the next time he sees Forrest James, it's going to be through a scope.

Poe keeps a collection of unnatural artifacts, files, photos, and documents—a carefully-curated archive of impossible nightmares—in a Cold War era fallout shelter on his property in the Allegheny Mountains of eastern Pennsylvania. The entrance is padlocked and all but invisible under thick underbrush. Poe enters by a tunnel beneath the house, hidden in a basement workshop behind a false wall (a trick picked up from Fairfield). The bunker also stores a wide assortment of heavy weaponry and a pallet of approximately eight million dollars in plastic-wrapped bricks of twenty-dollar bills: the Outlaws' operational budget, courtesy of the early exuberance of the War on Terror. Only Poe has access to the bunker.

His house is loaded with every kind of weapon known to man. Even in rural Pennsylvania, the arsenal would raise eyebrows. Poe goes to great lengths to avoid anyone taking an interest. A steel gate with a "Keep Out" sign discourages proselytizers, and barbed wire runs from either side of the gate around the property's perimeter. A small pack of guard dogs roams the grounds, trained to ignore ordinary forest smells and sounds but to raise havoc at the slightest hint of an intruder. By instinct, they stay away from the bunker.

Poe tries to never give the county sheriff or state police a reason to visit. He tries to stay out of trouble.

He doesn't always succeed.

Poe sees threats everywhere. Despite his best efforts, the old man has had meaningless confrontations and bloody fights in the nearest town. Worse, in 2015, two intruders wandered through his property one night, alerting the dogs. Poe, drunk and certain they were scouts for the Program, stalked them for a half an hour before killing both. Then he recognized their strange coats were varsity jackets from a nearby high school. He did what had to be done to cover it up. Philadelphia police found the teenagers' burned-out car later that month. The case went cold, and detectives stopped following up. Poe sometimes goes down to the river where he cut the boys up and buried them. He thinks about how far off the path he has gone, and what Joe Camp might think of him, now.

Still—there's the mission…

Donald Poe could once have been mistaken for the Minotaur, presuming his horns were hidden beneath a John Deere cap. At nearly 2.0 meters (6'5") tall and 136 kg (299 lbs), he could be said with charity to have a face like a fist and fists like boulders. A nasty, jagged scar runs down the side of his wrinkled, harsh face. Every year turns a little more muscle to fat and leaves him a little more stooped and hard of hearing. He can't run worth shit anymore, and a flight of stairs—which he used to take two at a time with a sixty-pound pack—are enough to leave him a wheezing mess. He wears his thinning white hair and thick white beard long. He prefers work boots, a black T-shirt, blue jeans and camo-fatigue jackets. He usually looks like he might be coming back from a deer blind, deep in the woods, and in fact he may have; he spends a lot of time hunting, thinking, and trying to soothe what's left of his long-battered nerves. His outfit is deliberate in another way. One of the best lessons the Viet Cong taught Donald Poe was that you should never, ever look like you are the one in charge.

Donald Poe

Agent Alphonse/Agent Charlie, age 73.

STR 15 **CON** 9 **DEX** 12 **INT** 14 **POW** 13 **CHA** 9

HP 12 **WP** 13 **SAN** 37 **BREAKING POINT** 26

BONDS: Curtis McRay (Agent Bernard), 5.

MOTIVATIONS AND DISORDERS: Living up to Joseph Camp's legacy.

Keeping the real Delta Green from being absorbed by the Program.

Doing this job right so nobody else has to.

Paranoia.

Sleep disorder.

Adapted to violence.

SKILLS: Alertness 69%, Athletics 41%, Bureaucracy 38%, Computer Science 20%, Demolitions 63%, Dodge 52%, Drive 44%, Firearms 93%, First Aid 41%, Foreign

Language (Spanish) 32%, Foreign Language (Vietnamese) 20%, Heavy Weapons 40%, HUMINT 44%, Law 41%, Melee Weapons 73%, Military Science (Land) 67%, Navigate 79%, Occult 20%, Science (Chemistry) 20%, Search 76%, Stealth 71%, Swim 42%, Survival 66%, Unarmed Combat 72%, Unnatural 26%.

SPECIAL TRAINING: Lockpicking (DEX), Parachuting (DEX), SCUBA gear (Swim).

ATTACKS: Ka-Bar combat knife 73%, damage 1D6+1.

Beretta M9 pistol 93%, damage 1D10.

M-40A5 suppressed sniper rifle 93%, damage 1D12+2.

MP5SD3 submachine gun 93%, damage 1D10 or Lethality 10%.

Unarmed 72%, damage 1D4.

UNNATURAL ARTIFACTS: Dust of the Thresholds (3 doses), Elder Sign (engraved on a 20-kg cement block), Powder of Ibn-Ghazi (5 doses).

UNNATURAL DOCUMENTS: *Azathoth and Other Horrors* (see page 156), Greg Mason's surveillance videos (see page 158), Gunter Frank's research notes (see page 159), Joseph Camp's grimoire (see page 160), Matthew Carpenter's Delta Green files (see page 161), *The People of the Monolith* (see page 162), *The Seven Cryptical Books of Hsan* (see page 163).

Emil Furst

Valedictorian of West Point's class of '75, Emil Furst went into the Special Forces, which was seen at the time—when the U.S. Army was at its nadir—as a bastion of warrior professionalism. Four years later, a covert special-operations unit, the Intelligence Support Activity, recruited him. His missions took him to Africa, the Middle East, and Latin America, doing intelligence work too secret for even the CIA. His career soared. In 1989, however, Lt. Col. Furst discovered a struggle far more primal than the Cold War.

Furst was leading an ISA team disguised as Ugandan soldiers in Uganda, searching for Joseph Kony, leader of the Lord's Resistance Army. They discovered thousands converging on a community on the shores of Lake Edward, where a "magical" cure for AIDS had been discovered. They encountered a cult of Glaaki, recruiting the terminally ill. The discovery cost the life of every member of the team except Furst.

Wounded and half mad, Furst wandered for weeks before he was found by Tutsi tribesmen in Rwanda. Over the next two years, he recovered, and studied at the feet of an ancient and powerful Tutsi shaman. With newfound power, he returned and destroyed the Glaaki cultists. But he failed to destroy the gate beneath Lake Edward that permitted Glaaki to manifest.

When Furst returned to civilization, he told his superiors what happened. Their response was a medical discharge and a trip to a V.A. mental hospital. He suffered six months of pharmacological restraint before Delta Green sprung him. Furst worked for them as Agent Matthew, but on his terms. He was in no hurry to return to being a "deniable asset." For a decade Furst was homeless, below the radar, only surfacing to cooperate with Delta Green when it suited him.

In 1999, Furst was pursuing Glaaki cultists operating as Bible Belt faith healers, and he needed extra firepower. He got the help of renegade Delta Green agent Forrest James, on a crusade of his own. Whatever happened between them, when James formed the Program out of MAJESTIC's wreckage three years later, Furst came into the fold at last—by joining A-cell and keeping its secrets away from the Program.

As A-cell's expert on hypergeometry, Furst is the man who decides what, if any, of such "technology" should be deployed during an operation. He sometimes guides Agents who encounter powerful secrets, and usually takes possession of those secrets.

By 2006, he began to see his personal mastery of unnatural rituals as Delta Green's only real hope—and then, he found the answer. A book was brought to him after one of the conspiracy's operations. This small journal, penned in a spidery script, contained several strange and intriguing things. Once he broke the initial code, the first line filled him with a greed he thought he could no longer feel. It read: "Of the First Secret. A book and instruction on the opening of the wall to free the sleeper, bane to the horned god, G'laak."

Furst spent ten years deciphering this new weapon against Glaaki. Twice he believed he was close, and each time, he found another layer of code. Finally, in 2016, without informing the rest of A-cell, Furst enacted the ritual of the First Secret. He communed with an intelligence that told him more about Glaaki than he could process. He has communed with the First Secret three times, and has used this intelligence to nudge A-cell in particular directions.

Furst has not yet noticed the string of spree murders that strike nearby each time he enacts the ritual of the First Secret. It is clear to all who know him that Furst is slowly coming apart at the seams, but Donald Poe—A-cell's leader and his only real friend—has no idea what action to take.

Col. Furst stands two meters tall (6'5") and weighs in at 104 kg (230 lbs) of muscle, bone, and scar tissue. He is missing his left eye and part of his ear, and ragged scars furrow his nose and brow. His dark skin throws those scars into stark relief. An eye-patch covers the ragged hole in his face. His personal grooming and attire tends towards the paramilitary, looking freshly pressed and starched, but with African occult fetishes hidden beneath his fatigues. He keeps his gray hair buzzed short. Delta Green acquaintances from his youth often have trouble recognizing the man who once resembled a homeless tramp in dreadlocks and a matted beard.

Lt. Col. Emil Furst, U.S. Army (ret.)

Agent Aaron, ruthless warrior-shaman, age 62.

STR 15 **CON** 12 **DEX** 10 **INT** 18 **POW** 16 **CHA** 11

HP 14 **WP** 16 **SAN** 39 **BREAKING POINT** 24

BONDS: Donald Poe, 7.

MOTIVATIONS AND DISORDERS: Correcting the mistakes of the past.

Saving the innocent from the Unnatural.

Obsession with the "First Secret."

Depression.

Totemic compulsion (expressed through African fetishes).

Adapted to violence and helplessness.

ASSETS: Emil Furst's Artifacts

Furst usually carries these tools at the bottom of an Army-issue duffle bag, underneath most of his other worldly possessions.

FETISH NECKLACE

Made of beads, claws, teeth, and feathers, this bulky necklace—it cannot be concealed except under something like a trench coat—causes arrows, thrown objects, and other low-velocity projectiles to miss the wearer completely. High-velocity projectiles such as bullets suffer a –20% chance to hit. Hand-held melee weapons are not affected. Each time an attack misses that would otherwise have hit, the wearer loses 0/1 SAN due to the Unnatural.

SCEPTER OF POWER

A short wooden scepter of indeterminate age, engraved with ancient symbols that defy anthropological or linguistic interpretation. Furst keeps it carefully wrapped in cloth to avoid accidentally touching it. Anyone grasping the scepter with a bare hand gains 3D6 WP and loses 1D4 SAN. The bonus WP last until used or, if unused, until the next sunrise. A wielder who has 10 or more SAN and succeeds at an Unnatural test also realizes instinctively that he or she may also choose to gain 1 POW, permanently, at the cost of another 10 SAN. After it confers the bonus WP, the scepter loses all power until the next sunrise.

SKYMETAL MACHETE

This broad-bladed implement, kept in a battered wooden scabbard, is made from intricately-engraved meteoric iron, with a handle of human bone. For the purpose of determining damage, every hit with it counts as critical, inflicting 2D8 rather than 1D8. (Rolling a critical inflicts no additional damage.) It has been found to harm some extradimensional entities that were otherwise immune to physical weapons. Harming such an entity with the machete costs the wielder 0/1 SAN due to the Unnatural.

SKILLS: Alertness 63%, Anthropology 34%, Athletics 86%, Dodge 54%, Firearms 73%, First Aid 39%, Foreign Language (Arabic) 22%, Foreign Language (Rwanda-Rundi) 25%, Foreign Language (Spanish) 44%, Foreign Language (Swahili) 63%, Heavy Weapons 50%, HUMINT 40%, Melee Weapons 88%, Military Science (Land) 52%, Navigate 63%, Occult 68%, Persuade 66%, Search 51%, SIGINT 50%, Stealth 82%, Survival 49%, Swim 57%, Unarmed Combat 63%, Unnatural 28%.

SPECIAL TRAINING: Parachuting (DEX).

ATTACKS: H&K P30 .40 pistol 73%, damage 1D10.
Skymetal machete 88%, damage 2D8+1.
Colt M4 carbine 73%, damage 1D12.
Hand grenade 86%, Lethality 15%.
Unarmed 63%, damage 1D4.

RITUALS: Call Zombies, The Closing of the Breach (Azathoth, Hunting-Horrors, Shub-Niggurath, Yog-Sothoth), Exaltation of the Flesh, Exorcism, The First Secret, Finding, Healing Balm, One Who Passes the Gateways, Release Breath, See the Other Side, Song of Power, Soothing Song, Speaking Dream, Speech of Birds and Beasts.

Chun-te Wu

The son of Taiwanese immigrants, Chun-te Wu earned degrees in computer science and law from the University of Southern California, and then landed a job as a special agent for the IRS Criminal Investigations Division in 1973. For twenty years, he was one of the top investigators of international financial crimes and an innovator of information systems. When the Financial Crimes Enforcement Network (FinCEN) was set up in 1990, Wu became one of its charter officers. He retired in 2016 as the Director for Information Technology for the Treasury Department's Office of Terrorism and Financial Intelligence.

Wu's eyes were opened to the existence of the unnatural in 1986, during an audit of a politically connected international corporation called Whole Earth Enterprises (WEE). After months of investigation, a company executive contacted Wu claiming that his employer's tax evasion, money laundering, and financing of international terrorism were directed by a diabolical inner circle of occultists. Doubtful, Wu went to meet this informant. He arrived just in time to see something impossible pull the screaming man through a hole in reality. Under congressional pressure, Wu's superiors disbanded his unit and reassigned him.

Exposing WEE became Wu's pet project. He hacked his way into their subsidiaries, and pulled their tax filings and articles of incorporation. He abused his power as an IRS agent. The inadmissibility of the evidence he gathered continued to frustrate him, until he encountered Delta Green agents working in parallel. The agents weren't concerned with legality or admissibility; they just wanted to know if Wu could "identify a target." When he showed them what he knew about WEE and pointed out what looked like targets, they took them out. It was never enough to shut WEE down, but it saved lives.

Wu was in.

For many years Chun-te Wu acted as a Delta Green Friendly. He didn't participate directly. Instead he conducted research, provided logistical support, and penetrated information systems. He used government resources to identify and recruit unwitting "tiger teams" of computer security experts to work for Delta Green. His recruits ranged from anarchist college kids to engineering professionals who'd become genuine computer criminals. Contacted through cut-outs, these mercenaries never knew who they were working for. To this day, he maintains these contacts.

That was as close as Chun-te wanted to get to Delta Green. When the Program launched in 2002, Wu kept his distance. The people he knew—among them Donald Poe and Curtis McRay—refused to come in from the cold, and he followed suit. He understood the critical importance of Delta Green's mission, but he had a family. He had normality.

All that changed in 2010 with a traffic accident that claimed the lives of his wife and two daughters. Their deaths left Wu hollow. He'd dedicated his life to keeping his family safe, and all it took to kill them was an underage drunk racing in her father's SUV. Since that day, the only meaningful thing in Wu's life has been Delta Green. Donald Poe and Emil Furst had relied on him from the beginning for information, illicit funding, and infrastructure, so they brought him into A-cell as Agent Anton. Wu sometimes meets

Agents in the field, acting as A-cell's representative. It would be smarter to restrict his involvement to missions that require his unique skills, but Wu becomes more bitterly careless with every year.

Chun-te Wu is a Taiwanese-American man with gray hair and black eyes, 1.7 m tall (5'9") and weighing 73 kg (160 Ibs). His once attractive, emotive features have collapsed into a limp, expressionless mask. His dead-eyed focus is intimidating, even to the hardened Agents. He joylessly chain-smokes unfiltered cigarettes. Anyone who asks him to stop smoking earns a withering stare, a face-full of smoke, or both. Once, when told that every cigarette was another nail in his coffin, Wu is alleged to have said, "That's the fucking point."

Chun-te Wu

Agent Anton, digital virtuoso who is all out of fucks, age 67.

STR 7 **CON** 8 **DEX** 10 **INT** 17 **POW** 14 **CHA** 11

HP 8 **WP** 14 **SAN** 41 **BREAKING POINT** 40

BONDS: None.

MOTIVATIONS AND DISORDERS: Making his own justice.

Ends, not means.

Uncovering secrets.

Depression.

Addiction (chain-smoking).

Adapted to helplessness.

SKILLS: Accounting 94%, Bureaucracy 63%, Criminology 87%, Computer Science 89%, Craft (Electronics) 93%, Drive 35%, Firearms 42%, Foreign Language (Mandarin) 95%, History 41%, HUMINT 61%, Law 88%, Occult 54%, Persuade 67%, SIGINT 81%, Unnatural 16%.

ATTACKS: Walther PPQ pistol 42%, damage 1D10.

Unarmed 40%, damage 1D4−2.

Curtis McRay

Curtis McRay joined the FBI as a special agent in 1985, straight out of law school at Rutgers. He cut his teeth in the Organized Crime Division in New York, New Jersey, and Rhode Island. In the 1990s, McRay discovered that the bed-time stories that New York's criminals told after last call were true. There was a second underworld called the Network, led by a cult called the Fate. McRay holds the unique distinction as the only man ever to kill Stephen Alzis and live. For his part, Alzis called the incident "a misunderstanding between two friends."

McRay would have gone the way of so many who'd previously interfered with Alzis if not for the intervention of Donald Poe and Joseph Camp. By ransoming Stephen Alzis's personal photo album (which included images of the unchanging Alzis as far back as the invention of the first cameras in the 19th century), McRay, Poe and Camp worked out an "armistice" with Alzis. When the Fate began to self-destruct less than ten years later, McRay and Poe were there as well. But they refuse to speak about it, even between themselves.

For a decade, Curtis McRay and Donald Poe—as Agent Cyrus and Agent Charlie—worked the deadliest operations that Joe Camp's Delta Green ever fielded. A strong bond of loyalty still exists between the two. When Poe took over from Camp in 2001, he put McRay in charge of B-cell to reorganize the conspiracy and root out the lingering influence of MAJESTIC.

When the Program launched in 2002, McRay faced a hard choice. Many of his trusted colleagues signed up—including fellow FBI Special Agent Abe Mannen (Agent Thomas), whom McRay recruited during a particularly bad operation in 1994. Poe saw the Program as a betrayal and would go nowhere near it, and McRay couldn't leave Poe behind. McRay and Mannen became the primary points of contact between the Program and the Outlaws. They know each other well enough to want to trust each other, but they're both experienced and cynical enough never to let that trust get too deep.

McRay has always acted as consigliere for A-cell, and is one of Donald Poe's few connections. As Agent

Bernard, he oversees the conspiracy's lists of storage facilities and its most reliable and experienced Friendlies. He checks backgrounds and keeps track of agents and Friendlies. He assists with tradecraft and cover-ups. For some cells, he is the point of contact with A-cell.

But he is spread so thin, and the Outlaws' communications are so slow, that he grows a little less effective at all those tasks with each passing year. Even relying on the other members of B-cell, who are a decade younger and who still have full bureaucratic access and contacts, only goes so far. McRay has warned A-cell many times that their rejection of modern communications is causing the dissolution of the conspiracy.

McRay turned 57 on 7 MAR 2017, and under FBI regulations he was forced to retire. Few of the fellow agents that ate cake at his retirement party had any idea of his real history. He had spent the last few years in the records department at FBI Headquarters in Washington, D.C. But his experience with the FBI would have been called "storied," if anyone knew enough to say so. Despite clearing many "impossible" cases for the FBI, he never brought in as many prosecutable cases as his superiors would have liked. For McRay, this became more a blessing than a curse. Seen as a has-been (or a never-was), McRay was able to move through the FBI like a shade. He learned FBI headquarters and Quantico inside and out, and developed excellent intelligence on the power players there. His access (authorized or not) to field reports put McRay in a unique position to look for new missions and potential recruits for Delta Green. Now, on the other side of retirement, he helps his B-cell colleagues swim in those waters.

Retired after 32 years in the FBI, McRay draws a pension that is more than enough to support him. Donald Poe reminds him often that he's now free to devote every hour of every day to Delta Green. McRay can't admit to Poe, or anyone else in the group, that he's not sure he can keep doing it. He is worn out. It has been decades since he had a stable relationship, or even maintained serious interests, outside Delta Green.

McRay long ago learned to substitute oxycodone for more time-consuming forms of stress relief. Two months after his retirement, Baltimore police pulled him over for erratic driving and found a stash that he'd boosted from drug dealers. "Ex-FBI agent caught with 10,000 painkillers." He pled down to a misdemeanor, but gossip rags had a field day. A-cell began keeping him at arm's length, leaving him with far too much time for reflection. But he has slowly regained A-cell's trust.

However, this addiction did not go away. Worse, he has worked out deals to use the storage facilities that he catalogs and maintains for the Outlaws as places for third-rate drug dealers to stash loads of pills. Most of these old Green Boxes (almost all located near the Canadian border) are long-emptied of their questionable contents, but that doesn't mean they couldn't be traced back to their previous renters. In exchange for access to this network of drug stashes, McRay receives an endless supply of "medicine," as well as various kick-backs from criminals that keep him comfortable. The world is too fucked up for him to feel bad about it for very long.

He sometimes thinks about faking his death, perhaps on a some half-assed operation where new, gullible agents can be convinced they saw it happen. He also wondered if chasing a few dozen painkillers with a tumbler of Scotch would be easier in the long run.

He often suspects that the agents who went to the Program had the right idea, after all.

Standing 1.88 m (6'2") and weighing 75 kg (165 lbs), McRay is a thin, gawky man with a slender face, topped with shaggy gray hair. His blue eyes are hidden behind thick-framed glasses. Even wearing his habitual suit and tie, he projects a kind of gracelessness. But he is intense, serious, and driven. He always wears a light Kevlar vest under his shirt and carries a pistol everywhere he can.

Curtis McRay

Agent Bernard, front-man for A-cell, age 57.

STR 9 **CON** 11 **DEX** 10 **INT** 16 **POW** 14 **CHA** 12

HP 10 **WP** 14 **SAN** 46 **BREAKING POINT** 40

BONDS: Donald Poe ("Agent Alphonse"), 8.

Mother, Dolores McRay, 4.

Younger brother, Leon McRay, 4.

MOTIVATIONS AND DISORDERS: Never letting Donald Poe down.

Finding a new generation to do this shit job.

Protecting Delta Green.

Addiction (opiates).

Anxiety disorder.

Adapted to violence and helplessness.

SKILLS: Accounting 59%, Alertness 67%, Anthropology 28%, Athletics 63%, Computer Science 36%, Criminology 54%, Drive 68%, Electronics 34%, Firearms 66%, History 39%, HUMINT 89% Law 57%, Occult 68%, Persuade 48%, Psychotherapy 42%, Search 71%, Stealth 51%, Unarmed Combat 60%, Unnatural 18%.

ATTACKS: SIG Sauer P228 pistol 66%, damage 1D10.

Unarmed 60%, damage 1D4−1.

Mossburg 12-gauge shotgun 66%, damage 2D10 (or 2D6 or 1D6).

Colt M4 carbine 66%, damage 1D12.

Edna Knotts

Edna Knotts joined the Air Force Office of Special Investigations soon after she graduated from the U.S. Air Force Academy in 1985, specializing in counterintelligence. She was seconded to the Central Intelligence Agency in 1990, ultimately joining in 1991 (a rare achievement in that age of post-Cold War budget cuts and organizational malaise). Once she was deployed overseas, she found herself having to invent work. In the decade before 9/11, Knotts spent her time recruiting and running unauthorized agents for the Agency. She nevertheless excelled at creating relationships, understanding what to be to her targets and how to give them what they needed. She was particularly adept at recruiting agents who never knew they were working for the CIA. Her agents thought that they were working for journalists, criminal organizations, corporate bagmen, political activists, missionaries and even international aid organizations.

During her stint at the CIA's Western Mediterranean operations center, Knotts had her first encounter with the unnatural. A team of Delta Green agents was pursuing one of her off-the-books assets, and she got caught in the crossfire. She kept her head, her sanity, and her job at the CIA, and Delta Green recruited her. In 1994, when Alphonse reorganized the conspiracy, Knotts became Agent Green, and worked closely with G-cell agents Graham and Grendel. A-cell soon came to rely on her ability to recruit. Many old hands remember "Agent Green" as their first point of contact.

When the Program launched in 2002, Knotts refused to join. Better to leave dealing with the unnatural to a tightly-knit brotherhood than an ever-shifting bureaucracy. A-cell had her take over C-cell, which it tasked with research. At first, Knotts thought that was a misuse of her experience, but that wasn't the case.

Knotts is still an ace recruiter, but her product is unnatural intelligence. She runs a network of informants throughout the U.S. government, academia, and the private sector. Some of them send word of weird events. Some debunk claims of the supernatural, and are interested in claims that can't be easily debunked. Some conduct deep, academic research into offbeat areas of anthropology, history, medicine, psychology, or parapsychology. Few of Knotts' spies think they're working with anyone but her. Most consider her a friend who has a keen interest in the weird. Only a handful know enough to even count as Friendlies. Knotts compiles tips, vets them, and sends the ones worth investigating to A-cell.

At the moment, her most puzzling source is an anonymous one. For two years now, she has been receiving encrypted data packages from inside the Program. They arrive without explanation. Whoever the source is, they keep finding her, even when she changes devices. Sometimes it's intel on disaffected Program agents. Sometimes it's intel on Program operations that are about to begin, or that ended inconclusively. Sometimes she is warned that the Program is interested in particular Outlaw assets or personnel. So far, the intel checks out. The questions Knotts can't answer are who, how and why. In the meantime, she has code-named the source "Secret Santa."

Knotts works often with Agent Bernard, whom she knows from the old days by his real name and by his old C-cell code name. At his request, she may help Agents determine whether a potential recruit is reliable. And there may come a day when Bernard, sensing A-cell's instability, begins deliberately trying to reduce their involvement. He'll need an intermediary of his own, and Agent Charlotte is his first choice.

She often observes that at 54, she's the youngster of Delta Green's leadership. Knotts suspects that slowly, year by year, the conspiracy is dying. It's not just that its average age keeps going up; the conspiracy has adopted a model of secrecy by which it cannot readily adapt. More and more, things slip. Public revelation of everything she has fought to conceal may be inevitable. If it is, then what has been the point?

Knotts is still a CIA case officer, but works mostly out of Langley. She lives in Chevy Chase, Maryland with her wife Maxine Isaacs, a State Department employee who has no idea about Delta Green. Isaacs blames Knotts' recurring, deepening depression on burnout from her demanding CIA career, and says retirement is long overdue. Knotts is deadly serious about not revealing the real reasons for her burnout. She would kill to keep her wife from knowing about Delta Green.

Edna Knotts looks a decade younger than her half-century. A dark-skinned African-American, with a broad, friendly face that encourages people to trust her, she stands 1.7 m tall (5'8") and weighs 60 kg (132 lbs). For the longest time, she wore her hair in long dreadlocks—after all, what kind of a spy wears dreadlocks?—but these days, she keeps her hair in short, tightly braided rows that are not so easy to grab.

Edna Knotts, CIA Case Officer

Agent Charlotte, researcher and recruiter, age 54.

STR 9 **CON** 12 **DEX** 11 **INT** 18 **POW** 15 **CHA** 16

HP 11 **WP** 15 **SAN** 50 **BREAKING POINT** 45

BONDS: Wife, Maxine Isaacs, 16.

Mentor, retired CIA case officer Ronald Abbot, 10.

Ex-girlfriend, CIA colleague, Mallory Klein, 8.

MOTIVATIONS AND DISORDERS: Understanding people's motivations.

Protecting her wife from the truth.

Staying ahead of the threats.

Excelling in spite of bureaucratic inertia.

Depression.

SKILLS: Alertness 58%, Athletics 71%, Bureaucracy 69%, Computer Science 33%, Criminology 75%, Disguise 92%, Drive 56%, Firearms 71%, HUMINT 86%, Persuade 89%, Search 66%, Stealth 71%, Swim 43%, Unarmed Combat 55%, Unnatural 23%.

ATTACKS: SIG Sauer P226 pistol 71%, damage 1D10.

Unarmed 55%, damage 1D4−1.

Grant Emerson, Ph.D.

Born in Epsom, England, in 1952, Emerson received a degree in zoology from Cambridge in 1973 and then did volunteer work for a year in Kenya. Having seen the problems associated with "exotic" diseases, he returned to Britain and gained a Ph.D. from Edinburgh University in 1977, studying the replication of rinderpest virus. In postdoctoral work, he studied dengue and yellow fever at the London School of Hygiene and Tropical Medicine, and later worked on hemorrhagic fever viruses at CBDE Porton Down. Eventually he received a traveling fellowship to Walter Reed Army Hospital in Bethesda, Maryland, where he gained a faculty position and worked on New World Arenaviruses. He accepted a chair at the Institute of Tropical Medicine at the University of North Carolina, Chapel Hill, in 1990, where he has been based ever since. His research remains focused on the mechanisms of pathogen transmission between species and the pathogenesis of hemorrhagic shock and fever.

Emerson first became involved with Delta Green in the summer of 1992. While investigating a suspected outbreak of viral hemorrhagic fever in rural New Mexico, he witnessed the attack of a gaseous creature which seemed to draw blood out of its victims through their skin. His assistance to the Delta Green team paved the way for his involvement in other operations, and he became a valuable ally.

Emerson has connections and clearances with biological research agencies around the world, including the CDC, USAMRIID, and Walter Reed in the U.S.; CBDE, CAMR, and PHLS in the U.K.; the WHO in Switzerland; and the Institut Pasteur in France. His experience with extreme biohazards is both unusual and invaluable, and he has at his disposal one of the few civilian biosafety level 4 laboratories in the nation. That makes unconventional research much easier.

When the Program launched in 2002, they tried to recruit Emerson by emphasizing the research and development that they would perform. Emerson had interviewed Forrest James before in a study of the so-called Deep Ones, and James expected him to join. But this argument was precisely what persuaded him to stay away. He trusted the Outlaws' old policy of studying phenomena only insofar as it advances the goal of eradication. As an expert in infectious diseases, Emerson is painfully aware of the risks involved in weaponizing even the natural viruses he has fought against his whole career. Weaponizing the unnatural promises a vastly more destructive spectrum of horrors.

Seeing the expansion of the U.S. biodefense industry, Emerson launched his own consultancy, Emerging Organisms Solutions (EOS), in 2008. EOS advises on biodefense, bioweapon inspection programs, and biocontainment lab design and operation, and trains medical and research professionals about the hazards of emerging microorganisms. Emerson remains an emeritus professor at UNC, but devotes most of his time to running EOS. He splits his time between Raleigh and a comfortable retreat in Maine, and frequently travels abroad for conferences and research.

Emerson rarely takes part in the Outlaws' operations, instead working in a support role from the laboratory. Following a messy divorce, his personal life is quiet. He still lives in Raleigh. When his two border collies, Watson and Crick, recently died, he replaced them with a trio of Rhodesian ridgebacks named Enders, Robbins, and Weller.

Dr. Grant Emerson stands 1.8 m tall (6'0"), weighs 71 kg (157 Ibs), and has blue eyes and a shock of thick, unruly white hair. He bears a broken nose and scars along his right arm from a baboon attack. He retains his strong English accent and frequently mutters to himself, perhaps contributing to a mild phobia of public speaking.

Grant Emerson, Ph.D.

Microbiologist and longtime Friendly, age 65.

STR 7 **CON** 10 **DEX** 12 **INT** 18 **POW** 16 **CHA** 12

HP 9 **WP** 16 **SAN** 72 **BREAKING POINT** 64

BONDS: Ex-wife, Jennifer Miller, 6.

Dr. Jasmine Lee, UNC postdoctoral fellow with whom he's having what he thinks is a secret affair, 12.

Dr. Rafael Colonna, research assistant, 10.

Mark Emerson, brother, 12.

MOTIVATIONS AND DISORDERS: Learning secrets that no one else has discovered.

Staying one step ahead of the Program.

Dealing with unnatural threats effectively and quickly.

Stopping the exploitation and weaponization of the Unnatural.

Preserving the mission of Delta Green.

SKILLS: Alertness 57%, Anthropology 16%, Art (Photography) 39%, Chemistry 50%, Computer Science 25%, Drive 35%, Forensics 30%, HUMINT 39%, Medicine 81%, Navigate 28%, Occult 21%, Persuade 66%, Pharmacy 19%, Science (Biology) 95%, Science (Genetics) 81%, Science (Microbiology) 89%, Science (Zoology) 75%, Search 72%, Survival 25%, Unnatural 18%.

ATTACKS: Unarmed 40%, damage 1D4−2.

TOMES: The files of Grant Emerson (see page 158).

James Derringer

James Derringer got his first taste of the unnatural while serving as a second lieutenant with the Marines in Quan Tri province, Vietnam, 1967. That makes him one of the few survivors of the Delta Green's first life under the Department of Defense. He served during the "Cowboy Era" of the 1970s and 1980s, and adjusted to the cell-structure of the 1990s. A model Delta Green and FBI agent—a balancing act few have pulled off—he was imaginative and dogged. He knew how to use the system, and to circumvent it when the situation demanded. Rising to the rank of Special Agent in Charge of the FBI office in Knoxville, Tennessee, he alerted the group to the first investigation into the Groversville incident. MAJESTIC's reach was long in those days, and after meddling in their affairs once, James Derringer saw his career trajectory at the FBI flatline.

But Derringer persevered. He had survived Viet Nam. He had survived a dozen Nights at the Opera. He survived losing his wife to lung cancer in 2001. When a recruiter from the Program sought him out, Derringer made it very clear that the Program was just another name for MAJESTIC. He retired from the FBI at the age of 57 in 2004. He even survived working as a Friendly following his retirement. Some people in the Outlaws thought James Derringer was just fucking unkillable.

In 2012, Derringer suffered a massive stroke that resulted in a coma and extensive loss of motor function and memory. It took a year of therapy for him to claw back to something resembling functionality. His three children helped him recover, despite the fact that their relationships had eroded over the years, especially after his wife's death.

By 2013, Derringer insisted that he was fit for duty, despite the cane he needed to get around. At first A-cell refused, but Derringer proved his capacity by attending a Night at the Opera he wasn't even invited to. Since then he has participated in several more in an advisory capacity.

These days, the real James Derringer inhabits the Great Library of Pnakotis. He uses a curious heated stylus to etch the story of his life and the history of Delta Green into huge copper plates, slithering from room to room on his enormous, armored, gastropod-like foot. He consults with other intelligences gathered from across time and space. Back in the 21st century, his body houses the time-traveling mind of a member of the Great Race of Yith.

The new tenant in James Derringer's body seems to be primarily observing and reporting. It appears willing to participate in operations, particularly those that might brush up against the Program. Derringer's new tenant has a particular interest in March Technologies. In the guise of so respected an agent, it may someday enlist Agents to dig deeper into March Technologies than A-cell would prefer.

James Derringer always looked like he was auditioning to be Clint Eastwood's stunt double: 1.92 m tall (6'3"), 91 kg (200 lbs), with narrow eyes that disappear into the crags of a scowling face. His crew-cut is snow white, like his bushy eyebrows. He's still spry enough on his cane and gets around, but he won't be doing any five-mile runs. He's still clumsy from the stroke. Many former colleagues have noticed a difficulty manipulating or even recognizing common household objects. He sometimes speaks in a halting way, as if he is quickly figuring out which words to use.

James Derringer

Strange infiltrator, age 70.

STR 6 **CON** 9 **DEX** 8 **INT** 22 **POW** 18 **CHA** 7

HP 8 **WP** 18 **SAN** n/a

SKILLS: Total Knowledge 75% (see **TOTAL KNOWLEDGE**).

ATTACKS: M1911A1 pistol 75%, damage 1D10.

Unarmed 75%, damage 1D4−2.

Electric gun 75%, damage variable (see **JURY-RIG**).

JURY-RIG: Compared to the power of the Great Race, human science is pathetic. Agents of the Great Race can warp modern devices into far more effective technology. Sometimes, this can be accomplished in mere minutes. Often, these tools are rigged to explode or self-destruct after a period of time. The most common are:

- *Electric Gun:* This device can be as small as a garage-door opener, and can inflict damage of the user's choosing: a jolt of 1D6 or 2D6, or a bolt of lightning with Lethality 15%. It ignores body armor but can be blocked by cover.
- *Temporal Mine:* This can look like nearly any household object or device. Once activated, it causes everything within a small radius to be frozen in time, effectively isolating it from the Construct of spacetime. The scope and duration of the effect are up to the Handler.
- *Transfer Device:* When it enters the limited human mind, the Great Race cannot use its ability to jump to another form without first building a transfer device. This small box, composed of rods, wheels and mirrors, permits the mind of the Great Race to return to the Library at Pnakotis.

TEMPORAL IMMORTALITY: To an extratemporal being, death is only an inconvenient "blank spot" in the otherwise limitless expanse of four-dimensional spacetime. Even if the human agent form of the Great Race appears to perish, that entity persists on, somewhere in time.

TOTAL KNOWLEDGE: As temporal explorers, the Great Race have access to endless epochs of knowledge from all times and cultures. Knowing a challenge is coming, they can learn all they must know before it begins. Only occasional, strange variances in causality limit them. They have the equivalent of 75% in every skill, alien or human.

TEMPORAL OMNISCIENCE: At the beginning of any action in opposition with the Great Race (Human Vessel), an Agent must make a Luck roll. On a failure, all actions by that member of the Great Race are +20% for the duration of that conflict or contest, because the entity lived through the episode before and knows what is going to happen.

TEMPORAL TRAVEL (LIMITED): The Great Race can move their consciousness through time to inhabit creatures with sufficient capacity to support their intellect. Humanity, at its best, offers a dim vessel within which to hold the mind of a member of the Great Race. Once in human form, the Great Race agent must construct a device (see **JURY-RIG**) to move its consciousness back. Without this odd machine, the member of the Great Race is trapped within the human form. That form's death creates a "dead end" in the Great Race's awareness of spacetime. Whether they can occupy another nearby host is up to the Handler.

SAN LOSS: 0/1D6 (if its influence over time is revealed).

James Derringer

If returned to his body; age 70.

STR 6 **CON** 9 **DEX** 8 **INT** 14 **POW** 13 **CHA** 11

HP 8 **WP** 13 **SAN** 19 **BREAKING POINT** 15

BONDS: Two sons and daughter, 6.

Grandchildren, 6.

Fellow prisoners in Pnakotis, 11.

MOTIVATIONS AND DISORDERS: Recovering time lost to his possession.

Warning Delta Green of what he has learned.

Amnesia.

Anxiety disorder.

Fugues.

Adapted to violence and helplessness.

SKILLS: Alertness 75%, Athletics 59%, Bureaucracy 47%, Computer Science 32%, Criminology 69%, Drive 58%, Firearms 73%, First Aid 46%, Heavy Weapons 44%, HUMINT 60%, Law 38%, Melee Weapons 41%, Military Science 43%, Navigate 61%, Occult 47%, Persuade 61%, Search 78%, Stealth 66%, Swim 66%, Unarmed Combat 62%, Unnatural 12%.

ATTACKS: M1911A1 pistol 73%, damage 1D10.

Ka-bar knife 41%, damage 1D6−1.

Unarmed 62%, damage 1D4−2.

After I calmed a bit, I put the car in gear, pulled back onto the highway and went home. The fog quickly dissipated. I'd driven ten miles in three minutes at 55 mph. That wasn't possible. What happened to me?

Cases of missing time and distance are as common as they are confusing. The Internet is littered with tales of travelers entering a fog only to discover they're suddenly 300 miles away from home, or they've gone nowhere, but it's inexplicably hours later. Explanations range from time slips, to dimensional slips, to alien abduction. Whatever the case, Brandon White of Maryville, Missouri, has experienced missing time and distance; more than once. "The first time I was about ten and I was walking out in the front yard," White said. It was just after lunch.

As White went toward a thick ring of pine trees that surrounded his family's farmhouse, he saw something floating on the other side of the tree line. "It was pale, sort of translucent," he said. "It was passing between our house an

What the Program and the Outlaws Know

The question "What does Delta Green know?" (be it the Program or the Outlaws) must ultimately be resolved by the Handler. The conspiracy has changed in structure and membership many times over the decades. What's more, for years there have been two separate groups calling themselves Delta Green. What the Outlaws know may be very different from what the Program knows. All those additions and subtractions of institutional memory allow the Handler flexibility in setting up a campaign and providing the Agents with as much or as little information as desired. Remember, ultimately, what the Agents, their colleagues, and their superiors know about the unnatural is up to you—even then, it may be entirely wrong.

Uncommon Knowledge

Many basic facts are known by the Program and the Outlaws alike, gathered in their most important files and based on first-hand experience. Some individuals know specific issues in greater depth.

Other Dimensions

There are alternate realities and higher dimensions. Entities that exist in these dimensions attempt to enter our world, for reasons and with methods that are inimical to human life, and can be aided in doing so by humans. These entities have been identified in folklore as demons and gods.

The Deep Ones

Elements of the U.S. government first became convinced of inhuman intelligent life during the 1928 incident at Innsmouth Massachusetts. Both the Outlaws and the Program have extensive experience with the deep-sea humanoids encountered there, known colloquially as "the Deep Ones," and sometimes as "Aquatic Humanoids." They use humans as breeding stock. They use hypergeometry and/or technology unknown to human civilizations. They are secretive, and appear to have little interest in conquest or expansion; their primary goal seems to be simple propagation. They are known for corrupting isolated seaside communities, turning leaders toward the worship of strange aquatic deities, and encouraging the interbreeding of Deep Ones and humans. These hybrids appear human for their first twenty or thirty years, before they begin to transform them into Deep Ones. The current actions and plans of the Deep Ones are impossible to guess.

The Greys and Their Creators

The conspiracy theorists are right. In 1947, the U.S. military did indeed capture a flying saucer at Roswell, New Mexico, and its occupants were the so-called "Greys" of UFO folklore. Decades later, these entities offered technology in exchange for collaboration. The government projects that worked with them, organized under the code name MAJESTIC, went from being America's first line of defense against invasion to a distorted cargo cult which worshipped the Greys' technological gifts.

By 2000, the illusion collapsed. The small, childlike humanoids turned out to be marionettes controlled by some other non-human intelligence. The Program has very limited information on just what this non-human intelligence is. Witness descriptions suggest a race of large, winged creatures that appear to communicate via changing color, and who emit an unsettling, buzzing approximation of human speech.

The Insects From Shaggai

In 1999, agents of Delta Green discovered that an alien intelligence, capable of mentally controlling humans, had infiltrated the United Kingdom's government through the organization PISCES. Delta Green immediately broke contact in order to gather intelligence, but it made little progress before the Program launched. The Outlaws let it go. The Program maintained limited contact.

Necrophages, aka Ghouls

Both the Outlaws and the Program have had extensive contact with so-called "necrophages," referred to as "ghouls" in folklore. These entities were once human until they began to consume rotten human flesh. The Program's researchers hypothesize their transformation to be the result of an unidentified prion disease that facilitates a specialization for underground life, effective immortality, and the capability to survive on a diet of human remains.

Ghouls are extremely varied in habit and ability, ranging from the urbane to the savage. Some possess the ability to experience the memories of any brain they devour. It is known that some can transform their appearance to be exact doppelgängers of those they have eaten.

The number of known necrophages is thought to be low. There are two major necrophage population centers known in the United States. The surviving ghoul tribe living under Manhattan Island, the Keepers of the Faith, consider themselves "traditionalists" who remain hidden and avoid contact with humans, only consuming those long dead. The Keepers, descendants of original Dutch settlers in Manhattan, even cooperated with Delta Green during an operation to eliminate ghoul "heretics" preying on live humans.

A second population center for necrophages was the DeMonte Clan of New Orleans. The Outlaws spent five years breaking the three-century hold the group of ghouls had on the New Orleans mortuary business, using the cover of Hurricane Katrina to launch a three-day all out war against the ghouls while the city fell to pieces.

Cults

Throughout human history people have attempted to treat with unnatural entities. They are the source of many legends about sorcerers and covens, and they often gather allies together to form deranged cults. Delta Green has encountered and overcome many cults, eliminating some completely: the Karotechia (see page 30), the Network (with its central cult, the Fate; see page 71), the Disciples of the Worm (see page 124), the sprawling Cult of Transcendence (see page 93), the Skoptsi (see page 105), and Tong Shukoran (see page 84)—and, in its own way, MAJESTIC (see page 46). Today, the most dangerous threats come not from organized cults, which tend toward self-destruction and are subject to surveillance and disruption, but from isolated, desperate individuals. (See **LURKERS AND LONE WOLVES** on page 129.)

Hypergeometry

Non-human intelligences utilize a kind of technology misidentified as "magic," sometimes called "hypergeometry," to manipulate matter and energy. Humans can learn to use these processes, but prolonged exposure leads to insanity and sometimes to physical mutation and disease.

Delta Green has hunted to extinction most organized groups that have embraced hypergeometry. Disrupting the activities of a large, well-organized, and well-funded group is often simpler than sniffing out a lone wolf or a disorganized network. Countless individual threats remain and new ones emerge every day.

The Program's Research

The Program has collected and collated everything the U.S. government knows about the unnatural and isolated that knowledge within itself. It compartmentalizes unnatural intelligence, and only those at the peak of the Program have access to all the data. These rare individuals have risen to these positions simply because they are smart enough to study only what is necessary.

The Program possesses MAJESTIC's voluminous (if surprisingly useless) files, from the 1947 Roswell saucer crash up to the 2002 collapse of MAJESTIC. It has the Office of Naval Intelligence's files on the 1928 raid on Innsmouth and subsequent operations in the 1930s, as well as such esoteric texts as a translation of the *Book of Dagon*. It has the OSS's wartime Delta Green files from 1942 to 1945. It has the reinstituted

DISINFORMATION

YELLOW CARD

THE PROGRAM – WHAT IS THE THREAT?

The Program couches the threat in jargon. Class I self-referential thought-form tesseract. Lobachevskian-space string-based nonlinear consciousness. Self-resolving quantum anomaly. Language is the first battlefield of dealing with the unnatural. Naming a threat brings it into focus, gives it the appearance of having been parsed by science, and reduces the sense of mystery around it. Unfortunately, this couching of terms does nothing about the absolutely alien nature of the unnatural threat itself.

Those briefed on the threat that the Program faces are told that it is super-spatial intelligences. The jargon serves two purposes. First, non-briefed personnel who are accidentally exposed to Program records won't know what to make of them. Second, the term super-spatial intelligence can cover nearly anything and put it neatly in a box. It is a conscious choice to conspicuously avoid words such as extraterrestrial, paranormal, magic, alien, and monster.

Further questions very quickly hit a barrier of understanding. The Program strongly implies that it understands the threat in its entirety, but it is not forthcoming at all. How could it be? For all its technology and research, it truly understands very little.

CUT ALONG THIS LINE

Delta Green's files from 1947 to its dissolution in 1970, including dossiers on the Operation RIPTIDE tapes from 1963. It has what few records exist of Delta Green's operations as an illegal conspiracy from 1970 to 2002. And, of course, it has records of all the Program's operations carried out since then.

These records are kept on secure computers not connected to the Internet, in heavily guarded research rooms shielded against radio signals to prevent outside communications. They have no USB ports or other means of connecting with another computer. Input is strictly keyboard; output is strictly through a monitor and speakers. Researchers who take data out for reference must transcribe it manually, with orders to destroy that data as soon as it is no longer necessary.

This data is protected by a labyrinth of Top Secret clearances. Precisely three people are cleared for all of it: the Director of Intelligence, the Director of Operations, and the Director of Delta Green. The directors of Intelligence and Operations are allowed to read others in on particular files on a need-to-know basis, and only with the explicit authorization of the Director.

The Program has, in short, any tome or item or record of unnatural knowledge that you, the Handler, want it to have, and none that you feel it should not. When an operation requires that Agents have access to prior intelligence, you decide how much or how little they get. Of course, from the Agents' perspective, the intelligence they receive is never enough.

For all its files, the Program has no broad, concrete understanding of the unnatural. No Program researcher, working in isolation from the others, understands an organized cosmology—though some wild theories have been put forward.

The Program maintains extensive files on individuals that have used religion as a means of harnessing hypergeometric techniques, as well as the methods that they employed.

When it comes to folklore and mysticism, the problem is separating the myths from the fact. There are vast amounts of data available on traditional paranormal phenomena such as poltergeists, psychic powers, and the gamut of fringe weirdness. But how much is nonsense, how much is contradictory, and how much is just closely held belief with no evidence to back it up? With centuries of human superstition to wade through, who can tell what truly relates to the unnatural?

Nevertheless, the Program's researchers have studied rituals—though they use more technical terms—that dealt with gate technology, the barriers between dimensions, so-called psychic phenomena, and many other techniques. The one thing that they all have in common seems to be their debilitating effects on the human mind. The Program's security officers stay busy monitoring researchers for mental deterioration that can turn work into catastrophe.

Most researchers believe that the difference between a demon and a non-human intelligence, explainable in scientific terms, is little more than cultural expectations. They see "hypergeometry" as a fascinating new field of physics that has yet to be unraveled. That may be even more dangerous than taking up worship of the entities beyond.

A-Cell's Files

The Outlaws' information on unnatural activity is sketchy. A-cell keeps some files, books, and other media in a bunker on property owned by its leader, Donald Poe. More is scattered among dozens of Green Boxes: storage facilities maintained by agents to keep things they cannot take home.

After a disaster in 1955, Delta Green transformed into an oddly anti-science organization. This Orwellian double-think when it comes to science, intel on the unnatural, and hypergeometry—the science of magic—affects the Outlaws to this day. When some anomalous specimen is recovered, there is a limited inquiry, and not the kind of fascination one would expect such oddities to garner. The information is run up the flagpole to leadership.

Have the Outlaws seen it before? Are its methods, or methods to eliminate it known? If so, the specimen is discarded at the soonest opportunity. If not… many things can happen. A specialist (usually a Friendly) can be brought in, the specimen can be moved to a secure location for later study, or the leadership can fear the recovery so much, they immediately order its destruction.

Often, the motives of the Outlaws' leadership are difficult to discern and their orders, though clear, might mean many things. Once an entity or item is cataloged (and such catalogs are kept only in the possession of Outlaw leadership) this data sits and waits for another piece of intel to come in.

There is no passive comparison of data—no correlation of contents, as it were. Instead, pains are taken to pursue leads (science, intel or other) only to the one step Delta Green is interested in: the destruction of the unnatural threat. Any investigation past that is considered too dangerous.

Often, however, agents deviate from this path, particularly new agents or Friendlies confronted with something in their field which is so staggeringly mind-boggling, they can't seem to stop investigating it.

The Outlaws are clever. Under such situations, a watch is placed on agents or Friendlies the group feels may wander off the path. Another agent in the cell monitors the suspect for signs of odd behavior, and more often than not, they can be pulled back from the edge before the obsession goes too far. Or, if they do cross that line, they can be eliminated more safely.

There have been many Friendlies and specialists experienced with such traditional unnatural phenomena as poltergeists and psychic powers. But even within the domains of the Outlaws' knowledge, they rarely draw useful correlations among unnatural phenomena. Most have no real understanding of how unnatural powers define the structure of the universe. They assume that Deep Ones and other unnatural entities are part of a larger unnatural world that might well include things like the Loch Ness monster, Bigfoot, or vampires. They don't really care to know more; they just want to make certain that whatever reveals itself, they can make it go away.

DISINFORMATION

YELLOW CARD

THE OUTLAWS – WHAT IS THE THREAT?

As to what the threat the Outlaws believe they are facing, the answers are as numerous as its membership. Some believe the forces of the unnatural are literally demons or angels or other myth-based beings. Agents have such a limited perspective that, often, they do not even have a basic understanding of the situation, much less how it might relate to other threats. In fact, most have no idea there are other threats than those they have seen with their own eyes. The Outlaws are happy with this. Letting agents come to their own private conclusions has served the Outlaws very well for decades. The leadership are certainly not providing any real answers. Many agents suspect they have none.

To the Outlaws' agents, there is no consideration of facts beyond those directly involved in the operation. There is no threat analysis, no reports on the hierarchies of non-human cultures, no positional analysis of the motivation of Cthulhu cultists. There is only the mission. Once the operation is done, there is only the cover-up, and then back to the world.

ALONG THIS LINE

// The Opera //

I had been treating her for ten months when I realized whatever was in her was mocking me. It was never obvious. It never went out of it's way to do it. It just demonstrated through conversation that it was entertaining itself with me. I was simply a sparring partner, never a threat.

She was 11 years old when I began treating her. It was the day after her birthday. Head injury, catatonic stupor. All pretty standard.

Four months in, I realized she was still conscious somewhere in that still body — back when I thought there was a "her." Five months and I had my first successes with hypnosis. Eight months and I was certain I was on my way towards something significant, maybe a new type of treatment. And then, I realized all at once, that what was in her was not her. The girl was gone. There was something else.

Now, when we talk, it is an interrogation.

D "When will you tell me who you are?"

A "Soon."

D "Tell me something. Prove to me you are from somewhere else, like you say."

A "The city of New York is a ruin, filled with corpses."

D "No. No, it's not."

— Then, that smile. The smile again. The one you should never see on a child's face.

A "Wait."

Four weeks ago, it told me to invest in gold, and I did. I don't know why, but I did. I made a lot of money. A great deal of money. I wipe my lips, trying not to show my fear.

D "What's your name?"

— "Abd al-Hazrad."

---

mission Informa

the evidence subm
NA profile.
r DNA analysis ma

to consume any a

ove information ar
A Analysis

Decades ago, some unknown agent came up with a bleak euphemism for going on a Delta Green operation: a "Night at the Opera." The phrase stuck. Delta Green ops have always been lethally dangerous, and confronting the unnatural stresses the mind like no other investigation or special operation. But there's no need to dwell on it, right? "A Night at the Opera." Cop humor. Agent humor.

Agents put themselves in the way of death and madness to protect the world around them. As a Handler running *Delta Green,* your first goal is to make death and madness a constant in their lives.

The Essentials

The details of an individual Delta Green campaign are, of course, up to each Handler. Before we get into how to make *Delta Green* your own, let's look at the aspects of the game that *should never change.*

Sometimes, it's tempting to make *Delta Green* upbeat and winnable. That choice transforms it into science fiction, a thriller, or a military role-playing game. Why bother? Plenty of good games already accomplish these things. *Delta Green* without Lovecraft's essential hopelessness misses the point.

So what makes it uniquely Delta Green?

Humans Are the Main Threat

While the unnatural is the focus of Delta Green's operations, humanity remains the main threat. People willing to do anything for power, for understanding, for immortality—things only the unnatural can bring them. Mankind is forever pawing at the locks to release the hungry powers that howl beyond, and Delta Green is forever slamming those doors shut.

The Mundane Is the Backdrop

Delta Green is rooted in the mundane. The more you cement it among things that the players know, trust, and understand, the more striking the moments of terror become.

Have the phase-shifting horror manifest in a grocery store. Note the details of unnatural destruction by describing the tipped-over coffee table and blood-soaked People magazine with the starlet of the week on the cover. The threat is most horrific when it haunts our own world.

At the same time, moments that feature the unnatural should be infrequent. Your game is a symphony. The crescendo must come at the key moment. A symphony of crescendos is boring. Choose when the unnatural appears with care, make those moments count, and make them hurt.

Nothing Is Certain

If the Agents (or their players) are confident, you're doing it wrong. They should live in fear of the double-cross, of being hung out to dry, of being set up, or just of getting caught. Their first operation probably turns them into felons. Anyone could be compromised. Anyone could be a puppet for an inhuman intelligence. Any new lead could be a trap.

Explore the Incursion

A little unnatural in a game goes a long way. A Handler who attempts to one-up the unnatural threat over and over soon finds the Agents bored. When something horrific is behind every door, and there are monsters everywhere, *Delta Green* ceases being horror and becomes farce. Better to introduce a single incursion, and then explore the horrifying effects and side-effects of that one threat's interaction with humanity.

Unnatural Horror Is About Lack of Understanding

With the unnatural, the answers can only go so far. How did the book displace the agent's consciousness? How does a gesture cut a man in half? How can a thing composed of swirling glass pass through walls and speak?

The ultimate answers to these questions are beyond human conception, and they always will be. That's why it's the unnatural. Do not give the players enough information to let them think they truly understand an unnatural threat. Let them have a sense of it, but only enough to keep them fascinated and afraid.

Delta Green is built to establish a tone of fear. The antithesis of fear is understanding. Once a threat's stats, actions, and behaviors can be guessed, it loses the mystery that terror requires. Remember Lovecraft's adage: *The oldest and strongest emotion of mankind is fear, and the oldest and strongest kind of fear is fear of the unknown.*

Death Is Omnipresent

Do not protect the Agents. You are simply a mediator. Death is not only part of *Delta Green;* it is its foundation. This is a game about human frailty, about the struggle against the unknown despite the impossibility of victory. The most heroic moments are found when the Agents know they're risking everything—their families, their careers, their sanity, and their lives.

Let the game dictate the outcome. The rules are stacked in favor of the unnatural. Unless humans are careful and clever, they have little chance of survival. Players sometimes get impatient and rash. Let the consequences play out without malice and without mercy.

This game is not about winning. It is about surviving to fight another day. It is about Agents who show up for the next op knowing what's in store for them. Death and madness are the main outcomes of Delta Green operations. An operation that doesn't leave an Agent dead, crippled, or insane should be defined by that—by the negative space left by a disaster that everyone expected.

There Are Worse Things Than Death

There are worse fates than death. There are creatures that subsume an Agent's mind, methods to artificially prolong or restore life, and places where all the rules of life and death are removed completely. But the price is the death—or loss—of humanity.

It is important to show that price being paid so the players are forced to contemplate it. Agents should exist in mortal fear of such outcomes. They should be on the lookout for situations which can compromise the very thing they are fighting for: normal human existence.

Creating a Campaign

A campaign is a series of Delta Green operations, focusing on a single group of Agents. Agents come and go—they may die, go insane, or "retire"—but a central thread remains. At first, that could be the team's code-name or cell designation, the case officer who manages them from a distance, or a central NPC; but ultimately, the thread is Delta Green itself.

As Handler, it's not just about selecting unnatural threats to investigate. You make many choices in constructing a *Delta Green* campaign. You are required to understand the moving parts on a level which the players never see. So, what are the steps to create a new *Delta Green* campaign?

Pick the Decade

In what era is your *Delta Green* game set? The group has existed since 1942 in many different forms. The era that serves as a backdrop deeply influences the tone and style of gameplay.

Are your Agents with P4 in the 1930s, pursuing a global conspiracy of Cthulhu cultists and Deep One lairs unearthed in the Innsmouth raid? Or covering up the monstrosities that Nazi Germany unearthed, racing against the Soviets to find them in April 1945? Or hunting a time traveler in a Kansas town in 1951? Or closing in on a cult attempting to wake something horrible beneath Yellowstone in 1967, during the Summer of Love? Are they on the run from government black-budget outfits with access to technology from beyond in 1982—or 1999, 2009, or 2019? Examples and ideas are given throughout **PART TWO: THE PAST**, beginning on page 14.

The choices are endless, so it's best to start with a basic idea: What feeling do you want to explore? Every decade evokes a theme that serves as a backdrop in the campaign. That theme helps you explore how Delta Green's power and influence has ebbed and flowed over the years.

- **1930s:** The risk of exposing ordinary men and women to the unnatural as the officers, Marines, and cryptographers of the P4 naval intelligence unit discover the extent of the threat.
- **1940s:** Confronting what happens when humanity embraces the powers of the unnatural, as Delta Green gains its name and pursues the Karotechia in World War II.
- **1950s:** As America and the Soviet Union rise as enemies over the rubble of the world, unnatural secrets settle into society like tumors.
- **1960s:** The Cold War grows hotter, and the costs of confronting the unnatural too overtly become too much to bear.
- **1970s:** Investigating the unnatural not just without official cover, but without any organization whatsoever. Delta Green is dead, but a handful of Agents keep up the struggle, with no one to trust.
- **1980s:** The rise of the MAJESTIC threat and the paranoia of pursuit by the very government you serve.
- **1990s:** A cell-based conspiracy pursues the unnatural and the seemingly overwhelming MAJESTIC threat.
- **2000s:** Seeing how money and power make the mission even more fraught due to bad intelligence and politicized decision-making. Be careful what you wish for.
- **2010s:** The danger of public exposure in the era of ubiquitous communications and the surveillance state—and the strange mutability of truth.

Customize the Situation

Sometimes you want to create your own particular setting within the Delta Green universe. For example, you might decide to focus on the 1950s, at a secret Delta Green mental facility that treats agents who have seen too much.

Being Handler means shaping the *Delta Green* game into what you want it to be. Sometimes you can explore the game as it already exists before bringing anything new to it. Sometimes you begin with a clear vision of something fresh, but try to keep it in line with the nihilistic core of *Delta Green*.

Define the Threats

What threats will your Agents see in your *Delta Green* campaign? Some campaigns are a mishmash of the unnatural with no connections except the particular Agents sent to investigate them. Others are fraught with correlated contents. You can even connect what were once disparate investigations into a single unbroken thread at a later time, if an idea strikes you.

Building your first *Delta Green* operation is a good way to establish the scope of threat. Don't start with your Agents fighting all the vast range of the unnatural. A single entity or a single ritual is enough to fill a game with mystery and terror. Perhaps the Agents have discovered non-human, immortal entities that feed on the human dead, colloquially known as "ghouls." Explore the repercussions and horrors of that one incursion. If the players pursue a lead that takes them away from the heart of the "ghoul" mystery, reveal the next, limited layer of horror. They'll soon come to suspect that the layers never end.

Brief the Players

Inform the players of any details they need to know to create their Agents. If all Agents need to be in the Pacific Northwest, or need a background in federal law enforcement, let them know.

Answer any questions the players might have. Step through Agent creation, and make sure the Agents that the players imagine work in the campaign you're creating. If a player comes up with a great idea that doesn't fit, decide whether you can adjust the campaign or, more likely, the Agent needs to be adjusted. Discuss it with the players.

It is best to do this footwork for them ahead of time, and to have some notes on how, specifically, to make their Agent work in your campaign, before the players go through the whole process of making Agents.

Creating an Operation

Don't be daunted by the challenge of creating a *Delta Green* operation. A good operation has a lot of characters, situations, and challenges for the Agents to encounter, but everything spins off of one, central idea: the terror that the Agents must overcome or prevent. If you get that right, everything else falls into place.

The **OPERATION OVERVIEW** and **OPERATION STRUCTURE** worksheets, on pages 363 and 364, may prove useful.

A Word About Fear

What makes a *Delta Green* operation horrific? *Uncertainty, risk,* and *lack of control.* Without these essential elements, any operation, no matter how terrible the creature involved, devolves into a bug hunt.

Delta Green is not about beating monsters. At the highest level, as a Handler, you must consider how to make your operations elicit *fear.*

Uncertainty

When a thing is understood ("Deep Ones have 15 HP. Get the shotgun."), it ceases to be frightening. It can never truly elicit fear. This is the essential rule of horror. Agents must never feel certain of what they're facing or why. Their decision-making should never come down to evaluating the odds of dice-rolls. The threats should be more mysterious than that. You should never, ever, tell them *everything*.

Risk

It is very difficult to maintain a sense of fear if the players feel confident that you're looking out for their Agents, and they know their Agents can't die or go insane until a moment that everyone finds dramatically acceptable. Fear involves risk and consequences. The players should feel like any mistake can begin a spiral of events that will get their team exposed or killed.

IN THE FIELD: A Note About Control

People have very different experiences with horror games. Some play a horror game like a Michael Bay movie or a Marvel comic. It's their game, and they can do what they want, but they're missing out. *Delta Green* is about fear.

Fear of the unknown, of losing control, of *losing*. Control is the opposite of fear. Players yearn for control. This game is about their struggle to gain it, the toll that struggle takes on their Agents, and the terrible ways that control escapes them in the end.

At first, a lot of players don't understand this. For that matter, a lot of Handlers don't understand it. In a horror game—not an action game, not a thriller, but horror—control is not an option. Unnatural rituals, creatures, and sanity-rending books are stacked against the Agents from the first moment of the game.

Furthermore, *Delta Green* is about the players' lack of control. Players should feel some sense, some echo, of the desperation of their Agents. They should viscerally feel the way that their Agents are scrabbling, grasping for any thread or hint of security. The game is built to evoke that mood at the table.

Played in a purely mechanical fashion, *Delta Green* is a machine that produces frequent Agent deaths and sometimes miraculous stories of survival. It describes Agents' decline—moral, mental, and physical—with horror and death on all sides. It is not about winning. The victories that Agents achieve turn out to be fleeting. Doom is inevitable.

Having discovered that, why does your Agent keep struggling? That is the question every player should explore. Why do any of us?

Delta Green is not a power fantasy. The players' experience of terror through the eyes of their Agent is what makes it so much fun.

Lack of Control

Many role-playing games are player-driven: the players dictate their choices and the world moves around them. *Delta Green* does not operate this way. It is a Handler-driven game where the world occurs around the Agents and the players must react.

There is a fine line to be drawn here. Players, through their Agents, can alter the outcome, but not dictate it. Being prepared, making plans, researching, securing backup, these are all healthy things in a horror game. They show that the players are thinking. They show the players are worried. All these preemptive actions can make survival and success more likely. But they should never let the players feel certain of the outcome.

The Nature of the Operation

The first thing to decide is the scope of the game you're about to play. Is it a quick, standalone scenario—a one-shot with Agents the players are unlikely to visit again? Is it a more involved mystery where the players have room to flesh their Agents out? Or is the mystery only the first part of an ongoing, long-term campaign?

In Medias Res

Some games begin with the operation already in progress. Usually reserved for one-shot operations, In Medias Res games dictate location, time period, and often even the players' Agents. They often are relatively simple, with limited background exposition and self-contained investigation that leads quickly to the central horror.

> **EXAMPLE:** *You're all FBI agents at the Bremen Estate, cataloguing a crime scene, waiting for the first train back to Albany once the snow clears. Everyone picks characters from pre-generated agents. You play the current operation and then you're done.*

The Mystery

This can be part of an ongoing campaign or more like an In Medias Res game. The players have more time to create and personalize their Agents and establish the setting before they are presented with a mystery to solve. Exploring the clues around the mystery leads to the central horror, and perhaps to ways to overcome or survive it. A Mystery can easily connect to an Ongoing Threat. If the players are careful and clever, a series of Mysteries can give rise to Agents that change and grow over time and across multiple operations.

> **EXAMPLE:** *People are disappearing at Lesner Institute, and the university has called in the feds—your Agents—to check it out.*

The Ongoing Threat

The operation is part of a campaign of scenarios (these can be linked, or individual investigations like "movies of the week") connected by a skein of returning Agents.

> **EXAMPLE:** *F-cell is a group of likeminded Agents bent on one task: stopping the rise of the unnatural.*

Step One: The Hook

Build your operation around a single nugget of an idea, a hook. Start with something mundane (and preferably disturbing) and add a creepy, overtly unnatural twist: "a mirror which allows time travel." There's some inciting event, some appalling way that the unnatural incursion intersects with humanity. Follow the leads and ramifications out from the inciting event. Imagine the hook as something solid, a thing to which all the leads attach.

> **EXAMPLE:** *A janitor is found dead at the county hospital, covered in the fingerprints of a suicide victim who was brought in the day before. The suicide's body is now missing.*

That starts with something mundane but inherently disturbing: a janitor found dead at a hospital. And it adds a creepy twist: the body was handled by someone who was found dead the day before. It is a clean start with a nice bit of weirdness.

The mark of a good hook is that there are many ways for Agents to enter the mystery, a few bits of spine-tingling strangeness, and a clear path forward.

We don't have an explanation for it, yet—the central mystery of the operation. We'll get to that. It might be the last thing you decide, after all the other pieces fall into place.

Step Two: Non-Player Characters

Non-player characters are the lifeblood of a good *Delta Green* operation. Who are the movers and shakers? It is important to cover all the basics when writing them up. For example, if a crime was the inciting event, it's likely police or federal agents are involved. So are the victim's family, colleagues, rivals, and anyone the police already consider a suspect.

Who are these people? What are their motivations, hopes, and dreams? Who are they loyal to? What forces do they serve? What will they do to get what they want?

Here are some key players for our hook. What others can you imagine?

Hector Sandovar, Janitor

Dominican-American male, age 39 (deceased). Here's the dead guy. The initial entry point. He's innocent and dead. We'll give him a background that might become a red herring by making him a follower of Santeria—a syncretic mix of Catholicism and Afro-Caribbean spiritualism.

Elizabeth Tun, Registered Nurse

White female, age 41. The woman who discovered Sandovar's body. She's innocent, and horrified by the ordeal, but wants to help.

Abigail Vosh, Registered Nurse

White female, age 27. A nurse who has been sneaking narcotics from the hospital and has a lot to hide (she also sells them). Tun heard Vosh sneaking up to the roof to take drugs, but did not see her. Now the police are looking for the person on the stairwell in possible connection to the crime.

John Doe

White male, age 30 to 40, deceased. The suicide pulled from the river the day before Sandovar's death and now missing. The hook of the operation.

IN THE FIELD: Hookless!

Sometimes, it's tough to come up with a hook. If you find yourself at an impasse, try the Internet. Look for ingredients in weird news stories and Wikipedia articles, and add a dash of the unnatural. For example:

- The disappearances at Roanoke, Virginia: endlessly fascinating. A whole colony vanished with no proof as to where they ended up. What if that happened to a small town today?
- Read about the Texas Tower Sniper, Charles Whitman, and the controversies about his brain tumor. Is that what caused his rampage, or was it something else? What if something unnatural pushed a mass murderer over the edge?
- Judge Joseph Crater vanished in 1930 without a trace and was never found. What if he walked in the door of a local police station tonight?

And that was just ten minutes of poking around online. There's always a hook available. There are *millions.*

Eric Marini, M.D.

African-American male, age 52. The director of the hospital, bent on controlling the negative spin from a murder on the premises. To him, there's no such thing as the unnatural, even if it's chasing him down a darkened hospital corridor.

Detective Ken Deveraugh

White male, age 45. The officer in charge of the murder investigation. He's surprisingly open-minded, and might make a good ally if something obviously unnatural occurs. But for now, he's operating under the theory that someone killed the janitor to cover up theft of the John Doe body.

Step Three: Leads

Leads are chains of causality and action that reach from the hook out into the world. They are usually made up of actions by NPCs or of threats, and they leave behind evidence that Agents can investigate. Think of them as strings that connect the hook to the NPCs. Some leads help Agents complete the operation successfully. Others may hint at dangers the Agents might avoid. Others may lead to dead ends, adding temporary frustration that can make ultimately solving the mystery more satisfying.

Imagine how the hook affected the NPCs and the locations around them. What did the hook leave behind? What did it cause the NPCs to do? Once you know the central mystery—see **STEP EIGHT: RESOLUTION** on page 337—more leads may come to mind.

With each lead, it's critical to decide what actions the Agents must take to discover it—and how they can figure out those steps. Some leads simply require Agents asking the right kinds of questions or looking in the right places. Others can only be uncovered if an Agent is expert in a particular skill. That makes it doubly hard to uncover. If a lead is necessary for the Agents to complete the operation, add a couple of alternate ways they can find it. If they don't uncover it at one scene, they may have a chance to find it at another, perhaps using some other skill.

Our hook presents clear leads, so let's flesh some out. Feel free to add some more if you can.

The Crime Scene

The janitor was found in the hallway of the basement, near the morgue. Deliberate examination of the hallway floor can find the sheen of nude footprints leading from the morgue door, across the floor the janitor was waxing. They roughly match John Doe's foot size.

The Janitor's Body

The janitor, Hector Sandovar, was working alone, on the two lower floors of the hospital, mopping and waxing the floors. He was found at 6:35 A.M., face down, neck covered in ligature marks from strangulation. Fingerprints lifted from the neck match the John Doe suicide brought in the day before that is now missing.

John Doe

The suicide victim was found in a nearby river the day before the murder, and was determined to have been dead for several days. The unidentified body was labeled "John Doe" and stored in a slide-rack freezer. The freezer was later blown open from the inside, and the body is now missing.

Step Four: Dead Ends

There should be a few leads that don't help the Agents solve the mystery. If the players know that every source of information is valuable, there's less suspense and their problem-solving is less of a challenge. And it will be a short mystery! Here are a couple of ideas. Try to add your own—but not too many! A mystery that looks easy to the Handler might seem impossible to the players.

The Man in the Stairwell

The person who discovered the janitor's body, Elizabeth Tun, a nurse, reported hearing someone moving up the staircase towards the roof when she was walking downstairs. The "man in the stairwell" is in fact another nurse, Abigail Vosh, going up to the roof to take illegal medicine she routinely steals from the hospital. She is unconnected to the murder.

The Janitor's Religion

Sandovar practiced Santeria, "the way of the saints," an Afro-Caribbean syncretic religion. Though Santeria involves animal sacrifices and other elements Agents may find outré, it is not related to the mystery.

Step Five: Creepy Moments

A few creepy moments, unexpected touches of the unnatural, are key to a great Delta Green operation. What do you want the players to "feel"? Embed two or three memorable moments that will stick with them.

The Security Video

Agents who check the security cameras find strange footage from the night of the murder. The hallway has two cameras, and both cut to static, and the hall lights dimmed to emergency lighting, beginning at 1:31 A.M. Careful, frame-by-frame examination of the static around that time reveals three clear frames. One shows a shadowy form—it could be John Doe, but there's no way to be certain—leaping on the janitor. Another seems to show them caught in some sort of embrace, locked in a kiss. The third shows the janitor on the ground, dead, with no one else in the hallway. Subsequently checking the janitor's body finds foreign saliva on Sandovar's lips and mouth. The saliva does not match anyone in the hospital, living or dead. Where did it come from?

The Dead Homeless Man

Another body turns up in an identical condition to Sandovar's. The corpse's lips and mouth are covered in saliva as if he had been kissed, deeply. The fingerprints around the corpses' neck match the John Doe. The mystery expands.

The Janitor Comes Back

Exactly 24 hours later, Sandovar "wakes" and smashes his way free from the morgue in the same manner as the John Doe. He seeks a victim to embrace, kiss, and strangle, and then escapes.

Step Six: Events

The Agents are not the only people acting in the operation. What are the NPCs and threats up to? Here are some examples.

John Doe Makes an Appearance

John Doe is on the hunt for something. He (or it?) turns up at several nearby places concerned with books or burials. What is he doing?

Spreading Vector

Two new bodies show up, strangled in a similar manner as Sandovar.

Step Seven: Trouble and Interruptions

Throwing these in is easy. Look at the NPCs, imagine their motivations and the circumstances, and extrapolate. How do they react to the Agents' actions? Here are some examples. Try to invent some more.

Dr. Marini Steps In

The hospital director is fed up with all the shenanigans and tries to shut down the Agents' access to the hallway and the hospital. He's a giant pain in the ass, and threatens to bring the hospital's lawyers to the situation. He can be made to cooperate, but is very officious about it. He requires paperwork for anything, and that adds a layer of stress and tension to the Agents' investigation.

Another Body In a Chain

Another body turns up, strangled in a similar manner, with the same John Doe fingerprints. This can cause the Agents to split up, as some rush out to investigate the second death.

Deveraugh's Too Smart

Detective Deveraugh waits in the morgue the night after Sandovar's death, just because he has a feeling. Will he become the next victim? What happens if he and the Agents have the same plan?

Step Eight: Resolution

What is the source of this "infection"? Well, that depends. Some ideas are listed below, but it literally could be anything. Vampires. Space virus. A complex hoax. Use your imagination, and use this core threat to flesh out the operation. Here are some possibilities.

A Deeper Mystery

The Agents track John Doe to an apartment (this can be provided by a witness identifying him, his fingerprints getting a hit, or someone coming forward). The apartment was paid for with cash, using a phony name and address. It is packed with dozens of news clippings and printed articles dealing with missing or stolen bodies, and a large, handwritten book entitled *The Final Door*, which seems concerned with the chemical process of death in the human body. It lists no author.

A Closed Loop

When the Agents find and kill the janitor and John Doe, they collapse into a gray dust, leaving behind a single, spiked, silvery cluster of unidentified metal. What this is is unclear, but John Doe's mote is much larger and more complex than Sandovar's.

A Greater Threat

Even a mystery closed may begins to propagate. Is this the beginning of an epidemic? How long will it be until other forces at play notice?

Step Nine: The Cover-Up

The purpose of any Delta Green operation is to reduce human exposure to the unnatural. What steps will the Agents have to take to explain everything away so nobody else investigates it? How far will they have to go to obscure any crimes they committed while trying to save lives? Who is most likely to challenge their story?

Witnesses

Did anyone other than the Agents see the dead coming back to life, or see a killer suddenly turn to dust and a weird silvery shard? How would you react if you saw that happen?

The Police

The local police will be happy to let the case go as long as they have a suspect in custody or dead, and no reason to think there are more suspects at large. But if Detective Deveraugh died, that complicates things for the Agents. The police will be much, much more heavily involved.

The Hospital

Dr. Marini's first priority is protecting the hospital. That means reducing liability over anyone who got hurt or killed while in the hospital's care. And Marini is a hardened skeptic, unwilling to accept any notion of the unnatural. Even if he sees it with his own eyes, he'll explain it away. He'll be happy as long as the Agents produce a suspect to blame and show the hospital is not responsible.

The Families

Even John Doe came from somewhere. The families of the victims, and of whoever the Agents pin the blame on in their official story, want to know what really happened. If they think the police or the Agents are lying, they may call in lawyers or local reporters. The Agents may have to satisfy the families fast if they don't want their carefully-orchestrated cover-up to make the evening news and go viral on social media.

// Appendices //

INTO THE WEST

56

When there was nowhere left to go, I went west. Twenty-six days before, I saw my last road—nothing more than a dirt track, really—and I went past it, and up. Two mountains. A river so large I didn't think I'd be able to cross it. A field of yellowed grass as far as I could see. Now, here is here. And still the world goes west. My sat-phone stopped working somewhere before Rikaze and I threw it away. After all, I hadn't seen an outlet since Lhasa. I haven't eaten since the road, but I feel fine. The map said as much.

Seven years ago today, I received the book about the hidden plateau. It was written in 1903 by an Englishman whose name escapes me. A colonel in Nepal. Inside was a handwritten map with instructions. Go here, smoke this weed. Go here, drink from this stream. Sleep here, dream about the world. I did it all.

I should be in Kashmir by now, but I know I'm not. I know because at the second peak, the mountains stretched in all directions for as far as I could see. Endless. So I keep wandering west, certain I have slipped from the world of men forever.

Then, smoke on the far side of the valley.

The buildings there are clustered on the side of a mountain like goats gathered for warmth. The streets are empty, laid with rolling, perfectly colored stones. The sun is shining. I smell jasmine tea.

In the tea room, dozens cluster near to their ceramic cups, sipping. No one looks to me as I sit and tea is brought. Money is never spoken of, but I don't imagine the U.S. dollar would go very far here. I lose myself to the warmth of the tea, for awhile.

It is the first drink I have had in twenty-three days, but somehow it feels unnecessary.

The owner is a thin, prematurely old man with a wide smile. He goes table to table, pouring liquid and steam. At each, he stops and exchanges pleasantries in a language I can't identify.

"Abso elat, tende," he says to me, smiling. "Tende? Tende?" He pours more tea.

At the last table, the one farthest from me, he places the kettle on the wood, bows deeply from the hips, and mumbles something.

The figure there, covered in leather bib, is low and wide and in the dark. It stirs, and I think I see red hair. Then blue eyes. A white hand from beneath the dark leather waves the tea man off.

"Colonel," the tea man says, very clearly, and turns to the next table.

US MI

NAVY

NAME

Arehart, F

Bader, All

The FBI's Crime Scene A
profiling process These st
Crime Assessment, The C
A brief explanation of eac

Profiling Inputs:

This involves the collectior
specific case. This would ty

INVESTIGATOR'S GUIDE TO ALLEGATIONS OF "RITUAL" CHILD ABUSE

January 1992

Kenneth V. Lanning
Supervisory Special Agent

Behavioral Science Unit

Operation FULMINATE: The Sentinels of Twilight

IN THIS *DELTA GREEN* SCENARIO, THE AGENTS learn that not all those who are lost should be found.

Overview

Something is taking people from national parks, and it might not be precisely human. Since the inception of the national park system, over 1,100 people have been reported missing inside their confines, many of them children. Often, missing children are found far from where they vanished, with no shoes or other clothing. Some are found dead. Some are never found at all.

Operation FULMINATE begins in Yosemite National Park on the Sunday of the Fourth of July weekend: Sunday, 5 JUL 2015, or 3 JUL 2016, or 2 JUL 2017—pick the date to suit your campaign. It likely interrupts Agents' holidays with their families. The operation will likely last no more than a day or two.

If the Agents survive that long.

TESTS: Stat, skill, and SAN tests required of the Agents are in **bold** for easy reference.

Operational Briefing

1. The Agents must go to the Rancheria Falls Trailhead ranger station in the Hetch Hetchy region of Yosemite National Park. They are to investigate the unexpected recovery of a six-year-old child who was found wandering naked in a field by a ranger, early Saturday (yesterday) morning.
2. The child identified himself as Brandon McGill of Topeka, Kansas, and asked to call his parents. After a brief conversation, the parents were beside themselves with confusion and tearful excitement and said they would depart for Yosemite immediately. They purchased tickets on the next available flight, departing at 6:30 A.M. on Sunday morning (today).
3. After the confusing conversation with the family, the supervising park ranger contacted the FBI. He texted photos of Brandon McGill, and the FBI matched them with earlier photos. Much earlier photos.
4. Brandon McGill disappeared from the Hetch Hetchy area in 1980 at age 6. If still alive, he should be more than 40 years old.
5. San Francisco-based FBI Special Agent Delilah Sands—a Delta Green agent—noticed the bulletin, and used her credentials as a child psychology specialist to muscle her way into the investigation. She has disrupted it as much as possible, "accidentally" sending confusing messages that delayed the FBI's response. Other Delta Green assets in the FBI held up response with apparently inept legal and jurisdictional wrangling.
6. The Program hastily scrambled a team (the players' Agents) for Operation FULMINATE. The Agents get the call Saturday afternoon, with orders to depart at once for a briefing with their case officer.
7. Sunday morning, the Agents meet their case officer in a secure meeting room in a small office building that poses as an accounting firm. It is a CIA front company, and everyone there assumes the Agents are on some official CIA-related operation and knows better than to ask questions. The case officer conveys the team's orders:

- Locate the child.
- Identify the child.
- Determine whether an unnatural threat is in the area.
- Remove the unnatural threat.
- Make the outcome appear mundane.

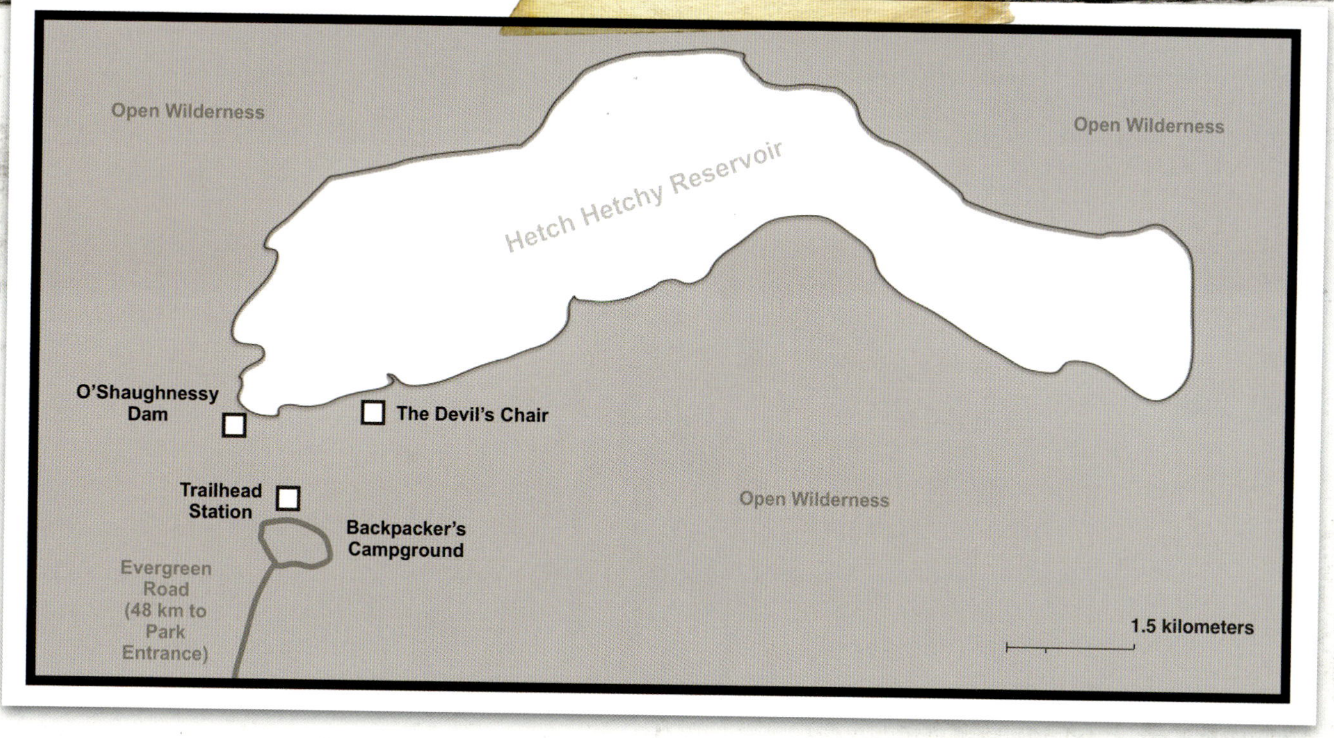

Resources

This operation came together as quickly as the Program could manage. They have had no time to get badges and false identities. The Agents have to talk their way through any trouble and improvise their cover-up. The case officer may have black-market weapons or other random supplies in a nearby safe house; that's up to the Handler.

The Truth

The found boy is Brandon McGill. He has spent most of the last 36 years in a dream-state, in hollow lava craters 5.5 kilometers beneath the Earth's surface, a prisoner of the K'n-Y'ani—a strange, advanced offshoot of humanity that has existed since time immemorial.

The K'n-Y'ani have struggled to use the humans of the surface (whom they consider "sub-beings") as breeding stock and food supplies. Their race is ancient and immortal, but also dwindling. What was once a civilization of hundreds of thousands is now, through time and circumstance, merely hundreds.

For centuries, since their retreat from the multiplying hordes of sub-beings, the K'n-Y'ani have snatched humans from the surface using their hypergeometric powers. They are the source of the legend of the "Moon-Faced People" fought by the Sioux in ancient times, as well as the giant, pale cannibals of Paiute legend. They may be responsible for the Serpent Mound and other structures built by the mysterious Adena "Mound Builder" culture.

In the modern world, the K'n-Y'ani have kept to places where they can stay well-hidden. Most of their structures are so deep that no human can encroach on them. Their powers allow them to move through spacetime in unnatural ways. There is no passage into their blue-lit caverns that a human may traverse, but the few K'n-Y'ani that remain move about the surface as needed.

With McGill, the K'n-Y'ani found something they long sought: human genetics compatible with their own. For decades, through communion with their god Ossadogowah, they have infected the boy with alien materials that caused him to produce the substance called *etzil iztac,* the "white blood." They have harvested enough stock from McGill to begin repopulating and feeding their once-great cities. McGill was a genetic sow, ever producing what they needed, and kept in a state of stasis which halted his memories as well as his aging. He woke only briefly, from time to time, to be fed special substances culled from Ossadogowah.

But the continuous ingestion of substances from Ossadogowah have transformed McGill, and awakened in him vast and terrifying powers. A simple child's nightmare was all it took for McGill to lay waste to dozens of K'n-Y'ani. The boy destroyed his captors and "thought" himself back to the surface. He stills seems like a child. He is actually a dangerous killing machine, vital to the resurrection of the K'n-Yani.

But it is worse. The K'n-Yani made duplicates of Brandon McGill. Many, many duplicates, some more "true" than others, serving as food, for ritual purposes, and for production of the substances the K'n-Yani require. These duplicates seem to be "awakening" like the first McGill. In turn, one by one, they escape.

The K'n-Y'ani are bent on locating and securing the "original" Brandon McGill, the first. The other Brandons are disposable.

Timeline

The Agents have 24 hours before the regular FBI arrive and things get much, much harder to contain.

Saturday Morning

National Park Ranger Tomika Gallegos finds a child, naked, wandering in a huckleberry field near the Hetch Hetchy Reservoir, about 2,000 meters from a rock formation known as the Devil's Chair. She is walking down to a backpacker's camp, collecting garbage, when she comes upon McGill. The child is coherent, though naked and filthy. He identifies himself and asks for his parents. Gallegos suspects the boy is lost from the backpacker's camp. She takes him to the Rancheria Falls Trailhead ranger station and gives him her cellphone. He is baffled by the phone, though he uses it readily enough when shown how. Gallegos speaks with his parents, Ann and Ian McGill, and learns they were not in the park and had not reported a child missing—but they were, and they had, in 1980. Their talk with the child and the ranger is brief, confusing, and near-hysterical. The McGills immediately buy tickets on the next available flight from Topeka, leaving early the next morning.

Saturday Mid-Morning

Park Ranger Douglass Keena, Gallegos' supervisor, calls the Sacramento FBI office, which covers Yosemite. Photos of the child are exchanged via text and a positive identification is made, but the FBI agents are baffled.

Saturday Afternoon

Hearing the strange details, Quantico-based FBI Special Agent Delilah Sands—a Delta Green agent in Behavioral Analysis Unit 3, which handles crimes against children—steps in. She alerts her case officer in the Program and forces herself into to the case. She calls in some favors, causing a jurisdictional dispute with Sacramento over which office will send agents, Sacramento or the national headquarters. That holds up the FBI's official response for a day, long enough for the Program to assemble the Agents' team for Operation FULMINATE. Sands does not join them, but remains in contact with the Agents as Agent Jace and runs interference to further delay the official response.

Sunday Morning

The Agents arrive as an unexpected rainstorm descends on the area, bringing thunder and lightning and reports of a water spout on the reservoir. A severe weather warning is issued for the area, restricting road travel.

Sunday Afternoon

Ian McGill (age 63) and his wife Anne (age 62) land at Fresno-Yosemite International Airport at about 12:30 p.m. They rent a car and depart for Yosemite.

Sunday Afternoon

Backpackers in the Hetch Hetchy area report a stranger poking around. Three separate reports come in within an hour, describing a strange, tall, pale "Indian" crouched in the trees and scrub brush, watching the backpackers from a distance in the pouring rain. The storm is severe, but comes and goes. Most backpackers fold up camp and take to the Rancheria Falls Trailhead ranger station for shelter. Ian and Anne McGill arrive at Yosemite about 3:00 p.m., but are held back from the Hetch Hetchy area due to severe weather.

Sunday Evening

After dark, four K'n-Y'ani "Strangers" launch an assault on the area during the rainstorm, looking for Brandon McGill.

Monday Morning

The regular FBI arrive.

Files on the Disappearance

Digital copies of the FBI's 1980 reports on Brandon McGill's disappearance are available from Agent Jace through an anonymous file-sharing link. They are relatively benign, but between the lines are bizarre implications.

Brandon F. McGill disappeared from the Hetch Hetchy area in Yosemite, near a natural landmark called "The Devil's Chair," on June 22, 1980. He was with his parents on vacation.

The Devil's Chair is a natural stone structure of shattered columnar basalt that happens to have cracked and collapsed to form a vague "seat" three meters tall and two meters wide. It is a popular tourist attraction.

Brandon McGill's parents—Ian and Ann McGill, ages 27 and 26 at the time—claimed the child was "right there with them" when he vanished. It was approximately 4:30 p.m.

The FBI became involved after an eyewitness claimed to have seen a man in black clothing following the McGills down the trail. Two independent witnesses volunteered this information. One described the man as tall and pale. The other described only as a figure in black.

Multiple searches—one of which involved well over 100 personnel and two helicopters—found nothing. Brandon McGill was officially declared dead in 1987. His parents did their best to get on with their lives...until the phone call from Brandon on Saturday morning.

Brandon McGill's father Ian was briefly investigated due to a domestic violence charge in 1979. This had to do with an infidelity. When the couple reconciled, his wife Ann dropped the charges.

Park rangers' reports mention other children disappearing in the park under similar there-then-not circumstances. Twenty-four children vanished in Yosemite over the last 40 years. The report of a long-retired park ranger named Walter Dellio mentions other oddities:

- Bad weather follows disappearances. The same thing happened here. On June 23, a huge squall hit the lake for two days, from out of a blue sky.
- Dogs could find no scent of McGill. That led many older rangers to conclude the boy wouldn't be found.
- When lost children are found, it is often miles from where they were lost. Veteran rangers encouraged a huge search radius. Often the child loses shoes or other clothing, but is found unharmed.
- Those that are recovered have high temperatures and are withdrawn and disoriented.
- The disappearances almost always occur late afternoon or early dusk. (McGill vanished at 4:33 p.m.)
- The disappearances tend to occur in areas overgrown with huckleberries. The Devil's Chair area is covered in huckleberry bushes.

Trailhead Station

The park rangers operate out of the summer-only Rancheria Falls Trailhead Station, a little more than a kilometer from O'Shaughnessy Dam on western end of the Hetch Hetchy Reservoir. The station is less than a kilometer from the Hetch Hetchy Backpackers Campground, and a kilometer and a half or so from the Devil's Chair.

The area is hot and dry in the summer. It is interspersed with many varieties of trees: California black oak, ponderosa pine, incense-cedar and white fir, with an occasional giant sequoia. The area has exposed rock faces, dirt, and scrub grasses which seem very desertlike in the summer. Small bushes cluster next to the trees: Oregon grape, Sierra coffeeberry, gooseberry, and pygmy rose. There are large open areas with only low shrubs, often screened by larger wind-break providing trees. It is hard to pick out human silhouettes at a distance.

The two-story Trailhead Station can sleep 19 (40 in a pinch), and has enough food and supplies for a week. It is a sprawling brown structure, obviously built and re-built over time, with reinforced snow roofs and a large free-standing radio tower. It is powered by the nearby hydroelectric dam.

The station has two four-by-four jeeps, three quadrunners, and enough open space for a helicopter to land. It is connected via telephone and radio to the main Yosemite station, which provides assistance when necessary.

Most of the rangers' job is making certain the backpackers in the area don't go too wild, don't light fires outside designated safe-burn areas, and, most importantly, don't interfere with the operation of O'Shaughnessy Dam. Fishing on the reservoir is allowed, but swimming is not. Backpackers see the rangers as a nuisance, and some call them "Pine Police" or "Pine Pigs." The rangers shrug it off. Being a National Park Ranger requires a certain level of detachment.

Trailhead Station has a staff of six, one or two at the station at any given time.

The Backpackers

The backpackers in the area (38 of them) are a smattering of normal people for a nice hike in Yosemite. On Sunday morning, they are either setting up or breaking down their camps. Due to the storm, most are in poor spirits. They were hoping for clear skies.

Brandon McGill

McGill speaks and acts like a normal six-year-old boy, but close examination with **Search** or **Medicine** at 40%, or a successful roll, reveals nearly invisible, seam-like scars criss-crossing McGill's body in bizarre, interlocking patterns.

He has a green tattoo on the back of his neck of three squares and what looks like a stylized ram head. Agents with **Archeology** at 40% or higher note it is similar to the Nahuatl (the Aztec language) character for "boy."

A tiny bump is detectable beneath the tattoo. If excised, the object in his neck is a small, transparent piece of quartz with a fleck of gold in its center.

If injured (including the surgery above), McGill heals almost immediately due to his regeneration power—as long as the quartz object remains in his neck.

If the quartz-object is removed, McGill seems to "lose" his apportation abilities and his regeneration, and is effectively neutralized as a threat.

McGill has an unusual dislike of heat. If exposed flame or placed in hot water, he goes into some sort of epileptic seizure, and a round or two later, the etzil iztac—the "white blood"—emerges from him and attempts to escape. It is a white, near-transparent blob that is extremely fast and motile. (Treat this as the shoggoth-weapon described in **THE THING IN THE STONE FACE** on page 352, at 1/4 the stats and damage.) McGill can produce one of these things every nine hours.

McGill remembers very little of his whereabouts. He remembers the Strangers, odd men who spoke without any voices. They were tall. *Very* tall. Taller than any other grownup. He remembers blue caves. He ate a grey paste that was made of mushrooms.

There were other children in the blue caves, Evelyn and Thomas. They were brother and sister. Agents who go online can find a record of two children

>> Park Rangers

Name	Age	Notes
Park Ranger Douglas Keena	35	In charge of the station
Park Ranger Tomika Gallegos	29	Found Brandon McGill
Park Ranger Maria Lemay	25	A trained medic, with First Aid 50%, Medicine 40% and Pharmacy 40%
Park Ranger Charles Nicholson	24	Pursuing a law degree at night and hoping to join the FBI
Park Ranger Christopher Devlin	22	A new recruit who just got his college degree; an Eagle Scout and proud of it
Park Ranger Naomi Blomberg	22	A new recruit who just got her college degree

>> Sample Backpackers

Name	Age	Notes
Elizabeth Bingham-Grant	60	A San Francisco hairdresser
Joyce Vasquez	40	A graphic designer originally from Connecticut; she took up hiking with her neighbor, Elizabeth Bingham Grant
William Bates Vasquez	22	A construction worker; Joyce Vasquez's adopted son
Paul Holding	69	An Oakland environmental lawyer, semi-retired
Lisa Gentry	31	A web designer, in a May-December romance with Holding after doing freelance work for his firm last year

missing in the Yosemite area from 1918, Evelyn and Thomas Yevetney.

When McGill sleeps, mild apportation effects occur. Doors shut without cause and things shift, ever so slightly. This is difficult to notice unless it is being looked for.

When the Strangers appear, McGill becomes hysterical, causing weird psychokinetic effects. Radios short out. Vehicles won't start, and worse. He might lash out with his Apportation Slam power, slamming things into the Stranger or (if a **Luck** roll fails) into an Agent or bystander who just happens to be in the way.

When he loses his temper or is truly terrified, huge apportation events occur. His Apportation Smash power lashes out, enough to inflict a Lethality 20% attack, lift and destroy a vehicle, or collapse a portion of a building.

The O'Shaughnessy Dam

The dam is closed to all but park rangers. The gate is locked and topped with barbed wire. Anyone attempting to climb over it to the spillway must make an **Athletics** roll at a –20% penalty. On a failure, the Agent suffers 1D4–1 damage and must make a **Luck** roll. If that fails, the Agent tumbles 40 meters into the water below, taking another 1D10 damage.

Operating the spillway controls requires **Craft (Mechanics)** at 50% or better, or an **INT** test at –40%. Those that do so can cause a flash flood in the valley so severe it momentarily overruns Trailhead Station, the Hetch Hetchy Backpackers Campground, and everything within five kilometers. Anyone on the ground when the flash flood happens must make a **Athletics** roll at –20% or a **Luck** roll, whichever is better, to climb to safety. A character who fails is swept away on the waves and smashed by trees and debris for 1D20 damage. Being caught in a flash flood costs 0/1D4–1 **SAN** due to helplessness.

This flood affects the K'n-Y'ani and their servants in this way as well, and most likely causes them to retreat.

The Moon-Faced People

The K'n-Y'ani are either the source or an offshoot of the human race. Where and why we split remains unknown, perhaps even to them. In most encounters, they are physically terrifying. They are extremely tall, some as tall as five meters, and have yellow-grey skin. They have broad noses, high foreheads, and pronounced cheekbones. A K'n-Yani has a large, wide skull which elongates strangely in the back. (In ancient times, certain Central American tribes used bands to force their skulls into such shapes in imitation of their K'n-Yani overlords.) Their teeth are broad and flat, and double rowed. Their hair ranges in color from black to wiry red.

Usually, they are nearly naked, wearing simple loincloths. They wear cleverly-made jewelry of copper, gold, and mica. Few carry anything more useful than a ceremonial knife.

Fleeing the Site (The Moon Children)

Agents can easily flee the site without McGill, suffering only the SAN loss described in **OUTCOMES** on page 349. Those who attempt to rush McGill from the site via vehicle find it more complicated than they had imagined.

In the bad weather, the only road out of the area—Evergreen Road—is treacherous and uncertain. Driving off-road, even in a four-wheel-drive vehicle, leaves the Agents immediately bogged down and stranded.

Worse, the Strangers wait with their servants, the Moon Children. These are the resurrected remnants of children who perished in experiments to create the genetic material the K'n-Yani require.

The Strangers order one Moon Child after another to leap into the road just as the car approaches. A **Drive** roll at –20% avoids a child-corpse, but they keep coming. If the vehicle moves too slowly to be stopped, dozens of Moon Children swarm it. Moon Children who have latched onto the car climb on top and smash their way in. The driver must roll **Drive** at –40% or go off the road. The Moon Children make fast work of the vehicle, ripping off panels, flattening tires and gaining access to the engine block.

Adjusting the Pace

The following notes should help the Handler in keeping the pace somewhat frenetic. The feeling of the operation should be one of survival and fear. The Strangers do not directly assault Trailhead Station for fear of terrifying Brandon McGill, and in turn, causing an "outburst"—unless the Agents protect McGill well enough to force them.

Speed It Up

If the operation seems to be slowing, any of these can ratchet up the intensity:

Increase the Storm's Intensity

The storm begins bad enough to limit visibility to a five or ten meters, but it can always be worse. Increase the storm intensity to cause –20% for all skills outside and –40% to try to see or hit anything beyond three meters. Rain and hail might pelt the ranger station, and trees might come down due to high winds.

Have the Backpackers Cause Trouble

The backpackers are normal people with normal worries. Many have cars parked near the backpacker area and might insist on going out to check on them. They may complain about Delta Green Agents doing any number of odd things, or they may take out their smartphones to take video of anything interesting.

Hint at the Moon Children

Have either a backpacker or a ranger see a Moon Child at a window momentarily and lose the appropriate **SAN**. Normal reactions follow.

Reveal the First Stranger

Worse, have someone see a Stranger, either as a *huge* silhouette at a distance, or standing or walking right next to a backpacker, ranger, or Agent who has no idea the Stranger is there. Apply **SAN** losses as usual.

Have the Strangers Destroy Vehicles

The Strangers may take a step to destroy the vehicles in the parking lot near the backpacker area to prevent escape. If they do, describe the smashing noises heard over the drumming rain, as well as the momentary flair or car alarms—which are nearly instantly silenced. Investigation reveals the cars as demolished by something huge (**SAN** loss: 0/1D4).

Slow It Down

If the operation seems to be rushing forward, any of these can bring focus to a single event, and slow it down:

Cause Conflict With the Park Rangers

Delta Green Agents who are not careful, or who begin doing odd things to McGill (such as excising his quartz implant), quickly find that National Park Rangers are not to be trifled with. Keena and the others question and even threaten the Delta Green Agents. They are armed and will do anything to protect the child.

Have McGill's Parents Arrive

Somehow, through the rain, McGill's parents arrive at Trailhead Station. When they see Brandon, they are apoplectic with joy, each losing 1/1D4 **SAN**. They do not leave his side from that point on for *any* reason—unless, of course, another Brandon shows up!

Show McGill's Susceptibility to Heat

Have the Agents discover etzil iztac—the "white blood"—when McGill reacts to heat. Have some of it "escape" through a cut or a bloody nose and get loose in the ranger station.

Display McGill's Apportation Effects

Have things get knocked over, doors slam, or people thrown when Brandon is startled.

Have McGill Remember

Agents trying to get McGill to tell what happened to him might get their wish. McGill describes his experiences in the blue-lit caverns of K'n-Yan: Its ghostly denizens half-visible and half-material. Their wishes appearing in his thoughts telepathically. Their awful, undead slaves formed of once-living human beings warped into bizarre shapes and kept animate by unknown means. Their souvenirs of human culture from the most ancient to the modern. Their horrifying experiments on young McGill himself. The nonsense word "OSSADOGAWAH" coming into McGill's head as he is fed the strange gray paste. (The word may sound disturbingly like "Tsathoggua" to an Agent who has **Unnatural** at 20% or greater or who succeeds at an **Unnatural** test.) All of that is filtered through McGill's six-year-old frame of reference, halting and confused.

Extensive details can grant an Agent +1 point in Unnatural, costing the Agent 1/1D4 **SAN** for hearing it. But it also costs McGill 1D4 **SAN** for remembering. That may require an Agent to succeed at Psychotherapy to keep McGill from shutting down in a fugue state.

Have Another Brandon McGill Show Up

Have a second, naked, terrified McGill show up at the door, spotted in the woods, or brought in by another ranger. This Brandon McGill is identical to the first Brandon except for a different mark on his neck, the meaning of which defies analysis. Those who have seen the first McGill lose 1/1D4 **SAN**, or 1/1D10 for his parents.

Have the Strangers Possess Backpackers

Have a backpacker be possessed by a Stranger and attempt to knock McGill unconscious and carry the boy outside. During this possession, the backpacker is under the influence of the Strangers and cannot be reasoned with. An Agent who kills a backpacker and later discovers the possession loses 1/1D8 **SAN** due to violence.

Outcomes

The Agents' mission is to end the unnatural threat. Some ways of ending the threat are more palatable—and difficult—than others.

Surrender McGill to the K'n-Yani

This horrific outcome may become necessary to save lives. If McGill is offered to the K'n-Yani, they immediately cease violence, take the child and vanish into the ground. McGill is never seen again. Agents who do this may be wracked by guilt for years. Each loses 1/1D8 **SAN**.

Murder McGill

An even more horrific outcome. If McGill's abilities are identified, and he is deemed enough of a threat, Agents may feel forced to "take him out." Murdering a child—even a duplicate McGill—takes an awful toll on the human mind. Each Agent loses 1/1D10 **SAN**.

McGill Survives

If McGill survives the incident and escapes the park, each Agent gains 1D4 **SAN** no matter what else happens. Each duplicate who dies in the process costs the Agents 0/1 **SAN**.

The K'n-Yani Are Killed and McGill Survives

In this difficult outcome, the Agents are triumphant and feel their choices have had an amazing impact on the situation. Each Agent gains 1D10 **SAN**. Each duplicate who dies in the process costs the Agents 0/1 **SAN**.

The Cover-Up

As the Agents confront Brandon McGill's strange powers, the Strangers, and all the Strangers' servants and tools, a dozen park rangers and backpackers are nearby. McGill's parents are waiting for the weather to clear so they can rush in. The regular FBI will drive in soon. The Agents could have a lot of witnesses to their operation.

If the weather allows it, careful Agents may avoid witnesses by sending the backpackers away, or by leaving with Brandon despite the park rangers' concerns about the weather and the closed road.

Most people don't believe what they don't wish to believe, and most bystanders would prefer not to believe in ghostly giants. Those that are certain often fear the ridicule they'd face telling the truth. With a plausible story, the Agents might convince witnesses that they did not see what they thought. Perhaps the Stranger seen through a stormy midnight window wasn't a Sasquatch, only a trick of light. Perhaps the Moon Children swarming the parking lot were wild dogs. Perhaps that invisible force that tore through a half-seen giant was just a flash of lightning and a tree falling. Perhaps that gunfire was just thunder. It happened so fast, after all.

Are you sure you're remembering it right?

Witnesses who stick to their stories may wind up on national news, probably the butt of countless jokes. Or they may be interviewed by a sympathetic seeker from Phenomen-X.com, putting a zealous citizen-journalist onto the Agents' trail. (For example, Lydia Kusuma, a 20-year-old Bay Area bike messenger who goes by the online nickname SueSueMe.)

If Trailhead Station and the surrounding woods become crime scenes due to the deaths of Agents, rangers, backpackers, or Brandons, the Agents have a much tougher task. If they come up with a plausible narrative, it may take a **Bureaucracy** or **Law** roll to stall the regular FBI another day, or a **Forensics** roll to falsify or conceal evidence, or a **Persuade** roll to talk Keena and his rangers into cooperating. Play it by ear. If the Agents are clever, it may be easier. Failing that, the Agents might face hard questioning.

If worse comes to worst, refer to **GETTING FIRED** and **PROSECUTION**, on page 80 of the *Agent's Handbook*, and explore the repercussions. Even if Agents lose their government jobs or go to prison, that only means they'll be civilians or ex-cons the next time the Program calls.

Characters

Each of these wants something different, and all their goals are at odds with those of the Agents.

- The park rangers want to protect the people and environment in their care.
- The backpackers want to enjoy the park and, when things go bad, to escape intact.
- Brandon McGill wants to go home.
- Brandon McGill's parents want to be reunited with their lost son.
- The Strangers want to take Brandon McGill back to their blue-lit, subterranean world.
- The Thing in the Stone Face and the Moon Children serve the will of the Strangers.

Park Rangers

National Park Rangers are college-educated and have standard federal law enforcement training and powers. The rangers assist Agents whose presence and actions seem official and legitimate. Most rangers, unless overcome by temporary insanity, will fight to the death to protect a lost child. They wear pistols, survival knives, pepper spray (used mostly to deter wild animals), and body armor, and have a few rifles and shotguns in a small, locked armory in the chief ranger's office at Trailhead Station.

Typical Park Ranger

Dedicated to protecting the public.

STR 11 **CON** 13 **DEX** 10 **INT** 10 **POW** 12 **CHA** 10

HP 12 **WP** 12 **SAN** 60 **BREAKING POINT** 48

ARMOR: Light kevlar vest (Armor 3).

SKILLS: Alertness 50%, Athletics 40%, Firearms 50%, First Aid 50%, Law 30%, Navigate 50%, Search 40%, Survival 50%, Swim 40%, Unarmed Combat 50%.

ATTACKS: SIG Sauer P228 pistol 50%, damage 1D10.

Remington Model 870 shotgun 50% (+20% beyond short range, firing shot), damage 2D10.

FN M16A2 rifle 50%, damage 1D12, Armor Piercing 3.

Pepper spray 50%, stuns target.

Unarmed 50%, damage 1D4−1.

Backpackers

These ordinary hikers are unprepared for what's coming.

Typical Backpacker

Prepared for nature, not the unnatural.

STR 10 **CON** 10 **DEX** 10 **INT** 10 **POW** 10 **CHA** 10

HP 10 **WP** 10 **SAN** 50, **BREAKING POINT** 40

SKILLS: Alertness 30%, Navigate 25%, Survival 30%.

ATTACKS: Unarmed 40%, damage 1D4−1.

Pocket knife 30%, damage 1D4.

Brandon F. McGill

Brandon appears to be a normal boy of age 6, though he is chronologically over 40. If he loses SAN, he must make a follow-up SAN roll or retreat into a fugue state, closing his eyes and tuning out the terrible world. His powers may emerge in deadly ways in that state. His duplicates use the same stats.

Brandon McGill

Haunted child.

STR 3 **CON** 6 **DEX** 8 **INT** 7 **POW** 10 **CHA** 10

HP 5 **WP** 10 **SAN** 35 **BREAKING POINT** 30

DISORDER: Fugues.

ARMOR: If McGill knows he is under attack, his powers deflect 3 HP damage per round.

ATTACKS: Apportation slam 30%, damage 2D10.

Apportation smash 45%, Lethality 20%.

DENIAL: McGill does not realize that he is utilizing strange powers. If forced to acknowledge his armor, regeneration, or apportation slam power, he loses 0/1 SAN. If forced to acknowledge his apportation smash attack, he loses 1/1D6 SAN.

REGENERATION: McGill regenerates 2 HP per turn.

SAN LOSS: Seeing McGill's powers at work costs 0/1 **SAN**, or 0/1D4 to see them lash out at a Stranger. Being attacked by Brandon's power costs 1/1D6 **SAN**.

The Four Strangers

The four K'n-Yani warriors are huge, silent, somber, and terrifying. They do not run, scream, or otherwise show alarm or emotional reactions—even if fatally injured. They fear open sunlight, and extremely bright light is enough to stun them for a round. They operate at no penalty in complete darkness.

A Stranger

More than human.

STR 22 **CON** 29 **DEX** 11 **INT** 19 **POW** 19

HP 25 **WP** 19

ARMOR: See **OUT OF PHASE** and **SCALE CONTROL**.

SKILLS: Alertness 60%, Anthropology (Human) 35%, Athletics 30%, Melee Weapons 50%, Swim 45%, Unarmed Combat 45%, Unnatural 50%

ATTACKS: Projection 55%, damage 1D6 (see **PROJECTION**).

Ceremonial knife 50%, damage 2D6.

Unarmed 45%, damage 1D10.

HUMAN OFFSHOOT: The K'n-Yani are genetically close to humanity, but not identical. Drugs and other chemical irritants sometimes work and sometimes do not. Any attempt to drug or chemically stun or disable a K'n-Yani succeeds only with a Luck roll.

OUT OF PHASE: K'n-Yani spend much of their immortal lives in a ghostly, immaterial state. A fully physical K'n-Yani can use its action in a combat turn to go immaterial, becoming immune to physical harm. Or one can go half-immaterial but still able to grasp physical things. When a K'n-Yani is half-immaterial, any attack that rolls an odd amount of damage or gets an odd number on a Lethality roll passes harmlessly through it.

SCALE CONTROL: The K'n-Yani can disassemble their physical form, and cause it to grow or shrink at will, by absorbing nearby matter or expelling it. While on the surface, the K'n-Yani often are five meters tall or more. A K'n-Yani at that great size is difficult to injure: a failed Lethality roll does not destroy it, but inflicts HP damage equal to the Lethality rating. Beneath the Earth, they assume human sizes, with half the listed STR, CON, and HP, and inflicting only 1D4−1 unarmed damage. Expelling mass causes a blue-white bright light that is visible at great distances.

MOTHER EARTH: A K'n-Yani touching earth with its bare skin can instantly vanish and return to their underground kingdom.

TRANSAPPORTATION: The K'n-Yani can step through physical obstructions as if they were not there; a single step transports the subject to the "other side" of the item, no matter the distance. Anyone they are holding is transported as well (and suffers 0/1 SAN loss).

PROJECTION, POSSESSION, OR ERASURE: The K'n-Yani can move objects, possess humans, or remove themselves from an individual's perception. Each attempted use of one of these powers costs 3 WP.

Projection allows the K'n-Yani to push objects with blunt force at a distance of about 10 m. This inflicts 1D6 damage, roughly the equivalent force of being struck by a stout club.

Possession is a mental onslaught of any one person in sight. The target gets a SAN roll in defense. On a success, the target loses 1 SAN and feels an alien presence. On a failure, the target loses 1/1D6 SAN and the K'n-Yani is in the target's mind. For one turn, the possessing K'n-Yani can see, hear and feel what the target does, and can sense and understand the target's thoughts and recent memories. The target can sense, feel, and do nothing. Once inside, the K'n-Yani can cause the target to take any single action of the possessor's choice, including suicide or murder. Then the possession ends. Normal SAN losses apply as the target realizes he or she has been possessed and recognizes what he or she has done.

Erasure causes a target to fail to see the K'n Y'ani or the effects of their presence. It only works on one target at a time. The target gets a SAN roll. On a failure, the K'n-Yani vanishes completely and remains unobservable by the target. The K'n-Yani can stand right in front of the target, root through the target's belongings, or even attack the target and not be seen.

THE STONE FACE: The K'n-Y'ani use this only as a last resort. Each stranger possesses one. It is an engineered shoggoth-weapon that will exist in the upper world for only several minutes before destroying itself in an out-of-control biological feedback loop. It appears to be a lump of white ivory the size of a human fist, carved with vaguely Mesoamerican patterns: a stylized K'n-Yani face.

SAN LOSS: 0/1D4.

The Thing in the Stone Face

The thing in the ivory-like stone is a shoggoth-weapon. Once thrown—this an action but not a roll—it hatches at the end of the turn. At the end of the second turn, it is the size of a small dog. At the end of the third, it is as big as a man. At the end of the fourth, it is full size, as large as an economy car. It is a mass of corded muscle and flesh with eyes like silver dollars. After 1D4 minutes, the thing disintegrates into a foul puddle of volatile chemicals. It does not attack the K'n-Yani or Brandon McGill.

Thing in the Stone Face

A shoggoth-weapon.

STR 30 **CON** 50 **DEX** 10 **INT** 4 **POW** 8

HP 40 **WP** 8

ARMOR: 5.

SKILLS: Alertness 50%.

ATTACKS: Grab 30%, damage 1D6.

Crush 25%, damage 1D10+2.

CRUSH: The shoggoth-weapon can use its crush attack only on a target it has already grabbed. If the crush attack succeeds, it inflicts damage once and then spits the target back out. If the grush attack fails, the target remains grabbed.

GRAB: If the shoggoth-weapon successfully grabs a target, the victim takes 1D6 damage from being squeezed and burned by strange chemicals, and is pinned. The target must escape the pin to break free. In each subsequent turn, the shoggoth-weapon can attempt another grab attack to inflict 1D6 more damage. If it fails, the target suffers no harm but remains grabbed.

SAN LOSS: 1/1D8.

The Moon Children

Up close, the Moon Children reek of a smell like cinnamon and chlorine. Their skin is pale and desiccated. Their eyes are sunken cataract-filled globes. They are obviously dead.

Moon Child

A failed attempt.

STR 9 **CON** 12 **DEX** 10 INT n/a **POW** 1

HP 11 **WP** 1

ARMOR: 2 points of unnatural toughness.

ATTACKS: Cling 30%, damage 1.

Bite 45% (only if clinging to the victim), damage 1D4−1.

CLING: The Moon Children clutch and bite. Once attached to a target, one does not release until it suffers 8 or more points of damage, or unless the target escapes (as if from being pinned). Having a Moon Child attached to an Agent reduces all skill use by −20%, or −40% for two or more.

NO PAIN: The Moon Children attack even if wounded so severely that attacks should be impossible. Broken limbs and twisted bodies do not slow them. At 0 HP, a Moon Child collapses, too damaged to function.

SAN LOSS: 1/1D6.

NPCs and Animals

DELTA GREEN WAS BUILT FROM DECADES' WORTH of percentile-based rules. There are hundreds of game books that can provide characters, monsters, and rules to expand your game. Here are a few essentials to get you started.

Generic Characters

Most NPCs don't require many details beyond a sense of their interests and one or two things that set them apart from each other. Those can be handled as "generic" characters.

A typical non-player character has average scores in most stats and the base ratings in most skills. Stats and skills may be higher if they're particularly important for the character's occupation. See **GENERIC NPCs** on page 354 for reference.

Animals

These animals' stats can be a useful starting point for designing new, unnatural entities.

An animal makes only one attack roll per turn unless its description says otherwise.

Unlike unnatural monsters, most animals flee gunfire unless cornered, enraged, or specially trained.

> **OPINT: Stats for Animals**
>
> Animals are not limited to humanity's narrow range of statistic scores. A cougar, for example, might have a DEX of 19, an elephant a STR of 35, and a great white shark a CON of 25. As a rule of thumb, nothing mundane on Earth has a stat that exceeds 100. No such restriction applies to unnatural entities.

Black Bear

For a larger bear such as a grizzly, add 1D6 STR.

STR 23 **CON** 16 **DEX** 10 **POW** 10

HP 20 **WP** 10

ARMOR: 4 points of fur and thick hide.

SKILLS: Alertness 70%.

ATTACKS: Bite 30%, damage 2D8.

Claws 50%, damage 2D6 and hold (see **HOLD**).

HOLD: A claw attack that rolls an odd number for damage also pins the target.

Boar

STR 12 **CON** 13 **DEX** 7 **POW** 7

HP 13 **WP** 7

ARMOR: 3 points of thick hide.

SKILLS: Alertness 50%.

ATTACKS: Gore 30%, damage 1D8.

Cougar

For a bigger cat, like a male African lion or Bengal tiger, add 1D6 STR. Cats of all kinds, including housecats, are acutely sensitive to the presence of the unnatural.

STR 17 **CON** 14 **DEX** 18 **POW** 10

HP 16 **WP** 10

ARMOR: 2 points of muscle and thick hide.

SKILLS: Alertness 50%, Athletics 80%, Stealth 80%.

ATTACKS: Claws or bite 50%, damage 1D10.

Crocodile

STR 25 **CON** 20 **DEX** 8 **POW** 10

HP 23 **WP** 10

ARMOR: 5 points of scaly hide.

SKILLS: Alertness 50%, Stealth 60%, Swim 70%.

ATTACKS: Bite 50%, damage 3D6 and hold (see **HOLD**).

HOLD: A bite attack that rolls an odd number for damage also pins the target. Crocodiles sometimes drag held prey into nearby water to drown or bleed out.

>> Generic NPCs

NPC Type	Most Stat Ratings	Important Stat Ratings	Most Skill Ratings	Important Skill Ratings
Child	5	7	None above 10%	20%
Youth	7	9	None above 30%	30%
Novice	10	12	Base	40%
Ordinary	10	12	Base	50%
Expert	10	14	Base	60%

>> Generic NPC Examples

NPC Example	Important Stats	Important Skills
Academic (humanities)	INT	Anthropology, Archeology, Foreign Language, Occult
Artist, author, or musician	INT, POW, or CHA	Art (choose one), Persuade, any two others
Bureaucrat	INT	Accounting, Bureaucracy, Law, Persuade
Computer expert	INT	Computer Science, Craft (electronics), Craft (microelectronics), SIGINT
Cult leader	POW, CHA	HUMINT, Occult, Persuade
Federal agent or police detective	CON, INT	Alertness, Criminology, Firearms, HUMINT, Persuade, Unarmed Combat
Firefighter	STR, CON	Alertness, Athletics, Demolitions, First Aid, Heavy Machinery
Gangster	STR	Alertness, Drive, Firearms, Melee Weapons, Unarmed Combat
Journalist	INT, CHA	Art (Journalism), Bureaucracy, HUMINT, Persuade
Laborer	STR	Craft (choose one), Drive, Heavy Machinery
Lawyer	INT, CHA	Bureaucracy, HUMINT, Law, Persuade
Nurse or paramedic	INT	Alertness, First Aid, HUMINT, Pharmacy, Search
Office worker or student	INT	Choose any three
Physician or coroner	INT	First Aid, Forensics, Medicine, Pharmacy, Science (Biology), Surgery
Pilot	DEX, INT	Alertness, Craft (choose one), Navigate, Pilot (choose one)
Police officer	STR, CON	Alertness, Drive, Firearms, HUMINT, Persuade, Unarmed Combat
Psychotherapist or social worker	INT	Bureaucracy, HUMINT, Persuade, Psychotherapy
Scientist	INT	Bureaucracy, Science (choose any three)
Soldier	CON	Alertness, Athletics, Firearms, any two others
Special operator or police SWAT team member	STR, CON	Alertness, Athletics, Firearms, Heavy Weapons, Melee Weapons, Military Science, Swim, Unarmed Combat
Terrorist	CON	Alertness, Athletics, Demolitions, Firearms, Persuade

Dog or Wolf

Guard dogs are enormously popular with police and special forces. Police-trained dogs can use their Track by Smell skill to identify things like explosives or drugs by scent. They are also trained to hold a target—knock it down and loom threateningly—and to bite only when ordered or if the target fights back. A smaller dog has lower STR and CON. Wolves and dogs are acutely sensitive to the presence of the unnatural.

STR 12 **CON** 13 **DEX** 13 **POW** 10

HP 13 **WP** 10

ARMOR: 1 point of fur and thick skin.

SKILLS: Alertness 70%, Track by Smell 80%.

ATTACKS: Bite 30%, damage 1D6.

Knock down 50%, damage special (see **KNOCK DOWN**).

KNOCK DOWN: If this attack hits, the dog attempts an opposed STR×5 test against the target. If the dog succeeds, the target is knocked prone.

Elephant

STR 60 **CON** 30 **DEX** 10 **POW** 12

HP 45 **WP** 12

ARMOR: 8 points of thick hide.

SKILLS: Alertness 80%.

ATTACKS: Stamp and trample 40%, Lethality 25%.

Trunk 50%, damage special (see **TRUNK**).

Tusk gore 50%, Lethality 20%, Armor Piercing 3.

HUGE: Do not roll for Lethality against an elephant; it simply takes HP damage equal to the Lethality rating.

TRUNK: A successful trunk attack pins the target.

Gorilla

STR 22 **CON** 17 **DEX** 10 **POW** 10

HP 20 **WP** 10

ARMOR: 2 points of thick skin.

SKILLS: Alertness 40%, Stealth 70%.

ATTACKS: Grab 50%, damage special (see **GRAB**).

Rend pinned target 70%, Lethality 15%.

Bite 50%, damage 1D10, Armor Piercing 3.

GRAB: A successful grab attack pins the target.

Horse

STR 28 **CON** 13 **DEX** 10 **POW** 10

HP 21 **WP** 10

ARMOR: None.

SKILLS: Alertness 50%, Dodge 40%.

ATTACKS: Bite or kick 20%, damage 1D6.

Trample 30%, damage Lethality 15% (see **TRAMPLE**).

TRAMPLE: A horse can only trample a target that is already prone.

Rhinoceros

This template could stand in for a hippopotamus by adding 1D6 STR and a Swim skill of 50%.

STR 40 **CON** 25 **DEX** 7 **POW** 10

HP 33 **WP** 10

ARMOR: 10 points of muscle and thick hide.

SKILLS: Alertness 60%.

ATTACKS: Gore or trample 50%, damage Lethality 20%.

Charge 50%, damage Lethality 30% (see **CHARGE**).

CHARGE: A rhino needs about 10 meters of running space to charge.

HUGE: Do not roll for Lethality against a rhino; it simply takes HP damage equal to the Lethality rating.

Shark

This represents an especially large predator such as a great white. For a smaller species, reduce STR and CON.

STR 25 **CON** 23 **DEX** 10 **POW** 10

HP 24 **WP** 10

ARMOR: 5 points of tough skin.

SKILLS: Alertness 90%, Stealth 90%, Swim 100%.

ATTACKS: Bite 70%, Lethality 10%, Armor Piercing 5.

Snake, Constrictor

STR 23 **CON** 17 **DEX** 13 **POW** 10

HP 20 **WP** 10

ARMOR: 2 points of thick scales.

SKILLS: Alertness 70%, Climb 80%, Stealth 90%, Swim 50%.

ATTACKS: Bite 60%, damage 1D10 (see **BITE**).

Constrict 50%, damage 2D6 (see **CONSTRICT**).

BITE: A successful bite pins the target.

CONSTRICT: The constrictor must pin a target to constrict it. A target who has suffered a successful constrict attack suffers a −20% penalty to attempts to all further escape.

Snake, Venomous

STR 5 **CON** 5 **DEX** 10 **POW** 5

HP 5 **WP** 5

ARMOR: None.

SKILLS: Alertness 60%, Climb 50%, Dodge 50%, Stealth 90%, Swim 50%.

ATTACKS: Bite 70%, damage 1 plus poison (see **VENOM**).

VENOM: A bite attack that rolls an odd number injects poison with a Speed of 1D6 hours and Lethality 10%.

Squid, Giant

STR 23 **CON** 15 **DEX** 19 **POW** 10

HP 19 **WP** 10

ARMOR: 2 points of slippery hide.

SKILLS: Stealth 70%, Swim 100%.

ATTACKS: Grasp 50%, damage special (see **GRASP**).

Bite 50%, damage 2D6, Armor Piercing 3.

GRASP: A successful grasp attack pins the target. If the squid hits a pinned target with another grasp attack, the target takes 2D6 damage from constriction.

Swarm of Pests

Small pests like rats, bats and spiders don't generally warrant stats, but they can be deadly carriers of disease or poison. Typically, an Agent can avoid infection or poisoning with a Luck roll, or perhaps an Athletics, Dodge, or Swim test to get to safety.

The threat depends on the swarm.

BATS OR RATS: disease (rabies).

VENOMOUS SPIDERS OR INSECTS: poison (equivalent to spider venom; see **SAMPLE POISONS** on page 61 of the *Agent's Handbook*).

JELLYFISHES OR PORTUGESE MEN O'WAR: venom inflicting 1D6 damage (halved on a successful CON×5 test, but doubled if the CON test is a fumble).

>> Rabies

The symptoms of the rabies virus appear 2D6 weeks after transmission. It can be cured by vaccination before then. After symptoms appear, the victim suffers the Speed and Damage effects and vaccination is no use.

Disease	Route	Speed	CON Test Penalty	Damage	Symptoms	Cure
Rabies	Bite, then 1D12 weeks of incubation	1D6 days	−40	2D6	Fever, headache, confusion, delirium, hydrophobia	Vaccination before symptoms appear

Recommended Media

Aronofsky, Darren (director). *Pi*. Santa Monica: Lionsgate Films, 1998.

Barron, Laird. *The Beautiful Thing That Awaits Us All.* San Francisco: Night Shade Books, 2014.

Campbell, Ramsey. *Cold Print*. New York: Tom Doherty Associates, 1987.

Carpenter, John (director). *The Thing*. New York: Universal Pictures, 1982.

Cook, Nick. *The Hunt for Zero Point*. New York: Broadway Books, 2002.

Flanagan, Mike (director). *Absentia*. Toronto: Phase 4 Films, 2011.

Goodfellow, Cody. *Radiant Dawn* and *Ravenous Dusk*. Seattle: Perilous Press, 2000 and 2002.

Harms, Daniel. *Cthulhu Mythos Encyclopedia*. Lake Orion, Michigan: Elder Sign Press, 2008.

Howard, Robert E. *Cthulhu: The Mythos and Kindred Horrors*. Wake Forest, North Carolina: Baen Books, 1987.

Howe, Linda Moulton. *An Alien Harvest*. Albuquerque: Linda Moulton Howe Productions, 1989.

Keel, John. *The Mothman Prophecies*. New York: Tor Books (reprint edition), 2013.

Ligotti, Thomas. *The Nightmare Factory*. New York: Carroll & Graf, 1996.

Lockhart, Ross E. (editor). *The Book of Cthulhu* and *The Book of Cthulhu II*. San Francisco: Night Shade Books, 2011 and 2012.

Lockhart, Ross E. and Justin Steele (editors). *The Children of Old Leech*. Petaluma, California: Word Horde, 2014.

Lovecraft, H.P. *The Call of Cthulhu and Other Weird Stories*. London: Penguin Classics, 1999.

Lovecraft, H.P. *The Dreams in the Witch-House and Other Weird Stories*. London: Penguin Classics, 2004.

Lovecraft, H.P. *The Thing on the Doorstep and Other Weird Stories*. London: Penguin Classics, 2001.

Lovecraft, H.P. and divers hands. *Tales of the Cthulhu Mythos*. Sauk City, Wisconsin: Arkham House, 1990.

Pellington, Mark (director). *The Mothman Prophecies*. Culver City, California: Screen Gems, 2002.

Powers, Tim. *Declare*. New York: HarperCollins, 2001.

Stross, Charles. *The Atrocity Archives*. New York: The Penguin Group (USA), 2004.

True Detective, season one. New York: Home Box Office (HBO), 2014.

The Unspeakable Oath. Seattle: Pagan Publishing, 1990–2001; Chelsea, Alabama: Arc Dream Publishing, 2010–present.

Villeneuve, Denis (director). *Sicario*. Santa Monica: Lionsgate Films, 2015.

Wheatley, Ben (director). *Kill List*. New York: IFC Films, 2011.

The X-Files. Los Angeles: Fox Broadcasting Company, 1993.

Other Delta Green books are available from Arc Dream Publishing, Armitage House, Pagan Publishing, and Pelgrane Press:

Delta Green, 1997.
Delta Green: Agent's Handbook, 2016.
Delta Green: Alien Intelligence, 1998.
Delta Green: Countdown, 1999.
Delta Green: Dark Theatres, 2001.
Delta Green: Denied to the Enemy, 2003.
Delta Green: Extraordinary Renditions, 2015.
Delta Green: Extremophilia, 2017.
Delta Green: Eyes Only, 2008.
Delta Green: Kali Ghati, 2016.
Delta Green: Music From a Darkened Room, 2017.
Delta Green: Need to Know, 2016.
Delta Green: Observer Effect, 2016.
Delta Green: The Rules of Engagement, 2000.
Delta Green: The Star Chamber, 2016.
Delta Green: Strange Authorities, 2012.
Delta Green: Tales From Failed Anatomies, 2014.
Delta Green: Targets of Opportunity, 2010.
Delta Green: Through a Glass, Darkly, 2012.
The Fall of Delta Green, 2018.

Index

a-Abhi 102, 237
a-Abhi Block 102
Aaron, Agent *See* Emil Furst
abominable snowmen *See* Metoh-Kangmi
Acéphale icon 249
Adam, Agent *See* Matthew Carpenter *See also* Gavin Ross
Agdesh, Emir 87, 98
Agua Verde, Nicaragua 25
Ahnenerbe 27, 32, 35
ai-apa 230
Akephaloi *See* Y'golonac
Al Azif (book) 154, 155
Alalu *See* Cthulhu
al-Hazred, Abd 72, 155, 232, 233
alien intelligences 96, 137, 146, 188–232
Allen, Zadok 18
Alphonse, Agent *See* Joseph Camp *See also* Donald Poe
Alzis, Stephen/Pariah 54, 57, 58, 63, 71, 72, 80, 81, 87, 98, 314
Anchongxiang, China 26
Ancile, Inc. 124, 295
Andrea, Agent *See* April Pleasant Crumpton
Angka 62, 66
Angleton, James 294
Antarctica 24, 25, 31, 40, 53, 79, 219
Anton, Agent *See* Chun-te Wu
Anzique tribe 44
Arizona naval station 22, 24
Arnold, Thomas 39
artifacts and alien science 143–145
Astarte *See* Shub-Niggurath
Atlantis 152, 219
Austin, Gilbert 102
Azathoth 44, 76, 103, 126, 142, 156, 162, 163, 187, 205, 230, 233–234, 237, 242, 244, 284
Azathoth and Other Horrors (book) 154, 156, 311
Baalberith 144
Balfour, Charles 64
Barris, Franklyn 26
Belial *See* Robert Hubert
Bell, Eustis 86, 89, 95, 270, 280, 293
Belmont, Keith 52
Bernard, Agent *See* Curtis McRay
Beyond-One *See* Yog-Sothoth
bhole-worms 76
bigfoot 51, 325
biomarker A, 274
Bishop, Z.L. 55
Bitterich, Olaf 42, 57, 91,
Black Buddha 308
Black Chamber 17, 19–22, 54
Black Cod Island 19, 129, 145, 147
Black Dragon Society/Kokuryūkai 37
Black Goat of the Woods With a Thousand Young *See* Shub-Niggurath
Black Ocean Society/Gen'yōsha 35, 37, 39, 60
Black Man *See* Dark Man
Black Pharaoh 153, 160, 242
Black Tuesday *See* Wall Street Crash
Blemmyes *See* Y'golonac
Blue Team, USAF 53
BLUEBLOOD 73
Book of Azathoth (book) 233
Book of Dagon (book) 19, 21, 22, 54, 55, 154, 156
Book of Eibon (book) 161, 183, 247
Bornless One *See* Y'golonac
Bostick, Charlie 89, 287–288
Brasseur, Engvald 131
Brichester, England 68, 69, 153, 239, 241
Bright, Alvin 68
Bromley, Wilbur 68
Bronk, Detley 49
Brown, Townsend 41, 52
Brunne, Arthur 95
The Bucket 6, 48, 49, 52, 53, 57, 68
Bush, George H.W. 94
Bush, George W. 94
Bush, Vannevar 31, 52
Byatis 151, 235, 237
Camp, Joseph/Agent Alphonse 34, 49, 59, 63, 73, 77, 79, 81, 86, 88, 160, 276, 277, 282, 299, 300, 301, 305, 309, 310, 314, 316, 317; grimoire 154, 160, 311
Campaigns: The Acquisition War 36; Cold War 51; Cowboy Years 70; Crucible 33; Fate 71; MAJESTIC, 47
Cap de la Hague, France 29, 30, 35, 38
Capone, Al 21
Carcosa 56, 108–110, 160, 161, 230
Carpenter, Matthew/Agent Adam 282; Delta Green files 154, 161, 311
Carter, Randolph 72, 102, 103
Cayce, Edgar 76
Cipher Bureau 19
Ch-em ch'og *See* Y'golonac
Chalmers, Amanda 27–28
Charlotte, Agent *See* Edna Knotts
Cheney, Dick 94, 95, 99
Chimagua, Lake 92, 239
Chimbote species 35
China: espionage 26
Chinnamasta *See* Y'golonac
Cho Chu-tsao 82, 84–85, 88, 93, 99, 104, 111, 116
Chorazin, New York 26
Churchill, Winston 28
Cimmeria 152, 153
Clinton, Bill 73, 94
Club Apocalypse 65, 80, 99, 113
Clulu *See* Cthulhu
Coatlicue *See* Shub-Niggurath
Cobb, Emmett 64
Codex Borgia (book) 232
Coffey, Robert 270
colours out of space 11, 188–189, 252
Coluinn gun Cheann *See* Y'golonac
Comte d'Erlette, Francois-Honore Balfour 157
Connelly, Joseph M. 41
Construct, the 78, 149, 201, 202, 320
Cook, Martin 32–33, 34, 35, 37, 46, 50, 54, 59, 60, 64, 157
The Cookbook, Grey treatise 69, 73, 94
Coolidge, Calvin 16
Cornwall, David 27, 39, 45
Correll, Victor 108
Cosmic Experience Acid Test 64
Courtis, Stephen 46, 52, 53, 289
The Courtis Paper (book) 46, 154, 157, 289
creating a campaign 330–331
creating an operation 332–337
creating new hypergeometrical effects 167–171
creating your own unnatural threats 252–255
Criss, Curtiss 62
Crumpton, April Pleasant/Agent Andrea 79, 104, 282–284
Cthulhu 19, 26, 29, 72, 106, 121, 142, 144, 145, 151, 152, 153, 156, 172, 182, 187, 191, 194, 215, 223–224, 230, 232, 234–236, 237, 247, 248, 252, 330,
Cultes des Goules (book) 154, 157
Cults: Azathoth 233; Bast 144; Brotherhood of the Ocean 29; Cthulhu 26, 72, 106, 121, 144, 215, 232, 235, 330; Disciples of the Worm 124, 129, 131, 322; Dorian Gray Society 128; Enolsis 80; Esoteric Order of Dagon 17, 19, 24, 25, 29, 106, 147, 160; Exalted Circle 106, 128, 129, 131, 133, 147–148; Ghatanothoa 103, 215, 236; Glaaki 162–163, 239; Kheshthogha 207, 244; Leng corpse-eaters 103; Mauti 64; Mule'le', 64; Nava Prayasa 128, 129; Salem witch-cult 243; Shub-Niggurath 65, 105, 179, 244; Skoptsi 105, 322; Stalin ("Great Provider") 29, 149; Starry Wisdom 242; Thuggee 39, 45; Transcendence 93, 126, 127, 128, 133, 147, 148, 233, 242, 322; Tsathoggua 110, 247; Y'golonac 248; Yig 250
Curwen, Joseph 251
Cybele *See* Shub-Niggurath
Cyrus, Agent *See* Curtis McRay
Dagon, Father 23, 38, 60, 148, 156, 160, 187, 223, 235, 237
Damballah 250
Danforth, Thomas 102
Daoloth 237
Dark Man 170, 184, 231
Darren, Agent *See* Forrest James
Dauthsnamjansboka (book) 41, 154, 155
de Zamacona y Nuñez, Pánfilio 55, 102,
Dean, Lester 25
Deep Ones 16, 18, 19–20, 22, 23, 24, 27, 29, 30, 31, 33, 38, 44, 46, 55, 106, 146, 147, 148, 151, 152, 156, 157, 159, 172, 175, 191–195, 221, 223, 235, 237, 252, 276, 277, 278, 318, 321–322, 325, 332; Claude 30; Greater Deep Ones 20, 23, 191–193; Henri 31; hybrid Deep Ones 17, 19–23, 49, 70, 147, 148, 192, 193–194, 273, 277, 322; Lesser Deep Ones 191, 192, 193–194, 252
Deep Ones Nicaragua colony 17, 18, 22, 25
Deep Ones Philippines colony 22, 24
Deep Ones reproductive element 19, 193, 195
Dekker, Mogens 148
Delta Green: Antarctica raid 53; Belgian Congo raid 35, 40; Cambodia operation

16; Cap de la Hague raid 35, 38; Executive Committee 58, 59–60, 67; Innsmouth raid 16, 17, 18, 19, 20, 21, 33, 35, 54, 70, 145, 147, 148, 156, 159, 235, 321, 323, 330; origin 16–18; war with MAJESTIC, 79
Delta Green: The Outlaws 8–9, 11, 12, 84, 85, 97, 100, 101, 104, 105, 107, 108, 111, 115, 125, 129, 131, 132, 137, 138, 139, 142, 258, 264, 274, 279, 282, 283, 284, 296, 299–325; agents 300–301; and other groups 302; and the Program 302–303; asking A-Cell 307–308; defection 142, 303; facilities 299, Friendlies 299, 300, 301; goals and beliefs 299; operations 303–305; organizational structure 299–300; recruitment 306–307
Delta Green: The Program 8, 9, 11, 12, 16, 69, 84, 85, 93, 96–97, 99, 100, 101, 104, 106, 111, 115, 117, 125, 129, 131, 132, 133, 135, 137, 138, 139, 142, 153, 195, 247, 258–298, 299, 300, 301, 302–303, 308, 309, 310, 311, 313, 314, 316, 317, 318, 319, 320, 321–324, 340, 341, 342, 349; agents 261–263; The Director 88, 89, 133, 137, 260, 261, 265, 271, 276–278, 279, 281, 286, 289, 293, 294, 295, 302, 324; facilities 259–260; foreign operations 269–271; goals and beliefs 259; operations 265–269; organizational structure 260–261; recruitment 264–265; Research 272–273; Security 271–272; specialists 262–263
Delta Green special access program *See* Delta Green: The Program
DeMonte clan of ghouls 105, 107, 129, 148–149, 296, 322
Derby, Edward Pickman 156
Derringer, James 125, 319–321
Devil's Reef 18, 19, 20, 21, 24, 61
Dho-Hna 61, 62
dog-headed men 58
Donnerschlag 39, 60
Donovan, William J. "Wild Bill" 32, 33, 34, 39, 40
Drake, John 296
dreamlands 56
du Nord, Gaspard 161
Dunwich 198, 251
Dunwoody-Smith, Sheridan 82
Durga *See* Shub-Niggurath
Dust of the Thresholds 160, 172, 178, 311,
Dweller in Darkness *See* Nyogtha
Dyer, William 24, 102, 103, 232, 233, 251
Dza-nGar Phan, U-Tsang Plateau, Tibet 57
Eihort 237
Einstein, Albert 28, 34, 56
Eisenbein, Wilhelm 39
Eisenhower, Dwight 53, 54, 59
Elder Sign (artifact) 178
Elder Thing City, Kadath 102
Elder Things 24, 102, 146, 151, 152, 158, 191, 196–197, 221, 223, 251, 252
Eldridge (ship) 40, 41, 42, 52, 64, 125, 126, 276, 281, 289
Eltdown Shards 154, 158
Emerson, Grant 78, 318–319; files 154, 158, 319
Enlil *See* Itla-shua
Esoteric Order of Dagon *See* Cults
La Estancia, Brazil 45, 90
Evers, Abdullah 64
Ewaipanoma *See* Y'golonac
extradimensional intelligences 149–150
Faber, C. Philippus 161
Fairfield, Reginald 58, 59, 67, 73, 79, 88, 277, 282, 308, 309, 310,
The Fate 54, 57, 65, 71, 80, 87, 92, 98, 129, 242, 314, 322,
feasters from the stars 197–198
Fécamp, France 39, 60
Federal Bureau of Investigation (FBI) 8, 13, 71, 84, 93, 104, 127, 138, 139, 158, 161, 260, 261, 262, 263, 265, 267, 268, 269, 278, 279, 282, 296, 297, 301, 304, 308, 314, 315, 316, 319, 333, 340, 342, 343, 345, 349
Fenton, Giles 76
Fisherman's God 237
Five Watchers 223
Forrestal, James 52
Frank, Gunter 45, 57, 91, 136, 159; research notes 136, 154, 159, 311
Friedrich II/ Frederick the Great 32, 42
Freis, Daniel 54, 55, 65, 46, 47, 57, 157; case file 154, 157,
Freyja *See* Shub-Niggurath
fungi from Yuggoth *See* mi-go
Furst, Emil/Agent Aaron 105, 137, 309, 311–313; artifacts 312
Galt, Reinhard 44, 52, 57, 64, 81, 90
Gates, George 86, 90, 261, 279, 280–281, 293
Geheimes Mysterium von Asien (book) 154, 158
Gen'yōsha *See* Black Ocean Society
Geoffrey, Justin 162
German Antarctic Expedition/Deutsche Antarktische Expedition 25, 27
Ghatanothoa 103, 151, 152, 211, 215, 236–237, 250
Ghorl Nigarl (book) 26, 158
Ghost Mound, Hydro, Oklahoma 55
ghouls 29, 30, 69, 93, 105, 107, 129, 146, 147, 148–149, 153, 157, 158, 172, 175, 198–200, 243, 252, 254, 296, 297, 298, 322, 331
Ghroth 76 *See also* Nemesis
Gibson Desert, Australia 40
Gilman, Walter 282
Glaakeen 180, 239
Glaaki 69, 92, 152, 153, 162–163, 172, 176, 180, 237, 238–240, 248, 249, 311, 312
Glasya-Labolas 144
Glenridge Chiropractor 80
Gnophkehs 67, 152
Goatswood, Wales 63, 64, 153
gravitors 41, 52
Great Old Ones 68, 75, 85, 87, 93, 109, 110, 121, 123, 142, 143–145, 146, 149, 150, 153, 161, 164, 176, 178, 180, 181, 186, 222, 223, 232–251, 252
Great Race *See* Yithians
Greist, Anton 48
Grey Men 25, 26
Greyman, Walter J. 65
Greys/extraterrestrial biological entities/EBEs 52, 68, 69, 70, 73, 74–75, 78, 79, 83, 88, 90, 94, 96, 146, 203–204, 217, 220, 275, 280, 293, 294, 322
The Group Dynamic in a Stress Environment (book) 64
GRU SV-8 8, 24, 27, 30, 36, 38, 42, 45, 49, 53, 88, 91, 113–115, 129, 135, 136, 149, 155, 244, 271, 276, 302
Haedi Nigritiae 204–205
Hali, Lake of 223
Handler (essential functions) 9–11
Hastur 103, 110, 144, 161, 237
Haumea *See* Shub-Niggurath
Haunter of the Dark *See* Nyarlathotep
He-Who-Swims-With-Corpses 23, 147, 223, 235
Headless Man *See* Y'golonac
Headless One *See* Y'golonac
Heinrich, Karl 44
Her Grey Song (play) 56, 110
Hermann der Cherusker 42
Hess, Rudolf 32
Hexenkartothek 25 *See also* Karotechia
Himmler, Heinrich 25, 27, 30, 31, 32, 42, 43
Hiroshima, Japan 47
Hirta, Scotland 45
Hitler, Adolph 27, 42, 43, 44
Hodge, Peter 53
Hong, Lawrence 81
Hoover, Herbert 19, 21
Hoover, J. Edgar 16, 21, 32, 37, 159
Hounds of the Angles 103, 151, 205–206
Hsan the Greater 163
Hubert, Robert/Belial 87, 92
human hybrids 148
Hunting-horrors 206–207, 252, 255
Hydra, Mother 23, 156, 223, 235
Hyperborea 67, 76, 150, 151, 152, 161, 237, 245, 247
hypergeometric addiction 166
hypergeometrical effects 164, 166, 167–174
hypergeometry 164–187
Ice Cave/YYII facility 24, 49, 70, 195, 272, 273
idol of Cthulhu 235
Ifrits 207–208, 244
Ina'hitelan *See* Itla-shua
inciting event 12
El Indio, Texas, UFO crash 52
inner space 56
inhuman Earthly intelligences 146–149
Inman, Bobby Ray 73, 117
Innsmouth, Massachusetts 16–22, 24, 33, 35, 37, 54, 55, 61, 63, 70, 79, 133, 145, 147, 148, 154, 156, 159, 235, 237, 273, 277, 308, 321, 323, 330; Innsmouth "plague" 19; Innsmouth "taint" 19, 23, 133, 194, 277, 278
The Innsmouth Report (book) 154, 159–160
introducing new agents 11–12
Interpreting the Rules 12
Irem of the Pillars 72, 152, 153
Ithaka *See* Itla-shua
Itla-shua 67, 103, 152, 228, 237, 240
Itoko, Congo 36, 229

James, Forrest/Agent Darren/Director John Smith 69, 80, 81, 82, 86, 90, 95, 276–278, 279, 280, 282, 285, 286, 287, 293, 294, 295, 296, 297, 298, 309, 310, 311, 318
Jenkin, Brown 231
Jermyn, Arthur 35, 38
Jermyn, Wade 229
Johnson, Lyndon 63
Kadath in the Cold Waste 102
Karotechia 25, 27, 29, 30, 31, 32, 34, 35, 36, 37, 38, 39, 40, 41, 42, 43, 44, 45, 50, 51, 52, 53, 57, 59, 60, 61, 80, 81, 88, 90, 91, 102, 113, 114, 129, 136, 155, 158, 233, 242, 271, 302, 322, 330
Keepers of the Faith 68, 148, 322
Kempeitai 35
Kennedy, John F. 58, 59, 60, 63
Keravuori, Michael 50, 51, 53, 59
King in Yellow 56, 109, 110
The King in Yellow (play) 56, 108, 109, 110, 154, 160–161
King in Yellow Tarot deck 44
Kingsport, Massachusetts 241
Kitchen Sink document 89
Klarkash-Ton 246
Kluge, Walter 24
Knepier, Johannes 77, 92
Knotts, Edna/Agent Charlotte 316–318
K'n-Yan/Xinaían 55, 120, 152, 209, 210, 222, 245, 247, 250, 347
K'n-Yani 55, 148, 209–210, 342, 347, 349, 351, 352
Kroft, Justin 64, 68, 69, 73, 86, 88, 89, 124, 273, 280, 293, 294, 295
Ktagoolik *See* Cthulhu
Kuen-Yuin/Quányòuyīn 26, 120–121
Kukulcan *See* Yig
Kyashi Uyeda 37
Kythamila *See* slime of Tsathoggua
L'gh'rxians 76
Ladeau, Alexis 42
Ladenburg, Rudolph 28
Lemuria 26, 103, 150, 151, 152, 213, 215, 219
Lemurians 26, 55, 103, 152, 211, 213, 215, 250
Leng 26, 57, 61, 76, 102, 103, 114, 158, 216, 240, 243, 246
Lepus, Adolph 64, 86, 88, 287
Lhosk 56
Liber Damnatus (book) 154, 161
Liber Ivonis (book) 161
Livre d'Ivon (book) 142, 154, 161
Libyan ruined city 34
liquivores *See* those beyond
liveliest awfulness 184, 210–211
Lloigor 26, 116, 118–119, 120, 121, 123, 149–150, 152, 211–215, 236
Lloigor-controlled quasi-dinosaurian construct 211, 213, 214, 215–216
Lodz, Poland 42
Lomar 55, 67, 150, 151, 152
Lomarians 55, 67, 152
Lord of the Abyss *See* Nodens
Lrogg 76
Lydney Park 241
M-EPIC, 8, 99, 271, 281, 302
MacArthur, Douglas 32, 35,
Macready, Arthur J. 17, 21
Magonia/Medieval Metaphysics Laboratory 45
MAJESTIC 31, 46, 47, 48, 49, 52, 53, 54, 56, 57, 58, 60, 63, 64, 65, 66, 67, 68, 69, 70, 72, 73, 74, 77, 78, 79, 80, 81, 82, 83, 86, 88, 89, 90, 91, 93, 94, 95, 96, 97, 98, 99, 102, 104, 111, 113, 115, 117, 124, 126, 129, 135, 146, 159, 161, 195, 204, 217, 220, 270, 273, 275, 276, 278, 279, 280, 281, 282, 285, 287, 288, 289, 293, 294, 295, 298, 299, 303, 308, 309, 311, 314, 319, 322, 323, 330
MAJESTIC OPORD 00001, 89, 154, 161
MAJESTIC-12 Special Studies Group 46
MAJESTIC Special Studies Group Two 52
MAJESTIC-12 Special Studies Project 93, 280, 293, 294
MAJESTIC-12 Steering Committee 68, 69, 82, 86, 88, 89, 90, 93, 94, 95, 96, 97, 273, 276, 280, 294
Makemake *See* Shub-Niggurath
Malbayam, Antonio 53
Man-With-No-Head *See* Y'golonac
Mannen, Abraham/Agent Thomas 261, 276, 278–280, 314
Marcel, Jesse 48
March Technologies 88, 97, 111, 125, 135, 245, 260, 272, 273–276, 278, 281, 283, 289, 290, 293, 294, 295, 296, 320
Marise, France 38
Marsh, Albert 159
Marsh, Obed 17, 19
Marsh, Robert 17
Másh-Ngi *See* Shub-Niggurath
Mason, Greg, surveillance videos 154, 158–159, 311
Mason, Keziah 230, 231
Matthew, Agent *See* Emil Furst
Mauti 61, 62, 64
McNamara, Robert S. 58, 59
McRay, Curtis/Agent Bernard/Agent Cyrus 80, 87, 138, 278, 279, 302, 303, 309, 310, 313, 314–316, 317
mermaids 58
metoh-kangmi 57, 216, 217
MI-6 30
MI-8, 19
MI-13 27, 28, 30
mi-go 55, 57, 74, 75, 76, 78, 80, 146, 147, 151, 152, 172, 175, 181, 187, 203, 204, 216, 217–219, 220, 236, 242, 245, 247, 250, 251, 273
Michaelson, Timothy 39
Mirage II device 34
Miskatonic University 72, 282; Antarctica expedition 102, 146, 251; 1935 Western Australian Desert expedition 36, 39
Mitchell, Marcus 60
Mnar 150, 151, 152, 153
Moon Lens 64
Moritaum, Arthur 57
Mors, Franz 30
Morse, Theodore 69
Mothman 51
Mu 120, 121, 150, 151, 152, 158, 211, 215, 236, 245
Mülder, Gottfried 26, 158
Muñoz, Javier 159
Muuruup 226
Myrlo, Michael 63
N-03 rocket 40, 41
Nagasaki, Japan 47
Nameless City 72, 223
Nancy, Agent *See* Jean Qualls
Narrative Concerning the Subterranean World (book) 55, 102
Naudabaum Castle 43, 44, 233
Nechustan/Nehustan 44
Necronomicon (book) 28, 41, 62, 72, 102, 103, 153, 154, 155–156, 232, 233, 234, 243, 246, 247, 251
Nemesis 76, 80
Nemmers, Harry 128
neotissue stain 274
Nephren-Ka *See* Black Pharaoh
Nicaraguan National Guard/Guardia Nacional 22, 25
Nick, Agent 111
Nietzsche, Friedrich 42
night at the opera 7, 303, 304, 319, 328
Ningal *See* Shub-Niggurath
Nitocris 153
Nixon, Richard 65
N'Kai 55, 151, 152, 246, 247
Nkulu *See* Cthulhu
NKVD 29, 43, 50; occult research program 29
Nodens 103, 237, 241
Nolan, Agent 93, 111, 296, 297, 298
Nori Onishi 37
Northam 19th Baron 72
NRO Delta 64, 68, 72, 73, 82, 86, 88, 98, 285, 287, 294
Nuada *See* Nodens
Nug 72
Nug-Soth 76
Nug-Yeb 237
Nyarlathotep 71, 76, 87, 103, 144, 145, 153, 156, 163, 172, 180, 183, 206, 230, 231, 233, 237, 241, 242, 252 See also the Black Man, the Dark Man, and Stephen Alzis
Nyhon 76
Nyogtha 243
Oakes, Katherine 260, 276, 277, 279, 284–286
ODESSA, 44, 52
Office of Naval Intelligence/ONI, 16, 17, 18, 19, 21, 22, 25, 33, 41, 60, 64, 67, 86, 159, 276, 280, 323, 330
Office of Strategic Services/OSS, 8, 16, 32, 33, 34, 39, 40, 43, 46, 59, 60, 73, 79, 299, 303, 323
Ohlendorf, Karl 31, 40, 41, 45
Oklahoma earthquakes 247
Olmstead, Lawrence 24
Olmstead, Robert Martin 18, 24, 159,
Omfalé *See* Tleche-Naka
ONI *See* Office of Naval Intelligence
Operations: Active Static 108; Advance Man 57; Aktion Eisschloss/Ice Palace 27, 31, 34; Aktion Götterdämmerung 43, 44, 45; Arc Light 67; Bakelite 25; Barrel Roll 67;

Bingo 66, 67; Black Mountain 102; Blue Fly 53, 70, 78, 86, 90, 270; Bristol 56, 60, 110; Caldera 72; Coral Nomad 85, 260, 261, 270, 290, 291, 292; Freedom Deal 67; Gladio 59; Good Look 67; Holstein 26; in China 1997–2008, 26; Kurtz 61, 64; Lancaster 235; Lifeguard 7, 38, 39; Looking Glass 65, 280; Lunacy 44, 45, 60, 155; Madchimp 237; Mallory 57; Northern Lighthouse 62; Obsidian 65, 66, 308; Osoaviakhim 43; Overdue 63; Paperclip 43; Porlock 64; Puzzlebox 18, 21, 70, 154, 159; Redbone 149; Riptide 61, 63, 324; Schwarzes Wasser/Black Water 27, 28, 29, 30, 31, 38; Sic Semper Tyrannis 50, 51, 53, 57; Skunked 51, 59; Somersault 133, 137, 277; Somersault II, 277; Southern Comfort 7; Southern Hospitality 50, 52, 53, 57, 102; Static 7; Sudden Sam 64; Summer Breeze 43, 45, 60; Talcum 24; Tarquin 36; Thimble 25; Threnody 60; Tiki Bar 132; Uproar 60
Organization Todt 38
Ortega, Robert Justin 124, 295
Osiris *See* Shub-Niggurath
OSS *See* Office of Strategic Services
Ossadagowah 67, 237, 247, 341, 342, 348
Ossendowski 26
Ossorronophris *See* Y'golonac
Outer Gods 114
Outlook Group 57, 68, 69, 81
P4 Desk (Office of Naval Intelligence) 18, 21, 22–25, 30, 32, 33, 34, 60, 156, 159, 235, 258, 330
Paragon Foundation 45
Payton, David Farragut 59, 60
Peaslee, Nathaniel 39, 72
Peaslee, Wingate 39
Peis, Erwin 45, 50, 53, 54
The People of the Monolith (book) 154, 162, 311
Perón, Juan 41, 50
Phenomen-X 74, 104, 105, 115, 272, 287, 349
Philadelphia Experiment *See* Project Rainbow
Pieda Negra 24
PISCES 8, 28, 30, 34, 35, 36, 38, 39, 40, 45, 48, 49, 54, 64, 68, 69, 72, 81, 110, 271, 302, 322; archaeological intelligence operation in Borneo 48
Pnakotic Manuscripts 28, 36, 67, 102, 154, 162, 232, 246
Pnakotis 36, 319, 321
Poe, Donald/Agent Alphonse/Agent Charlie 80, 88, 90, 97, 100, 104, 159, 163, 282, 299, 308–311, 312, 313, 314, 315, 316, 324
Point 102, Queen Maud's Land, Antarctica 102
Point 103, Antarctica 27, 31, 34, 40, 41, 45, 50, 53, 79
polyps, spectral 36, 122, 151, 152, 201, 225–227
Ponape 19, 235
Powder of ibn-Ghazi 311
portraying the Deep Ones 23
Princess Martha Coast, Antarctica 25
Prinn, Ludwig 163, 194, 204, 242
Projects: Aquarius (MJ-1) 53, 54, 65, 68, 86, 293; Artichoke 56; Blue Book 53, 60; Bustle 273; Contrail 273; Copper Mask 273; Drought 273; Dulcimer 95; Empty Mountain 273; Garnet (MJ-3) 69, 80, 285, 287, 294; Grudge 52, 53, 60; High Day 273; Lambent 273; Looking Glass 65, 280; Mainframe 273; Mirage 31, 34, 39, 40, 41, 52; MKSearch 56; MKUltra 56; Moon Dust (MJ-5) 53, 280; Nacre Python 273; Outlook 56, 273; Parsifal 35, 38, 39, 40; Phi 34; Pluto (MJ-6) 68, 273, 280; Puzzle 41, 64; Rainbow 28, 31, 34, 42; Red Pendulum 273; Redlight 68; Sign 49, 52; St-Barnum 57; St-Circus 57; Sharp Atlas 273; Subsume 56; Suzerain 273; Tell 111, 281, 289, 290; Wells 111, 125, 126, 273, 281; Zero Rapid 273
Propavsheye 136
protomatter 78, 220, 274
psychotic opera 7
Punta Gorda, Nicaragua 18
Qualls, Jean/Debra Constance/Jean Qualls/ Agent Nancy 69, 81, 111, 279, 296–298
Quányòuyīn *See* Kuen-Yuin
Quetzalcoatl *See* Yig
Qu-tugkwa 207, 208, 237, 244
R'lyeh 151, 164, 234, 235, 236
Ramsey, Lt. Commander Frederick 30; Ramsey's Talents 30, 39
Rathke, Franklin 39
Reagan, Ronald 68
Red Cross Pocket Bible (book) 43, 154, 162,
Red Orchestra spy network 27
Redman samples 57
Reich, Wolfgang 102
Revelations of Glaaki (book) 76, 77, 154, 162–163, 239, 248, 249
Rhan-Tegoth 67, 152, 237
Ringwood, Abner 65, 68
Rituals: activating 166; combining effects 174; costs 166–169; duration 171; effects 166–171; flawed 169; learning 165–166; witnessing 174
Rituals, cultural: African and Caribbean 170; Ancient Chinese 170; European, Judaic, and Islamic Occultism 179; psychic powers 170
Rituals, sample: Ageless Banquet 44, 172, 174; Call Forth Those From Outside 157, 163, 172, 175, 225; Call Forth Those From Outside (Azathoth) 163, 284; (dimensional shambler) 284; (Glaaki) 163; (Feasters from the Stars) 163; (Great Race) 158; (Haedi Nigritiae) 157, 163; (Ifrits) 163; (Itla-Shua) 229; (Mi-Go) 163; (Nyarlathotep) 163, 284; (Nyogtha) 157, 161, 163; (Qu-Tugkwa) 208; (Shub-Niggurath) 163; (Y'golonac) 163; (Yog-Sothoth) 284; The Call of Dagon 156, 160, 172, 175, 278, 284; Call Zombies 157, 172, 175, 313; The Calling of the Goat 166; Changeling Feast 172, 175, 199, 200, 220, 298; Charnel Meditation 157, 160, 163, 172, 175, 200, 298; Clairvoyance 172, 176; Closing of the Breach 157, 161, 163, 172, 176–177, 243, 284, 313; Closing of the Breach (Azathoth) 284, 313; (Haedi Nigritiae) 157; (Hunting-Horrors) 313; (Nyogtha) 157, 161; (Shub-Niggurath) 284, 313; (Yog-Sothoth) 284, 313; Consciousness Expansion 157, 172, 177; Create Stone Gate 160, 172, 177, 182; Dho-Hna Formula 62, 158, 161, 162, 172, 177, 225; Dust of the Thresholds 160, 172, 178; Elder Sign 158, 160, 161, 172, 178, 278, 284, 311; Elixir of Infinite Space 163, 172, 178; Exaltation of the Flesh 163, 172, 179, 313; Exchange Personalities 172, 179, 284; Exorcism 172, 179, 313; Fascination 160, 163, 172, 180, 220; Finding 172, 180, 313; The First Secret 137, 163, 172, 180, 311, 312, 313; Healing Balm 163, 172, 180, 313; Immortal Messenger 163, 172, 180; Infallible Suggestion 172, 180, 220, 284; Knife of Ibn-Fedel 169; Leaves of Time 162, 163, 172, 181; Lure the Hungerer 163, 172, 181; Meditation Upon the Favored Ones 160, 163, 172, 181; Mountain and Sea 163, 172, 182; Obscure Memory 157, 160, 172, 182, 220, 284; Of the Shadowe 167; One Who Passes the Gateways 162, 172, 182, 225, 313; Open Gate 161, 172, 177, 182; Pentagram of Power 161, 163, 172, 175, 182; Petrification 161, 172, 183; The Powder of Ibn-Ghazi 160, 172, 183, 311; Prayer to the Dark Man 163, 172, 183, 231; Preserve Living Brain 159, 172, 184; Primal Lay 162, 172, 184; Raise From Essential Saltes 159, 161, 163, 169, 173, 184–185, 210, 284; Reanimation Formula 136, 159, 173, 185; Release Breath 157, 173, 185, 313; See the Other Side 161, 173, 185, 278, 284, 313; Song of Power 173, 185, 313; Soothing Song 173, 185, 313; Speaking Dream 160, 161, 173, 186, 313; Speech of Birds and Beasts 173, 186, 313; Stone of Life 174; Storm and Stillness 156, 173, 186; Swarm 156, 173, 186; Touch of Saval 174; Vach-Viraj 243; The Voorish Sign 160, 161, 162, 163, 173, 186, 225, 278, 284; Whispers of the Dead 163, 173, 186–187; Whispers of the Dead (Cthulhu) 156; Whispers of the Dead (Tsathoggua) 161; Winged Steed 161, 163, 173, 187, 230; Withering 160, 161, 163, 173, 187, 220; Zombie 157, 161, 173, 185, 187
Roosevelt, Franklin Delano 32
Ross, Gavin/Agent Adam 68, 69, 82, 86, 94, 95, 116, 124, 278, 282, 285, 287, 294–296
Roswell, New Mexico, UFO crash 46, 47, 48, 49, 52, 68, 74, 83, 89, 161, 288, 322, 323
Saaktog *See* Tsathoggua
Sadogawh *See* Tsathoggua
Sadogua *See* Tsathoggua
Sadoguë *See* Tsathoggua
Saima Yoshimura 37
St. Bernard Parish raid of 1907 26, 72, 235
St. John Philby, Harry 72
St. John Philby, Kim 72
St. Valentine's Day Massacre 19
San Francisco, California 37

Sandino, Augusto 22
Sarkomand 56
Sarnath 153
SaucerWatch 74, 81, 82
Shaeffer, Denton 81, 82
Seaton, Samuel 229
Secret Intelligence Service, British 32
The Secret Room 32
Secret Service, American 26
serpent people/serpent-folk 55, 146, 147, 148, 149, 151, 152, 215, 219–220, 250
servitors, winged 173, 187, 230
The Seven Cryptical Books of Hsan (book) 103, 154, 163, 170, 311
Shaggai insects 63, 64, 76, 81, 153, 208–209, 233, 273, 322
Shalin, Mikhail 53
Shamballah 152
shambler, dimensional 172, 181, 194–196, 252, 255
Shea, Ronald 63
Shelton, Dana 261, 292–294
shoggoths 24, 146, 147, 151, 197, 220, 221–222, 223, 251, 252, 255, 345, 351, 352
Shonhi 76
Shtemyenko, S.M. 49
Shub-Niggurath 65, 93, 105, 172, 174, 179, 180, 183, 204, 209, 236, 237, 244–245
Shuba-Nigur-Urash *See* Shub-Niggurath
Sigil, anti-gravity 48
Sila *See* Itla-shua
Siringo, Joe/Agent William 278
Slater, Joseph 76
slime of Tsathoggua/Kythamila 222–223
SMERSH 38, 45, 51, 53
Smith, Director John *See* Forrest James
Smyth, Arthur Emery 56
Somoza, Anastasio 22, 25
Sonderkommando-H, 25, 27
spawn of Cthulhu 172, 223–224
spawn of Yog-Sothoth 198, 224–225
star-spawn *See* spawn of Cthulhu
Stalin, Josef 29, 43, 49, 50, 53, 54, 59, 149
Stillman, Michael 39, 60, 67
Stimson, Henry L. 21
Strange Ones 122, 202
Strater, Lewis 57
substance K 56
Sumatra Queen (ship) 17
Tadjbegskye Bratva 115
Tapham, Gregory 261, 279, 288–290, 291
Tawil at-'Umr *See* Yog-Sothoth
Tcho-Tchos/Tochoa/Yueh-Chi/Chauchuas/ Tachoans 54, 61, 62, 65, 66, 67, 82, 84, 85, 88, 103, 104, 116, 121, 125, 129, 148, 152, 158
Tchortcha 26
Tectonic Agitator 45
Temple of Winds 240
Tenebrosa Aqua (book) 27, 28, 29, 30
Tess, Jürgen 25
Theissen, Ernst 43
Thing That Should Not Be *See* Nyogtha
Thomas, Agent *See* Abraham Mannen
Thornhill, Rebecca Kaur 290–292
those beyond 227–228, 252; disc-shaped liquivore 227–228; ophidian liquivore 228; tumbleweed liquivore 228
Thresher (submarine) 61
Thule/Itoko, Belgian Congo 35, 36, 229
Thule, Yithian Queen Maud's Land city 36
Thule, Yithian Australian colony 36
Thule Generator 31, 45
Thulians 34
Tiger Transit 82, 84–85, 104, 129, 268
Tillinghast radiation 81, 227, 273, 274, 289
Tillinghast resonator/Mirage III, 39, 40, 42, 64, 125, 126, 227, 276, 289, 291
Tipler, Arvin 65
Tiráwa *See* Tsathoggua
Tlaloc *See* Cthulhu
Tlatlecuhtli *See* Tsathoggua
Tleche-Nacha/Tleche-Naka 237, 245–246
Tokio Club 37
tomes 142–143; skimming 143
Tong Shukoran 82, 84, 88, 93, 99, 104, 105, 111, 125, 130, 322
Tonya, Agent *See* Victoria Winstead
travelers/EBE2 78
Truman, Harry 46, 49, 59
Trump, Donald 138
Tsadogwa *See* Tsathoggua
Tsan-Chan 26, 119, 121, 150, 153
Tsath 55, 247
Tsathoggua 55, 67, 76, 110, 132, 152, 161, 172, 180, 183, 222, 223, 237, 243, 245, 246–248, 348
Tseche-Nako *See* Tleche-Naka
'Tulu *See* Cthulhu
Tunguska, Siberia, blast 43, 233
Turner, Arthur 31, 34, 35, 39, 40, 41
Tutula *See* Cthulhu
Ubar 72
Ultima Thule 162
Uluumil-Naga 150, 152
Unaussprechlichen Kulten (book) 36, 42, 76, 103, 153, 154, 163
unhistory of Earth 150–153
unnatural entities 10, 132, 174, 175, 178, 181, 188–232
Unnatural skill 142, 143, 145, 146, 147, 166, 174, 181, 186
unnatural threats 150, 252–255
unnatural tomes 153–163
USAMRIID 8, 92
U.S. Marine Corps 16; 42nd Marine Battalion 18
Valusia 150, 151, 219
van der Heyl, Claes 26
van der Heyl, Dirck 26
Varney, Robert 86
Vault of Souls 67
De Vermis Mysteriis (book) 154, 163, 167, 204, 242
Versailles negotiations 1919, 19
Vietnam War 26, 32, 59, 62, 64, 66, 67, 84, 276, 308
Vodou 250
Volturnus 144
von Bismarck, Otto 42
von Junzt, Friedrich Wilhelm 26, 42, 103, 158, 163, 236, 247
Voorii/Voormi 67, 152, 216, 237
Wade, Satchel 66
Waite, Ephraim 63
Wall Street Crash 21
Warren, Augusta 60
Warren, Harley 60
Washington Naval Conference of 1922 19, 21
Wendigo/Wendigowak 228–229, 240
West, Herbert 159, 231
Wexler, Dr. 53
what Delta Green knows 321–323
Whateley, Elijah 251
Whateley, Lavinia 251
white apes 36, 229
William, Agent *See* Joe Siringo
Wilmarth report 76
wind-fed intelligent fungi of Neptune 76
Windigo *See* Itla-shua
Winstead, Victoria/Agent Tonya 279, 280
Winters-Hall, Arthur Brooke 158
witches' familiars 184, 230–231
World War One 17, 19, 22, 27, 44, 156
World War Two 8, 16, 27, 30, 31, 33, 42, 44, 47, 51, 54, 70, 79, 83, 162, 289, 299, 302, 330
Wormius, Olaus 156
Wu, Chun-te/Agent Anton 114, 313–314
Xada-Hgla *See* Azathoth
Xin 26, 158, 211
Xinaían *See* K'n-Yan
Xing Tian *See* Y'golonac
Xinjiang, China 26
Xiuha, Lord *See* Qu-Tugkwa
Yabou 247
Yaddith 76
Yang-tze River, China 25, 26,
Yeb 72
Yekub 76
yeti 57, 150, 216
Y'Golonac 68, 92, 163, 237, 248–249
Y'ha-nthlei 18, 24, 63
Yhe 150
Yhtill 109, 110
Yian-Ho 25, 26, 120, 121; Song of Thirty-Thousand Calamities 26
Yig 151, 232, 237, 250
Yithians 26, 36, 67, 72, 76, 78, 122, 123, 149, 151, 153, 158, 164, 201, 202, 226, 229, 273, 320; cone-shaped vessels 23, 200–201; human vessels 122, 202–203, 320
Yog-Sothoth 62, 72, 144, 172, 173, 175, 179, 180, 184, 198, 224, 225, 237, 251
Yoth 55, 151, 219, 222, 247
Yrjo, Albert 58, 63, 64, 68, 69
Yue-Laou 26, 120
Yuggoth/Pluto 74, 76, 134, 146, 151, 204, 217, 219
YY-II facility *See* Ice Cave facility
Zobna 67
zombies/resuscitated casualties/poyavlyatsya 41, 42, 45, 53, 136, 172, 173, 175, 185, 187, 231–232
Zuilphagua 248
Zvery, P.E. 229

>> Operation Overview

Name	Hook

Nature (In Media Res, Mystery, or Ongoing Threat)

NPCs

Unnatural Threats

SAN Rewards

>> Operation Structure

Leads, Dead Ends, Creepy Moments, Events, Trouble, and Resolution (Draw the Connections)

>> Unnatural Entity Details

Name and Description	Sources of Information

STR	CON	DEX	INT	POW	CHA	HP	WP

Armor, Skills, Abilities, and Other Notes

Attack Name or Description	Chance to Hit	Damage or Lethality	Other Effects

SAN Loss

>> Ritual Details

Name(s)	Known Sources

Complexity (Simple, Complex, or Elaborate)

Study Time, Costs, and Requirements	Activation Time, Costs, and Requirements

Effects

>> Personal Pursuits Summary

In a "Home" scene, each player chooses and describes one personal pursuit for their Agent. Determine how it affects the Agent's Bonds, skills, and Sanity. No personal pursuit can raise SAN higher than POW×5 or a Bond's score higher than the Agent's CHA. Record the results on the character sheet or on a separate page for notes.

Pursuit	Cost	Roll	Effects
Fulfill responsibilities	None.	SAN.	» *Fumble:* Reduce a Bond by 1D4. » *Failure:* No effect. » *Success:* Improve a Bond by 1D6. » *Critical:* Improve a Bond by 1D6 and gain 1 SAN.
Back to nature	Reduce a non-DG Bond by 1.	SAN.	» *Fumble:* Lose 1D4 SAN. » *Failure:* No effect. » *Success:* Gain 1D4 SAN. » *Critical:* Gain 4 SAN.
Establish a new Bond	Reduce a non-DG Bond by 1D4.	CHA×5.	» *Failure:* No effect. » *Success:* Gain a new Bond with a score of ½ CHA.
Go to therapy, sharing truthfully	Reduce a non-DG Bond by 1.	Luck or the therapist's Psychotherapy skill.*	» *Fumble:* Lose 1 SAN. » *Failure:* No effect. » *Success:* Gain 1D6 SAN. » *Critical:* Gain 6 SAN. A disorder goes into remission. Gain a Bond with the therapist at ½ CHA (or add 1D4 to an existing Bond with the therapist).
Go to therapy, not sharing truthfully	Reduce a non-DG Bond by 1.	Luck or the therapist's Psychotherapy skill.	» *Fumble:* Lose 1 SAN. » *Failure:* No effect. » *Success:* Gain 1D4 SAN. » *Critical:* Gain 4 SAN. A disorder goes into remission. Gain a Bond with the therapist at ½ CHA (or add 1D4 to an existing Bond with the therapist).
Improve a skill or stat	Reduce a non-DG Bond by 1.	The skill or stat to be improved.	» *Failure:* Add 1 to a stat or 1D10 to a skill. » *Success:* No effect.
Indulge a personal motivation	Reduce a non-DG Bond by 1.	SAN.	» *Fumble:* Lose 1 SAN. » *Failure:* No effect. » *Success:* Gain 1 SAN. » *Critical:* Gain 1D4 SAN.
Special training	Reduce a non-DG Bond by 1.	None.	Gain special training with a skill or stat.
Stay on the case	Reduce a non-DG Bond by 1 and add 1D6−3 SAN.	Criminology or Occult; the Handler rolls secretly.	» *Fumble:* Uncover a dangerously wrong clue. » *Failure:* No effect. » *Success:* Uncover a pertinent clue. » *Critical:* Uncover an especially valuable clue.
Study the unnatural	Reduce a non-DG Bond by 1D4.	Depends on the source.	Depends on the source.

* If the Agent describes criminal or unnatural events and the therapist thinks they are delusions, the roll is at a −20% penalty. If the therapist does not think they're delusions, there's a risk of criminal investigation or further exposure of the unnatural.

Open Game License v. 1.0a

The following text is the property of Wizards of the Coast, Inc. and is Copyright 2000 Wizards of the Coast, Inc ("Wizards"). All Rights Reserved.

1. **Definitions:** (a) "Contributors" means the copyright and/or trademark owners who have contributed Open Game Content; (b) "Derivative Material" means copyrighted material including derivative works and translations (including into other computer languages), potation, modification, correction, addition, extension, upgrade, improvement, compilation, abridgment or other form in which an existing work may be recast, transformed or adapted; (c) "Distribute" means to reproduce, license, rent, lease, sell, broadcast, publicly display, transmit or otherwise distribute; (d) "Open Game Content" means the game mechanic and includes the methods, procedures, processes and routines to the extent such content does not embody the Product Identity and is an enhancement over the prior art and any additional content clearly identified as Open Game Content by the Contributor, and means any work covered by this License, including translations and derivative works under copyright law, but specifically excludes Product Identity. (e) "Product Identity" means product and product line names, logos and identifying marks including trade dress; artifacts; creatures characters; stories, storylines, plots, thematic elements, dialogue, incidents, language, artwork, symbols, designs, depictions, likenesses, formats, poses, concepts, themes and graphic, photographic and other visual or audio representations; names and descriptions of characters, spells, enchantments, personalities, teams, personas, likenesses and special abilities; places, locations, environments, creatures, equipment, magical or supernatural abilities or effects, logos, symbols, or graphic designs; and any other trademark or registered trademark clearly identified as Product identity by the owner of the Product Identity, and which specifically excludes the Open Game Content; (f) "Trademark" means the logos, names, mark, sign, motto, designs that are used by a Contributor to identify itself or its products or the associated products contributed to the Open Game License by the Contributor (g) "Use", "Used" or "Using" means to use, Distribute, copy, edit, format, modify, translate and otherwise create Derivative Material of Open Game Content. (h) "You" or "Your" means the licensee in terms of this agreement.
2. **The License:** This License applies to any Open Game Content that contains a notice indicating that the Open Game Content may only be Used under and in terms of this License. You must affix such a notice to any Open Game Content that you Use. No terms may be added to or subtracted from this License except as described by the License itself. No other terms or conditions may be applied to any Open Game Content distributed using this License.
3. **Offer and Acceptance:** By Using the Open Game Content You indicate Your acceptance of the terms of this License.
4. **Grant and Consideration:** In consideration for agreeing to use this License, the Contributors grant You a perpetual, worldwide, royalty-free, non-exclusive license with the exact terms of this License to Use, the Open Game Content.
5. **Representation of Authority to Contribute:** If You are contributing original material as Open Game Content, You represent that Your Contributions are Your original creation and/or You have sufficient rights to grant the rights conveyed by this License.
6. **Notice of License Copyright:** You must update the COPYRIGHT NOTICE portion of this License to include the exact text of the COPYRIGHT NOTICE of any Open Game Content You are copying, modifying or distributing, and You must add the title, the copyright date, and the copyright holder's name to the COPYRIGHT NOTICE of any original Open Game Content you Distribute.
7. **Use of Product Identity:** You agree not to Use any Product Identity, including as an indication as to compatibility, except as expressly licensed in another, independent Agreement with the owner of each element of that Product Identity. You agree not to indicate compatibility or co-adaptability with any Trademark or Registered Trademark in conjunction with a work containing Open Game Content except as expressly licensed in another, independent Agreement with the owner of such Trademark or Registered Trademark. The use of any Product Identity in Open Game Content does not constitute a challenge to the ownership of that Product Identity. The owner of any Product Identity used in Open Game Content shall retain all rights, title and interest in and to that Product Identity.
8. **Identification:** If you distribute Open Game Content You must clearly indicate which portions of the work that you are distributing are Open Game Content.
9. **Updating the License:** Wizards or its designated Agents may publish updated versions of this License. You may use any authorized version of this License to copy, modify and distribute any Open Game Content originally distributed under any version of this License.

10 **Copy of this License:** You MUST include a copy of this License with every copy of the Open Game Content You Distribute.

11. **Use of Contributor Credits:** You may not market or advertise the Open Game Content using the name of any Contributor unless You have written permission from the Contributor to do so.
12. **Inability to Comply:** If it is impossible for You to comply with any of the terms of this License with respect to some or all of the Open Game Content due to statute, judicial order, or governmental regulation then You may not Use any Open Game Material so affected.
13. **Termination:** This License will terminate automatically if You fail to comply with all terms herein and fail to cure such breach within 30 days of becoming aware of the breach. All sublicenses shall survive the termination of this License.
14. **Reformation:** If any provision of this License is held to be unenforceable, such provision shall be reformed only to the extent necessary to make it enforceable.
15. **COPYRIGHT NOTICE**

Open Game License v. 1.0, © 2000, Wizards of the Coast, Inc.

Legend, © 2011, Mongoose Publishing.

Unearthed Arcana, © 2004, Wizards of the Coast, Inc.

Delta Green: Agent's Handbook, © 2016, Dennis Detwiller, Christopher Gunning, Shane Ivey, and Greg Stolze.

Delta Green: Handler's Guide, © 2017, Dennis Detwiller, Adam Scott Glancy, Kenneth Hite, Shane Ivey, and Greg Stolze.

PRODUCT IDENTITY: The following items are hereby identified as Product Identity, as defined in the Open Game License Version 1.0a, Section 1(e), and are not Open Game Content: the intellectual property known as Delta Green; all trademarks, names (including the name Delta Green), artwork, and trade dress; and all text not explicitly identified as Open Game Content.

Main Con

sign out

Copyright

- Account
- Groups
- Settings
- Phone
- Block or Allow
- Privacy

TOP CODE

There are entire towns under water, there since the Thirties, down, drowned, in the dark. I grew up on the lake next to one and never knew it. Grandy told me, out at his trailer, after his fourth bottle was chucked and smashed at the tin wall covered in chicken wire. About Danvers and the Donnels, and the devil.

Danvers Lake was called Danvers, Arkansas, back in the day. Then the WPA showed up and blocked the Tuft River with the dam. The Donnels ran booze, and guns before that, and had a bunch of money stashed in the town. Gold. Silver. That was the rumor. Anyhow, the sheriff buddied up with the Feds and ripped up a bunch of the town as it was evacuated, all the while waiting to scoop up the Donnels if they showed. They didn't. And the sheriff didn't find shit.

The town flooded, treasure and all.

Before the war, Tommy Donnel drowned out there in the lake, looking for his gold. His brother Taft quit the town and joined up and spent three years in some Pacific hellhole. He came back and built a shack out on the lake. I grew up looking at that tar shack from my window. I'd see the man who lived there from time to time. Strange. Big and gangly and without age. Bald and slick like a seal.

He'd swim out there in the lake and dive. I remember this clear. He's dive and not come up for minutes. Always in the same place. Straight across from my house. Gold down there in the dark, waiting.

One time, Taft Donnel shook his fist at my dad when he was a boy, and Grandy went out there with a shotgun and had words. Grandy says Donnel lost it in the Pacific. That he was soft. Donnel told him the devil was named TULU and that the devil's time was at hand. Nothing could stop the devil, who would work his ways on him.

Taft Donnel died like he lived, drinking paint thinner. Years later, when I was about ten, they found him. The county buried him. His shack was knocked flat by Moe's pickup truck and dragged off. No great loss.

I dream now of spires and doorways and empty windows alive with fish. Murky water floating in what once were kitchens. Winding staircases that lead up to, but never reach, open air. Green plants growing from the peaks of roofs like waving hands, barely touched by the dim light. Walls and boxes and safes, filled with gold in the black.

I can hold my breath a long time, now.

[redacted]

The FBI's Crime Scene Analysis involves six steps that collectively make up their profiling process These steps include Profiling Inputs, Decision Process Models, Crime Assessment, The Criminal Profile, The Investigation and The Apprehension. A brief explanation of each step shall be discussed below.

Profiling Inputs:
This involves the collection and assessment of all of the materials relating to the specific case. This would typically involve any photographs taken of the crime scene and victim, a comprehensive background check of the victim, autopsy protocols, other forensic examinations relating to the crime, and any relevant information that is necessary to establish an accurate picture about what occurred before, during or after the crime. This stage serves as the basis for all others, and should incorrect or poor information be provided, the subsequent analysis will be affected.
Decision Process Models: This stage simply involves arranging all of the information gathered in the previous stage (Profiling Inputs) into a logical and coherent pattern. This might also include establishing how many victims were involved, for example, with the purpose of establishing whether the crime was the result of a serial offender.

Crime Assessment:
This stage would typically involve the reconstruction of the sequence of events and the specific behaviors of both the victim and perpetrator. This will aid the analyst in understanding the "role" each individual has in the crime and should assist in developing the subsequent profile of the criminal.

The Criminal Profile:
This is the process of providing a list of background, physical, and behavioral characteristics of the perpetrator. In the FBI model, this stage may also involve providing th
requesting agency with directions on how to most appropriately interview the indivi
al. This stage would also inform investigators how to identify and apprehend the pe
trator.

The Investigation:
Here, the actual profile is provided to requesting agencies and incorporated into
investigation. If no suspects are generated, or if new evidence comes to light, the
is reassessed.

The Apprehension:
It is stated that the purpose of this stage is to cross check the profile produced
characteristics of the offender once they are apprehended. This would